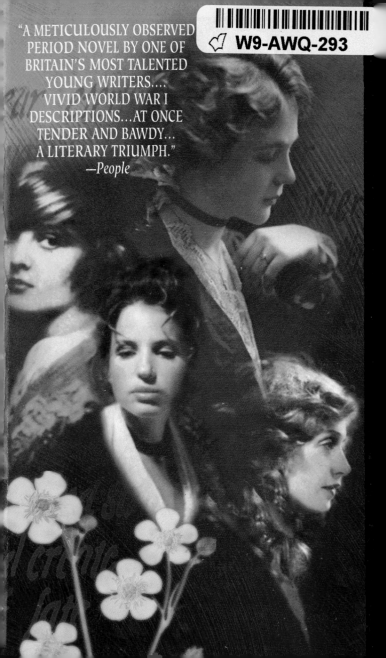

Plan your summer dream vacation with the
⊘ Signet/Onyx ℗
BOOKS THAT TAKE YOU ANYWHERE YOU WANT TO GO Contest

GRAND PRIZE $5,000 in CASH!
3 – 1st Prizes $1,000 in CASH!
25 – 2nd Prizes $100 in CASH!

To enter:

1. Answer the following question: **WHY WAS THIS BOOK THE IDEAL SUMMER READ?**
2. Write your answer on a separate piece of paper (in 25 words or less)
3. Include your name and address (street, city, state, zip code)
4. Send to: **BOOKS THAT TAKE YOU ANYWHERE YOU WANT TO GO** Contest
P.O. Box 844, Medford, NY 11763

NIGHT
SHALL
OVERTAKE
US

Kate Saunders

AN ONYX BOOK

ONYX
Published by the Penguin Group
Penguin Books USA Inc., 375 Hudson Street,
New York, New York 10014, U.S.A.
Penguin Books Ltd, 27 Wrights Lane,
London W8 5TZ, England
Penguin Books Australia Ltd, Ringwood,
Victoria, Australia
Penguin Books Canada Ltd, 10 Alcorn Avenue,
Toronto, Ontario, Canada M4V 3B2
Penguin Books (N.Z.) Ltd, 182–190 Wairau Road,
Auckland 10, New Zealand

Penguin Books Ltd, Registered Offices:
Harmondsworth, Middlesex, England

Published by Onyx, an imprint of Dutton Signet,
a division of Penguin Books USA Inc.
Previously published in a Dutton edition.

First Onyx Printing, July, 1995
10 9 8 7 6 5 4 3 2 1

REGISTERED TRADEMARK—MARCA REGISTRADA

PUBLISHER'S NOTE
This is a work of fiction. Names, characters, places, and incidents either are the
product of the author's imagination or are used fictitiously, and any resemblance
to actual persons, living or dead, events, or locales is entirely coincidental.

To Eleanor, Francesca and Jenny,
who kindly lent their names for old times' sake.

Life, after the first warm heats are over, is all downhill: and one almost wishes the journey's end, provided we were sure to lye down easy, whenever the Night shall overtake us.

—Alexander Pope

Aurora

Letter to my Daughter, 1935

I am writing at the desk in my bedroom window, and I can see you, kneeling beside the border, grubbing up weeds, and looking so much like your father that it gives me a turn even now.

My darling, you tell me you despair of your "ugliness" when you compare yourself with Flurry Fenborough. Well, Flurry is divine—that heartbreaking little face of hers has been wreaking havoc in London, since she came out. I expect my boys to fall in love with her as soon as possible, and get it over with, like the measles.

But you fail to see your own special beauty. You are tall and graceful, with straight black hair like a jay's wing. It's true, your nose is too long and too sharp—and it doesn't matter, because your eyes, thickly lashed and as dark as Egypt, are as remarkable as his were.

I rather miss the little wild animal I first brought home to Ireland. I could not have foreseen that you would grow into such a cultivated and elegant young woman.

My four boys—Pierce, Tark, Giles and little Roland— are my delight, and the jewels of the Mater's old age, as she often says. (We like to think that Pierce, despite his gangling limbs and russet hair, has a look of Tertius about him.) I love them all devotedly, but you are my special pearl.

I couldn't bear you to think, after you have read this, that I only love you from a sense of guilt. No, no, no— guilt is far too dreary and barren to sustain the tenderness I have for you. I'm so proud of you. I know you will do your very best to understand what I did, even if you can't forgive me for it. I had to tell you, but I'm delaying the awful moment when I write my last full stop, and take this bundle of papers to your room, for you to find and read.

Resurrected from memory, the ghosts of the past are crowding around me one last time, all mutely imploring me never to forget them, and what they might have been, without the tragedy that overtook us all.

Once, these shadows loved and were loved. Let that be said in mitigation for any sins we committed. But love can't be all. If there was nothing beyond, life would be too cruel to bear.

I am telling you this, because you, of all people, have a right to know. I never told you the whole truth—not because I meant to hide anything, but because I felt you were too young to understand. Oh, how hard this is. I suppose by "understand," I really mean "forgive."

Prologue

Surrey, 1907

"Aurora Carlington, you are, without a shadow of a doubt—take the end of your plait out of your mouth and stand up straight—quite the worst girl ever to pass through this school." Miss Maud Westwood was enthroned in angry majesty behind her ponderous, heavily carved mahogany desk. The Punishment Ledger lay open on the blotter in front of her.

Rory flicked her long red plait over her shoulder, thrust out her chest, and fought a nervous compulsion to paw the Persian carpet with the toe of her shoe. Sometimes, it seemed that her entire career at Winterbourne House had been spent under heavy cannon fire in the headmistress's stifling, over-furnished study. But it really wasn't so bad, she told herself sturdily, if you made yourself think about something else. She stared at the jet bugling on Miss Westwood's blouse, fascinated by the way it caught the light as the corseted bosom heaved.

"Over the past year, Aurora, I have made endless allowances for the irregularity of your upbringing, and the fact that you have no mother. I had hoped to fulfill my promise to your aunt, and fashion you into something resembling a gentlewoman. Yet you are as rude, untidy and undisciplined as the day you stepped through this door. Your clothes are a disgrace—a positive disgrace—and your accent and grammar would shame an Irish stableboy, let alone anyone calling herself a lady."

Rory's gaze traveled downward. She hypnotized herself with Miss Westwood's pince-nez, gently swinging on a long silver chain against the ironclad waist.

"I have written to Miss Veness, regretfully stating that it

is beyond even my power to make a silk purse out of a sow's ear. Have I said something amusing?"

"No, Miss Westwood."

"No indeed. I should think not." Miss Westwood snatched her spectacles in mid-swing and fastened them on her nose, to scan Rory's face for signs of secret levity.

God had intended fourteen-year-old girls to be tidy, meek and obedient; softly pure, yet steeled by a sense of duty, preparing themselves to be the wives and mothers of Empire builders. Aurora Carlington, in shameful contrast to this ideal, was wild, clumsy and opinionated. Her hands were inky. The hem of her blue serge skirt was tacked up with pins. Her white blouse was smudged with dirt, and her black stockings drooped over the tops of her scuffed shoes. Despite endless black marks for posture, her tall, comically skinny figure was slouched and ungainly.

Once Miss Westwood had believed that Aurora had possibilities, if only she would brush the tangles from that burning bush of red hair, and iron out her shocking Irish brogue. Now, she knew the child was a lost cause. All the black marks in the world could not prevent her from repeating blasphemous superstitions or calling down the names of saints at moments of excitement. Clearly, this was what happened to Protestant children when they were brought up among the savages. Miss Westwood had never been to County Galway, but she knew that the West of Ireland was a heathen wilderness, populated by Roman Catholic barbarians.

Certain members of her staff persisted in liking this dreadful child. Miss Scott, who was artistic, actually maintained that Rory's brilliant coloring held the promise of future beauty. But Miss Westwood failed to see what was beautiful about threadbare elbows and unkempt hair, or why any girl's appearance should be offered as an excuse for bad behavior. In an ecstasy of solemn indignation, she rose behind her desk.

"In forty years of teaching, you would imagine that I have learned something about the nature of girls, but you are quite beyond me. I have tried patience and forbearance. I have tried punishments. Nothing has had the slightest effect, and I am forced to conclude that you will never be an asset to Winterbourne House. Your aunt, Miss Veness— deeply grieved—has agreed to withdraw you from this school at the earliest opportunity. You will travel to London with Miss Curran tomorrow morning."

Rory's eyes were round with astonishment. "You—you mean," she whispered, "I'm expelled?"

"I do. I realize what a bitter blow this must be to you."

"You mean—I'm to go—home?"

"Yes." Miss Westwood was slightly taken aback by the child's flurried breathing and agonized look of suspense. "I have to consider the other students at this school. When you made friends with Jean Dalgleish and Eleanor Braddon—both excellent girls—I began to hope they would exert some sort of influence over you. However, I very much fear it has been the other way around." From the drawer of her desk, she drew a tattered exercise book, blackened as if by a storm of ink. "You recognize this, I presume? Miss Curran found it behind a cistern in the junior cloakroom."

Rory choked, and hastily hid her face in her hands. Miss Westwood felt she had dealt her masterstroke.

"I am glad to see you are ashamed of it. Perhaps you do have a shred of decency, after all." Holding the book delicately, she read from the cover: "*Passionate Hearts* by Aurora Mary Carlington. And I am astonished that you dared put your name to anything so depraved and revolting. If I found a servant girl reading such stuff, she would be instantly dismissed. You even had the temerity, I see, to dedicate it to me with a line of verse." Clipping her pince-nez back on her beak, she read in a deep, sorrowful voice: "'Maudibus satibus/ On the deskilorum/ Deskibus collapsibus/ Maudie on the floorum.'"

Fastidiously, she dropped the book and folded her hands. She had not wasted her wrath. The girl was positively shaking with remorse, and the tips of her ears were as red as her hair. Lowering her voice still further, Miss Westwood intoned: "Aurora, you will eat your tea in the pantry, and any girl found talking to you will earn herself a black mark. You may leave."

From the window of the governesses' sitting room on the floor below, Miss Curran and Miss Scott watched Rory dashing away across the lawn.

"Poor Rory!" exclaimed Miss Scott. "How I shall miss her! I do hope Miss Westwood let her down lightly."

"Wholesale slaughter, by the looks of her," commented

Miss Curran. "Serves her right. It's hard on me, having to cart the horrid little beast back to London on my day off, but I'll be glad to see the back of her. Another term and we'd all have been in a sanatorium."

"Oh, Dinah," protested gentle Miss Scott, "she's really such a darling."

"Well, it looks as if old Maudie's given the darling one of her specials. She won't forget that in a hurry."

Below them, Rory suddenly launched into a series of perfect cartwheels, in a whirl of white petticoats and blue serge bloomers. Her great whoop of triumph could be heard all over the garden.

Jenny, Eleanor and Francesca had bagged the mossy stone seat below the terrace of the gray, ivy-covered Victorian gothic mansion; a relic of its former life as a gentleman's residence. The seat commanded a smiling view of the school grounds, set in the trim, domesticated lanes and fields of the Surrey countryside. Late afternoon sunlight filtered through the interlacing branches of the oak trees above them, dappling the girls' full-sleeved white blouses and waist-length hair. They had been waiting here for Rory since her arrest at the end of prep.

From the nets on the other side of the dense shrubbery, they could hear the First Eleven being harangued by the Games Captain after practice.

Jenny sat on the bald, trodden earth around the seat, where several generations of schoolgirls had worn away the lawn. She had brought out Macaulay's *History of England,* because she was determined to spend every spare moment cramming for the History Medal at the end of term, but the book lay forgotten beside her, as she picked the corpses of last year's leaves from her black stockings. Eleanor lay sprawled on her stomach, chin resting on her cupped hands, dreamily paddling her feet in the air. They had spread their handkerchiefs on the stone bench for Francesca.

"She ought to be out by now," Jenny remarked in her calm voice, with its crisp Scottish accent. "Maudie's never kept her this long before." She consulted the gunmetal watch pinned to her breast. "What time d'you make it, Eleanor? I think mine's slow again."

Eleanor lolled sideways to look. She also wore her watch on the front of her blouse, but hers was gold, fastened with a seed pearl bow. "Ten past five. I do hope she gets out before the bell goes for tea."

"Priscilla Floyd fainted once, when she was up before Miss Westwood," Francesca said. She was meditatively eating lemon drops from a paper bag.

"Really honestly fainted?" asked Jenny, with a flicker of interest. "What had she done?"

"Borrowed someone else's galoshes and went to church in them, and Maudie said it was stealing. It was ages ago."

Francesca Garland was an authority on school history. She had come to Winterbourne House six years before, at the age of eight, and it had been her only home ever since. Her father was dead, and her mother lived permanently on the Continent. A gentleman known as "Uncle Archie" paid Francesca's fees and lavishly supplied her with pocket money. Her mother occasionally sent parcels of underclothes, beautifully embroidered by the nuns at Mentone. Matron did not like her to wear these scanty chemises and camisoles. With the curious lip-pursing that always accompanied the mention of Francesca's mother, she remarked that warm flannels would be more suitable for such a delicate child.

Francesca was the reigning belle of the school; a fragile sylph with huge, wistful dark eyes and a waterfall of glossy chestnut ringlets. She was tiny and underdeveloped for a girl of fourteen, and her frail beauty seemed to have been made for petting and caressing. Everyone spoiled her, from the mistresses, who were reluctant to criticize her badly spelled work too harshly, to the little first formers, who fought for the privilege of shining her dainty shoes. Francesca's locker was like an altar, filled with offerings of wilted posies and squares of chocolate, and she accepted all tributes with grateful sweetness.

Miss Westwood herself had given Francesca permission to lie in bed after rising bell on frosty mornings, because she was so susceptible to feverish colds. And artistic Miss Scott was painting her as an Italian flower girl. Francesca liked posing in Miss Scott's cozy study-bedroom, clutching a basket of artificial lilies and clad in a gauzy rag that exposed her shoulders. Scottie said she was utterly Burne-Jones, and she had promised to send a photograph of the finished picture to her mother.

Most people, she knew, thought it a shame she never

saw her mother. But Francesca was happy to contemplate
this sparkling, dimly remembered figure from a distance.
She was used to Winterbourne House now. The only thing
she had disliked was staying on during the holidays with
the handful of girls whose parents were in the colonies. The
deserted dormitories seemed so ghostly and forlorn, and
you had to sit through frightening dinners with Miss Westwood, remembering all the right forks and conversing in
French. However, for the past three years Francesca had
been best friends with Eleanor Braddon, and that meant
spending all her holidays in the comfortable bosom of Eleanor's family.

Eleanor, chewing absently on a wisp of grass, gazed up at
Francesca in soulful adoration. The way Francesca's shining
lashes hovered over her cheek entranced her. It was a
cheek as white and soft as a petal torn from the heart of
a rose. Eleanor knew, because she kissed it reverently every
night. Being Francesca's best friend—the darling's chosen
one—was simply wonderful. She yearned to express her
undying love in a grand, noble gesture. Exactly what, she
was not sure—the kind of sacrifice that would bind the little
beauty to her side forever.

The fact that she was no beauty herself Eleanor considered the great tragedy of her life. Her dull blond hair was
as straight as a ruler. Her face was a flat, poignant dish,
with a wide, shapeless mouth, an unromantically turned-up
nose and small, grayish eyes. Worst of all, she had to wear
hideous horn-rimmed spectacles. She hid them in the leg
of her bloomers as often as possible, but the world was
blurred and confusing without them. It was so unfair. Viola,
her older sister, currently being "finished" in Paris, was of
a legendary loveliness, still recalled with awe by fifth- and
sixth-form girls who had brought her flowers and left gushing poems on her desk.

Perhaps, Eleanor thought, she would one day meet a
man who loved her for her soul. She was sure she would
never be loved for her body. Over the past year, it had
constantly betrayed her. She marked the onset of her
monthly periods, and the humiliating, furtive ritual of asking Matron for piles of linen squares, as the beginning of
the end. The sturdy figure of her childhood was thinning
out in some places, and acquiring soft deposits of fat in
others, almost overnight. She haunted mirrors, hoping for

a miracle, and unable to decide whether to admire or dislike the small, hard breasts blooming under her liberty bodice.

"I don't know how much longer we can wait," Jenny said anxiously. "We're sure to get order marks if we're late for tea."

"It won't hurt you to get a mark for once," said Eleanor.

Jenny shook her head. "I haven't had a single one this term, and Mother and Father will be so disappointed if I miss the Order Medal again."

"Well, I don't know how you can bear to be so virtuous," remarked Eleanor. "You've already got more medals than Lord Kitchener."

Jenny smiled to herself resignedly. It was no good trying to make Eleanor or Francesca understand. When they ran out of money, they wrote home for more. When they finished with school, they would slip into lives of comfortable idleness. Only Rory, brought up on a semi-ruined estate in Ireland, knew about the blackness that lay beyond the last shilling; the wolf that perpetually bayed at the doors of the genteel poor. Jenny Dalgleish's father was a clergyman in Edinburgh. His living was a modest one, and Jenny's mother pinched and scraped to maintain standards. She had explained to her daughter that it was necessary to buy inferior cuts of meat and to melt the ends of candles together so that they could have a carriage on Sundays, keep two servants, and generally fulfill their proper station in life.

In Mrs. Dalgleish's house, every lump of coal was reckoned, and every crumb of bread accounted for. She had somehow managed to pare dancing and music lessons for Jenny out of her allowance, and she had declared that her only child was to have the very best schooling, even if she had to go without sugar in her tea for the rest of her days.

Jenny knew what was expected of her and repaid the sacrifices made at home by turning herself into a model daughter and model pupil. "Jean is an ornament to the school," wrote Miss Westwood in her yearly reports. The walls of the Reverend Mr. Dalgleish's study were lined with Jenny's prize certificates and medals. These had less to do with the getting of wisdom than the earning of a future living. One could not rely on the possibility of a suitable husband, Mrs. Dalgleish said. And it was better to be independent than to say yes to the first penniless curate who happened along. Jenny sometimes felt years older than Eleanor and Francesca. The small privations she had witnessed throughout her childhood had given her a realistic view of life. Rich and stylish people were admired; poor and shabby people were not. Being detected in an economy was the worst shame one could suffer. There were certain standards, and if one failed to meet them the world was a hostile place.

Jenny had been rather a stodgy child, but she was growing very pretty in adolescence, almost as if she had made a conscious decision to add good looks to her armory of accomplishments. Her soft, wavy brown hair had golden lights in it. Her large, gentle hazel eyes and broad cheekbones gave her face a madonna-like serenity, and the freckles were fading from her complexion, leaving it as white as porcelain. She liked to pull her Russian leather belt to the last notch to show off the small span of her waist. Month by month, her short, plump figure was developing into graceful curves, which tapered to admirably neat, slender wrists and ankles.

Jenny was fond of Eleanor and Francesca, flattered by the way they sought her advice, and—very deep down—mindful that they would be useful social contacts in the future. However, her deepest loyalty belonged to Rory. By some strange attraction of opposites, correct and temperate Jenny loved wild Rory with an intensity that sometimes surprised her.

"Here she is!" She straightened expectantly when Rory came tearing across the lawn toward them. "What happened?"

Rory struck a dramatic pose. Her blouse had come adrift from her waistband, one stocking was twisted around her ankle, and her heavy plait looked as if it had been used to sweep the garden paths. "My dears—I've been sacked!"

"No!"

"Oh, Rory, how putrid!"

"You poor angel!"

She collapsed breathlessly on the grass beside Jenny, laughing at their shocked faces as she hitched her stocking over her bony knee. "Isn't it marvelous? I nearly shrieked right out loud with joy. I'll be home at Castle Carey by the end of the week!"

"But what did Maudie say to you?" demanded Eleanor.

"Well," Rory paused, relishing their rapt attention, "well—she was in the most terrific state, and she chucked the fire shovel at my head. But she was so rolling drunk, she missed. You could smell the gin on her breath from ten paces."

Jenny and Francesca began to giggle. But Eleanor, who had a literal mind, and never knew how to take Rory's extravagant fictions, persisted: "No, honestly, what did she say?

Sighing, Rory confined herself to dull truth. "It was the novel that did for me in the end."

"What!" gasped Jenny. "You can't mean she's found *Passionate Hearts*?"

"My own heart just about dropped into my boots when she whipped it out of her desk. Just imagine her reading it. I didn't know whether to laugh or cry."

There was a short, dismayed pause, while the others took in this blow of blows. Rory's novel had been a source of forbidden thrills for three whole terms. Even Jenny had risked sneaking into the cloakroom, to pry up the loose floorboard under which it was hidden, to read the latest installment.

"However did she find it?" wondered Eleanor.

"Oh no!" Francesca wailed suddenly.

Rory pinched her knee affectionately. "You little chump, I guessed it was you. Why'd you have to shove it behind the tank? You know Curran always looks there."

"I—I—oh, Rory, the bell was going, I was in such a rush—" Tears welled up in her eyes, and her little pointed chin began to quiver pathetically. "And now you've been expelled, and it's all my fault."

"Well, don't cry about it, blossom. It can't be helped."

"Your wonderful story!" Francesca wiped her nose on Eleanor's handkerchief.

"I wanted to read the proposal again," Eleanor said disconsolately. "I think about it every night in bed. It's a simply divine story."

"I'll write you another one," Rory promised. "I get ideas all the time."

"What will happen to you now?" To Jenny, expulsion was the worst possible calamity, and she could not understand why Rory was taking it so lightly. "Will your people be furious?"

Rory leaned over on one elbow and began digging her fingers in the dirt. "Aunt Hilda will moan and lament, but I shan't have to put up with that for long. I'll soon be out of dismal London and her dull old house."

"Perhaps your aunt will make you stay, and have a beastly governess," suggested Eleanor gloomily.

"Not she. I drive the poor soul demented. She'll give me up as a bad job and shoot me back to Papa. And he doesn't care what I do. As for the darling old Mater, she'll welcome me back with open arms. She doesn't believe in girls going away to school."

"Don't you think," Jenny continued soberly, "that it's rather a pity to break off your education?"

"Shan't be breaking it off," returned Rory. "I'll go back to having lessons at the rectory with Tertius. Didn't that always do me fine before? Aren't I better at Latin and Greek than any of you? Our rector is heaps cleverer than some of the old biddies here."

"They'll say you're too old to go around with those boys of Lady Oughterard's now," Jenny pointed out.

"Why? I've always gone around with them."

"You'll have to put your hair up," Francesca chimed in, "and pour the tea, and pay calls."

Rory rudely snorted with laughter. "Pay calls! There's no 'gintry' for miles, and if I called on them, they'd think we'd had a death in the family. I can't wait to shake off this poky place and breathe some real air again."

"When do you have to leave?" Jenny asked.

"Tomorrow morning. Curran's taking me." Rory's face clouded for the first time. "I say, I shall hate saying good-bye to you all. You will write, won't you?"

"Absolute screeds," Eleanor assured her warmly. "You don't need to worry about being so far away because we'll be friends forever."

Francesca became tearful again. "It will be so dull without you."

"I'll come to London when I'm old enough." Rory was trying to sound cheerful. "But that won't be for ages."

There was a silence, as the four of them digested the fact that the circle was about to be broken.

"I've just remembered," Rory said, "I'm s'posed to be a prisoner, and you'll get black marks if you're seen with me. I'd better go—I don't want to blemish Jenny's record."

"That doesn't matter." Jenny, normally undemonstrative, put her arm around Rory's waist. "We won't let you go without a proper goodbye. Let's have a farewell banquet."

"At midnight!" Rory brightened. "The witching hour, when even Curran's beady eyes are veiled in slumber, and Maudie sits alone stirring her cauldron, and the miserable specters of starved boarders haunt the tennis courts."

Jenny and Eleanor were laughing, but Francesca looked plaintive. "Does it have to be midnight? Can't it be after prayers? I hate getting up in the dark!"

"I'll lend you my quilted dressing gown, darling one," Eleanor coaxed. "You won't feel the cold a scrap."

"All right." Francesca always gave in gracefully when she was overruled.

"We'll make a vow of eternal friendship," Rory said, "signed in blood—the boys showed me how."

There were approving murmurs, rather doubtful from Francesca, who did not like the sound of the blood.

"And—I know," Eleanor cried, "we each have to seal the vow by burning our dearest possessions."

"Someone would see the fire," said Jenny, "and then there'd be the most almighty row."

"We can bury 'em instead," put in Rory. "I'll bring my Japanese box. The catch is broken anyway. And I'll fetch the spade, too."

From the house, a bell clanged discordantly. Rory scrambled to her feet. "See you at midnight. I've got to go, or we'll all catch it." Agile as a monkey, she climbed up the wall of the terrace and vaulted over the balustrade to deliver herself into custody. Mrs. Sedge, the housekeeper, was waiting grimly in the hall.

"There you are, Miss Carlington. I was just going to report you. Your bread and butter and milk are in the pantry."

"Oh, Sedgie, couldn't you get me a piece of cake, and some jam? I'm so ravenous, I'll die."

Mrs. Sedge grabbed Rory's wrist. "Oh no, miss, you won't get round me this time. You'll do as you're told for once." And she marched Rory off to the pantry, just as the other girls began to file into the refectory.

Jenny surfaced from a cave of delicious, velvety sleep, aware that someone was shaking her. "Go away!" she mumbled aggressively. The shaking began again, just as she was falling back into weightless oblivion.

"Wake up!"

"Eh?" Suddenly conscious, she propped herself on her elbow.

"Shhhh!" Rory was beside her bed; a wild, bundled figure striped with shadows. She had a talent for getting up, fiendishly alert, at any hour of the night.

Blinking stupidly, and suppressing a desire to moan self-piteously, Jenny swung her legs out of bed and reached underneath it for her raincoat. As she pulled it on—in breathless silence, so she would not wake the girl in the next bed—she felt the bread and butter she had saved from tea lying, clammy and disagreeable, in her pocket. During her imprisonment in the pantry, Rory had taken the opportunity to raid the tins for stale cake. The faintly acidic odor of elderly currants floating from her bag made Jenny feel queasy, but she knew that in half an hour she would be devouring them with relish. Midnight escapades made one so hungry.

Eleanor and Francesca were waiting for them further down the passage, outside their dormitory. Eleanor was already wide awake and eager for adventure, but Francesca was languid and peevish. Eleanor had lovingly bundled her up in two dressing gowns and a woolen hood.

"You were ages!" she whispered.

Hearts thudding, the four of them made their way down the first flight of stairs.

"Cave!" hissed Rory, who was leading. They were instantly still. The lower passage was where the mistresses slept, and one of the doors stood half-open, spilling out a solid bar of yellow light. From within, they heard Miss Curran, speaking in a low, continuous murmur. Motioning to the others to stay where they were, Rory boldly crept to the edge of the light, and looked into the room.

Miss Curran was sitting in a basket chair, reading aloud from a book of poetry: *"For a day and a night Love sang to us, played with us, Folded us round from the dark and light; And our hearts were fulfilled with the music he made with us—"* She was stroking the head of Miss Scott, lying against her knee. They were both totally absorbed, sealed in their golden circle of lamplight.

Rory beckoned, and one by one, the girls flitted dry-mouthed past the open door. This small success made them euphoric. Francesca let out a nervous giggle and was pinched reprovingly by Jenny. Downstairs, the hall was a ghostly cave of shadows. In the long refectory, the break-fast things laid out on the tables had a menacing gleam in the half-light. The next part was easy. Rory slipped the catch on the window at the end of the kitchen passage, and they clambered over the sill.

"Ow—be careful—ow!" Francesca had to be pulled through by the other three.

The night air, cool and intoxicating, assaulted them. They began to shake with laughter as they skirted the lawn, away from the eyeless slab of the house. The inky stillness of the shrubbery was thrilling and terrifying. Francesca grasped the back of Jenny's raincoat for protection. Rory drew a candle from her pocket, and lit it with a safety match. Expertly ducking the low branches of laurel and rhododen-dron, she led the way to their secret meeting place, a small patch of earth behind the potting shed.

"Right," she said, no longer bothering to whisper. "First the hole." She planted the candle in the ground. In its feeble light, her hair was like hot coal in a dying fire and her eyes were chips of emerald.

"You know, Rory," Francesca piped up, "you'd be quite pretty if you washed your face."

"Wouldn't be worth the effort," Rory said amiably. "I haven't time to waste in the mornings, trying to lay hands on a washcloth."

"Let's have the grub first," said Jenny. "I'm famished."

"All right, you start. I'll get the spade." Rory was swal-lowed by the blackness as she dived into the bushes. The others heard clumping and rustling on the other side of the shed. When she rejoined the circle, they wolfed the clods of bread and butter and the moist bricks of fruitcake, pausing between bites to giggle until they almost cried. Francesca produced a bottle of ginger beer, and they took turns to drink.

Digging the hole took a surprisingly long time. Everyone except Francesca took turns with the spade, and Jenny re-marked that whenever someone in a book decided to make a hole, it appeared just like that. They stopped at eighteen inches, enough to cover the box with earth and stamp it down flat.

"Now," said Eleanor, "let the ceremony commence."

The hollow solemnity of her voice brought on another attack of mirth, and Rory was still weakly sniveling with laughter when she opened her dilapidated lacquered box to take out a darning needle and a scroll of paper. They suddenly became serious, gazing at each other's faces, mysterious in the fitful candlelight.

"I composed this during tea. I made it as legal as I could." Rory unrolled the paper, and read aloud:

"We, the undersigned, do most solemnly swear eternal friendship. From this day, May the 3rd, 1907, we vow to love one another until the end of our lives. We undertake to help one another in times of sickness, suffering or poverty, even if we are at the four corners of the earth. We sacrifice our dearest possessions to seal this binding oath.

> *Let these four maidens in the spring of life*
> *Remember Love through suffering and strife.*
> *Let this great vow a lasting bond create,*
> *Though we are parted by the seas of fate.*

> *Signed*
> AURORA MARY CARLINGTON
> JEAN ALICE DALGLEISH
> ELEANOR BEATRICE BRADDON
> FRANCESCA PATRICIA ALEXANDRA
> GARLAND."

In the awed silence that followed, they joined hands around the stump of candle and listened to the wind stirring the boughs above them.

"The poem's good, isn't it?" said Rory. "I wrote out a copy for each of us so we won't forget."

"I'll carry it with me always," Eleanor breathed. "Isn't it romantic? We all have to come to each other's aid. In ten years' time, or twenty, even. What do you suppose we'll be doing in ten years' time?" Her eyes narrowed, as if blinded by the brightness of the future. "In 1917. We'll be twenty-four."

Ten years yawned before them, tantalizingly unspoiled, infinitely rich in promise.

"As soon as we put our blood on the paper," Rory explained, "we can never break the oath without something dreadful happening."

"It had better not be too dreadful," said Jenny, "because one of us will break it."

"Jenny!" Eleanor was shocked. "What on earth made you say that?"

"As if any of us would break a binding oath of friendship!" Rory cried indignantly.

Jenny looked around at them all, apologetic but stubborn. "I don't know, but I know it's true. It was when you said ten years—I suddenly saw it. I do sometimes see things before they happen."

"What do you see?" asked Eleanor.

Jenny sighed, trying to explain. "It isn't like a vision, or anything. It's more of a feeling—a taste of the feelings I will have about something in the future. I've had it before."

There was an awed hush, broken by Francesca. "Oh, Jenny, is it me? Am I the one who breaks it?" She began to cry, her mouth full of cake. "It's just the sort of thing I always do—like getting Rory sent away because I didn't hide the book!"

"Now look what you've done," grumbled Rory, while Eleanor hastened to fold Francesca in her arms. "You might have known it would set her off."

Jenny relented. "Don't take any notice of me. Father gets dreadfully angry when I say I see things. He says it's doubting Providence."

"Exactly!" declared Rory. "And how can it come true, when we're the best friends in the world? Wipe your nose, baby, and stop fussing." She held the darning needle in the candle flame, and watched it blacken. Then, with her face taut and apprehensive, she smartly drove the needle into the pad of her thumb.

"Oh no—" Francesca murmured.

A fat, vermilion bead of blood bloomed on Rory's flesh. She held it there for a moment, twinkling like a jewel, before she tilted it onto the paper, and smudged it into the letter A.

"There you are. Easy—doesn't hurt a bit."

Jenny took the needle from her, and bravely repeated the process without a tremor of pain. Eleanor, with a look of glorious martyrdom, pricked herself too hard, and bled so heroically that she was able to write both her initials.

"We'd better let Francesca off," Jenny said. "She'll only faint, or something."

"I'll do it for her with my other thumb," Eleanor offered.

"But I want to do it myself," insisted Francesca surprisingly. "Otherwise I won't count. Give me the needle. I won't faint, I promise." A thin silt of obstinacy lay at the bottom of Francesca's sweet nature. She happily gave in over small things, but she always got her own way when it really mattered. Snatching the needle from Eleanor, she quickly jabbed her thumb, and blended her blood with that of her friends. Also her tears, because she did so detest even the littlest amount of pain.

"I call that jolly plucky," announced Rory.

Francesca beamed around at them, sniffing back the tears. "We're just like sisters now. You all have to come to my aid."

They laughed, and Rory produced the last slice of cake. The four of them settled themselves comfortably, to finish the feast.

"Of course, in ten years' time, you'll all be married," Rory said.

"Won't you?" asked Eleanor.

"Not likely."

"Oh but, Rory," Francesca said sweetly, "I told you, you could be quite pretty if you tried. If you'd only brush your hair and make sure your stockings are nice—"

Rory snorted unkindly. "You really are the most complete ninny sometimes."

"What did I say?" Offended, Francesca turned to the others for support.

"I meant that I don't want to get married."

"But getting married is—is just what people do."

"You'll change your mind," Jenny said wisely.

"Oh no I shan't." Rory energetically brushed crumbs from her mouth. "I'm going to live alone, writing my poems, and giving parties for famous and distinguished people. The brilliance of my salon will be renowned throughout society. And when they let women into Parliament, I'll get myself elected as the Home Rule member for Oughterard, and stand on the hustings with a little picture of Parnell in my hatband."

"Women won't ever be allowed to vote," Jenny said.

"Oh yes we will. Any time now, Christabel says." Rory, as they all knew, was an ardent admirer of Christabel Pankhurst. She cut photographs of her out of illustrated magazines and pasted them inside the lid of her desk.

"But don't you want to fall in love?" Eleanor asked.

Rory frowned. "No. I'm never going to get married. Men always want to be in charge."

"I'm going to be just like Mummy in ten years," announced Francesca. "I'll have lovely Paris gowns, and Uncle Archie will take me to theaters and cafés. And then I'll get engaged. I'd like a man who looks like my postcard of Henry Ainley playing Hamlet. Wouldn't it be divine to be engaged, and have a trousseau and a diamond ring?"

"I wouldn't care about any of that," said Jenny, her face softening wistfully. "My husband wouldn't even have to be especially handsome, as long as he had a nice big house in the country. I'd organize all the shoots and dances, and drive around visiting all the poor people—oh, it would be heavenly. But I'll probably end up working as a teacher. Maudie says I can get a scholarship to college."

"You don't want that!" exclaimed Eleanor.

"No, not really."

"Don't let them make you do it."

Only Rory saw the look, half-cynical, half-amused, that Jenny shot at Eleanor. She guessed that Jenny was thinking of the difference between wearing a gunmetal watch and a gold one.

"Do tell us where we'll be able to find you in ten years," she said quickly, "in case we have to call in the vow."

"Well," Eleanor considered the question seriously, deaf to the irony in Rory's tone. She never could get any kind of joke, unless the joker sent up a flare in advance. "I don't know, exactly. Marriage seems so—so ordinary. Like Mother and Father—you know—ordering kippers for breakfast, and sending complaining letters to the laundry. There must be something more." At the moment, the dearest wish of Eleanor's heart was to grow out of wearing spectacles, but she had misty ideals beyond that, and she struggled to put them into words. "I should like to love splendidly. To do something noble and beautiful for the sake of love. I shall have a grand, tragic love affair, where my heart almost breaks with anguish. It just sends shivers down my spine to imagine suffering for love—think how divinely romantic it would be."

They all brooded over this, until Francesca said plaintively: "I'm sitting on something awfully hard, and my feet are freezing. Let's do the dearest possessions and go back to bed."

"All right." Rory held out the box. "You first."

"My silver ring with the real carnelian." Francesca drew it proudly off her finger, savoring the moment, and dropped it in.

Eleanor fished a dull bronze disc attached to a blue ribbon out of her pocket. "My music medal." She had won it for playing a Schubert piano sonata in the school's Exhibition Concert at the beginning of term.

"I would have given my Exhibition Medal, too," Jenny said hastily. She had sung "Ye Banks and Braes" in her sweet contralto, and reduced an elderly colonel on the board of governors to tears. "But I sent it straight home. Mother and Father like to have my prizes." Something clattered into the box. "Here's my penknife, and blow me if I know what I'm going to do without it."

All eyes turned expectantly toward Rory, who was bristling with impatience, and exulting over some private joke.

"I never win any prizes," she said proudly, "and most of my things are broken. So I'm sacrificing a little something I made myself."

"Do get on with it!" Francesca cried.

With a magnificent flourish, Rory whipped out a pair of sewing scissors.

"Oh, you cheat!" gasped Eleanor. "Those are Edith's— I saw you borrow them!"

Rory grabbed the end of her long plait. The scissors flashed in the nape of her neck and her severed hair slithered into her lap like a red snake.

Francesca let out a thin scream. Eleanor and Jenny were frozen in horrified disbelief. For a few seconds, Rory gaped down at her hair, shocked by what she had done. Then, with a delighted laugh, she picked up her plait, spun it around in the air and flung it to the bottom of the box.

"My pledge of eternal friendship," she said triumphantly, "and may the seas of fate never part us."

PART ONE

1913

Aurora

When you were little enough to sit on my knee, you used to ask again and again for the story of the blood vow the four of us made at school. I can see you now, lying against my arm with your eyes pinned to my face, eagerly tracing your destiny back to the shadowy time before you were born. For the story of your mother and her friends is your story, too.

One

County Galway, Ireland

The ragged elms fringing the Careys' parkland cast their noonday shadows across turf of a green so piercing bright, it made the retina ache. The heathery slopes of the mountains, golden in the sunlight, were garlanded with fine clouds of mist, like wisps of silver chiffon.

Rory was standing on top of the mossy, crumbling wall that divided Marystown, her father's estate, from the wild, unprofitable acres of Castle Carey. Slowly, her eyes traveled across the soft folds of landscape, from the flat, black peat bogs to the silver waters of the lake. Drops of yesterday's rain still hung from the fuchsia hedges, turned by the sun into necklaces of mercury.

"Don't move!" ordered Tertius, as she unthinkingly shifted her foot. He was astride a branch of the huge beech tree, pouring concentration into his drawing. Rory rested her eyes affectionately on the top of his dark head. She always liked to watch him working. It was the only time one could ever catch him being remotely quiet or serious. His hand swept over the paper in fluent, confident strokes. Occasionally, in an absent, sleepwalking manner, he flicked back the heavy skein of curly hair that spiraled across his brow. In her fever to get away, Rory had not properly admitted to herself how much she would miss him.

The pencil hovered impatiently. "Rory-May, why to God can't you ever keep still?"

"Sorry." She eased herself back into position. Half an hour before, when she had climbed onto the wall to gaze at the view, he had been seized with a desire to sketch her in profile. "Like an eagle looking out of its nest," he had said, "Caitlin ni Houlihan's farewell to her kingdom."

Rory surveyed her kingdom. It was beautiful. Wherever

she went, part of her would always long for the lake, with its swirling curtain of mist, and the endless vista of mountains, changing from green to black as the clouds charged across them. Sometimes, the winter torrents obscured them altogether, and turned the whole land into one treacherous bog. Impossible to imagine now, when the bees were droning in the sweetbrier, and everything hummed with the promise of May.

But she was ready to leave. For all its beauty, Ireland seemed to her a sad, poverty-racked, elderly place, now that the heroic days were over, and the hillside men had all vanished into the hills of heaven. She thought of her battered trunk, waiting packed and corded in the hall, and her veins tingled with anticipation. By this time tomorrow, she would be on her way to London and freedom—escorted by Fingal, who did not in the least want the responsibility, but she was not going to let his carping spoil her enjoyment.

The breeze whipped short strands of red hair against the nape of her neck. She had never let it grow in the six years since she had left school. However, the gawky, stooping schoolgirl of fourteen had changed into a tall, lean young woman of twenty, with bold eyes, a curved, high-bridged nose and a fine, strong jaw. She was still skinny, but years in the saddle had given her the ramrod spine of the typical hard-riding Anglo-Irish woman—"grenadier guards in tea gowns," as Fingal scornfully described them.

Fingal was home on a short visit, and he had already nettled Rory by informing her that she was too tough and sinewy to be considered a beauty—as if she had asked him. He did concede that her complexion was goodish. In fact, Rory's coloring was as clear and pure as stained glass; flashes of scarlet and emerald against a skin as milkwhite as the inside of an oyster shell.

She smiled suddenly, as she wondered what Eleanor, Francesca and Jenny would make of her when they met again after all this time. Eleanor's weekly letters had lately echoed her own doubts and yearnings, but they also contained detailed descriptions of the latest London fashions. She kindly assumed Rory needed such information. If she could see me now, Rory thought, glancing down at her shabby whipcord breeches and cracked riding boots. These articles, and the open-necked white flannel shirt, were cast-offs outgrown by Tertius and his brothers. She only ever wore a skirt when she rode into town with the eggs. John the Baptist in his goatskin had less need of fashion than she did.

"All right. Got it." Tertius stretched himself luxuriously. "You can move now." He leaned against the tree trunk and lit one of the crumpled cigarettes he kept in the pockets of his homespuns.

Rory walked along the top of the wall, flexing her cramped muscles, and climbed into the tree beside him. "May I see?"

"If you like." He lost passion for his drawings as soon as they were finished.

She studied the sketch. It was hasty and impulsive, and the angles were curiously sharp, as if he had broken her to pieces and rebuilt her in a jigsaw of geometric shapes. Yet, in some way she could not define, it was truthful. Tertius obsessively drew everything he saw, from clouds to cattle, and was mostly content to reproduce nature. This harsher, more experimental style was reserved for Rory alone, because she required interpretation, so he said.

"It's good." She exchanged the paper for the cigarette. "Really, it's marvelously good."

"It'll do."

"If only you'd work at it harder."

"Don't lecture me, there's a darling."

She ignored this. "It's high time you took something seriously."

"You know what I care about. Ah, Rory-May—" His voice, with its lilting local accent, was warm and coaxing. "Why d'you have to go away?"

Rory drew on the cigarette and passed it back to him. "I've told you. I can't stay here. There's nothing for a girl to do."

"There's getting married."

"If you start all that again," Rory said sharply, "you'll have to take the consequences. Beware of Rory of the Hills, who always warns before she kills."

"All right. But what can you do in London that you can't do here?"

"I'll be where things happen. You know I've planned it for ages, and now I've got my mother's money, I can be independent. You won't catch me staying long at Aunt Hilda's."

"What if I tell your father you're planning to run off and live by yourself?"

"Just you try it."

"Why can't you smash windows in Dublin, with Mrs. Sheehy-Skeffington and her harpies? You'll get the vote just as quick."

"Too near home. I need room to maneuver."

"I'm telling you," Tertius said severely, "you won't like it. You'll be back on the next boat."

"I suppose you think I'd be lost without you?"

"Well, you will. We've always done things together."

Rory's eyes had the distant, calculating expression Tertius hated. It meant she was immovable, and deaf to any appeal that might deflect her from her purpose. "I wouldn't expect you to understand," she said, "because you don't have any convictions. But we are on the brink of the greatest revolution in a hundred years—Home Rule for Ireland, votes for women, an army of workers ready to fight against ignorance and poverty—there's a wonderful age coming, a golden age, as long as we're prepared to pull together for our freedom."

Tertius had heard this speech before. He was well used to being harangued by Rory as if he were a public meeting, and he blew smoke rings while he waited for her to finish.

"You've got all the freedom you want already," he said reasonably, when she paused for breath.

"I'm after fun, too. I want to see the girls from school, and have a little intelligent female conversation."

"Are you tired of us boys?" He squeezed her thigh gently.

"Don't be an ape," Rory snapped, brushing his hand away. "I've told you not to paw me about. You never think of anything else."

"How can I, with you sitting so close and making my blood race?" His impersonation of injured innocence was remarkably realistic. Rory was not fooled for a moment, but she smiled at him before she knew what she was doing. Tertius had the face of an angel, and his deceptively soulful blue eyes were sweet enough to melt sterner natures than hers.

"There's something dreadfully peculiar about your

blood," she said teasingly. "You should ask it to turn around and race to your brain for a change."

He laughed. "You can't blame me for trying."

"Yes I can. I just wish you'd put as much effort into your painting." She leaped neatly out of the tree into the muddy, rutted road below. "Let's go and ride Baucis and Philemon."

"Right-oh." Tertius threw her his portfolio, and jumped down beside her. He tried to take her arm, but she ducked out of his reach.

"Seriously—" she began.

"Not seriously. I don't want to be serious."

"That's just your trouble. If I'd a tenth of your talent, I'd slave day and night."

Tertius lazily shifted his portfolio under his arm. "What for?"

"Fame, money—"

"Don't want 'em."

"To achieve something, then." Rory was earnest. "To let people see what you can do."

"People don't want to see the sort of things I paint. They want naked virgins reclining on feather pillows, and that's not art."

"But if you had one spark of ambition—"

"You know what my ambition is." The portfolio slid to the ground as he seized both her hands. "Marry me!"

"Certainly not. Of all the silly ideas."

"I'll go right on asking until you say yes."

"No! The answer's no!"

His grip tightened. "Do you realize I've been desperately in love with you since I was three? I'm nearly twenty-one, so that makes eighteen years. Eighteen long years of suffering and pining for you, Rory-May, and I'll go on adoring you until I'm old and white-haired—"

Rory snatched away her hands. "What nonsense! You never suffered or pined in your life."

"I did too! And imagine what will happen to me when you leave. I'll perish from neglect—there'll be nothing left of me but a heap of dust in the churchyard. Cruel girl, imagine how distraught you'll be, watering the daisies on my grave—"

She tried to dodge past him, but he blocked the path, dancing in front of her like a boxer. Although his weekly proposals made her want to cry with irritation, she could not help laughing. "Oh, Tertius, for pity's sake!"

"Marry me!"

"And live on what?" she demanded. "Grass? Air?"

"I'd work like a slave if I could have you."

"You'd carry on just as you do now, lounging around at O'Dwyer's still, and painting people's prize cows in exchange for poteen. What on earth makes you think I'd give up my whole life before it's even started, to tie myself to you and raise a tattered brood in the middle of nowhere? What are you laughing at?"

"God, Rory-May, what a tongue you've got. It'll wear out two heads before you die."

Rory sighed, exasperated. "I wish you'd listen to it sometimes. I'm never going to marry you, and well you know it, so let's talk about something else."

"Darling," coaxed Tertius, "it's our last day together. Can't you be nice to me for once?"

Solemnly, Rory looked at him, and wondered—not for the first time—whether she had a heart at all. Here he was, young, ardent and bright-eyed; as full of spring vitality as the warm breeze that ruffled the velvet backs of the bees in the sweetbrier, and she absolutely could not fall in love with him. He was her best friend, her twin, her right arm. That was all. It was quite baffling when half the girls in the countryside were mad for him.

"I'm always nice to you," she said.

"Give us a kiss, then."

"No!"

"One kiss—Jesus, it's not much to ask!"

"All right then, if you leave me in peace afterward." Rory turned a cold white cheek toward him. She loathed being kissed by anyone, but supposed it would be mean to refuse him on her last day. "Just one, mind."

Tertius was in no hurry. He folded his arms around her, drawing her close. She felt his heart thudding as he pressed her against his chest.

"Do get on with it!"

Slowly and deliberately, he fastened his lips on her cheek, holding them there to breathe in her scent for a long moment, and drawing away with a sigh.

"There—" Rory began, and as soon as she moved her face around toward him, he stopped up her mouth with his hot tongue. Outraged, she struggled and kicked, and rained down blows on his back, but Tertius only held her tighter, and devoured her as if he were starving.

Then, suddenly, a spasm ran through his body, his head jerked back, and he moaned up at the sky. Rory saw her advantage. In an ecstasy of fury, she freed herself with a smartly aimed smack on his ear, stamped on his foot for luck, and scrambled over the wall.

"Wait," he gasped. "Rory, please—"

She was pelting away toward the house, her fists clenched and her head down.

Reeling from the blow, Tertius decided he was in no condition to run after her. She would not tell on him in any case, because she never did. And, fortunately, she was very unlikely to realize how far he had gone. He was amazed, and then slightly amused by his lack of control. Jesus, his ear hurt—Rory's thrashings were no joke.

The taste of her lingered in his mouth. He was hard again, and desperate for the comfort of female flesh. He grabbed his portfolio and started down the shortcut to the village.

"Mother? Oh, here you are." The Honorable Fingal Carey glanced around the dank, stone-flagged scullery of his ancestral home, as if amazed that such a room existed. Although irritated out of his usual exquisite dignity, he was languidly elegant in white jodhpurs and a showily cut gray tweed riding jacket. "Mother, you absolutely must do something about the sheer ghastliness of Aurora. If you don't, I shall simply refuse to travel with her tomorrow."

"Wicked little hoyden," his mother said comfortably. "What's she done now?" Lady Oughterard was busy putting the family wash through the mangle. It was heavy, monotonous work, and she was going at it in a determined but amateurish fashion. One by one, she had to fish the clothes out of the boiling copper with wooden tongs and feed them through the rollers, turning the heavy cast-iron handle until all the excess water ran into the bowl beneath. She bent down to retrieve a pair of combinations, which she had dropped in a slack, steaming heap on the dirty floor, and Fingal had to address his grievances to her back.

"Well, she's a horse thief, for one thing. I had Philemon all saddled up and ready, I virtually had my leg over the back of him, and she snatched the reins right out of my hands and galloped away. Paddy Finnegan simply stood there laughing. I insist that you say something—what on earth is the matter?"

Lady Oughterard had dropped the handle of the mangle to stare at his clothes. "I haven't seen this before, have I? Another coat! Brand-new, not a thread gone! And a real gold pin in your stock, how beautiful! It's a good thing you didn't go riding got up like that. You'd be up to your ears in mud by now."

"I don't think you recognize the seriousness of the situation," snapped Fingal. His monocle was fogging over in the steamy atmosphere. He let it fall, and the thin gold circle bounced against his yellow vest. "Aurora is appallingly spoiled. She's every bit as loutish as Tertius, only it's ten times worse in a girl. Seldom have I witnessed such a coarse display of temper. Really, one can't be seen with her—she barely looks like a lady."

"Oh, but you must be seen with her!" protested Lady Oughterard, beginning to be alarmed. "You promised to take care of her in London!"

"Who's to take care of me?"

"Look here, I'll get Lucius to grind some manners into her." Lucius was her eldest son, known to everyone except his mother as Muttonhead. "She usually listens to him."

"A shining example," Fingal said sarcastically. "The perfect person to tell her how much manure should be worn on the boots at mealtimes."

Lady Oughterard was slightly in awe of Fingal, but she could never bear any criticism of Muttonhead. "Nonsense. He'll probably tell you to stop finding fault wherever you look. No wonder Rory and Tertius tease you."

"Tertius is a thoroughly bad influence," Fingal declared. "One hopes, for the sake of one's poor nerves, that Aurora will be more manageable away from him."

"She's a charming child, she always was." His mother resumed her mangling, taking care not to crack the buttons on Muttonhead's scratchy woolen undergarments. "All she needs is a chance to meet some nice people."

"And marry one of them, you mean. *Mon dieu,* the idea of anyone wanting her ... Mother, forgive my asking, but don't you employ Una to do the washing?"

"Una has her hands full making tonight's dinner," said

Lady Oughterard. "The chickens only came over from Marystown half an hour ago. I daren't ask her to do anything else in case she flies off into one of her rages."

"How too Irish!" Sighing, Fingal tapped his riding crop on the palm of his gray leather glove. "One does detest being cross—it's so harming to one's equilibrium. I shall give up all thoughts of riding, and seek serenity in literature. I've discovered the most divine bound volume of old Police Gazettes in the library. Perhaps reading about a brutal murder will make me less likely to commit one." He replaced his monocle. "If I ask for a fire, may I assume that a servant will materialize to light it? Or shall I discover you bearing logs into the hall yourself?"

"Ask Paddy," Lady Oughterard said shortly.

"Thank you." He made a graceful exit.

His mother tried not to be annoyed by his tireless superiority. Fingal seldom came home these days, and she felt guilty about not being better pleased to see him. If only he would stop criticizing Rory and Tertius. Whenever poor Tertius opened his mouth, Fingal shuddered over his accent, and he could hardly look at Rory without his lips puckering in disapproval.

Admittedly, Lady Oughterard had been uneasy about Rory for some time. The girl was her responsibility. Had Tertius really been such a bad influence? It was difficult to judge them individually. They had been inseparable since childhood. Now that they were children no longer, however, Lady Oughterard saw her duty. It was high time Rory left Castle Carey.

There were other advantages to the London plan. The neighboring families were already looking askance at Rory, because of her boy's clothes and short hair. A certain amount of eccentricity was tolerated. Peculiarities flourish where people are isolated and hard up, and absurdly grandiose into the bargain. Rory's loudly voiced opinions of Women's Suffrage and the labor conditions in Dublin might have been swallowed more kindly if she had shown that she wanted to be part of their society. But they all knew how she laughed at their tea-fights and horse-meets and endless drawing-room politics. She was too impatient to reject all this and throw herself into what she supposed to be "real" life.

Lady Oughterard smiled as she remembered driving over

to Marystown on the day Rory was born. The nurse had brought her the lusty, red-tufted scrap on a lace pillow, and she had run upstairs to congratulate poor Charlotte. She could see her now, her long auburn hair spread against her white nightgown, saying she had dropped the baby like a cat and meant to have a dozen now she knew it was so easy.

Charlotte had been English, a beauty and great fun. What she had seen in Justus Carlington was still a mystery to Lady Oughterard. He was one of those men who look as if they have grown up in a dark bureau drawer; dusty and desiccated, with a complexion as sallow as old parchment. An avid scholar, with a first in Classics from Trinity, his abiding passion was Celtic history and culture.

He was a Nationalist in the old, romantic mold, and the fall of the mighty Parnell had almost broken his heart. The country people thought him quite mad, because he took down their anecdotes in a notebook. The gentry found him criminally dull because he took no interest in horses or entertaining, the twin pastimes that fueled the social life of the county.

There had been Carlingtons at Marystown since Cromwell's time. In its heyday, it had been a fine property, with six thousand acres of good farmland. An earlier house had been burned down in the troubles of 1798, and a charming, neoclassical manor had risen in its place. By the 1890s, despite the inroads of the Land Acts, it was still a fine property. Ready for a bride, people said, and Justus duly brought home Charlotte Veness, whom he had met during a visit across the water, in Somerset.

Charlotte died of pneumonia eighteen months after her wedding, during a terrible January when the rain turned the whole countryside into one treacherous bog. She was interred in the family vault at the Protestant church, and the parson said it smelled like the very breath of Tophet in the reeking damp. Lady Oughterard, who had seen Charlotte in her bridal finery, watched the rain battering the funeral wreaths and wondered what Justus would do next.

He did his best to revert to his old, reclusive ways, reading and writing in a dusty house kept quiet by elderly servants. One thing, however, ruined his peace: Charlotte's baby girl was manageable enough while in the arms of her nurse, but she grew into a two-year-old imp who baffled him with her sudden rages and her thirst for danger. Lady

Oughterard had yearned to interfere. Something should be done before the imp killed herself eating rat poison or climbing up on the roof of the conservatory. Boldly, she offered to take Rory into her own nursery at Castle Carey.

Sitting in Justus's study with the grimy baby in her lap, she had explained that it was bedlam already, and one more could hardly make a difference. Tertius, the youngest of her three boys, was just a year older than Rory. Later, they could share a governess. Justus, almost speechless with gratitude, had offered to pay for the governess. Remote as he kept himself, he knew the Oughterards were chronically short of money.

From that moment, Rory grew around Lady Oughterard's heart like ivy. By the time the child was a cheeky brat of six or seven, her father occasionally asked for her to be sent over to Marystown because she amused him and reminded him of Charlotte. However, Castle Carey came to be considered her real home.

Castle Carey was not a castle at all, but a gray Georgian cube, handsome in its classical simplicity. Huge sash windows stretched from floor to ceiling, flooding every room with light. A gravel walk ran the half-mile between the park gates and the semicircular steps leading up to the front door. At the back, French windows opened onto a broad terrace. Stables and offices stood a hundred yards from the house, screened by elms. Behind the stables were the paddocks, and two walled kitchen gardens. Around this domain, five thousand acres had once lain like a mantle.

Most of this, however, had been sold off after the Land Wars of the 1880s. Taxes had risen, and the succeeding Land Acts had whittled down the great estates all over Ireland. Only the home farm was left now, along with the worthless tracts scarred by an ancestor searching for copper. These raped, marshy acres had hazed over with viridian grasses, but their beauty could never be converted into anything as useful as hard cash. Once, the Carey family, Lords of Oughterard for two hundred years, had been rich and powerful. Now, with their fortune swallowed by the fictitious copper and the land parceled out among their former tenantry, the threadbare title was almost the only relic of that ancient grandeur.

The top floor of the house was boarded up because parts of the roof had fallen through the ceilings. Only owls lived there these days, and mice nested in the rotten stuffing of the old brocade chairs in the attics. Preserving pans, footbaths and derelict tubs lined the bare upstairs passages to catch the rain, which seeped through every crack, bringing the ornamental plasterwork down with it. The ranks of Grecian maidens on the wall-friezes had been decimated by the damp. The outside walls had rusty stains where the guttering had given way. The family inhabited the lower two stories.

Around them, they saw their parkland, once attended by six gardeners, reverting to the wild. The rose garden, lovingly designed and planted by a Victorian Lady Oughterard, was a riot of blooms in the summer, invaded by dog roses from the hedgerows. The circular beds of Gloire de Dijon were almost hidden beneath great fountains of honeysuckle, overpoweringly sweet in the warm twilight. At night, badgers and hares danced on the lawn in front of the ballroom windows where the bucks and belles of the county had waltzed years before.

The Careys themselves were also reverting to the wild, camping in their own house like tinkers. When her boys were young, Lady Oughterard had appeared at local entertainments in a silk gown trodden ragged around the hem and a dingy diamond tiara. Lord Oughterard, a huge, looselimbed, genial man, had managed to hunt four days a week in the season in a coat that was nearly transparent with age.

Oughterard had been a silent sort of man, but his wife had enough of a voice for the pair of them—a massive voice, which seemed to issue from lungs like a giant's leather bellows. Small and stocky, with curly black hair threaded with gray, keen blue eyes and a high pink complexion, she was the self-appointed magistrate, sage and busybody of the district.

When Oughterard died in 1904, a year after the Wyndham Act had put the last of his salable acres under the hammer, his widow had devoted herself bravely to her boys, selling everything that was not nailed down to pay for their education. Lucius, the present Lord Oughterard, now thirty, was her shelter and mainstay. Two years before, during yet another financial crisis, he had resigned his commission in the army to manage the farm.

The nickname "Muttonhead" had stuck to him as a child because of the slow, considered way he moved through life.

He was a terse, deliberate man, as undemonstrative and impenetrable as a slab of granite. When he removed his pipe from his mouth to speak, his utterances were brief, but sensational in effect. His word was absolute law. Tertius and Rory—although unable to resist teasing him—held him in awe. As his mother said, Muttonhead was as true as steel and as sound as a good nut. The whole countryside looked up to him—literally, since he stood four inches over six foot. He was very handsome, in a rough-hewn way, with heavy-lidded dark eyes and hair like thick brown furze. His face was tanned by his two years with his regiment in India, and lined by the Irish winds. When he stood in the drawing room in his hairy, locally made tweeds and muddy gaiters, he looked like a great oak tree hastily transplanted, with the soil still clinging to its roots.

His brother Fingal, now twenty-six, could not have been more of a contrast. Lady Oughterard had never understood him, and she often wondered if she had failed him in some way. As an infant, Fingal had been sickly and fretful, scared of his own shadow. As a child, he had been acidulous and secretive, always buried in a book. He had got himself to Cambridge on a scholarship, and now lived in London, where he earned his living as a barrister. Lady Oughterard assumed it was a good living—how else could he afford his silver cigarette cases, or his elaborate "country" outfits, which looked as if they belonged in a musical comedy? At the back of her mind, she sensed she was not getting the whole story. Muttonhead seemed to know more, but whenever she said: "Lucius, do you suppose anything is wrong?" he briefly removed the pipe from his mouth to grunt: "Leave him. He's all right."

Fingal was all elegance; thin as a whip, with long, fastidious fingers and slender limbs that automatically found graceful poses. His sharp white features were delicately chiseled, and he had fine hazel eyes, thickly lashed. Only his mouth, thin-lipped and peevish, marred his sleek good looks. Vulgarity outraged him, and during this brief stay at Castle Carey, he had taken great exception to the antics of Tertius.

At the very thought of Tertius, Lady Oughterard's heart contracted with love. He was his mother's darling, and lately, her torment. Her irresistibly delightful boy had grown into an irresistibly delightful, spoiled and idle young

man. If ever there was a human lily of the field, it was the
Honorable Tertius Carey. He certainly never toiled or
spun, but Solomon in all his glory could not compare with
him for beauty. He was the handsomest Carey for ten generations. Not one of the oily ancestors lining the drawing
room walls could match his eyes, blue as forget-me-nots,
his shining curls of black hair, or his fresh, seraphic face.

But what use were his looks, except to get him into trouble with the local girls? Lady Oughterard was still waiting
for him to settle down to something practical. Muttonhead
said he was worse than useless on the farm because he
spent all his time sketching, or lying asleep under hedges.
His mother suspected, although she would never have put
it into so many words, that his main interest was fornica-
tion. What was to become of him? Whenever she allowed
herself to worry, Lady Oughterard always ended up worrying about Tertius.

Muttonhead and Fingal had both been sent away to Upping-
ham, but by the time Tertius was old enough, there had been
no more money for an English public school. He had got his
education from Mr. Phillips at the rectory. It had been a
good, if somewhat old-fashioned education, too. Yet there
was no getting away from the fact that beside his brothers,
Tertius lacked a certain gentlemanly varnish. He had
scarcely set foot out of Connemara. As Muttonhead said,
he had "gone native." When Lady Oughterard had been a
girl, waltzing away the winter at the Viceregal Court in
Dublin, she had never imagined that she would produce a
son who spoke with a strong local accent, and chatted to
the villagers in Gaelic.

However, as Muttonhead also said, times were changing.
The previous January, they had lit tar barrels on Carey Hill
to celebrate the third reading of the Home Rule Bill. It
was doubtful what would become of the old Protestant gentry, when Ireland finally won a measure of independence.
There were fewer and fewer great Anglo-Irish estates and
fortunes, and hardly a family in the county that was not
feeling the pinch. We're being forced off the land, Lady
Oughterard thought sadly, until all we have left are these
ridiculous great houses we can't afford to live in or leave,
and our ridiculous social positions.

Fingal and Rory were right to look for their futures elsewhere. In the quiet hour before dinner, while the color

rapidly bled out of the sky and the shadows darkened, Muttonhead retired to the gun room. This supremely uncomfortable stone-flagged cell at the end of the kitchen passage was his private territory. He spent most of his spare moments here, among the fishing baskets, rods, guns and boxes of cartridges. The shelves were filled with damp-bloated farm ledgers and game books dating back fifty years. Beneath the high barred window was a battered rolltop desk cluttered with pipe racks, unpaid bills and jars of live bait.

On this evening, the usual smell of mildew was leavened with coal tar soap. Muttonhead was sitting in a tin bath, smoking his pipe and reading the *Cork Examiner* by the light of the fire. He did not look up when Tertius crashed in without knocking.

"Muttonhead, can you do us a favor?"

"How much?"

"Enough to get me to London."

Tertius perched on the edge of the desk while the wheels of Muttonhead's brain turned. The pipe came out of his mouth several times, before he said: "She'll never have you. No good chasing her."

"So you won't cough up?"

"I didn't say that. What do you intend to do?"

"The only thing I can do. I'm going to be a painter."

Muttonhead grunted disgustedly. "Better than nothing, I suppose. Do you good to get away. You're no bloody use here."

After this long speech he sealed himself up with his pipe to consider further. Tertius lit a cigarette, not at all offended by the response. There was an amused gleam in the depths of Muttonhead's dark eyes, which those who knew him well recognized as affection. They sat in a silence broken only by the shifting of the peat on the fire.

Tertius thought how enormous his eldest brother looked without his clothes. His hard, hairy limbs were sprawled over the rim of the bath, and the water barely reached his navel. His long penis, in its thick black hedge of pubic hair, swayed in the gentle current made by his breathing.

"The Mater will be a problem," he observed finally. "She won't like losing you."

"You can settle her, Mutt. Hasn't she said herself it's time I found something to work at?"

"She's a woman. Don't expect logic. Still, she'll come

around." Another spell of silence. "Is Rory your only reason?"

"Yes, of course. She's been on at me to take my painting seriously."

"You've been out screwing," said Muttonhead. "I can smell it on you."

"Who, me?" Tertius tried to look injured.

"Haven't got anyone in the family way, have you?"

"Certainly not!"

"Glad to hear it." Muttonhead rarely mentioned his brother's sexual adventures. Tertius was desperately curious to know how he got his own satisfaction. He can't be going without, he thought; not a man like him, with a cock that size. But where and with whom? In a countryside where the gossips could spy out a grain of sand, Muttonhead had seemingly achieved the impossible—perfect discretion.

"What do you say?" Tertius asked him. "Will you let me have the cash for the boat?"

"Depends when you want to leave. Things'll be tight for a week or so."

"Fine. Don't tell anyone yet. Keep it under your hat."

"Suit yourself. How will you manage?"

"You know me. I'm always fine."

"True." Muttonhead raised his pipe, then lowered it again. "Don't expect Fingal to look after you."

"Why not?" Tertius was startled. What were brothers for, if you could not sponge off them?

"Because—well, he can't afford you, for one thing. Now, go and dress for dinner. The Mater wants a good show. Rory's last night, and all that."

"Right-oh. Where is Rory?"

"Upstairs," Muttonhead frowned suddenly. "She was in a fearful state earlier. Nothing to do with you, I suppose?"

"No, Mutt, I swear."

"Listen here—" Slowly and carefully Muttonhead stood up in the bath, letting the water run off his body. It was an impressive sight. "Pass me that towel. Thanks. Now, you listen. If ever I get to hear about you pestering Rory, I will give you the mother and father of all hidings. You won't have a whole bone left. Is that clear?"

"Yes."

"All right. You can bugger off now."

Tertius dashed upstairs, to change into the rusty, soup-stained evening clothes he had inherited from his father. He was late. While he was straining his neck into the unfamiliar stiff collar, he heard carriage wheels crunching the weedy gravel of the drive, and the loud voice of his mother trumpeting greetings downstairs.

Lady Oughterard loved to entertain, though the great days of her hospitality were over. To mark Fingal's visit and Rory's last evening at home, she had invited her three nearest neighbors: Justus Carlington, the Reverend Mr. Phillips and old Emma Billinghurst. Miss Billinghurst was a disagreeable spinster renowned for her eccentricities—she slept in a tent in her garden in all weathers, and could be seen on her lawn in the mornings doing deep knee-bends in a flannel bathing suit. When Rory and Tertius were children she had been their sworn foe, and Tertius still groaned inwardly at the thought of being civil to her for a whole evening.

The dinner would, in any case, be unbearable unless he made it up with Rory. She was not to know about his plan to follow her to London, but it was essential to soften her up in advance, so that she would be pleased to see him. Mentally preparing an apology of the utmost poignancy, he went down the long passage to her bedroom.

The door was open, and a gramophone was wheezing out the overture to *Mignon.* Rory could be heard laughing as Fingal's high-pitched voice cried: "The gold, darling, the gold—it's too divine with your hair."

The shabby velvet curtains had been drawn against the twilight. Dozens of candles flickered on the chimneypiece and dressing table. An old trunk lay open on the floor, spewing out a tangle of antique clothes, relics of long-dead Lady Oughterards. Fingal was hooking Rory into a dress of deep yellow silk, brittle with age, dating from the 1830s. Its tight waist, full sleeves and billowing skirts softened Rory's sharper angles and gave her slenderness an unexpected grace. Her shoulders rose white as bone above the scooped-out neckline, and her bobbed hair, set against the rich fabric, was almost wine-red.

Tertius stood in the doorway gazing at her, sick with love and praying not to get an erection. The dress seemed to symbolize Rory's escape into adulthood. It put more distance between them than the Irish sea. He was so stunned

that it took him a second to nótice that Fingal was also
wearing a dress. His was blue, with a collapsed bustle and
sweeping train. The back gaped open, showing his evening
shirt and white braces. There was a bottle of gin on the
bureau, and Rory had a glass in her hand. They were
both laughing.

"Look what he's done to me!" Rory cried, seeing Tertius. "I can't possibly go down like this!"

"Tell her, Tershie," urged Fingal. "Doesn't she look sublime?" They waltzed around the room, treading on each
other's skirts, and collapsed on the bed giggling.

"Gin, is it?" Tertius came in and took a swig from the
bottle. "Have you had this all along and never told us?
Jesus, you're a mean little shoneen."

"Dear heart," shrieked Fingal, "who is 'Jaysus'? Really,
the pair of you—I've met Irish laborers with a better grasp
of English. Oh, how glad I shall be to get back to
civilization!"

Tertius and Rory made their "Fingal face" at each
other—a hideous grimace with their chins retracted and
their lower lips drawn up behind their front teeth—and
began laughing so helplessly that eventually Fingal joined
in.

"Fiends," he said amiably, "give me the bottle. I need
sustenance for the awful evening ahead." He gulped down
another shot of gin. "Hours and hours of politics and rustic
tittle-tattle. Mind you"—he paraded in front of the glass,
expertly manipulating his long train—"if I wore this down
to dinner that old sapphist Emma Billinghurst would probably think I was rather a peach."

"I suppose we should go down," Rory said, wiping her
eyes. "Now, seriously, boys—aren't I a complete guy in this
moldy old gown?"

"I insist that you wear it!" Fingal stepped out of his
own frock. "It's a thousand times more becoming than that
shudder-making Suffragette sack you were putting on when
I came in. Just you thank heaven fasting that I remembered
the Mater's dressing-up box."

"Do wear it, Rory-May," begged Tertius. "You don't
know how lovely you are."

Fingal took his jacket off the bedpost and settled the
bow in his black silk tie. "She is lovely, but it's not your
place to say so, you wicked boy. Aurora has told me all

about your licentiousness this morning. She asked my advice, as one versed in affairs of the heart, and I was simply appalled."

"Liar!" exclaimed Rory. "You said only shopgirls made a fuss about their purity these days."

"Well, I may have, but you mustn't let him know he's forgiven so soon."

Rory finally met Tertius's hungry gaze. "I always forgive him. You won't tell on him to Muttonhead, will you?"

"My justice is tempered with mercy," declared Fingal. "Wild horses couldn't drag it out of me—not if they were on their bended knees and had beautiful long eyelashes."

Tertius kissed Rory's hand. "I'm sorry, I truly am. I'll never take liberties again—" The other two hooted so loudly at this that he decided to shelve the rest of his apology.

"Now I really must take this silly dress off!" said Rory.

"No you won't! Take a hold of her, Tershie."

Fingal and Tertius grabbed an arm each and dragged Rory down the stairs. They exploded into the drawing room, bright-eyed and boisterous.

The Reverend Mr. Phillips, the white-haired, red-faced Protestant clergyman, had been holding forth beside the fire. He broke off to stare at his former pupil.

"Aurora, my dear—well, this is a transformation. The butterfly unfolds her wings at last. Dear me, how fast these children grow up."

"Darling, how pretty you look!" Lady Oughterard appealed to Justus Carlington, who was sitting hunched on the window seat like a bespectacled praying mantis. "Isn't she the image of poor Charlotte?"

"Yes, there is a resemblance," Justus conceded, peering at his daughter curiously. "But aren't your shoulders cold?"

"Papa, don't be a fusspot." Rory felt color mounting in her cheeks. She had worn the silk dress as a joke, yet the faces around her were full of a new respect. It was gratifying, and a little disturbing.

Muttonhead looked her up and down in such grave silence that she was afraid he disapproved. Finally, he whistled, and pronounced: "You're a corker."

Embarrassed, Rory hurried through her greetings, shaking hands with Mr. Phillips and Miss Billinghurst, and giving her father a brief, dutiful peck on his lank cheek.

Mr. Phillips turned back to Muttonhead, to resume his speech. "Bad feeling is what we must avoid at all costs, Oughterard. Doyle has great influence over these people. He's constantly stirring them up from his pulpit—"

"Openly inciting them to be disrespectful," interrupted Miss Billinghurst, in her gravelly voice. Being feared and disliked, she always got the best that was going, and she was sitting now at the easiest end of the old Hepplewhite sofa. She wore a shapeless gown of brown velveteen, studded in odd places with brooches—"Like the shrunken heads of her enemies," Rory whispered to Tertius—and every time she moved, there was a smell of mothballs.

"Home Rule will be the thin end of the wedge," Mr. Phillips said, shaking his head. "If men like Doyle have their way, there won't be a single Protestant left in Ireland from the center to the sea."

"Nonsense," snapped Justus. "The Irish peasant doesn't understand the first thing about religion or politics. All these people care about is land. You have to understand their historical relationship with the soil. Doyle can talk at them until he's blue in the face, but anything abstract simply sails over their heads."

"They would murder their own mothers for half an acre," agreed Miss Billinghurst. "I don't need another Home Rule Bill to persuade me to keep a loaded gun beside my bed. I remember the Land Wars."

"Dear me, yes," said Lady Oughterard, "what dreadful times those were. The rents went down to nothing, and if you evicted you couldn't get another tenant to come near the place for fear of the hillside men. Look what happened to our Paddy Finnegan—he moved into a vacant cottage, and the Land-Leaguers came in the night with their faces all blackened with soot, and sliced off one of his earlobes. Terrible."

"Criminal," supplied Miss Billinghurst. "Absolute daylight robbery, and the government blackmailed into going along with it. Phillips is quite right—Home Rule is nothing short of betrayal."

"But who's being betrayed?" demanded Rory. "We're Irish people. Why should we submit to being governed by another country?"

Mr. Phillips was shocked. "It's not another country. It's England. You don't seem to have thought, my dear, of what we will lose if Ireland falls into the hands of the Catholics. I don't know what Doyle imagines will become of his little black rose, without a class of educated Protestants."

"Well, if we ever had anything to lose, it seems to me that we've lost it already," Rory said with the brutality of youth, glancing around at the dilapidated grandeur of the drawing room. "The English don't think we're English, and the Irish don't think we're Irish, so it's up to us to decide where we belong. If we simply go on telling each other how civilized we are, with no money and our houses tumbling down on our heads, we'll be nothing but a laughingstock."

Everyone watched Muttonhead. The local gentry were constantly trying to squeeze out his political opinions, but it was difficult to know exactly where his sympathies lay. He stood, massive and inscrutable, surrounded by the smoke-blackened portraits of his forebears. His own image, painted by Tertius, gazed down at them between the two long windows. All he said was: "We must adapt or die." Forgetting he was in evening dress, he stamped on one of the logs in the grate, sending up a storm of sparks.

"I'd rather die," said Miss Billinghurst grimly. "If the government won't protect us, we must protect ourselves."

"From what?" Rory persisted. "There aren't any ribbon societies or Land-Leaguers or hillside men left these days. More's the pity."

Lady Oughterard laughed. "She's a born Fenian."

"But a very pretty one," Mr. Phillips said gallantly. "Before you know it, she'll be coming home with a grand English husband in her pocket. Don't you say yes to any of those swells without asking our permission first."

"Don't you start, too," sighed Rory. "I can't hold another drop of advice. Papa has been on and on at me, though he hasn't been in London since the flood. And Muttonhead has been positively loquacious. He gave me such a lecture last night—the first time I've seen him open his mouth long enough to let the flies in." Enjoying the arrogant rustle of her long skirts, she reached for the whiskey decanter.

"Leave that alone, miss," said Muttonhead, relighting his pipe.

"Be a sport—my last day!"

"Sherry."

"Honestly, you're so old-fashioned." But she obeyed him, and poured herself a small glass of the pale sherry.

"Muttonhead may be something of a dinosaur," Fingal said, "but I think his antediluvian attitudes rather suit him. Every family should have one thoroughly traditional type."

"So you'll be staying with your aunt?" asked Mr. Phillips.

"Charlotte's sister," Justus told him. "Nothing like her. She claimed to have washed her hands of Aurora after the sorry business at that boarding school, but her sense of duty always prevails in the end. She means well."

"There you are, Muttonhead," cried Rory, "I told you Aunt Hilda was horrid. What a thing to have on one's tombstone: 'She Meant Well.' " Muttonhead gave a brief grunt of laughter. "Hope she takes a slipper to you for cheek. You deserve it."

Una came in, wiping her hands on her apron. "Dinner is served, my lady." Una was a tall Irish beauty, much given to drama. Now over sixty, she was still square-shouldered and high-colored, with a youthful gloss to her heavy coils of black hair. She had been in service at Castle Carey since girlhood, and deeply resented the decline of its fortunes. "Come in quick, before the sauce cools to a blanket. It's seldom enough I get my hands on anything decent and I'd like it appreciated."

Everyone brightened, for Una was an excellent cook. Fingal, who had been yawning in a corner, said: "Do let's eat it without another helping of politics. There must be something else to talk about."

"That shows how long you've been away," said Tertius.

Justus gave Lady Oughterard his arm. "I'm sure you've done wonders, Una. I only wish our Mrs. MacNamara could roast chickens as you do, instead of boiling them."

"I can only do my best," Una said haughtily, "with the house at sixes and sevens, and everybody leaving, and the banshee crying her heart out under the eaves."

Muttonhead gave a short but expressive snort of disgust.

"I know you don't believe in her, Mr. Muttonhead, and very ungracious you are when she loves every hair of you. The night your father died, she wailed so you could hear her in the kitchen."

"And have you heard her tonight?" Lady Oughterard had been battling against local superstitions for years, but she could not conquer a sneaking interest in the Carey banshee. According to Una, this ghostly creature haunted the family for the sole purpose of mourning its misfortunes.

"Some might say it was the wind. I say it was the banshee."

"Wish to God we could sell her," said Muttonhead. "If she could mend the roof instead of camping under it she'd be worth something."

"May you never live to repent those words," Una snapped at him, over the general shout of laughter.

They moved across the hall to the dining room. Una had done her best with the table, placing the candlesticks to hide the darns in the old damask cloth. The candlelight had the effect of softening their faces, and cruelly bringing out the whitening seams of their clothes. Fingal, in his dazzling linen and gold cuff links, seemed to come from another world. His hair, carefully oiled, was sleek as patent leather beside the rough, curly heads of his brothers.

He was destined to be disappointed about the politics, for they started up again as soon as Una had removed the soup plates and taken around the vegetables.

"You're poorly defended here," announced Miss Billinghurst. "Anyone could get in through these French windows."

Rory, Fingal and Tertius, already in a hilarious mood from the gin they had drunk upstairs, dared not meet each other's eyes. Miss Billinghurst always made them howl.

"Who would want to?" wondered Lady Oughterard. "Everyone knows the front door is always open."

"If it comes to a fight," Miss Billinghurst told the table, "I'm prepared. For hand-to-hand combat, if need be."

This was too much. There were sounds of smothered giggles, quelled by a stern look from Muttonhead.

"Guns," said Miss Billinghurst, loading her fork with chicken, "that's what you need. Take those old flintlocks off the wall."

"It will never come to that," Justus said. "The Bill has put paid to it. We won't see another '67."

"The Protestants are arming themselves in Ulster," barked Miss Billinghurst. "The question is, when are you going to join them, Oughterard? The Ulster Volunteers need men like you, with army experience."

Rory was not having this. "Mutt doesn't want to waste

his time drilling a lot of old Ulstermen with rolled umbrellas! They're just bank clerks playing at soldiers."

The smell of mothballs around Miss Billinghurst intensified. "One day, Aurora, you'll bless those bank clerks for their protection of your country."

"Do they admit ladies to their ranks?" Tertius asked suavely.

"Don't imagine I wouldn't join them if I could, young man! I'd defend the Union to the last drop of my blood! Fortunately, they have no need of me. Unlike your brother, there's many an officer willing to give himself to the cause. And then let them try to force the Bill through. What British officer would consent to fire on his own comrades?"

Muttonhead was frowning. "I'm not a British officer anymore. I'm a Galway farmer. That's all."

"All? You'd let other men do your fighting for you?—Oh!"

There was a loud crack. Miss Billinghurst screamed and crashed to the floor in the fragments of her chair, treating them all to a display of knee-length flannel bloomers.

"The bad chair!" Lady Oughterard cried in anguish. "I knew one of them was unsafe and I prayed it was mine! Oh, Emma, Emma!" While Muttonhead and Mr. Phillips leaped up to pull Miss Billinghurst to her feet, she dived for a severed leg, riddled with woodworm like a hail of fairy bullet holes. "My mother's swan-backed chairs—oh, what a pity! Emma, are you hurt?"

"You three!" Muttonhead raised his voice threateningly above the shrieks of laughter. Rory, Tertius and Fingal were in purple-faced hysterics, clutching their stomachs and choking helplessly. "Out!"

"You little horrors!" Lady Oughterard admonished them with the chair leg. "How could you be so unfeeling and rude?"

Miss Billinghurst was mottled with fury. "Grace Carey, you have the most vulgar, unmannerly children in this county—everyone knows it but you. Carlington will live to rue the day he ever left his daughter in your care. Don't look to me for pity when they bring your gray hairs down in sorrow to the grave. I'm going home this instant."

"I'll see you out." Muttonhead offered his arm, taking a sideswipe at Tertius with his napkin.

"Please don't trouble, Lord Oughterard. I thought I had

an officer and a gentleman for a neighbor, and not a Galway farmer too selfish to defend his country's flag!"

Out she swept, like the bad fairy at the christening. Muttonhead, looking furious, followed her, to perform the polite but unlovely task of helping her into her jaunting car.

"Lord!" said Fingal, still tittering nervously. "We'll catch it now."

"And so you should." Lady Oughterard was troubled. "Lucius is quite right to be angry with you."

Rory refused to be daunted at the prospect of Muttonhead's rare and terrible anger. "Don't take any notice of her, Mater darling. We mightn't be much of a credit to you, but it's not your fault. And she was only getting at Papa because of the row they had when Parnell died."

"Elephants and Billinghursts, you know," Justus said vaguely. "She never can forget."

They heard Muttonhead's heavy footsteps returning. Mr. Phillips and Justus hemmed and stared down at their plates. He took his place with a brow of thunder. They began to eat again, in agonizing silence.

Then Rory said: "It's getting awfully dark. I hope her broomstick has lights on it."

Everyone winced. Muttonhead swiveled his eyes toward her very slowly, emitting a bass growl.

Her gaze did not waver. "These May breezes can be so cruel. What a comfort it is to know she's got her warm underwear on."

Muttonhead slammed down his knife so hard that all the glasses jumped. "Drop it."

" 'An Ode to Miss Billinghurst,' " Rory announced. She rolled her eyes and extended a hand theatrically.

"O, Old Billinghurst is come out of the West!
Through all the wide borders, her bloomers were best!
So thick and so hairy, so dauntless in wars!
Not one knight could breach those impregnable
    drawers!"

Muttonhead looked for a moment as if he would explode, then suddenly let out a great bellow of laughter.

Immediately, as if he had released a spring, they all went into convulsions of laughter—even Una, listening behind the door—and could not stop for several minutes.

After this, the evening became uproarious. Muttonhead poured the wine himself, kindly allowing his mother and Rory more than he normally considered good for them. Lady Oughterard was still laughing over the poem when the pair of them were exiled to the drawing room.

"You are a bad girl. I don't know why we encourage those saucy rhymes of yours."

"I used to think I was going to be a great poetess," Rory sighed, stretching herself out on the sofa to ease her aching ribs. "But saucy rhymes is all it's come to. I accept that my talent for doggerel will never set the Thames on fire. So much for the literary salon of my youthful dreams."

The men did not leave them alone for long. Rory and Lady Oughterard spent only twenty minutes pretending not to hear all the pipes groaning in concert, as they took turns in the downstairs lavatory. Then Muttonhead appeared, carrying the heavy silver tray of coffee himself, to save Una's back.

Fingal, in a rosy flush of high spirits, brought down his gramophone and taught Rory "Shaking the Shimmy" and the two-step, filling the drawing room with the tinny grind of ragtime. When he was breathless, Muttonhead put on a waltz, and Rory stood on his feet while he danced her around the room, just as they used to do when she was small.

All this time, Tertius watched her quietly, leaning over the back of his mother's chair. Rory was aware that his eyes were pinned to her, and through her laughing and romping she felt a chilly void opening in her stomach at the idea of leaving him the next morning. If only he could be made to understand.

Under cover of Justus and Mr. Phillips' leaving, she went to him and laid her hand on his sleeve.

"Tershie—"

"Oh God, Rory-May, please don't say it!" His warm hand covered her cold one. "I can't bear it twice in one day. It hurts me to look at you, I love you so."

"And I love you—you know it perfectly well. But not in the way you want, that's all. Goodness knows, I've tried and tried."

"Have you?"

"Yes, and it simply doesn't work. There's nothing wrong with you, so it must be me."

"Couldn't you keep trying, just a little longer?" His voice was at its softest and most dangerously persuasive.

"I don't think it's much use."

"I can wait. You have a good time, and think of me sometimes."

The innocent blue eyes misted piteously, the corners of his guileless mouth lifted in a smile of heart-rending melancholy. Perversely, Rory had the smallest twinge of suspicion. No—she was instantly ashamed of herself. "Of course I will, old thing."

She did not know that Lady Oughterard had been observing the whole scene.

When Fingal had gone to bed, exhausted by drink and hilarity, and Tertius had joined Muttonhead for a smoke in the gun room, she asked, "Rory—have I been a good mother to you?"

The question was so odd and so unexpected that Rory did not know how to reply. "I—you've always been—I mean, you're the only mother I've ever had."

"But not your real mother. It didn't seem to matter when you were a little girl."

Rory spoke gruffly. Emotion always made her uncomfortable. "Is this because of what old Emma said?"

"I took on a very special responsibility with you. I'd never forgive myself if my upbringing of you had been—wrong, in any way."

It was bewildering to see her so doubtful. Rory noticed, with a stab of pain, how deep the lines were around her eyes.

"Papa wouldn't have done it any better," she said.

"I think of you as mine. And I shouldn't."

"You must! I am yours!"

"I never told you, darling—" Lady Oughterard was struggling to find the right words. She was equally inept at expressing her deepest feelings. "I never told the boys—a few months after you were born, I lost the baby girl I was carrying. Oh, she was only as big as that"—she measured a pitiful little space in the air—"but I wanted her so much. And there you were, over at Marystown. I know I behaved as if I was doing a noble thing, taking you off your father's hands, but I do sometimes wonder now if it was really a form of stealing."

"Nobody else wanted me," Rory muttered fiercely.

"You've been a comfort and a joy to me, I hope you always will be. But, Rory dear, the fact remains—it's an important fact—that my boys are not your brothers."

"They are to me."

"No." Lady Oughterard was recovering her firmness. "You've got to stop believing it."

"Because of Tertius?" They had never spoken about this openly before. Rory was afraid. The wind of change was blowing, and its breath was icy.

"Yes. He really is in love with you."

"What if he is? I've never given him any encouragement."

"I know, I'm not blaming you." She took both Rory's hands in hers, shaking them gently for emphasis. "But he's so stubborn, he can wear down a stone. And he has such a way with him that you feel like a monster if you refuse him anything. I may be his doting old mother, but even I can see that you'd be throwing yourself away. I have to remember that he is a grown young man, and you are a grown young woman who is in my care. You must remember it too. If I kept you here with him, I'd be doing you a real injury. You do see, don't you, that I'm sending you away for your own sake? It isn't that I want you to leave."

Rory stood up, with the folds of gold silk falling around her, and went to the window to look out at the stars. The night was clear and beautiful. Reflected in the dark pane, she saw another Rory; a grown woman, standing alone in a long dress. And it seemed as if that shadow on the other side of the glass was her real self, staring back at the childish Rory in the drawing room.

It was true. The change must be made, and the old ties seen for what they were. She turned to face Lady Oughterard.

"You're right. You and the boys will always be my family, but I can't go on pretending in the old way. When there's a sea between us, Tertius might even forget me."

"Don't—don't forget us, though, will you?"

Rory saw what it had cost poor Lady Oughterard to set her free. Kneeling at her feet, she took her in her arms.

"No sea is wide enough for that, Mater. Many waters cannot quench love."

Two

Scottish Borders

It was only three o'clock but Jenny's head was already aching with frustration. Rosalys and Gertrude Kentish had been staring at the same French verb for one solid hour and every time she tried to make them repeat it after her, they gaped at her like a pair of slow-blooded fish. Mrs. Kentish had been forced to take them away from their boarding school at very short notice because of an epidemic of measles. Jenny, temporarily engaged as their governess, had been warned to watch for signs of ill health. Unkindly, she wondered now if they had contracted measles without anyone noticing, and suffered irreparable brain damage. She had never met such stupid children.

"Do try it again, Rosalys," she said gently. "I'm sure you can say it nicely if you make an effort."

"I hate French," said Rosalys, a sullen, whey-faced ten-year-old. "And I hate Scotland. I want to go home to London." She glared accusingly out of the schoolroom window. "It's always raining here. There's nothing to do." The hills and woods outside were half-obscured by a drooping gray cloud of drizzle.

Jenny was pining for the velvety caress of the dampness, and a lungful of the earth-scented air. "When you can both say *Etre* without your books, we'll go for a walk."

Both children set up a wail of protest.

"Walking's beastly," said Gertrude, a sour twelve-year-old. "I wish I'd stayed at school and caught the measles."

"I don't see why we can't have a holiday," Rosalys muttered rebelliously. "It's beastly mean, making us work all day."

"You were complaining a moment ago that you had nothing to do," began Jenny. Then she sighed and shut the

French grammar. "Hasn't your mother said anything about leaving yet? I thought she had only taken the lodge for a month." Much as she needed the money, she was counting the days until she could return to Edinburgh.

"She won't budge, because she thinks Mr. MacNeil is going to propose to Isola," Gertrude said, unconsciously imitating her mother's fussy, self-important tones. "And I wish he'd hurry up about it."

"He's ever so spoony on her," piped up Rosalys. "He whispers to her behind the curtains for ages."

Jenny summoned up her strength, willing herself to shake off the headache. Governessing was loathsome, Gertrude and Rosalys had been rendered unbearable by a combination of neglect and spoiling, and Mrs. Kentish's exuberant vulgarity pained her every nerve. But each week that Mr. MacNeil failed to propose to Isola helped to lift the burden of her college fees from her parents. She must try to be grateful for that, at least, and stop fretting because the Kentishes refused to leave the rented lodge for their home in St. John's Wood.

"Let's put our French books aside for the moment," she said briskly. "Rosalys, get down *Lamb's Tales* and show me how well you can parse."

Rosalys scowled and gnawed the end of her hair ribbon. The words "I hate parsing" were on her tongue, but Jenny was spared hearing them. Mrs. Kentish, clad in a silk tea gown with trailing sleeves, came sweeping into the room. She was handsome in a larger-than-life fashion, like a gleaming, newly painted tailor's dummy in a West End shop. Her jutting bosom was a tangle of gilt chains, from which keys, eyeglasses and lockets depended. Numerous lace handkerchiefs, heavily scented, sprouted from various openings in her dress.

"How are my busy little bees?"

"Mummy, we're so tired of lessons!" whined Gertrude.

"Poor precious." Mrs. Kentish hardly heard her. The main occupation of her life was marrying off her eldest daughter. Jenny had been hired less to teach her younger children than to keep them out of the way.

"Can't we come downstairs?"

"Later, poppet. I'm busy getting ready for the party, and I don't want you cherubs in my way. Miss Dalgleish, give them something to do, and come down to the morning room." She swept out again, with a firm, royal tread, which made the windows rattle.

Jenny rose calmly, smoothing her gray tweed skirt and mentally gritting her teeth. The servants, all but the lady's maid, were rented with the lodge, and they had not taken kindly to Mrs. Kentish. She had fallen into the habit of using Jenny to fill the gaps left by their insubordination. "Girls, you may read your storybooks."

"I hate—" Rosalys began.

"Then do what you like. Only for heaven's sake, stay up here and don't bother Cook." *Or it will be left to me to placate her afterward,* she added to herself. She went downstairs, hoping she was not expected to spend the rest of the afternoon brushing leaves and burrs from Peek-a-Boo, Mrs. Kentish's fierce Pekingese.

In the morning room, where the bay window commanded a weeping, khaki view of the hills, Isola Kentish, wrapped in a pink silk kimono, was lying on the sofa flicking through the *Strand Magazine.* Isola was undoubtedly the beauty of the family, with her wandlike figure, alabaster complexion and thick knot of waving chestnut hair. But she was lazy and peevish, and her voluptuous lips were usually curled into an expression of scornful boredom. She lifted her drowsy blue eyes only briefly when she saw Jenny.

Mrs. Kentish was paddling her ringed fingers in a pile of papers at the escritoire. "Miss Dalgleish, I left all the place cards for tonight at the stationer's and I simply can't make that awful little coachman understand that I want the carriage again. You're such a sturdy walker, I'm sure you won't mind trotting into town to get them."

"Not at all," Jenny said eagerly. "I'll go now, if you think the children will be all right."

"Poor little pets," said Mrs. Kentish absently. "You might look into the hotel, too, and remind them to send the waiters up on time. I'm frantic, absolutely frantic, and Isola won't do a thing."

"Nobody forced you to throw a party," murmured Isola. "You don't even know most of the people you've invited."

"My darling, I'm doing this for you!" She turned back to Jenny with a patronizing smile. "I'm sure the children have told you that Isola is about to be married. Little tongues will wag, and it's no good expecting them to be discreet in front of outsiders. Poor Mr. MacNeil is utterly smitten with her, but he can't get up the courage to pop the question. The surroundings are all wrong, of course. He can't feel romantic in this depressing countryside. But when the house is full of flowers and music—"

"There's no need to launch me at his head like a torpedo," Isola said, from the depths of her magazine. "Why can't you let me manage my own proposal?"

Mrs. Kentish decided not to notice the interruption. "You've heard of Mr. MacNeil—the laird—of course? He lives up in that splendid castle on the hill and owns all the land for simply miles. When we called on him yesterday, he insisted on whisking Isola away all by herself to show her the new storm drains."

"It was madly romantic," said Isola.

"And you should have taken an interest!" snapped Mrs. Kentish.

"Can I do anything else while I'm in town?" Jenny asked, anxious to end the conversation.

Isola focused upon her languidly. "Goodness, Miss Dalgleish, how very energetic you Scotch people are. I suppose you're used to this ghastly weather."

"Here's the note for the stationer." Mrs. Kentish waved a hand sparkling with diamonds. "Make it clear that I sent you personally. I find that my name has a magical effect among these simple folk. Oh, and I do hope you will join in our modest festivities. I shall rest easy if I know you're there to keep an eye on the little ones. There's no need to dress up—that white thing of yours will do very well."

"You're very kind, Mrs. Kentish," Jenny said dryly. She knew exactly what the invitation meant. She would be carrying coats and handing around coffee all night, like a glorified parlormaid, when she had hoped to catch up on some work in her room.

"Don't mention it!" trilled Mrs. Kentish graciously. "Now, run along."

Jenny ran along, delighted to be released. Ten minutes later, dressed in her gray tweed Norfolk jacket, with a scarlet tam-o'-shanter pulled over her soft brown hair, she was striding away from Craig Lodge and the Kentishes as fast as she could. After six weeks of walking off her impatience and her wounded pride among the misty umbers and greens of the Borders countryside, she was beginning to love Glen Ruthven. It was such a shame, she thought, that Isola Kentish, who was soon to own it, was so blind to its beauties. Her spirits rose as she took the shortcut through the forest.

Reveling in the cool May air and bathing her face in the filmy drizzle, she thought of the letter she had received that morning from Eleanor. *Viola will be married at the end of the season,* she had written. *Why don't you come to us now and enjoy a month or two of dissipation? Mother would be so pleased.* Eleanor was a dear girl, but it had not occurred to her that girls who were working their passage through college were unlikely to drop everything and dash down to London for a society wedding. Rory was apparently coming over from Ireland and Jenny yearned for a sight of her: She had met up with Eleanor and Francesca the previous summer, during a holiday in the Lake District, but she had not laid eyes on Rory since the morning she had left Winterbourne House six years before.

It was quite impossible, of course. Her savings would have covered a modest season's worth of gloves, gowns and stockings. Such a small sum of money would have meant nothing to wealthy Eleanor Braddon or spoiled Isola Kentish. However, it was Jenny's only hope of independence. After two weary years of governessing, she had built up enough to pay her expenses at Somerville, over and above the scholarship she had won. And after that she supposed she would earn her living as a teacher. Miss Maud Westwood, still firmly at the helm of Winterbourne House, had written to her promising to keep a position open. Dreaming about London seasons, parties and concerts, and other delights reserved for rich girls, was simply useless. Jenny had learned long ago to accept the situation, and to make the best of it.

The exercise sent the blood racing through her parched veins. Her small hourglass figure strode lightly and nimbly over the bracken.

Then, as if she had looked into a mirror but sensed rather than seen something moving behind her, Jenny suddenly halted. A cold hand was around her heart, and the quiet woods screamed with a terrible urgency. The certainty of a future grief flooded through her. Something terrible would happen unless she did something immediately.

Listening, she heard a hoarse cry near her, a creature in danger. She followed the sound to the edge of the clearing. Beyond the shelter of the trees, the ground suddenly dropped into a small ravine. A shallow stream foamed over rocks, some twenty feet below. Driven by the inexplicable sense of urgency, Jenny looked down. The edge of the ravine was ragged and naked roots wormed out of the loose earth. The cry came again and she found what she was looking for. A dog, a large brown terrier with a rough coat, had fallen into the ravine, catching its collar on a branch on the way down. It was struggling in its piteous final agony, its legs reaching for footholds in midair.

Jenny's panic receded, and was replaced by determination. She did not care for heights, and avoided risk when she could, but this was something she had to do. Kneeling down, she calculated that by balancing one foot on a solid-looking rock, and gripping one of the exposed roots, she could reach down with her other hand and pull the dog free.

"I'm coming," she said aloud, buttoning her leather gloves. And with her pulse beating in her dry throat, she gingerly climbed down. Her palm ached with the effort of holding the root and the glove split across the back. Stretching out her other arm, she reached the dog's collar and, with a mighty effort, unhooked it. The weight of the animal was pulling her bones out of their sockets. The pair seemed certain to fall, and although the drop was not deep, she could easily break something and lie there for hours. She had risked her limbs for a dog's life as if her own depended upon it.

All this took only seconds. Miraculously, the dog jumped onto a shelf of rock and climbed back to the top of the ravine, scrambling over Jenny's head and shoulders and spraying her with loose earth. Breathlessly, with sweat collecting under the band of her hat, Jenny began to pull herself up while the dog barked out its triumph above her.

"Inky, where in God's name have you been, you imbecile? Great Scott—" A hand closed around Jenny's wrist and heaved her back to firm ground. "What on earth are you playing at? Did you fall?"

Jenny sedately brushed the dirt from her jacket, and fleetingly regretted the torn glove. She took pride in the neatness and rightness of her appearance.

"Your dog did," she explained. "He got his collar caught. He would have been strangled."

The man she assumed to be the dog's owner stared at

her in amazement. She could not blame him. The rashness of the exploit was extraordinary when considered in cold blood. No attempt could be made to explain her moment of premonition.

"Do you really mean to tell me you climbed down of your own free will, just for the sake of this idiotic creature?"

He was not, in Jenny's twenty-year-old eyes, a young man—perhaps thirty-seven or thirty-eight. His pale blue eyes looked out of a net of fine wrinkles. Fifteen years before, he would have been a bonny, red-cheeked, fair-haired lad. There was enough of the youthful roundness and color left in his face to suggest this. It was not a handsome face, but it was friendly and attractive, and Jenny unconsciously warmed to it, even though the man evidently thought her quixotic to the point of madness.

The line of his close-cropped yellow hair was beginning to recede, and his exposed forehead balanced a chin that was a shade too broad. He was tall and thin, but radiated good health and easy good nature. More important, as the hawk eyes of Jenny's mother would instantly have discerned, his plus fours and jacket were expertly cut from the kind of superfine tweed that Mrs. Dalgleish sighed over in Princes Street before settling for something a shade less perfect. His brown leather gaiters were polished like toffee. His stance was confident and soldierly, and his voice was just faintly tinged with the Borders accent. He was a gentleman.

"I couldn't let him die," she said. "Could I?"

"My dear girl, you might have killed yourself—" He broke off as the dog gave a comical sort of gasp and dashed for the trees. "Inky! Come back here." The dog, who had evidently scented rabbit, returned reluctantly to his master's heels. "What manners. I apologize for him. Look here, we've not met before, have we?"

"No, I'm only visiting the neighborhood."

The lines around his eyes deepened into a smile, and Jenny relaxed as she sensed that this was his habitual expression.

"Do you like it?" he asked.

"It's very beautiful," she said seriously. "I'll be sorry to leave."

"You're from Edinburgh?"

"Yes. I'm staying at Craig Lodge."

"Are you now?" He was thoughtful. "What is a smart Scottish lass like you doing at La Maison Kentish?"

Jenny's pride urged her to get the confession out of the way. "I'm the governess."

"The—oh, yes. Two little brats. I forgot about them."

"Everybody does, poor things." She was more comfortable now that her position was clear. "Do you know the Kentishes?"

"Most certainly. I am their landlord." He squared his shoulders. "I beg your pardon. I am Alistair MacNeil, of Ruthven."

"Of course, I should have guessed! You're the Mr. Mac-Neil who—I mean—" Appalled, Jenny stopped herself mentioning Isola. Love affairs were none of a governess's business. "I am Miss Dalgleish."

"I'm honored, Miss Dalgleish. And even though you were crazy to do it, I'm immensely grateful to you for saving my dog's life."

"Behold, the handmaid of the laird," Jenny said lightly.

MacNeil punched the dog affectionately. "This is Inkerman."

"Named for the battle?"

"Now, there's a good schoolroom memory. I bet you remember the date, too." He was teasing.

She laughed. "The Crimean War."

"Correct. My grandfather distinguished himself there, and I was hoping young Inkerman would live up to his reputation."

Jenny caressed Inkerman's head. "He's a beauty. Put a slipper in his mouth and he'd be pure Landseer. I couldn't think why you were calling him Inky when he isn't black."

"Yes, it is confusing," MacNeil agreed cheerfully. "I have a Labrador, black as a tar barrel, and he's called Parker."

"Parker Quink," she said. "The blue-black ink."

"That was quick of you. Most people have to think about it."

His hand rested near hers on Inky's unresisting head. He wore a gold signet ring on his little finger, with the crest half rubbed away. "Fond of dogs, are you?"

"Oh yes. All but one."

"Don't tell me. That fanged rat Madame Kentish dresses up in ribbons."

They laughed. He's nice, Jenny thought, he's really very amusing and nice. How odd it was about nice men. They invariably chased after women like Isola.

"Do you keep a dog at home, Miss Dalgleish?"

"We had a collie when I was a child. My father had a country parish in those days."

"Pater a parson, eh? That explains it."

"What?"

"It's rude of me, but I was wondering why a lady like you has to depend on Kentish gold. I ought to have guessed."

This was blunt to the point of impertinence, but Jenny sensed that he meant to be kind. And although she was ashamed of it, the fact that he recognized her as a lady was healing ointment to her wounded pride. "Yes, I'm afraid poor church mice must always put their daughters out to scrub."

"I wouldn't have put it like that."

"But you don't approve?"

He was regarding her with a humorous curiosity that was pleasantly unsettling. "No, I don't. Perhaps there are some cases where it can't be avoided, but I can't approve of gentlewomen going among strangers. I have one little sister left at home, and I'd break stones at the roadside before she had to work for her living."

Jenny smiled wryly and assumed a cool, cynical tone to hide her wistfulness: "Perhaps your sister would not thank you for breaking stones. She might prefer to use her own talents to make her living."

"I don't think the poor child's talents are of the lucrative sort," MacNeil said, gazing at her intently.

"Very few young ladies are brought up to cultivate their true gifts."

"What do they need to know that can't be taught at home? They should be preparing to get married and run homes of their own."

"I'm afraid some of us have to earn our bread, even though you disapprove," said Jenny.

"You're educated to the hilt, I suppose?" he asked teasingly.

"Oh dear me, yes—full of dates and verbs and dead languages until I can barely hold any more. I'm fearfully clever. Except," she added, "when I jump over cliffs to save dogs."

"And stupid dogs, at that. But it's worth owning such a daft creature to meet you, Miss Dalgleish. Will I see you at the lodge this evening?"

"This evening?" Jenny repeated vaguely. Then place cards and inquiries after waiters rushed into her mind, extinguishing her enjoyment. "I'm afraid I must be away, Mr. MacNeil. Goodbye. I'm so glad poor Inkerman wasn't hurt."

As she hurried toward the town, she regretfully decided that Mr. MacNeil would not be half so informal or jolly when she met him again in her role of governess.

When Jenny finally escaped to her room, with barely ten minutes left to change into her evening dress, she opened the casement and made herself take in a few healing breaths of fresh air. For three hours, she had been working furiously. Although she had told herself that the party was beneath her notice, meeting Mr. MacNeil had somehow made her anxious to remove the worst absurdities from Mrs. Kentish's arrangements.

The Japanese lanterns, for instance. It was no use telling her employer that the idea of hanging colored lanterns in the gloomy pines outside a rugged Scottish shooting lodge was ridiculous. Instead, she had managed to persuade Mrs. Kentish that there was about to be a downpour, which would mash the lanterns into pitiful smears of pulp and dye. She was glad to note now that she had been a true prophet about the rain, which was coming down in buckets. Mrs. Kentish was childishly disappointed that, after all her trouble and expense, Craig Lodge failed to be anything but what it was—a square, gray stone house with old-fashioned, anonymous furniture and tarnished rented silver. It refused to be transformed into the romantic bower she had imagined for her daughter's engagement.

Jenny had tried to divert her attention toward the more successful features, such as the magnificent hothouse flowers, sent by train from Glasgow and arranged impeccably by Jenny herself. Exotic lilies, orchids and tuberoses bloomed in all the downstairs rooms, filling the lodge with a breathless scent of heated flesh. Mrs. Kentish could not complain about Jenny's skill, but she could and did complain at very great length about the lack of decent vases. Instead of taking pleasure in the waterfalls of blossom

Jenny had created, she fretted about the washstand jugs and kitchen jars that contained them.

Everything else was wrong too. A glistening slug had been discovered on the trailing ivy that decorated the dinner table. The drawing room carpet had faded patches. The fires smoked. The waiters from the hotel were rude and inattentive. The musicians—a pianist and violinist who had come down on the train from Glasgow with the flowers—smelled powerfully of beer. They had turned out to be shifty septuagenarians with unshaven blue chins, rusty dinner jackets and dingy celluloid collars, who seemed to know nothing newer than the Savoy Operas.

Before she dashed upstairs, Jenny had seen Mrs. Kentish and her daughters installed in the drawing room, waiting stiffly for the guests. Mrs. Kentish wore rich purple satin in the style of some ten years before, cut low across her monumental bosom, with a long train at the back. A pearl choker with a heavy amethyst clasp embraced her neck, and she carried a fan made of peacock feathers. Gertrude and Rosalys shivered in identical pale blue accordion-pleated silks—their summer "bests" from school—belted low on their hips. Huge blue bows nested in their lank brown hair. They were squabbling in whispers, and warming their white-stockinged legs at the inadequate fire.

Isola, reclining in the most comfortable armchair and nonchalantly playing with the tassel on her beaded bag, was the one indisputable triumph of the evening. She was perfectly exquisite in her filmy gown of coral chiffon, even though she did not exactly suggest a fluttering maiden whose fate was about to be decided. Jenny had enviously studied the details of her ensemble—the intricately draped and daringly short hobble skirt, the sleeves that stopped just above the elbow, the cobweb thin silk stockings and high-heeled shoes of coral satin. It would not have been Jenny's style, but it somehow expressed and underlined Isola's peculiarly languid, snake-like charm.

Her own evening dress was a tired-looking white silk that had been made for the grand prize-giving at the end of her schooldays. And although some alterations had been made to the prim neckline, it was still unmistakably a schoolgirl's frock. Jenny brushed out her abundant brown hair and quickly rolled it into a bun at the nape of her neck, despising herself for wanting to cut a figure at Mrs. Kentish's silly

party. She might not have cared so much if she had not
been thinking of Mr. MacNeil. It was depressing to have to
appear before him in the obvious guise of a poor parson's
daughter. Fortunately, he was unlikely to pay much attention to her when he had Isola's loveliness to distract him.
As an afterthought, Jenny fastened her gold and enamel
locket—her one presentable piece of jewelry—around her
neck, and was comforted by its gleam in the hollow of
her throat.

Then the bell rang, and she hurried downstairs to take
her place with the children. Mrs. Kentish stood to attention
in the middle of the drawing room, as if someone had
played the National Anthem. The first guests were having
their wet wraps peeled off in the hall, and advancing with
gloved hands extended. There was a moment of awkward
silence when the formalities ran out. In the hall, the musicians suddenly burst into a bilious rendition of "Braid the
Raven Hair."

"Miss Dalgleish," gushed Mrs. Kentish, "would you
move the fire screen in front of Mrs. Laing's chair?"

During the next half-hour, Jenny heard her own name
endlessly punctuating her employer's unstemmable tide of
small talk. Mrs. Kentish rapped out orders like a sergeant
major. Her high color steadily deepened to a florid flush
and her eyes lost their critical gleam, for things were shap-
ing well. The rooms looked better when they were full of
people, and the musicians sounded less dismal beneath the
chatter of conversation. A plain spinster, grudgingly invited,
had unexpectedly brought along a dashing young cousin in
the navy, whose dark blue, gold-braided mess jacket definitely added cachet, and whose charming manners were
rousing Isola into something like animation. Relieved that
the evening was going so smoothly, Jenny obediently fer-
ried cups of fruit punch, nagged the hired waiters, sent the
children to bed with compensatory plates of trifle, and
showed ladies up to Mrs. Kentish's bedroom to preen.

There were a few last-minute alterations to be made in
the dining room. Mrs. Kentish wished the young naval officer, Lieutenant Mackendrick, to have a prominent place at
the table. While Jenny was hastily writing out a new card
for him, she caught a snatch of conversation through the
open door.

"—a vast city fortune, probably deeply dubious," a female voice was saying. "And what they're doing up here is anybody's guess. What can have possessed Alistair?"

"The girl is a stunner," replied her male companion. "But he should take his eyes off her long enough to look at her mother. That's what she'll be like in twenty years."

Jenny froze, wondering if she should cough to warn them that they were being overheard.

"—that dress and those great staring jewels—" the woman was saying. "And I bet she's the most fearful tartar. I don't envy that poor little mouse of a governess."

They moved away, leaving Jenny smarting with anger. For the rest of her life she would be at the mercy of snobs like these, who felt they had the right to laugh at anyone with new money and patronize their miserable dependents. She was just as cultivated, just as much of a lady as anyone here. The humiliation of being a servant washed over her in a great sick wave, then passed as it always did. One must make the best of things, as her mother said. Happiness was not having what one wanted, but wanting what one had.

A honk of joy from the hall told her that Mrs. Kentish's satisfaction was complete. "My dear Mr. MacNeil! No, not late at all. And Miss MacNeil—so sweet of you to come. A terribly informal affair, as you can see, but you must take us as you find us. Isola! Come and look after Mr. MacNeil—Isola? Oh, where has she got to? Miss Dalgleish, would you take Miss MacNeil upstairs?"

MacNeil had brought his sister, the girl he would break stones for. She was a tall, uncoordinated beanpole of fifteen or sixteen, with wispy yellow hair and knobbly red elbows. Clearly she was terrified of Mrs. Kentish and she clung defensively to her brother's arm. Jenny sympathetically remembered her first forays into adult parties as a schoolgirl. Even at that awkward age, she had managed a certain poise, but poor Miss MacNeil was in agonies of shyness. Worse, she was a blusher. The dread of being spoken to had turned her scarlet to the tip of her snub nose.

"Here she is Effie," MacNeil said, smiling at Jenny over Mrs. Kentish's shoulder. "Now you can thank her in person. Miss Dalgleish, may I present my sister, Euphemia?"

"How do you do, Miss MacNeil."

"Well, you have apparently already met our governess," Mrs. Kentish said, unsheathing her most lethal voice and sending a chill of foreboding through Jenny's bones. "Such

a talented young woman. I don't know what we would do
without her."

"I—we're so grateful to you for rescuing Inky," blurted
out Miss MacNeil. "He might look big, but he's really only
a puppy. He isn't awfully clever, but he's—he's very loving
and good—"

"I'm so sorry to interrupt you, Miss Dalgleish," said Mrs.
Kentish, with ominous suavity, "but perhaps you could
carry on your conversation while you are taking Miss Mac-
Neil upstairs? Isola has been pining to see you, Mr. Mac-
Neil. Shall we go and find her?"

"Go on, Effie," MacNeil said. "She won't bite, I guaran-
tee it. I'll be waiting for you." As soon as he released his
sister's arm, Mrs. Kentish took him into custody and
dragged him away toward Isola.

Effie, tripping over the hem of her unbecoming cream
lace frock, stumbled upstairs behind Jenny. She looked
around Mrs. Kentish's bedroom in awe, staring at the frilled
cushions, silver-framed photographs and gold-stoppered
jars and bottles.

"Your hair is slipping down at the back," Jenny pointed
out. "Shall I put it up for you?"

"No—I mean—you mustn't trouble." Painful color
surged up Effie's neck like a tidal wave.

"It's no trouble. Sit down at the dressing table."

The girl sat down, hunching her shoulders and making
the vertebrae stand out along her skinny back above the
fastening of her dress. Jenny set about pinning the slithery
fair plaits more securely. When she had finished, Effie
gazed at her reflection in the glass, shaking her head
experimentally.

"Thanks. You're awfully kind. I'm not very good at it
yet."

"I wasn't at first," Jenny assured her. "My mother had
to do it for me."

"Oh, but Mother's ill, so I have to do everything myself."

"I see."

"Miss Dalgleish—I—I really am so grateful to you about
Inky. Alistair says I'm silly about him. But he was frightfully pleased, too. He said it was the pluckiest thing he
ever saw."

"You're making me feel quite a heroine," Jenny said,

laughing. "Perhaps I should apply for a medal from the Humane Society. Shall we go down to the drawing room?"

"Couldn't I just wait here?" Effie's voice began to wobble perilously. "I've hardly ever been to a party before—Mother can't go out, you see—and I never know what to say. I didn't want to come, only Alistair thinks it's good for me."

"He's right," said Jenny encouragingly. "You'll soon forget to be shy. It's only local people, so you'll find plenty of familiar faces."

"They won't be familiar to me. I don't know anyone." Effie fumbled with the clasp of her embroidered bag, and fished out a limp handkerchief.

Jenny decided to take a firmer line. Mrs. Kentish was already absolutely furious with her because the laird had noticed her. She would not take kindly to Jenny ensconcing herself with MacNeil's sister. "Don't you know that everyone is nervous when they walk into a roomful of people? When I went to my first dance in Edinburgh, I wished the floor would open up and swallow me. But by the end, I was enjoying myself so much I didn't want to go home."

"Really?" gulped Effie.

"Honor bright. I even accused my father of being early when he came to fetch me."

Effie sniffed, and gave Jenny a watery, trusting smile. "You're awfully nice."

"Nonsense. Now, I'll just put some powder on your face"—Jenny dabbed at the childish, round cheeks with Mrs. Kentish's swansdown powder puff—"and you're all ready."

"Gosh! Mother never lets me have powder." The dewy blue eyes were fixed admiringly on Jenny's face. "You know, you're not at all like a governess. You don't mind my saying so, do you?"

"I'll take it as a compliment."

"I meant it for one."

Jenny, partly touched and partly irritated, realized that Effie was now prepared to follow her around like a shadow. The poor girl was at the age where a little kindness precipitates a rush of devotion.

"Let's go down," she suggested.

"Oh yes, I'm not nearly so scared now."

On the stairs, Effie clumsily managed the skirts of her frock and chattered happily to Jenny about the dogs at the castle. Jenny, unconsciously relaxing far more than she had intended, found herself describing Slipper, the beloved collie of her childhood, and her grief at having to leave him behind in the country.

Effie took this very seriously. "Yes, I don't know what I shall do when we go to London. I want to stay here, but Mother has to see the specialist, and Alistair says we must leave the dogs behind."

They had reached the drawing room. To Jenny's dismay, Effie went straight to her brother, who was standing in the window with a bored-looking Isola, and tucked her hand into his elbow. "Alistair, wouldn't it be nice if we asked Miss Dalgleish to come up to the castle? She could meet Parker, and she likes horses, too—"

"And for goodness' sake," drawled Isola, "don't forget the drains. I simply loved those."

To Jenny's astonishment, one of her eyes narrowed in the faintest suspicion of a wink, and she looked significantly over at the fireplace, where Lieutenant Mackendrick was entertaining the Laing sisters.

MacNeil noticed nothing of this. His face showed how fond he was of Effie. "Yes, why not? And if she likes people as much as horses and dogs, perhaps she could meet Mother."

"Silly, of course I meant Mother, too. You will come, won't you, Miss Dalgleish?"

Jenny decided that action was called for. This would not do at all. She was only too aware of Mrs. Kentish glaring at her across the room. "Yes, it would be lovely. Have you met Miss Mackendrick's cousin? He'll be taking you into dinner." Ignoring Isola's sour look, she hauled Effie away to introduce her to the young officer. Effie blushed fiercely, but made an effort to smile. She did not seem to see that though Mackendrick's ears followed her stammering small talk, his eyes were pinned to Isola.

Mrs. Kentish pounced on Jenny in the hall. "If you can bear to tear yourself away, perhaps you could tell me where you have put that Mackendrick boy at supper?"

"Between Miss MacNeil and Isola—"

"Oh yes, that would suit your purposes very well, I dare say. Go and change the cards again. I want him as far away from her as possible. He can take you in."

"Yes, Mrs. Kentish."

Jenny shook with anger as she returned to the dining room. How dare the horrid old woman hint that she was plotting and planning to entrap MacNeil? The sheer vulgarity of it made her feel unclean. And there was no denying that she also felt a twinge of triumph. For despite all Mrs. Kentish's efforts to diminish her, MacNeil evidently did like her.

"May I come in? I don't want to disturb you." MacNeil himself was at the door.

"You're not disturbing me," she said. Her pulse heightened nervously. If Mrs. Kentish chose to fill her head with ideas, she had only herself to blame for the consequences. Jenny decided to give herself up to the enjoyment of his attention, reasoning that she might as well be hanged for a sheep as for a lamb.

MacNeil came in and leaned against the chimneypiece.

"You've made quite a hit with Effie. I wanted to thank you for being so kind to her."

"Is she all right?"

"Chattering away like a little magpie last time I looked. I worry about her sometimes."

"Why?"

"It's a lonely life for her out here," he said seriously. "She's the last one left at home, and our mother simply hasn't the strength to take her out. I do what I can, but it's feminine company she needs. That's why I'm being so firm about taking her down to London with me—although she thinks I'm a monster of cruelty for separating her from her animals."

"She'll forgive you," Jenny said, smiling.

"Well, I hope so. It's true that our mother does need to see a specialist, but we're going down in the season mainly for Effie's sake. She's such a dear little girl."

"Yes." Jenny waited warily to hear what he was leading up to. It was beginning to sound depressingly like a spot of governess-hunting.

"I can't help wanting to look out for her," he continued. "I'm pretty well old enough to be her father, you know. There are five more sisters between us. All pretty, and all married. Poor Effie hasn't really grown into her looks yet." Absentmindedly he fingered the dusty chenille fringe around the chimneypiece. "She never seems to have anything to say to girls her own age. I was wondering if the

Kentishes are planning to take you back to London with
them."

"I don't think so."

"That's a shame."

"Is it?" asked Jenny.

"For us, I mean. If you do find yourself in London during
the season, I wish you'd look Effie up."

Jenny, realizing he was not offering her a job but paying
her the compliment of begging her friendship for his beloved little sister, blushed with gratification.

MacNeil straightened, and took a step nearer to her. "I
was going to say she needs an older friend, but you can't
be much more than a schoolgirl yourself. You seemed so
self-possessed this afternoon, but seeing you in that
frock—"

Oh, this awful dowdy dress, Jenny thought. When will I
ever have decent clothes? "I'm nearly twenty-one."

"That means you're just twenty," said MacNeil, his eyes
laughing at her. "You're not such a parcel of sophistication
as you look, are you?"

"Dinner will be announced in a few minutes, Mr.
MacNeil."

"May I take you in?"

"Certainly not," Jenny said crisply. "You're taking in
Miss Kentish. It's all arranged."

"Mustn't upset the arrangements." He held the door
open for her respectfully as she left the room.

Jenny told one of the waiters to announce dinner, which
he did, in an impenetrable, wine-smelling mumble. Mrs.
Kentish, moving among her guests wearing a bright smile
of murderous rage, was slightly mollified to see MacNeil
claiming her daughter. Graciously, she paraded into the
dining room on the arm of an old white-whiskered Justice
of the Peace. Mackendrick, reduced to the ranks for flirting
with Isola, brought up the rear of the procession with
Jenny.

"I say, Miss—er—I say, isn't Miss Kentish a corker of
a girl?"

"Yes, Mr. Mackendrick."

"Isn't she simply a peach? I say, you'll tell me—she's not
engaged, is she?"

"Not yet."

"Good-oh."

The rather austere dining room had sprung into life. Silks, laces, feathers and black jackets jostled around the long table to read the place cards.

"I don't think you want to sit next to me," Isola coolly informed MacNeil. "I'm really not in the mood for talking about things on four legs. I'd much rather hear the end of the Lieutenant's story about Bermuda."

"Isola!" shrieked Mrs. Kentish.

"It's quite all right, Mother. All I have to do is swap places with Miss Dalgleish. There, isn't this cozy?" And she whisked neatly into the chair Mackendrick was about to tuck under Jenny.

There was nothing to be done. Jenny, her cheeks hot with embarrassment, subsided into the place next to Mac-Neil as inconspicuously as possible, avoiding Mrs. Kentish's accusing, outraged eye. At the other end of the table, beyond her mother's reach, Isola was smiling serenely, and beckoning the waiter back to fill her glass to the top. Mrs. Kentish tried to put a good face on it, but the best face she could manage was that of a gorgon. All her plans were going wrong.

Jenny found it impossible to be shy with MacNeil. Soon she was more herself than she had been during all her time at Glen Ruthven, talking about her parents, her history, and her plans for the future. He listened seriously, hardly taking his eyes from her face. And as soon as he realized that his questions were making her uncomfortable, he began to entertain her with stories of his ancestors.

By the time Mrs. Kentish coughed, to signal that it was time for the ladies to retire, Jenny was conscious of a peculiar warmth in her blood that came from a sense of power and confidence. There was no mistaking the fact that she had made her first conquest. And deep, deep down, buried far below the sheer pleasure of talking to him, nestled the knowledge that her conquest had a great deal of worldly value. She was smiling dreamily over the laird of Ruthven and his acres as she strolled back into the drawing room, arm in arm with Effie.

"Miss Dalgleish, will you have the extreme goodness to serve the coffee?"

"Yes, Mrs. Kentish." Jenny no longer cared what her employer thought. It was simply too late to repair the damage.

"I'll help you," said Effie, eagerly seizing two of the cups. "We'll do it in half the time. You know, you were absolutely right, Miss Dalgleish—parties are great fun, aren't they?"

With Mrs. Kentish immured in her anger, conversation among the ladies fell into familiar local lines. Isola lounged on one of the sofas, sleepily contemplating the toes of her satin shoes and openly yawning. However, Mrs. Kentish had another shot left. Over the general flurry of animation that greeted the arrival of the gentlemen, she called: "Sit down, everyone. Miss Dalgleish, will you ask the musicians to bring in the piano from the hall? Isola darling, I'm sure you'll sing to us."

"Dancing would be more fun," Isola said, making room on the sofa for the smitten Lieutenant. "I wonder if they know any twosteps?"

"I find something so fresh and moving about a young girl's voice, Mr. MacNeil," confided Mrs. Kentish loudly. "And Isola sings beautifully."

Jenny had found the two musicians furtively drinking the dregs of the claret bottles under the stairs. She shepherded them into the drawing room with the upright piano, and after lengthy negotiations, it was established that they could play "It's Quiet Down Here" in Isola's key.

An after-dinner resignation settled on the guests as they distributed themselves on the available chairs. Isola certainly looked lovely, standing beside the piano in her delicate sunset-colored gown. Mrs. Kentish took her by the shoulders, aimed her at MacNeil and—having metaphorically lit the fuse—retired.

Isola's voice was thin and flat, and a little tinny in the high phrases. The guests rewarded her with polite applause, and enjoyed the spectacle of Isola's graceful curtseys. MacNeil clapped enthusiastically.

"Absolutely charming, Miss Kentish. Delightful. Perhaps one of the other young ladies would favor us?"

"I shouldn't dream of imposing—" began Mrs. Kentish in dismay.

But MacNeil was already leaning over the back of Jenny's chair. "I know you can sing, Miss Dalgleish."

"No—really, not at all—"

"But you told me you won a prize for it at school."

"Did you?" exclaimed Effie. "Oh, I should love to hear you sing something! Won't you ask her, Mrs. Kentish?"

Forced to give in, Mrs. Kentish said disagreeably: "Well, there's no end to your accomplishments, apparently. Do something brisk and short, and don't send everyone to sleep."

Jenny got up and went to the piano. She had too much taste to drag out the scene with a show of reluctance. "I don't know any of the new songs," she whispered to the pianist. "Can you play 'Auld Robin Gray'?"

The mist lifted from his bleared eyes. "Of course I can, miss."

He touched the keys softly and a hush fell as the old Scottish melody stole through the room. Jenny's voice was low and sweet, with an indescribable poignancy that contrasted surprisingly with her matter-of-fact tone of speech. The moment she began, MacNeil froze, as if she had pinned him to the wall with an arrow through his heart.

"Young Jamie loved me well, and sought me for his
bride,
But saving of a crown, he had nothing else beside . . ."

She had never sung as well as she did now, half-frightened as she was by the unguarded expression of tenderness in his eyes. When she got to: *"I dare not think of Jamie, because that would be a sin,"* she noticed Effie fumbling in her bag for her handkerchief, her lip trembling. *"—and a good wife I will be,"* she finished demurely, *"for Auld Robin Gray is a kind man to me."* The last chords of the song were followed by a gratifying hush, so profound that she could hear the gentlemen's starched shirtfronts creaking. During these few seconds, Jenny met MacNeil's eyes, suddenly feeling very young and confused under such a barrage of conflicting emotions. There was something about the way he looked at her that made her want to run away, as if from a trap. But this was underpinned by a kind of guilty curiosity, and a sense of victory.

The applause was sincere and prolonged, and after one rapid bow she did her best to deflect the attention. Mrs. Kentish immediately started a loud conversation, as if to remind Jenny that she had had all the notice she deserved.

MacNeil was making his way toward her, but Effie got

there before him. She laid a baggily gloved hand on Jenny's sleeve. "That was simply lovely. You do have a nice voice. But oh dear, why did it have to be so sad? If only she'd waited for young Jamie, instead of marrying Auld Robin— even if he was kind."

"Perhaps she was happier," Jenny suggested, deliberately not turning to MacNeil, although he was obviously impatient to speak to her. "You don't find kind men lying beneath every stone."

"I think everyone should wait for their true love," Effie declared, sublimely confident. "No matter what. Alistair, why are you laughing? Don't you agree with me?"

"Effie, you're beyond everything. You know less about love than Inky."

Mrs. Kentish broke in, "Miss Dalgleish, tell Jessie I shall want her for the cloaks, and then take the coffee around again."

Jenny did as she was told. Her triumph was beginning to deflate. As soon as the guests had gone, Mrs. Kentish would repossess her dominion, and her offensively obtrusive governess, princess for an hour, would find herself back in the land of mortals.

Jessie, the elderly parlormaid, was merrily entertaining the waiters and several coachmen in the kitchen. "Cloaks," Jenny said briefly, "and you'd better find William for the carriages."

"Had I, indeed?" grumbled Jessie. "You'd better tell the old besom I cannot be in two places at once."

Knowing this meant yes, Jenny hurried back down the kitchen passage. The door to the servants' quarters swung open, and she almost collided with MacNeil. He put his hands on her shoulders to steady her, and did not remove them.

"Got you."

"Mr. MacNeil—"

"You dashed away before I could pay you any compliments for your singing."

"You're very kind. Now, if you would let me through, I have to serve the coffee."

"Damn the coffee," MacNeil said cheerfully. "You've been running away from me all evening—you even had to be forced to sit next to me at dinner—and I'm tired of trying to catch you for a decent conversation."

"Couldn't we"—began Jenny, flustered by the warmth and weight of his hands through her dress—"couldn't we have a conversation in the drawing room?"

"No. Now look here, I want you to tell me what's going on. Come on, Miss Dalgleish. Something's up."

"It's really nothing—"

"Oh, nothing my foot. Why is Mrs. Kentish being so beastly to you? Have I got you into a hole?"

This was such an understatement that Jenny laughed. "You weren't supposed to pay any attention to me," she explained, deciding that he might as well know the truth. "We've been waiting for you to propose to Isola."

"To what? Good Lord!"

"Wasn't that your intention?"

"So that's what the old—what Mrs. Kentish has been hinting at! Great Scott, at last it becomes clear!" He chuckled to himself, then gazed down at Jenny with disquieting gravity. "Miss Dalgleish, I want you to understand something—do you have a first name?"

"Jenny. But Mr. MacNeil—"

"I say, that's awfully pretty, and it suits you. *Jenny kissed me when we met, Jumping from the chair she sat in—*"

"Mr. MacNeil, really!"

"It's only a poem, you impossibly proper little girl. A beautiful poem, with not a single sentiment in it to sully the hem of that sweet white gown. *Say I'm weary, say I'm sad, Say that health and wealth have missed me, Say I'm growing old, but add,*" his voice had become very soft and low, *"Jenny kissed me."*

Unable to help herself, Jenny stared up into his face as if hypnotized. She had never been in such a situation before, but she sensed the strength of his emotions, and was suddenly afraid of the unknown power in herself that had aroused them.

"Jenny, this is important. I have flirted with Isola, I admit it. But I'm not the bounder you must think me."

"Oh, but I don't—"

"She's the sort who flirts with everyone, and she was only having her game with me until something younger and more handsome came along. Nothing more serious than that, upon my honor. Say you believe me."

"Yes, of course." She knew already that MacNeil's honor

was not the sort to be doubted for a moment. How her mother would have thrilled to such a gentlemanly speech.

"And will you now take a compliment or two, from a foolish old fellow who loves a sentimental song?"

"You may say anything you please, Mr. MacNeil," Jenny said, gazing up into his face and thinking that in the dim light of the passage, he did not seem nearly so old.

He thoughtfully squeezed her shoulders. "That was the sweetest thing I've heard in a long, long while. And the singer is every bit as fresh and wholesome as the song. You're a sprig of bonny white heather among all these hothouse bouquets. Looking at you rests my tired old eyes."

The voices beyond the door seemed to come from an immense distance. They stood in a private world of shadows and breathless silence. MacNeil broke the tension by chuckling softly. "You see, I can be quite a poet. Aren't you glad you let yourself be caught?"

"I—I should go—"

"When may I see you again?"

"I don't know. I'm not in a position to make plans for myself."

"Then I'll make them for you." He leaned so close to her that his breath stirred her hair, and she could smell his shaving soap. "I don't intend to lose you, Jenny."

"Where is Miss Dalgleish?" shouted Mrs. Kentish, dangerously close to the other side of the door.

Jenny broke away from him and hurried out, knowing her cheeks were pink and her eyes unfocused.

"I will see you in the morning room," whispered Mrs. Kentish meaningfully, "directly everyone has gone." And she added, in a loud, unpleasant voice: "Ah, there you are, Mr. MacNeil. Thank you so much for honoring us this evening. I only wish the house was more suitable for entertaining. I do assure you, our style at home is quite, quite different."

"It was a charming evening, Mrs. Kentish."

"Two of the sinks are still blocked," Mrs. Kentish said disagreeably. "I wish you would tell your factor to see to them tomorrow. And the piano seems to have left marks on the parquet. I freely admit responsibility. You can put it on the bill."

In the flurry of farewells, Effie pushed a scrap of paper

into Jenny's hand. "Just in case you can't come to see us, it's our address in London—my sister's house in Hyde Park Gate. We'll be there in a fortnight."

As the house emptied, the hour of reckoning approached. Only one guest was left in the hall—the plain spinster who had brought the young naval officer. Mrs. Kentish's black scowl and tapping foot were making her twitter with nerves. "Goodness, what can be keeping Douglas? Perhaps I had better go and have a look ... ? I did tell him it was time to leave. I told him twice."

The Lieutenant emerged at last, thick-tongued and as red as a peony. The shoulders of his mess jacket were spangled with rain.

Mrs. Kentish shooed him out of the house with the barest, scantiest covering of civility. Jenny noticed Isola gliding away upstairs, beads of rain sparkling in her hair like diamonds.

"Right." Mrs. Kentish jerked open the door of the morning room. "In here, if you please."

She positioned herself splendidly before the embers of the dying fire. Jenny faced her on the hearth rug, trying not to look cowed.

"I wonder what you can possibly have to say for yourself, Miss Dalgleish?"

"I beg your pardon, Mrs. Kentish?"

"There are no men to witness your performance now, Miss Dalgleish. I am the only person in this room, and I am quite impervious to your wiles. So you needn't play the innocent. Never—never—have I seen such shameful, flaunting behavior from someone in my employ."

Jenny's blood was drumming in her ears. She was afraid of the woman, but she was determined to preserve her dignity. "I'm afraid you will have to explain."

"Very well. Your open intriguing with Mr. MacNeil has deeply shocked me and embarrassed my guests."

"I have done nothing of the kind," Jenny said, making an effort to raise her head. "I have done nothing wrong. You can't complain about my behavior. I won't stand for these accusations."

"Very affecting, I'm sure," sneered Mrs. Kentish. "You're quite a talented little performer—all injured purity. I have been very much mistaken in Mr. MacNeil, who is certainly not the gentleman I took him for, but I have been even more mistaken in you. I have a good mind to dismiss you on the spot."

"Thank you," said Jenny, in a sudden rush of exulting, righteous anger, "that won't be necessary. I shall leave on the first available train."

"You'll do nothing of the kind!" shrilled Mrs. Kentish. "We made an agreement! I refuse to be left here without a governess. You'll stay till you've worked out your notice, or not a penny will you get from me."

"Since you are so disappointed in me, I shan't require payment."

"You won't be so grand when you have to come crawling to me for a reference!"

"And I shan't require a reference either," Jenny returned scornfully.

"How dare you!" Mrs. Kentish's bosom swelled wrathfully. "Of all the pert, forward—

A white-hot flash of anger burned away the last of Jenny's fear. No longer an employee, she simply walked out of the room, and left Mrs. Kentish fuming impotently among the smeared punch glasses and wilting tuberoses. It was a moment of exquisite satisfaction, which carried her upstairs on feet of thistledown.

"What—?" On the threshold of her bedroom, she halted, bewildered.

This was too much. Isola was lying on her bed in a limp cloud of chiffon. Her unpinned hair flowed across the counterpane in rich, scented waves. She was smoking a cigarette, and flicking the ash into the water glass.

Jenny banged the door smartly behind her, wishing the entire Kentish family at the bottom of the sea. "What do you want?"

"Just a word," Isola said, "before you go the way of all governesses."

"I can't say that I see any necessity."

"Oh, for goodness' sake," Isola said wearily, "do get off your high horse. I'm not going to accuse you of stealing my beau, if that's what you're afraid of."

"Good." Jenny pointedly jerked open the window.

"Really, it's just this. You've played your cards awfully well."

"I—I beg your pardon?"

"You've been meeting MacNeil on the sly, haven't you? And to think we never suspected."

"I've been doing nothing of the kind!" Jenny was horrified. "We met for the first time this afternoon."

"Then you're an absolute genius. That white sack thing you're wearing is just the kind of vestal garb to appeal to a boring old stick like him. If Mother wasn't such a fool, she'd have put me in one just like it. And the locket is a masterstroke. I suppose it has a wee picture of your mamma inside, and even if it hasn't, who's going to look? Really, my dear, with your gifts you're wasted as a governess."

It was the longest speech Jenny had ever heard from Isola's lips, and she was too astonished to reply. Her father had once warned her that the minds of the wicked worked in different and unfathomable ways, but she had never believed it until now. She was insulted and hurt, and suddenly so lonely that she wanted to cry.

"We're both in disgrace," remarked Isola, "but I'll get off lightly, thanks to you. You realize, of course, what a frightful scrape you've got me out of? If MacNeil had proposed, and I'd said no, she would have cut off my dress allowance. She's quite desperate for me to marry some strict old man because she thinks I'm too naughty to be trusted on my own. And actually," she added, casually dropping the end of the cigarette into the glass, "she's quite right. But I've no intention of tying myself down until I've had some fun. So I'm very grateful. If ever you come to London—and you'd be mad not to after your triumph tonight—I'll stand you tea at Gunter's."

Jenny, in a turmoil of disgust, pain and anger, amazed herself by suddenly laughing. The foundations of her world were shaking, and in the upheaval fresh absurdities were positively raining down. During the course of one evening, she had somehow transformed herself from a frumpish children's governess into a scheming adventuress. Her dignity was deeply wounded, but it was exciting, too.

Isola watched her dispassionately. "She sacked you, I suppose?"

"I resigned." Jenny stopped laughing as she realized what she had done. She had taken leave of her senses. How was she to explain leaving her position without a reference if a future employer happened to find out? For the sake of

her dignity, she had made a mighty blemish on her only
asset—her professional character. Years of work were
blown away, and a small mouthful of humble pie might
have saved them.

"Two and a half cheers for you," Isola said. "There's a
Bradshaw on the bureau, so you can look up the trains. It's
been thumbed by many a Kentish governess in its time."

"You're quite wrong about me," said Jenny.

"No I'm not." Isola dragged herself off the bed, leaving
a perfumed chasm in the feather mattress. "I'm never
wrong about people. And I'll eat my garters if I'm wrong
about you. Goodbye."

When she had gone, Jenny dazedly sat down on the end
of the bed, knowing she should begin to pack her trunk at
once, but hardly able to analyze her feelings. Isola's pre-
sumption made her furious, but could she be right? Jenny
remembered her surge of excitement as she thought of
MacNeil's money and rank, and her face burned with
shame. For a moment, she almost believed herself to be as
tawdry and degraded as Mrs. Kentish supposed.

And then she began to think about the future. She could
return to Edinburgh, humiliated and disgraced, and look
for another job. But why should she? Cultivating her mind
had brought her nothing but endless drudgery. For the first
time, it occurred to her that there were greater prizes to
be gained if she cultivated her looks.

It would be a gamble, of course. But the odds were in
her favor. MacNeil had promised to come to find her and
all she had to do was make it easy for him. He was kind,
he was reasonably handsome and, since she liked him so
much more than any man she had ever met, surely falling
in love with him would be a simple matter? If she could
pass exams in Latin and algebra, she could make herself
love Alistair MacNeil.

Trembling with eagerness, she rapidly ran through the
practicalities, realizing that it could be done provided she
attacked the project with total determination. There were
her savings. Her father would be aghast, but she knew she
could play on her mother's ambitions; Mrs. Dalgleish would
immediately recognize this as the sort of chance that came
once in a lifetime. She took Effie's scrap of paper out of
her pocket. Using Effie as a road to her brother was a base

thing to do, but she knew she could do it with hardly a twinge of guilt.

Instead of beginning the tiresome work of packing her belongings, Jenny seized her inlaid traveling desk and whipped out her fountain pen and a sheet of paper.

Dear Eleanor, she wrote, *I was delighted to receive your invitation. I should love to come down for the season. Unless I hear from you I shall aim to leave Edinburgh on the 11th . . .*

Three

Hampstead, London

Pale afternoon sunlight flooded the drawing room, dazzling as it caught the silver frames of the photographs that crowded the chimneypiece, and the glass doors of the inlaid display cabinets. A breeze snatched at the tassels of the brocade curtains, and gently agitated the crystal pendants of the chandelier. Both sets of French windows stood open, framing a vista of striped lawns and immaculate parterres.

Eleanor was at the grand piano, idling her way through a palpitating Chopin Fantasie, enjoying the peace. The garden was as stiff and artificial as the house. But beyond the shrubberies and tennis courts lay Hampstead Heath, a wilderness of white hawthorn and rambling musk roses. It was just possible to shut out the distant rumble of London traffic, and the drowsy scent of beeswax polish baking in the sun, to imagine oneself in Arcadia.

Spring intensified Eleanor's craving for romance and poetry—the craving that had lately made her so dissatisfied with the ordinariness of her life. Her emotions were manageable, as long as she harnessed them to music. If they broke out anywhere else, her mother accused her of "sulking." Mrs. Braddon had a depressing talent for reducing everything to dull prose. Really, what was the use? Lazily, Eleanor skipped a difficult passage. Then, because there was no one to complain, she abandoned Chopin for the noisy two-step of "Ragging the Baby to Sleep."

It sounded marvelously incongruous in the choking splendor of her mother's drawing room. Mrs. Braddon favored the Waring and Gillow school of taste—no expense spared, and the maximum return for one's money in the way of show. You could not accuse her of vulgarity, exactly, but there was too much gloss, too much plump comfort. The

Braddon house had been built in the 1890s, and the architect, influenced by the Arts and Crafts Movement, had designed a rambling mansion of tesselated red brick, with sloping mansards and tall ornamental chimneys. Mrs. Braddon cared less for Arts and Crafts than modern conveniences. Eleanor would have liked more ancient inconveniences—furniture with the brittle charm of antiquity, and pictures of something other than horses and food.

She stopped playing and stretched luxuriously. How tranquil it was without Mother. Only when she was absent did Eleanor realize how much their running battle tired her. Mrs. Braddon was always urging her to "make something" of herself, as if she could help being put in the shade by Viola and Francesca. "You're not trying" was her great refrain. But as Eleanor knew well, no amount of trying could turn her into a beauty. She was vaguely appealing, with her wide mouth and upturned nose, and that was all.

Mrs. Braddon also complained about Eleanor's behavior. "It's all very well to spend your days mooning over books and music when you haven't anything better to do, but there's no need to behave like a tragedy queen when we go out. Yes, you do—you drift around with a martyred look as if ordinary social duties were beneath you. I'm sure you think you're very clever, but it puts people off. Especially men." Meeting men and eventually getting married to one of them was the sole point of a girl's existence. Eleanor had nothing to say to the red-faced boys who shuffled her clumsily across dance floors. She was waiting for the true purpose of her life to reveal itself. However, this was not the sort of thing one said to Mother.

Reaching for her spectacles, Eleanor wandered out into the spring sunshine. Mrs. Braddon and Viola had driven off in the Daimler after lunch, to attend Lady Gaisford's At Home, and to make a surprise raid on the Bond Street milliner who was working on Viola's trousseau. Viola was engaged to Lady Gaisford's son, the Honorable Gus Fenborough, and since the announcement her mother had been running a high fever of delight. She never could forget that her grandfather had made his money by manufacturing ointment. Marrying a daughter into the peerage seemed to confer the scepter of gentility on that vulgar fortune.

With Mrs. Braddon's troubling energies directed elsewhere, the whole house had loosened its corsets. From the open kitchen window, Eleanor could hear the two parlor-maids laughing as they set the tea trays. They were taking their time over the rolled cucumber sandwiches and sponge cakes. Cook had stumped up to the attic for her rest. Sharp, the butler, was studying the racing pages in the pantry. All was serene below stairs.

Above stairs, poor Aunt Flora Braddon, safe from the eagle gaze of her sister-in-law, had fallen asleep in a basket chair on the terrace. Even as she slept, there was a harassed look on her faded, rabbity face. Her thin lips were parted, and brittle strands were escaping from her gray bun.

Francesca was an altogether lovelier spectacle, curled picturesquely on the terrace steps, scanning Jenny's letter.

"Won't it be fun when we're all together again?" she said contentedly. "I knew Jenny could come if she really tried. Poor thing, she does sound tired of teaching."

Eleanor sat down on the step beside her. "Mother's as pleased as punch. You know she loves a house crammed with people. And if she could write off to Whiteley's for a perfect daughter, Jenny would be exactly the pattern she'd order."

"And funny old Rory, coming to London at last. She must be as wild as an Irish chieftain by now. I still have her poem in my glove box—the one she gave us when we made the vow."

Eleanor laughed. *"These four maidens in the spring of life.* Yes, I kept my copy, too."

"Don't laugh. I mean to hold you all to the vow so I can be sure of a divine summer full of larks."

Eleanor squeezed her hand affectionately. "Poor darling. You've been so blue recently."

"Only because of Mummy," Francesca faltered. "I was so looking forward to her coming back, and us having that little house together—I couldn't help being disappointed, though I do love staying here. Your mother is so kind to me."

"We all adore having you."

"Do you, honestly? I was afraid I would be in the way when Mummy changed her mind so suddenly. But you know, I've been thinking. Maybe it's better for her to stay in New York after all. Uncle Archie says the house in Long Island is lovely, and it would have been so awkward—nobody would have called on her, even though she's married to Uncle Archie now."

Eleanor did not know how to reply to this. Not for the first time, she was taken aback by Francesca's streak of practicality. There was a virginal sweetness about her that made such hard-headed statements seem rather shocking. Yet her long-lashed brown eyes were as dewy and cloudless as ever, and her rosebud lips looked as if they could drop nothing but diamonds and pearls.

"Uncle Archie was a perfect dear about it all," she continued, smiling. "Wiring me such a stupendous lot of money, as well as sending that darling pearl set and the velvet wrap. It's all for the best, I'm sure."

In her white voile gown with its lace fichu collar and ankle-skimming skirt, she was as delicate as a camellia. Her chestnut hair lay in a shining coil on the nape of her neck, with little ringlets escaping around her temples. Eleanor knew that this lovely creature cast a cloak of invisibility over her when they were out together in public, and loved her far too much to mind. Francesca needed her, and she longed to be needed. She knew at twenty, just as she had known at fourteen, that she had an almost limitless capacity for emotional sacrifice.

Far away, muffled in the depths of the sleeping house, the front doorbell clanged.

"Bother and blast it," Eleanor sighed. "Who would think of paying calls on a day like this? I expect it's the Vicar. Mother shouldn't encourage him."

"Too late," said Francesca. "He knows when we have tea now."

"He's always trying to get me to do 'useful' work," Eleanor complained, "because he thinks I'm serious."

"But dearest, you are serious."

"I'm not! Not in the dull way he means."

Margaret, the elder of the two parlormaids, came onto the terrace with two cards on a silver salver.

"Miss Flora." She bent over the basket chair. "Wake up, Miss Flo."

Flora guiltily jerked awake. Her ball of crochet wool rolled off her lap. "What?"

"Two young gentlemen to see you, miss. I put them in the library."

"Dear me, there must be a mistake," Flora exclaimed,

dismayed. "Eleanor, do you know anything about this? You surely wouldn't ask anyone to call while she was out?"

"Not while I'm dressed like this," Eleanor said, glancing down at her white flannel tennis skirt and plain white silk blouse.

"Margaret," said Flora anxiously, "you shouldn't have told them we were at home. I don't think we're supposed to be in, or Mrs. Braddon would have said."

"But they asked for you, miss, most particular."

Margaret had come down firmly on the side of the two young men. She held out the salver, and Flora picked up the cards, straining to read the names without her glasses. "For me? Oh, well—"

"Shall I ask Mr. Sharp to bring the table out, miss? Shame to have your tea indoors on such a beautiful afternoon."

The servants loved and humored Flora, mainly because she always did as they told her. She said: "Thank you, Margaret, that would be very nice," and was secretly flabbergasted that she had managed to invite two strange young men to tea without even seeing their names. What on earth would Sybil say?

Very flustered, she hurried into the library to meet them.

"Mr. Carr-Lyon and Mr. Hastings, miss." Margaret announced them with an approving flourish.

Their names made absolutely no impression on Flora, and she instantly forgot them. She simply stood and gaped at the two young men. One was dark and one fair, and both seemed dangerously tall in their light summer suits. Young men as a class were so big. They loomed, and left footmarks, and at least three fierce duennas were required to keep them in order when there were girls about. Sybil would be furious about this.

Flora was wondering what to do when the fair one said in a gentle, coaxing voice: "Now, Aunt Flora, don't say you've forgotten me."

"I—I'm sorry—" she stammered, appalled.

"Well, who can blame you? I would insist on growing up."

His smile suddenly poured light into a secret corner of Flora's memory. She saw a sunny room, and a little golden-haired boy in a sailor suit leaning against her shoulder, as she read aloud from *Peter Parley's Annual*. The picture was

so vivid that for a moment she felt his sharp elbow boring
into her stays, and smelled his freshly soaped neck and silky
yellow mop.

Unconsciously, she held out her arms. "Can you be little Stevie?"

The dream child grasped her hands, laughing. "I told you
she'd know me," he said to his companion. "Let's look at
you, Aunt Flo—and I can't call you anything else. You
haven't changed at all. Do you remember how you used to
sneak me slices of cake?"

"Stevie—Mr. Carr-Lyon—oh, if only you'd told us you
were coming!"

"It was a mad impulse. And actually I was rather hoping
you still had some cake on offer."

"Yes, of course. You must stay to tea." Flora was beaming. Once upon a time the Carr-Lyons and the Braddons
had lived in the same Kensington square, and Stevie had
been unleashed on the Braddons' nursery to play with Eleanor. What a sweet child he had been—so much more
willing to accept her stores of unused love than her brother's family. The fact that he had remembered her filled her
with warmth. People so seldom did. Of course, he had really come because he knew the house was full of girls, but
his smile was still genuine enough to irrigate her dried-up
affections. And, best of all, it was perfectly all right to ask
him to tea because Stevie's mother had been at school with
Sybil and she was rich. Instead of being blamed for care-
lessness, Flora would be garlanded with praises for her sensible management.

"Are any of the girls at home?"

"Eleanor is out in the garden, and she'll be so pleased
to see her old playmate—she always was your favorite,
wasn't she? Viola's gone out with her mother—she's about
to be married, you know—and Nancy, baby Nancy, well,
she's a great thing, away at boarding school—" As she babbled, Flora wistfully looked Stevie up and down, searching
for the golden boy she had so often secretly dreamed was
hers.

He must be twenty, she calculated, perhaps twenty-one,
and the passing years had neither tarnished nor darkened
the pure blond of his hair. In the shadowy room, he almost
shone. He was at least a foot taller than her now, with a
man's hard jaw and high forehead. But his eyes were the

same soft blue and his mouth was still ripe and relaxed like a child's. Little Stevie had grown up dashing and gallant, just as she used to imagine Sir Galahad when she had been young and silly enough to read Tennyson and have dreams.

Her chinless face alight with excitement, she led him—and his silent friend—out to the terrace.

"Eleanor dear, you'll never guess—"

Eleanor had no trouble recognizing Stevie, though her heart gave an unexpected jump of surprise at finding him so handsome. For a minute or two she was flustered. Stevie, however, reconstructed their old friendship as easily as if they had still been sharing a tree house in the square gardens. He had a graceful, easy charm, which shone as impartially as the sunny weather. Eleanor could see exactly how he had conquered Margaret: when he smiled, you felt his whole attention wrapping you in its warmth. Within five minutes, they were all basking.

"You haven't changed a bit," he told her.

Eleanor guessed that he had wondered if he would find her pretty and had now ascertained that she was not. His eyes kept traveling over her shoulder to where Francesca watched him warily. She liked him, Eleanor could see, but was far too shy to speak.

He had the sense to include her in the conversation without expecting a reply, until she finally found the courage to murmur: "I know who you are now. You gave Eleanor the little sickle-shaped scar on her knee."

"What a horrid little brute I was," Stevie said. "Did she tell you I did it with her own penknife? We were playing surgeons and it was better than mine."

Eleanor blessed him for the tactful way he ignored Francesca's crimson face. Poor darling, she was so frightened of strangers that most social events threw her into agonies.

"You were a naughty pair," Flora said happily. "I miss the old house sometimes, but it never was the same after you all left, Stevie dear."

She hovered ineffectually while Sharp and Margaret laid the cloth and unloaded the two crowded trays. Then, in the middle of arranging herself behind the silver teapot, she suddenly remembered Stevie's companion, who had been silent all this time.

"Mr.—I'm awfully sorry, I don't seem to—"

"Lorenzo," Stevie interrupted cheerfully. "We all call

him that, because he looks so much like an Italian organ-grinder. Which, of course, leaves a glaring vacancy for a monkey—that's the only reason he can bear to be seen out with me. Please don't waste your small talk on him."

"Why ever not?"

"Light conversation makes him savage. Just toss him a bun from time to time. He never bites if he's fed."

Lorenzo sighed, and said: "You're an idiot" with such obvious boredom and exasperation that Flora was embarrassed.

Stevie, neatly whisking into the chair beside Francesca before Eleanor could reach it, only laughed. "Sit down and eat something. If my frivolity shocks you so much, talk to Eleanor. She always was the clever sort."

Eleanor, cast into despair by this awful description of herself, immediately whipped off her spectacles, reducing the bright garden to a gaudy blur. Nobody ever wanted to talk to a girl who was clever.

Her aunt, as usual, made it worse. "She certainly is devoted to music, Mr.—er—" she offered, as Lorenzo sullenly lowered himself into a chair and accepted a sandwich from Margaret. "Serious music, naturally. And poetry. Are you interested in poetry?"

He stared ahead, without a flicker of response. Flora, in her lowly position as unmarried aunt, was used to rudeness; but nothing like this. She gazed helplessly around the table.

Stevie whistled sharply. "Larry!"

Lorenzo turned to face Flora. "Did you speak to me?"

"Yes," she whispered.

"I didn't hear. I'm partly deaf. You've got the wrong ear."

"Oh, I see. Oh dear." Flora was so disconcerted that she scalded herself on the teapot and set the cups afloat in the saucers. There was something about Lorenzo which, to borrow an expression of Margaret's, fairly gave her the creeps. For a moment, his face was associated with something uncomfortable at the back of her mind. Could she have seen him somewhere before? What was his real name? She could hardly ask again.

"Let me, Miss Flo." Margaret gently tugged the teapot from her hands. "You'll have the whole cloth underwater."

Flora subsided into the depths of her chair, far too frightened to attempt another assault on Lorenzo's deaf ear. She dreaded the silliness of having to shout at him.

Across the table, Stevie had managed to overcome Francesca's nervousness. Really, as if he had waved a magic wand, Flora thought. Sybil, who had virtually given up on the child, would be amazed to see her so animated.

"Hold still, Miss Garland—there's a bee near your hair."

"A bee! How too terrible!"

"Don't you like them?"

"No! Suppose it stings me! Is it very big?"

"Gigantic. Want me to whop it away for you?"

"Oh, would you, please?"

"Bees adore flowers, you know."

"Do they?"

"Rather. They always scent out the prettiest ones."

"How clever, when they don't even have proper noses."

Eleanor could not listen to much more of this. She was also impressed with the way Stevie had gained Francesca's confidence, but wondered why they both seemed so pleased to be having such a foolish conversation. She put on her glasses to draw Lorenzo's dark face into focus. He was picking the currants out of a piece of fruitcake and swallowing a yawn.

"How do you know Stevie?" she asked.

"We were at school together. Now we're up at Cambridge."

"Oh." She had assumed, somehow, that he would be older than Stevie. His voice had the bitter flavor she associated with wisdom. Now that she could see him properly she thought him very striking. Perhaps he did have some Italian blood, as his nickname suggested. He was as swarthy as a Florentine, with thick smooth hair, the color of molasses, and magnificent, intense dark eyes—eyes like night, as black as ebony or Whitby jet. They dominated his thin, clever face, with its large, sharp nose and prominent cheekbones. He was not handsome, like Stevie. But he was interesting. He sat very still, a statue of boredom, but Eleanor could tell he was all needles and pins underneath. Cautiously, she made another bid for his attention.

"Are you at the same college?"

"I'm at Trinity. He's at King's."

"And do you like it?"

"As much as I can like anything."

She persisted. "I thought term had started. Shouldn't you be there now?"

"I've been in a nursing home."

"Oh. Were you ill?"

"Amazingly, yes. It ruined my whole stay."

His languid sarcasm mortified her, but she knew she deserved it. "What was wrong with you?"

"I had my appendix removed. Stephen made me promise not to talk about it in polite society, which I suppose this is. But you asked. And if I hadn't told you, you might have thought it was something even more unspeakable."

"Did they show it to you after they had taken it out?"

He showed the first rustle of interest. "What on earth made you ask that?"

"I'd rather like to know what an appendix looks like."

"No you wouldn't. They did show it to me, actually, swimming in a jar of formaldehyde, and I found it quite repulsive."

"But weren't you interested?" she asked.

"I was surprised. If you really want to know, it looked like the most vulgar sort of pickle—disappointingly small and commonplace for something which had given me such heroic amounts of trouble."

"It would be so useful," Eleanor said earnestly, "if doctors could take out anything that was uncomfortable or painful, and put it in a jar, like an appendix."

This was the kind of remark that made most men run away from her at dances. Lorenzo, however, was considering it seriously.

"One's faults, you mean. Or one's worst memories. Anything that poisons the system. But one could never risk it, in case they turned out to be too awful to contemplate after all."

"Could anyone's faults be that awful?" she wondered. "Unless they had done something horrible—if they were a murderer, perhaps. I shouldn't think Charlie Peace's conscience would fit in one jar."

"Quite." The muscles in Lorenzo's jaw tensed, and he looked away from her angrily. "How colorfully you put it."

Stevie had caught some of this exchange. "You are a ghoul, Larry. Do stop going on about your operation. Talk to Eleanor about music, or something."

Obviously, Eleanor had said something wrong, just when

they were beginning to get somewhere. Afraid that she had
hurt him, she took Stevie's hint and changed the subject.
"Music? Do you play?"

"Yes."

"So do I."

"Are you any good?" His interest was minimal.

"I'd like to be better. My mother doesn't understand
how much it means to me. She can't see any purpose in a
musical daughter, beyond always having someone who can
get up a dance from scratch after a supper party."

"Whereas your aspirations are far loftier," suggested Lorenzo. "You utterly reject *The Merry Widow,* despise the
two-step and abominate ragtime."

Eleanor recalled her earlier performance of "Ragging the
Baby to Sleep," and hoped he was not making fun of her.
"I try to study properly, but my parents like something
with a jolly tune."

"Philistines. How they must wound your sensitive soul."

She had often thought this, and was crestfallen because
he had guessed it so easily. "Please don't laugh at me. I'm
sure you play so brilliantly that no one ever asks you to
roll back the carpet and thump out the cakewalk."

His thin lips twisted into a lopsided, rather rancid smile.
"Quite the opposite. Dance music is all I wish to play these
days. It's my one claim to popularity."

"Dance music?" The smile had caught Eleanor completely off guard. It set off a frightening, delicious shudder
in the pit of her stomach. Then, to her embarrassment, she
felt a hot, damp blush between her legs that swept right up
to her hairline. She rushed back into the conversation. "I
thought you'd be more interested in the more serious
composers."

"By 'serious' I take it you mean sickening Victorians
such as Chopin and Brahms, quivering with unctuous piety
and emotionalism."

"But great music is meant to be emotional," Eleanor
protested. She was still tingling, and had to make an effort
not to sound too excited. "It expresses the kind of universal
passions that can't be put into words."

"Nonsense. You can find the words for that sort of rubbish in any penny love story. The rhythms of the new
American music are infinitely greater because they express
the true spirit of the modern age."

"But they're so—so brash and unfeeling!"

"Exactly. Feeling is the death of art."

"Art," Eleanor said passionately, "should be beautiful."

"No. It should be brutal and uncompromising."

"What I mean is, art should be beautiful enough to arouse the emotions. I recognize great art because it makes me cry."

"Life makes you cry," he corrected her. "You're a sensualist, evidently."

"Am I?" She was mesmerized. "Does that mean I've been taken in by all the wrong things? Are you saying that if a thing is too easy to like, it isn't any good?"

"There should be no question of liking or disliking. Great art simply Is."

Flora was straining to keep the thread of their conversation, because Sybil would expect a report later. She did not understand a word of it, and could only pray that it was proper. Eleanor was probably not aware that she was leaning eagerly toward this young man they were all supposed to call Lorenzo, or that the color had deepened in her sallow face. If you didn't listen, you would swear she was flirting with him. More than ever, Flora wished she had caught his real name. Those peculiar dark eyes of his disturbed her with a nagging sense of familiarity. It was like the aftertaste of a bitter memory, and it faded before she could pin it down. No, she really could not say she had seen him before.

She was searching her memory when Stevie stood up, saying: "Aunt Flora, you've been an angel, but Lorenzo and I must dash for our train."

Lorenzo, to Eleanor's dismay, leaped out of his chair with unmistakable relief and shook her hand without meeting her eyes. She hardly heard Stevie's lavish thanks and goodbyes, and invitations to May Week, which left Francesca and Flora laughing together over the remains of the tea. Neither of them noticed Eleanor picking up Lorenzo's plate, and reverently eating the currantless crumbs of cake he had discarded.

"I'm insanely in love!" Stevie shouted, snatching off his college boater and hurling it into the air. "She's the sweetest, the most divine, the most adorable, the most peerless little jewel I ever saw in my life!"

"Is she?" asked Lorenzo. "I didn't look."

Stevie retrieved his hat from a gorse bush. "No, of course not. You're too infinitely lofty, too far above us all."

"Well, what good would it have done me? You were all over her. It was a revolting spectacle."

They were walking down East Heath Drive toward the cab rank in Hampstead High Street, smoking Lorenzo's Turkish cigarettes.

"I don't know how you can be so impervious to beauty," Stevie said reproachfully. "That gorgeous, ridiculous little nose, that wicked little mouth—"

"That totally empty little head," supplied Lorenzo.

"Delightfully empty. Girls shouldn't know anything. They should be restful and refreshing. Look at poor old Eleanor—just about as dry as a government report. You were a hero to keep her occupied."

"I wasn't doing it for you," Lorenzo said. "I rather liked her. Girls with turned-up noses are always kindhearted."

"What on earth were you talking about?"

"Art. I could have done without her opinions, which were quite amazingly silly. Like all these earnest women, she's coated in a sort of sticky glue of romance. It's a pity, really. All she needs is prolonged and intense fucking. Then she might be intelligent."

"Larry, you couldn't!" exclaimed Stevie. "She's a good sort . . ."

"I'm only writing out the prescription. I don't propose to administer the medicine."

Stevie stopped in front of Lorenzo, and placed his hands on his shoulders. "What's the matter?"

"Nothing."

"I keep forgetting, you're supposed to be an invalid. Are you all right?" Affectionately, he smoothed back a lock of Lorenzo's black hair. "Have I tired you out?"

Lorenzo jerked his head away and walked on. "You make all this fuss about coming down from Cambridge to fetch me because you decide I'm an invalid, and then you drag me across town to drink tea with a lot of bloody women."

"I thought it would cheer you up!"

"Stephen, your obsession with cheering me up bores me beyond measure. It's so simpleminded."

"Come on," Stevie coaxed, "what's up?"

"You might have told them my name. None of them knew who I was."

"I sent in your card. What more do you want?"

"The old trout couldn't read them. You should have said something—they'd never have let me in if they'd known."

Stevie, trying to keep pace with him, caught Lorenzo's arm. "Look here, what harm can it do? You're always saying you despise the conventions. I think you make too much of the whole business. It's never mattered to me."

"No, because you're so nice," Lorenzo said. "So appallingly, unremittingly nice—it's like being stuck in a heatwave without any shade. Nothing much matters to you."

Stevie laughed. "Thanks."

"It's a gift. Cultivate it."

"For God's sake, Larry, what's the use of torturing yourself over something you can't change?"

"Other people do the torturing. You can't imagine what it's like to be treated as a live exhibit from the Chamber of Horrors."

"Oh, it was all ages ago," Stevie said breezily. "You're far too sensitive. When poor old Eleanor started talking about murderers, you looked as if you were going to bite her. Actually, I think she was rather smitten with you. What did you really think of her?"

"She's all right." Lorenzo considered for a moment. "Better than most, I suppose."

Sybil Braddon, a middle-aged, dried-up gimlet-eyed caricature of Eleanor, was replete with the triumph of her afternoon. Viola's splendid, glacial blond beauty had created a sensation at Lady Gaisford's, and hearing about the reappearance of Stevie added the final flourish of delight.

"Nice boy, how dear of him to look us up," she said to Flora. "Marian Carr-Lyon wrote to say they were back from India, but what with Viola and Gus, I never got around to calling. We must go tomorrow. You'll come with me."

"Yes, of course," Flora said meekly.

"He seems to have cast a spell on Francesca. Poor little thing, she's usually so terrified of strangers. And with that dreadful mother of hers, who can wonder at it? Oh, she says Stevie brought a friend with him. Was it anyone we know?"

Flora braced herself. "I'm afraid—you see, in the confusion, I didn't quite catch his name."

She waited for the heavens to fall, but Sybil continued to smile. Her mind was on the handsome Carr-Lyon fortune, and the possibility of another engagement in the house before the end of the season. "Never mind. I'm sure he's suitable if Stevie knows him."

"Yes," beamed Flora, "that's just what I thought."

"Really, Flora, what a good thing you had your wits about you and thought of making them stay for tea. Send Stevie a card for Viola's dance, dear, and put in a note to say that Mr. Whatshisname can come too. There are never enough young men to go around."

Flora decided that if she could earn this much approval without even trying, things were really looking up. She would forget all about those vague feelings of recognition and foreboding she had had concerning Lorenzo the Innominato. Sybil would only demand one of her grand inquisitions, and one should never go looking for trouble. There was enough in the world already.

PART TWO

1913

Aurora

Letter to my Daughter, 1935

There we are, the four of us, faded to sepia in the photograph I keep on my desk. Caught for all time in clothes that have gone through fashionable and grotesque, and now merely seem quaint. It is the summer of 1913, and we are on the terrace of the Braddons' house in Hampstead. I am on the right, with my arm around Eleanor. Why am I laughing? I can't remember. But we laughed all the time in those days.

That summer seems as strange as a foreign country now. The way we talk about it, you'd think it was an age of gold. Mr. Asquith was Prime Minister and, rain or shine, he left the nation to govern itself for two hours every evening while he played bridge. The newsboys, with their perpetual litany of "Extra! Extra! Read all about it!" had not yet become urchins of doom, because the news never seemed very bad.

In fact, it wasn't a golden age at all. There was a civil war brewing up over Ulster. The suffragettes were at the height of their militancy, slashing paintings and planting bombs. The workers were on the rampage, and there were strikes and lockouts. Plenty to worry Papa and Mr. Phillips over their morning kippers.

But it was an age of innocence for us, because we were innocent. We lived at the heart of a wealthy Empire, safe in the protective wadding of our gender and social class. We believed in honor and chivalry, and the nobility of a just war. People talked knowingly of "sending a British gunboat" to trouble spots, as if the mere presence of our flag could make right prevail over might. Our generation was young and idealistic, and like all younger generations we secretly believed we would never grow old. The tragedy was that so many of us turned out to be right.

At the time, however, it was wonderful fun. London was a sooty carnival, under a warm May sky. We danced and gossiped, and drove our elders mad by bashing out the latest rags on the piano. I considered myself a serious, intellectual person, but my political obsessions did not seem to interfere with the ceaseless round of organized frolics. Tennis parties were all the rage, and I spent hours on the Braddons' tennis court, teaching the other girls my unbeatable overhand serve.

Mrs. Braddon didn't much like me. Who can wonder at it? My voice was loud and unrefined, and so Irish that it sounded as if I had been marinading it in a bog for the past six years. I never wore a corset, and affected a "bohemian" style of dress that mortified my poor friends. You must picture me in my favorite Russian blouse of vivid lizard green, loosely belted over a shapeless black skirt, to understand what a scarecrow I made of myself. I dare say I was rather an embarrassment.

There was nothing delicate about my innocence. A velvet bloom it was not—it was more like a brazen suit of armor, which clanged hideously whenever I opened my mouth. I fancied I knew everything, and assumed happiness was my birthright. In short, I was as raw as a newly lifted turnip.

Mind you, having to stay with Aunt Hilda damped down my high spirits. Aunt Hilda Veness lived in a gloomy, gravy-colored Bayswater mansion, with four dotty old servants and nine parrots. These peevish, molting birds gobbled and raved all night, like nine demented Mrs. Rochesters, and I wished they had not been encouraged to fly around the house—I never could get used to their scaly little feet suddenly landing on my shoulder.

Poor Aunt Hilda, how cordially we disliked one another. Her white puffiness reminded me of a two-day-old blancmange, and she reeked of cabbage. She was a very strict vegetarian, so the food was unspeakable. After a week of it I had such a craving for meat that I could have eaten the coalman's dray horse, blinkers and all. She was also a spiritualist and hosted a séance in her dining room every Tuesday afternoon. This obsession with the dead made a grievously depressing atmosphere for a lively twenty-year-old girl. I'm not ashamed to tell you that I howled with homesickness for the first few nights, and I would have bartered my soul for a sight of Tertius.

However, I had my blood-sisters of the vow to comfort me. I had not known, until I met them again, the value of female friendship. Men are all very well in their proper places, bless them, but you will only find true sanity in the company of women. I had grown up regarding myself as a failed boy. Thanks to Eleanor, Francesca and Jenny, I learned to be proud of my womanhood. The old love between us proved to be as strong as ever, though there were one or two initial frictions. For instance, it took me a while to get used to the immaculate young ladyhood of Jenny, whom I loved most of all. Frankly, I thought she had become disappointingly stuck-up. And so I told her.

"You don't have to be tepid and genteel with me," I said. "What are you up to?"

"Up to?" Jenny echoed vaguely.

"I remember that look of yours from school. You're after another prize medal." I had got her on her own. We were strolling around the pond in Kensington Gardens, watching the little boys sailing their toy boats. "I want to know why you're dressed like a fashion plate all of a sudden," I persisted, "and turning up your exquisite nose at working for a living. Have you come into a fortune?"

"Wish I had."

"In that case you must have blown the entire contents of your piggy bank on a ridiculous load of gloves and stockings. And I can't believe you'd be so daft without a good reason."

Jenny, who was rarely moved to bluntness, retorted that I had no right to lay down the law about other people's clothes—had I seen myself lately? We had quite an argument, which ended with her spilling out all her matrimonial plans and making me swear not to tell the others. I can't say I approved. The bare idea of marriage was enough to make my blood run cold.

If you are to understand anything at all about us, you must understand our desperate ignorance. Our grasp of sexual matters was pitifully vague. All we knew was that it was disastrous to let a man go "too far." The four of us used to have long discussions about what "too far" meant. Being a country girl, I had seen animals mating, but nobody had given me the slightest reason to believe the human act might be similar. Nobody told girls anything.

For unmarried girls before the war, life was a web of petty restrictions—all designed to shield us from the truth. Where have you been, dear? Whom were you with? Were they our sort of people? I had a hell of a time squeezing my own latchkey out of Aunt Hilda. "When I was a gel, Aurora, young ladies never went anywhere alone." We were young ladies. And young ladies were supposed to be guarded and spied on until they were handed into the custody of a husband, or until their virginity turned so old and sour that it was no longer a temptation to the opposite sex.

Men, of course, could do anything and go anywhere. The unfairness of it drove me crazy. For I was ambitious to change the world and I didn't see how I was to do it, when I had to fight just to go on a tram by myself. You couldn't pick up a newspaper that summer without reading about suffragettes attacking politicians, smashing windows or pouring treacle into pillar boxes. I longed to be one of them.

Looking back, the injustice of denying women the vote amazes me. Don't ever forget the heroines who suffered and struggled so that you could have a voice in the government of your country. Don't forget the prison sentences, the hunger strikes, the cruel forcible feeding. When I arrived in London, the Liberal Government had just devised the ingenious torture of the Cat and Mouse Act. Up to then, if a woman had gone on hunger strike and endured forcible feeding, the Home Office released her for the sake of her health—so she was free to go back into battle. Under the Cat and Mouse Act, she was released into house arrest and taken back to prison to resume her sentence as soon as she recovered. Mrs. Emmeline Pankhurst went in and out of Holloway Prison so many times under Cat and Mouse that the *Daily Mail* calculated she would not finish her sentence until 1930.

Her daughter Sylvia also knew the inside of a prison cell. Christabel Pankhurst, head of the Women's Social and Political Union, was hiding in Paris. Meetings of known militant organizations had been banned—the police had instructions to break them up and arrest the ringleaders. This

was the climate surrounding the WSPU when I joined—
dangerous, violent and utterly bewitching.

But how could I become a part of it with Aunt Hilda
on my back? She was always threatening to write to
Papa, and I knew that if I went too far I would be
whisked back to Ireland as fast as a weasel up a drain. I
had to find a way in, before my yearning for action exploded like a volcano.

One

London

Perhaps this was the place for her first grand political gesture, Rory thought. She could carve "Votes For Women" into that silly canvas of the execution of Mary, Queen of Scots. Then the police would haul her out screaming. She would be sent to prison for desecrating a National Treasure, after giving a stirring speech in court about the iniquities of the Cat and Mouse Act.

Impatiently, she sighed and dragged her boots resentfully across the parquet floor. What good would it do in the end? There was no fun in being militant all by yourself. She was only wandering around the National Gallery because she had nothing to do, and nowhere to go. Eleanor, Francesca and Jenny were at a charity bazaar, and it was séance day in Bayswater. Aunt Hilda had ordered her to make herself scarce "Because I will not have Madame Gerlinska's aura damaged by your skepticism and rudeness."

She could have disobeyed and stayed to laugh at Aunt Hilda's gullible circle of ladies and their fat Polish medium, but where was the fun in laughing alone? For the thousandth time, Rory longed for Tertius. Lord, how intensely she missed him, though she would never have told him so. He was conceited enough already.

"Aurora?" A hand suddenly touched her sleeve. "I knew it was you! Dinah, look—"

"Well, I'll be damned."

Startled, Rory turned to face the two women who had crept up behind her. They were in their mid-thirties, with the kind of intellectual drabness that conveyed gentility, high thinking and frugality. The woman who had greeted Rory was small and plump, in a shapeless dress of blue tussore with an appliqué of rust-colored fruit around the neck, and a long string of amber beads. Under her large, rather sagging hat—blue straw embroidered with orange raffia—her wispy brown hair was drawn into an artistic bun at the nape of her neck. She had moist, eager hazel eyes and slightly protruding front teeth.

Her friend, in sharp contrast, had the look of a leathery Romany, incongruously forced into a tweed jacket and skirt. Above the masculine collar and tie, her sallow face was lined and bitter, but her black eyes glittered with humor.

"Miss Curran—Miss Scott!" Rory recognized her former teachers from Winterbourne House and had to stop herself checking her hands for ink stains.

Dinah Curran gave a short bark of laughter, enjoying her confusion. "Aurora Carlington, I might have guessed we hadn't seen the last of you. You're the sort who's born to curse a schoolmarm's life. And good grief, child, hasn't your hair grown yet?"

"I prefer it this way," Rory returned, reminding herself that Curran no longer had the power to give her a black mark for untidy shoelaces. "That long plait was such a burden to me. Do you remember taking me home in the train after I was expelled? You nearly lectured my ears off."

"Yes, but how we laughed over it afterward," cut in Miss Scott, tilting up her mild face under the brim of her drooping hat. "You looked so dreadfully funny, just like a porcupine."

"How is old Maudie—Miss Westwood, I mean? Are you still at Winterbourne House?"

"No, thank the Lord," said Curran. "We left two years ago. Cramming erudition into ignorant little girls was beginning to curdle my milk of human kindness. I'm scraping a living writing articles now, and Cecil does woodcuts."

"You've grown into your looks, dear," Scottie murmured. "I always said you would. What a strong face she has, Dinah, with that high-bridged nose."

"Hmmmm," Miss Curran said dryly. "What brings you to the National Gallery? It can't be love of art, since you've spent the last ten minutes staring at quite the worst picture in the room."

Rory laughed. "I was trying to pluck up the courage to put my penknife through it."

Curran and Scott glanced at each other significantly.

"So," Curran said, "you cherish dreams of suffragette martyrdom, do you?"

"Yes. But I haven't done anything about them yet. And it's too quiet here, anyway. Who'd notice?"

"Aurora, you're priceless. You always did manage to commit your crimes in a blaze of glory."

"Excuse me, Miss Curran"—Rory was transfixed by a discreet strip of green, purple and white ribbon, pinned to her lapel—"are you a member of the WSPU?"

"Have been for years," Curran said proudly. "You might as well know. Why shouldn't I tell you? I didn't leave Winterbourne House. I was sacked."

"Why?" Rory was thrilled. "What did you do?"

"Marched in a WSPU procession to Hyde Park. Maudie would never have known about it if my picture hadn't appeared in the *Illustrated London News.*" "Large as life, and twice as handsome," put in Scott. "Miss Westwood doesn't approve of the vote and she made a fearful scene—well, I dare say you can imagine that, dear."

"I was requested to tender my resignation," Curran continued, "and I tendered Cecil's as well."

"How splendid of you!" Rory cried.

"Wouldn't call it that." Curran was gruff, but obviously pleased by her admiration. "Not much of a sacrifice."

"Look at her brooch," urged Scott, her eyes glistening with pride.

"Oh, Cecil—honestly!"

Curran's only piece of jewelry was a small gold brooch, set with a piece of flint. It took Rory a moment to work out what it was, but when she did she was filled with envy.

"The stone-thrower's badge! You've—you've been to prison!"

"Fourteen days for putting a brick through the window of the National Provincial Bank in Regent Street," Curran admitted, smiling.

"And did you"—Rory was breathless—"did you go on hunger strike?"

"Oh yes. Released after five days. But that was before forcible feeding, and long before the Cat and Mouse Act." Curran frowned. "I wouldn't do it now."

"This is so lucky," blurted Rory. "I'm so glad I met you—"

Curran suddenly laughed. "Are you hoping to pick up a few hints?"

"I never met a real suffragette before. I want to hear everything. Would you and Miss Scott come out to tea with

me?" Taking in the shabbiness of their clothes, she added:
"I mean, won't you let me take you out to tea?"

Curran and Scott looked at each other cautiously. There
was such a long pause that Rory was afraid she had said
something wrong. Presently, Miss Scott began to flutter politely that they must go. Curran interrupted her.

"The fact is, we haven't a brass farthing between us beyond our omnibus fare home. But if you're really offering
a free tea, we'll gladly accept."

"Dinah!" groaned Scott.

"My dear girl, there's no shame in being poor. Why
make it harder by being proud as well? Lead us to the
grub, Aurora, and don't take any notice of Cecil. She won't
admit it, but we're both ravenous. We did without lunch to
save the bus fare, but I'm not on hunger strike now."

Rory was intrigued. Old Curran always had been a character. She had feared her tongue as a schoolgirl, but now
she was beginning to appreciate the honesty and humor
behind the acerbity. This meeting was the best bit of luck
she'd had since she stepped off the boat.

They found a teashop with dimly artistic pretensions in
a turning off the Strand. It was decorated with beaten copper jars full of bullrushes, and the waitresses were genteel
types in crumpled smocks and Venetian glass earrings. Curran and Scott, having got over their spasm of pride, looked
around happily. They were savoring every crumb of this
unexpected treat. When the cake stand arrived, they fell
upon it voraciously.

Evidently the independent life Rory hankered after had
its harsher side. Curran and Scott—or Dinah and Cecil, as
Rory was told to call them—had won a measure of freedom. But as Dinah frankly said, with her mouth full of
Chelsea bun, very little stood between them and absolute
indigence. Cecil's meager private income paid the rent of
their attic. They ate, dressed and traveled out of whatever
they could earn from writing and drawing. Sometimes, Rory
gathered, they were actually hungry.

"I don't need much," explained Dinah, "but Cecil isn't
strong, you know. I do get rather wretchedly worried about
her."

"People are so kind to us," Cecil said, spooning rasp-
berry jam on her scone. "The lady we lodge with sent us

up a beautiful ham last week. Someone had given it to her, and she's Jewish, so she couldn't eat it herself—"

"That was her story anyway," interrupted Dinah.

They both laughed, and went on to tell Rory how lucky they considered themselves. Dinah edited a suffragette magazine called *Atalanta,* owned and distributed by her landlady, Miss Berlin. Cecil designed posters and cards for the Suffrage Atelier, a group of artists dedicated to getting the vote. She also sold textile designs to an arts and crafts shop in New Oxford Street. It was a precarious existence, but a happy one.

"Miss Berlin knows we wish to be alone and independent," Cecil was saying, "but she is wonderfully generous about inviting us downstairs to dinner."

"Too generous, I sometimes think," Dinah said. "Her guests have a miraculous knack of begging off at the last minute, just when we're at our hungriest. And always in pairs."

"Yet she is so tactful one couldn't possibly refuse her."

Dinah briefly covered Cecil's round hand with her veined brown one. "It's the spirit behind the offer rather than the help itself that matters."

They exchanged an oddly expressionless look as if they had gone beyond ordinary intimacy and were each drawing strength from an invisible current that flowed from the other's eyes. It was only the briefest moment before Dinah attacked the last scone, but Rory suddenly remembered seeing the two of them at school, reading poetry, enclosed in an intimate circle of lamplight. The memory was oddly embarrassing. She quickly ordered another pot of tea and pushed Dinah onto the subject of the suffragettes.

Dinah immediately became stern and businesslike. If Rory was serious about the cause, she said, she had chosen a critical moment to join it.

"The long and short of it is that after so much progress, we seem to be at a standstill."

"But the bombing, the stone-throwing—" Rory protested. "The militants have never been so strong. And so many people sympathize—"

"Three little words, dear," Dinah shook her head grimly. "Cat and Mouse. Do you know what it means to be a mouse? Scores of us simply can't afford it. How on earth would Cecil manage on her own while I popped in and out of the clink?"

"Dinah—" Cecil cut in gently.

"All right, I'm speechifying. I'll get off my soapbox. But I can't help despairing sometimes. Because we all know the reasoning behind the Act—it's so they can round up all our leaders and clap them back in prison at the least sign of trouble. And now even some people in the WSPU are saying it's all because of the extreme militancy."

"And I bet others are saying it hasn't been extreme enough!" Rory declared.

Dinah gave Rory one of her bitter smiles, which wrinkled her brown face like a walnut. "Is that what you think?"

"Yes," Rory said. "The government must see that they can't stop women fighting—that if they make it harder, we'll fight harder."

Dinah nodded appreciatively. "One of these days, someone will bundle Asquith, Lloyd George and Churchill into a motorcar and drive it over a cliff. Serve 'em right."

"But then the Conservatives will get in," Rory pointed out. "And that'll be even worse. We should be joining forces with the Labour movement, so that when women get political power they can use it to do some good!"

Instead of being annoyed, Dinah and Cecil grinned at each other.

"She ought to meet Frieda, she really ought," murmured Cecil.

"How the old girl would love her!" Dinah agreed. "Look here, Aurora—are you free on Friday evening? Miss Berlin is holding a meeting of our committee and I'm sure I can bag you a place at supper."

"I'd love it." Rory lay back in her chair, so happy she felt immortal. It was as if a wall had come down, revealing a shimmering landscape of possibilities. The crowd inside the teashop had thinned, and the waitresses were brushing down the abandoned tables. Outside the sky was deepening to dusk. Rory, enchanted by the lights blooming along the windows opposite, and the seething tide of people and traffic, wished this moment could last forever.

"You'll find all the bad influences you're obviously longing for," said Dinah. "It's the least we can do after stuffing ourselves at your expense." She waved an empty plate at a passing waitress. "Now, how about another go at those scones?"

Two

Jenny took a tiny mirror out of her bag and checked as much of her appearance as possible. Yes, she looked perfect. And so I should, she thought, settling back in the taxi. Everything she had brought with her to London, down to the buttons on her gloves, was virginally new. When Rory accused her of blowing all her savings on a load of gloves and stockings she had scored a bull's-eye. Jenny and her mother had assembled an entire trousseau, taking the husband on trust. But once you decided to take such a risk, half-measures were pointless.

At home in Edinburgh, Jenny had felt an occasional twinge of panic. The last doubt had vanished, however, on her very first evening at Hampstead when she laid out her new eau-de-nil dinner dress on the satin eiderdown of her superlatively comfortable bedroom. This was where she truly belonged; this world of cat-footed servants and hothouse flowers. The old life already had the strangeness of a disagreeable dream.

For the last three days, she had been finding her position in the Braddon household. And, as usual, she had judged it to a nicety. She wrote letters for Mrs. Braddon, sang to Mr. Braddon after dinner, listened patiently to Flora's ramblings, and never rang her bell when it was inconvenient for the servants. Mrs. Braddon could not do enough to show her approval. "That child," Jenny had overheard her telling her husband, "was born to be a comfort to others."

However, she had plans for her own comfort. She was here to cultivate poor little Effie MacNeil, with a view to marrying her brother, and she did not intend to let the grass grow under her feet. Checking her hat for the last time, she stepped out of the taxi and into the huge, chilly porch of number five Hyde Park Gate—the London house of MacNeil's sister, Mrs. Hamish MacIntyre.

It was a ponderous, six-storied mansion of yellowed stucco on the best side of the park. Jenny had to breathe deeply several times to compose herself for the opening of the campaign. There was no need to be nervous, she reminded herself, because she was unlikely to find any of the family at home now. All she had to do was leave a card.

A footman in a striped vest showed Jenny into a hall tiled with black and white marble and overshadowed by a huge staircase. It seemed magnificent, but it had a reassuringly lived-in air. The end of a pram was visible under the stairs, and the chasing on the footman's salver was clogged with old polish.

Telling her to wait, he whisked open a tall door. Through it shot Inkerman, barking energetically, his paws skidding on the marble.

Effie ran out behind him, grabbing his collar. "Miss Dalgleish? Is it really you? Oh, how nice!"

Jenny was slightly taken aback by how young she looked. Her lank floss of fair hair hung loose to her waist, tied with a wilted red ribbon, and she wore a schoolgirl's white blouse and navy serge skirt. Her round, button-nosed face beamed with such unaffected pleasure that Jenny was both warmed and ashamed.

"I said I'd call if I found myself in London, Miss Mac-Neil, though I didn't think it likely at the time."

"Have you got a job down here?"

"No, some friends very kindly invited me down for the season."

"I see." Effie was sensitive enough to realize that she had said something wrong, but had no idea how to put it right. The painful crimson bled into her cheeks and ears. "I'm sorry—I thought—I shouldn't—"

"Two girls I was at school with," Jenny said quickly, with a sideways glance at the footman, who was eyeing her shrewdly. "My oldest friends."

"I saw you getting out of the taxi," Effie said, gazing at Jenny's suit with round eyes, "but I didn't recognize you. I thought you must be someone terribly grand, coming for Cornelia. What a perfectly lovely hat!" She remembered her manners. "I—won't you please come into the drawing

room? Cornelia's upstairs, in the nursery. It's not her day
for receiving."

"It's you I meant to call on, Miss MacNeil. I was going
to leave a card, while you were out—"

"Oh, I'm never out."

Awkwardly, Effie did the honors of her sister's house.
She led Jenny into the faded, somewhat old-fashioned
drawing room, and invited her to sit in the extreme corner
of a long sofa beside the empty fireplace. She perched herself on a hard chair about twenty feet away, and frowned
at Inkerman when he tried to jump on her knee. The footman shut the double doors behind him, and they were left
in a rigor of politeness.

"Are you enjoying your stay in London?" began Jenny.
She noticed a chewed, grubby tennis ball beside her foot,
and laughed. "I interrupted your game, didn't I?"

Effie blushed again, but joined in the laughter. "Yes, I
was rolling it under the furniture for Inky to chase. He's
not supposed to be in here—that's why the servants are so
cross with me. But I haven't anything else to do." She came
over to take the ball from Jenny's hand and stayed kneeling
on the rug beside her, stroking Inkerman's head. "To tell
you the awful truth, I'm not enjoying myself at all. I
wouldn't mind if only I could take Inky out more, but I'm
only allowed in the park with Alistair, or the nursemaid
when she takes the children. And anyway, it isn't the same
as Glen Ruthven."

"No, it certainly isn't," Jenny agreed. "But surely you're
going out and meeting people?"

"Cornelia's friends are so old," said Effie disconsolately.
"All they talk about is babies. It's not so bad when Alistair's here—he took me to the theater to see *The Mikado*
last week, and I loved that. But he's out most of the time.
At his club, I think."

"You haven't been here long. You'll find it's a lot more
fun when you get out more."

"I bet you're having fun." Effie's wistful eyes were once
more devouring Jenny's clothes. "You look simply gorgeous. I hope it's not rude to say so."

Jenny felt a stirring of genuine sympathy, which slightly
irritated her because she had not anticipated it. Poor little
thing, she could not help thinking, it really must be as dull
as a tomb for her here. Why had MacNeil made such a

fuss about bringing her to London if he meant to leave her alone all day? She began to describe the Braddon household and its entertainments. Her sympathy increased as she saw how blissful the dinners, dances and wedding preparations sounded to Effie.

"There's to be a party, the night before the ceremony, and I'm to be one of the bridesmaids."

"Lucky, lucky you," Effie said, with her whole heart. "Alistair knows Mr. Fenborough—he showed me a beautiful picture of Miss Braddon in the *Bystander*. Are your school friends her sisters?"

Jenny found herself explaining about Eleanor, Francesca and Rory, and the blood vow they had made at school. It was the last thing she had intended to do, but it was only too easy to expand before such a rapt audience.

Effie, drinking it all in enviously, had gradually collapsed onto her stomach, propping her plump chin with incongruously skinny hands. "I could tell you weren't a real governess," she declared, "not like the ones I had, anyway. And Alistair agreed. We thought you must be in disguise, like a witch in a fairy tale. Oh, I'm so glad you came! You're the first visitor I've had."

"Don't you have any London friends at all?"

"No, Inky's my best chum, aren't you, laddie?" She cuffed the dog affectionately. "I should have listened to Alistair, and left him at home. He doesn't think much of any place where he can't chase rabbits."

Her cheerfulness touched Jenny. "I can't bear to think of you having such a dull time—and there's really no need for it. You said Mr. MacNeil knows Mr. Fenborough, so perhaps your mother and sister would let you come out to Hampstead one afternoon?"

"Gosh—when?"

"Well," Jenny paused. It was essential to manage the affair properly. "Mrs. Braddon loves a full house, and she seems to have guests at most meals except breakfast—but I really should ask your sister, before I invite you anywhere."

"Yes, I suppose so."

Jenny was sorry to see Effie deflating. "We're holding a tennis party tomorrow—very informal, just us and some neighbors. It doesn't matter if you can't play. None of us is much good—"

"I'd love it!"

"But, Miss MacNeil, you must see how awkward it is since I haven't been introduced to your sister. Perhaps another time would be more—"

"Wait, I'll ask her now." And before Jenny could object, Effie dashed out of the room with Inkerman panting at her heels. Silence descended as the sound of her scampering footsteps faded up the stairs. Jenny smoothed her gloves, and marveled at her newfound capacity for acting on impulse.

Heavier-sounding footsteps were heard in the hall. Jenny rose and turned toward the door, trying not to feel defensive.

"Miss—Dalgleish? I am Euphemia's sister." She was a fair, handsome woman in her late thirties, with her brother's small, steel-blue eyes and square jaw.

"How do you do, Mrs. MacIntyre?"

Jenny saw at once that Mrs. Hamish MacIntyre was normally an easygoing, smiling woman. She was not, however, smiling now. Suspicion gathered on her face as she duplicated Effie's performance of scrutinizing Jenny's clothes.

"Forgive me, Miss Dalgleish, but this is all most irregular. That silly child is upstairs nagging Mother about some sort of tennis party. I felt sure there had been a misunderstanding, and I wish you would tell her so."

Jenny knew she was at a disadvantage. It happened rarely, and was humiliating. "I'm sorry. You see, I was assuming that because I met Mr. MacNeil in Scotland—"

"Yes," Mrs. MacIntyre interrupted sternly. "You were a schoolmistress, weren't you? Or was it a governess? I do recall hearing something about you."

Evidently it had not been a pleasure. Jenny held her head higher. She had not foreseen that MacNeil would have an armed guard of female relations ready to defend him from designs like hers.

"I was temporarily employed by Mr. MacNeil's tenants. I'm staying in London with friends."

"How nice. We should be glad to see you on our day, Miss Dalgleish, which is Thursday. However, I'm sure you appreciate that I can't allow Euphemia out with strangers—"

"They wouldn't be strangers!" Effie had caught the end of this speech. She ran into the room breathlessly. "Alistair

knows Mr. Fenborough, and Mr. Fenborough is engaged
to—"

"I thought I told you to leave that animal in the pantry,"
complained Mrs. MacIntyre, whisking her skirt away from
Inkerman's nose.

"Cornelia, please, please let me go!"

"Don't be foolish, dear. You're embarrassing Miss Dalgleish. You know Mother would never hear of it."

"But I never go anywhere!" Effie was tearful. "What
harm could it do me? If I could have the car I wouldn't
even have to put a toe on the pavement!"

"How can I possibly spare the car?"

"Oh, please! Just this once!"

Out in the hall, the front door slammed. Someone whistled, and Inkerman streaked toward the sound.

"Down, laddie—down, Inky. For the Lord's sake, get
down, you blithering nuisance—"

The moment she heard Alistair MacNeil's voice, Jenny's
heart fluttered painfully with suspense, as if she were moments away from foreclosing a vital bargain. Yet when
MacNeil came into the drawing room with Inkerman caper-
ing around his legs, her first emotion was keen disappointment. Unconsciously, she had improved him in her
imagination. He was older and balder than she remembered; an undistinguished, sandy, middle-aged gentleman in
a morning suit and spats.

When MacNeil saw her he halted, stared, and visibly
changed color. The solid red blush turned his eyes into
vivid chips of blue, and the lines around them melted.

"Je—Miss Dalgleish—"

This was so much more than she had allowed herself to
hope for that Jenny was exultant. She was also slightly dismayed by the way he gazed at her. At the Kentishes' party,
he had made her feel as if she had wounded him by mistake
with some invisible weapon she did not know how to handle. And here was that same look—glistening, wistful, horribly unguarded.

Effie broke the spell. "She came specially to see me.
Wasn't that decent of her?"

"Yes indeed." MacNeil recovered his usual expression of
quiet amusement as Effie took hold of his attention.

"They're having a tennis party tomorrow and she's asked
me to go but Cornelia says I can't. And I do call it mean."

"Oh, for heaven's sake, Alistair," Mrs. MacIntyre said crossly, "do put it out of her head. Mother will get so agitated."

"Why does she have to find out about it? What's the objection?"

Mrs. MacIntyre became embarrassed. "I know it's terribly kind of Miss Dalgleish, but I don't think Mother would be at all happy about Effie going to a stranger's house."

"She won't mind if I'm with her."

Effie flung her spindly arms around his neck. "Oh, you saint!"

"Steady on, old lady. Don't throttle me. May I invite myself, Miss Dalgleish?"

"Of course you may." Jenny smiled, ignobly enjoying Mrs. MacIntyre's discomfiture. "If you'd really like to—though our game is simply awful. Three o'clock at Laburnum House in East Heath Drive."

"Splendid. That's settled, then. No need to get into a state, Corney. It'll do the child good to get out."

"Yes," Effie broke in eagerly, "I'm sure I've been looking pale lately."

"Pale—oh, really!" Reluctantly, Mrs. MacIntyre laughed. "We spoil you horribly."

She shook hands with Jenny quite graciously, and Jenny noticed that MacNeil, for all his geniality, took it for granted that his sisters would obey him. Her triumph was complete when he insisted on seeing her into a taxi.

Descending the front steps on his arm, Jenny had the peculiar sensation that she was standing aside and watching something she had invented herself—as if she had fallen asleep at her desk in Edinburgh, and woken up in one of her own dreams.

Once they were alone in the street, however, it was MacNeil's masculine reality rather than his symbolic value that held her attention. She was overpoweringly aware of the brisk smell of his sandalwood shaving soap, and the tufts of fair hair on his wrists under the cuffs. She was not sure that it was pleasant.

He cleared his throat several times, before saying awkwardly: "Thank you for coming—to see Effie, I mean. I'm sorry if my sister seemed—she needs to get out among people nearer her own age. Cornelia and I are too old for her."

Jenny, to her surprise, felt entirely in control of the situation. "It's always difficult to know what to do with girls when they're in between the schoolroom and being presented. But frankly, Mr. MacNeil, I do think you could have done a little better. She looked so aimless, my heart went out to her."

"What should I do?"

"You shouldn't ask me. I don't want to interfere."

"Nonsense. I am asking you. You're the ideal person since you're still a flapper yourself. Her clothes, for instance?"

Their pace had slowed. Jenny smiled up at him.

"Honestly?" she asked.

"Be brutal."

"Awful. Far too young for her."

MacNeil laughed. "Then we'll take her shopping."

Instinctively, Jenny veered away from this implied intimacy. She was not sure how serious he was. "There won't be much point buying her clothes unless you intend to take her out in them. She didn't tell me in so many words, of course—but I did get the impression that you leave her alone a great deal."

They halted in the middle of the pavement. Out of the corner of her eye, Jenny saw a vacant taxi rattle past. MacNeil was staring down at her again with the expression that made her long to run away.

"Jenny." His fingers were warm on her glove. There was no escaping now. "Can't you guess what I've been doing since I last saw you?"

"I—I don't know—"

"Searching for you."

"What?"

"Don't look at me like that. Don't be angry. Every time I close my eyes, there you are in your white gown. I dream of hearing you sing until I think I'm taking leave of my senses. I even made Mrs. Kentish give me the address of the agency she got you from. You poor little girl"—he gave a short, rueful laugh—"you look absolutely scandalized. Was it so dreadful of me?"

"Oh no!"

"Of course, the damned agency wouldn't give me your address—I suppose they thought I was a white slaver—so I've been at my wits' end. Before I saw you this afternoon, I was on the point of composing an advertisement for the

Edinburgh papers. Wanted, young governess from Morningside area, must have sweet voice and hazel eyes."

"Mr. MacNeil—"

"No, you mustn't say anything. It wouldn't be fair of me to expect it. But I had to tell you. I won't mention it again, if it upsets you."

"I'm not upset," Jenny muttered, but it was not true. She was wild to get away from him. "Look, here comes another one."

"Another what?"

"Taxi."

MacNeil seemed to shake himself awake. "Good Lord, what must you think of me?" He waved the taxi down, bowed to her gravely and handed her into it as if attending Cleopatra in her barge.

Jenny risked glancing behind her as the taxi pulled away, and saw, with a peculiar mixture of annoyance and gratification, that he was still standing on the curb, his hat in his hand, watching her. Thank heaven he had not kissed her. Preparing herself for the awful moment when he did would be her next task.

Meanwhile, she had made excellent progress. There would be no need to set snares for Alistair MacNeil. If you wanted to be coarse about it, you could say he was not only shot and bagged, but practically trussed and cooked. A sprig or two of garnish, and he would be ready for the table.

Yet the taste of success was unexpectedly sour. A man of honor, upright and kind, a man who deserved the sort of woman he innocently believed Jenny to be, had fallen in love with her. All she had to offer in return were chilly things like respect and esteem. She despised herself, but what good would that do anyone? Scruples were expensive and far beyond her means.

Intensely weary, Jenny looked down at her white kid gloves, the best that could be got for money. All her pleasure in them had vanished. For there was one glaringly cheap, tawdry item that spoiled her crisp new trousseau completely. It was, of course, herself.

Three

She heard the front door slam, she heard him dropping his cane on the hall floor, and his breath thickening as he bent to pick it up.

How had he got in?

No house in the world, no power on earth, was strong enough to keep him out. Francesca's limbs stiffened and chilled to stone inside the warm sheets, and her tongue swelled with panic. His footsteps were coming up the stairs. He stumbled, and cursed to himself absentmindedly. He was on the landing, winged like a great bat in his evening cape.

Her eyes were tight shut, but she could see him. She curled into a ball to make herself invisible, hugging her knees under her chin. The whole room reeked of evil. It was no use crying out for Mummy, because she was far away, and nobody would tell her when she was coming back.

His hand was turning the handle of the door, and the yeasty smell of alcohol was already in her nostrils. This time, she must scream—for Mummy, for God, for anyone—before his shadow fell across her bed. Her throat was dry, and there was a sickening weight on her chest.

He was in the doorway, staring at her. Horror poured over her, unending, utterly engulfing. Oh, please, please— Then the sinister angles became straight. She was awake, mantled in a film of sweat, tears stinging her lips. And she was safe, because Mrs. Braddon was beside her; a comfortable figure in her lacetrimmed dressing gown, with her gray-streaked hair in a long plait down her back.

"My little lamb."

The mattress sagged under her weight. She smelled of sleep and lavender. Her hand was cool on Francesca's forehead.

"Mother?" Eleanor was in the doorway, blinking drowsily.

"She was dreaming again, that's all. Go back to bed, dear. I'm here."

Francesca shut her eyes, making herself concentrate on the hypnotic rhythm of Mrs. Braddon's hand stroking her hair. She could not look at Eleanor because of the terrible, spider-legged shadow she made.

Stevie's shadow sprawled across the grass, thin and gangling in the slanting rays of afternoon sun. Francesca was tired, and suddenly gnawed by a sharp anxiety to get home. She edged closer to Eleanor, who was waiting with Viola and Gus while the young men argued over how they should divide in the punts.

"I'll take Miss Garland, but not the tea basket. And not you, Squeakie—there isn't room. Twisden can have you."

"No fear. Twisden's hopeless. And you had the girls last time. It's not fair."

Eleanor, with her perpetual hunger for anything beautiful, was watching Stevie. His hair was ethereally golden where the sun struck it. In his white flannel trousers and open-necked white flannel shirt, he was the living spirit of youthful gallantry and grace. Dashing, she thought. Like a painting of a young cavalier in a lace collar and breastplate, equally at home in a drawing room or a battlefield.

And Stevie was only the centerpiece of a scene that should have been idyllic. Green willows wept into the sparkling waters of the Cam. Silky ripples smacked against the three punts moored among the reeds. The air smelled of high summer, yet the leaves still had a springlike sheen that reflected shifting diadems of light onto the young grass.

But Eleanor had seen the day through a rimy fog of disappointment. Stevie had invited them up to Cambridge for this picnic tea on the river. He had promised friends, and she had assumed Lorenzo would be among them. He was not. Instead, she had to make do with a thin, pale and generally weedy youth named Hilary Twisden, and a pair of identical twins, introduced as Miles and Cedric Burlington, but always addressed as "Bubble" and "Squeak."

She had a terrible suspicion that Mr. Twisden had been specially invited with her supposed earnestness in mind. He had sat beside her all through tea, talking about Norse myths and Tennyson. Of course, he was going to be ordained. He was one of nature's curates. Bubble and Squeak teased him relentlessly. They were as lively as a pair of puppies; tall and skinny, with innocent, surprised brown eyes, and springy clumps of dark hair like the dots on exclamation marks.

"Look here," Bubble piped up now. "If I take Fenborough and Miss Braddon—"

"Dearest," Gus said to Viola, "are you cold?"

Viola, standing immobile beneath her parasol, shrugged. "No."

"Can I get you a shawl or something?"

"A shawl? I'm not a grandmother."

Eleanor unkindly thought that it would take more than a shawl to warm her sister. She was as cold as an icicle, and it was amazing that dear old Gus had not turned blue, after a day of dancing attendance on her.

Viola was the family miracle; a pale gazelle with a cloud of white-blond hair and eyes of an unusual blue-green, like flawless aquamarines. People who had seen photographs of her were unprepared for the shock of her extraordinary beauty. She exuded a silvery aura of separateness that no picture could capture. All the young men were frightened of her, and obviously wondered how Gus had ever got up the courage to propose.

You could not help liking Gus. Viola's brilliant match was a short, thick-set man of twenty-seven, with sparse light brown hair, a small mustache and an unremarkable round face. He did not look like a brilliant match—particularly not now, when the sun had baked him as pink and shiny as a glazed ham—but there was kindness and good nature in every line of him. He loved Viola to desperation, and Eleanor always tried to be nice to him when her sister rebuffed his attempts at romance.

"Were you good at punting, Gus, when you were here? I do think they might give you a turn."

He grinned at her. "Never really got the hang of it."

"It's all settled," Stevie announced. "Twisden gets the tea basket, Eleanor and Squeakie. Bubble will take you and Viola, Fenborough—"

Francesca plucked at Eleanor's sleeve. "That means I'll be alone with him!" she whispered. "And I can't!"

"Oh, darling, you're not afraid of Stevie! I thought you liked him."

"Not all by myself."

The disappointment of the afternoon had worn away Eleanor's patience. Of course, she would do anything to protect Francesca, but this time she was just being silly. Perhaps Mother was right about not indulging her peculiar terrors. "You won't be by yourself. He isn't going to abduct you. And if you make a fuss about it, we'll be standing here forever."

"All right." Francesca seemed to shrink back into herself, and Eleanor felt mean.

"I'll tell Mr. Twisden to stay close," she said reassuringly. "It's not as if I won't be looking after you."

She felt meaner when she saw the limitless trust in Francesca's eyes. It reminded her that Francesca's total reliance upon her had meant less since she met Lorenzo. Did the fact that she seemed to be outgrowing this old love mean that she was clearing emotional territory for a new, a greater one? Eleanor's ideas about falling in love had been largely culled from romantic novels, and she could not see how her one meeting with Lorenzo had anything to do with conventional courtship. She was aware, however, in a confused way, that she responded powerfully to unhappiness.

But if Francesca feared being alone with poor Stevie, who had probably arranged the whole day around the chance of a few minutes' unchaperoned flirtation, it must not happen.

"Tell you what," Eleanor offered, "I'll get into Stevie's boat with you. He can hardly say anything once I'm actually there."

"Oh, would you?"

At last, they were moving toward the punts. Squeak threw the plates and cups into the tea basket, while Hilary Twisden and Gus conscientiously buried the champagne bottles and stamped on the embers of the fire. Stevie leaped into his punt, holding out a hand for Francesca.

This was Eleanor's cue. She imitated his agile jump off the bank, caught her foot on the rope and hit the water full-length, in an undignified belly flop. The river—unexpectedly freezing and far less pleasant to be in than on—rushed up to meet her so fiercely that her glasses were sucked off her nose and the hatpins torn out of her hair. Fighting to find the surface, she panicked, and the current tugged her out of her depth.

Within seconds, Stevie and Gus had jumped in after her. Even in this extremity, Eleanor knew she would be mortified afterward to think of the parts of her body they had touched in their attempts to grapple her back to the bank. She was carried to the shore in Gus's arms, and deposited, shivering and plastered with green slime, beside Viola.

It was a disaster. If Eleanor had not been so cold, she would have blushed with shame.

Viola regarded her with a scornful little half-smile. "Oh, Eleanor. Really. How typical."

"Say you're all right," Francesca implored tearfully. "Please say it!"

"Yes—I'm fine—oh, Gus, I'm so dreadfully sorry. You can let go of me now, really—"

"Got the hat!" Stevie shouted. He was treading water, holding Eleanor's wilted, dripping straw hat aloft like a trophy.

Gus's attention veered back to the river. "She's lost her specs. Anyone see where they went down?"

"Let's dive for 'em!" yelled Bubble, jubilantly flinging off his blazer.

"No, you mustn't—" began Eleanor.

But Bubble and Squeak plunged into the water, sending up tremendous fountains of splashes. Gus, unable to resist, dived after them.

"Well, that's that," Viola said. "We'll never get back to London now. Look at them—they're having a divine time."

Stevie, Gus and the twins, all roaring with laughter, were spraying and ducking each other, and vanishing under the punts with hands clamped over their noses. Eleanor bit her wobbling lower lip. She might have drowned, and they were using it as an excuse for playing about in the water. The wearing of spectacles apparently made one's every action seem ludicrous. If she wore them on her deathbed would they all stand around hooting with merriment?

"Here, put this on." Hilary gently draped his cricket jersey around her. "You shouldn't be standing still, you know. You'll catch the most fearful cold."

Eleanor gave him a grateful smile. "Thank you." His solemn, vulnerable face radiated sympathy, healing ointment to her ruined dignity.

"Your teeth are chattering. Walk around a bit—take my arm."

"I'm all right, honestly."

Francesca, still tearful, was making ineffectual passes at Eleanor's dress with her handkerchief. "That was horrifying. I hope I never have to live through anything like it again. I thought you were drowning. Is the water poisonous, Mr. Twisden? Did you swallow any, darling?"

"Mother will have apoplexy," remarked Viola. "You are an idiot."

"Could have happened to anyone," Hilary defended her. "I fell in last term, when I was cycling along the banks. It was beastly."

He encouraged her to hobble up and down the bank, clutching his arm, until she could draw a proper breath without shaking.

Cheers and more extravagant splashes came from the river. Bubble was wearing her spectacles comically on the end of his nose. The four divers waded to the bank, and hauled themselves onto the grass, where they lay spitting out fronds of weed in between shouts of mirth.

Stevie was the first to recover. Snatching the glasses away from Bubble, he wiped them carefully on Hilary's jersey and gave them back to Eleanor.

"Poor little thing, you look like a plucked chicken."

Eleanor forgave him for laughing, for he wrapped her in his own blazer, and put his arm around her in a protective, brotherly fashion that was very soothing, despite the fact that he was now wetter than she was.

"Look here, what on earth are we going to do?" demanded Gus. "We can't go back in the boats like this. And Eleanor ought to take those things off. She'll catch her death."

"We all will!" Squeak was running on the spot.

"Who lives nearest?" Gus asked. "Does anyone know exactly where we are?"

"Newnham," said Stevie. "I think we'd better try Lorenzo's. He can't be more than a quarter of a mile away."

The twins groaned loudly. "Not old Prussic Acid," protested Bubble. "I'd rather catch pneumonia."

The sound of Lorenzo's name, and the sudden hope of seeing him, sent a twitch of nervous anticipation through Eleanor's body. Stevie misinterpreted this and tightened his grip around her shoulders.

"It's not your pneumonia I'm worried about, you ass. Come on, Eleanor—it isn't far."

Eleanor stumbled awkwardly beside him, her sodden skirt flapping against her legs like a sheet of lead. "He—he won't mind, will he?"

"Course not. Don't take any notice of them. Lorenzo's a bit of a recluse these days, that's all. He's living out of college."

"On a Parnassian eminence," supplied Squeak. "With only the muses—the Naughty Nine—for company. Won't he be furious to see us poor mortals?"

"You don't have to annoy him. He isn't such a bad sort."

"Blood will out," Squeak said serenely.

"Shut up!" Stevie was angry. Eleanor, without understanding the reason, felt his muscles tightening in a sudden surge of violence.

Bubble and Squeak went through an elaborate pantomime of buttoning their mouths and Stevie relaxed into a smile. "Only one brain between them," he said to Eleanor. "It's so sad."

"Keep her circulation going," called Hilary. He trotted alongside them, jerking his knees and elbows encouragingly. "You should run, Miss Eleanor—like this."

"Nobody could possibly run like that!" Bubble said derisively.

"You liked Lorenzo, didn't you?" Stevie asked Eleanor. "Yes."

"I asked him to come today but he hates going out. He refuses to see any of us at the moment."

"Oh." She sifted this in her mind, trying to discover a nugget of hope for herself. At least it was not her presence that had put Lorenzo off the picnic.

"Twisden's right." Stevie gave her a rough squeeze. "We're not going fast enough. Your mother will put me through the mincer if you catch cold."

The straggling, dripping procession was winding along a rutted track on the outskirts of Newnham village. Flat fields, drowsy in the last of the golden light, were visible through the gaps in the hedgerows as the line of dilapidated cottages petered out into open country.

Bubble and Squeak dashed ahead to the last house in the row; a long, two-storied farmhouse, with untidy satellites of outbuildings—a cowshed, a henhouse and an unashamed outside privy like a little sentry box. The whitewash was peeling from the walls and the mossy tiles on the roof of the cottage were sagging.

"Lord," Viola murmured rudely.

"Any port in a storm," said Gus.

The twins were shouting at the upstairs windows. "Windy! Lorenzo! Are you there?"

From inside a voice called: "What angel wakes me from my flowery bed?" A casement opened, and a rough brown head, sucking an empty pipe, appeared.

After a confused barrage of explanation, the head vanished, and its owner came out into the farmyard. Eleanor, shivering again, wished the young men were readier with their introductions. She gathered that this was Lorenzo's co-tenant, an American undergraduate named Windrush. He seemed older than the rest of them—possibly in his late twenties; a portly, genial-looking man with a walrus mustache and a day's growth of beard; haphazardly dressed in darned tweed plus fours and a football jersey.

He chuckled behind his pipe. "I guess Hastings had better overcome his objections to hospitality."

"This is most frightfully good of you," Gus said, absurdly polite in his drenched flannels.

Eleanor hastily gathered together her last few shreds of dignity. Lorenzo was standing in the doorway, an open book dangling from his hand. There was another explanatory clamor, through which he frowned silently at Stevie. He was unshaven, and his thick black hair fell chaotically over his forehead. His eyes were suspicious; his body was as tense as a stretched wire. He would not look at her.

Mrs. Fuller, the owner of the cottage, had now run out and was apparently delighted by the drama, for she circled them exclaiming: "Oh, you poor things! And the poor young lady! You come inside with me, dear. I'll get you some hot water and put them clothes in front of the kitchen fire."

The party split up. Mrs. Fuller led Eleanor, Viola and Francesca into her dark, cabbage-smelling entry, while the men squelched up the narrow staircase after Windrush.

"Tea," Mrs. Fuller was saying knowledgeably. "Nice hot cup of tea. That's what you need."

"We've just had tea," Viola whispered crossly to Francesca.

Lorenzo made no attempt to move to allow them through. As Eleanor squeezed past him, she risked looking up, and saw that he was quietly laughing at her.

"You've got things growing on you," he said, picking a strand of river weed out of her hair. "This must be the result of a fertile imagination."

The shock of his touch set off a tingling in the pit of her stomach. She was so close that she could smell him, and see the gloss on the thick lashes around his ebony eyes.

"I say, Lorenzo!" Hilary's reedy voice broke the spell. "You might come and dig out some dry clothes!"

"Coming."

He went upstairs, and Eleanor dazedly followed the others into Mrs. Fuller's soot-blackened kitchen. Francesca instantly began to unhook her dress.

"Goodness, you're chilled to the bone. You really ought to take off everything."

"I can't!" Eleanor felt she had had enough embarrassment for one day. The rafters of the low ceiling were creaking under the feet of no less than seven men, inches above her head. She could hear drawers opening, and the rumble of their conversation, seasoned with yelps of laughter.

"Every stitch," Francesca insisted. "Mrs. Fuller will find you something." She had assumed an air of motherly capability. Eleanor was never prepared for these flashes of strength in Francesca's timid character. Before she could protest any further, she was peeled down to her skin, and Mrs. Fuller was arranging her clammy underwear on a clotheshorse in front of the range while Francesca rubbed her naked body with a towel.

Viola perched herself on one of the deal chairs, eyeing Mrs. Fuller's scrawny red elbows disdainfully. "That dress is absolutely ruined."

"What about these, miss?" Mrs. Fuller held up a dingy print gown and a pair of knitted stockings for Francesca's approval.

"Perfect. You are kind." Francesca wrapped the towel in a turban around Eleanor's head. "Are you warmer now, darling?"

"Much." The combination of Lorenzo's smile and the kitchen fire had turned Eleanor's skin a delicate pink.

"Do get dressed," Viola said. "I'm sure I can hear them coming."

Eleanor glimpsed the setting sun through the thick, sweet wreath of clematis around the kitchen window, and experienced a sudden rush of happiness; a lifting of the heart almost religious in its intensity. The beauty of this moment in Lorenzo's house possessed her totally, as if she had cheated time and could live in it forever.

Life was glorious, and falling into the river was a marvelous joke. When Gus and Windrush came down, with Hilary and the twins, she paraded in her ridiculous costume and joined in the laughter over the clothes provided by Lorenzo and Windrush. They were a troop of harlequins, in a rainbow motley of ill-fitting jerseys and flannels.

Even Viola laughed. She was not without a sense of humor, though it had an edge of malice. "Oh, Gus! What a sight you are!"

"A thing of shreds and patches." He grinned, showing off his borrowed trousers that were too small in the waist and too long in the leg. "If you like it, I'll get married in it."

"Kettle's on, Mr. Windrush," cried Mrs. Fuller. "Will it be tea all around, dear?"

Upstairs, Lorenzo was gathering armfuls of wet clothes from the floor and furniture. The room looked as if a cyclone had rushed through it.

"Oh God." He lifted a shirt off a chair, and found the chamber pot underneath, nearly full. "How disgusting."

"Bubble and Squeak." Stevie was apologetic. "They do everything together."

"They must have loved peeing all over my room, the little bastards. You should have drowned them while you had the chance."

"Don't be warped, Larry. They're all right. Why do you have to dislike everyone?"

"It saves trouble." He checked the papers strewn across his desk. "Oh, look. They've left a message on the blotter: *Thanks for the togs, Prussic.* How screamingly hilarious. I assume it's addressed to me."

"Honestly, they don't mean any harm."

Lorenzo flung the clothes over the iron bedstead. A muscle twitched angrily in his cheek. "And you ask me why I want to be left alone."

Stevie was lounging naked on the bed, smoking a cigarette. The dying sunlight lay across his flat, tight stomach in bars of gold. "It's a rum place, though. Aren't you lonely with nobody but Windrush?"

"No."

"I've missed you. Pretty badly, actually."

"Have you, precious? Well, one little tiny kiss, then. But if you're naughty, I'll scream."

The sneer in his voice stung like acid, and Stevie flushed. "Oh, shut up. You know what I mean."

"I'm only trying to stop you being sentimental. It makes you so dreary."

Stevie smiled. "You can't put me off. I still insist on liking you."

Reluctantly, suspiciously, Lorenzo allowed his scowl to fade. "I think I must quite like you, since I saved you the most presentable clothes. You can hardly seduce that Garland creature if you're got up like a tinker." He threw a pair of flannels at Stevie, and peeled off his own jersey, revealing a frayed, collarless shirt.

"Larry, you're a brick." Stevie pulled the jersey over his damp fair hair. "How can she possibly resist me now?"

They had moved out of Mrs. Fuller's cramped kitchen into the garden. The warm summer evening was heavy with the smells of the country, but the cows were almost canceled out by the clematis, and there were fragrant beds of cottage flowers, pale and ghostly as the deepening twilight bleached out their gaudy colors.

Mrs. Fuller had provided tea as brown as gravy, and heavy slices of musty fruitcake. They sat cross-legged on the grass, suspended in a bubble of contentment, and unwilling to pierce it with the practicalities of getting back to Cambridge.

Viola had thawed enough to allow Gus's arm around her waist. She rested her head against his shoulder, her eyes dreamy. Eleanor had not seen Gus so replete with happiness since the day he had proposed to her. She knew how it was with him—he loved these moments so much that he believed them to be the truth. All the rest could be dismissed as irrelevant; unreal.

Francesca, she was glad to notice, had overcome her twinge of panic about Stevie; perhaps because he looked so young in Lorenzo's jersey. He was leaning on one elbow, saying something to make her smile. Only his hands, absently plucking blades of grass, betrayed his eagerness.

"What a night for love this is." Lorenzo, lying on his back beside her, was also watching them. His voice was sour. *"In such a night Stood Dido with a willow in her hand Upon the wild sea-banks—"*

"*—and waft her love To come again to Carthage,*" Eleanor finished, savoring the quotation's tragic sweetness.

"Of course, you're the clever type. I forgot." In the semi-darkness, he made a peculiar, rasping noise, which Eleanor recognized as a laugh. "A naiad in blue stockings and spectacles." He sat up. "You look nice like that."

"Do I?" She was enchanted.

"Girls like you shouldn't try to be fashionable. It's different for your sister, because she's beautiful. Oh for God's sake, take off that wounded look. I suppose you think I'm insulting you. But you must know you're not beautiful—or doesn't your house have any mirrors?"

Eleanor was mortified, yet there was something delicious in the mortification. She craved his attention, even if it meant grasping thorns and being singed by live coals.

"I wonder," mused Lorenzo, "why it's considered rude to tell women the truth?"

"I don't think you're rude," she said hastily. "Wasn't there a compliment in there somewhere?"

"What? Can't hear."

"I said—"

"Don't bawl at me. I'll give you my good ear." He scrambled around to her other side.

Flattered, Eleanor risked a personal question. "How bad is your deaf ear? Does it hear anything at all?"

"Not much. Muffled, underwater sounds."

"Were you born like it?"

"No," he said shortly.

"Was it a childhood accident, or a—"

"You do love to know the gory details, don't you?" he snapped. "Last time we met, you were interrogating me about my appendix."

"I'm sorry." Eleanor was humble. "Curiosity is a fault of mine."

"Because knowing all about someone gives you a handle

to grasp them by. One fact, and you'll gallop off with a whole sackful of assumptions."

"I won't if you tell me the truth," she said boldly.

Lorenzo tensed into absolute stillness. She knew he was furious, and the thrill of danger made her light-headed with elation.

"What can you possibly want to know?"

"Your name."

His silence was charged, like electricity. "Hasn't Stevie told you?"

"No."

"Hastings." He spat it out. "Laurence Hastings."

"Laurence Hastings." Eleanor tried it. For a fraction of a second, it seemed vaguely familiar. She decided this was because it had the ring of destiny. Possibly this was one of those moments when the scales of life turned on two words that carried the weight of the future. "The Laurence doesn't suit you," she pronounced. "I'll go on calling you Lorenzo."

"I don't answer to anything else."

The expression in his eyes was unfathomable—wariness, puzzlement and relief; almost tenderness. Eleanor longed to bombard him with questions, but was held back by a merciful impulse not to hurt him. Before she could make up her mind, they were drawn into the conversation, which had become general.

"Well, let's ask Lorenzo," Bubble was saying hotly. "I don't think we'll be like forty-year-olds when we're forty, do you? We'll be just as we are now, and the fact that we're forty will be nothing more than a ghastly coincidence."

"You won't," Windrush said, his eyes wrinkling with amusement. "You'll have wives and hordes of children, and you'll tell yourselves you've changed because you've grown wiser. How could anyone stand it otherwise?"

"It ought to be possible to hold onto certain values," Lorenzo protested. "Surely people only reject the ideas of their youth because they are forced to conform to a society that prizes dullness and suburban prudishness above everything?"

"In twenty years, we'll be society," Stevie pointed out, "and we'll set the standards."

"Wait till you get to forty years," chuckled Windrush, "with whiskers down to your knees."

"Imagine the awfulness of being forty!" Squeak groaned. "The sheer, awful Victorianism of it—of waking up one morning to find one has turned into an alderman, who shouts at his cook and fumes over the letters in the *Morning Post*!"

"Whither is fled the visionary gleam?" Hilary murmured. *"Where is it now, the glory and the dream?"* "There wouldn't be a way out," added Stevie. "Unless you could find a way of recapturing the Vision Splendid."

"But you could, technically." Lorenzo lit a cigarette, inhaling hungrily. "If you were ruthless enough, you could capture another twenty years of youth. Assuming that youth is partly a state of mind. We could decide now to meet at a certain place in—let's see—1933. No matter what we were doing, or however many wives, concubines and kids we had. We would vow to leave it all behind, and arrive at the rendezvous divested of all our accumulated habits and assumptions."

"Rather drastic," commented Gus, glancing fondly at Viola. "You can count me out."

"I think it's marvelous!" Bubble cried. "We'll do it! All of us except Fenborough—and you won't want to come, will you, Twisden?"

Eleanor considered this a somewhat brutal dismissal, but Hilary only laughed gently. "I doubt it," he said. "It would hardly be suitable for a clergyman. They'd think I'd absconded with the parish funds."

"Well, why don't you?" asked Stevie, who—unlike the twins—seemed genuinely fond of Hilary. "You could turn your collar the right way around, change your name and have a whale of a time tasting fleshpots. Whatever they are."

Bubble was quivering with enthusiasm. "So that's you, me, Squeak, Lorenzo and Windrush—meeting on January the first, 1933. All whiskers to be shaved off beforehand."

Eleanor was beginning to dislike this discussion. Not only were women not included in this plan—they were seen as encumbrances, to be left behind; the ivy that wrapped itself around a man, choking his youthful aspirations and leaving him nothing but the journey to the grave. Was it one of the laws of nature, that men should want to make for the horizon, and that women should wish to tie them down? How did they know that she would have nothing to escape from on that blue, distant morning in 1933?

Stevie, aware of Francesca's soft brown eyes, noticed the omission. "What about the girls? Are they invited too?"

"Yes," Lorenzo conceded, "if they don't bring any luggage and don't expect an escort. Terms of equality only."

"I'll come," Eleanor said promptly.

"I shan't," declared Francesca.

"Where shall we meet?" asked Squeak.

"Havana," suggested Windrush. "Or Cairo, maybe. All the fleshpots we can eat."

"Lake Como," Squeak said decisively.

"And Eleanor can fall in!" cried Bubble.

The conversation splintered into screams of laughter. When these had died down, Gus regretfully released Viola and said that if they intended to return to the center of Cambridge by river, they had better do it before the light went completely.

"Let's get our clothes from upstairs, and leave the girls alone, to get ready down here," Stevie said, referring with characteristic tact to the shamefully public position of the outside privy.

There was a drift back to the cottage. Eleanor, hardly able to bear breaking the moment, lingered beside Lorenzo.

"I'm glad we met again," she ventured.

"Are you?"

"Perhaps another time I could hear you play. Did Stevie tell you that you're invited to Vi's dance?"

"Oh yes."

She was careful to keep the yearning out of her voice. "And you're coming?"

"No. Kind of you and all that. But of course not."

"Please," she coaxed. "I should like it so much."

He sighed. "Well, I'll think about it, if I'm in London."

"Larry," Stevie called from an upstairs window, "come in!"

"Yes, yes. What a perfect gentleman. An example to us all." Lorenzo stood up, holding out his hand to Eleanor. "I hope you're a better host than I am."

Eleanor could not take his hand. The loose cuff of his shirt had parted, and she saw, with an icy, paralyzing wave of shock, that the skin on the inside of his wrist was whitened and puckered by a long, deep scar.

He knew she had seen, but he did not take his hand away. She clasped it, and his fingers tightened around hers, unexpectedly warm.

The voices of the twins floated through the casement into the dusk: "We'll never be old—we'll never be old!"

Four

The Berlin sisters were the ugliest women Rory had ever seen; a trio of wrinkled tortoises, with knowing, curranty black eyes, and slits of mouths pursed under huge, bony noses. When Dinah and Cecil led her into the dark, over-furnished back parlor of the Berlins' house in Notting Hill, they found Frieda, Berta and Dorrie sitting around a table sewing. They looked up, their scissors open and their needles frozen in midair, and Rory felt as if she had been ushered into the cave of the three Fates to watch them spinning and cutting the thread of all human lives.

Over supper, she found it difficult to tell the sisters apart. They all wore black dresses, very plainly cut, and teased their hair into identical wiry plaits around their witchy heads. Gradually, however, she realized this was because Miss Berta and Miss Dorrie had deliberately submerged themselves in the personality of the eldest sister, Miss Frieda.

Frieda Berlin (named after her father's friend, Friedrich Engels) was the driving force, the heart and mind of the household. To say that she devoted herself to progressive causes was a pale understatement. She was a principle made flesh; a woman consecrated to her beliefs. Or rather, the beliefs she had inherited from her father, an exiled Viennese revolutionary whose memory she held in absolute veneration.

Dr. Berlin had been lying in Kensal Green Cemetery for twenty years, but Frieda, now in her late forties, kept his work alive with intense, almost religious devotion. Berta and Dorrie, though individually vigorous and practical women, looked to her for leadership.

Rory got her first glimpse of their solid rallying power at the meeting of the Suffragist Committee, which took place in the dining room after the remains of the cold salt beef and sauerkraut had been removed. Frieda took the carver's chair at the head of the table, and Berta and Dorrie flanked her like staff officers with a trusted, well-beloved general. Dinah took the other end of the table.

For once, Rory's tongue was still. She was all eyes and ears, immersing herself in the intoxicating climate of high ideals and political activism. Simply being here, in this cluttered, foreign-looking room, with large portraits of Engels and Dr. Berlin glaring at each other from opposite walls, was excitement enough. If Muttonhead could only see her now!

The committee members arrived in twos and threes, peeling off their gloves, scattering papers and talking so determinedly that the room was soon vibrating with noise. Finally Becky, the maid, came in with the coffee and shut the door. She was a sharp-faced, undersized Jewish girl from the East End, and she did not wear a uniform because the Berlins did not believe in the social gulf between mistress and servant. Rory had not been too surprised by Becky's habit of interrupting the conversation as she dished up the supper, being used to the intrusions of Una at home. But she had been astonished when Becky sat down to eat with them. It appeared that she was also a member of the committee, for she poured herself the last cup of coffee and took the vacant chair next to Cecil, who was taking the minutes.

"The meeting will come to order." Frieda's mild voice cut through the hubbub, and her smile included all thirteen women packed around the table. "Are you ready, Cecil? I would like to welcome a new comrade, Aurora Carlington, from Ireland."

There were polite murmurs of greeting, and Rory felt herself being scrutinized through hat veils and steel-rimmed spectacles.

She reveled in the agenda—pickets for Holloway while Mrs. Pankhurst was inside, representation at the next illegal WSPU rally in Hyde Park, and most thrilling of all, weapons of self-defense against policemen and organized anti-suffrage rowdies. This was truly living.

The women loved to disagree, and to rage over their disagreements, but the meeting ended amicably, with coffee and spiced cakes in the drawing room. Becky handed around plates with her mouth full, and Rory was hemmed in by friendly committee members eager to introduce themselves properly.

"Thank you for bringing me," she said to Dinah, as soon as she could catch her alone. "It's been splendid."

"Thought you'd like it. But don't speak as if it's over. The question is, what can you do for us? Do you have any cash?"

"I beg your pardon?"

"I mean, do you need to earn your living?"

"Well, no." Rory felt self-conscious about this. "I'm not at all rich, but I live with my aunt, and I have some money of my mother's—"

"Wonderful! Couldn't be better! Do you want to work for us?"

"Oh, rather!"

Dinah smiled at her enthusiasm. "I need an assistant editor for *Atalanta*."

Rory, who had been prepared to do anything heroic, from whacking the Prime Minister with her riding crop to bombing the Houses of Parliament, returned to earth. "Are you sure I could do that? I mean, I don't know anything about magazines—"

"You don't have to," Dinah explained. "You see, we all give our services for nothing, and most of us can barely afford the time. I need someone to correct the proofs, answer correspondence and see the plates made up at the printers."

This sounded simple enough—and how grand to be able to tell Jenny and the girls she was an assistant editor. "I'll try, though you'll have to be patient—you remember my punctuation from school, and it hasn't improved."

"As long as it hasn't got any worse," said Dinah, "you may consider yourself hired, Miss Carlington, for the staggering remuneration of absolutely nothing."

Rory laughed. "Miss Curran, you overwhelm me. However shall I spend it all?"

This, Rory decided two weeks later, is the happiest time of my life. She wondered how many people could identify the happiest times of their lives when they were actually in them, and sighed with contentment. Her work for *Atalanta* was far harder than she had expected. It took up hours of her time, and mostly involved the drudgery of poring over

very dull articles and making tiny symbols in the margins—
but she loved every moment, for it brought her into the
Berlins' house nearly every day.

The more she saw of the Berlins, the better she liked
them. Once you got used to it, their reptilian hideousness
was strangely appealing. Every twist and wrinkle of the
family face was radiant with intelligence and kindness. Rory
thought of Mr. Phillips saying "by their fruits shall ye know
them." If you judged the sisters by their deeds, rather than
their appearances, they were surely as beautiful as angels.

Frieda had inherited some money from her mother, and
used it to turn her house into a haven for anyone whose
ideas coincided even vaguely with her own. She was also
charitable, and individual cases of hardship never failed to
awake her sympathy. Her hands were always open, whether
she was nursing a forcibly fed suffragette back to health,
or assisting the family of a crippled docker. Berta and Dorrie were similar mixtures of idealism and tenderness.

There was also, to Rory's slight surprise, a Berlin
brother. Joe Berlin was the child of the Doctor's old age;
a reminder of a brief second marriage. His mother had died
giving birth to him, and Frieda—fully twenty-five years his
senior—had brought him up. He was just down from Oxford, and working as secretary to a Labour MP. All the
sisters worshiped him, but he had a special love for Frieda.
"My eldest," he called her. Berta was "Medium" and Dorrie was "Dot."

The family lived in a constant upheaval, for the house
hummed with industry. Cecil and Dinah wrote and painted
together in their airy attic room. The other lodger was a
homeopathic doctor, who used her second-floor front room
as a consulting room. Rory dealt with the day-to-day business of *Atalanta* in the small back parlor. And a swarm of
comrades and sympathizers called at all hours of the day
and night—usually hot from some soapbox or other, and
waving a pile of pamphlets.

Rory had met Mr. Keir Hardie, the rough-knit Scot who
spoke for the Labour interest in Parliament. She had also
met Mr. Bernard Shaw, and his fellow Fabians Sidney and
Beatrice Webb, who disagreed violently with everything
Frieda said, but who nevertheless ate enormously and
stayed for ages. The conversation was astonishing and often
alarming. Among the talk of empires crumbling and palaces

in flames, Rory sometimes felt she was moving further and further away from Jenny, Francesca and Eleanor. Yet she made sure she kept up with them, for fun and frivolity were in rather short supply at the Berlins'.

This was awkward, because her high spirits would keep breaking out. The previous evening, an angry author had called to complain to Dinah because Rory had scribbled what she termed "a disrespectful poem" across the corrected proofs of her article on Scottish militancy:

> *A sweet suffragette named Miss Brady*
> *Refused to act like a young lady.*
> *She went out to tea*
> *With a Scottish MP*
> *And shoved a bomb under his plaidie.*

Fortunately, though she managed to keep a straight face in front of the author, Dinah had found this funny. "But for pity's sake, child," she had said afterward, "you're not working for *Punch*. We don't consider militant tactics a laughing matter."

Yes, life at this Olympian level was a serious business. Rory yawned and forced her attention back to the proofs. Dull as they were, they had to go back to the printers that evening. She was annoyed when the doorbell rang. The blasted thing seemed to go every two minutes, and answering it was her responsibility. Everyone else was too busy.

Rory had learned by now that many of the comrades were desperately tedious. She went down the hall to open the door, resigning herself to doing her share of duty with an East End garment worker, or a Balkan exile packed with grievances about the war, or some crank who believed the whole world should wear lock-knit Jaeger knickerbockers—she had met them all.

The caller turned out to be a young man, tall, pale and intensely shabby, with a rolled-up manuscript sticking out of his jacket pocket.

"Good afternoon," Rory said. "May I help you?"

"I've come for Miss Berlin. Is she there?" His eyes were the color of wet slate, unnaturally large in his attenuated face and circled with exhausted violet shadows. He took off his tweed cap and tried to smooth his tawny hair, which was sprouting untidily where it wanted cutting.

"She is, but she's busy in one of her meetings."

"Oh. I'll go then."

"No, please come in. She won't be long." Rory, who had difficulty identifying the various English accents, placed him somewhere in the north. He was as thin and ascetic-looking as a medieval saint, she thought; his flesh worn away by an excess of spirit.

He glared at her accusingly. "I've not got time to waste. Tell me when she'll be free and I'll come back."

"I told you, she won't be long. You can wait in the—"

"I don't wait for anyone." He rammed on his cap and turned away.

"Suit yourself," said Rory crossly, shutting the door.

A second later she heard a peculiar noise—as if someone had dropped a sack of coals on the front steps.

She jerked open the door again and found the young man lying unconscious. Appalled, she gaped down at him. He looked like a limp suit of clothes with nothing inside.

Pulling herself together, she dropped on her knees beside him and began to unfasten the studs in his frayed paper collar. "Becky!" she shouted. "Come up here quickly, and bring some water!"

Frieda, who had a way of materializing whenever there was trouble, emerged from the dining room to see what had happened. Half a dozen members of her "No Votes, No Taxes" committee crowded into the hall behind her, treading on each other's feet and calling out advice.

"Smack his face—"

"No, no, burn some feathers under his nose—"

"Rub his hands—"

"Women, wait for me inside, please," Frieda said firmly, shooing them away. "It is only poor Mr. Eskdale."

"Shall I run for the doctor?" asked Rory, frightened by the young man's lead-colored lips. "He looks awful."

"No, dear child, he's not ill. Go down to the kitchen and ask Becky to cut up the cold chicken into a good plate of sandwiches."

"You mean he's just hungry?"

"Just hungry," repeated Frieda, with grave emphasis. "Yes."

"I'm sorry—I didn't mean—"

"Don't be sorry, dear. To tell you the truth, Mr. Eskdale

is rather foolish about taking care of himself. Tom, can you hear me? See what you have done now."

Eskdale blinked stupidly and raised himself on one elbow. "I've finished it—my book—I was up all night, and I walked from Queen's Park—"

"Later, later." Frieda patted his threadbare arm reassuringly. "Always in such a hurry."

Rory hovered, fascinated by this starved Chatterton who had apparently nearly killed himself slaving in a candlelit garret. Frieda glanced at her shrewdly. "Run along, Aurora. I'll look after him."

Reluctantly, Rory left to get the sandwiches. When she returned with them, she found Eskdale in the drawing room, haranguing Frieda while she spooned sugar into his coffee. The room was crowded. The committee members had adjourned for refreshments, and were clustered around the grand piano, arguing in low voices across the ranks of silver-framed family photographs.

"I know you'll want to publish it!" Eskdale blindly gulped his coffee and bit into a sandwich, as if filing them away for future reference.

"Tom dear," Frieda said, "you are very clever, and your ideas are undoubtedly important, but where would I be if I paid for everyone's books to go through the press? Leave it here. I will read it."

"When?"

"When I have the time. Or I will give it to Aurora and she will tell me what she thinks."

Cramming down another sandwich, Eskdale turned his attention to Rory. "Does she know anything about politics?"

"I know the difference between good writing and bad," she returned. "And that's what matters."

He looked at her properly for the first time, and suddenly smiled. A poignant crease appeared in one of his lank cheeks; the burned out crater of a childhood dimple. "I've not seen you here before, have I?"

"Aurora Carlington." She helped herself to a sandwich. "I work with Dinah and I'm from Ireland. A product of the tyrannical classes, and not an honest peasant, before you ask."

He was severe again. "It's not a laughing matter."

"Well, I'm sorry. But I'm so tired of things that aren't

laughing matters. And I'm sick to death of being lectured about Ireland. If there was anything really wrong with me, would I be here? Nobody chooses where they're born."

"Ah, but you can't just deny all responsibility," he said. "A person is shaped by their social class, like it or not. Look at you. Anyone can tell you're a so-called lady. If you'd been born down my street in County Durham, you'd not make smart remarks about peasants, and you'd sooner die than wear that bloody awful green shirt."

"Tom!" warned Frieda.

"It's all right. I don't mind." Rory was mesmerized.

"Everything about you tells me you come from a class that's used to doing as it pleases. Only a lady thinks she's above dressing like everybody else."

The committee women were draining their cups and filing out of the room. Frieda stood up, looking doubtfully from Rory to Tom. "Are you feeling better now, dear boy?"

"Yes. I'm sorry about that," Eskdale said. "The functions of the body shouldn't exercise such tyranny over a man. For instance—" He was evidently about to expand on a favorite theme.

Frieda neatly cut him short. "Don't move until you have finished the sandwiches, and be civil to Aurora." As his mouth opened again, she added: "Even though you don't believe in the bourgeois tyranny of civility."

"Yes, she's a good old sort is Miss Berlin," said Eskdale, when she had gone. "One of the best. What are you laughing at?"

"Don't you believe in anything ordinary?"

He was not offended. He smiled at her in a friendly way. "We're looking at 'ordinary' from opposite ends of the scale, Miss Carlington."

"Is that what your book is about?" she asked.

"Certainly. It's a manifesto for turning the world upside down. I've called it *The Phoenix of the New Order*. The ruling classes imagine that capitalism is something under their control, but it's not—it's a juggernaut, moving on its own momentum toward mass destruction. I'm predicting a gigantic war between the Imperial powers, which will result in international bankruptcy and the triumph of the worker state. Oh, it'll be a splendid spectacle."

"You call war splendid?" she demanded indignantly.

"Yes, if it brings about the desired change. You look at

the Germans, building up their navy. Look at the Balkans, and Parliament voting to use our taxes for killing machines—"

"But it won't come to a war! Nobody thinks the Kaiser would dare take on our navy!"

"Don't they? Ordinary people can't stop wars starting, but they can refuse to fight them. The way I see it, there'll be a mass refusal among working men to aid the Imperialist fighting machine. When the traditional cannon fodder refuses to take up arms against brother workers, the whole system will collapse."

"Sounds pretty far-fetched to me."

"Maybe."

Rory had never heard anyone speak with such sublime conviction. It was extraordinarily compelling. "How did you become such a prophet, Mr. Eskdale?"

"Want to know about me, do you? Trying to place me on the social scale, hoping you can explain away my ideas? Well, I could tell you things I've seen you wouldn't believe. My dad was a miner, see. Seven of us in two rooms. Only chance him and my mam had to conceive another one was Sunday afternoons. They packed us all off to Sunday school, see. And the Vicar saw I was a likely lad and persuaded them not to send me down the mine." The wording was aggressive, but he explained all this with perfect amiability, while pouring them both more coffee from the pot Frieda had left beside him. "Now, he's a good man, is this Vicar. Yes, I'll give him that. He wanted to save one from the heap, and he did. Tutored me for an Oxford scholarship and paid my expenses."

"So you've been at Oxford?"

"There, you see—you're surprised. Knew you would be."

"I didn't mean—"

"That's all right. You don't mean any harm, unlike some of the chaps at my college. I might as well have come off the moon. Got my first, though; no thanks to anyone but myself."

"And your Vicar," Rory reminded him.

"Yes, though we had our differences. He believed in God as a reason for maintaining the hierarchy. Couldn't stomach my socialism. Naturally, I wasn't going to keep quiet about that."

"Naturally," she murmured, trying not to laugh.

"That's how I came to know Miss Berlin. Her brother, Joe, dragged me out of the river one night, after I'd been handing out my pamphlets in St. Giles. They were always dunking me in water. I've been in more college fountains than a stone cupid."

This time Rory could not help laughing in his face. "You like a difficult life, evidently."

"I see it this way, Miss Carlington: a man in my position is faced with a clear moral choice. He can either forget all about his background and shore up the bourgeoisie by joining it. Or he can use his education to organize his own people. Do you see?"

"Yes."

"Dangerous nonsense, you'd say."

"No I wouldn't. I think it's admirable. To most educated people, poverty and injustice can only be ideas, without experience."

"Now, there's a sensible woman," Eskdale declared. "I might be able to get something out of you."

"Not money. I'm not rich enough to be anyone's patron."

"Work, then." He smacked his manuscript on the cushion beside him. "Read this and tell Miss Berlin she's got to publish it. I'm not too proud to beg for what I believe in."

Rory picked up the uneven, blotted bundle of papers with respect. The singleness of his purpose made one breathless. "I'll read it tonight, Mr. Eskdale."

He gave her one of his bright, shadowless smiles. "Tom."

"I might not understand it all."

"A child could understand it."

Rory laughed. "Is that your estimation of my intelligence?"

"We'll have to see about that," he said seriously. "I know you suffragette types—you reckon you can outthink anyone. Nine times out of ten, you can't see beyond the ends of your own umbrellas."

"Oh charming!" Rory exclaimed. "Don't you care about votes for women?"

"Votes for everyone. You've got to tackle social change on the broad scale—and it begins and ends with the working man. He's the one with the load on his shoulders."

"What about the working woman?"

He did not reply, for Joe Berlin had breezed into the room, bringing with him his sisters and their visitors.

He was a cheerful, energetic soul; very like his sisters only less ugly, because the Berlin face looked better on a man.

"Tom! So you've finished it, have you? Pour us a cup of that coffee, Rory, there's a good fellow."

Rory poured him a cup of coffee. She liked Joe—he was the only person in the house who ever dared to make fun of the comrades. As soon as he kissed Berta and Dorrie, and exchanged greetings, in German, with their party of visiting Austrian socialists, the atmosphere noticeably brightened. There was even laughter when he rattled off an account of his day's work, and did an imitation of his Labour MP addressing the Commons in a broad Yorkshire accent.

"So," said Tom, when the conversations had splintered again, "you still believe in the parliamentary solution, do you?"

"Has he been bending your, ear Rory?"

"Rather. I'm going to read his book for Frieda."

"Are you now? Hope you haven't put a date on this war of yours, Tom. You'll look a terrible idiot when it doesn't happen."

"You're using ridicule as a shield to deflect reality," Tom said calmly. "But you'll be laughing on the other side of your face when you see I'm right."

Rory could hardly tear her eyes away from him. He seemed so strong and brave; the still center at the heart of a mighty storm. He spoke to them as if he could see over their heads to the distant spires of the future.

Joe shook his head. "I've never been able to see things in black and white, as you do. You're for chucking the whole world away, and starting again. But there's some good in it, which ought to be saved. A little leaven, to help the new order."

"Decency!" Tom said scornfully. He stood up, his back to the mantelpiece. "Is that what you mean? Common decency, they call it, because it's a common sort of thing for the common man. The empires of the rich are forming and dissolving alliances, and there'll be no decency left when they set their armies marching."

Joe, still laughing, made parliamentary heckling noises.

"No," said Tom impressively, "there's something in the air." He suddenly glared down at Rory with such intensity that she felt he could see right into her soul, with all its dusty inherited prejudices and shameful, ladylike frivolity.

"Something so great, so mighty, that it will crush the old order into atoms. My Vicar would say that princes and kings shall bow down before it, and so would I. But he'd mean God. And I mean Death."

Five

"Awfully good of you to come." Alistair pressed Jenny's hand eagerly. She had never seen him so nervous. "Mother's longing to meet you."

"She hasn't been at all well," said Cornelia MacIntyre. "So I'm afraid she can't come down. We're expected upstairs." She began to lead the way, coldly avoiding Jenny's eye.

"I know she'll like you," murmured Alistair, sounding as if he was trying to convince himself.

"Her heart has been very bad lately," Cornelia said, shooting Jenny a resentful little glance over her shoulder. "I must ask you not to excite her."

"For pity's sake," Alistair said testily, before Jenny had a chance to reply. "What do you expect her to do—scream and tear her hair like one of the wild girls of Bacchus?"

"You know what I mean. The smallest little thing sets her off." Briefly, she turned to face Jenny on the landing, taking in her gray moiré suit, a copy of one of Viola's Paris models. "You're very elegant today, Miss Dalgleish. I should have warned you what a very quiet, unfashionable occasion this is going to be. It's just us and Mother. Effie's spending the day in Epsom with some cousins."

"I won't have the poor little thing wilting in an atmosphere," Alistair muttered between his teeth. "Even if she doesn't understand it."

Ignoring this, Cornelia led them down a short passage and halted in front of a closed door. There was only the fraction of a pause before she knocked, but it was enough to show Jenny how frightened she was of her mother. And yes, Alistair was frightened, too, though he showed it by squaring his shoulders and frowning determinedly.

The door was opened by a gray-haired, uniformed nurse, with beads of sweat glinting on her upper lip. As soon as

Jenny entered the invalid's room, she saw why. It was as hot as a Turkish bath. The heavy velvet curtains were drawn against the summer afternoon and a coal fire burned in the grate.

A feeble, wavering voice issued from a bundle of blankets beside the fire.

"Alistair darling, is that you?"

"Yes, Mother. How are you?"

"The worst of the pain has gone, thank heaven."

"Mother, I've brought her." He gently tugged Jenny into the circle of lamplight. "Here she is. This is Miss Dalgleish."

Jenny held out her hand to Mrs. MacNeil. "How do you do?"

The old lady let her stand there with her hand extended, while she scrutinized her from neck to hem. Jenny, in her turn, wondered how such a wasted, frail bundle of bones managed to keep her two middle-aged children in such a flutter of nerves. Her face, framed in soft white hair, was pitifully thin and lined, but her blue eyes were shrewd. Eventually, she offered Jenny the tips of her bony fingers.

"Sit down. Bates will give us our tea." She spoke so softly that everyone had to crane forward to listen. "Put Miss Dalgleish in the armchair, Alistair. I want to see her face."

Jenny sank into a stifling pile of feather cushions on the other side of the grate. Sweat was creeping through the roots of her hair. Alistair mopped his balding dome with a handkerchief.

"It is a curiosity and pleasure for me to see a young face," Mrs. MacNeil whispered, "when I spend all my days shut up inside four walls."

"What nonsense, Mother!" Cornelia cried, with rather desperate heartiness. "You can see Effie and the children anytime you like!"

"They tire me so. But Miss Dalgleish seems reposeful."

"I told you she couldn't possibly disturb you." Alistair was eager. "She's as gentle as a dove."

"Oh no, dear, not a dove," said Mrs. MacNeil sadly. "Doves are supposed to bring peace."

Alistair flinched as if stung, and Jenny—still smiling her dovelike smile—marveled at the old hawk's rudeness. It was remarkable what you could get away with if you looked pathetic and laid a trembling hand upon your heart.

Bates, the nurse, began to pour cups of tea from a trolley. The sight of the blue flame of the spirit lamp under the silver kettle made Jenny feel like a lump of melting butter. When Bates leaned over the back of her chair, she had to hold her breath to block the smell of starchy armpits.

"Good God, Mother"—Alistair ran his finger around the inside of his collar—"you could steam a pudding in here. It can't possibly be healthy."

"I'm so sorry, darling," his mother whispered, "but cold of any kind brings back the pain. Drafts, breezes"—her face creased into a martyred smile—"even cold hearts."

Alistair's face fell. He looked like a snubbed schoolboy. Jenny felt sorry for him, but was impatient too. Why couldn't he stand up to her?

Mrs. MacNeil accepted her cup of tea with shaking hands. "Now you must leave us. I want to have a private chat with your Miss Dalgleish."

Alistair and his sister exchanged silent telegrams of alarm.

"Are you sure?" asked Mrs. MacIntyre. "Will you be all right?"

"Of course I will. Do go upstairs, Cornelia, and keep the children quiet. Why must your boys wear such thick boots? The noise goes right through my head."

Alistair and Cornelia obediently crept from the room. Jenny's pulse began to gallop uncomfortably, but she was not going to be afraid. For it was all obvious to her now—this dear little white-haired Whistler's Mother was the one obstacle to her success. It was his mother Alistair had remembered on the several occasions when he had stopped short on the brink of a proposal. And the old lady clearly imagined she could fiddle any tune she fancied on his tender heartstrings. Jenny, however, was not so sure. She had learned a tune or two herself.

"You too, Bates."

"Yes, madam." Bates looked disappointed. "Call if you need me —I'll only be outside."

They were alone. Jenny sipped her tea demurely, waiting for Mrs. MacNeil to begin. The barely concealed rudeness of this woman and her daughter was a sign that daggers were out and gloves were off. Good, she said to herself. That means I must have the advantage. Deliberately, she shut down her conscience. There would be time enough to feel shabby later.

A sullen red coal shifted in the fire.

"Alistair and Euphemia talk about you a good deal, Miss Dalgleish," said Mrs. MacNeil with honeyed sweetness.

"They've been very kind to me. I don't have many London friends."

"You're from Edinburgh, I believe?"

"Yes."

"Before my husband died, I knew the Edinburgh set rather well. But I don't think I recall meeting any Dalgleishes."

"You wouldn't have been likely to meet them." Jenny was determined to show that she had nothing to hide. "My father is a clergyman and can't afford to go into society. I have been brought up to work for my living."

"Most admirable," Mrs. MacNeil said. "My son is far too sentimental about ladies earning their own bread. I think it an excellent thing."

"So do I."

"Yes, I told Alistair you wouldn't thank him for making a fuss over you. He thinks you're quite a heroine."

Jenny smiled. "How nice of him."

"He's the soul of chivalry, the dear boy, but I told him he mustn't waste his sympathy. She's perfectly happy being a governess, I said. She doesn't require a knight in armor. We can't all be fine ladies." The dim, sighing voice took on a note of pathos. "You appreciate, Miss Dalgleish, what a good man he is. I want to tell you about him—that's why I had to speak to you alone. I sometimes think Alistair is all that keeps me in this world. I can't describe his devotion, his consideration for my smallest wishes. You see, Miss Dalgleish, my wretched heart condition means I must never be unhappy, I must never be agitated—oh, it's all very tiresome."

"It must be," said Jenny, thinking what a useful condition this sounded.

"I know he has sacrificed his own wishes for mine. He has never married because he thinks it would upset me. But he does me an injustice, Miss Dalgleish. Alistair's happiness is the only thing I have left to wish for. I know I could rest easy as long as he found the right sort of woman."

There was a long pause while she drew a handkerchief from her sleeve and lifted it to her eyes.

"He's too romantic, too good," she said. "He tells me I'm hard and worldly. But you're a sensible girl—you can see that he must marry someone with breeding, or at least money. Someone who shares his background, and could love him for himself. To see him entrapped by a designing person who only wanted his wealth and position would absolutely kill me. You do understand?"

"Of course," Jenny soothed, inwardly raging. "It's only natural that you should be concerned. What a comfort your son must be to you."

"Oh yes," Mrs. MacNeil continued earnestly. "And you can imagine the terrible shadow that would fall across my life if someone were to come between us. Surely, surely, nobody could be cruel enough to force Alistair to break his mother's heart?"

"Mrs. MacNeil, he'd never dream of such a thing!"

"Men can do some extraordinary things, you know. They lose their heads so easily." Her hand fluttered and came to rest on her thin bosom.

There was another silence. Jenny felt sweat trickling between her breasts. Then the papery, rustly voice began again.

"Alistair doesn't know what a catch he is. I often warn him that it's dangerous for a man in his position to make too little of himself. People will take advantage."

"I dare say," said Jenny.

"My dear, I'm glad to find you so sympathetic. I can see you would be simply aghast at the mere prospect of setting a family at odds. And I'm sure you would tell Alistair so."

"Tell him?" Jenny echoed carefully.

Mrs. MacNeil stopped to consider. She was in a corner now, for if she came right out and demanded to know whether Alistair had said anything, she risked letting Jenny know she had a hold on him. And that would spoil her present tactic of lofty disdain.

"It was so kind of you to come," she finished. "Thank you for letting me unburden myself." She smiled, sinking back into her cushions. "I do hope we'll meet again some day. May I trouble you to send in Bates?"

Jenny bowed herself out of the room, relieved to get back into the cool passage. Bates was hovering outside, looking so furtive that you could almost see the impress of the keyhole on her ear.

She scurried in to her employer immediately. To talk

about me, Jenny thought, and what an evil, jumped-up, calculating young woman I am. She suddenly felt weary and near tears. Honestly, she had not meant to stir up such terrifying emotions. If only she could squeeze them all back into the box and close the lid, but it was too late for that.

Her throat contracted with a great pang of guilt when she found Alistair waiting for her in the hall. He took both her hands.

"My dear," he murmured. His eyes, in their fine web of wrinkles, were full of pain. They stood like this in silence for a minute or so. "I will see you again."

He was not speaking to her. This was a statement to himself, and the world at large. Jenny lightly returned the pressure of his fingers, and saw how her touch could lift years off his brow. She would make it up to him.

"It's just as Cornelia said. She's using you to get herself a fortune."

"Mother"—a muscle was leaping in Alistair's cheek—"I won't let you speak of her like that."

Mrs. MacNeil had moved to her bed, and lay beneath a heap of Indian shawls, clutching her eldest daughter's hand. Tears were pouring down her face. Alistair was on the other side of the room, with his back to her.

"My darling, oh, my darling—she's an ambitious little nobody, anyone can see it. How can you let her make a fool of you?"

"She's not doing anything of the kind—and she's a perfect lady."

"She's a governess," Cornelia said sharply. "A pretty one, I grant you. But it's written all over her. Imagine what people would say."

"What could they say?" growled Alistair, whipping around to face them. "I dare anyone to breathe a word against her!"

"They're bound to infer some sort of schoolroom scandal, Alistair. It's such a penny-novelettish scenario."

"People may think what they please. The plain fact of the matter is that I am in love with her."

Both women knew he was speaking from his heart—he looked a foot taller as he said it. There was a spell of shocked silence. Then Mrs. MacNeil broke into high, anguished sobs.

"Mother!" Frantically, Cornelia grappled for the smelling salts. "Oh, dear heaven—"

The color was draining from the thin lips, and her skin had a deathly, grayish tinge.

"Fetch Bates!" shrieked Cornelia. "Fetch the doctor!" She leaped up to tug at the embroidered bellpull, nearly overturning her chair. "Look!" she hissed at her brother. "Look what you've done to her!"

The words plunged into him like daggers. He knelt beside his mother's bed, taking her hand with fearful tenderness.

She was struggling for air, each breath dragging and painful. But she managed to gasp: "Alistair—"

"Don't talk, Mother. It's bad for you."

"A little more time—"

"What?" He put his ear closer to her mouth. "Corney, what's she saying?"

"Not yet," choked Mrs. MacNeil. "Don't ask her yet—"

"But I must ask her! I can't leave her thinking I've acted like a cad!"

"Promise me—"

He had gone very white and still.

"Promise her!" begged Cornelia.

"I can't. It's not a fair thing to ask."

"For God's sake, do you want to kill her?"

Mrs. MacNeil began to groan. "Aah—Aaaghh—promise— Ohhhh!"

Alistair and Cornelia gaped at one another, panic-stricken.

"Yes, yes!" Alistair said hurriedly. "I promise, Mother. I promise anything!"

Much later, when the doctor had been and gone, and a cab had been sent to fetch a second nurse, Cornelia stole into the study.

"Alistair—"

He was at the window, holding a glass of whiskey. "Well?" He would not turn around.

She sank into one of the leather-covered armchairs. "They think she'll be all right. But the doctor says I must send the children down to Bournemouth to keep the house quiet." Intensely weary, she pushed a loose hank of hair off her hot forehead. "How can I let them go without me? I'll miss Peterkin's birthday. But how can I leave Mother?"

He was silent.

"Alistair, I—I wanted to speak to you."

"Haven't you done enough?"

"I wanted to say I'm sorry I blamed you for her attack."

"I forgive you," he snapped. "Now leave me alone."

"I could almost hate that girl for what she's done to us. My house is upside down. My servants are giving notice. My children have to creep around the nursery in slippers, and my husband is spending every waking hour at his club. I'm at my wits' end!"

"None of it's Jenny's fault," he said. "Mother wouldn't have got into such a state if you hadn't filled her head with nonsense in the first place."

Cornelia was reproachful. "You know that's not true."

"Drop it, Corney, eh?"

He could not hide the miserable break in his voice. She hastened over to him. His eyes were red-rimmed and there were tears on his cheeks.

"Poor old boy!" She laid her arm gently on his sleeve. "She shouldn't have made you promise."

"What else could I do? Whichever way I look at it, I'm bound to hurt one of them."

"She had no right to do it to you. It was cruel of her."

This was an incredible thing to say. Forty years of tyranny lay exposed between them. They stared at each other, amazed.

Cornelia's eyes were large with awe at her own daring, but she could not stop. "She doesn't want you to be happy. She's never wanted to share you with anyone. But she can see you're head over ears in love with that girl."

He took her hand. "How does that song go—about the old bachelor? *When he thinks that he is past love, it is then he meets his last love; And he loves her as he's never loved before.*"

"Alistair darling! I'll do my best to be civil to the creature, for your sake. But can't you see why I was so against her?" Cornelia's lip trembled. "She doesn't love you!"

"No." He smiled ruefully. "I know. But I'm afraid that doesn't matter."

Aurora

Letter to my Daughter, 1935

Just as I had begun to congratulate myself for striking out on my own, Tertius shot back into my life like a streak of summer lightning. He had walked all the way from Liverpool, earning his meals as an itinerant sign-painter, and (having just enough sense not to present himself at Aunt Hilda's) had turned up unannounced on Fingal's elegant doorstep in the Albany, Piccadilly.

I had only seen Fingal once since my arrival in London. He had not told any of us that his rooms actually belonged to a rich and cultivated gentleman named Aubrey Russell, and he was very annoyed with Tertius for finding him out. After a row (those two had always fought like cat and dog) Mr. Russell, who was a great patron of modern art, had packed Tertius off to lodge with one of his painters.

The first I heard of all this was a crumpled postcard, summoning me to Torrington Square, Bloomsbury. There I found Tertius, in a vast, dirty attic studio, horribly pleased with himself for following me to London. I knew I should have been annoyed, but I was so glad to see him—I never could survive without him for long.

I wish I could make you see Tertius as he was before the war, in all his youthful energy and impertinence, with the shine still on his hair, and smears of oil paint congealing on his hands. His co-tenant, a bearded, barrel-chested giant of a man named Arthur Quince, was painting a mural of the Holy Grail for a provincial Town Hall, and Tertius modeled for Sir Percival. It's funny to think of that portrait now, gazing down on some council chamber in the West Country. I haven't seen it for years, but I remember thinking it too melancholy to be an exact likeness. Tertius said it was because he felt such a fool in the breastplate.

And there are photographs, of course. Take a good look at the one I have pinned to this page. It was taken in a raffish Soho cellar called the Wormwood Club, where we used to dance, drink, talk about the Second Renaissance in art, and generally feel very sophisticated. I forget the occasion, but what a slice of history it is now.

The handsome dark man at the back is Duncan Grant. Next to him are Percy Wyndham Lewis and Henri Gaudier-Brzeska, who were casual cronies of Q's, though they didn't think much of his daubs. Q is the bearded leviathan looming over the rest of us. I'm on the floor at the front, wearing the famous Russian blouse. Tertius is beside me, grinning from ear to ear. That's how he usually was in those days, and when I look at the picture for too long it just about breaks my heart.

Beloved Tertius, what I wouldn't give to turn the clock back to that forgotten party, to touch his hand and listen to him bawling out a song—for when the drink reached a certain level in his gut he fondly imagined he was musical, though he had the original tin ear. If I hear that racket at the hour of my death, I'll know for sure there is a God.

Within days of his arrival, Tertius had woven himself into the center of my new life. His charm could work its way through keyholes and cracks in floorboards. He was one of those rare men who truly enjoy the company of women, and he took to my three friends as if he known them all his life. Very soon, he had won himself the status of a favorite brother, to be alternately teased and spoiled.

Mrs. Braddon took a tremendous shine to him. Firstly, his brother was a lord, and she always had a soft spot for a title, even if it was only an Irish one. Secondly, she had decided he was a great artist—"a young Leonardo," as she put it. Ma Braddon knew as much about art as I know about brain surgery, but she fancied herself as a patron. And she was madly impressed with the sketches he made of her family. These were miraculous, spur-of-the-moment things, often bordering on caricature. Fortunately, the old barnacle had no sense of humor at all and it never crossed her mind that her magnificent household could be a subject for satire.

"Look at this one of poor Flora," she would proclaim, as she waved the gallery under the noses of visitors. "Flo to the life—he's even caught the dotty look in her eyes! Dear Tertius is such a remorseless observer!"

It was Mrs. Braddon who made Gus commission the

wedding portrait of Viola. She negotiated the price (forty guineas), too, because she thought Tertius too careless about money. And she was right about that. He was quite content to scrape along on Fingal's handouts and whatever else he could scrounge—he borrowed from Gus with breathtaking audacity.

"I need all the cash I can lay my hands on, Rory-May," he said, when I remarked on this. "And I don't care where it comes from. Oil paints don't grow on trees."

Wonder of wonders, Tertius was working. And harder than he had ever done in his life. The studio was so crammed with canvases in different stages of stretching and sizing that you could hardly turn around. I was delighted, though I must confess, I found some of his paintings hard to understand. Not the portraits, for anyone could see how brilliantly he captured a face.

But his true passion went into violent, baffling sunbursts of color and fantastic geometric shapes. They were profoundly odd. Q, who was devoted to Tertius, admitted he could not understand them either.

"But try taking your eyes off them—I have to turn them to the wall at night."

"Are they any good, Q?"

"Good?" bellowed Q. "If he believes in them, they must be. The boy's a bloody miracle—but don't you go telling him I said so. He's conceited enough already, and it might make him lazy."

The London Tertius was never lazy. He played as hard as he worked, and through him I discovered an unconventional new world of garrets, chimneypots, area steps and cellars—bohemian life in those days was lived either far above or far below the pavement. When I got too weary of politics, he would whisk me off to the Wormwood Club, or to the pit of a music hall, followed by fish and chips and bottled porter. Now this was what I called living—the other girls could keep their dainty suppers and boxes at the opera. We agreed it was a shame they missed so much fun.

When Q finally finished his town hall mural, Tertius decided they should throw a party at the studio. And he was determined to invite Eleanor, Jenny and Francesca. Mrs. Braddon was not to hear about it. Much as she loved Tertius, she would never have allowed her girls to mix with a lot of artists' models who were no better than they should be. In the end, Gus fixed it by pretending he was escorting them to a concert. He brought them all in together—Jenny, Eleanor, Francesca and queenly Viola—and Q declared that their evening dresses lent "tone" to the occasion.

What a night that was. Beer and porter flowed abundantly, and the men passed around bottles of whiskey. I'm sure we drank most of Q's town hall earnings. The studio was crammed. They had invited everyone, including their Irish landlady and the three Indian law students from the floor below. It was funny, seeing my schoolfriends perched on the bed, cautiously sipping beer. Only Viola held herself aloof, looking around her with chilly, detached interest. Tertius had found a drunken old fiddler in one of the Irish pubs in Somers Town. The floor was cleared and we had jigs and reels. The other girls had to be taught, but my feet flew away by themselves the moment the first note sounded. Soon, everyone was dancing. It was grand to see Gus in his evening clothes, jigging away with the landlady, and timid little Francesca laughing as mighty Q swung her around like a piece of thistledown.

Viola turned into a pillar of salt and gave withering looks to anyone who dared to ask her to dance.

"She's not going to get away with it," Tertius declared. His curly hair was damp with sweat, and his eyes were sparkling. "Paddy, give us 'The Blue-Eyed Rascal.' "

Boldly he went up to Viola and extended his hand.

"I don't care to," she murmured.

"Ah, come on now, Miss Vi! It's a fine stately step."

She hesitated, then suddenly smiled up at him and accepted his hand. He led her out into the middle of the floor, and we watched in amazement—toffee-nosed Viola, her cheeks pink, dancing "The Blue-Eyed Rascal" with the rascal himself!

When it was over, he kissed her hand and said: "You danced that like an empress. Now we'll have one especially for you—'Haste to the Wedding'!"

Afterward Viola all but reduced poor Gus to tears of happiness by kissing him and saying she had had the best evening of her life. Tertius had a talent for breaking ice, and everyone liked him.

That is, nearly everyone. His only failure was with Tom Eskdale, who said he couldn't stand "renegade gentlemen posing as artisans."

"I do wish you'd stop calling him 'The Honorable Tertius,' " I complained. "It's just snobbery in reverse. He never uses the title himself, and if you could see how poor his family are—"

"Poor?" snapped Tom. "You mean, poor for aristocrats. You think it's noble and tragic for the likes of them to have to live like ordinary human beings. Whereas the beggars at their gates—"

"No, I won't let you lecture. He's like a brother to me."

"Sentimental claptrap," Tom said. "He wants to sleep with you."

"Tom!" I wasn't really shocked. I had got used to his way of talking.

"It flatters your female pride to have him dancing around you." He laughed unkindly. "You won't be satisfied until the Honorable Tertius's balls are as blue as his blood."

I hadn't a clue what he meant, and innocently repeated the remark to Tertius, who was furious.

"I'll give him blue balls, the self-righteous humbug—"

"Tershie, he's not a humbug!" I swung into the reverse position of defending Tom. "His work is vitally important."

"Glory to God, Rory-May, I don't believe how green you are! Can't you see what he's after?"

No, I couldn't. I was green, all right. I honestly did not realize that the instinctive animosity between Tertius and Tom had anything to do with me. And I had other things on my mind.

On June 4 the suffragette agitations of that summer reached a tragic climax. Emily Wilding Davison threw herself under the King's horse at the Derby, and died of her injuries four days later. Whether she intended to make a martyr of herself or not, her death was widely seen as the crowning symbol of our desperation to win the vote. The whole movement plunged into elaborate mourning.

It made a deep impression on me. I had seen Miss Davison on the very eve of the Derby, laying a wreath on a statue of Joan of Arc at a WSPU bazaar in Kensington. Afterward, she came over to our committee's stall to exchange a few hurried but cheerful words with Dorrie Berlin. I struggled to reconcile my image of this tall, smiling woman with the marble heroine, chilled and dignified by her great sacrifice for our cause. And for the first time, I began to understand the true seriousness of the fight I had joined so lightheartedly.

Something else occurred at the 1913 Derby to enlarge my understanding of the world. Fingal played truant from Russell, with the excuse that he was going to his chambers. Instead, he took several young laborers down to Epsom and treated them to beer and bets at Tattenham Corner. They were only a few yards from the tragedy, and Fingal fainted. He was carried back to Albany by two unemployed gasfitters, and Russell—with no sympathy for his swooning condition—promptly threw him out.

He ended up in Q's studio, where he cried continuously for a week. I'm afraid Tertius and I were too caught up in the preparations for Emily Davison's funeral procession to pay him much attention. His tears, and his peevish demands for impossible things to eat and drink, drove Tertius and Q nearly crazy. Poor old Fingal. It can't have been much fun for him, banished to a corner of the dirty attic, because Tertius and Q had covered the floor with an enormous banner.

Eventually, one afternoon when I was at the studio, helping to paint in the banner's purple background, Russell arrived to fetch him. He was a middle-aged man, with a supercilious, lined face. Awesomely grand and elegant, I thought—so I was amazed when he launched into a screaming, fishwifely quarrel with Fingal on the stairs. There were tears, then embraces, and a touching third-act curtain of mutual forgiveness.

After they had gone, arms affectionately twined: "Well," said I, "what was all that about?"

Tertius did not believe in hiding the facts of life from women. He put down his brush, took the cigarette out of his mouth, and explained the love that dare not speak its name in crude detail. I was stunned and revolted—not by the fact of homosexuality, as much as the universal human shame (as it seemed to me) of the sexual urge itself. How repulsive and ungovernable our bodies were, with their goatish yearnings and oozings. I was so distracted that Tertius lost patience with my clumsiness and sent me out for fish and chips. I remember leaning on the greasy zinc counter of the fish shop and vowing to keep my own virgin flesh under the strictest control.

One good thing came out of this blush-making episode.

The following evening, a penitent Russell took Tertius, Q and myself out to dinner at the Savoy, to efface the bad impression he had made on us. I didn't want to go, but Tertius told me not to be so silly. We mustn't hurt Fingal's feelings, and anyway, Aubrey Russell owned an important gallery.

At first, the embarrassment was appalling because, for some reason, Tertius and Aubrey could not look each other in the eye. But Aubrey's good breeding, and several quarts of equally well-bred champagne, quickly thawed the atmosphere. Aubrey and I took to each other greatly, and it was the beginning of an odd but warm friendship that persists to this very day. Apart from a few hungry glances at Tertius (who was fairly ravishing when shaved and in evening dress) his behavior that night was perfect, and he sent us home in a state of tipsy good-fellowship.

Because I battered his ears with my politics, Aubrey began to take an amused interest in women's rights. He was among the watchers of Emily Davison's funeral procession on June 14. He stood on the roof of his Bentley in Piccadilly Circus—with a luncheon basket, which perhaps wasn't quite in keeping with the somber tone of the occasion. Jenny, Francesca and the Braddon girls watched from a window in Buckingham Palace Road, and had a magnificent view of the coffin coming out of Victoria Station. It was draped in a purple pall appliquéd with silver arrows—a tribute to Davison's spells in prison—which glinted in the fitful sunshine.

Those of us who were marching took our places behind the bier. I was among the London members, who had all been told to turn up in white dresses. Frieda handed us crimson madonna lilies to carry.

Thousands lined the streets, all the way to St. George's Church in Bloomsbury. There had been scattered hisses when the coffin first appeared, but this gradually settled into a respectful hush. Heads bowed as we passed, a ripple went through the crowd as the men removed their hats. Perhaps they were awed by the magnificence of the spectacle; perhaps the noble sight of the suffragette sisterhood mourning its first martyr roused genuine sympathy.

Sylvia Pankhurst, pale and ghostlike, paced behind the flower-laden bier of her friend. She was the only Pankhurst present. Christabel was still hiding in Paris, and their mother's carriage, circled by a guard of hunger strikers, was empty. She had been rearrested that morning under the Cat and Mouse Act, and carted back to Holloway.

Over our heads, the huge banners floated like the sails of galleons. Cecil and Berta Berlin carried the banner painted by Tertius and Q: the words "O Deed Majestic!" wreathed in shining laurel. I held my head high, burning with divine purpose. The idea of sacrifice was sacred and beautiful to us young ones then. If Emily Wilding Davison had laid down her life for us, what a future we would build for our unborn daughters!

And we soon had a chance to temper our romance in the fire of reality. This was the summer when the Liberal Government came down on the suffragettes like a wolf on the fold. Tom and I were drawn into a whirlwind of activity—chalking slogans on pavements, distributing handbills and rallying supporters for demonstrations. I stood in Hyde Park, with half of London treading on my feet and shoving umbrellas into my back, pressed against Sylvia Pankhurst's platform, listening enthralled as she urged us to shake the government so hard that all the change fell out of its pockets. What an orator! I could have stormed the Bastille singlehanded with Sylvia to lead me.

At the climax of her speech, the rally was broken up by a gang of roughs and rowdies. The men in the crowd, and many of the women, started to fight with them and we were engulfed in a flood of policemen. Now here was a lesson. I had been brought up to believe that policemen were my friends and protectors. When one of them whacked Tom to the ground with his truncheon, I grew up ten years in as many seconds.

I did not behave like a grown-up. Tom was arrested and bundled into a van with barred windows. I burst into tears, and would not be consoled until Joe Berlin persuaded him to be bound over to keep the peace, and paid his fine.

For all his revolutionary ardor, Tom was not a strong man. He suffered from asthma, and the poverty of his childhood had permanently undermined his health. The thought of him bleeding and bruised, languishing in a cold prison cell, drove me nearly wild with anxiety. He complained about my fussing over him afterward, but I think he liked it really. At any rate, he let me put iodine on his wounded head.

The experience toughened me up. By early July, when we were down in the East End as part of a vast bodyguard protecting Sylvia from arrest, I could face a line of police-men without flinching. We linked arms around her drab, stocky little figure, and I lost my shoes and tore a sleeve in the struggle. The detectives won the first round, and off she went to join her mother in Holloway. After a hunger and thirst strike that nearly did for her, she was released under Cat and Mouse.

Sylvia was back on the platform before you could say "Votes for women," and hundreds of us were involved in shielding her from the police. Tom and I spent many a July evening on the tram back from Bow, tattered and ex-hausted, but in a state of fiery exhilaration.

At the end of the month, I was ready for my first taste of real violence, though I didn't expect it. Frieda, Dinah and I were attending a WSPU meeting in the sedate Lon-don Pavilion. Mrs. Pankhurst, on release from Holloway, was due to make an illegal appearance, and several dozen beefy supporters were packed around the platform in readiness.

We had arrived late, and were just inside the door of the hall when I turned and saw a small, elegantly dressed el-derly lady in a velvet toque hat. Dinah nudged me, and I realized with a shock that I was looking at Mrs. Pankhurst herself—standing just inches away from me. I couldn't have been more impressed if I had seen Queen Boadicea in her chariot.

Suddenly, she was surrounded by plainclothes detectives. The bowler-hatted oafs had appeared from nowhere.

"Women!" she cried, in her clear voice. "Women, they are arresting me!"

Dinah and I, hardly knowing what we were doing, leaped to the rescue. I don't recall how many other women threw themselves into the fray, but I have a chaotic impression of feathered hats all squashing together, elbows every-where, and someone's Gladstone bag making a handsome dent in one of the bowlers. The detectives opened a door and hustled Mrs. Pankhurst into a side room. In we rushed after them.

The light snapped out, and I found myself in a black confusion of shouts, shrieks and flailing limbs. I felt the rough jacket of one of the policemen seconds before his fist rocketed into my chest, sickening me with the impact. While I was still gasping for breath, the entire universe collapsed on my head in a searing flash of pain, and I lost consciousness.

I came to on the floor of the emptying auditorium, with my pounding head resting on Dinah's arm, and her smelling salts under my nose. A motherly stranger gave me some brandy from her flask, and I was taken home to Aunt Hilda's in a very sorry condition. Half my face was swelling like a pudding and I soon had a beautiful black eye. Aunt Hilda nearly had a fit when she saw me. She was even more furious the next morning, when she read in the paper that five women had been arrested for assault. Dinah had dragged me out just in time.

For the next few days, I lived in miserable purdah among the parrots. If it hadn't been for the girls, I think I might have died of unhappiness. Eleanor, Francesca and Jenny (in the teeth of Mrs. Braddon's intense disapproval) took turns keeping me company and rubbing raw beefsteaks on my eye. They were bricks, Lord bless them. Tertius treated me like a heroine and Aubrey Russell sent me a huge basket of white grapes. But all the time, I was pining and fretting for one word, one message, from Tom. It never came. Of course not. How dared I imagine I had any claim on his attention? I told myself it was the bourgeois frivolity of my heart that made it ache so, and tried with all my might to be more serious.

When my eye had faded to a more presentable palette of colors, the girls took me up to Hampstead for a taste of fresh air and suburban splendor. I sat on a basket chair on the lawn, covered with shawls. Jenny sat beside me, sewing a lace collar for one of her new frocks.

It was always soothing to watch her at work. She looked so pretty and serene, with her soft eyes bent toward her needle, and the brown curls framing her heart-shaped face. Yet she seemed tired. There was something careworn in the line of her lips.

"How are you, anyway?" I asked, trying to forget my own concerns for once. "And how's—" Vainly, I grappled for the name of the ancient, bald man she wanted to marry.

"Alistair?" she supplied, looking hard at her work. "Very well." A closed subject, evidently. She smiled at me. "You shouldn't be thinking about anything but yourself.

Honestly, Rory, you might have been badly hurt. Poor Tertius was as white as a sheet when he came to tell us."

"I dare say."

"He's such a dear. No wonder you're so fond of him."

"But not fond enough," I said ungraciously. "That's what you're trying to say, isn't it? I wish he'd keep his feelings to himself. Next time he starts, you just box his ears."

"He's dreadfully smitten with you," Jenny said, laughing.

"Don't! I've just had Ma Braddon lecturing me about what a sweet, sensitive boy he is. The old dragon had the nerve to talk about love in a cottage, and a dinner of herbs being better than a stalled ox. I tell you, Jenny, I nearly threw up."

"But he's such fun," she coaxed. "None of us can see how you manage to resist him."

"It's surprisingly easy, thank you."

There was a hair's-breadth pause, during which I felt Jenny changing gear, to slip into difficult territory.

"I can't help thinking," she said carefully, "how much nicer he is than Mr. Eskdale."

To my annoyance, I reddened. "Tom doesn't have to be nice. He's useful, and Tertius is only ornamental."

"Rory, don't get into a state."

"I wish you'd all stop shoving Tertius down my throat!" I cried. "He pesters me enough as it is."

"Do admit, his devotion's awfully touching."

"I thought you would be immune," I said accusingly. "You always disapprove of ne' er-do-wells."

"I never disapprove of people who are whole-hearted and honest," she returned. "Tertius might not be as full of himself as your Mr. Eskdale, but he knows how to give as well as take. There's a very good nature under all that blarney."

Captured by her seriousness, I asked: "Am I too hard on him?"

She shrugged, and looked down at her hands. "I don't know. What I'm trying to tell you—and I have no right at all, except that I'm your friend—is don't be impressed by the wrong qualities. You know the saying about turning an angel away from your door—"

"Oh, draw it mild!" This was a bit strong.

"No, listen to me." She was earnest. "I only feel it would be such a shame for you to—to invest your love badly, when you could put it where it would reward you a hundred times over. Believe me, I know"—her voice trembled a little—"that a truly loving heart beats all the cleverness in the world. I couldn't bear to see you surrendering yourself to someone who doesn't deserve you."

What exactly was she trying to tell me? I was as scarlet as a peony by now, but I did have an eerie feeling that she was addressing someone else.

She saw my surprise and smiled wryly. "I'm not trying to make you marry Tertius. Actually, I'm warning you not to fall in love with Tom Eskdale."

I couldn't reply, for, of course, I was already in love with Tom. Fathoms deep, and falling further every day.

Six

"Jesus, this is awful," Tertius complained. "I've seen sardines with more room to move."

He had dragged himself out of bed with a terrible hangover, to squash himself into this tight, sweaty crowd in Trafalgar Square. He had heard some speeches, eaten a pack of sandwiches, and frightened the woman in front of him by pressing against her with a bottle of stout in his pocket. Now he was bored.

"Do stop grousing," Rory said. "Nobody forced you to come."

Tertius saw the flash of joy in her face as Tom said something to her, and jealousy sank its poisoned fangs into his soul.

Rory had no idea how cruelly she was hurting him by being so entirely happy in a world he could not share. She should not have been at this demonstration. Tertius had begged her not to come. It was barely a week since she had got that clump on the head at the London Pavilion, and her black eye still looked like one of Turner's sunsets. But Tom Eskdale only had to whistle and Rory jumped to his side.

"What a spectacle!" Quince rumbled beside him. "Trafalgar Square covered in a seething carpet of radical humanity! I'd paint it ten by twenty—a sort of socialist version of Frith's *Derby Day*—with the East End workers pouring in from the Strand under their banners, and Sylvia Pankhurst on the platform."

"I don't believe that Pankhurst woman will turn up," Tertius said scornfully, hoping Rory could hear him. "She's supposed to be in hiding, and the place is crawling with police. I bet you ten bob they arrest her before she even gets a toe on the platform."

The plainclothes detectives were making no attempt to

blend into the crowd, and the side streets leading into the square were solid blocks of blue serge uniforms. Officially, the demonstration was being held in the name of the Men's Federation for Women's Suffrage, but it was common knowledge that they were covering for the militant suffragettes of the banned WSPU. It was also common knowledge that Sylvia—currently the most sought-after "mouse" in London—would dodge the cats-in-blue yet again, to rouse her supporters with her rhetoric.

"Bet you a pound she'll make her speech," said Quince.

"Done."

Sylvia's name was announced from the platform in tones of triumph. A breathless lull of suspense fell upon the crowd, then a woman in a hideous tartan suit leaped from behind one of Landseer's stone lions and ripped off her wig.

"Women! Workers! Friends of Freedom!"

An outburst of hysterical cheering. The crowd surged forward so violently that Tertius and Quince had to clutch at each other to stay upright.

"Told you!" Quince bellowed above the din. "That's a quid you owe me."

A few policemen near the platform flailed through the sea of heads toward Sylvia, but her unofficial bodyguard had already linked arms around her. Evidently, the police had had orders not to stir up too much trouble in the packed square. They fell back, and left Sylvia to speak. Her voice was small, but sharp as a blade in the breathless silence.

"Again and again," she cried, "we have been told that public opinion is against us. But the tide is turning. The men and women of this country will not stand aside and do nothing, while hunger strikers are being dragged in and out of prison. Listen to what they are writing about us now." She read from a newspaper: *"The women are winning again. What they lost by window smashing has been restored to them and multiplied a hundredfold by the government's Cat and Mouse Act.* That, by God, we can't stand!"

The cheers rang out, deafening and dangerous. People had come prepared to fight. Rory grasped a sharpened umbrella, and Tom carried a weapon known as a "Saturday nighter"—a thick length of tarred rope. The woman in front of them took a large stone out of her handbag and cradled it in her gloved fist.

Tertius felt the tension in the air, the collective rush of adrenaline, and his pulse began to gallop uncomfortably. Sylvia was holding up a roll of paper, her "Women's Declaration of Independence," and proposing a resolution to carry it to Downing Street. There was an explosion of assent, as if the four stone lions around the Column had opened their great mouths to roar, and a sweep of movement in the crowd like a gust of wind across a barley field. Buffeted on all sides by elbows and shoulders, Tertius tried to keep his eyes on Rory's red head as she was borne away from him toward Parliament Street.

He had to run or he would have fallen. They were streaming after Sylvia so fast that the police had no time to move from their vantage points in the side streets. By now, the cheers had subsided into a low, simmering growl. Around him, Tertius saw blank faces with fiery eyes, and hands holding up sticks and stones. He was pouring sweat. Rory and Tom were being swept farther away.

Two ranks of mounted police managed to form at the top of Whitehall. Sylvia's bodyguard tried to push between the flanks of the horses, and for a moment, it looked as if they would burst through. Then, from behind Tertius, came screams of: "Coppers behind! Watch out behind!"

Tertius risked looking back over his shoulder, and saw what seemed to be a vast army of police closing in on the tail of the procession. They were trapped, and the fighting had begun. He heard the sound before he identified it— the dull, rhythmic thud of police truncheons laying into unprotected heads. He almost tripped over the groaning body of a young man. Quince dived out of the maelstrom and helped him to carry the man to the relative safety of the pavement.

"Where's Rory?" Tertius shouted. "We've got to get her out of this!"

Rory had charged along in the herd, thinking of nothing but fighting her way through the cordon of police guarding the end of Downing Street. She was covered in bruises, and her throat was hoarse from shouting, but a blissful energy had possessed her. A policeman's hand closed around her wrist, and she shook him off like a fly. He grabbed her arm, twisting it viciously behind her back.

"Votes for women! Votes for women!" There was no pain, just the extraordinary lightness and warmth of her anger. She struck at him with her umbrella. "Down with the Cat and Mouse Act!"

The policeman was dragging her toward a waiting van. She was about to be arrested. At the very edges of her consciousness, she was aware of Tertius and Quince running through the thinning crowds toward her. None of it was real.

The ambrosial, cheap-tobacco scent of Tom's clothes suddenly blotted out her senses. He whacked the policeman's restraining arm with his Saturday nighter, threw him roughly to the pavement, and hauled Rory back into the cover of chaos.

Blood was oozing from Tom's nose. One side of his collar had come adrift, and flapped absurdly under his ear. He flung his arms around her waist. His lips closed on hers, his tongue invaded her mouth. It was only a moment, before they were pulled apart by two policemen and clapped into two separate vans.

Rory was boxed in a dark space, partitioned off from the other prisoners. She was breathless and reeling, and barely registered the woman in the next space thumping the walls of the van and screeching: "Votes for women!" Her center was the warmth of her mouth, numb and tingling from the ferocity of Tom's kiss.

The next few hours were a slow, depressing return to earth. Rory, Tom and the twenty-three other prisoners were crowded into Cannon Row Police Station, where a harassed sergeant tried to enter them in the charge book over the zoolike shrieks of defiance.

Sylvia Pankhurst, with nothing to look forward to but another hunger and thirst strike in the grim fortress of Holloway Prison, snatched up a glass tumbler and hurled it through the window. She was led away in a barrage of cheering. That part had been fun. Rory met Tom's eye, and felt worthy to stand beside him at last. He loved her. She was his elected partner. Together, they would storm the palaces of the mighty, and suffer unimaginable torments for the cause of freedom.

The elation died away, however, when she was charged with a minor breach of the Public Order Act, and bundled into a subterranean cell, with a dozen other women protesters.

"Votes!" someone called bravely. "Death to the Cats!"

"Death to you, you fucking bitches!" They had woken a drunk and disorderly, sleeping it off in a corner, and she began to mumble slurred insults at them. "Fuck you ... bleeding posh cows ..."

It was disgusting. The place stank of slops and Lysol, and God knew what might crawl into your hair. Rory sank onto one of the wooden benches bolted to the wall. She was exhausted. Her bones ached and her eye throbbed, and she would die if she stayed here. Swallowing a foolish rush of yearning for Muttonhead and the Mater, she shut her eyes and struggled not to cry.

Two hours later, she was hustled out and told she had been let off with a caution. Aubrey Russell, with a great show of elegant disdain, was waiting for her at the desk.

"Well, you are a pickle. I've had to weep and beg, and swear you'll never do it again, and I don't know what."

"Aubrey, you brick!" Rory hugged him fervently. "How did you know I was here? Did Tertius bring you?"

"Alas, no. The blue-eyed rascal has flown, we know not whither. Quince is out hunting for him, I believe—he scurried away the minute he'd told us about you."

The memory of Tertius's face, glimpsed out of the corner of her eye at the moment she was separated from Tom, tugged at Rory's conscience. She decided to change the subject.

"I hope I didn't cost you an absolute fortune."

"We won't talk about money. I shall consider myself sufficiently repaid if you give us all the details. Fingal desperately envies you your skirmish with the policeman. He would have come himself, but he hasn't been well. I left him at home ordering in the champagne."

"Champagne?"

"To celebrate, of course—my dear, your first arrest!"

Tertius had barricaded himself in behind the piano at the Wormwood Club. He was falling-over drunk, and singing loudly.

"Time gentlemen, please," Quince said. "We're going home." He put Tertius's limp arm across his shoulder and caught a blast of his breath. "God Almighty, boy! How much have you had?"

"I'm so in love that I can't deny it," sang Tertius forlornly. *"My heart lies smothered in my breast—"*

Quince lugged him into a taxi and took him home to Torrington Square. Halfway up the stairs to the attic, Tertius stopped singing and turned aggressive.

"Fuck you . . . lemme go . . . I'm going out to kill the bastard . . ."

"Kill him tomorrow," Quince suggested placidly, "when you're feeling better."

"She let him kiss her . . . I can't touch her, oh no, but that prick's allowed to kiss her . . ." Tertius slid down the wall and collapsed in a slack heap on the dusty coconut matting. "Just leave me . . . leave me to die . . ."

"You can't die here. Come on now."

"No!" His head sagged to the floor, and he exploded into passionate tears.

His abandoned howls brought one of the Indian law students from the third floor out onto the landing.

"What is this racket, please? We are endeavoring to work." He peered curiously at Tertius. "Your friend is ill, perhaps?"

Quince, unperturbed by Tertius's whooping sobs, took a firm hold of his shoulders. "My friend is tight, and no perhaps about it. Take his legs, Kapoor, there's a good fellow."

They carried him up the last flights of stairs, and dropped him on the couch in the studio.

"The maudlin stage," Quince pronounced, when they were alone. "Oh, the extravagant grief of youth." He lit the gas under a saucepan of scummy coffee. "I can't believe I'm living with someone young enough to be getting his first lesson in romantic disappointment." Ruminatively, he stirred condensed milk into the coffee. "Someone still young enough to have wet dreams, too. All that mad energy. Left ball doesn't know what the right ball's doing. It's overrated, is youth."

He sat down beside Tertius and mopped the tears and snot from his face with a corner of a blanket. "Sit up and drink this."

Tertius blearily raised himself on one elbow, and drank the coffee. Presently, he mumbled: "Q, I'm sorry."

"Nothing to be sorry for."

"It wasn't him kissing her—it was the look on her face.
I felt like someone had stabbed me. Did you see it?"

"Yes. Afraid I did."

"I wanted to murder him," Tertius said. "I could've
strangled him with my bare hands."

"For God's sake, boy, what good would that do? I don't
much care for Eskdale—"

"He's a piece of shit!"

"Well, he may be. But if Rory likes him, it's none of our
business, is it?"

"I can't stand by and watch her loving someone else!"

Quince sighed. "You think that now. It all seems too
much to bear. But nobody ever died of love. If you have
to get over it, you will."

"How do you know?"

"Because I've done it, that's how. I met a girl last year
when I went home to Hull. Nice girl, too. Draper's daughter. Didn't know a thing about art and didn't care. Oh, she
was an angel. I almost lost my mind, dreaming about the
happiness I might have had with her."

Tertius blew his nose on the blanket. "Wouldn't she
have you?"

"I didn't ask," Quince said sadly. "There wasn't any
point."

"Why?"

His brow darkened. "Because I'm married already."

"What?" Tertius sat up, amazed. "Since when?"

"I met her when I was about your age—fifteen or so
years ago. Big breasts, she had. Wouldn't let me touch them
until it was legal and decent. So I married her—and she
still wouldn't let me. Haven't seen her for ten years. She
went back to her mother. It was a disaster at the time. But
I've had to live with it, and that's that." He ruffled Tertius's
hair affectionately. "No use moping for what you can't
have. Tell you what—as soon as you're feeling better, we'll
go out and treat ourselves to a couple of whores. You need
a distraction."

"I don't want a whore. I only want Rory. If I can't have
her, I don't care about anything."

"Oh yes you do. You care about your work. That's the
most important thing in your life—and so it bloody well
should be." Quince gestured toward Tertius's half-finished
portrait of Viola Braddon. "Look at that."

"Conventional," Tertius said. "Chocolate-box stuff."

Quince picked the stub of a cigarette out of a dirty saucer, and lit it. "My God, you can be arrogant. It's too easy for you, that's your trouble. Do you have any idea how many years some men have to work to produce one painting like that? It's going to be magnificent—I don't know how, but you've made her look like a woman instead of an iceberg. Wait till you get to my age—you'll realize that your talent is worth more than any bit of skirt in the world."

Seven

Tom had fallen silent, and was pacing to and fro in the Berlins' small back parlor, deep in thought. Rory took the opportunity to flex the cramped muscles in her back. She had been bent over the typewriter since supper, while Tom dictated his article: "Why Britain Should Not Rearm—The Anglo-German Imperial Conspiracy."

"Tom?"

"Where was I?" he asked vaguely.

"Are you all right?"

"Course I am."

"Perhaps you're tired," she suggested. His mind had been wandering away from the threat to international socialism all evening, and this was not like him.

"You mean you're tired," Tom snapped. "Why don't you just come out and say it?"

"It's just that I've still got some proofreading to do for Dinah, so if you felt like finishing—"

"You're right, we're not getting anywhere." He stopped pacing, and looked down at her crossly. "I can't work when I'm distracted. It's your fault." Brisk and businesslike, he pulled out a chair and sat at the table beside her.

Rory's pulse quickened. He had dragged his attention away from politics, and was focusing entirely on her. Shamefully, she lived for these moments.

"My fault?" she echoed hopefully.

"I've been thinking it over. At first, I decided I should stop seeing you. But it's too late. The chemical reaction has already set in."

"Tom darling, what are you talking about?"

"I'm physically attracted to you."

Rory, totally against her will, blushed violently. "I know. You—you kissed me, at the demonstration."

"Yes, and what a bloody silly thing to do. I had far more

important matters to attend to." He took her hand. "This is exactly what I mean about distractions. No, don't say anything. I want to explain. I've always sworn I'll never allow myself to be governed by the urges of my body. That's why I thought it would be safe to work with you. Carrot hair and as skinny as a broomstick, I said to myself, no danger there. But for some reason, I haven't been able to stop thinking about you. What's so funny?"

Rory had started laughing. "Is this your idea of a declaration?"

"That's another thing—the way you're always laughing," Tom complained. "Levity belongs—"

"—in a drawing room," Rory finished for him. "I know. I'm sorry. Please go on."

"Well, I've tried masturbating last thing at night to get you out of my system. But it hasn't worked, and in any case, it's bad for the chest—all right. I'll go out of the room, and give you ten minutes to stop sniggering."

The word "masturbating" had sent Rory into nervous hysterics. Ashamed of her immaturity, she tried to pull herself together. "Tom, I'm sorry, really—"

"Bloody hell!" Tom squeezed her hand angrily. "Will you listen to me, woman? I've decided there's only one way to get myself back to normal, before I ruin my work— not to mention my glands. I've got to start sleeping with you."

The laugh died in her throat. The first feeling to hit her was hurt. How could he speak of the consummation of their love as the solution to a physical problem, as if he had been lancing a boil? But no, she scolded herself a moment later, this reaction was proof of her unworthiness. She realized she had been entertaining bourgeois fantasies about romance and courtship. And, of course, as Tom had told her many times, these were ridiculously primitive and restricting. As usual, his rationality exposed her inbred upper-class silliness. She would be modern and rise to the occasion.

"Once our relationship becomes physical," Tom explained, "we will have achieved the perfect balance. You're a sensible woman, Rory, and I know you'll want to meet me as an equal. You won't revert to type and start tormenting me about marriage. I'm assuming, by the way, that you feel a corresponding attraction to me."

"Yes," she said tremulously.

"Good." He folded both her hands in his own, and fixed her with his intense gaze. "Because I don't mind telling you, the chemical disturbance is driving me crazy. I can't even swallow my dinner properly when you're in the same room."

"Oh, Tom!"

"Stand up."

He pulled her to her feet, and held her ceremoniously at arm's length, considering the way the overhead light made a bonfire of her hair.

"I shan't sleep with anyone else when I'm with you," he announced sternly. "And I'll expect you to be my girl—I won't have the Honorable Tertius sniffing around you."

"I am your girl," Rory assured him. The blood was singing in her veins. "I could never look at anyone else."

"Are we agreed then?" he demanded.

"Yes—"

Immediately he jerked her toward him, sank a hand between her breasts and plunged his tongue into her mouth.

Rory's knees buckled under her, and she felt a surge of delicious, debilitating heat in the pit of her stomach, and between her legs.

The door opened and they sprang apart.

It was Miss Berta, with a tray. "Frieda told me to bring you both a nice cup of Bovril."

"Thank you," Rory said breathlessly, not looking Miss Berta in the eye, and not daring to think what color her face was.

"Aurora, *liebling*, it is getting fearfully late. Perhaps you had better get a cab home?"

"I'll see her home," said Tom.

"Oh. Very well." Miss Berta seemed uneasy. "I'll tell Frieda."

She pointedly left the door open when she left, so that they could hear the murmuring of voices in the Berlins' drawing room.

"This is hopeless," said Tom. "Let's go back to my place."

"Tonight?" Rory was suddenly frightened. "We can't! It's impossible—Aunt Hilda's expecting me—"

"Telephone her. Say you're staying here."

"No!"

"Rory! I can't bloody well wait!" Frowning, he snatched her hand and pressed it against the hard bulge in his groin. She recoiled as if he had bitten her. "See what you're doing to me?" He groaned, and his tone softened. "Rory love, don't start playing with me now! I thought you wanted to—"

"I do, but—"

"Nobody will know, and nothing will—you know—happen. I've made all the arrangements. You know."

Rory did not know, but squared her shoulders and made up her mind to be brave. She was not the type to go back on her word. If this was the price of being Tom's girl, she must go through with it.

"Wait here."

Making sure she was unobserved, she crept upstairs to the telephone used by the homeopathic doctor and whispered the number to the operator. She was answered by Aunt Hilda's parlormaid.

"Motson? It's Miss Aurora. Will you tell Miss Veness I shan't be coming home tonight? I'm—I'm staying with my friends the Berlins."

"Very good, miss."

And the deed was done. Rory walked out of the house on Tom's arm, and descended into a dream of strangeness as she followed him onto the tram for Queen's Park.

What was she doing? What on earth was she doing? She had laughed at words such as "honor" and "reputation," but they clanged like great warning bells now. Tom was leading her away from the safe territory of virtue and gentility, along dismal, ill-lit streets, crammed with mean little red-brick houses and smoky pubs. An awful picture loomed into her mind—Muttonhead's face if he ever found out. God help her, she would be a lost woman in his eyes. Honor and reputation were all in all to him.

She glanced at Tom for reassurance. She was proving her devotion to this man. He could still make everything right.

"Here we are," he said, digging his latchkey out of his pocket. "Keep quiet on the stairs—the landlord'll charge me extra if he thinks I'm bringing a woman in."

They went through a dirty front garden full of cats and dustbins into a pitch-black hall that smelled of stale food and oilcloth. Gripping Tom's hand, Rory crept up the stairs, wincing over every creak.

Tom locked the door of his room behind them before he put a match to the gas. It was like a monk's cell, with bare walls covered in white distemper, a narrow bed, a desk, a washstand and heaps of books and papers.

They were still for a moment, staring at one another gravely. Rory ached to be in his arms again, but he did not kiss her. Instead, he began to take his clothes off. She watched, mesmerized at the matter-of-fact way he hung his tie and vest over the back of the chair.

Hesitantly, not wanting to do anything wrong, she slipped off her coat, and unhooked her blouse with numb, clumsy fingers. A lead weight of embarrassment lay on her chest. Only her growing sense of unreality prevented her from panicking.

Tom was naked. His long limbs were white and thin, and his ribs jutted painfully over his concave stomach. His erection was enormous, leaping up toward his navel. Rory could not look at him; she had not seen a naked male since she was five, and still small enough to share the nursery bathtub with Tertius.

He helped her off with the rest of her clothes in silence, and she automatically covered her pubic hair with her hand. Tom moved it away.

"Red," he whispered. "I thought so. Lie down on the bed."

Very self-conscious, Rory did so. The counterpane was scratchy, and smelled of him. Once again, she felt the rush of heat between her legs. It subsided, however, when Tom took something out of his desk drawer—a length of whitish rubber lying in a tin full of French chalk. He blew away the chalk, and, amazingly, fitted the rubber sleeve over his engorged penis.

Now, she could not take her eyes off it, for she had never seen anything so bizarre. Tom climbed onto the bed, straddling her body so that the twitching, rubber-covered truncheon almost rested on her pubic bone. More amazing yet, he spat on it until the whole surface glistened with saliva.

Then he pried her knees apart, and guided the thing to the opening of her vagina. She tensed, feeling its hardness, and gripped the sides of the bed.

Fiery pain plowed through her. She was being torn apart. Her mouth opened in a silent scream.

Tom clamped a hand on each of her breasts, and stabbed himself into her, frowning with concentration. The bed lurched violently five or six times. His face took on a look of abstracted astonishment, then twisted, as if in anguish. His back arched convulsively, his head shot up, and he cried out at the damp-stained ceiling.

It was, apparently, over. He sagged on top of her, panting.

"Good God, the relief of it!"

He pulled away from her, and the rubber flopped wetly off his penis.

Rory gulped back a cowardly impulse to weep. She was scorched and smarting. Thank heaven it had not lasted long.

"Look—" Tom held up the rubber. It was smeared with blood. He grinned at her. "You're a real woman now."

And then he washed the frightful object, dried it meticulously with his handkerchief, and replaced it in the tin.

"Let's get some sleep," he said. "I've a meeting down in Stepney first thing." He turned off the gas, and the room sank into shadow. "Shove up, hen."

There was comfort in his warm body, squeezing into the bed beside her.

"Tom—"

"What?"

"I love you."

"Aye, that's right." He kissed her forehead. "You may be on the skinny side, but you'll do."

Five minutes later, he was snoring.

Eight

There was nothing like a dance, Sybil Braddon thought, for luring young people into doing their duty. Girls forgot any silly ideas about independence, and men forgot their fear of marriage. Give them plenty of champagne, turn a blind eye to kissing on the stairs, and everything settled itself naturally. Viola's engagement was bound to encourage the others.

She had provided a perfect setting for flirtation. The band, behind their screen of potted palms in the corner, was quietly warming up with a medley from *Floradora*. A rose-scented breeze was wafting through the open French windows. The terrace outside was lit by a ripe harvest moon, and the polished parquet floor was already thronged with lovely young creatures, all eager to tango and two-step until "John Peel" and carriages.

Sharp, the butler, was announcing names at the door, as guests handed in their cards.

"Mr. and Mrs. Danvers and Miss Danvers ... Sir Arthur and Lady Burlington ... Colonel and Mrs. Carr-Lyon ..."

Marian Carr-Lyon, a bony woman tanned like leather from fifteen years in India, grasped Mrs. Braddon's white-gloved hand.

"Sybil, my dear, what a delightful occasion. How happy you must be!"

Mrs. Braddon gave her standard reply. "Happy for Viola, of course, but it isn't easy to part with one's daughter. I positively dread tomorrow."

"Dread my foot," Mrs. Carr-Lyon muttered to her husband, as soon as they were out of earshot. "She can't wait. Nobody thought she'd pull it off—but poor young Fenborough is absolutely silly over the girl, so I've heard."

"Don't wonder at it," said the Colonel, staring across the room at Viola. "She's a marvel."

"Oh, she's the beauty of the season, no question about it." Mrs. Carr-Lyon assessed Viola's dramatically simple yellow gown with an expert's eye. "Paris," she pronounced. "A real Poiret, and it must have cost a king's ransom."

"His family'll be glad of her money," the Colonel remarked. "Old Gaisford hasn't a bean. Patent medicine, wasn't it? On Sybil's side?"

His wife snorted with laughter. "Sybil's grandfather invented Rutherford's Balm—"

"Good God! Not the stuff I smear on my piles?"

"Harry, keep your voice down! We used to tease her so dreadfully at school."

He was still staring at Viola. "Not very bride-like, is she, the young ointment princess? Bit of a cold fish."

"Oh, I don't believe there's much to her—nobody has ever heard her speak. I wonder if she's happy?"

"Daughters must be hard work," mused the Colonel. "Having to bag fellows for them, and all that."

Mrs. Carr-Lyon took a glass of champagne from a tray offered by the footman. "Sons are bad enough. Where's Stevie? He promised he'd be here."

"He's picking up young Hastings."

"He's what?" Mrs. Carr-Lyon almost shrieked. "You can't mean he's bringing him?"

"He was invited, apparently."

"Nonsense, Harry. Sybil would never dream of it. You must have made a mistake."

Mr. Bartholomew Braddon, on the other side of the room, was busily carrying out his wife's orders, and writing his name in the dance programs of plain girls who were likely to be short of partners. He was a stout, whiskered man; once as fair as Viola, now bleached with age and money-making. Nancy, his youngest daughter, home from boarding school, pranced up to him, fanning out the skirts of her pink silk dress.

"Darlingest Dad, do tell Mother I can't go to bed before supper —it's too cruel!"

Fifteen-year-old Nancy was plump and freckled, and allowed to take all kinds of liberties because she was her father's pet.

"You know the rules, old lady. Behave yourself, and I'll give you a waltz."

"A two-step!"

"At my age?"

"Oh please—"

"The Honorable Mr. Carey," announced Sharp, "and Miss Carlington."

Braddon's attention swerved to the doorway. "I say!"

Jenny nudged Eleanor. "Gracious, look at Rory!"

"Disgraceful," Mrs. Braddon said under her breath. "Absolutely disgraceful."

An emerald-green chiffon gown decorated with panels of scarlet beading sheathed Rory's slender body like the skin of a snake. The neckline plunged front and back, revealing her startlingly white skin. The skirt was slashed to the knee. Her arms were bare, except for a thick silver bracelet clamped above one elbow.

"They're all gaping at me," she whispered to Tertius. "Philistines. Haven't they ever seen the Russian ballet?"

Aubrey had insisted upon giving her the gown, a copy of one of Leon Bakst's designs for the *Ballet Russe,* because he said he could not bear to see a beautiful woman who did not know how to dress. Rory thought it a great lark. She loved to shock, and being considered a beauty was a novelty.

"They're too busy looking at everything else to think about ballet," Tertius said. He was hypnotized by the way her breasts and hipbones moved under the fabric when she walked. "Are you wearing anything underneath that?"

She grinned at him. "None of your business."

"What does Eskdale think of it?"

"That's none of your business either." The reply had come out more snappishly than she had intended. "I wish you'd stop being so jealous."

"I love you."

Rory rudely made snoring noises.

"All right. But how am I supposed to feel, when you're standing there half-naked?"

"Tershie darling," she took his arm. "We haven't seen each other for ages. Don't let's argue."

Tertius did his best to swallow a raging pang of jealousy; Rory not wanting to argue was a very bad sign.

"Sorry," he said. "So tell me what you've been up to. Without mentioning Eskdale's name more than three times—it's a new parlor game."

She laughed. "For that matter, what have you been up to? I haven't seen you for ages."

"Oh, working."

"Working at what?"

He looked down at his cuff, and said distantly: "The portrait of Viola, mostly. Gus wanted it in time for the wedding."

"But you began it ages ago! Why has it taken so long?"

Tertius frowned. "Can't imagine."

Obviously, he did not want to talk about it. Rory, hating the idea of secrets between them, scrutinized him closely for the first time that evening and saw—to her surprise—that his ears were reddening above his stiff collar. Before she could interrogate him, however, they were joined by Eleanor.

"You've done it now," she told Rory. "I thought Mother would faint when she saw that dress."

"Like it?"

"I adore it. I think you look absolutely lovely."

Rory squeezed her hand. "You look fairly lovely yourself."

Eleanor was, she realized, a chameleon who changed according to her feelings. Tonight, in her cloud of pale blue tulle, she was a beacon of happiness, radiating a secret light that gave her sallow face a piquant charm, entirely individual and delightful. She was keyed to a pitch of excitement that would end either in bliss or despair. But it had not made her selfish.

"Tertius, I know how kind you are or I wouldn't ask—but will you please let me put you down for a couple of dances with Francesca? I'm filling her card because she's hiding upstairs. She might come down if she's knows it's only you."

"Poor little thing, anything you like," he said. "I won't frighten her. What about you?"

"Oh, I'll fill my card later." Eleanor had no less than three programs dangling from her wrist. "Would you be a real saint and dance with Aunt Flo? Nobody ever asks her and she does so love it. Only Gus and Father have agreed so far."

"Don't you worry, I'll keep the old girl moving."

"You're a dear."

Rory spotted Jenny gliding away into the conservatory. "Excuse me."

She hurried after her, aware that men were staring at her dress. Or rather, the spaces where her dress should have been. Perhaps she should not have worn it. She had no right to make a spectacle of herself now that she belonged to Tom.

Belonging to Tom was lonely. She could never tell the girls about the real nature of their relationship. Tom had taken to carrying his French letter around in his pocket so that he could relieve his chemical disturbances whenever he felt the urge. The day before, he had actually taken her on the sofa at Aunt Hilda's while the old lady held a séance in the next room. Fortunately, it never took long. Rory worshiped Tom and lived for his rare expressions of affection, but she did not enjoy the physical part of it at all. She could not imagine why people made such a fuss about it.

"Jenny?"

Paper lanterns had been hung in the rich, damp foliage of the conservatory, and the leaves and flowers glowed with tropical intensity. They made an ideal background for Jenny's eau-de-nil silk dress, immaculately cut to emphasize her tiny waist and generous breasts. She wore no jewelry. Her only ornament was a knot of white camellias in her thick golden-brown hair.

Rory kissed her. "You're the real beauty. None of us can hold a candle to you."

Jenny's gentle eyes were full of amusement. "I shouldn't be seen with you. That frock is an absolute scandal."

"What are you doing in here? Don't tell me you're hiding, too."

"Oh, people keep asking me to dance and I don't want to fill my card too soon."

"You're expecting your laird," Rory teased. "Rob Roy, or whatever his name is. Will he be wearing his sporran?"

Jenny did not smile. "I'll tell you the truth, but you must swear not to breathe a word to the others."

"I swear!"

"I'm tired of waiting and worrying. By the end of the evening, I intend to know my fate."

She did not look as if the prospect pleased her.

*　　*　　*

"God, the little darling," Stevie breathed. "She's exquisite."

Stevie and Lorenzo were leaning against the wall, watching Francesca through the crush of dancers. They had arrived too late to be announced, and too late for the welcoming champagne. Lorenzo had a silver hip flask of whiskey, which they were passing between them.

"Her card'll be crammed by now," complained Stevie. "I wish you hadn't made me wait so long."

"You could have come alone."

"Oh no. I promised Eleanor."

Francesca whirled past them in Tertius's arms. Her white dress, a mass of tiny pleats in the Grecian style, was a real Fortuny, sent by her mother. Diamonds sparkled in her dark hair and around her delicate throat. She was the epitome of virginal grace, but she seemed uncomfortable and kept her eyes cast down to the floor. When the dance finished, she clung to Tertius's arm and ran to Eleanor and Jenny with evident relief.

"Three little maids from school," said Stevie.

"Four little maids," Lorenzo corrected him, as Rory joined her friends.

"Oh yes. Four toothsome young virgins."

"Three." Lorenzo was staring at Rory. "If that redhead's a virgin, I'll eat my hat. Who is she?"

"A school friend, I believe," Stevie said stiffly. "Bit of a hoyden by the looks of her."

Lorenzo snorted scornfully. "A hoyden! Stephen, if you could hear yourself sometimes. She's the only passable female in the room."

"She's half-naked." Stevie was reddening.

"Which is not nearly naked enough. Would you introduce me?"

With rare firmness, seeing Eleanor's hopeful face, Stevie said: "No, I won't. You promised not to make trouble."

Across the room, Rory was snared in the challenging gaze of Lorenzo's dark eyes. There was something very impertinent, she thought, in the way he was looking at her. She gazed back, with the oddest feeling that he could see right into the marrow of her bones.

"Eleanor, who is that man?"

"Never you mind." Tertius clasped her waist possessively. "This is my dance and I want some attention."

Mrs. Braddon's social antennae were telling her something was wrong. The older guests were giving her peculiar glances, puzzled and slightly contemptuous. With the bright smile glued to her face, she took a rapid look around. Were her girls all behaving? Yes. The servants? Yes. On the surface, everything was running like clockwork. She followed the glances to the dark-haired young man beside Stevie.

A memory stirred at the very back of her mind. An ugly, painful memory that resisted being dragged into the open.

"Flora, who is that man?"

"Why, you told me to invite him!"

"Did I? What's his name?"

"Why—why"—Flora stammered—"I don't know. He's the friend Stevie brought to tea. Eleanor liked him so much."

At that moment, Lorenzo turned his head, and Mrs. Braddon saw his face properly. Those eyes. Large, fiendishly beautiful and as black as night. They were exactly like—

"Merciful heavens!" The color drained from her lips, and she was stilled by a thunderclap of recognition.

"Sybil," Flora asked timidly, "are you all right, dear?"

Mrs. Braddon snatched her sister-in-law by the wrist and dragged her out of the crowd into the darkened library, where Viola's wedding presents were displayed ready for the following day.

"You fool!" She was trembling with anger. "Do you realize what you've done?"

"No, I—"

"As soon as I saw him, I felt as if a goose was walking over my grave. It's the eyes. I'd know them anywhere. I'd stake my life that's Sir Laurence Hastings."

The name struck Flora like a hammer blow. She backed nervously away from Mrs. Braddon. "But he—he's dead!"

"Not the dead one, you halfwit! There was a son."

"Oh, but it couldn't be—he was just a little boy!"

Mrs. Braddon fought to control herself. "Do you know, Flora, I seriously wonder sometimes if you are quite all there." Her voice broke out in a suppressed scream. "It was seventeen years ago!"

"Lizzie's boy," whispered Flora. "Yes, of course. That was it. He looks just like her. Exactly like her. I forgot about her boy—"

"Yes, you forgot. And you invited Sir Laurence Hastings to Vi's dance." She fanned herself furiously. "Why stop there? Why not Sweeney Todd and Jack the Ripper?"

"No!" pleaded Flora. "It's not as terrible as that!"

"Just think what people will be saying about me—that I'm so desperate to marry off my girls, I'll push them at anyone, with not a thought for decency or reputation!"

"What are we going to do?"

"You're not going to do anything, Flora, except keep your mouth shut." She was calming down now, as she cast about for ways to control the damage. "What Bartholomew will say, I can't imagine. I've a good mind to tell him it's all your fault."

"Oh no!" Flora quavered tearfully. "Oh please don't!"

"Now listen. You said Eleanor liked him."

Flora mouthed: "Yes."

"I can hardly ask him to leave, so don't let her out of your sight. Do you hear?"

"I won't. Oh, Sybil, forgive me. I can't endure it when you're cross!"

"I forgive you. Now stop fussing." Mrs. Braddon minted a fresh smile, and they returned to the drawing room.

It was a struggle to pretend nothing was wrong, for she was acutely aware that people were talking.

"It is, I tell you. Don't you remember, there was a little boy? Well, he's up at Cambridge now—"

"Good heavens, the son of the Beastly Baronet. Bad blood all around, I'd say. What's he doing here?"

Marian Carr-Lyon said: "How extraordinary of you to invite the Hastings boy. Stevie's very attached to him, but nobody else asks him anywhere."

"Marian dear," said Mrs. Braddon, "won't you go through to the dining room?"

Frantically, she searched for Eleanor.

This was disastrous. She was dancing with young Hastings, and anyone could see she was thoroughly infatuated; Eleanor had always worn her heart on her sleeve. Mrs. Braddon blamed herself. If only she had not been so caught up in Viola's wedding she might have noticed the signs earlier.

She was not an unjust woman, and she fully saw what a pity it was that Laurence Hastings should be blamed merely for his name. It must, of course, be awful for him. But

blood was blood, and one could not change the past. She
had worked hard for the social triumph of Viola's marriage,
and nothing was going to spoil it. She would die before she
allowed one drop of Hastings blood to stain her family.

Francesca curled her knees under her chin and shrank into
the shadow of the wall. She wanted to be tiny; a dot, a
speck. She wanted to be invisible. The babel in the drawing
room roared in her ears, tearing at her nerves.

Everyone would be annoyed with her, but she had endured it as long as she could. Whenever she raised her eyes
from the floor, she had seen them gaping at her in their
black evening clothes. The whole room smelled of them—
hair oil and shaving soap, and the alcohol on their breath.

When one of them had loomed over her chair, claiming
that Eleanor had put his name in her dance program, it
had been more than she could bear. She had panicked, and
dashed away to this dark recess behind the green baize
door. But suppose he was angry and came to find her?

"Don't chase me! Don't chase me!" she whispered. She
chanted it like a spell. "Don't chase me! Don't chase me!"

Tears were stealing down her face. How stupid she was.
Mrs. Braddon would give her such a telling off, and quite
right, too. It was unreasonable of her, and hysterical, and
silly, and all the things they always said. She could never
explain the fear. She just had to be where it was quiet.

There was a sound of churning water, and a door opened
suddenly, spilling yellow light into the passage. Francesca's
heart swooped, and sweat prickled under her arms. How
awful. She had forgotten that the downstairs cloakroom had
been set aside for the male guests. And now one of them
was coming out. How too awful.

"What on earth—I say, I'm frightfully sorry. I had no
idea there was anyone here."

The embarrassment was agonizing. Of course, it would
have to be handsome Stevie of all people who found her
huddled on the floor in such a shameful place.

"H—hello," she said lamely.

"Francesca—Miss Garland." Stevie reddened up to the
roots of his fair hair. Are you all right? You're not ill or
anything?"

"Oh no!"

He crouched down on the dusty floorboards beside her. "Why, you poor little thing, you've been crying."

She risked meeting his eyes. They were as kind and clear as the blue day.

"I'm hiding," she explained. "I ran away. I was so scared, I couldn't help it."

"Who scared you? Should I punch anyone's nose?"

"Oh no, it's only my silliness. I hate parties so much—I always end up hiding somewhere."

He settled himself comfortably against the wall. "I can't say I blame you. It is rather a madhouse in there."

"Everyone gets cross with me when I do it. Even Eleanor."

"Well, I'm not cross. You gave me a start, though. I nearly tripped over you."

"You think I'm peculiar," Francesca said disconsolately.

He smiled. "I think you're heavenly."

"Oh don't, please!"

"Don't you like compliments?"

"It makes me feel all squirmy."

Stevie laughed softly. "In that case, have my handkerchief instead."

"Thank you. I mean, are you sure? It isn't just tears. I have to blow my nose."

"That's all right. You can keep it. Here." He put the handkerchief into her hand.

"How nice you are!"

"Steady on. You'll make me feel all squirmy too."

Francesca giggled and blew her nose loudly. "I'm better now."

"Good, because you can't hide here, you know. Let me take you into supper."

"No!"

"Aren't you hungry?" he coaxed.

"I can't!"

"Not even if I take care of you and swear never to leave your side for a single moment?"

"Well—" Francesca considered. It was true, she felt safe with Stevie. She trusted him, and it was strange, since the thought of being alone with a man usually terrified her. But Stevie wasn't made of the same material as some of those others; the beastly, hairy ones. With the light from the doorway striking a halo out of his hair, he was more like an angel than a man. Nobody could be terrified of an angel.

She smiled. "All right."

The dining room was thronged. People were crowding around the table two and three deep; the younger ones making bold lunges for the chicken galantine, and shrieking with laughter when they dropped blots of mayonnaise on the white cloth. Poached salmon lay in silver dishes on beds of parsley, their pink backs glazed with jelly and jeweled with strings of capers. There was a centerpiece of fruit, crowned with a pineapple, and vast cut-glass bowls of trifle, bristling with blanched almonds. Margaret and the second footman dashed to and from the kitchen with fresh plates, their faces scarlet from the heat. Below stairs, a dance meant long hours and grindingly hard work, yet all the servants appeared to be enjoying themselves. Like everyone else, they were caught up in the bustle and hilarity, dazzled by the colors of fruit and frocks, dizzied by the scents of rose and patchouli wafting from the warm flesh of the women.

Jenny, watching from the doorway, marveled at the way a dance always seemed to stretch into a lifetime. You walked from room to room for hours, the shifting kaleidoscope of faces gradually becoming as familiar as your own family. You learned every picture and ornament, every tuft of carpet, by heart. You watched silks wilting and flowers turning brown at the edges. You felt as if you had been born in your evening dress.

Dawn was another era, too far off to worry about. Jenny pretended the future did not exist, and stubbornly stuck her mind in the groove of the present. How odd it was, she thought, to see her school friends as grown-ups, airing their party manners. Here was Rory, transformed from a bundle of bones into a siren, with at least five young men fighting to eat supper at her feet, while Tertius looked daggers at them all. Eleanor, at Lorenzo's side, was in such a state of bliss that Jenny felt a twinge of envy. To be carried away to the isles of the blessed, simply because you were eating your supper next to a particular man—that was something she would never know.

Even Francesca seemed enviably happy, clinging to one of Stevie Carr-Lyon's coattails while he stretched across the table to bag her a nectarine. For once, apparently, she had managed not to run away. Restlessly, Jenny cast around for some social duty to distract her. She had devoted a great deal of energy to looking after Effie, who was a natural wallflower. Now, however, she had been taken under the wing of kindly Mr. Braddon, and was rosily eating trifle and giggling over his elephantine jokes. But there was always a casualty in a crowded dining room. Flora sat forgotten, one picked bone upon her plate, and the fringe of her shawl trailing in a glass of punch cup someone had left on the floor. Poor old thing, she did look miserable. Jenny started toward her.

"No, you don't!" Alistair's hand suddenly closed around her wrist. "Are you doing this to me on purpose?" He was smiling, but his grip was so tight, it hurt a little.

"Doing what?"

"Every time I come near you, you dash off somewhere else. Damn it, I've only had one dance with you. Are you trying to avoid me?"

"No!" She had been avoiding him, she realized. It was extraordinary the way her instincts kept working against her own best interests. "But I promised Mrs. Braddon I'd make sure all the ladies got enough to eat, and I really must get something for poor Miss Flora, so—"

"You're doing it again." His fingers gripped harder. "Hang Miss Flora. I wish she was at the bottom of the sea."

"I beg your par—"

"Burn and sink the lot of them. I've had enough of chasing you, my little Morningside violet, and I'm not releasing you until you talk to me. I can't wait any longer."

"All right, but you don't have to take me into custody. I'll come quietly."

This must be it. Jenny kept her tone light, but her heart was thrashing wildly. She had become used to the way her feelings divided over Alistair, as if she had two selves. One of these was eager to see a return on her investment. The other, her better self, dreaded having to deal with his emotions.

Mistaking her flicker of repulsion for maidenly modesty, his face softened into undisguised yearning. "I'm sorry, my dear. I'm making you nervous and that's the last thing I meant to do. It's this army of braying youths—they set my teeth on edge. I'm too damned old for dances. I should be in the card room, playing whist with all the other relics."

"Alistair, you are silly." She took his arm. "Let me guide your tottering steps to the terrace. It's a heavenly night, and I'm pining for some air."

They stepped into a warm summer night, lit by stars and perfumed with roses. As if on cue, the musicians in the drawing room began to play "I'll Be Your Sweetheart" in a slow waltz time. The setting was ridiculously perfect. If Alistair had been a few years younger, the two of them would have made an admirable illustration for the lid of a chocolate box.

He cleared his throat, and she watched dispassionately as the color deepened in his neck.

"Jenny, I have behaved dishonorably to you. I've tried to conceal my feelings from you, when I should have spoken out. I dare say I've managed it all very badly. When a man waits till he's my age to go off his head, he's bound to make an ass of himself."

She decided to help him. "You had your duty to your mother to consider. And I know she doesn't like me."

"No, she—she doesn't understand you. She hasn't had a chance to know you. But she depends on me so."

"You're a good son to her, Alistair. I've always admired you for that."

"My darling little girl." He grasped both her hands. "Have you any idea how wretched I've been because of you? I'm horribly in love with you, and it's reached a pitch where I can't bear the thought of living without you. I believe I'd die for you if I had to."

Jenny was silent, full of shame. How could she match such emotions without lying to him?

"My mother knows my feelings. I told her last night that I intended to speak to you. She may not have given her blessing, exactly"—(Blessing! Jenny could just picture the selfish old woman's dismay.)—"but she knows. I haven't broken any promises. So you needn't think you're doing anything improper or deceitful in listening to me."

She felt mean and humbled now because Alistair was assuming that she was as honorable as himself. It would have been easier if he had loved her less. His terrible goodness softened her into something like love.

"I know that when I listen to you, I'll never hear a word

that isn't thoroughly kind and good. You could never be deceitful."

He smiled. "You do like me a little, then?"

"Oh, just a little. You're only the nicest man I know. I feel dreadful for causing you all this trouble, and making you unhappy."

"My angel," he murmured, "you have it in your power to make me very happy indeed. You only have to say you'll marry me."

"Yes, Alistair. I'll marry you."

"I'm forty next birthday. Nearly twenty years older than you."

"That doesn't matter," she said. "Young men are silly."

"I get lumbago in wet weather. I fall asleep after dinner. I want to be sure you won't find it dull, living with a man who's already set in his ways."

"I like your ways," Jenny said.

"Yes, I think you do. You belong in the countryside, like the sprig of white heather that you are. With you beside me, I'll be as brisk as a puppy. You'll see me leaping over stiles when I'm eighty."

Happiness had sponged every line from his face. He shone with it, breathed it, sweated it. He had said he would die for her. She did not deserve it. To her amazement, tears rushed into Jenny's eyes.

"You're not old, Alistair. I won't let you say it. You're just you—I wouldn't have you any different for the world."

"Oh, Jenny, Jenny, my ain bonnie lass!" He caught one of her tears on the end of his finger. "I don't deserve your tender heart."

She laughed shakily. "How idiotic of me—"

"I wish I could set it in gold and hang it on my watch chain. It's selfish of me, but I'm desperately proud of myself for making you cry. You're so cool and collected—so pure—a chap feels a brute for wanting to touch you."

He dug into the pocket of his white vest. "I've been carrying this around for a week." A ring lay in the palm of his hand; a hoop of diamonds and sapphires.

"It's lovely!" Jenny's baser self rejoiced in the bauble.

She had done it. She would never have to do another day's work in her life. She was engaged.

Alistair slid it onto her finger, and turned her hand so that the jewels caught the light. "Pretty," he remarked.

"Far too good for me."

"Nothing is too good for the future Mrs. MacNeil. I say, I hope your father won't think I've been impertinent—I haven't even written to him."

Jenny smiled. "Nobody writes to fathers these days."

"Nevertheless, I shall ask his permission before I rob him of his pearl."

He put his arms around her waist. Jenny stiffened defensively, before she had had time to think. Immediately, he drew away from her.

"Jenny"—his face was unbearably kind—"are you afraid of me?"

"Oh—oh no," she faltered, "how could I be?"

He tilted up her chin and searched her face for a long time, before saying: "It's not me you're afraid of. Have you ever been kissed?"

"No."

"No," he murmured, "of course not."

She saw that her hesitation pleased him, because he mistook it for something else. His red face moved toward her. She closed her eyes. His smell overwhelmed her. His sweat was unexpectedly strong and horsey, mingled with the sandlewood soap he used for shaving. His lips pressed against hers.

This was not so bad. She could endure it.

He drew away. When she opened her eyes, he was looking at her humorously.

"My sweet girl!" With great gentleness, he pulled her lips apart.

Jenny was totally unprepared for the shock of his thick, wet tongue invading her mouth. She could hardly breathe, and his saliva, trickling down her throat, made her want to retch. Was this what people meant by kissing? It was disgusting—and now she had said yes to him, she had no power to stop it.

Alistair came up for air, moaning: "Oh God, I've waited so long—"

He crushed her against him, and his mouth swamped hers again, his rough chin rasping against her lips.

Rory's voice, amused and challenging, shattered the spell: "What has got into you tonight? I might as well dance with Father Doyle!" She had come out to the other end of the terrace with Tertius at her heels.

Alistair released Jenny, tensing with annoyance. "Damn!" he whispered.

Jealousy and alcohol had loosened the Honorable Tertius's grasp of grammar. "I won't have them fellers eyeing you up like you was meat in a butcher's window!"

Rory replied: "Lord, how provincial you sound. It's fine for you to talk grandly about ignoring convention, but when I do it, out comes the moralist of the bogs—"

"I've had enough of it!" shouted Tertius. "You look like a whore, so you do!"

Alistair threw a proprietorial arm around Jenny's shoulders and hurried her indoors. "I'm surprised at Mrs. Braddon letting that Irish chap hang around her house. He's disgracefully tight. And as for that girl! I know she's a friend of yours, my dear, but—"

"Don't let's worry about them." Jenny wanted to get him off the subject of Rory. "May I go and show my ring to Effie?"

"How like you to think of her! Yes, by all means. There's one member of my family who'll welcome you with open arms, bless her."

He was radiant. Jenny smiled, swallowing away the taste of his kiss, and trying to ignore the persistent little voice at the back of her mind, saying over and over: "What have you done?"

"You seem determined to make a mission out of me," Lorenzo said peevishly. "Any minute now, you'll hand me a blue ribbon and urge me to sign the pledge. Or perhaps it'll be an improving tract and a hot meal."

Eleanor sighed. "I'm asking too many questions again. I don't mean to pry."

"Of course you mean to pry. You're the nosiest girl I've ever met. And then you have to discover the moral reason for everything."

He dropped the end of his cigarette into the grass. They were walking among the ghostly blue shadows of the shrubbery. The house was a lighted ship, far away across a sea of moon-blanched lawn.

"I want to know you." Eleanor took his arm. In this eerie, rose-scented darkness, she felt his terrible, spiked loneliness. She knew it was his fear of being found hideous that prevented him revealing himself to her. "Why won't you let me like you?"

"Because you'll make demands. You're doing it already. I shouldn't have come tonight."

"I'm awfully glad you did."

"I didn't do it to please you," he said harshly. "I had an irresistible urge to annoy everyone."

"To annoy everyone?" Eleanor was baffled. "I'm sorry—"

Unexpectedly, he laughed. "I forgot, you haven't got your spectacles on. A case of the blind leading the deaf."

"What should I have seen?"

He was silent. She let a moment go by, then plucked at his sleeve. "Lorenzo? What?"

"It's why I had to get out—I'm attracting more attention than your sister. You might as well exhibit me in a cage."

"Why?"

"Why, why, why? There you go again."

"It's because I hate mysteries." Eleanor tried to keep the pleading note out of her voice.

"You adore mysteries," he corrected her. "That's the only reason you're interested in me. You have some romantic notion that my reluctance to tell you my life story masks something thrilling. You're too silly to realize that when people refuse to talk about themselves, the reason is usually disgusting."

Eleanor ached for him. His misery seemed to deepen the darkness around him. His rudeness only aroused a rush of longing in her. It was no use trying to reach him with words. She had to beat down the door of his cell.

Impulsively, she flung her arms around his neck and pressed her lips against his.

They were cold, and tightly closed. His body was an iron pillar of anger.

She fell away from him, hurt by his lack of response, but not ashamed. She was never ashamed when she acted from her heart. Their silence stretched painfully into minutes.

Eventually, Lorenzo asked: "Why did you do that?"

With no pride left to lose, Eleanor replied: "Because I love you."

"Well, well."

Another silence.

When he spoke again, the quiet nastiness of his voice

crept into her veins like poison. "I shouldn't be surprised, I suppose. Ever since I met you, you've been begging me to fuck the nonsense out of you. Call it love, if it suits you. How much do you love me, I wonder? As much as this?"

His hand suddenly dived between her legs, crumpling her dress. He squeezed and she gasped with shock.

"Oh no," he murmured, "don't scream. That's not playing fair. If young ladies go around making declarations of love, they ought to know what happens. Or perhaps you do know. Is this what you wanted?"

Paralyzed with disbelief, Eleanor felt him lifting her skirts. This could not be happening; it was not possible. His hand fumbled with the buttons on her underwear. Impatiently, he ripped the damp silk covering her crotch.

His finger slid along her split to her clitoris. "Yes— you're wet."

"No!" she whimpered. "Please—"

"My God, you're dying for it."

"Lorenzo, no—"

"Shut up." He sealed her mouth with his own.

It was not a kiss. He was biting her tongue hard enough to make her eyes water.

Eleanor had never known such fear, or such bewilderment. She was a stranger inside her own body. Her heart seemed to have plummeted down through her stomach, and was throbbing against Lorenzo's fingers. She was writhing instinctively against his hand before she realized what she was doing. Shudders of delight, so intense that they were almost indistinguishable from horror, charged through her.

He pulled his face away from hers and still she could not move. His touch had made her a prisoner, though he held her so lightly, she could easily have stepped away. Consumed by a terrible, debilitating sweetness, she gazed up into his shadowed face.

His breathing was hoarse and disordered, unnaturally loud against the distant chatter and music from the house.

"That's all you're getting," he said, taking his hand from her clitoris. "Enough to teach you not to fall in love."

Eleanor dazedly smoothed down her creased taffeta skirt. He was walking away, leaving her alone with an agonizing urgency in her body that she had no idea how to relieve. And somehow, she had done something dreadful to him.

"Lorenzo—" She ran after him. "Wait!"

"All right, I'm sorry," he snapped. "Tell your mother. Have me thrown out. Summon the police."

"Please! Wait just a moment! I didn't mean to make you cross. It's all my fault—"

Lorenzo stopped, turned back to her and gripped her arms fiercely. "What do I have to do to keep you away from me?"

"I—I thought you liked me—"

"Oh dear God!" he groaned.

"Don't you?"

He let her go. "Look, it's not a question of whether or not I like you. Though I suppose I do in a way."

"Oh, Lorenzo!" Eleanor felt her insides opening for him, like the petals of a fleshy flower. She was giddy with the yearning to be in his arms.

"Stop making cow's eyes at me. I simply don't know how to carry on with nice girls. What do you want from me?"

Eleanor could not decide whether she had lost her senses, or suddenly come into them. The words simply jumped off her sore tongue. "I want to marry you."

"You want to what?" A stunned pause, then he laughed unkindly. "Miss Braddon, this is so sudden. Are you sure you can afford to keep me?"

"Don't laugh!" she begged. "I can bear anything else, but I hate it when you laugh like that!"

"I beg your pardon, but I thought it was customary for the gentleman to do the proposing."

"I don't care." Eleanor's instincts had taken over, and she felt a reckless pleasure in pouring out her feelings. "I know I could make you happy. Until I met you, I didn't know what to do with my life—it seemed so frivolous and silly. For years, I've been looking for a purpose, something or someone I can devote myself to—"

"Why don't you join the Salvation Army?"

"You don't understand. Loving is the only thing I'm good at. I have so much love, Lorenzo, and the minute I saw you, I knew I had to give it to you."

"Well, it's awfully kind, but I'm afraid I must decline the offer."

"I'm not pretty enough for you," she said wretchedly.

"You're not bad. But it doesn't make any difference because I'm not on the market." He sighed, exasperated, but spoke quite kindly. "I don't owe you an explanation, but you'd better have one or I'll never get rid of you."

Taking her hand, he led her into the summerhouse, an opensided, damp-smelling structure behind the shrubbery. Its wrought-iron curlicues made an elaborate net of shadows in the moonlight.

Lorenzo pulled her down onto an uncomfortable rustic wooden bench and lit a cigarette. She glimpsed his great dark eyes in the momentary flare of the match and felt a surge of moist heat between her legs. If only he would touch her again—she did not care how angry he was, or how much he hurt her.

He exhaled a plume of smoke. "Have you ever heard of the Hastings Case?"

"No." Eleanor braced her arms across her stomach to stop herself trembling.

"You're too young, I suppose. In its day, the Hastings Case was the delight of every illustrated newspaper. A music-hall comedian only had to mention it to raise a laugh." The bitterness in his voice made Eleanor wince. "When you want entertainment, there's nothing like a good murder."

"A murder?" She was instantly still.

"One of the very best. Only the other day, I read an article deploring the modern shortage of classic lady poisoners. Where, it asked, are the Florence Bravos and Lady Elizabeth Hastingses of yesteryear? Where are the heroines who can spike their husband's claret with prussic acid and calmly watch him dying in horrible agonies over his dinner?"

Eleanor's heart was beating so hard that she could see it knocking against the fabric of her dress. She stared at his dark profile as if hypnotized.

"Lady Elizabeth Hastings," Lorenzo said, "was my mother. On Valentine's Day 1896, she murdered Sir Laurence Hastings, my father."

She had just breath enough to ask: "Why?"

"She didn't need a reason. She was insane. It should have been easy enough to prove to the jury. Two of her brothers are still locked up in asylums, I believe. And her counsel revealed certain juicy facts about my father that would have sent any woman off her head. Oh, everyone loved those—he was given the posthumous title of 'The

Beastly Baronet.' If that had been all, she would have been treated more leniently. As it was, there was a good deal of sympathy for her."

"What—what happened to her?"

"She was hanged. Public opinion could not forget or forgive the fact that before she dispatched the Beastly Baronet, she hit her four-year-old son on the head with a fire shovel, and left him for dead in the cellar."

He related the facts with such cold detachment that it took Eleanor a moment to realize exactly what he was telling her. When it came, the revelation pierced her to the soul.

"You," she said softly.

"Yes."

Now she understood. She had been afraid at first, because she had never known that in real life tragedy had such a hideous face. But the beauty of Lorenzo's innocence illuminated the whole sordid tale. How dreadful it was, yet how romantic. She felt so tender toward him that a breath could have bruised her. Of course, she told herself, it was the child who called to me; it was the child looking out of Lorenzo's eyes that made me love him so.

She took his hand. "Do you remember it?"

"No."

"Nothing at all?"

"The dark," Lorenzo said through gritted teeth. "I remember lying in the dark, and the pain in my ear, and thinking nobody would ever come. And the looks people gave me afterward—the cautious way they handled me, as if I might bite them."

"How mean of them, when you were so little."

"Oh, I can quite understand it. They were watching me to see which parent I resembled most. Would I inherit the paternal depravity, or the maternal lunacy? It has fascinated people ever since. They're absolutely convinced I'm about to go around the bend and poison someone. If ever I want to frighten people, I simply invite them to dinner."

"Don't joke about it!"

"What else can I do?" he demanded, turning on her angrily. "Imagine it. Just try to imagine what it's like to be me, going through life with my father's name hanging around my neck like a bloody millstone, and my deaf ear—the mark of Cain—thoughtfully provided by my mother."

He threw down his cigarette, and seized both Eleanor's hands, shaking them for emphasis, the words pouring out of him in a desperate, furious torrent. "Imagine being Sir Laurence Hastings at school. No, you can't—because you don't know that a boys' school is the cruelest place on earth. Of course, I was immediately rechristened 'Prussic Acid.' Or just plain 'Beastly' to my most intimate circle of friends. Imagine other boys' parents writing to the headmaster because they didn't want their precious sons in the same dormitory as Sir Laurence Hastings, just in case he turned into his dirty old father after lights out. Just imagine the whole world knowing that you're a freak, a ghastly aberration—someone who should never have been conceived, let alone born."

"Lorenzo, don't!" Her sympathy was so violent, so intense, that she was taking on his pain. "I can't bear it!"

"No, no—you wanted to know everything. Well, you shall." He dropped her hands and pulled back his cuffs. "See these?" He tilted his scarred wrists, so that a silver bar of moonlight fell across them. "I did that when I was at school. Go on, look at them properly. Doesn't it make your flesh creep?"

Eleanor thought she saw it all. She felt the loneliness of the outcast. She would descend with him into the valley of the shadow. The horror of what he had told her, combined with the upheaval in her body, convinced her that she had come to the turning point of her life. This was surely what she had been born for—to shield him from suffering, bearing the agonies herself. The beauty of her destiny filled her with a kind of ecstatic awe.

Lorenzo, however, had become prosaically conversational now that his spasm of anger had passed. "Stevie found me before I bled to death. He saved my life. I think that's why he loves me so much."

Stevie loved him. Yes, Eleanor thought, it was only natural that he should.

"But I don't like being loved," Lorenzo said. "Sentimentality is the curse of the age. I detest being slobbered over quite as much as I detest being stared at. If only people would leave me alone. The anonymity of death was what attracted me. Now, let's go back inside. I'm boring myself, and I could do with another drink."

"Thank you for telling me, Lorenzo."

He stood up. "Something to tell your grandchildren. And I'm truly sorry for what I did. It was good of you not to make a fuss. I won't do it again."

She was longing for him to do it again, but had just sense enough to know what a dive she would take in his estimation if she said so. Keeping in his good graces was such a delicate business.

He did not offer his arm to her as they walked back to the house, but he did not protest when she took it.

"Lorenzo—"

"Hmmm?"

Eleanor was so drunk with exultation, she had to say it: "When may I see you again? I know you told me about your parents because you wanted to put me off. You thought it would make me change my mind, but it hasn't. I could only love you more after hearing it. I promise not to make any demands on you. But it can't do you any harm to know that I'm here whenever you need me, ready to give you whatever you choose to take."

He did not reply.

"Lorenzo?"

They stepped into the light at the foot of the terrace steps, and she was deeply disappointed to see his expression of sour boredom. She had offered to sacrifice herself on the pyre of his sorrows, and all he could do was shake her hand off his arm as if she was nothing more than an irritation.

"The most tiresome thing in the world," he said, "is when people make long, involved speeches into my bad ear, and then expect me to answer them. It's something you will have to learn if ever we happen to meet again."

He strode ahead of her into the house.

"Let me handle this," Mrs. Braddon told Flora. "If we act fast enough, Bartholomew need never know."

The last guest had departed half an hour before, and they were supervising the dismantling of the dinner table. It was past two, and Viola's wedding was only hours away, but the girls were still up, and could be heard laughing behind the library door. Mr. Braddon had insisted upon opening another bottle of champagne in honor of Jenny's engagement.

"Oh, Sybil, do you really think it will be all right? I've been feeling so dreadful!"

"Go to bed."

"Yes, dear, thank you. But, Sybil—"

"What?"

Flora screwed up her courage. "Please don't be too hard on her. I mean, she's so tenderhearted, and how was she to know that—"

"Thank you very much, Flora," her sister-in-law said royally, "but I think I know how to manage my own daughter."

"Yes, dear. Of course."

Mrs. Braddon went into the library. "Really, Bartholomew, do you know what time it is? You are naughty, keeping them all up so late."

"Special occasion," Braddon said, through a veil of cigar smoke.

Mrs. Braddon softened as she turned to Jenny. What a dear, charming girl, she thought; I'm sure she's never given her mother a second's anxiety in all her life. If only Eleanor could find someone as solidly suitable as Mr. MacNeil.

"I shall write to your mother, dear, the moment I get upstairs. I couldn't be happier if you were one of my own girls."

Jenny smiled, and self-consciously fingered her ring. Mrs. Braddon had been too flurried to examine it closely, but she recognized handsome jewels when she saw them. They must have cost a small fortune. And the child had such a pretty color, too. She loved the man. Why couldn't all girls invest their feelings sensibly?

"Isn't it romantic, Aunt Sybil?" demanded Francesca. "She'll be shooting grouse, and tossing cabers, and dancing about in a tartan sash—"

"Yes, my duckling, it's perfectly lovely." Mrs. Braddon caressed Francesca's soft white neck. "But Jenny must be a bridesmaid before she's a bride—and so must you. Off to bed, children."

Not for the first time, she nursed the guilty knowledge that she loved Francesca more than she loved Eleanor. This cuckoo in her nest roused a maternal passion she had never felt for her own daughter. Eleanor's tumultuous, quivering emotionalism had always been a thorn in her flesh. She was clever, but it was an impractical brand of cleverness. Mrs.

Braddon did not trust it. As far as she was concerned, when it came to the really important things in life, Eleanor was as harebrained as Flora.

"Bartholomew, if you must smoke that thing, take it out on the terrace." She put a restraining hand on Eleanor's arm. "Wait a moment. I'd like to speak to you."

She shut the door behind the others. Eleanor stood under the glare of the overhead light, waiting for the inquisition with the look of tragic martyrdom Mrs. Braddon dreaded. She braced herself for a scene.

"Have I done something wrong, Mother?"

"Goodness, no. There's no need to be so dramatic. Have you enjoyed yourself this evening?"

"Yes, thank you."

"Let's sit down. My poor feet are ready to drop off." Mrs. Braddon sank into a leather armchair with a sigh of relief. Eleanor pointedly remained standing. Her cheeks had a hectic flush, and there was something else in her face besides defiance—voluptuousness, her mother decided, suppressing a shiver of revulsion. Lord, how she maddens me, she thought. Look at her, standing there like Sarah Bernhardt, all ready to play the star-crossed lover. Well, let her. Eleanor was not going to be allowed to ruin everything.

"I was so busy tonight, I hardly saw you. Whom did you dance with?"

"You know perfectly well, so why don't you just come out and say it?" Eleanor's chin was trembling. "I danced with Sir Laurence Hastings. And then I walked with him in the garden."

"Did you, indeed? I think I had better explain something to you, dear—"

"If it's about his parents, please don't trouble. He told me the whole story."

Mrs. Braddon clung to her patience. "And what did you think?"

"It's the saddest thing I've ever heard."

"Yes. It was a dreadfully sordid business. I'm very sorry for the young man. But it goes without saying, I can't possibly have him in the house again."

"Why?"

"Don't annoy me, Eleanor. No decent woman could possibly have anything to do with him—not when you think about his father—"

"But what exactly did his father do?"

"Never you mind!" snapped Mrs. Braddon. "Isn't the fact that there's insanity in his family enough for you?"

"I don't care." Tears were brimming in Eleanor's eyes. "I—love him."

"What nonsense. It's another of your silly phases, like wanting to be a nun, or pestering your father to let you study music in Leipzig. You'll get over it—you always do, thank goodness."

"Not this time." Eleanor raised her head proudly. "It doesn't matter what anyone says about him. I love Lorenzo and I want to marry him."

"Marry him!" shrieked Mrs. Braddon, letting go of her temper. "Over my dead body you'll marry him!" Forgetting her aching feet, she leaped out of her chair. "Are you too stupid to realize what it would mean? It's hereditary, you know. Your children would all be mad as hatters, and locked up in lunatic asylums like half his mother's family! He should know that, if you don't! Has he dared to make love to you? Because if he has—"

Eleanor subsided into sobs. "No. I only wish he would."

"I forbid you to see him again. Do you hear?"

"I will see him!" Eleanor sobbed. "I'd run to the ends of the earth to see him! But you don't have anything to worry about. He doesn't love me. He told me so himself, and I'm so unhappy, I wish I were dead. There—aren't you pleased?"

And she ran off, stormily and door-slammingly, to her room.

Aurora

Letter to my Daughter, 1935

Everyone said Viola's wedding made a lovely end to the
season, and I dare say it did look pretty if you weren't
standing close enough to see how swollen Eleanor's face was
above her blue organdy bridesmaid's frock. Viola was as pale
as death, and Gus was so dreadfully nervous that he nearly
dropped the ring. Spots of rain began to fall as we waved the
bridal pair off in their carriage. Eleanor caught the bouquet,
and Mrs. Braddon's brow became as black as the sky. The
rain turned into a downpour. Summer was over.

A few days later, the Braddon family shut up their house,
put the servants on board wages, and decamped to Deau-
ville. Jenny went up to Scotland for a fortnight, as a guest
of the MacIntyres, to watch Alistair and his brother-in-law
shooting grouse. Aubrey and Fingal departed for Italy, in
search of great art and dark-eyed gondoliers, and Tertius
and I scraped together enough cash for a visit to Ireland.

I did not want to leave Tom, but Aunt Hilda had booked
a holiday at a vegetarian hotel in Bournemouth, and she
would not let me stay in Bayswater without her, so I had
no choice. Home I went, cursing my lack of freedom, and
full of secret fantasies that Tom and I were married, with
a flat of our own.

Going home was odd. Tertius and I agreed that we felt as
if we had been away for centuries, instead of a few months.
Paddy Finnegan met us at Galway and told us a momentous
piece of news. We already knew, because we had seen it in
the newspapers, that the Home Rulers had set up their own
citizens' army, the Irish Volunteers, as a defense against Sir
Edward Carson's Ulster Volunteers. But had we heard, Paddy
demanded, that the Captain (as he always called Muttonhead)
had joined them? Half the families in the county were now

refusing to speak to him. Mr. Phillips had apparently nearly had a stroke when he heard, and Emma Billinghurst had publicly denounced him as a Fenian traitor.

Muttonhead in the Volunteers! Tertius and I thought it was splendid. Paddy had joined, too, and so had Papa. I couldn't help laughing to think of poor old Papa learning to march and stand to attention. There were about fifty of them, mostly farmers, armed with pitchforks and hoes, and sharing five old shotguns between them. Muttonhead drilled them in the big paddock three evenings a week.

We went to watch and were very impressed with the soldierly figure Muttonhead cut in his hairy tweeds, barking orders at his motley army. Otherwise, everything at Castle Carey was exactly the same.

"Nothing ever really changes here," Tertius said. "The politics makes for a bit of excitement, but it's three parts Guinness and flannel, as usual."

We fished, rode and walked together, as happy and dirty as a pair of tinkers. The barrier was still between us, but with Tom on the other side of the Irish Sea, it did not seem important. And neither Tertius nor I had the heart to spoil the Mater's happiness by quarreling.

"God bless her, it's overjoyed she is to hold her boy in her arms again," Una told me. "She'd have slain every animal in the place for the prodigal's return, so she would, if I hadn't put my foot down."

The Mater decided I looked thin and pale, and I made the most of this.

"It's the food at Aunt Hilda's," I complained to Papa, as pathetically as possible. "No milk, no butter, no meat— just beastly black toadstools, and boiled greens."

"She can't stay there, Justus!" exclaimed the Mater, alarmed. "She'll go into a decline!"

"And the séances send ice water down my spine," I continued, avoiding Muttonhead's suspicious eye as I piled on the agony. "Would you believe it, Papa, she keeps nagging me to contact my mother!"

"Table-turning, is it?" cried Una, who was more staunchly Catholic than the Pope. "The profanity!"

"Charlotte wouldn't speak to Hilda when she was alive," Papa commented dryly. "I don't imagine being dead has made her change her mind. Still, it's all in very poor taste. Perhaps we should try to find somewhere more suitable."

This was what I had been waiting for. "Couldn't I have a flat of my own, Papa?"

There was a horrified babel, and a low growl of outrage from Muttonhead, but I kept on. "Lots and lots of girls do it. It's perfectly respectable these days. Miss Curran and Miss Scott, my two old governesses from school, would keep an eye on me if I found a place near them—"

I could always get around Papa, and by the end of the visit, I had his grudging permission to look for rooms. I took care to avoid Muttonhead while this debate was raging, but I could taste his disapproval. He cornered me at the back of the field during a splendid day out hunting with the Galway Blazers, and warned me to behave myself, or else.

"Don't you trust me?" I asked. Suddenly painfully conscious of what I had been up to with Tom, I pretended to watch the huntsmen and the Master drawing a cover up ahead.

"No," said Muttonhead.

"Charming."

"I don't want the Mater worried."

"I've no intention of worrying the Mater."

"Rory—"

It was the tone of voice that meant you had to look at him. I did so. He was particularly impressive on horseback, even though his coat was as old as Noah, and a strong breath of wind would have shivered his boots to pieces. He had the best seat and straightest back in the whole of Ireland. His tanned, handsome face was stern, and meeting his dark eyes made me quail a little.

"Rory, you were born a lady, and you're damned well going to remain a lady. Get your idiotic ideas out of your system if you must —but if I hear about anything unworthy of your father's name, I'll be down on you like a ton of bricks."

"You have no right to dictate to me," I returned, as boldly as I could manage.

"You were brought up in my house," Muttonhead said. "As far as I'm concerned, you're still under my protection, and I expect you to behave as if you were my sister." His face remained grave, but his eyes softened. "Ungrateful brat. I have a right to dictate to you because I care for you."

That made me feel awful. For the first time I realized how securely Muttonhead's love and my so-called reputation were bound together. Could I bear to lose them, even for Tom's sake?

I set about finding a flat as soon as I got back to London. Aunt Hilda made shocked noises, but she was so glad to see the back of me that she proved unexpectedly helpful. One of her séance friends, a Miss Thompson, let rooms in her South Kensington house, and her attic set was free—a landing with a gas ring, a tiny bedroom, a large sitting room with a sloping roof, and a bathroom shared with Miss Thompson's maid. The stairs were endless, the house was full of aspidistras and the cistern groaned like a soul in torment. I thought it was quite perfect.

I painted the walls white, covered the furniture in brightly colored shawls, and hid all the nasty china ornaments in the broom cupboard. Tertius gave me one of his paintings (a still life of fruit—it often made me feel hungry), which I hung above the gas fire. I had my own latchkey and was free at last.

Miss Thompson was deaf and elderly, and never looked out of her ground-floor rooms to see who was going upstairs. When Tom was able to sneak in for an hour or two in the evening, I was in heaven. I'd pretend we were married. Once or twice he stayed the night, though he had to be careful to leave before dawn. I would watch him sleeping beside me, his lashes making spiked shadows on his pale cheeks, and I would cry because I loved him so.

Poor Tom, he never really guessed how desperately I loved him. His head was too stuffed with socialist ideals to accommodate romance. He assumed that we were working partners, sharing a vision of Utopia. He did not know that he was my Utopia. Sometimes he would put down his papers, take my face between his hands, and tell me I was his best girl, and I would dine on joy for a week. Tom could not dine on joy. It's thanks to him I can cook a little. I thought my disgusting attempts at meals were hilarious, but he told me that if I had been born poor, I would find nothing funny about spoiled food. Very seriously, he showed me how to make Welsh rarebit and boiled eggs. I became self-sufficient—a great thing, in the days when it was assumed there would always be servants.

A few weeks after I had set up on my own, Jenny came

to tea. She brought Alistair, which surprised me very much.
I knew he did not like me, and he looked very uncomfortable, perched on one of Miss Thompson's rickety basket
chairs. Jenny went over every corner of the flat, and bom-
barded me with questions about hot water, and laundry
arrangements.

"Will it suit, madam?" I asked jokingly.

And Jenny amazed me by replying: "Yes, if you'll have
me. There's plenty of room in the small bedroom, and I
can help you with the rent."

"Jenny—" Alistair groaned.

She put her hand on his arm. "This is what I can afford.
You know I can't go on imposing upon Mrs. Braddon, kind
as she is."

"But here! I mean—can't you go back to your parents?"

"Will my staying in London make your mother's heart
condition worse?" Jenny was smiling, but I realized that
she was extremely angry.

"Oh God." Alistair slumped wearily. "If only you'd let
me help you—"

"No. You know it's out of the question. I'll be perfectly
happy waiting for you here—if Rory will have me."

I could not refuse her. Tom would have to be considered
later. "Darling, of course. I'd love to have you. But what
on earth is going on? I thought you were getting married
in a couple of months."

They exchanged significant glances. Alistair hung his
head as if ashamed.

"Alistair's mother," Jenny explained carefully, "has had
another relapse. It happened just after we set a date for
the wedding. Her doctors say she must spend the winter in
the South of France and she won't go without Alistair."

"Can't you get married first and both go with her?" I
asked.

"She wouldn't hear of it," Alistair said heavily. "She only
consented when I promised she'd have me to herself. You
do see, Miss Carlington, that I—that we—couldn't refuse.
She's put me in an impossible position."

He was so miserable that Jenny relented. "Not impossible, Alistair. Don't be so gloomy. We'll just have to wait a
little longer. Now, you leave me with Rory. I've a hundred
things to ask her, and I don't want to bore you."

He left unwillingly, with an adoring look at Jenny and an uneasy look at me.

Giving myself time to digest the situation, I made more tea, while Jenny examined all the drawers and cupboards. Finally, when we were crouched on the hearth rug in front of the gas fire, I said: "Well, you have had a time!"

Jenny chuckled softly. "You can't imagine the row. The old horror is being perfectly outrageous. Cornelia took my side, and now her mother won't speak to her. Cornelia's not a bad sort, actually—she even asked me to stay with them while Alistair's away."

"Why did you refuse? Isn't Hyde Park Gate more your style?"

"Not really. She meant to be kind, but I knew I'd end up helping with the children. And to tell the absolute truth, Rory, in a way I'm quite relieved not to be getting married just yet. You don't know how I envied you your independence."

No, I certainly didn't—Jenny could always surprise me. There was, however, something she should know. Stammering and turning beet red, I told her about Tom.

She was silent for such a long time that I was afraid she would never speak to me again. I took her cold hand.

"Are you furious with me? D'you think I'm very wicked?"

"Is he going to marry you?"

I tried to sound sophisticated. "We don't believe in it."

"Oh, Rory!" Another silence. "And have you really— have you—done it? You know, as if you were married?"

"Yes."

"What was it like?"

"Rather awful at first," I admitted, "but you get used to it."

"How do you know you won't have a baby?"

I began to describe the rubber thing Tom used, and before I had finished, we were both rolling around on the rug weeping with laughter. Under Jenny's Protestant, daughter-of-the-manse correctness, there was a fine sense of humor.

It was one of those arrangements that suited everyone. The Mater was inexpressibly relieved that I was living with another girl, and wrote that Muttonhead had said Jenny sounded like "a sensible little woman"—the highest possible praise. Tom complained at first, but Jenny was good about disappearing during his visits. After one taste of Jenny's cooking, Tertius and Q haunted us like a pair of disreputable ghosts. Poor old Alistair still did not care for me, but was only glad to see his beloved so contented.

For Jenny did not look like a girl whose wedding plans had been upset. On the contrary, she was a blossoming rose. She smiled and sang, and generally behaved as if a weight had been lifted from her shoulders.

"If I ever had to go back to work again—" she began one day.

"—You won't," I interrupted. "Not now you're engaged to Alistair."

"No, but if I did, I wouldn't be a governess again," she said decisively. "I'd like to nurse. I know I'd be good at it. I rather wish I'd become a probationer at a hospital instead of taking all those exams."

"But you'd never have met Alistair," I pointed out.

"I suppose not." She brushed this aside. "If there's another war, they'll need nurses."

I should say here that Tom was by no means the only person talking about a war with Germany. The Kaiser was seen as our natural enemy, and there were articles in the press about why our two cultures could never be reconciled. Cornelia MacIntyre took it all very seriously, because her eldest boy was a cadet at the Royal Naval College in Dartmouth. A friend of hers had started first-aid classes at her house in Knightsbridge, and she persuaded Jenny that it was her patriotic duty to go along and do her bit.

Jenny, in her turn, persuaded me. And that is how I met Lady Madge Allbright. She was a short, round tub of a woman, with buck teeth, and tiny hands like a hamster's paws. She had assembled a dozen ladies in her ballroom, and bounced around among us in a dainty little nurse's uniform that had been run up by the best dressmaker in Bond Street.

"Oh no!" I heard Jenny say under her breath.

"I quite agree," said I. "Did you ever see such a collection of overdressed old peahens?"

But Jenny was staring at an amazingly pretty girl with a mass of chestnut hair, who was leaning against the shrouded grand piano in a semi-swoon of boredom. She saw Jenny and roused herself enough to stroll over to us.

"Miss Dalgleish, what a shriek to find you here!"

"Miss Isola Kentish." Jenny introduced us through pursed lips.

"How do," Isola drawled at me. "I say, Miss Dalgleish, did you finally bag your laird?"

Fortunately, before Jenny could reply, Lady Madge clapped her paws for silence.

"Ladies, please! Sister wants to begin." ("Sister" was the grim-faced professional nurse she had hired to teach us.) "Now, who'd like to be bandaged?"

Nobody wanted to be bandaged. After a long argument, Lady Madge volunteered the parlormaid, and routed an unwilling footman out of the kitchen. Then Cornelia MacIntyre arrived, very flustered, with her two youngest children in tow.

"Madge, I'm so sorry—their wretched nurse has a toothache, as if I hadn't troubles enough."

"They're rather small," Lady Madge said, eyeing three-year-old Peterkin and five-year-old Meggy as if she was thinking of eating them, "but they'll do. Come along, darlings, and let Sister put you in splints."

Both children wailed in alarm, but Lady Madge (as I was to learn) had a formidable talent for making people do what she wanted. She bent down to them with a broad smile that made her plump face unexpectedly lovely, and said: "You shall have a piece of chocolate afterwards. And we'll use red ink and pretend you're covered in blood." They were as good as gold after that.

We spent two hours bringing the children and Lady Madge's servants around from faints and strapping up their broken limbs, and were then led into the drawing room for tea. Appearing not to notice Jenny's chilliness, Isola attached herself to us.

"I really think," she said, "that in the event of war, I could do more for the army than put their arms in slings. Isn't Madge's footman divine? I must ask her about his afternoons off."

Cornelia heard this, and was so shocked that she nearly spilled her tea. Later, she cornered Lady Madge.

"Who is that awful girl?"

"Isola is full of possibilities," Lady Madge said, with one of her seraphic smiles. She laid her little hand on my sleeve. "And you, Miss Carlington—I feel you're full of possibilities, too. I hope you'll come next week."

I had not meant to, but I did. Madge threw herself into her nursing classes with white-hot enthusiasm, and those of us with "possibilities" ended up taking our Red Cross First Aid and Home Nursing examinations. Tom, surprisingly, approved. I think he thought my skills would come in handy on the barricades, come the revolution.

Jenny adored it all. The stern professional Sister told her she was a born nurse: "It's a pity you're engaged to be married, Miss Dalgleish. You're admirable material—admirable." Madge and Jenny began to discuss the possibility of setting up a Voluntary Aid Detachment, and going out on maneuvers with the Territorial Army. Isola, needless to say, was extraordinarily keen on this idea.

For most of us, however, the Red Cross classes remained a game, a lark, a spree. I see us all, laughing and gossiping in Madge's ballroom. Each of us is secretly making plans. Our minds keep wandering away from what Sister is saying, to the men we imagine make up our real lives. Outside the tall windows, the autumn afternoon is darkening into dusk. Soon, the men will emerge from their clubs and offices, and we will lay our bandages and iodine aside. We look pitifully silly to you, I dare say. Most of us are only here to get ourselves through the manless desert of the daylight hours. We are passing time.

But don't be too hard on us. For us and those we love, time is passing faster than we know. There is so little time left.

PART THREE

1913–1914

One

"The nerve of the woman!" Mrs. Braddon raged. "Coming back to London, after all these years. As if I hadn't troubles enough, what with Viola expecting a baby and refusing to let me near her—me, her own mother! And Eleanor still sighing over that murderer—now I shan't be able to sleep for worrying about poor little Francesca. I don't know how that woman dares to show her face. Why couldn't she stay in New York?"

It was three weeks before Christmas, and Sybil Braddon was prowling around the drawing room, whisking her long velvet skirts behind her like the tail of an angry dragon. Francesca was upstairs, prostrate in the arms of Eleanor after an hour of hysterical weeping.

Flora was reading the letter that had whipped up this long-distance storm—a semiliterate scrawl from Francesca's Uncle Archie, containing the date their ship would dock at Southampton, and announcing that Francesca was expected to live with her mother and stepfather at a rented house in Half Moon Street, Piccadilly.

"Leaving us so soon! Oh, Sybil—"

"Don't you dare start crying!" Mrs. Braddon lashed out at her sister-in-law, trying to overcome the terrible bleakness that had settled around her heart. She had allowed herself to love Francesca more than her own daughters, and this was her punishment. The delicate creature she had sheltered so carefully would be exposed to the withering blast of scandal, and she would be forced to stand by and watch. "Think of that highly strung child in a house full of foreign servants. Think what she'll have to see and hear—"

"But after all," Flora ventured, "she is Francesca's mother."

"Oh yes!" snorted Mrs. Braddon. "She remembers she's a mother now, when Francesca is grown-up and out in society, and she won't have the bother of running a school-room. But what does she know of a mother's feelings? She doesn't deserve to be one."

Flora was dismayed to think of the gap Francesca would leave in the house, but felt she should play devil's advocate. "We always knew we'd have to give her up someday."

This brought on another tirade. "This is the only home she knows. Monica Garland—or Monica Templeton, as we're supposed to call her—won't have the slightest idea how to manage such a shy, difficult girl. Why, you know as well as I do what a business it is to get Francesca into a room full of strangers—and I'm talking about nice people, our sort of people, not the kind who would mix with the Templetons." She groaned. "I'd set my heart on finding her a suitable husband and giving her a wedding. What does Monica Templeton know about marrying off a nicely brought-up young girl? I shudder to think whom she'll meet, and Stevie Carr-Lyon was practically on the point of proposing. Well, that's all ruined now."

"It won't make any difference to him," Flora protested, speaking up for her favorite. "Stevie isn't the sort to change his mind."

"No, but his mother will change it for him. He's completely under her thumb."

"It won't be so bad. It's not as if Francesca's leaving the country."

"My dear Flora, she might as well be on the moon. Nobody in our set can possibly call on them. When I think of all the trouble I've taken, introducing the child to the right people, and now that outrageous woman proposes to throw it all away."

"I wonder," mused Flora, "what Mrs. Templeton looks like these days? She used to be so pretty. Do you remember when Sargent painted her, and the road outside the gallery was blocked for absolutely days?"

"An, but that was years ago," Mrs. Braddon said, with fierce satisfaction. "She must be over forty now, and look at the life she's been leading. Racketing about on the Continent, swilling champagne, staying at casinos until dawn—"

Flora's pale eyes widened behind her spectacles, dazzled by this Arabian Nights picture of the wages of sin.

Mrs. Braddon hastened to add the proper note of retribution. "It can hardly be good for the complexion. I shouldn't be surprised if Monica Templeton turned out to be absolutely raddled."

"So this is Stevie."

In one graceful, sinuous movement, Monica Templeton rose from the sofa and stepped out of the shadows toward him.

Stevie gaped, too confused to reply. He had expected Francesca's mother to look wanton—a painted harridan, whose face proclaimed her scandalous past like a theater billboard—but this woman was ravishing.

She had the same small-boned slenderness, the same melting brown eyes, milky skin and rich dark hair as Francesca. But where Francesca was dewy and fresh, her mother was hard and polished; a work of art rather than nature. Her lips were startlingly scarlet in her white face, and her fabulous, exotic eyes were outlined in black.

How old was she? It seemed impossible to apply any age to her. She wore a wisp of black chiffon, clasped under her small, firm breasts with a single diamond brooch. Her arms, shoulders and three-quarters of her breasts were bare. In the soft lamplight, her flesh had an opalescent gleam. Stevie tried not to stare.

"How do you do, Mrs. Templeton?"

She smiled, showing a provoking dimple. "I've already decided to address you as Stevie, so you must call me Monica. I do so loathe my official title—it has such tiresome associations."

Stevie was overwhelmed by a sizzling blush.

Monica pretended not to notice. She lit a cigarette. Stevie disapproved of women who smoked, but was hypnotized by the way her red lips caressed the cigarette's cork tip.

"So nice of you to see in the New Year with us. I positively couldn't bear to spend New Year's Eve at home. Too depressing. Francesca and Archie won't be long. It's just the four of us, if you don't mind. Archie insisted we must have someone to keep Francesca company, and I couldn't face spending the evening with some dreary, well-brought-up girl." She laughed. "Which is just as well, since I can't think of any well-brought-up girl who'd dream of spending an evening with me. How is your mother? You are Marian Hopwell's boy, aren't you?"

"Yes, she—very well, thanks."

"Good old Marian, I bet she's furious with you for accepting my invitation. Give her my love, and tell her I dare her to visit me. God," she exclaimed, "it's so priceless, finding England as stuffy as ever. That old trout Sybil Braddon looked as if she'd like to handle me with tongs when I called at her horrid suburban palace."

Stevie's attention had veered to the doorway, where Francesca stood, celestial in white silk. He felt his faculties loosening in the idiocy of worship.

Monica's eyes became shrewd and thoughtful as she followed his gaze. "Ah yes, here you are, darling. I've been entertaining Stevie for you. Why didn't you tell me how handsome he is?"

"Oh, Mummy, please—"

"For heaven's sake, don't look so shocked. Anyone would think you were still in the nursery. Has Sybil Braddon been keeping you in a cupboard all these years?"

"Monica—" Francesca's stepfather bustled into the room, fastening his cuff links—"why are those bloody decanters always empty? I'm parching for a drink." He was a slight, gray-haired man, sleekly handsome. Rather a bounder, Stevie thought.

Templeton briefly shook his hand. "How d'you do, young man. I say, Monica, that dress is a bit much."

"Not enough, you mean." She shot an amused glance at Stevie. "What do you think?"

"Leave the boy alone," Templeton said sharply. "If you want to go out in public looking like a damned tart, that's your affair."

They drove the short distance to the Ritz in a Rolls-Royce, which, Stevie gathered, was hired by the month along with the chauffeur. The whole Templeton ménage had a rootless, temporary feel to it, which made him very uneasy.

He did not enjoy walking through the restaurant behind Monica, and seeing the other diners staring and whispering. Francesca's hand trembled on his arm. She was in agonies and he longed to protect her. It was appalling that a disreputable pair like the Templetons had the right to make a spectacle of his innocent white rose. When they sat down, he kept hold of her hand under the tablecloth, and she hung onto his fingers for dear life.

Templeton had also noticed her discomfort. "I would like

to remind you," he muttered to Monica, through clenched teeth, "that you have someone besides yourself to consider. Perhaps you could make an effort to behave respectably, for the child's sake?"

"I'm all right, Uncle Archie," Francesca murmured.

Monica laughed. "Oh, Archie, I do adore it when you talk about respectability. Wherever did you learn it? But you mustn't worry. Nobody will take any notice of me when they have my beautiful little girl to distract them."

Stevie loathed the idea of Francesca being gaped at by strangers, but it appeared to mollify Archie. He was very fond of his stepdaughter, and anxious that she should have a good time. It was all kindly meant, but his idea of a good time was drinking vast amounts of champagne. He fussed when Francesca did not touch her glass, and did not seem to know that ladies were not supposed to drink. Not in public, at any rate. Well, how could he, thought Stevie, when his own wife was funneling the stuff down as if it had been lemonade? Stevie gulped his own glass, and swapped it with Francesca's full one. He was not used to knocking back alcohol so fast, but was rewarded by her heavenly look of gratitude.

He gallantly continued to drink for two, until a bubble of unreality closed around him. Fresh bottles marched to their table as if some sorcerer's apprentice among the waiters had uttered the wrong spell. A band was playing. There were festoons of flowers and ribbons around the walls. People at other tables were wearing paper firemen's hats and tinsel crowns.

Of course, it was New Year's Eve. Stevie felt a fizzy, champagne-flavored rush of sentimentality. The dawn of a new age of romance. He would sweep Francesca away from her parents on the back of a white charger—never mind what his mother said. He could face her for Francesca's sake. What an angel she would look in a chaste bridal crown of orange blossom.

The gunshots and shrieks startled him, until he realized they were firecrackers and cries of laughter. They were on their feet, and the band was playing "Auld Lang Syne." Above them, a banner printed "1914" unfurled lopsidedly, to loud cheers. He was saying something about love to Francesca under cover of the noise, and her eyelashes drooped so adorably that he could have fallen on his knees there and then.

Instead, before he was properly aware of what he was doing, he was following Archie through a glittering jumble of colors and lights. Then they were standing side by side in the gentlemen's lavatory.

"Thought we'd never get here," Archie said amiably. "Monica sits over her food till you're ready to piddle on the carpet. No consideration." He fastened his fly, suppressing a belch. "Coming for a smoke?"

Oh God, Stevie thought with horror, I'm drunk.

Archie found some acquaintances, but Stevie hurried back to the table. One did not leave ladies without an escort. Mercifully, with Archie out of the way, it was possible to sober up a little over coffee.

Archie returned briefly, clutching a glass of brandy. "Monica, you'll never guess who's here—old Buckie Van Helsing, all the way from Boston, and he knows where we can find a poker game. The boy will see you home."

Stevie was disgusted with his manners, but Monica did not seem to see anything untoward in the arrangement.

"Yes, Stevie will look after us. Give my love to Buckie, darling, and don't lose too much money."

Outside, the night air was deliciously crisp and cold. Monica paused with one foot on the running board of the Rolls.

"I think I'll let you two walk, and keep the car to myself. It's a shame to waste all these stars on a dilapidated old party like me."

Stevie, who had given up hoping for a few seconds alone with Francesca, could hardly believe his luck. For the first time, he could savor the company of his unattainable angel, without the danger of a chaperone cutting in at the crucial moment.

He felt the bones of her hand inside her kid glove, and smelled the delicate perfume on her hair. Her eyes were soft and trusting above the high collar of the magnificent sable wrap Archie had given her for Christmas. One long earring tapped the sleeve of his coat as she huddled closer to him.

Piccadilly was full of revelers. A noisy group of men in top hats and tails were piling into a row of taxis, with half a dozen screaming, painted girls. Some East End types, up

West on a spree, were drinking bottled beer under a lamp-post and eyeing the passing dandies as if they had been exhibits in a zoo.

A policeman patrolled the park railings. He saluted briefly as Stevie and Francesca strolled past. Stevie felt as if he had swallowed a balloon, which was swelling inside him until he was breathless with happiness. The stars in the clear sky, the streetlamps and the lantern the policeman was shining into the park bushes were all veiled in ethereal white mist.

They did not speak until they had reached the front steps of the house. Half Moon Street was deserted, and striped with ghostly gray and indigo shadows. Reverently, Stevie took Francesca into his arms.

"My darling girl." He was ready to die for her.

"Please don't—" She was shaking, and trying to back away from him.

"You mustn't be scared," he murmured. Very gently, he touched her eyes and mouth with his lips. "Darling one, I won't hurt you."

Her tense muscles relaxed a little. She allowed him to draw her head against his shoulder. It was like holding a bird that had to be stroked and reassured with painstaking tenderness to prevent it flying away.

He breathed into her ear: "Will you marry me?"

Another charge of fear ran through her body. "No, please!"

"Don't you like me?" he whispered. "Even a little?"

"Oh, Stevie, I like you such a lot, but I'm so frightened!"

"Of me?"

Her voice was muffled in his shoulder. "Of—of what you might do."

Stevie was enchanted. How pure she was, how untouched and inexperienced. "You angel, all I want to do is take care of you. Say yes."

Francesca said: "Yes," and instantly bolted out of his arms to ring the front doorbell.

A shifty-looking Italian manservant let them into the hall. Stevie lifted her hand to his lips.

"Happy New Year."

She searched his face apprehensively. Something in it re-assured her. She smiled. "Happy New Year, Stevie dear."

He watched her picking up her skirts with one hand and

climbing away from him upstairs until he was left alone in the hall gazing at his own fatuous reflection in the mirror.

"Now you can come and wish me a happy New Year, too, Stevie dear," said Monica's voice.

Stevie started guiltily. The drawing room door was open. He went in, hoping he did not look sheepish. When a man was about to make a formal pitch for a daughter's hand in marriage, he needed all his dignity.

"Shut the door." Monica was lying on the sofa by the fire. A thin blue column of cigarette smoke rose from its cushioned depths. She broke into a teasing laugh. "Well, you do look pleased with yourself."

"Mrs. Templeton, I—"

"The starlight worked, I see. Oh, how touching a thing is young love!" She threw the cigarette into the fire and stood up, stretching languidly. "I'm going to have a whiskey and soda. Will you join me?"

"No thanks."

"Don't be silly, of course you will. Goodness, how tall you are!" She raised her black-rimmed eyes to his face. "I wish you'd sit down."

"I—I've asked Francesca to marry me."

"And she accepted?"

"Yes."

"Bully for you. Perhaps you can sit down now the formal part is over?"

Stevie sat down on the sofa while Monica poured the whiskey.

"So," she said over her shoulder, "you're really prepared to take my poor little girl off my hands?"

"I know it must seem awfully sudden," Stevie began.

She handed him his drink, and sat down beside him, apparently unaware that her knee was pressing against his thigh. "I wonder if you know what you're doing?"

"I'm terribly in love with her."

"Oh, you chivalrous boy. I meant, what on earth will your parents say about it? Have they any idea?"

"No. But they must love Francesca when they get to know her properly."

"Sweet Stevie, I do feel mean, pushing you off your lovely pink cloud so soon. Of course, nobody could help loving Francesca. But don't you think they might find my reputation somewhat hard to swallow?"

This was so true that he could not reply.

Monica sighed and patted his leg. "It wouldn't be such a problem if only we'd managed to stay in New York. I may as well tell you because you're bound to hear the gossip eventually: we left because we had to. I got entangled with someone, and it was all rather unpleasant. The United States simply became too small for us. His vulgar horror of a mother actually offered me money to leave the country—can you imagine? I wanted to go back to the Continent, but Archie doesn't like the political situation there. And he longed to see Francesca."

"He's awfully good to her, isn't he?"

"Well, he would be," Monica said calmly. "He is her father, after all."

Stevie almost choked on his whiskey. "Her stepfather, you mean."

She patted him again, and left her hand on his thigh. "No, darling. Her real father. It isn't generally known, but I know you won't say anything."

"Oh no, of course not." He wondered if he dared twitch his leg away. "Never."

"But it does rather put a different complexion on the matter, doesn't it?"

Stevie thought of Francesca asleep upstairs, and his heart contracted with the longing to preserve her innocence. "No," he declared forcefully, "it doesn't change anything. I don't care what my parents say. I'm over twenty-one and I'll marry her as soon as I'm finished with Cambridge."

Monica ruined the effect by laughing. "I forgot. You're terribly in love with her."

"I adore her."

"And what do you think you'll do with her when you've brushed away all the confetti, and carried her into your rose-covered cottage?"

"I'm sorry?" he stammered.

Her jeweled hand was rhythmically stroking his leg. He had to fight an impulse to retreat to the back of the sofa.

"Stevie, have you ever made love to a girl?"

He could have run away, but her musky scent and the nearness of her exotic dark eyes made his senses reel.

"No," he said helplessly.

"God preserve us all from English men. And do you have the remotest notion how it's done? Don't bother to answer. My daughter is as ignorant as a baby. A fine mess you'd make of it between you."

There was a moment of intense relief when she removed her hand from his leg, then appalling disbelief. Monica plucked open his fly buttons and reached for his penis. It lay in her hand like a damp prawn. He dropped his glass, spraying the cushions with whiskey.

"No!" he moaned. He could not move. She began to pull the limp folds of his foreskin to and fro very gently.

"You're such a beautiful boy," she whispered. "You'll like it if you just relax." She was laughing at him. "Lie back and think of the honor of the school." She tightened her grip. "Do you play with yourself?"

Stevie was beyond blushing. "I try not to."

"You should. It's excellent practice. Archie says he did it all the time when he was at Eton. But Archie was so depraved—he had wild affairs with half his house. Were there any wicked boys like him at your school? I do think it's odd the way English men have to fall in love with each other first, before they can do it with women. Boarding schools are hothouses of passion, so Archie tells me. Did you have a fearful yen for some cricketing hero?"

He had an erection. Monica's fingers worked expertly around his pulsing glans. "That's nice, isn't it?"

"Yes," he said feebly. Numbed with desire and incapacitated by alcoholic languor, he allowed her to push him down on his back.

She stood over him, smiling at him as he took hold of his penis and began fisting himself mechanically.

"That's it. You just keep on thinking of something very, very nice." She raised her skirts. He saw a pair of ivory silk drawers drop to the floor.

The black chiffon brushed his aching groin, light as a cobweb. Monica sat astride him, lowering herself slowly onto his erection. She arched and sighed, and her eyes closed in ecstasy.

Stevie was afraid. He felt himself being drawn into the moist warmth as if she were a witch draining away his soul. Monica moved her hips, slowly at first, but gathering momentum until she was riding him ferociously, pulling him into the vortex against his will. He grabbed her waist. The approach of his orgasm was terrifying, and it was too late to stop. She shouted. The fiendish shape of her red mouth disgusted him.

Too late. His hands dug into her flesh. He came and came, his heart bursting.

Monica climbed off him as soon as he stopped twitching. She was breathing hard, and her eyes were alight, but she smoothed her hair and pulled on her drawers with remarkable serenity.

Stevie lay among the soft cushions. His groin was uncomfortably cold and wet, and he was wrung with shame. He wanted his mother. He could not trust himself even to think of Francesca in case he started to cry.

Monica put a fresh glass of whiskey into his hand.

"There you are, darling. We've managed to lose your innocence and I don't think we'll miss it. Happy New Year."

Two

Dinah pulled her watch out of her vest pocket. "Five more minutes." The furrows in her dark brow deepened. "Let's hope we get off lightly. The closer we come to the moment of reckoning, the less I fancy doing another stretch in Holloway."

Rory squeezed her gloved hand. "What can they do to us? It'll probably be nothing worse than a night in the cells and a fine."

Dinah let out a hiss of impatience. "You're right, you're right. It's this waiting that's making me so twitchy."

They were sitting in the back of a large car, borrowed from one of the Berlins' friends. It was parked in a narrow alley off the high street of West Surfleet, a semirural South London suburb. There was to be a by-election here the following week, and the Liberal candidate—supported by no less a person than the Rt. Hon. David Lloyd George—was holding a meeting at the Temperance Hall across the road. Crowds of men, eager to see the Chancellor of the Exchequer in person, were swarming into the hall through the ranks of policemen.

"But can we do it?" Dinah asked, in a rush of last-minute doubt. "Can we really get away with it?"

Rory chuckled. "You certainly can—you look wonderful." Because no women were to be admitted to the meeting, and the police had their eyes peeled for suffragette troublemakers, Rory and Dinah were disguised as men. Rory, in a pair of Tertius's trousers, a loose jersey and flat tweed cap, would just pass as a lanky adolescent boy, provided she kept her head down. Dinah's transformation, however, was uncanny. She wore a brown suit borrowed from Joe, complete with boots, bowler hat, stiff collar and tie. Her hair was clipped short, and she had painted a five o'clock shadow on her upper lip and chin.

Rory, who had been looking forward to this adventure for weeks, thought it an absolute scream. "I say, isn't this a lark?" she blurted out. "Aren't you dying to see their faces?"

Dinah, instead of joining in her exultant laughter, became stern. "This isn't a game."

"Oh I know!"

"Rory, listen to me. We're not here for a lark. Do you understand? You've got to be absolutely sure what you're doing."

Rory shrugged, annoyed to be brought back to earth. "Of course I'm sure."

"For heaven's sake, stick to the plan. I know you'd rather be fooling around with bombs, but the object of this exercise is simply to prevent Lloyd George from opening his mouth. We're not getting ourselves into hot water just for the sake of it. Action of this kind demands discipline."

"You sound just like you used to at school," Rory complained. "Of course I'll stick to the plan—wasn't it all my idea? There's no need to lecture."

Dinah sighed, exasperated. "I'm not suggesting you're not brave enough—goodness knows, you've enough audacity and cheek for the whole WSPU. But you confuse rashness with courage, and that worries me. You're such a one for taking things on without thinking of the consequences."

Joe, who was at the wheel of the car keeping lookout, blew through the chauffeur's speaking tube.

"Off you go, girls. Good hunting!"

Instantly forgetting everything except the task ahead, they slipped out of the car and went to the mouth of the alley, waiting for the best moment to fold themselves into the crowd of men. Rory pulled her cap low over her eyes and Dinah nervously checked her tiepin.

Their pulses beating uncomfortably in their dry throats, they stepped into the file of men shuffling into the Temperance Hall.

Rory dug her hands deep into her trouser pockets to hide their trembling, and stuck close to Dinah as she elbowed her way boldly to the front. Only when they were seated on the hard wooden chairs did she dare to look up.

The hall had pitch pine walls and bare rafters, and religious texts stenciled around the walls in Old English lettering. The platform, framed in dusty red curtains, was furnished with a table and chairs, a carafe of water and some bleary glasses. Along the back wall, beneath an immense assertion that God was Love, someone had tacked a row of posters, urging a vote for Francis Oxleigh, Liberal.

Around them surged the murmur of five hundred male voices. The scent of so many male bodies prickled in Rory's nostrils. She had not realized how peculiar it would feel to be hidden among men who had no idea that women were present. And this was only one of the sacred gatherings, from working men's clubs to the House of Lords, that men were so anxious to defend from female intrusion. How extraordinary to be a man and take for granted one's right of entry into these forbidden places.

The door at the side of the platform opened, and the men around them sprang to their feet, cheering raucously. Lloyd George acknowledged the applause with a lazy wave, taking his seat at the table.

Rory stared at him while a fat man in a frock coat made a speech. He sat with one leg crossed over the other, his face fixed in an expression of earnest attention, easy and relaxed as if power fitted him as naturally as a pair of old slippers. Lloyd George was smaller than she had assumed, and more disheveled. His hair was a mad professor's thatch, and his gray-sprinkled mustache hung across his mouth like a ragged hedge. How, Rory wondered irrelevantly, did he drink his tea?

The fat man, after a long waffle about the great part played by the voters of West Surfleet in the affairs of the nation, introduced the candidate. Rory could not help a twinge of sympathy for Mr. Francis Oxleigh, for he looked as terrified as she was. He was a young man, prematurely bald, with an Adam's apple that traveled up and down his long white neck like a mountain train.

"Men of West Surfleet—" he began.

"I'll give the signal," Dinah whispered. "Don't move until Lloyd George stands up."

From somewhere behind them, a voice shouted: "What about Home Rule for Ireland?"

The cry was taken up in other parts of the hall.

"What about Ulster?"

And, directly in front of Rory, a man with a brogue that sounded as if he had just stepped off the boat, roared out:

"How do we know we won't be betrayed by the army? Whose side are you on if it comes to civil war?"

There was a fierce outbreak of applause, and a palpable tensing of the atmosphere. Rory, bold enough now to study faces, realized that the hall was full of Irish immigrants, all obsessed with the latest obstacle to the passing of the Home Rule Bill—the declaration by certain British officers that they would refuse any future order to fire on Edward Carson's Ulster Volunteers.

Mr. Oxleigh took out a handkerchief and wiped his forehead, but bravely launched into assurances that the Liberal Government stood solidly beside Mr. Redmond and his Nationalist MPs.

A flash of anger ignited the gunpowder in Rory's veins. Swatting away Dinah's restraining hand, she sprang to her feet and shouted: "Don't listen to him! They'll break their promises to Ireland, just as they broke their promises to women!"

"Votes for women!" Dinah yelled, gamely overcoming her surprise. "Give women the vote!"

The hall exploded into a turmoil of laughter and catcalls.

Out of the corner of her eye, Rory saw—and was further enraged by—Lloyd George's humorous, infinitely patronizing shrug of resignation. Policemen popped through various doors like cuckoos in clocks, and Dinah was quickly pinned to her seat by several pairs of arms.

Rory, however, was already in the aisle. She had wriggled and scrambled along the row of men, quick and supple as an eel, bawling for Home Rule so determinedly that some of her countrymen had actually helped her past. Now she was running up the steps to the platform, yelling: "Down with the Liberal traitors! *Erin go bragh!* Votes for women!"

Mr. Oxleigh jumped in front of Lloyd George and roughly seized Rory's arm.

Instinctively, Rory rolled her free hand into a fist and swung it into Mr. Oxleigh's chin. This was the mighty right uppercut that she had used against Tertius and Fingal as a child, and she put all her strength and fury behind it. The Liberal candidate for West Surfleet fell backward, hitting his head against a corner of the table.

Rory scarcely had time to register the pain in her knuckles. She felt her feet lifted from the floor, and hard hands pulling all her limbs in different directions. The noise was indescribable—animal yells of rage, gusts of laughter, scattered outbursts of cheering, threats and curses. She thought she was about to be killed. As they dragged her through the hall, the tableau on the stage—Mr. Oxleigh being helped to his feet and Lloyd George appealing for calm—receded and was blotted out by the blue serge uniforms of policemen. She heard her own screams above the shrilling of police whistles and the cries of "bitch" and "whore" from the onlookers.

For the fraction of a second, the wall of blue serge shoulders parted, and she saw Dinah's back being bundled through the doors of a police van. Then all light was extinguished and she was boxed in the moldy darkness of a Black Maria.

Nausea swelled in her stomach as the van lurched over the cobblestones. She drew a breath to yell again and found her throat too swollen to make a sound.

"Rory! Aurora!" Dinah was calling to her through the wooden partition. "For pity's sake, child—say something! Are you all right?"

With her last scrap of energy, Rory managed to croak: "Yes."

"Oh, you little idiot!" groaned Dinah. "You'll get three months' hard for this!"

"... You may count yourself extremely fortunate that Mr. Oxleigh, with a chivalry as misplaced as it is admirable, has refused to press charges for assault ..."

The magistrate was a retired major with a red face and a high, overheated voice. He was working up to his sentence—clearly wishing he had the authority to hang her—and Rory did her best to concentrate. Overnight, her right hand had painfully doubled in size and turned purple, making sleep impossible. It had been the longest night of her life.

Now, still wearing her boy's clothes, she was standing in the West Surfleet Magistrates' Court, trying to persuade herself that this was really happening. The small, paneled room was packed, and the atmosphere was so dangerous that one could almost taste the tension. The newspaper reporters, delighted by Rory's boyish appearance and the fact that she had felled a prospective MP with a single blow, had interrupted the proceedings with roars of laughter.

"... No sentence, in my opinion, is severe enough to punish a woman who has deliberately outraged the sacred veneration due to her sex ..."

Cecil, wedged between Frieda and Joe, was weeping quietly into a handkerchief, giddy with relief that Dinah had been let off with a fine. Rory did not trust herself to look at Tertius and Jenny, who had driven out here with Aubrey and Fingal. Tertius's face was white, and there were dark circles under his eyes. She was terrified that meeting his compassionate gaze would make her cry—and suffragettes never cried. But where, where was Tom? If he had been in her place, she would have walked barefoot over flints and stones to be near him. Perhaps something awful had happened to him—a train crash, an overturned bus? Horrible to contemplate, but more bearable than the possibility that he had failed to turn up because he did not care.

"... time to show that this country will not be terrorized by acts of violence. When women overstep all bounds of modesty and ladylike behavior they must be punished accordingly. I therefore sentence you to twenty-one days' penal servitude."

Part of Rory's mind detached itself from the babel of protest in the courtroom, to consider the length of twenty-one days. Three weeks. It meant nothing to her, and might as well have been three years. She was conscious of a wild, primitive longing to struggle for freedom.

But as she was led out of the dock, she looked at Jenny and the dark panic lessened. Jenny was strained and anxious, but she managed a smile of encouragement that put some starch into Rory's soul. She grinned back, and found reserves of determination that took her to the police van with her head high.

Penned into the stifling space, she was overcome by merciful sleep. She was still foggy and giddy when the van thundered through the gates of Holloway Prison, and she was pushed into a reception cell with the clang of doors and the grinding of keys ringing in her ears.

Her stomach rumbled loudly. Lord, what she would have given for something to eat—one of Tertius's huge sandwiches, a plate of the Berlins' sauerkraut and raisins, even one of Aunt Hilda's mushroom messes. She had touched no food since the previous day. What time was it? They had taken away her watch, but it felt like lunchtime. Far away at Castle Carey, Una would be sending one of the boys out to the fields with Muttonhead's bread and cheese. Papa would be sitting down to trout and potatoes in the dining room at Marystown—but she must stop thinking about food. This was no way to start a hunger strike—she would be crazy after two days of it.

Tom loomed up in her mind as she had last seen him yesterday morning, whistling as he flung his clothes on—

"No," Rory said aloud, her voice echoing flatly off the walls. She curled up on the hard wooden bench, hugging her knees, and tried to distract herself by reading the words other prisoners had scrawled across the whitewashed bricks: "Bert Harris is a bastard who will go to hell." "I only dun it for the baby."

The door sprang open. Rory flinched, unused to the sensation of being intruded upon without warning. A wardress, her bunch of keys jingling formidably at her waist, came in holding a bundle of coarse gray material.

"Stand up."

Rory stared at her. The woman was squat and ugly, and vulgar to the last degree. No such person had ever dared to shout an order at her before.

"Stand up, girl!"

Dazed, Rory obeyed.

"Put these on."

The bundle of material turned out to be a prison uniform, painted with white arrows a foot long.

"No," Rory said. "I'm under rule 243A." She had often imagined herself making this grand statement, and was disappointed by the indifferent way it was received. "You have no right to search me and I'm permitted to keep my own clothes."

The wardress pursed her lips sourly. "Suit yourself. Only don't come crying to me if you get tired of them trousers. Now you follow me and look sharp about it."

Cold. Cold. Cold. After eight days, it was not the hunger that tortured you, but the bitter, unremitting cold. It gnawed at Rory's feet and fingers and empty stomach, and her blood felt as if it had thinned to a trickle of freezing water.

This was her world; her narrow cell, with a plank for a bed and a high window, far out of reach, covered with a rust-caked metal grille. No reality existed beyond it. Sometimes, in the uncountable hours of light-headed dozing, the pale phantoms of Tom and Tertius and Jenny flitted across the back of her consciousness, but they could not penetrate the great glass slab of cold that covered every thought and dream.

She had passed the stage of groaning over the food she could not touch. Today, they had stopped bringing the prison rations, and attempted to seduce her out of her hunger strike with grapes and cutlets. But the smell of the hot meat pinched at her salivary glands so cruelly that she only wanted to retch.

Rory searched her numb brain for something to take her mind off it. During her captivity, she had kept herself sane by remembering the poetry they had made her learn at school.

> *"Nobly, nobly Cape St. Vincent to the North-west died away,"* she muttered;
> *"Sunset ran, one glorious blood-red, reeking into Cadiz Bay;*
> *Something mid the something-something, full in face Trafalgar lay . . ."*

She suddenly saw Francesca, as clearly as if she had been in the room, reciting this poem in front of the fourth form. Dinah Curran had caught Eleanor trying to prompt her.

Rory's restless mind shuttled to Dinah. She could not regard herself as a heroine when she knew that she had disobeyed Dinah's orders. She had been foolish and irresponsible, and criminally undisciplined. It would serve her right if Frieda never trusted her again.

Damn Dinah and her lecturing, she thought angrily. Why did she always have to be right? She had predicted that Rory's hotheadedness would spoil the symmetry of their plan, just as she was always predicting the grief she was storing up for herself in her entanglement with Tom: "A man like that has no space in his life for love, Aurora . . . He'll soak up your affection like a sponge and never give you anything back . . ."

Rory drove her nails into her palms, furious that she had

once more tricked herself into thinking of Tom. She had not shed one tear so far, and she was not going to begin now.

The metal spyhole on the door slid back and a cold gray eye gleamed upon her. Whenever this happened, Rory had to fight a sensation of culpability and an impulse to cringe. She drew her aching limbs bolt upright on the bed and wrapped herself in her last few shreds of pride.

The wardress bustled in, her healthy energy setting all Rory's raw nerves on edge. She held open the door for the two doctors who had bandaged Rory's hand on her first day in prison; a tall one with iron-gray hair and a closed, impassive face; and a younger one who looked at Rory as if she smelled bad.

Without a word, the older doctor put his chilly fingers on her pulse. He nodded to the wardress. She bounced forward and whisked up Rory's jersey and vest, exposing her breasts, which were still bruised from the struggle at the Temperance Hall. She winced as the stethoscope met her goose-pimpled flesh.

"Hmmm," the doctor said. "How long has it been now?"

"She come in eight days ago, sir," supplied the wardress.

"And she has refused all nourishment?"

"Yes, sir. We've been weighing her meals before and after, sir, and she ain't touched a morsel. Just a drop or so of water."

For the first time, the doctor addressed Rory directly. "You are still determined not to eat?"

"Yes."

"You are aware that you may permanently undermine your constitution?"

"I—I don't care."

He folded his stethoscope. "You have until tomorrow morning to come to your senses. After that, I shall have no alternative but to feed you by force."

Rory felt as if a stone had dropped into her chest. She braced herself, so that they would not see her shudder of fear. She had been expecting this, but that did not make the prospect easier to bear.

"The trouble these women put us to," the doctor grumbled to his colleague, "just because they want to make martyrs of themselves." He turned to the wardress. "Take that tray away and bring her a fresh one."

"Very good, sir."

After the doctors had gone, the wardress picked up the untouched meal, and lingered for a moment in the cell. Rory waited for her usual diatribe against the wanton waste of good food and public money.

Instead, she whispered hurriedly: "Try and get something down, dearie, for your own good. Forcible feeding ain't a joke."

This unexpected kindness brought a rush of tears to the back of Rory's eyes. For one perilous moment, she was weak and near surrender. She longed to raise her voice and cry for food, if it would bring the woman back to comfort her. She hadn't an ounce of strength left to endure the horror of forcible feeding. She was sure she had heard of women who had been killed by the ordeal.

But the long, terrified night ahead would be the ultimate test of her courage. Somehow, she was going to get through it with all her guns blazing. Forcing herself to take deep, steadying breaths, she wrapped her single blanket around her legs, stretched herself on the bed and fixed her eyes on the ceiling.

In the loudest voice she could summon, she chanted:

> *"My good blade carves the casques of men,*
> *My tough lance thrusteth sure,*
> *My strength is as the strength of ten,*
> *Because my heart is pure . . ."*

The moment she heard the footsteps clattering along the stone corridor outside, Rory began to tremble uncontrollably. Since dawn she had been listening to the prison cacophony of slamming doors, shouts, whistles and people marching past her cell. But she knew these particular footsteps were meant for her before the spyhole swung back and the key turned in the lock.

She was stiff, but she stood up. Throughout the endless night, she had mentally rehearsed this terrible moment so often that its coming was almost a relief. Her most haunting fear, she had discovered, was the fear of being unequal to the ordeal and revealing herself as a coward. A hunger strike and forcible feeding had not been part of the original plan, but she had courted this horror with what Dinah called her "rashness." Now, she must prove to herself that she could follow up rashness with genuine courage.

The door opened. The doctors entered, and six wardresses, grimly indistinguishable in their dark uniform dresses and white caps, pressed in after them. The cell was crowded to the point of claustrophobia, and eerily silent. Nobody would meet her eye.

Rory need not have worried about surrendering at the last minute, for she was given no chance to speak. They flung her onto the bed so quickly that she was surprised into panic, and struggled fiercely.

Nobody, nothing, could have prepared her for the terror of this helplessness. The wardresses held her arms, legs and shoulders with a grip of iron, and she could not have moved a muscle even if she had still had all her strength.

The older doctor tied a waterproof sheet under her chin, and said to his colleague: "Get her mouth open."

Not being able to see what they were doing made it worse. The faces of the wardresses blocked Rory's vision, and she found herself noticing, with peculiar clarity, that one of them had a mole on her cheek that sprouted two gray hairs.

She clamped her jaw shut until it ached, and pursed her lips tightly. The younger doctor forced her lips apart—his finger tasted salty. "There's a gap here," he announced.

Vicious pain tore into her mouth. They were digging a sharp instrument into her teeth, tearing at the nerves and slicing into her gums. Rory fought to twitch her head away, but they were holding her too firmly. The glitter of steel was in front of her eyes. The doctor turned a screw, and each turn forced her jaw open, clawing deeper into her gums.

The pain was outrageous, unimaginable. Her whole body was a red-hot flame of agony. Above her, she saw the brown rubber tube snaking down toward her, and she retched convulsively when it touched the back of her throat.

The doctor muttered: "T-t-t!" when she coughed up the end of the tube. Rory suddenly had an enlarged view of the broken veins in his nose when he leaned close to her and held the tube in place until she swallowed it.

Now she began to struggle like a madwoman against the horrible sensation of the tube traveling down to her stomach, seeming to bruise every rib and lighting searing coals of pain in her chest.

The next few minutes were the most purely disgusting of her life. A wardress poured a jug of warm milk and raw eggs into the funnel at the end of the tube. It gurgled down to her stomach, flooding her with nausea to the very ends of her hair. There was an upheaval in her chest, as if her entire body was being pulled inside out, and her throat contracted as the tube came out. The doctor unscrewed the steel gag and wrenched it away from her bleeding mouth. The wardresses released her and stepped back.

Immediately, Rory vomited up the contents of her stomach, in violent spasms that rocked her body against the bed. The sight and smell of the regurgitated milk, steaming on the cold brick floor, were so revolting that she spewed until she had nothing left to bring up but a few threads of saliva.

"It generally happens the first time, before they get used to it," the older doctor said, with his back to her. "We'll try again this evening. She won't have the strength left to struggle."

Humiliated and exhausted, with the blood dribbling from her lacerated mouth, Rory drew a breath and exhaled it in a sob. Her aching eyes smarted as the tears spilled out. She wept and wept, each hiccup lashing her bruises like the stroke of a whip.

Tom had not come to the court because he had seen no reason to rearrange his own all-important timetable. And he never, ever would. This was what she had tried so hard not to face, during these days of enforced loneliness. He did not love her enough. He had given her all the love he had to spare, and she knew that it was only her weakness and selfishness that made her want more. But it was breaking her heart, all the same.

Morning. She knew it was morning, because of the daylight filtering through the dirty window. Any minute now they would be surging up the corridor toward her and crowding around her with the gag and the feeding tube. Had it been four times so far, or five? She had lost count, but she spent all the hours in between curled on the bed, too weighed down by the anticipation of pain even to walk across her cell. It seemed ages since she had cried over Tom. She lay in a dreary limbo, feeling the flesh shriveling on her bones.

Her mouth hurt. Each one of her teeth sang its own discordant note of anguish. Her cracked gums shrieked when she took a sip of water. Idly, she wondered if she would get used to it one day. Perhaps her mouth would harden, as a horse's mouth hardened when it got used to the reins.

Here were the approaching footsteps. Rory did not move. What was the point? She could not be bothered to look up when they came into the cell.

"Miss Carlington."

The voice was unfamiliar and surprisingly courteous. Her head swimming, she dragged herself upright. There were only two people today—her wardress, and a tall man with yellow hair.

The wardress snapped: "Stand up for the governor!"

"That won't be necessary." The governor motioned to Rory to stay where she was. "The doctors tell me that you have not succeeded in taking any nourishment from the enforced feeding. They have informed me that a further attempt may weaken your heart. I have, therefore, told them to stop the treatment."

Rory gaped at him. The news was so unexpected that she was afraid she had misunderstood.

"You have only served thirteen days of your sentence," he continued dryly, "but we can take no more responsibility for your health while you refuse to take nourishment voluntarily. You are aware, no doubt, that the Home Secretary has the power to release you under the Prisoner's Temporary Discharge for Ill Health Bill. Owing to your youth, however, and your relatively unblemished record, it has been decided to grant you an unconditional discharge."

Still, Rory could do nothing but stare at him, her mouth hanging open.

"You will be released at four o'clock this afternoon."

The wardress curtseyed as the prison governor left the cell. Then she shut the door behind him, and took a step toward Rory.

"There you are, dear," she said, with a smile. "It's all over. How about a nice cup of tea?"

Rory feebly burst into tears. "No! Go away! You're trying to trick me!"

"Don't be silly, girl!" the wardress reproved her, affronted by this reaction to her kind offer. "The documents are all signed. One cup of tea won't hurt you!"

Seeing that Rory could not stop crying, her voice softened. "They can't keep you locked up anymore. I shouldn't really be the one to tell you, but there's been ever such a fuss made about you outside. You've been in the papers, and everything. The minute he got into Parliament, he stood up and made a speech all about you and how you never should have been put inside in the first place."

Rory wiped her nose on her sleeve. "Who—who did?"

The wardress suddenly laughed. "Why, Mr. Francis Oxleigh, of course! And he sent you a lovely basket of roses this morning. Next thing you know, he'll propose."

The first breath of freedom was as sweet as a draft of champagne. Rory filled her thirsty lungs, and her head reeled with euphoria. Outside the gate of Holloway Prison everything was one vast, white, gleaming sky. She took one step, almost expecting to fly.

"Rory! Oh my good God, what've they done to you?"

She was in Tertius's arms. His warm cheek was pressed against her cold one, and he was hugging her wasted body as if he would never let go.

Dazed, Rory allowed him to cover her face with kisses. She was already looking over his shoulder with a wild hope that Tom had come to meet her.

He had not. The disappointment was acute, but she pushed it away from her. One thing at a time—she had little enough energy to spare. At least Jenny was here, draping a coat around her shoulders, and saying something about ointment for her poor, cracked lips. A huge, gleaming car was parked at the curb, with a chauffeur holding open the door. Beside him stood Fingal, and beside Fingal—

The pavement turned to sponge under her feet. There, unfamiliar in a dark suit and bowler hat, was the massive, granite figure of Muttonhead.

"Mutt—" She heard her own voice, a bat's squeak above the rushing in her ears.

His eyes met hers, and she felt the force of his solid, immovable anger. Now she saw herself as she must appear to him and knew that she was barred from his heart by gates of stone. In her desolation, Rory could have howled like the Carey banshee. She staggered toward him, with some mad idea of throwing herself at his feet, and fainted.

She returned to consciousness with a scrambled impression that someone had removed her brain and put it back the wrong way round. She was lying on a sofa, under a pile of scratchy blankets. Jenny was kneeling beside her. Why was Jenny holding a glass of brandy, and why was she apparently trying to tip it into her ear, like Hamlet's uncle? Rory tried a smile, and could not understand why everyone looked so solemn.

Then she saw Muttonhead, standing to attention on the hearth rug, and realized where she was. This was Aunt Hilda's drawing room in Bayswater, and here—with her favorite parrot enthroned upon her shoulder—was Aunt Hilda herself. Rory moaned softly. The big guns were ranged against her. She was in the profoundest, murkiest depths of disgrace.

"Why did you bring me here?"

"Now, Rory, keep calm," Jenny soothed. "Miss Veness can take proper care of you. It's only for a few days, until you're strong enough to come back to the flat."

"Flat!" barked Muttonhead, so ferociously that Rory, Tertius and Fingal winced. "Ha!"

"Please, Lord Oughterard," Jenny said reproachfully, "she mustn't be upset."

"Nonsense," Fingal cut in. "She's behaved appallingly. She doesn't deserve to have a fuss made of her now."

"You mean little weasel!" snapped Tertius. "Hasn't she been punished enough?" He turned to Rory, and his blue eyes filled with tears. "Look at her!" Pulling out an incredibly dirty handkerchief, he noisily blew his nose. Rory suspected that he had been drinking, and hoped he had the sense not to let Muttonhead smell his breath.

Muttonhead glared down at Rory. "You will rest here for two days. Then I'm taking you straight back to Ireland."

"You can't!" Rory sat bolt upright, her tangled red hair bristling like a fox's brush. "I won't come!"

"You'll do as you're told, miss." His tanned complexion deepened to mahogany. "Good God, I've never been angrier in my life. How dare you brawl in public and drag your father's name through the newspapers?"

"It's her name, too," Aunt Hilda said. "Really, Lord Oughterard, this is the twentieth century, not the Dark

Ages. Women are no longer chattels—and Aurora is no relation of yours so far as I'm aware. You have no right whatever to dictate to her."

There was an astonished silence, during which Rory wondered if she had heard correctly. A triumphant little smile lifted Aunt Hilda's pasty jowls. The light of newfound passion was in her eyes.

"It is one of the few privileges granted to our sex," she continued grandly, "that we are allowed to change our minds. True, in the past, I have been unable to see the advantage of granting the vote to women. But this whole affair has given me pause for thought. I pay this government shocking sums in income tax—yet I did not vote for this government and have no power to remove them. I only wish that Aurora had managed to strike the Chancellor of the Exchequer himself, because you may as well be hanged for a sheep as for a lamb, and that Mr. Lloyd George is no better than a highway robber. Stop it, Lascar," she added to the parrot, who was nibbling at her earring.

Jenny's lips were twitching, but Rory was too stunned to laugh. Aunt Hilda was the last person she had expected to convert.

"My niece was only doing what she thought to be right," Aunt Hilda told Muttonhead. "Strong principles are a characteristic of our family—she and I are alike in that respect at least. And I won't allow her to be carted back to Ireland like a brown paper parcel just because her father wishes it."

Muttonhead's neck was swelling wrathfully. Rory could no longer endure being on the wrong side of his anger. There must be some way of smoothing him down.

"Mutt darling—" she began.

It was at this moment that Tom chose to erupt into the room, holding a bunch of violets and still wearing his hat. Without even glancing at the others, he dropped down on the sofa, scooped Rory into his arms and gave her a smacking kiss on the lips.

"Look at you, love, you're a bag of bones—but you're a brave lass and I'm proud of you."

"Oh, Tom!" Rory's pale face flooded with painful color. She dared not look at Muttonhead now.

"What's the matter?" Tom eyed Tertius sharply. "Oh, I see. The Honorables have been getting at you. I should've been here sooner. Never mind, I'm here now and I've come to take you home."

"You've no right to take her anywhere!" hissed Tertius.

Very slowly, Tom stood up. Tertius did so too, rolling his hands into fists.

"Tershie!" Fingal murmured nervously.

"It's up to Rory where she goes," Tom said, "and she wants to come with me."

Muttonhead's voice was dangerously quiet. "What is your business with Miss Carlington?"

"She's my girl. That's my business with her. Now what's yours?"

Rory's pulse was drumming in her parched mouth. Her flaming cheeks and Tom's proprietorial swagger told the whole story.

"Aurora," Muttonhead said, with a thunderous scowl that made her quail, "you can come back to Ireland with me and I'll never ask you about this man. Or you can stay here with him and never speak to me again. It's your choice."

"No, Mutt," Tertius said urgently, "for the love of God—"

Frozen with disbelief, Rory stared at Muttonhead. He couldn't mean that he would cast her off forever. It wasn't possible. This was Muttonhead, whose love was one of the most constant facts in her world. She could not imagine her life without it.

"Well, you heard him," sneered Tom. "The lord giveth, or the lord taketh away. It's up to you."

Tertius's fist shot out, but Muttonhead had lightning reflexes. Barely seeming to move, he grabbed Tertius by the belt and held him at arm's length as if he had been a squirming kitten.

"Manners. We're with ladies."

"So we are," said Tom, flaunting his unpunched chin at Tertius. "We can't thrash peasants in front of ladies."

Rory stared at the man she thought she was in love with and a terrible, sick realization crept into her bones. Tom's eyes were narrowed slits and his smile had a savage glitter. He was enjoying the situation—reveling in it. Infatuation had blinded her to this part of his character, but she saw it all now. He had not come here to claim her because he loved her, but because he hated Muttonhead and all he stood for.

He never really loved you for yourself, said a hard little voice in her head. He wanted you because of what you represented. He wanted to take something from the oppressors.

The desolation was ghastly, but it was mixed with fury.

Now Muttonhead had betrayed her too. These two men, who were supposed to love her, were each prepared to withdraw their love the minute she chose the other. They didn't consider her a real person with real feelings. They didn't give a damn about her, unless they could possess her on their terms.

"Tom," she said, "shut up."

She knew she had been right when he turned toward her and she saw the disdain in his eyes. "Tired of playing socialists now, are you? A bit keener on being a lady, now that you see what you've got to lose? Well, it's a bit late for that, love. You should have thought of it before you came to bed with me. You're not a lady anymore. Just a common or garden whore."

Muttonhead uttered a bellow of rage, hurled Tertius aside, and knocked Tom across the room. The parrot screeched, and fled to the ceiling in a whirlwind of dropped feathers.

Anger poured strength into Rory's limbs. Leaping off the sofa, she hurled herself upon Muttonhead, pounding his chest with her fists.

"Go away! Get out! I hate you! I don't ever want to see you again! Never!"

Fingal and Jenny pulled her, still punching feebly at the air, back to the sofa. Part of her was horrified by the hurt and bewilderment she saw in Muttonhead's eyes, but fury had her in an iron grip.

"You should all be thoroughly ashamed of yourselves," Jenny said icily. "Don't any of you care that Rory is ill?"

The silence seemed to stretch into minutes. Jenny put her arms around Rory, stilling the tempest with her steady strength. Tom picked himself up, massaging his jaw.

Muttonhead squared his shoulders.

"Miss Veness," he addressed Aunt Hilda. "I beg your pardon. Please accept my apologies."

Without looking at Rory, he left.

Tertius was gazing down at Rory with a sympathy that made her ache all over.

"Come on, Tershie," Fingal said softly. "Yes, come on." They followed their brother.

Rory buried her face in Jenny's shoulder. She did not trust herself to meet Tom's eyes.

"Rory," he said, "I'm sorry I called you a whore. But what do you think you are? Just because a chap tries to persuade a girl it doesn't mean she has to listen to him. Not if she has any self-respect. There's decent factory girls would look down on you because you slept with me. I thought you understood that."

And he was gone.

Rory spent her first evening of freedom weeping into Jenny's blouse, and sobbing Muttonhead's name between mouthfuls of beef tea.

Three

Lorenzo was playing Beethoven's "Appassionata" on an upright piano in the parlor window of Mrs. Fuller's cottage. The cascades of music, ethereally sweet in the summer air, expanded Eleanor's soul into a kind of sacred rapture.

He played wonderfully, with wrists of steel and a technique so flawless that the notes sparkled around her like a shower of diamonds. Bewitched, enchanted, transported, she followed the siren's song along the muddy lane. Instead of knocking at the front door as she had planned, she walked right through the flower bed to the open casement.

This was more romantic than her most extravagant daydreams. Her heart hammering, she stared at his shining dark head, bent over the keys. Any moment now, he would look up at her, and she would catch his hypnotizing jet eyes while they were still filled with music.

Then he did look up at her. The dream faded into embarrassing reality. His hands froze, and his eyes narrowed in anger. Eleanor was suddenly aware that she was standing with her mouth open in a patch of marigolds, listening to nothing but the prosaic scratchings of Mrs. Fuller's hens.

"Hello." She knew she sounded ridiculous, and cursed her fatal habit of being seduced by her own wishful fantasies. Why was it that whenever she went off in blind pursuit of beauty, she always ended up making a fool of herself?

"What," asked Lorenzo, "can you possibly be doing here?"

It did not occur to her to lie to him. Telling the truth about her emotions was another of her fatal habits. "I had to see you again."

"Well," he said disagreeably, "now you see me."

Her words tumbled out in a nervous torrent. "I didn't even know if you'd be here. I just got on a train this morning, and found a cab to take me as far as the village. I couldn't bear the waiting any longer, and you haven't written or—"

"Why did you have to see me?"

"Lorenzo, I'm sorry. I know it was foolish of me. But don't you know what today is?"

"Should I?" To her relief, his annoyance was beginning to give way to reluctant amusement.

"Today is the anniversary of the day we met."

"Good God." Now he was startled. "Is it? How on earth do you know? Wait a minute—don't tell me—you keep a diary." His lips curled into a sour smile. "Dear diary, oh ever-to-be-remembered day! A strange man came to tea and filled me with divine intimations of I knew not what!"

Eleanor's face was beet-red, but he had captured the style of her diary so cleverly that she could not help laughing.

"How did you guess? Am I so predictable?"

To her delight, he laughed too. "You're not predictable at all. I thought I was hallucinating when I saw you looming at me through the window. What am I supposed to do with you now?"

"Ask me in?"

"I can't. Mrs. Fuller's gone to market, and Windrush is out at a lecture. I'm alone here."

"I don't mind."

His eyes, more lustrous and disturbing than she had remembered, were taking her in thoughtfully. "Do you really not mind being alone with me?"

"No," she said. "I'm not afraid of you."

"You damn well should be. Look what I did to you last time we met."

"I forgave you," Eleanor said nobly.

This time, his laughter had an unkind edge. "You mean, you liked it." He stood up. "All right. If you don't care about your reputation, I'm certainly not going to worry about it. Come around to the kitchen door. It's open."

Eleanor hurried around the side of the cottage. She found him in the musty little kitchen, pouring red wine into two teacups. He was dressed in ancient white flannels and a cricket jersey held together by darns, and she thought he carried his poor scholar's rags with wonderful elegance.

"I'm not making you tea," he said, handing her one of the cups. "The fire's gone out."

She saw a covered plate on the table, with a note on top of it: *Mr. L—corned beef for yr dinner. Do not let the range go out!* The plate was untouched, but there was an empty wine bottle beside it.

Lorenzo drained his wine in a single gulp, and his eyes raked over her critically. "You have saved me from falling into a stupor of drunken boredom," he announced, "and I think I may be quite glad you're here. But there's something the matter with you."

Eleanor lowered her face, surrendering herself to the delicious humiliation of his attention.

"I know. It's that ludicrous hat. Take it off."

With shaking hands, she pulled the pins out of her flower-decked straw hat—six guineas from the best milliner in London—and laid it on the table.

"Hmm. Better," he said. "But do you always truss yourself up in silk for a day in the country? I suppose you intended to fascinate me. How touching." He did not sound touched. "Well, you can stay and amuse me if you like—on one condition."

"Yes?" she asked.

"That you don't propose to me again."

"I won't."

"Because," Lorenzo said languidly, "if I find that's the reason you came here, I'll throw you straight into a cowpat, run inside and bolt the door."

She giggled, deciding to take this as a joke. "I promise."

"Good. Let's go into the garden. It's the only place in this pigsty that has any pretentions to charm." Snatching up the bottle, he led her outside.

To Eleanor's enchanted eyes, the garden was a golden paradise of birds and butterflies. Lorenzo stretched himself out on the grass. She sat beside him, careful to get his good ear.

"You play marvelously," she ventured.

"Don't I just? And couldn't you hear my soul vibrating through every divine phrase?"

"You're teasing me," she said reproachfully, "but you couldn't play like that—with such tenderness and passion—if you didn't feel it."

"I was drunk, and I didn't think anyone was listening. I expect I committed all kinds of vulgarities."

"Oh, Lorenzo, are you cross with me because I heard you playing? I'm sorry—but it was so lovely."

"Don't apologize. You're here to amuse me."

Eleanor had managed to finish her wine, and her blood felt pleasantly warm. Lorenzo was rather alarming when he had been drinking, she thought, but easier to talk to than usual. She leaned over on one elbow, idly stroking the daisies in the grass. "How?"

"Just talk," he said. "I feel like hearing someone talk. Tell me about your life."

"It's not very interesting. Girls' lives aren't."

"Any old tattle will do. Stevie used to keep me supplied with nonsense, but I've hardly seen him since he got trapped by that designing female."

"She didn't trap him!" Eleanor did not mind how rude Lorenzo was to her, but she could not allow him to be mean about Francesca. "That's not fair! She's the most innocent and undesigning person in the world. She says she'll wait for Stevie any amount of time because she's so afraid of spoiling his prospects."

"My God," Lorenzo murmured, "you sound just like him—that surge of outraged loyalty. You're both such sweet souls, friends of all the world. But when you love someone you grip like the jaws of death."

"There isn't any other way of loving someone."

"Yes, that's what Stevie always says. Neither of you have the faintest idea when you're being tiresome, because you're sure other people need your love, whether they know it or not. A drunken beggar might refuse a sovereign, but you're going to make him take it anyway—he'll be *so* glad to find it when he comes to his senses."

The bitterness in his voice made Eleanor ache for him. "Lorenzo, I wish you wouldn't talk as if I wanted to take something away from you. I'm not making any demands— I only want to give to you. As much or as little as you please."

He turned his face toward her. "You don't understand, do you? I wish you'd try to see it from my point of view." He sat up to pour them both more wine, spilling a little. It splashed across the face of the daisies like blood. "You're a nice girl, Eleanor. I like you."

Eleanor felt herself dissolving as a great sunrise of happiness surged across her body.

"I really was ashamed of myself," he continued, "after I treated you so badly at that party. You could have had me arrested, and you behaved like a saint." His brow knotted ominously. "So thank you. Thank you intensely, utterly, from the bottom of my black heart." He lashed out the "thank yous" like insults. "But gratitude is the limit. It's not going to lead to anything else."

"I wasn't expecting—" she began.

"Spare me. Your expectations are your own lookout, and I don't want to know about them."

"But, Lorenzo," she said gently, "I only want you to know that I do understand why you—what made you do those things to me. You were trying to warn me off. Because of who you are."

"Oh God," he said, exasperated, "I was afraid you'd embroider it into something like that. Now, will you listen to me? Say that you're listening."

"I'm listening."

He spoke with exaggerated slowness, as if to a halfwit. "I behaved wickedly because I am wicked."

"Oh no—"

"Eleanor, I didn't have any other motive. And when I didn't make any effort to see you again afterwards, it wasn't from a sense of shame. I simply didn't want to."

The light drained from her face.

He sighed. "Don't make me feel as if I'd stabbed you. I'm trying to make you see that you're wasting your love on someone who doesn't want it. I'm never going to ask you to marry me. Do you hear me?"

From the frozen wastes of desolation, Eleanor breathed: "Yes."

"Say 'I hear you, Lorenzo.' "

"I hear you, Lorenzo." But her mind was already squirming away from reality and desperately searching for some hope. Perhaps he didn't mean it. Perhaps he was still trying to protect her. There would be time enough to mull this over later. All that mattered now was immersing herself totally in the present moment and relishing every second of being near him.

"You mustn't take it personally," Lorenzo said. "You'll soon find some other man to throw yourself at. There's nothing wrong with you. You're very sweet and very kind, and not at all bad-looking."

He brushed her cheek with the backs of his fingers and all her senses leaped to meet his touch.

"You have such a fresh, pink face." His eyes were laughing at her. His breath smelled strongly of wine. "You look just like an innocent milkmaid, got up in fashionable clothes for a bet. You see? I can be perfectly civil to you now that you understand I'm not going to marry you. The less you love me, the more I shall like you. Tell you what, I'll play you the rest of the Beethoven and you can romanticize him instead. Stay out here—Mrs. F's piano's rather tinny at close quarters."

Staggering slightly, he heaved himself to his feet, and went into the cottage. Eleanor rolled over on her back. The sky was dazzling. She closed her eyes, listening to the rustling of insects in the grass, and the whining of the midges in the shadows under the trees. His offhand compliments had made her dizzy with joy, and she ran through them again. As she did so, she edited out the things he had said about not wanting to marry her, and almost managed to forget that he had said them at all.

Presently, the music stole out toward her. Stretching luxuriously, she gave herself to it. The sun covered her in a golden blanket of warmth. Lorenzo was playing specially for her, as he had done so often in her dreams. Please God, she prayed, let me have Lorenzo. I don't care what he does to me—just let him accept my love and I can bear anything.

She felt the chill of his shadow falling across her.

"I've sent you to sleep."

Eleanor opened her eyes. He was kneeling over her, his face inches away from hers. If he touches me, she thought, I shall faint.

"You want me to kiss you," he said. "Well, why not? I'll show you how nicely I can do it when I choose."

Very slowly, he lowered his mouth to hers, and when his tongue slid between her lips, Eleanor thought she was about to die of bliss. There was a fierce, indecent heat between her legs, and she was ashamed of the dampness spreading in her drawers. But although she was frightened, she could not stop herself from moaning, and arching toward him.

The movements of Lorenzo's tongue became firmer. He made a sound between a sigh and a hiccup, squeezed her in his arms, and rolled on top of her. Eleanor clutched at the back of his jersey, feeling the muscles moving around his spine. The heat was building to a terrible urgency. She wanted it to go on forever.

He pulled his head away. "Better stop," he said breathlessly.

"No!"

"I'm getting carried away. Must be the wine."

"Please—please—" Eleanor did not know what she was begging for.

"More?" he asked, smiling.

"Oh, please—please—"

"A little, then, since you want it so much."

She kept her eyes on his face as he shifted to unfasten his trousers. Then his hand went up her skirt to her drawers.

"How do you get these bloody things off?"

With shaking, clumsy fingers, Eleanor undid the little pearl buttons across her crotch. Part of her was horrified by what she was doing. She was more horrified when she saw Lorenzo's penis, hard and flushed in his hand. Dimly, she remembered her mother's guarded words of warning about the unpleasantness of "the marriage act," but it was too late to stop now.

Lorenzo parted her legs, and speared her in a single thrust that cut right into the center of her yearning. The pain made her catch her breath, yet it was wildly relieving, like having a wound cauterized.

Propping himself above her on his elbows, Lorenzo watched her, his face expressionless.

"Do you like it?" he asked.

"Yes—" Hardly knowing what she was doing, Eleanor pushed her hips toward him, trying to take in as much of him as possible.

"Keep still." He pinned her arms back and began—with the same blank face—to thrust rhythmically against her womb. The pain mounted to wave upon wave of ecstasy, which subsided just as it seemed about to kill her. Hot, voluptuous tears collected under her eyelids.

"My darling—" she whispered.

Suddenly a door slammed in the house, and Mrs. Fuller's voice shrilled: "Mr. Lorenzo! Are you there, dear?"

Lorenzo twitched convulsively. His eyes widened with shock, and he collapsed on top of Eleanor, groaning: "No—oh God, no! No!"

He leaped off her immediately, and Eleanor felt a trickle of hot liquid oozing out of her vagina into the grass.

"Damn! Damn it to hell!" Lorenzo pounded the earth furiously with his fists.

Inside the house, Mrs. Fuller began to sing: "If I could plant a tiny seed of larve, in the garden of your heart, would it grow tew be a great big flower one day or would it die and fade away—?"

Eleanor sat up, bewildered. "Lorenzo—"

He whipped around to her, shaking with anger. "Get out!" he hissed. "Go away and leave me alone! And God help you if I ever see you again!"

"But—"

"Pull your bloody skirt down."

He charged away from her into the cottage, and Eleanor hastily stood up, smoothing her clothes. Sense was coming back to her and she was terrified of being seen by Mrs. Fuller. Lorenzo reappeared a moment later, just long enough to throw her hat at her before diving back inside and banging the door behind him.

Numb with anguish, Eleanor fled, stumbling against the deep, muddy ruts in the lane. It was not until she had turned the corner and lost sight of the house behind a tall hedge that she realized she was crying.

Lorenzo paid off the taxi in Piccadilly Circus. Pulling his hat down over his forehead, he began to walk quickly along Piccadilly toward the park. He had drunk another bottle of wine over supper, but the alcohol had only inflamed his hatred. He was hard all over with rage, aching and trembling. And he had learned by now that it was never any use fighting for control.

He halted briefly at the mouth of an alley, unlit and barely noticeable, and glanced around before ducking down it into the shadows. There was an unmarked door, just visible in the gloom. He knocked three times. It opened a few inches, and he hurried into the dark, bare passage. At the top of the uncarpeted stairs, he knocked again.

A stooped elderly maid let him into the hall. He blinked in the sudden, dazzling light. He was standing on a thick red carpet, in a blue haze of cigar smoke. Through his anger, he was aware of the uproarious male voices in the drawing room. A gramophone was playing somewhere.

Dozens of silk top hats were lined up along the ornate mahogany sideboard.

He took off his own hat and held it out to the maid, but she would not take it. Her eyes were fixed doubtfully on his face.

"Wait here a minute, sir." She scurried into the drawing room.

"Shit," Lorenzo muttered. He could leave, he supposed. But the rage would not let him. Gritting his teeth, he looked up at the row of whips, riding crops and canes that decorated the walls. There were engravings, too, in the classical style, of fat naked maidens being chastised by strapping young warriors. The sight of their rosebud lips, pursed in exaggerated fear, stiffened the anger into pulsing urgency.

Mrs. Watson emerged from the drawing room, upholstered in an electric blue evening dress with a train, and holding a glass of champagne.

"You." Her face was grim. "You've got a nerve."

The maid whispered something in her ear.

"All right," she said, "I'll take care of him. Go and find Alf."

"Yes, madam." The maid vanished through a baize-covered door.

Mrs. Watson took a step nearer Lorenzo and murmured: "I don't want trouble. Just turn around and go. We don't want your kind here—not after what you did last time."

"I thought that was supposed to be your stock in trade."

"You took a bloody sight more than you paid for."

"I see." Lorenzo reached for his wallet.

"Put your money away." Mrs. Watson's voice became a suppressed snarl. "I've got my goodwill with the police to consider. Alf!"

The baize door opened, and an enormous, shambling man with a broken nose came out. He placed himself behind Mrs. Watson, eyeing Lorenzo with sulky detachment.

"Get out," Mrs. Watson said. "And if you ever come back here again"—her eyes were slits of contempt—"I'll have Alf do to you what you did to that poor girl."

Lorenzo left in a volcanic, desperate state of fury. It was late. The streets were dark and deserted. He strode through them, not caring where he was going. His limbs were aching with fatigue, but the terrible energy possessed him and drove him on.

In Shepherd Market, a solitary policeman shone his lantern into Lorenzo's face, saw that he was a gentleman in evening dress, and said: "Mind how you go, sir."

Listening to his footsteps echoing away along the street, Lorenzo was gripped by a sudden spasm of fear, which brought the sweat out on his upper lip. Go home, he told himself.

Then he saw her.

She was watching him from a doorway, in the bleary light of a lamp set in the wall above. She was thin and threadbare and past her best, with deep grooves on either side of her painted mouth.

"Looking for a friend, mister?"

Slowly, Lorenzo walked over to her. She smiled up into his shadowed face.

"Only seven-and-six, love."

He put his hand in his pocket, and drew out a handful of coins. She gave a hungry little gasp as she caught the glitter of gold sovereigns. But she also caught the glitter of his eyes, and though she kept smiling, her skinny shoulders twitched with fear.

This one did not need a friend. He was looking for an enemy.

Four

" *'Long live the great art vortex sprung up in the center of this town!'* " declaimed Rory, reading from the crudely printed, puce-covered book. *'A VORTICIST KING! WHY NOT? DO YOU THINK LLOYD GEORGE HAS THE VORTEX IN HIM?'*

"Well, if anyone can put it in him, darling, you can," said Aubrey, deep in his own copy of *Blast.* "Oh, listen to this—*'We only want Humor if it has fought like Tragedy. We only want Tragedy if it can clench its side muscles like hands on its belly, and bring to the surface a laugh like a bomb.'* " He looked over the top of the book at Tertius. "It's quite brilliant—a manifesto for the modern age, and the death knell of the Victorians. You're a genius."

"Too funny for words," put in Fingal, who was giggling over the lists of Blasts and Blesses. *"Blast years 1837 to 1900.* I do so agree. And how sublime to bless hairdressers."

Tertius shrugged. Despite the success of *Blast,* the new quarterly that had set half of London talking about the artistic revolution of Vorticism, he was not in a good mood. "Wyndham Lewis wrote all that stuff. I just signed my name to the manifesto, and did a couple of woodcuts."

Aubrey drew out his gold cigarette case. "But my dear boy, they're utterly miraculous—I haven't seen anything as exciting in years. And I'm still reeling over the paintings. Why, why haven't you shown me your work before?"

"I didn't show it you."

"Bloody hell, boy," bayed Quince, from the other side of the room, "you're not still sulking because I showed Russell your canvases? How else do you expect to sell them?"

Tertius and Quince were painting explosive images of machinery on the walls of the Wormwood Club, over a

previous mural of fruit, which had fallen out of favor with
the management. It was only five o'clock, but Aubrey, Fingal and Rory had descended on the club to baptize the
Vortex with champagne, after an evening of shrieking and
exclaiming over *Blast* into the small hours. The excitement
and exhaustion had dyed Fingal's wasted cheeks with an
unhealthy flush. His fingers trembled as he lit a cigarette.

"I don't know what's got into him lately," he told Aubrey. "It's not at all like him to turn up his nose at an offer
of money. He must be going into a decline."

Aubrey turned to Rory. "I appeal to you, darling. If Tertius lets me buy those canvases, he'll be able to paint what
he pleases and stop wasting his time doing tiresome society
portraits. Can't you persuade him?"

"I'm not ready to sell 'em," Tertius said.

"There won't be any more cash from Muttonhead," Fingal reminded him, "not after you took Rory's side in the
great Vortex of wrath."

Tertius scowled. "I warned you not to mention that."

"Well, I don't see why I should keep forking out just
because you and Mutt aren't on speakers—" Tertius leaned
over and smeared a blob of blue paint over Fingal's monocle. "Ow! You beast!"

The action cheered Tertius up, and he laughed so much
he had to lie down on the floor, covering his shirt with
paint. Eventually, Fingal joined in.

"Blast Tertius," he shrieked, "for being an ungrateful
little upstart with the manners of a laborer!"

"Blast Fingal," shouted Tertius, "for being a stuck-up
shoneen!"

Rory refilled their glasses. "Bless this champagne. And
all who sail in her. Come and have some, Tershie, and stop
being a bear. Aubrey's only trying to help."

Tertius rolled himself up and came to the table, kissing
Rory's forehead as he sat down. Since the row with Muttonhead, and the heartbreaking split with Tom, Tertius had
been very tender to her.

"So," he said to Russell, "you think my portraits are
tiresome, do you?"

"No, of course not. They're brilliant, like everything else
you do. If you wanted to, you could buy a top hat and a
ghastly villa in St. John's Wood and turn yourself into Sir
Luke Fildes or Lord Leighton, and all the Margot Asquiths

and Lady Madge Allbrights would come flocking to your door waving huge checks. But is that what you want?"

Tertius laughed. "Does it look like it?"

"Then what on earth is the point?" Aubrey was serious. "You know and I know that your real work is far more important. When Q showed me those paintings, I saw it all. Dear boy, for the first time in God knows how long, I experienced the authentic tingle. It's more than Futurism, or Cubism, or Vorticism—if you work hard enough everyone will have to talk about Tertiusism."

"Hmmm." Tertius stared down into his drink, not at all shaken by this barrage of praise. "I'll think about it."

Quince could not stand much more of this. "What's the matter with you?" he roared. "He'll stump up hard cash, and he'll give you an exhibition when you're ready. Don't make him beg, boy. Why should he? You're lucky not to be painting labels for jam jars."

Tertius's brow cleared. "Poor old Q, I've been drinking the proceeds of those bloody jam labels faster than you can paint them. It's time I brought in some money for a change. Well, as I said, I'll think about it." Draining his champagne in one gulp, he went back to his wall.

Rory and Fingal, now decidedly tipsy, began composing lists of blasts and blesses, but Aubrey stared thoughtfully at Tertius, painting with such fierce concentration. When the next bottle was opened, he took him over another drink.

Tertius stiffened defensively when Aubrey touched his shoulder. "Thanks."

"You're still cross with me," Aubrey observed.

"No. It was Q who made me so mad—he's such a fucking nursemaid sometimes."

"Tertius, why won't you let me help you? I simply don't understand. London is full of young artists perishing for want of recognition, who would shed blood for the chance I'm offering you. I have money and a gallery. I can get you the success you deserve."

"What's in it for you?"

Aubrey glanced over his shoulder to make sure Fingal was not watching. "Could it be," he suggested gently, "that you're afraid I'll take liberties again? No, dear boy. I'm not doing this for the sake of your blue Irish eyes. I give you my word, my only interest is in helping you with your work."

Tertius went on painting, but turned briefly to smile at him. "I know. And I don't want to sound ungrateful. You're absolutely right, I'd like nothing better than to stop daubing queens of society. Trouble is, I've other obligations besides art."

"Nothing," Aubrey said, "should be more important to you than art. Can't you get out of these other obligations?"

"I don't know." Tertius painted an angry slash of orange across his harsh, black-edged abstract. "It's not going to be easy."

Five

The sobs were high and anguished, wrenched from the absolute pit of despair. Margaret, listening outside Eleanor's door, wondered if she should knock again, or take the supper tray back to the kitchen. Poor little beggar, she thought. Eleanor was a favorite in the servants' hall, and they had all been saying for weeks that there was something wrong. Miss Flora had noticed too—night after night, she told Margaret, she heard her through the wall, sobbing her heart out. Today, Eleanor had gone off somewhere in a taxi and returned hours later, ashen-faced, with pouches under her eyes the size of Gladstone bags. She had said she wouldn't have dinner downstairs because the heat had given her a headache.

Headache my foot, Margaret thought. God knew, it wasn't her place to speculate about Miss Eleanor's character, but twenty years of sharing attic bedrooms with other parlormaids had taught her that only one thing in the world made a girl cry like that.

With a sudden surge of resolution, she went into the room and set the tray down on the chest of drawers. Eleanor had evidently thrown herself straight across the bed the moment she shut the door. She had not even taken off her hat, and its wide brim was buckled against the pillows.

"Miss Eleanor—"

"Go away!"

Margaret, who had known Eleanor since she was a baby, calmly pulled the pins out of the wrecked hat. "Tell Margaret all about it, lovey."

"Oh go away! Please!"

"I might be able to help, and a trouble shared is a trouble halved, so they say."

Eleanor lifted her swollen, tear-sodden face. "Nobody can help me. I wish I was dead."

Margaret decided it was time to be firm. "Sit up—that's a good girl—and rest your head on my shoulder. There, isn't that better?" She took her own handkerchief out of her sleeve and pressed it into Eleanor's sticky hand. "Whatever it is, it's not the end of the world."

"It is," Eleanor said bleakly.

"Nonsense. That's only what you think now. There are always ways and means."

"Are there? I've tried and tried, but I can't think of a single thing to do, except drown myself. I used to wonder why girls in novels drowned themselves and now I know."

Margaret saw then that she had been right. Well, well, she could not help thinking, this'll be one in the eye for Mrs. Braddon—pride goeth before a fall. "Just answer me this, dearie. Have you been doing something you shouldn't with your young man?"

"You—you won't tell Mother? Swear you won't?"

"Not if she put me to the torture," Margaret declared, privately thinking that Mrs. Braddon would have to find out sooner or later, but that it was better for poor Miss Eleanor to work out this fact for herself. "You can trust me."

Eleanor blew her nose. "I haven't dared to tell anyone. They'll all think I'm so wicked."

"How late are you?"

Eleanor turned crimson, and whispered: "I've missed two. That means I'm going to have a baby, doesn't it?"

"Yes, love, it looks that way."

"Margaret," she looked pitifully young and scared, "what on earth am I going to do?"

"The fellow you went with—if he's a gentleman, he'll see you right."

"He won't." She shook her head mournfully. "He doesn't want me. He told me he never wanted to see me again."

Damn him, Margaret thought angrily, damn the lot of them. "He'll have to want you now, my love, or your Pa will have something to say to him."

"I hate the idea of forcing him into anything."

"Don't talk so soft. If he liked you enough to take liberties in the first place, he'll want to take care of you now. Have you told him?"

Eleanor broke into fresh sobs. "I went to tell him today.

I went all the way to Cambridge, and he'd gone. He doesn't live there anymore and his landlady couldn't tell me where to find him."

"Someone must know."

"I won't be able to find him until the beginning of term, when it's too late. And he'll hate me because I've ruined his life. What shall I do?"

Margaret frowned. "We'll have to act sharpish before the old cat gets wind of it and makes it worse by shoving her oar in. Your Auntie Flo would help, bless her, if I could only make her understand the ins and outs. The poor old dear still thinks kiddies grow on gooseberry bushes." She sighed. This was a tough one. "No good going to Mrs. Fenborough, not in a million years. What about your young lady friends?"

"I couldn't! They don't know anything about it. I'm not fit to go near them now."

"Rubbish! They're only girls like you, and girls should stick together at a time like this." Margaret brightened. "They'd walk through hot coals for you, those young ladies. You tell them to meet you tomorrow. It's my half-day so I can come with you, no questions asked."

She was glad to see the first glimmer of hope on Eleanor's innocent, woebegone face. "Oh, how kind you are—"

"Don't, you'll have me crying, too. And then we'll be a right pair, won't we?" Margaret patted her shoulder and stood up, straightening her starched white cap. "Now, I'd better run downstairs to serve the veg, or Mr. Sharp'll have my guts for garters."

When she had gone, Eleanor went to the open window, to catch the evening breeze wafting over the garden. Everything ached. At first, she had thought her breasts hurt so because her heart was broken. Only gradually had it dawned on her that she might be pregnant. She had listened to her mother's delighted monologues about the birth of Viola's daughter, Fleur, and winced at the cruel contrast between herself and her sister.

But there was some comfort now, in the thought of her friends. She had been foolish not to ask them for help. Hadn't they sworn in blood to love her forever?

It was time to call in the vow.

*　　*　　*

"There's only one thing she can do," Rory declared. "She'll have to marry the man."

"I thought you didn't believe in marriage," Jenny said acidly. She had been thin-lipped since Eleanor broke the disastrous news, and sat on the hearth rug buttering scones as if they had done her an injury.

Rory raised her chin aggressively. "What a time to chuck my principles in my face. I may not believe in marriage for myself, but it's the obvious solution for Eleanor. What else can she do?"

Jenny murmured: "If you had more respect for marriage, Rory, you'd know how foolish it is to push someone into it. She has to live with the man for the rest of her life."

"But she's mad about him!"

"First impulses aren't always the right ones—as you should know. What would you have done if someone had forced you to marry Tom Eskdale?"

Touched on her raw wound, Rory blazed: "This has nothing to do with Tom!"

"We must put Eleanor's future happiness above everything," Jenny persisted, "and consider all the possibilities."

The four of them, with Margaret, had gathered at Rory and Jenny's flat. They were all subdued and anxious, and awed by the seriousness of the problem. Eleanor was pale and puffy-eyed, clutching Margaret's hand like a submissive child. But she had found a kind of still dignity, which seemed to set her apart from the others.

Francesca, with Stevie's pearl and diamond engagement ring twinkling on her finger, was of course in tears. Nobody had expected her to be much use except as a kind of Greek chorus, giving voice to the collective woe.

Margaret found herself turning automatically to Rory, who had seemed to grasp the essentials faster than the others. "You'll excuse me for speaking freely, miss, but there might be another way around. I've a sister who's a lady's maid, and when her young lady got into trouble they found a doctor to fix it. Not cheap at fifty guineas, but safe. And nobody ever needs to know—that's the beauty of it."

The four girls took a minute or two to work out what she was suggesting. Then Jenny said, with unusual vehemence: "No. It's wicked and immoral, not to mention illegal. I won't be a party to it."

"There's too much risk," said Rory. "We can never be

absolutely sure it's safe—I've read the most awful stories. We'd never forgive ourselves if we put poor Eleanor in any danger. And why should she suffer while he gets off scot-free? No, I'm still for making him swallow the consequences."

"Nobody has asked me what I want," Eleanor said quietly. "You mean to be kind, Margaret, but nothing would induce me to harm Lorenzo's child. I shall have it anyway, no matter what happens, and I shall love it as much as I love him. The one thing I have decided is that not being selfish is the only way I come out of this feeling clean. I refuse to be foisted on Lorenzo like a punishment."

Rory groaned impatiently. "Don't be such a ninny. Why should you take all the responsibility? Why should you be the only one to pay?"

"Because the last thing I want to do is spoil his life. I dreamed of helping him and making him happy. I still think I could—but not like this. If he has to be bullied into marrying me, simply for the sake of respectability, I'd rather have my baby in the poorhouse."

"Well, darling," Rory said, "it certainly sounds wonderfully noble, the way you put it. But what about the child? It won't thank you for bringing it up without a name. It mightn't take the same view of cleanness."

Eleanor looked stricken. "What do you mean?"

Rory knelt down beside her. "God knows, I don't want to be mean to you. But are you sure you're not letting your pride get in the way? Aren't you really saying you won't take your Lorenzo unless he suddenly falls madly in love with you? And isn't that driving rather a hard bargain? It looks to me as if you'll be lucky to get him at all—the damned villain."

Eleanor bit her lower lip to stop it quivering. "I—I hadn't thought of it like that. I can't seem to help wanting wicked things, even when I try to be good."

"You're not wicked," Jenny said. "But Rory's right. It isn't Lorenzo's feelings you should be sparing now."

"It's no use. I don't even know where he is."

"Stevie will tell us," Francesca said suddenly. "What a silly I am, not to think of it before. He was writing to Lorenzo only the other day."

"No!" cried Eleanor. "You can't tell Stevie—I'd never be able to face him again!"

"I'll face him," said Rory. "He introduced you to the man."

Francesca briskly wiped her eyes. "He's taking Mummy to a concert this afternoon. Come home with me and we'll wait for them."

"You leave it to me." Rory was cheered by the prospect of action. "I'll do all the blush-making bit."

"Rory, will you promise me something?" Eleanor caught at her hand. "When you see Lorenzo, don't bully him into marrying me. If he doesn't offer to do it freely, I won't have him forced."

Reluctantly, Rory said: "I promise."

Rory stretched out her long legs and shifted restlessly against the plush cushions of the first-class compartment. It was as hot as Vulcan's forge, and the sight of the sun-parched fields flashing past the sooty windows made her feel as if she were being slowly grilled over charcoal. She had never known a summer like it. Too hot to read, or to eat the grapes Stevie had bought at Paddington, she had nothing to distract her from her gnawing anxiety for Eleanor.

It was pretty ghastly, whether she married the man or not. Why, she fretted, did I humor her by making that silly promise? She had no intention of sticking to it. The piercing mortification she had suffered at the hands of Tom fed her determination to ride down Sir Laurence Hastings like a Valkyrie. This one was not going to get away.

She contemplated Stevie, who was sitting opposite, ostensibly reading *The Times*. He had not turned a page for ages. Obviously he was as anxious as she was, but not for Eleanor. All his thoughts were for his friend. Give him his due, however. Through all his embarrassment and distress, Stevie had behaved admirably. His sympathies were in the wrong place, yet he had not said one unkind or indelicate word about Eleanor. He had only blamed himself for bringing the ill-fated pair together. Rory and Francesca had gone straight around to Half Moon Street after their meeting the previous day. To their surprise, Stevie and Mrs. Templeton had been there already—the weather was too warm for Wagner, Mrs. Templeton had said, so they had decided to give the concert a miss and stay at home.

Rory had thought that Stevie looked dismayed to see

Francesca back so early. He was certainly dismayed when he discovered why they had come. But he had told them at once that Lorenzo was at a reading party in North Devon, and that he would go down the next day. He had not even protested when Rory announced that she was coming with him, though she was not the sort of woman he was used to being seen with in public.

Hatless and gloveless as usual, Rory had dressed for comfort rather than elegance, in a loose dress of emerald green. Stevie wore the summer uniform of his caste—pristine white flannels, a blazer, a college tie and a stiff straw boater. His fair face was flushed with heat—at least, Rory assumed it was the heat. He had been one flaming blush ever since they barged in on him yesterday. She longed to tell him to take a few clothes off, but decided not to alarm him more than necessary. The more uncomfortable she made him, the politer he became.

He lowered his newspaper. "Miss Carlington, would you mind terribly if I opened the window?"

"Not at all. And for the last time, call me Rory."

"Right-oh. Sorry." He opened the window, letting in a rush of warm, soot-flavored air. "Gosh, it's hot, isn't it?" He drew a silver cigarette case from the pocket of his blazer. "Would you mind awfully if I—"

"Darling, I don't care what you do," Rory said irritably, "but please stop treating me like a maiden aunt or we'll detest each other before we get to Exeter. It's too hot for manners."

For a moment, he was startled. Then he grinned, and offered her the cigarette case. "Want one?"

"Thanks." The case was engraved: *To Darling Stevie, from his "Little Mum,"* and as she took a cigarette, Rory was fleetingly surprised that the leathery warhorse she had seen at the Braddons' party should describe herself in such a fashion.

Stevie lit their cigarettes. "I didn't mean to annoy you. To tell you the truth, I hardly know what I'm doing. This whole affair has rather knocked me sideways."

There was a silence, in which Rory mentally exclaimed "Poor Eleanor," and knew that Stevie was thinking "Poor Lorenzo."

"You're very fond of him," she said accusingly.

"Yes."

"One of those sacred male friendships—Damon and Pythias, David and Jonathan. Passing the love of women."

"Something like that. Don't girls have them too?"

Rory thought of her three friends and the blood seal that bound them all together, and was almost surprised by the ferocity of her loyalty to them. "I couldn't love Eleanor more if she was my sister."

"So you're here to keep an eye on me," he said, "because you don't trust me to manage it properly."

Rory thought this bright of him. There was more shrewdness inside that radiant golden head than she had allowed for. "Eleanor needs someone to bat for her. You're so sorry for him. You won't be able to help making him think he's doing something noble on Eleanor's behalf—when it's all his fault."

Stevie opened his mouth to say something and changed his mind.

"You don't think it is all his fault," she prompted sternly.

He looked down at his hands, and muttered: "It'll destroy his career. He'll have to leave Cambridge. It's the end of all his chances to overcome his past."

Rory did not care about Lorenzo's past. "Too bad. Eleanor's life is destroyed already."

"I know, I know." Stevie was unhappy. "But if only she hadn't encouraged him—"

"If only he hadn't been encouraged." She was merciless. "If an innocent, ardent girl threw herself at you, Stevie, without the least idea what it could lead to, would you take advantage of her?"

His lingering blush flared up to painful scarlet. "I'm not trying to excuse him, honestly. But it will be a blow to him." He leaned toward her. "I'd be so grateful if you'd let me tell him. Just me, alone. I'm used to him, you see."

There was something so appealing in his earnestness that Rory, despite her avenging mood, was softened. "All right, you do it. You know him best, after all."

"Thanks." He favored her with an enchanting smile, which softened her still further, and retreated behind the grim headlines in *The Times*.

At Exeter, they changed to a lurching little branch-line train, full of farmers' wives, which took them as far as Barnstaple. Then they traveled the next ten miles in the local carrier's noisy old motor van, together with the milk, a crate of live chickens and a new iron bedstead. He dropped his passengers at a remote crossroads, surrounded by endless, baking fields and dust-whitened hedgerows.

"It's another three miles," Stevie said. "Can you walk that far?"

"What would you do if I said no—carry me on your back? Back home in Ireland I've walked twice and three times as far. Just let me step behind the hedge to take my stockings off." She scrambled up the poppy-spangled bank and crashed through the brambles without a thought for her dress. "Thank God I'm not fool enough to wear a corset."

Stevie laughed. He had overcome his wariness of Rory by deciding to forget that she was female and treat her as a boy, and he did not feel he needed to apologize or explain when he went behind the opposite hedge to pee.

When they were both ready, he lit them each fresh cigarettes and they set off through the noonday glare and stillness.

"Will he marry her?" Rory asked.

Stevie considered this. "I don't know. Most chaps would mind what other people thought of them. But Lorenzo's such an Ishmael already that it mightn't make much difference to him."

"You can assure him that money won't be a problem. Eleanor will be twenty-one in a few weeks, and then she'll have complete control of her share of the ointment."

He smiled ruefully. "Money will be the last thing on his mind. He's rather rich, you know. The slumming is only a pose."

"I wish he'd pose nearer town," Rory complained, wiping her face with one of her discarded stockings. "He doesn't want to be found, does he?"

At a second set of crossroads, they followed a finger post into a dense wood. It was shady here, among the mossy trunks of the oaks and beeches, but patrolled by such armies of midges that it was a relief to emerge into the fiery sunlight. The sea was suddenly before them, flat and turquoise, melting in the sky. They had come out in a fishing village—one steep, winding street, and a scattering of small white cottages in the crevices of the cliffs. Nets and lobster pots were heaped beside each front door.

Rory wondered if they had come to the wrong place;

there did not seem to be one dwelling commodious enough to accommodate three gilded Cambridge men. However, Stevie took directions from an old woman in a sunbonnet, and went up a narrow path to the square, whitewashed cottage that crowned the village like a lopsided hat. Pouring sweat, they stepped through the open garden door and surprised Hilary Twisden and Windrush, who were drinking bottled beer under a tree on the lawn.

"Stevie!" Hilary jumped up. "What on earth are you doing here?"

"Dying," gasped Stevie, casting himself into the shade. "Here, Rory, sit down." He introduced her to the others, and Hilary ran into the house to fetch them drinks.

"A newspaper!" crowed Windrush, making a dive for Stevie's crumpled *Times.* "News, give me news, for the love of heaven! I'm starved of tidings of the outside world."

"The outside world doesn't matter down here," Hilary said, coming out with a jug of lemonade. "We only care about tides and seasons—the really important things. This is my part of the country," he explained to Rory. "My father has a parish near Bideford."

"Has the war started yet?" Windrush spread the newspaper on the grass, and rolled over on his stomach to study it. "Has Austria declared war on Serbia? Goddammit, Europe's in turmoil and I'm stuck down here."

"Oh, Europe's always in turmoil," Hilary said breezily. "If we don't worry about it, why should you? You're an American."

Stevie, revived by the lemonade, propped himself up on one elbow. "Austria's mobilizing along her borders, apparently. And my father has a letter in today about the recruiting crisis. He thinks the Kaiser will invade France, and then we'll all be for it. He's been saying so ever since the Archduke was murdered at Sarajevo—but he's army, you know, and he starts predicting war if they put up the price of coal. I shouldn't take any notice."

"You may be right," said Windrush, "since your Liberal Government is such a lily-livered bunch of swine. They'll lick the Kaiser's boots and offer him the Isle of Wight to moor his battleships if it means he'll leave them alone."

Rory said pointedly: "I didn't come here to discuss the Serbian crisis."

Stevie sat up. "Where's Lorenzo?"

"Down on the quay, watching the old salts at their work," said Hilary. "But I'd leave him alone, if I were you. He's in one of his moods."

"I have to see him." With one supplicating look at Rory to remind her not to follow him, Stevie left.

"Oh dear," said Hilary.

Windrush cocked an eye at Rory. "What's up, ma'am? Don't tell me you were just passing."

"Shut up, Windy," protested Hilary. "It's none of our business."

Rory sighed. "You're bound to find out eventually, I suppose. But you're not to tell anyone—on your honor."

Briefly, without mentioning Eleanor's name, she told them.

"Oh, poor little Stevie," said Windrush. "I didn't think his idol had any further to fall."

"It won't matter to him." Hilary was indignant. "No matter what Lorenzo does, Stevie always sticks to him. He was just the same at school."

"Why didn't he come down here with you?" Rory asked.

Windrush raised his head from the newspaper. "Lorenzo told him to stay away. He likes to escape from Stevie sometimes. He says his goodness depresses him. He needs to enjoy his sulks and revel in misanthropy without being jollied out of it."

The garden door opened, and Rory found herself staring at the saturnine young man she had glimpsed at Viola's dance. She had an impression of seething nervous vitality held in check by a tremendous force of will.

This thin, sunburned Saracen, who had so enslaved poor Eleanor, took in Rory and said: "There's a woman here. Take it away. I never want to see another of the creatures again."

Stevie was a few steps behind him. "Sorry, I forgot to tell you. This is Miss Carlington. She's—she's a friend."

Rory registered that Lorenzo had extremely handsome, glittering, thickly lashed black eyes, and remembered how peculiar she had felt at the dance when he stared at her. Now, through his anger, she sensed the same ruthless intimacy in his gaze, as if he had turned a searchlight on her most secret thoughts. It made her almost afraid of him, until she recovered her pride.

He was no more compelling or frightening than a villain

in a bad melodrama, she decided, and Eleanor was a ninny to fall for something so obvious. Fine dark eyes were all very well, but fancy ruining your life for the sake of them. She stood up.

"Well?"

"You want to know if I'm going to cast your friend into the snow, like the village maiden."

She was not amused. "Are you going to marry her?"

"Yes," Lorenzo said shortly. "I shall break the habit of a lifetime and commit an act of decency. And Stephen"—he turned on Stevie with sudden ferocity—"if I hear one more moan about my ruined prospects, I'll chuck you over the cliff."

"But, Larry—"

"For the last time, I never had any prospects to ruin. So why not marry the girl? I've nothing to lose."

Rory recalled her promise to Eleanor and, for the first time, saw the sense of it. The withering contempt in his voice made her feel she was throwing her friend to the lions.

"Please—please don't blame her." For Eleanor's sake, she was prepared to beg. "Don't do it, if you can't at least try to make her happy."

"I shall do nothing of the kind," Lorenzo said. "She knows the kind of man I am. If she wanted someone who would make her happy, she'd never have got me into this mess in the first place."

There was nothing to say to this. Rory had to admit it was true.

"You can tell her," he continued, "that I will do my best not to add to her misery. She can have my name. She knows it's more than she has a right to expect."

"Shut up," Hilary blurted out desperately.

"There's no need to take it out on Rory," Stevie reproached him gently. "She's only trying to help."

"Help? She wants to punish me for the wrongs of her sex. What the hell does she know about something like this?"

"I know about rubber goods," snapped Rory, "which is more than you do, by the look of things."

Lorenzo froze, and glared at her as if he would have liked to hit her. Stevie and Hilary were scandalized, but Windrush let out a great shout of laughter.

"Rubber goods! You wicked little harpy! She's got a point, though, Hastings."

Lorenzo's lips had hardened into a thin, angry line. He stalked away from them into the cottage, slamming the door so hard that the windows rattled.

"Larry—" Stevie glanced around at the others, then rushed after him.

Windrush was still chuckling. "Rubber goods, indeed. You're no lady, are you, you Irish termagant?"

Rory, loathing all men and spoiling for a fight, turned her fury on him. "And you're no gentleman, you filthy Yankee. You call me names and you'll feel my fist, so you will!"

This made him laugh even harder. "My God, the idea of Sir Galahad Stevie going on his quest with you on his back! But look, we're wounding poor old Twisden. Let's remember he's a future man of the cloth, and spare his feelings."

Hilary had retreated against the trunk of the tree, where he sat with his knees huddled under his chin.

"Miss Carlington, I know this is frightfully impertinent of me, but—but the young lady who—is it Miss Braddon?"

He was so far out of his depth, so grieved and bewildered by this sudden tempest of human weaknesses, that Rory felt sorry for him. "Yes."

"Oh," he said miserably. "I see."

"Sit down, Irish," Windrush advised her, "and don't get mad. You've got what you came for—now let them talk it over."

Rory sat down. Her temper had deflated and she was tired. She would let Stevie make all the arrangements, as he had promised. She had done all she could. They would return from their joint embassy with concrete plans for the future of Eleanor and her unborn child.

But why was it taking so long? The shadows were lengthening, the grass around her feet was littered with cigarette butts, and still Lorenzo and Stevie talked.

At last, Stevie emerged from the house alone. He looked exhausted and Rory wondered if he had been crying.

"I'm sorry." He would not meet her eye. "I didn't realize how late it was. Hilary, how on earth are we going to get back to Barnstaple?"

Hilary shook himself out of his silence. "There's only the bike, I'm afraid. Not at all comfortable—but you should know that because you sold it to me. It's down in the boathouse."

Rory was wild to know what Stevie and Lorenzo had been discussing. All her instincts told her that something was bothering Stevie. If he had not been so transparently good, she would have said he looked shifty. But she could not interrogate him in front of Hilary and Windrush.

There was no chance to talk during the journey to Barnstaple. Rory had never ridden in a motorcycle sidecar before, and discovered it was like being a bell on a Salvationist's tambourine—holding on and not spewing took all her concentration. Hilary and Stevie hauled her out more dead than alive and then there was a rush for the train, caught with seconds to spare. As soon as they were on it, Stevie fell asleep.

Rory did not get her opportunity until they were facing each other in the dining car of the London train from Exeter, over supper and a bottle of Great Western claret. Stevie was as courteous as ever, but sober and preoccupied.

"It's all settled," he told her. "If I can get a license—and I haven't the remotest idea how to go about it—he'll marry her in about three weeks."

"Not sooner?"

"It seems awfully soon to me."

"And where will they live?"

This question seemed to make him uncomfortable. "I'm to look for a furnished flat wherever Eleanor pleases. Lorenzo will pay for it. He's writing to his solicitor to take care of the money."

Perhaps, Rory thought, it was the responsibility of finding the flat that dismayed him. "Leave the flat and the servants to Jenny," she advised. "She loves prodding mattresses and interviewing cooks, and asking when the butcher calls."

"Does she? It would be a weight off my mind."

But that was not, thought Rory, where the real weight lay. She was getting suspicious. "And when is Sir Laurence planning to make his appearance? When should the wise virgins start trimming their lamps for the bridegroom?"

Stevie was scoring patterns on the tablecloth with his knife, and staring at them earnestly. "He—he'll come to London for the wedding."

"Not before? Not even to speak to Eleanor before he marries her?"

"He has things to do."

"What things?" Rory pulled his sleeve to make him look at her. "Stevie, I smell the most enormous rat. You're up to something, the pair of you."

He squared his shoulders defensively. "I give you my word, Lorenzo will marry Eleanor."

"But what—"

He leaned toward her, and said with sudden desperation: "Rory, you have my word. Now please don't ask me any more."

Six

In the split second before the storm broke, Eleanor had an eerie sense of detachment, in which she almost felt sorry for her mother. Mrs. Braddon sat at her desk in the morning room, surrounded by bills, invitations, menus and laundry lists—all the marks of her queenly status as a rich, impeccably organized woman with pretensions to high society. And now, in one short sentence, her least favored daughter had turned all her dreams to dust.

"No." She clutched at the edge of the desk, breathing hard. "I don't believe it."

"I'm very sorry to have to tell you like this, Mother. But I couldn't think of any other way. And I'm sorry that I've managed it so badly—so stupidly." Eleanor had rehearsed this speech many times, and found it easier—or rather, less dreadful—than she had expected. It was the truth, and honesty was her home ground. "I hate to make you and Daddy unhappy. But I can't apologize for marrying Lorenzo, because I love him."

Very quietly, almost to herself, Mrs. Braddon said: "You slut." Then, as if the word had been a spark to gunpowder, she leaped out of her chair and struck Eleanor across the face. "You filthy little slut! You don't even care what you've done! You've disgraced us all—ruined us—and you don't even care!"

There was a hair's-breadth pause. Mother and daughter gaped at each other, trembling and appalled.

Eleanor held her stinging cheek and fully realized what she had always known in her heart of hearts—that this woman did not love her, nor even like her. They were strangers. The sense of loneliness was piercing, but in that fragment of a moment, Eleanor was conscious of a peculiar sense of relief. She no longer had to work to please someone who never could be pleased with her. She was, in a way, free.

"Get out," Mrs. Braddon said. "I want you out of this house. I never want to see you again."

And it was over. During all the turmoil caused by Mrs. Braddon's passion, Eleanor steadily packed her trunks. She had chosen the road that led to Lorenzo, and she knew, because she was not a fool, that it was unlikely to lead to happiness. But there was no love for her here, and Eleanor could not live without the possibility of love.

Margaret, who helped her to pack, did not understand her serenity, and was frightened by it. All hell was breaking loose around them: Mrs. Braddon, mad as a dancing dervish, was berating Flora for her foolishness and incompetence, Flora was in hysterics, and poor Nancy, only just home for the holidays, was rushing around in tears, vainly imploring the servants to tell her what Eleanor had done. Yet Eleanor folded nightgowns and selected clothes as if she was simply going away for a visit. The strength she always found when she followed her heart had risen up around her like a protective shield.

She spent the next three weeks at the Templeton house in Half Moon Street. Despite Francesca's tenderness, it was not a comfortable time. Monica Templeton treated her situation with a levity that grated dreadfully on Eleanor's nerves. She relished a lost reputation, and now that Stevie had gone to join Lorenzo, she had nothing to do but lounge around in a kimono, telling stories that made Eleanor red as a radish with embarrassment. The two of them were in the same boat now, she implied. Privately, Eleanor decided that no boat was large enough to contain the two of them, and shuddered at the idea that other people might bracket her and this disgraceful woman together.

She had no word from Lorenzo to sustain her, unless she counted the curt letter from his solicitor, informing her of the income he proposed to settle on her. Jenny told her it was a handsome one, and chose a furnished flat for her in Clarges Street on the strength of it. Eleanor dutifully admired the drawing room, the dressing room and the nursery, without being able to believe that they could have any connection with her or Lorenzo. She was in limbo, like a piece of unwanted luggage waiting to be claimed.

On the morning of her wedding, she woke at dawn, with

a heavy heart and churning stomach, and solemnly promised all the gods and fates that she would devote the rest of her life to Lorenzo. From this day forward, his wishes were hers. It was too much to hope that one day he might come to bless the awful mistake that had forced him to the altar, but she would make sure he did not regret it too deeply.

Knowing he did not like to see her dressed grandly, she intended to wear a plain suit of navy blue. Francesca, however, would not hear of it. She persuaded Eleanor into a summer dress of ivory silk and a large hat of white straw. Monica kissed her and handed her a bouquet of pink roses and orange blossom. Archie, who had agreed to give her away, wore a wedding boutonniere in the lapel of his morning coat. The slovenly servants of the Templeton ménage assembled on the front steps to throw rice and old tennis shoes as the Rolls pulled away. Now that she was on the point of being respectable, they were all doing their best to infuse a little conventional joy into the blush-making occasion.

Still, Eleanor could not make herself believe it was really happening. In the porch of St. James's, Piccadilly, she took Archie's arm, thinking how strange it was to stand here in the gloom while the weekday traffic thundered past outside as if the morning were quite ordinary.

Archie was leading her into the shadowed nave. She had taken off her spectacles, and she could barely make out the few figures dotted around the bare pews. Rory and Jenny were here, of course. And here was Margaret, in a fantastic hat covered with birds' wings. She had someone with her—Aunt Flora, weeping softly, and constantly looking behind her, as if the police were after her.

Now she could make out the Vicar, poised at the altar-rail with his prayer book open. Her pulse drumming in her ears, she looked for Lorenzo.

Two figures in drab green coats and riding breeches stepped out of the front pew—two young subalterns, with gleaming boots, razored hair, and swords hanging at their sides.

"Well, I'll be damned," whispered Archie. "They've gone and joined the army!"

The moment she recognized Lorenzo's face above the uniform, Eleanor was engulfed by a nauseous wave of shock. She saw the petals scattering on the stone flags as her bouquet dropped to the floor.

Archie felt her swaying, and hissed: "Oh God, you're not going to faint, are you?"

"No—no, I'm perfectly all right."

Someone put the damaged flowers back into her hands. Swallowing hard, she stood at the altar steps beside Lorenzo.

"Dearly beloved," the Vicar began.

Afterward, Eleanor thought it typical of the whole, luck-less affair that she was too busy trying not to be sick to concentrate on the ceremony. All she felt when Lorenzo placed the gold band on her finger was terror that she would vomit all over the flashing insignia on his sleeve. She hardly knew what she scrawled in the register. The girls and Flora pressed around her to kiss her, and she only longed to be outside.

It was over. The new Lady Hastings stumbled down the aisle on her husband's arm, and drew a long, thankful breath as soon as he led her into the fresh air.

"Here, have some of this." Lorenzo pushed a silver flask into her hand. "It's cognac."

Eleanor took a sip, and the fiery liquid scorched away the sickness. She belched. "Gosh, sorry."

He was smiling down at her quite kindly. "Better?"

"Yes, much. Oh, I felt so dreadful! Did it show?"

"Indeed it did. You looked as if you were being burned at the stake."

They were formal and awkward with each other; distant strangers thrown together in a crisis that now seemed to have very little to do with either of them. Eleanor did not know how to begin to mention the fact that he was in uniform. Lorenzo glanced at his watch and took a few steps away from her.

The others were coming out of the church, blinking and blowing their noses, and full of the brittle gaiety that takes over after weddings and funerals.

Flora, her faded face haggard with anxiety, stole to Elea-nor's side. "We daren't stay a minute longer, dear. Your mother doesn't know I'm here."

Eleanor felt a pang that she had not loved Flora more, as if she had died and could never make it up. "Thank you for coming, Auntie."

"It's horrid without you. Bartholomew looks years older, and poor little Nancy cries for you every night, I know she does." Flora began to gabble. "And I'm sure your mother misses you, though she's too proud to say so. You know it's nothing more than pride, Eleanor. If you could only try to see her, she wouldn't have the heart—"

"I can't go back," Eleanor said firmly, "unless she asks me herself."

"No, dear. Of course not," Flora sighed. "Oh, Eleanor, this wasn't the wedding I wanted for you, but I do wish you joy—yes I do—" She ducked away from Lorenzo as if he had been a cobra, nervously clutching Margaret's hand.

"Good luck, Miss Eleanor," Margaret said, "your ladyship, I should say. I told you it would all come out in the wash."

"It was very good of you to come, Margaret."

"I wouldn't have missed it for a week's wages, love. You take care of yourself. Come along, Miss Flo." She shepherded Flora into a taxi.

Stevie came to kiss Eleanor, with Francesca hanging on his arm. She was beaming.

"Don't they look handsome? And aren't they clever, to go away and join the army without anybody noticing?"

"Fiendishly clever," Rory commented, with an acidity that made Stevie flush guiltily.

Monica took possession of his free arm. There was a sour drag to her rouged mouth. "Can the war wait while you come back to the house with us? Archie's whining for a drink."

It was a dismal gathering. Monica had provided enough champagne for a regiment, and hastily added a few plates of salmon sandwiches at the last minute. Nobody except Monica and Archie were in the mood to drink, and there were not enough sandwiches to go around.

Stevie made strenuous efforts to be sociable, but Lorenzo sat grimly over his untouched glass, answering every attempt at conversation with a scowl, and frequently glancing at his watch. Eleanor sat at his side for form's sake, smiling around her with wavering uncertainty.

Eventually, she stood up. "Well, I suppose I should change."

Lorenzo held open the door for her with indifferent formality. She did not even try to look at him. All she wanted was to go home, though she had no home to go to except the polished, barren new flat.

In her room, she let the bouquet she had been clutching fall from her cold hand, and stared for the first time at the shining gold band on her finger. This was all. Had she expected any more?

The taxi would be here soon. She began to unhook her wedding dress, thinking that she never wanted to see it again and pausing—as she always did now when she took her clothes off—to feel her stomach. Soon it would bulge out grossly, as Vi's had done when she was expecting Fleur.

"Eleanor."

Lorenzo was in the doorway, watching her.

"Oh—" Automatically, she pulled up her dress to hide her liberty bodice.

He shut the door behind him. "Well. It's done."

"Yes."

"Go on changing. Don't stop on my account. You have no reason to be modest. We're a married couple now."

Eleanor self-consciously let her dress fall. "Lorenzo, let me say this now: I'm very sorry about what's happened, and so grateful to you for—"

"Drop it," Lorenzo said abruptly. "The last thing I want is one of your scenes. Let's just agree to make the best of it." He retreated to the window, turning his back. "I owe you an explanation."

"Oh no—" she began.

"Don't I? Weren't you surprised to see me in uniform?"

"Yes."

"Stevie and I were commissioned a week ago. The Colonel pulled the strings with the War Office. He doesn't consider me much of an ornament to his regiment, but he's got a bee in his bonnet about the officer shortage when the war starts."

"The—the war?" Eleanor echoed stupidly.

"The war, Eleanor, the European war, for God's sake. Don't you read the newspapers?"

"Not lately."

He laughed ruefully. "I suppose not. Well, Russia has mobilized. So, apparently, has Germany. When the Kaiser declares war on France—as he's bound to do—we'll be in it too. So Colonel Carr-Lyon was prepared to forget whatever he might have known about my bad ear, and take me on the strength of my OTC certificate from school. Stevie helped, too, of course. Nothing would stop him chucking Cambridge and going with me."

Through her misery and confusion, Eleanor was beginning to grasp that these far-off political developments might have some effect on her.

"I think it's splendid of you," she managed to say, through a tightening throat. "And, of course, I understand. If we need soldiers, it's everybody's duty to go, isn't it?"

"I was expecting it to be frightful," Lorenzo said coolly, "so I'm not finding it too hard. All it seems to consist of is learning the correct way to load a camel onto a troopship, and being snubbed in the mess. But I had to get away and do something."

"So you wouldn't have to live with me," murmured Eleanor, biting down on the truth at last.

He faced her. "Let's understand one another. I don't want to live with you—or anyone, for that matter—any more than I did the last time we met. I'm happy to observe all the outward forms of propriety. You have my name. Your child will be born in wedlock—"

"Our child," she interrupted him gently.

"All right, our child. But don't imagine I'll change, Eleanor, because I won't."

Eleanor found that her courage was coming back to her, and thawing the numb loneliness that had frozen her since she left her home. Of course, his sharp manner and his evident lack of love for her hurt fiercely. Yet she admired his honesty. More than admired it—she recognized it as something she could understand and live with.

"I don't want to change you," she said.

His expression became sadder and softer. "You make me feel a hound."

"You've done your best."

Lorenzo looked at his watch again. "Flat all right?"

"Aren't you coming to see it?"

"No. Stephen and I have to go straight back to Salisbury."

"Oh." Eleanor fastened her teeth to her lower lip, to stop it trembling. She wasn't going to make him say it out loud because she could not bear to hear it, but she knew he had made up his mind never to make love to her. He

did not even intend to spend his wedding night with her.
"When—when will I see you again?"

"I don't know. When I get leave, I suppose."

"I see."

"I'll write, if you like."

"Please."

There were already vast distances between them. Lorenzo put his hands on her shoulders, and still she felt they
were calling to one another from opposite sides of a can-
yon. He gazed down at her, his expression a curious mix
of kindness and impatience.

"You're a brave little thing," he pronounced.

She found she could hardly bear the kindness because it
contrasted so cruelly with everything else. "No. If I was
really brave, I'd never have let them make you marry me.
Were you very angry?"

He gave her one of his lopsided smiles. "Bloody furious."

"Oh, Lorenzo," she cried out impulsively, "I know you
don't like me to apologize, but I'm so dreadfully sorry. You
were drunk, and I made you do it. It wasn't really your
fault at all ... Why are you laughing?"

"Because you're so priceless, calling me a drunken liber-
tine and blaming yourself for it all in the same breath." He
became serious again. "But I knew I couldn't get out of
my share of responsibility because of the child. And the
kind of child I might produce."

"He'll be a beautiful child," Eleanor declared.

Her sublime assurance darkened his face with pain. He
seemed years older. "You know what I mean. You might
as well prepare yourself for the worst. There's poison in
my blood. I always swore I'd never—"

"I'm not afraid." Eleanor's cheeks were tinged with pink
and her gray eyes shone. "Let's not condemn him before
he's even born."

"I shan't like the baby," Lorenzo said fiercely. "And
you're not to try and make me."

"I won't. Please, Lorenzo—I understand. I'm not going
to expect anything."

"You poor girl." He picked up her left hand, and
frowned at it. "What a terrible wedding you're having. I
haven't even kissed you, have I?" He brushed his lips
against her forehead. "There."

*   *   *

Running upstairs, Rory met Lorenzo coming down. He did not stand aside to let her pass. Instead, he folded his arms, and trapped her in one of his black stares.

Rory stared back. So close to him, she suddenly found herself wondering how he had looked when he made his fatal love to Eleanor, and felt her face turning hot. Don't blush, she ordered herself. "Is Eleanor ready?"

"I don't know."

"I was just going to see if she needed any help."

"How kind." Still, he did not move. "What loyal friends she has."

"She needs them."

"Not anymore, Miss Carlington. She's got what she wanted. I'd take it as a kindness, if you would now withdraw your nose from my business."

Rory, whose best behavior was wearing thin, returned: "That would suit you very well, I dare say. If you'd had your way, we'd never have interfered at all, and you'd have made for the horizon."

"Oh, how right you are about me, as always. You wouldn't have seen me for dust."

"My God," she blurted out, "I've never seen anyone fulfill a duty with such bad grace!"

"Good grace is an extra. It wasn't part of the agreement."

The unwavering insolence of his gaze was making Rory uncomfortable. She lowered her eyes. The danger she sensed in him was turning—she was alarmed to discover—into a nagging, reluctant attraction. She was sure Lorenzo was aware of it, too.

"You might at least consider her feelings," she said. "It's worse for her than it is for you."

"Really."

"Yes, because she's in love with you." For the first time, she could see why, and gave Eleanor credit for taking the risk.

"Would you believe me," he asked coolly, "if I made all the noble vows you want to hear?"

"No."

"You'd better settle for what you can get, then, hadn't you?"

He was enjoying himself. Rory could not endure this. "If you make her any more unhappy than she is, I'll—I'll—"

"You'll what? Challenge me to a duel? Punch me on the nose?" Lorenzo picked up one of her wiry, businesslike fists. "With this little lily-white hand?"

Rory snatched it away, and he grinned down at her, with real humor. "Drop it," he said. "It's all over. Eleanor is an honest woman again, and although she richly deserves to be beaten like a gong, promptly on the hour, I shall leave her to grow fat at my expense, and withdraw to wait for the war to start. Perhaps—who knows—a tactful bullet will resolve everything. I certainly hope my funeral is better fun than my wedding has been."

Rory was surprised and annoyed by an unholy desire to laugh. "I'm sure we'll all bear up wonderfully well," she said. "At least you won't be there to spoil it."

She had meant to be crushing, but Lorenzo chuckled appreciatively, and stepped aside to let her pass.

Insufferable man, she thought. But she had to suppress a pang of irritation with Eleanor. No wonder he was so rude to her, when she made a doormat of herself. Lorenzo needed a woman who could answer back.

Stevie had taken Francesca into the empty dining room across the hall. He was holding both her hands, and she was gazing up at him with a face full of love and loyalty.

"I hope there is a war," he was saying earnestly, "because it'll be such a tremendous chance for me to do something good and clean. I shall feel I'm fighting to make myself worthy of you."

Francesca smiled, her brown eyes taking in the novelty of his uniform. "Oh, Stevie, what a thing to say! Why shouldn't you be worthy?"

"I'm not. I'm not half good enough for you. But I will be. You're very sweet not to be cross with me."

"I couldn't be prouder—though I'll worry about you dreadfully."

"You little angel! Will you honestly?"

"Every second."

"My darling." He folded her in his arms. "And will you still love me if I come back minus an arm or leg?"

Francesca tentatively ran her hand down his upper arm, as if trying to imagine him without that strong limb with the blood pulsing through the muscles and veins. "I'll always love you. But you won't get hurt, will you?"

Stevie laughed. "I'll do my best."

"I know you'll be brave. Just don't be too brave."

"Here you are." Monica breezed into the room, holding a glass. "Eleanor's coming downstairs, darling, so I'm afraid I shall have to break up the soldier's farewell."

Francesca broke away from Stevie's embrace. "I must go to her."

Stevie started to follow her, but Monica placed her hand on his chest, and kicked the door shut behind her. "Don't I get a share of the warrior's kisses?"

"Monica, for God's sake," he muttered desperately, "not here."

"Where, then?" The angry set of her mouth made him notice the fine lines etched around her lips. "I suppose you've been showing off your fine military feathers to my poor babe, and telling her what a noble boy you are, rushing to the colors in your country's hour of need?"

"Please—"

"I know the truth. You did it to escape from me, didn't you?" She put the glass down on the dusty table, and her hand reached for the stiff fly of his cavalry twill riding breeches. He twitched away from her.

"Well," she said, "it really is a suit of armor, isn't it? And you really believe it has the power to restore your purity. The truth is, you're not a noble boy at all. You're very ungrateful, after all I've taught you."

"It was despicable of me," Stevie said. "I should never have allowed myself to do it. I wish you'd try to understand—this is my chance to redeem myself."

"To shed a little blood, so you can wipe off the stain of contact with me?" She leaned toward him, enveloping him in a cloud of musky scent. "How convenient this war will be for all the hundreds of men who want to get away from women. I wish we girls had a little war we could go to, whenever things get hot."

He was deeply wounded. "You'll never understand."

"On the contrary, I understand much more than you think. But I forgive you, my lamb, because you know so little about yourself. You'll come back to me. You'll have to. I may not conform to your knightly ideas of a lady, but I'm the only woman on this earth who can make you hard."

"Shut up!" Stevie hissed, scarlet with anger. "I tell you, it's absolutely over—over and done with forever!"

Pushing her roughly aside, he escaped into the hall, where Jenny, Rory and Francesca were grouped around Eleanor.

"Let us come with you," Jenny was pleading softly. "We can't leave you all alone!"

Eleanor smiled, calmly and even cheerfully. "I must get used to that. It's my home now, don't forget. And the servants are there."

"I feel as if we'd lost you," Francesca said. "Why must weddings be so sad?"

Lorenzo, now visibly struggling to contain his impatience, held out his arm to her. "Stevie and I have a train to catch. If you're going to hang around, we'll take another cab."

"No, Lorenzo, I'm ready. My darlings—" Hastily, she kissed her friends, and whispered, too quietly for Lorenzo to hear: "You're not losing me. I need you more than ever."

She took her husband's arm as if they were the happiest couple in the world.

Jenny, Francesca and Rory were left standing disconsolately on the front steps, watching Eleanor driving away into her forlorn new existence as Lady Hastings.

"Why?" Jenny blurted out despairingly. "Why did she do it?"

"Because she wanted to suffer for love," Rory said bitterly. "Don't you remember her going on about it at school? She's got her wish now—may all the saints in heaven help her."

Seven

EXTRA!!!! EXTRA!!!
READ ALL ABOUT IT.
A PARTY TO CELEBRATE THE END OF
CIVILIZATION,
TO WHICH ALL
VORTICISTS
HEATHEN CLOWNS
GRAVE BOOTH ANIMALS
CYNICAL ATHLETES
AND NEUTRAL COUNTRIES
ARE INVITED
AT 16 TORRINGTON SQUARE,
AUGUST 4, 1914.
NEWSPAPER HATS WILL BE WORN. ALCOHOL
WILL BE CONSUMED.
THIS ULTIMATUM TO TAKE EFFECT AT 9 P.M.
AFTER WHICH A STATE OF INTOXICATION
WILL EXIST IN EUROPE.

Over the door of the studio, someone had tacked up the latest editions of the papers, with news of the invasion of Belgium and Britain's ultimatum to the Kaiser, and painted across it: "Welcome to the Brink of the Vortex."

Rory, Jenny and Francesca had to fight their way into the packed room. The babble of conversation almost drowned the din of two rival gramophones, pounding out different pieces of ragtime. Rory wore a scarlet gypsy blouse embroidered in green, and a loose skirt made even more shapeless by the wine bottles in her pockets. Jenny and Francesca were in evening dress. They all wore cocked hats made from that morning's *Daily Mail*.

Francesca grabbed the back of Rory's skirt. "Oh, I

shouldn't have come! I should have stayed with Eleanor!" She was pink-cheeked and giggling because Rory had made her drink two glasses of wine before getting into the taxi.

The studio looked like a sea of bobbing paper boats. The more artistic souls had folded their newspaper hats into intricate fans and peacock tails. One of the models was dressed entirely in a tabard of Late Extras.

"Hello, girls." Tertius squeezed through the crush to meet them. "Glad you could come."

Tertius and Quince were wearing chamber pots, covered with newspaper and adorned with papier-mâché German spikes. Tertius had painted a huge Kaiser Wilhelm mustache on his upper lip, and he left smears of burned cork on the girls' cheeks when he kissed them.

"What an appallingly frivolous occasion," Jenny said, with mock severity.

"We've decided it's going to be an appallingly frivolous war," said Tertius. He put an arm around Francesca's waist. "Don't you run away and hide from us, darling. I'll take care of you."

"Oh, Tertius, promise you won't leave me—" Francesca was helpless with laughter. "I'm so frightened of that lady with no clothes on!"

Rory pushed her way to the corner where Aubrey Russell, in white tie and tails and incongruously drinking stout straight from the bottle, was holding forth to a group of homosexual friends.

"It's the triumph of the Philistines. Culture will simply perish overnight. You should have heard the overfed brutes at my club today—positively blaming the war on suffragettes and vorticists and striking workers, and drooling at the idea of slaughtering the lot, the fat fools—" His face cleared as Rory embraced him. "My darling girl. What a horrendous blouse."

"Is Fingal here?"

"I'm afraid so. I tried to make him stay at home, but he never listens to me." He pointed to the opposite corner where Fingal was entertaining three authentic, and very drunk, soldiers. "And now that he has found Thomas Atkins, I doubt if wild horses will drag him away."

There was laughter from the group around him.

"You'll have to put him on a leash the minute the ultimatum expires at eleven o'clock," one man said. "My dear,

London will be thronged with achingly attractive creatures in uniform—sheer heaven for us sodomites."

"Small consolation, I fear." Aubrey was tight-lipped. "Nobody seems to realize how ghastly it will be. Someone put a brick through the window of my gallery today, just because we weren't displaying a portrait of the King. I've had to hang Union Jacks all over my Gaudier-Brzeskas."

"And they're going to cancel German nights at the promenade concerts," someone else put in. "No more Beethoven and Wagner—too barbaric."

"I'm already sick of the flag-waving," Rory declared. "I think London's gone crazy. I went around to my aunt's today and found her telling some poor old biddy to have her dachshund put down. Thank God it'll all be over soon—we'll be bored to death by Christmas."

"Seriously, though," one of the men said, "it's rather exciting, isn't it? In a hideous sort of way."

Rory could not help agreeing with him. In theory, she was opposed to the idea of war. Yet there was something thrilling about the charge of electricity in the air, and the sense of the whole country focused upon one objective. The city seemed to have been taken over and overrun by youth. This was their hour and the elderly were suddenly obsolete and dull, with no function except to cheer at the sidelines.

The gaiety at this party reflected the fever that had broken out in everyone under thirty. They were all reeling from the heady scent of gunpowder. Rory could not imagine ever sleeping again. It had become extraordinarily important to drink as much as possible. She left Aubrey to lecture and went off to find a corkscrew.

What a shame, she thought, that Eleanor was stuck at home with her feet up. She was glad Jenny and Francesca were here, though she was still slightly surprised that they had agreed to come. Jenny, in particular, had been in an odd mood all day, determined to snatch every shred of enjoyment without really appearing to enjoy it.

The woman next to her stepped back suddenly, treading on Rory's feet, and jerking the bottle from her hands. There was a general babble of alarm, followed by a breathless hush. Aubrey lay sprawled on the floor with a thin ribbon of blood trickling from his nose.

A plump, brawny young man stood over him, breathing

heavily. "Stand up and fight, you bloody pansy coward. You limp-wristed pacifists make me sick!"

Aubrey raised his head. "All I said was, British honor can't possibly depend upon kicking a few Germans off a tiny corner of Belgium."

"You'd refuse a cry for help to save your skin, would you?"

"My skin, your skin—the skins of all these poor young men." Aubrey coughed as his friends dragged him to his feet. He pulled out a silk handkerchief and applied it to his nose. "Yes, I would. Nobody should have to die for the sake of a few trampled cabbages."

"Why, you little traitor—you beastly, Teutonic little invert—" The angry patriot seized Aubrey's starched shirt-front. "It's because people like you have pansified this country—"

Tertius choked off the rest of the sentence by grabbing the back of the man's collar and thumping his chin. Several of the women started screaming, and the onlookers began to take up the quarrel among themselves. For a moment, the excitement in the room flared to danger point. Then Quince waded in. He picked up the young man, hustled him out of the door, and the tension melted in a burst of laughter.

"No, no, darling," Aubrey assured Rory. "Perfectly all right—no need to inflict your Red Cross skills on me."

"One can't express an opinion now," said Fingal, who had torn himself away from the soldiers, "without the most awful sort of person feeling he has the right to thump one."

Tertius picked up his chamber pot and put it back on his head. "Then why express an opinion at all?"

Aubrey was shocked. "Because it matters."

"No it doesn't. Let them as wants it have their bloody war. Why should I care?"

"Oh, my dear boy," Aubrey said earnestly. "With all my heart, I hope you'll never have to."

"Don't fret about me, Russell. I'm not taking the shilling until they improve the food."

Around them, people were becoming glassy-eyed with alcohol and adrenaline. A few couples were trying to dance on whatever floor space they could find. Foreheads gleamed with sweat, and the men had damp circles under their armpits. Tertius's burned cork mustache was running down his face in stripes.

"Come on," he murmured into Rory's ear. "Let's get out of this zoo."

"Out where?"

"You'll see."

"I can't leave the girls."

"Bring 'em too. And something to drink."

They scavenged among the smeared bottles covering every surface, and found half a dozen unopened beers. Rory rounded up Jenny and Francesca, and they followed Tertius's curly head through the hot press of bodies.

Out on the tiny, cobwebby landing, he climbed up a ladder set against the wall and flung open a trapdoor.

Francesca gazed up at the clear night sky, soft as a swathe of dark blue velvet and studded with stars. "Where are we going?"

"The roof!" Rory cried, enchanted. "How divine!"

"You're not seriously expecting me—" Francesca began indignantly.

To Rory's surprise, it was Jenny who cut her short. "It'll be an adventure," she said, "and beautifully quiet and cool, I dare say. Tertius, will you help me up?"

He was already outside, looking down on them like a dirty-faced angel. "Give us your hand."

Jenny was very nimble on her feet, and she vanished through the trapdoor in a flurry of skirts. "It's wonderful!" she called. Her voice had a wild, open-air quality.

"Now, blossom," Rory soothed Francesca, "I'll push and he'll pull. It's as easy as pie."

"Oh, I can't!" Francesca had started to giggle helplessly. "It's worse than the pantry window at school!"

Somehow, she was hoisted up through the door. Tertius kept a tight hold of her when she shrieked at the sight of the steep slates, and the sheer drop into the square below.

Rory erupted out like a jack-in-the-box, her skirts full of beer bottles. They chivvied and coaxed Francesca until she could move, and perched themselves securely on the brick parapet behind the chimney stack, "like birds," as Francesca said. The fresh night breeze lifted the damp strands of hair around her face, and whipped at the fragile lace of her dress. She had conquered her nerves, and was catching the mood of exhilaration.

"The city at our feet." Rory surveyed the twinkling carpet of London lights. "It's another world up here."

Jenny's hazel eyes stared out toward the distant Kentish heights. "One day," she said, "when we're all dead, we'll sit in heaven like this."

Rory chuckled. "If they let us in."

"Tertius will pull us up."

The remark shot a chill through Rory's heart. She shivered, and moved closer to Tertius, suddenly eager to feel his sweaty warmth, and the tension in his body as he pulled the corks out of the beer bottles with his teeth. "What has got into you?" she asked crossly. "You've been acting strangely all day."

The veil over Jenny's eyes lifted. "I don't know." Her voice had hardened. "Perhaps it's because Alistair's coming back."

"How lovely!" exclaimed Francesca. "Will you be married now?"

"Probably. Unless his mother decides to be ill again. I got the telegram this morning, Rory, while you were out. They'll be arriving in Dover any moment. Mrs. MacNeil kept him in Nice as long as she could, but even she couldn't compete with the Imperial German Army. And I can't imagine how it will feel to be engaged to him again after all this time."

Tertius put the bottles into their hands. "Tell you what, let's drink confusion to the old trout."

They held their bottles in the air, and shouted "Confusion to the old trout!" in ringing, triumphant voices, which soared up to the stars.

Underneath them, a great burst of cheering broke out in the studio. In the same moment, they heard it echo down in the square, and roll away across London in a diminishing wave. There were lights in windows, and people spilling into the streets. Motor horns began to hoot at each other. Church bells jangled and pealed in the still summer air.

"Eleven o'clock," whispered Jenny. "We're at war."

They sat frozen in silence, listening to one another's breathing.

Tertius asked: "What should we drink to now?"

"Victory," suggested Jenny.

Rory raised her beer bottle ceremoniously. "To us."

ties in the first place, he'll want to take care of you now. Have you told him?"

Eleanor broke into fresh sobs. "I saw if—saw him today

PART FOUR

1914–1915
The Winter
of the World

War broke: and now the Winter of the world
With perishing great darkness closes in.
                                Wilfred Owen

Aurora

Letter to my Daughter, 1935

And so the old world—the world we had loved and taken for granted—vanished. It glowed for a moment in the last evening rays, seemingly as solid and unchanging as ever, then slipped away below the horizon like the setting sun. At the time, few of us realized what we had lost. If anyone had told me in those first days that over the next four years I would taste such bitterness and despair that I wished myself dead; that I would cry till there were no more tears left—well, I simply wouldn't have believed it possible.

Afterward, we read that gray-haired statesmen wept for the sorrow and wickedness of mankind, as they handed over their ultimatums, and set their armies marching over the fat farms and basking summer resorts of Europe. But at the beginning, we knew nothing of sorrow or wickedness. The cacophony of brass bands and stirring speeches drowned out the sound of the old reaper sharpening his scythe.

Before the war was an hour old, a telegram arrived at Castle Carey, summoning Muttonhead back to his old regiment. He took with him all the able-bodied troops from his squad of Irish Volunteers. The Mater fired off bulletins to us in London, taking to ink in her hour of crisis, like one of Richardson's heroines. I think she must have slept with a pen in her hand.

With a sinking of the heart that was to become all too familiar over the next four years, I read the names of the boys I knew who had gone for soldiers: *The two O'Donnell brothers, Andy Sheehy, Ned Gallagher and young Gerry Molloy. Half the countryside rode down to Galway to see them off, and our people sang "Oh, Missis Gallagher, the captain said/ Would ye like to make a soldier out of your*

boy Ned?" *without the least trace of irony. They are wild
lads, and Lucius thinks it will be the making of them.*

Muttonhead, prudent creature that he was, had been prepared. *He took his uniform out of mothballs the moment
he heard the French had mobilized,* wrote the Mater. *The
smell of camphor was dreadful, but only the tuft had been
eaten.* (Mutt's regiment, The Kilkennies, wore a little tuft
of rabbit fur on their collars, which had something to do
with the Battle of the Boyne.) *Now that he is Captain Carey
again, it is hard to imagine him as anything else. I would
give the very blood out of my heart to keep him safe, but I
am as proud as Punch too. He cuts a fine figure in his
uniform, and says it's a mercy it still fits him so well, for the
harvest money won't run to a new one. The villagers have
showered him with holy medals for luck. Lucius says he
would rather they offered to help with the plowing. We don't
know what is to become of the farm while he is away. Paddy
is too old to manage on his own, and Lucius says not to
ask Tertius to come home—though I don't for a minute
think the bad boy would stir his idle self if I did.*

If tears rushed to my eyes when the Mater wrote that
she would "give the very blood out of her heart" to keep
Muttonhead from harm, just think how this next bit of her
letter made me feel: *My darling Rory, I don't know exactly
why you and Lucius have quarreled so bitterly.* (How typical
of him not to have told her!) *I do know, however, that he
loves you in the same old way. He won't say so, because he
is so stubborn—just like the Pater, who used to drive me
mad. But feelings go very deep with him, and once he loves,
he loves forever. So, though he might have been in the
wrong, please, Rory, forgive whatever there is to forgive, and
pray for him as hard as you can.*

Well, I cried buckets over that letter. Of course I did.
No, I had not forgiven Muttonhead for the way he had
betrayed and humiliated me (as I saw it) after my release
from prison. I still associated him with the death of my first
love and the pain of the split with Tom—a pain so ferocious
that it had turned my heart to stone.

At last I admitted to myself that Muttonhead had behaved as he did because he lost his temper. I could hardly
blame him, since I had lost mine, too. And now he was
going into battle, perhaps to die, without one kind word
from me.

Jenny, after sitting patiently through my torrents of self-reproach, took the opportunity to deliver one of her lectures. "I could have told you all this ages ago, Rory, if you hadn't bitten my head off every time I mentioned it. You have worked out that you didn't mean what you said. Well, I'm sure Lord Oughterard knows that too. As for Tom Eskdale, I don't think you ever loved him as much as you thought. The trouble was, you didn't stop to consider your true feelings for him. You do have a way of galloping off after your first impulse and never thinking about anything properly until it's too late."

So people were always telling me, and I never could see what they meant—until it was too late. I blew my nose, and went to church to pray for Muttonhead. I was not on very familiar terms with the Deity. I began by trying to be holy and humble, and ended on a burst of anger, imploring him not to ruin my life.

At least it was honest. After that, I went into a Roman Catholic church, and lit five candles for the boys. Mr. Phillips would've had a fit if he found out, but I knew those boys thought our Protestant God as unholy as a fat bull of Bashan, and probably an Ulsterman to boot. They wouldn't want any favors from him.

It was the middle of the day, yet both these churches were full of women, huddled and silent, praying for the men they loved. It was all a woman could do. War was men's work. I was wild for action, and could have fought with the best of them, but though Lord Kitchener soon appeared on countless posters, pointing outward under the slogan "Your Country Needs YOU!", he didn't mean me.

"They should form a special regiment for women," I declared to the other three girls, one afternoon when we were all around at Eleanor's. "A monstrous regiment."

Jenny laughed. "Poor old Rory, it's a shame you can't enlist. Alistair says the thought of you with a bayonet almost makes him feel sorry for the Huns."

"It's not fair, that's all. Here I am, sound in wind and limb, and there's nothing for me to do."

"Why don't you apply to the Red Cross, to be a VAD, as Jenny's doing?" asked Eleanor. "They need gentlewomen like us, who don't have to be paid. I'd gladly volunteer, if I wasn't going to have a baby." She sighed. "I'd like to think I was helping Lorenzo and Stevie."

"I wrote to Stevie, and asked him what he thought I should do," Francesca said. "And he told me he always wanted to have a picture of me in his mind, safe at home, far away from all the horrors and dangers. He said it would make him feel he was fighting for me."

Jenny and I tried not to look at each other. We had agreed that we were getting rather tired of hearing quotations from Stevie's endlessly noble letters.

"He mightn't even get to France before it's over," I pointed out unkindly. "The worst danger he faces at the moment is eyestrain, from sweating over Army Regulations every night."

Francesca ignored this. "And think of the horrid things nurses have to do—think of the blood!"

"I'm not sure I'd have the patience to nurse," I said.

The others, to my annoyance, agreed. The fact was, only women with womanly skills—cleaning, knitting, bandaging—seemed to be required. I would have been terrific at aiming a rifle or lobbing a grenade. I had often shot rabbits and hares in Ireland, and was a useful fast bowler at cricket. But the awkward fact that I was female meant all these talents went for nothing. I sound dreadfully bloodthirsty to you, I dare say. Any man who got through the war would tell me I was damned lucky.

But in those early days, when the air was full of promised glory, women like me, who had organized to win the vote (and successfully terrorized the powers that be) were only too keen to turn over our collective strength for the good of the country. Some of the government must have privately blessed the Germans, for effectively silencing troublesome suffragettes.

Poor old Frieda Berlin, it was very hard on her. "I have my principles," she told us, during a tempestuous meeting of our WSPU committee, "and I cannot change them. My conscience tells me that this war is wrong."

Berta and Dorrie, on either side of her, emanated silent waves of agreement.

"I'm sorry, Frieda," Dinah said, "but my conscience won't allow me to turn my back on my country. I can't stand by and watch those Prussian brutes marching across Europe."

"We're fighting for fairness, and decency, and everything we value," Cecil put in hotly. "They'll be gone forever if the Germans win."

"Don't you see," demanded Frieda, "that they are all the same? Germans, French, British, Russians—they're all part of the same system that will crush us all if we let it? What are we really fighting for?" Her soft voice trembled. I had never seen her so passionate. "The old order, of princes and kings, and rich people who make slaves of the poor! Why have they all poured millions into the science of killing? The great men are waving their flags, but whose blood will be spilled? When this war is over, you'll find they have turned the clock back a hundred years! The true honor lies in the workers opposing them all!"

"You won't find many workers ready to oppose the war," Dinah said. "Ask those roughs who broke your window."

Frieda winced at the reminder. The previous day, a group of boys had chucked a brick through her drawing room window, shouting: "German witches! Go 'ome and eat sausage!"

Doubly unfair, as Berta had said, because they were Jews, and had never eaten sausage in their lives. I disagreed with the Berlins' stubborn pacifism, but hearing about that incident made me boiling mad. Were people so stupid that they couldn't recognize real goodness when they saw it?

The gift of prophecy is no blessing. Looking back now, I wonder if Frieda had guessed the personal suffering the war would bring her, and clung to her iron principles all the more staunchly, knowing it was the only way to save herself from despair?

We voted to reform our committee into a charity for refugees, and an organization center for women's war work. Only the three Berlin sisters voted against.

Frieda stood up and made a little speech that made us all rather ashamed. "Women, we accept that we are out-numbered. We are happy to do everything we can for refugees and the distressed families of soldiers. That is only common humanity. But we cannot allow our house to be used to promote or aid the war in any way. On the contrary. Our brother, Joe, has put his strength behind Ramsay MacDonald, who has said he will raise the working classes against the war. I tell you this knowing many of you will disapprove. You are all welcome in our home, but you may not care to visit us once we have turned it into a refuge for those you would call cowards."

It hurts me to remember the way her soft voice broke over those last words. If I had been wiser, I'd have set my face against the coming slaughter there and then, and cast my lot in with the Berlins.

But I was so far from being wise that I happily plunged feet first into an adventure that was little short of madness. I've never told you about it before, and to this day, I don't know whether to laugh or cry when I think of how it happened.

A week into the war, Jenny and I received an urgent summons from Lady Madge Allbright. It was evening, and we found Madge in a silver tissue cloak and diamonds, ready to go out to dinner. As usual, she was in a state of high excitement.

"My dears, now is the hour for you to make the most of your possibilities!"

Watching from the sidelines was not enough for Madge. She had the entrée to every ballroom in Europe, and she was equally determined to get a ticket to the smartest enclosure of the war. She had bought two large Wolseley lorries, and was having them fitted out as private ambulances. By pulling every string and nagging every War Office connection, she meant to leave for the front line on the first available boat. Would we go with her?

I was ready there and then. Jenny, however, refused. She preferred, she said, to work under proper supervision in a Red Cross hospital. She doubted the usefulness of a small "flying column" of nurses, and felt it would be more productive to keep her war effort in the conventional channels.

On the way home, she did everything she could to dampen my enthusiasm. "It'll be dangerous, Rory. And irresponsible. The army has better things to do than take care of well-meaning amateurs. Besides which, you don't know nearly enough about nursing to do much good."

None of it had the slightest effect. I spent the next few days in a whirlwind of preparations. Madge had the ambulances stocked with dressings and medicines. Also boxes of rose soap and glycerine for our hands, and hampers of selected tinned goods from Fortnum's. "Emergency rations," Madge said gaily, showing me the potted pheasant, "just like the tommies in the field!"

We were kitted out with nurses' uniforms, Burberry mackintoshes and round felt hats. Madge had designed our hat badges herself—a red cross outlined in gold and the words "Allbright Ambulance Brigade." Jenny laughed until she cried when she saw it. She laughed even harder at the white veil of starched lawn, which floated gracefully to my waist, and the dainty lawn oversleeves to protect my cuffs from flecks of blood. True, they were not going to be awfully practical in the heat of battle, but Madge thought they looked charming.

She simmered down a fraction when we were joined by our two professionals. Sister Ethel Harrow, tall and sleepy-looking, with a bulky, shapeless body, was to act as our Matron. She had been a ward sister at Guy's, until retiring three years before to nurse her mother, now dead.

Isabel Beech had been recruited as our doctor. She was a thin, sharp-faced woman in her thirties, whose struggle to educate herself in the male world of medicine had been the stress-equivalent of several wars. She had qualified in Scotland, and managed to observe (though never to practice) some surgery in America and France. Madge's unofficial ambulance represented her only chance to try out her skills in the front line—the Royal Army Medical Corps had already told her they had no use for her unless she chose to retrain as a nurse.

Dr. Beech introduced a much-needed note of discipline to the Allbright Flying Angels. She told Madge that she was to have the final word of authority, and insisted that the cases of champagne were left behind, to make way for more morphine. Madge was to drive one of the ambulances, and Sister the other.

Isola Kentish, to Jenny's intense disapproval, completed the party. I had never really got to the bottom of Jenny's dislike for Isola. Actually, I rather liked her. The studied indifference of her manner could be irritating. But she had stuck out the Red Cross classes when many other women fell by the wayside. In her way, she was efficient and clever. I suspected Madge was right about her "possibilities."

I do have to admit, however, that her reasons for following the British Expeditionary Force overseas were anything but heroic. In fact, you'd have to sift through the motives of all of us Flying Angels for quite some time, before you found a nugget of real heroism. At this distance, our naïveté and sheer wrongheadedness amazes me. I don't want to disparage the work of other private ambulances at the front—but compared to them, we were, as Tertius rudely said, "a bloody concert party."

In a matter of days, we were ready. Madge had set her heart on landing in France with the BEF—possibly arriving on the arm of Field Marshal Sir John French himself. This was not to be. Despite all Madge's pleadings with her contacts, and her pesterings of everyone from Mr. Winston Churchill to Lady Haig, there was not an inch of deck to be had in Portsmouth or Southampton.

Never mind. Each day, the newspaper accounts from Belgium were more terrible. We would go there instead. Madge went back to work on her various bridge partners at the War Office, and squeezed out passports and letters of introduction. She was treated indulgently because there was still a feeling of holiday optimism in the corridors of power.

In bright sunshine, we drove our gleaming, perfectly appointed ambulances onto a channel steamer at Dover and set sail for Ostend.

"One last look at the white cliffs," cried Madge, beaming around at us all, "and then the work begins in earnest. Farewell the tranquil mind."

I had no way of knowing, as I breathed that heady mixture of salt air and youthful exultation, that I was saying farewell to tranquillity forever.

One

"My dears, it's all fixed." Madge, sleek with triumph, bustled into the salon of the hotel, where the Allbright Ambulance Brigade were waiting for her over coffee and pastries. "That delightful French doctor has arranged everything. I have the papers and letters of introduction, and we're to leave this afternoon."

Rory sprang to her feet. "Oh, Madge, well done! Where are we going?" They had spent an interesting few days in Brussels, admiring the spotless boulevards, cobbled old quarter and medieval town hall. This was Rory's first visit to the Continent, and she had reveled in every detail, from the mechanical figures in the town hall clock to the foreign flavor of the coffee. But she had come prepared for the dangers and privations of war, and even with refugees steadily flocking north to Antwerp, the city was disappointingly calm. More disappointing still, you could not move for nurses.

"Where we are really needed, my darling child," Madge said, settling the airy folds of her white veil. "The front line."

"There you are, Isola," said Rory. "I told you Madge could wangle it. How too splendid."

Dr. Beech glanced up from the letter she was writing. "I hope you've arranged it properly this time." Her ferrety dark eyes were skeptical. "Could one of you nurses, for instance, take the trouble to glance at a map before we start?"

"Oh, Doctor," Madge said tenderly, "we may have had one or two little upsets on the way, but we're all seasoned campaigners now."

"Good, because I'm not walking five miles in the blazing heat when we run out of gas again."

"Fancy bringing that up! Poor Sister Harrow forgot, that's all. It could have happened to anyone."

Dr. Beech dropped her pen and whipped off her wire-rimmed spectacles. "It's simply not good enough. So far, we've been more like a plate-smashing scene in a panto-mime than a medical unit on active service. I don't hold out much hope for the wounded in the front line when we've no notion where we're going, and our every move precipitates a tempest of breakages."

"Well, those cobblestones were so slippery." Madge's voice was reproachful. "We know Sister Harrow was doing her best. She didn't mean to drop the iodine."

Sister Harrow took another eclair and began to eat it mechanically, like a cow chewing the cud.

"Is that what you'll say to our patients—God help them?" demanded Dr. Beech. "I'm sorry, we've broken all our medicine bottles, but we were doing our best?"

Rory and Isola exchanged meaningful glances. They had been waiting for the moment when the Doctor's patience finally snapped. She had been getting frostier and tighter-lipped with every fresh disaster.

Madge was sensitive about her arrangements. Her eyes misted sorrowfully, and her rosy mouth quivered. Only a heart of stone could bear to criticize her.

Dr. Beech had the necessary heart of stone. "Quite honestly, Lady Marjorie, if we continue to muddle along in this fashion, we'll do more good pointing the ambulances in the opposite direction, and heading straight back to Ostend."

"You wouldn't desert us! You wouldn't be so mean!"

"I stipulated that I was to be in charge."

"But my dear, of course you're in charge!" Madge had switched to her soothing tone. "We'd be absolutely at sea without you."

Dr. Beech was not the type to shout. Her voice was thin and high with anger. "Then let me make a few things clear. This is the last time you will do anything without consulting me. You will remember—all of you—that you are nurses under my command, and not each other's dears and dar-lings. Or mine."

"Yes, Doctor." Madge folded her hands meekly and gave her best impersonation of a ministering angel.

"Carlington and Kentish," Dr. Beech said, "I want you to check every inch of those vehicles. If we're missing so much as one needle, or one inch of gauze, then tell me. Allbright, since you're so good at wheedling things out of people, you can help me find some more iodine."

"Yes, Doctor. And what shall Sister Harrow do?"

Behind Dr. Beech's back, Isola puffed out her cheeks and imitated Harrow's relentless chewing. Rory had to struggle not to laugh.

Dr. Beech's voice was lethal. "Harrow will help us all by staying where she can't do any more damage."

Licking the crumbs off her lips, Sister Harrow fixed Dr. Beech with a look of sullen loathing. The two had been sworn enemies since the very first day, when Dr. Beech had asked suspicious questions about references, and Harrow had muttered that she didn't hold with being "under a lady doctor." Madge's diplomatic skills were being tested to the limit.

"Let her eat cake," Rory said to Isola later, when they were checking the contents of the ambulances against the inventory. "That's all she's good for, the clumsy old bat." She had removed her veil, and the August sun, slanting through the open canvas flap of the lorry, kindled her red hair into a blaze.

"I think Harrow tipples." Isola lounged against one of the folded stretchers, lighting a cigarette. "Slippery cobblestones my foot. She was lurching about like anything when she dropped that crate of iodine. Didn't you nearly die of laughing?"

Rory flipped open the polished box of surgical instruments, gleaming in their bed of baize. "Come on, Kentish, do some work for a change. And put that cigarette out, or Beech will kill you."

By two o'clock, the Allbright Ambulance Brigade was in marching order. The four nurses, crackling with starch, were lined up beside the ambulances. Rory allowed herself to feel proud. Every box and locker contained its quota of bottles and bandages. The very wheels of the lorries sparkled. Dr. Beech inspected everything minutely, determined not to show satisfaction. But there was not a spot or speck to be found.

"Number one. Harrow, Carlington and myself," she said. "Number two. Allbright and Kentish—and Allbright, don't you dare stop without asking me. Right, nurses. Let's go."

The corners of Harrow's mouth drooped. She did not enjoy having the Doctor "spying on her," as she saw it.

"Keep the peace, dear child," Madge whispered to Rory. "Don't let them kill each other."

Rory and Isola cranked the starting handles of the lorries. Harrow pulled out of the hotel courtyard first, narrowly missing the gatepost, and deliberately clashing the gears. Rory strongly suspected her of exaggerating her motoring experience. It was maddening to have to sit by and say nothing when she scraped the hubcaps against the curb. Rory had fallen in love with the ambulance and spent all her spare moments deciphering the mysteries under its khaki bonnet. She found Harrow's lack of respect for the engine almost heartbreaking.

Once clear of Brussels, she applied herself to the map. They were headed for Chaussonville, a village a few miles outside the town of Namur, near the French border. And they did not need to be told they were approaching the front line. For the first few kilometers, the flat countryside seemed reassuringly peaceful. It was harvest time, and the peasants were bent over in the fields like figures by Courbet. Presently, however, the file of refugees became such a flock that they had to slow down and drive right up against the grass divider.

Rory stared into the resigned, exhausted faces of the people fleeing from the Germans. Some families had cars, with tin baths and rocking chairs lashed to the roofs. Some traveled in haycarts, clutching cats and birdcages. Many were on foot, dragging their bundles of bedding and crockery—all they owned in the world—as best they could. Mothers, powdered with dust, carried babies in their arms. Fathers struggled along with tiny children on their shoulders.

They halted, patient as cattle, to let the ambulances pass. Rory choked on her useless sympathy and impotent anger. War had swept these people out of their cottages and farms like a giant reaper swinging a scythe across a cornfield. She imagined their deserted gardens, heavy with ripe fruit, and their carefully worked acres with the harvest left to rot on the stalk. You could labor and slave to squeeze a living from a little plot of land, never thinking once of politics or foreign treaties, never doing anyone harm. And the plans of distant kings and statesmen could undo it all in a day.

The village was roughly fifty kilometers from Brussels,

and the journey had been estimated at two hours, but the crowded roads stretched it out to three and a half. It was nearly seven o'clock when the ambulances braked in the deserted square.

The sky was fading from blue to white and the shuttered houses cast long shadows across the cobblestones. Nothing stirred. Three flags—Belgian, French and British—hung limply from a statue of King Leopold in the center of the little square. The engines shuddered to a halt, and they sat for a moment in eerie silence, which was broken by Madge's plaintive voice.

"Well, I do think someone might have been here to meet us."

Dr. Beech briskly jumped out of the ambulance. "I suspect we passed the welcoming committee on the road. They've all cleared out."

Madge was never at a loss for long. "The Mayor will be here." She tooted her horn.

A few minutes later, a door opened. A thin, elderly man with a gray goatee beard stepped out cautiously, shading his eyes against the evening light.

"Bon soir, monsieur," called Madge. *"Etes-vous Monsieur Dupont? Nous sommes les soeurs anglaises, qui—"*

"Thank God," interrupted Monsieur Dupont. "I thought the Germans had arrived."

His vest gaped open over his collarless shirt, and he was wearing bedroom slippers, but he bowed to Madge with the grace of a courtier, and told them they were to set up their hospital in the empty school.

"All very well," Madge said, glancing around, "but who on earth are we going to nurse?"

"It's true, madame, many have departed. The Germans are only a few kilometers away, so we are told."

Rory tried to imagine the gray ranks of Germans, waiting beyond the poplars on the horizon. It did not seem real in this sleepy rural silence.

"I shall not leave," the Mayor told them. "Somebody must stay to protect the village. If we cooperate, if we are reasonable, they are far less likely to harm us."

"I'm sure you needn't worry," Madge said, with one of her winning, dimpled smiles. "I know scores of Germans— poor, dear Prince Lichnowsky, the Ambassador, was a particular crony of mine—and I really can't imagine them doing half the frightful things one reads about in the newspapers."

"One hopes, madame," Monsieur Dupont said grimly.

He led them to the school, a one-story building at the edge of the village. Dr. Beech assessed it shrewdly. There was one large schoolroom, with windows set high in the whitewashed walls. Forms and desks had been hurriedly pushed to one side or dragged out into the grass-covered yard. A dozen or so beds, of all ages, shapes and sizes, stood about at odd angles in the middle of the floor. A door led to the teacher's flat, now unoccupied, which had two rooms, a small water closet, and a kitchen with a stone sink and a pump. There was an earth closet outside for the children, and a tiny cellar full of mildewy textbooks.

"Such small time to prepare," explained Monsieur Dupont. "If there is anything else we can give you, please ask. Better you should have it than the Germans."

Rory would have loved to sit down with a cup of tea after the hot journey, but Dr. Beech set them to work immediately. The inside lavatory and kitchen were to serve as the "sink" room. They would all sleep in the teacher's bedroom, and the other room would be the Doctor's dispensary and consulting room. Their first task was to clean every inch that could be cleaned. Madge, who had scarcely seen a scrubbing brush in her life, gaily attacked the lavatory. Rory and Isola washed the walls and floors in a solution of soap and Lysol.

"There go our hands," said Isola, pausing to survey her reddened knuckles.

Dr. Beech and Sister Harrow unpacked the medicines and instruments from the ambulances. It grew dark, and they worked in thin pools of electric light. Once the schoolroom was clean, they arranged the beds in two neat rows, propping the uneven legs with books.

By ten o'clock, Rory's stomach was growling with hunger, and she ached as if someone had put her through a mangle. She nearly wept with relief when the Mayor returned, accompanied by his wife and daughter. They had brought extra supplies of linen—beautiful stuff, with a ghostly aroma of oak presses and lavender—and a large cast-iron pot of stew, wrapped in cloths. The shy daughter carried a steaming coffeepot and a bottle of red wine.

The rich smells of the coffee and meat, delicious after

hours of slopping around disinfectant and brown soap, made even Dr. Beech decide they had done enough. They spread newspapers across the ward table, and sat down to eat with groans of joy. Rory thought she had never had such a feast in her life. As her tiredness lifted, she felt a thrill of pure exhilaration. Raw hands and aching joints were a small price to pay for this adventure. The sense of actually being on active service was like champagne.

Dr. Beech decided to rob the wounded of the bottle of wine, and they each had a glass—except Harrow, who primly declined. Madge produced a box of crystalized fruits for pudding, and they drank their coffee in a blissful state of sticky repletion.

"Do you know," Madge said, "I've never had so much fun in my life. Won't my servants be surprised when I tell them the proper way to clean a lavatory bowl?"

Far away, across the dark fields, they heard the rumble of summer thunder.

"Weather's breaking," said Dr. Beech.

The thunder went on and on, swelling into a roar. Rory sat stock still, watching her wineglass trembling on the table.

There was a rushing sound, like an approaching train. It crescendoed above their heads, then burst in a tremendous explosion that made the overhead lights dance madly on their long wires.

In the silence that followed, the five women stared at each other's white faces. The shock had frozen them into cowering statues, crazily illuminated by the swinging bulbs.

It began again, with a force that shook the tiled floor. The rumble accelerated, and the sky above them was blasted apart by a series of merciless crashes. The lights went out. Rory was under the table, clutching Madge's hand, before she had time to digest the fact that the village was being shelled.

The noise was obscene. It seemed to suck the air from her lungs and drain all strength from her limbs. She curled herself into a ball, hugging her knees against her chest, wishing she could retreat inside her own body.

"Cellar!" Dr. Beech shouted into her ear. "Get to the cellar!"

Rory did not want to move, but discovered that she

could. In the darkness they scrambled for cups, pillows and matches, clumsy with fear, flinching with every blast.

The pounding of the German field guns kept them in the cellar for two days and nights. Rory's nerves were on wires. The cramping, the claustrophobia and the suppressed hysteria of the other women were enough to drive her to screaming madness. But as long as Madge and Isola could keep up the pretense of being calm, so could she. It took every ounce of concentration.

Madge braved the shelling to fetch her cards from her luggage, and they eked out their collective sanity by playing bridge. Harrow refused to take a turn, or to have anything to do with any of them. She pressed her bulk into the corner, away from the light, and flatly refused to relieve herself into the bucket as the others did, even when Beech managed to screen it behind a blanket. Instead, she insisted upon going upstairs to the water closet. Each time, she stayed away a little longer.

"She's up to something," Rory said. "Signaling to the Huns, I shouldn't wonder."

"Your call, partner." Beech played bridge with unshakable determination. Occasionally, the cards trembled in her hand when there was a particularly loud explosion. Otherwise, she behaved as if she was in a drawing room.

After her excursions, Harrow would stumble down the ladder, breathing thickly, and fall into a doze in her corner. Rory was amazed that she could sleep with hundreds of shells whistling over her head on their way to Namur. It was, as Madge said, like living in a tunnel on the London Underground.

Then, at the end of the second night, the noise suddenly stopped. Limp with exhaustion, their heads reeling with the ecstasy of silence, they waited for it to begin again. With every moment that ticked past, Rory felt the silence deepening and spreading around her in a great wave of peace. She was dizzy with the longing to sleep.

Blinking and swaying, they crept out into the light. A delicate summer dawn was breaking over the fields. All the schoolroom windows were shattered. Their feet crunched broken glass, and they coughed in the fog of plaster dust. Beech hurried to the dispensary. Fortunately, most of the breakables were still safely packed in wooden boxes.

The silence hummed on.

Isola said: "I wonder if they've come yet."

They went out to the square, and found a bizarre mixture of chaos and normality. One house had been destroyed, and the cobbles were carpeted with glass, rubble, and the shattered bones of furniture. But the remaining residents were sweeping their front steps and hanging feather mattresses out of upstairs windows. Monsieur Dupont was out surveying the exposed guts of the destroyed house. The interior walls were intact, with pictures and photographs still hanging on them at mad angles. Someone's life, Rory thought, staring at a shattered print of the Sacred Heart. Someone's privacy, turned inside out.

"It was empty, thank God," the Mayor told them. "She left last week to stay with her son in Bruges."

Nobody had been hurt. They returned to their hospital to begin the weary task of cleaning up.

Rory was ready to fall over where she stood and sleep for a year. Only her determination to show Beech her mettle kept her driving her broom across the floor. Once the room had been swept and tidied, however, and the worst of the dust had been laid with water, Beech sent them all away to rest.

"I don't care if the Germans do come," Isola said, yawning noisily, "as long as they don't wake me up."

In the nurses' room, Harrow lay sprawled across the largest bed, snoring fit to beat the band. Tired as they were, they could not bear to sleep anywhere near her. Rory threw herself onto one of the beds in the ward, and immediately dropped into oblivion.

"Rory! Wake up! The wounded!"

Madge, blowsy with sleep and wildly excited, was shaking her impatiently. Rory leaped off the bed, snatching at her apron and veil, and pinning them on as she ran outside. Their first patients had arrived—Belgian and French soldiers, and civilians from the surrounding villages. The worst cases lay in farm carts. Others limped behind, clutching each other's shoulders, or leaning on improvised crutches.

Rory froze, stunned by a sickening sense of inadequacy. Then, before she properly knew what she was doing, she was moving to help a French soldier whose left leg ended in a filthy, misshapen mass of bandages. Beech was rapping out commands, and she obeyed them like an automaton.

Privately, she had been afraid of touching the wounded, of seeing and smelling real blood. Now, there was simply no time to be squeamish or indecisive. Within twenty minutes, every bed was occupied, and the overflow lay in the nurses' room and on the floor. There was hardly a chance to draw breath as she dived from one task to another— cutting off the soiled red *pantalons* of a French poilu, running for fresh gauze and disinfectant, dragging rags off wounds that looked like freshly butchered meat, murmuring *"Soyez calme, soyez calme,"* into faces twisted with fear and pain.

All you cared about, she discovered, was doing things properly and promptly. Years of careful upbringing and young ladyhood were blasted away into oblivion. The same Rory who had blushed to see Tom naked could now hold the penis of a strange man while he urinated into a bottle, without a tremor of embarrassment. She could hold a bowl filled with blood, and wipe vomit off the floor. It was a nightmare, but curiously liberating.

The wounds were terrible. Fragments of shell had plowed through soft flesh, exposing white bone. Beech, impervious to screeches for mercy, picked out shards of metal with tweezers, and dropped them into a kidney dish. Sister Harrow swabbed the wounds with Lysol, and applied strips of gauze soaked in tincture of iodine. Rory, Madge and Isola ripped off clothes, changed stained bed linen and took around the cocktail of aspirin and brandy, which was the only available painkiller. Morphine made the patients unconscious, and Beech was saving it for the most serious cases.

Harrow moved slowly, wrapped in a strange remoteness, as if operating on a different timescale to the rest of them. Fleetingly, Rory noticed that she made several trips to the dispensary, and returned empty-handed and slower than ever.

The day had worn on into afternoon, and the confusion had subsided into something like order. Patients who could walk had been sent to houses in the village. The others slept, or fought silent, internal battles against pain. Madge brewed coffee in the sink room, and they took turns to sit down for five minutes, easing their shoes off swollen feet.

Only Beech, her white apron spotted with blood, kept on working.

"Carlington," she called, "go into the dispensary and fetch some more brandy."

Rory opened the door of the dispensary in time to catch Sister Harrow holding a brandy bottle to her lips, like a herald with a trumpet. When she saw Rory, she choked and tottered against the desk.

"Who told you to come in here? Get out!"

Rory folded her arms belligerently. "Dr. Beech."

"Ha!" said Harrow. "Dr. Bitch."

If the situation had not been so desperate, Rory would have laughed. As it was, she could not help remembering the time Tertius gave Una's hens tipsy-trifle to see what would happen. Sister Harrow, with her fluted cap tilted rakishly on top of her bosomy body, reminded her irresistibly of those cockle-topped old biddies staggering around the chicken coop.

"I'm to get some brandy," she said, "if you can spare it."

Harrow drained the bottle. "All gone."

"I'll open another one."

Rory went to the wooden case in the corner, and pulled out one bottle after another. They were all empty, with the stoppers neatly replaced. She turned to Harrow in disbelief.

"What am I supposed to do with these?"

Harrow chortled unpleasantly. "Put ships in 'em."

Rory's self-control broke its moorings, and she flew into a rage. "So this is where you've been sneaking off every five minutes—you drunken old cow! That brandy was meant for the patients, and I'd like to break every single bottle over your fat head, so you'll know what it's like to lie there in pain—"

"How dare you speak to me in that way!" Absurdly, a sense of her own dignity as a trained nurse seemed to be Harrow's one unfuddled faculty. "Get out of this room at once. You will be disciplined—sheverely dishiplined—"

"Don't you go telling me what to do, you boozy old eejit. I'd eat me apron sooner than take an order from you."

"Nurse Carlington." Beech was in the doorway, pale and rigid with anger. "Have you gone mad? Stop that bawling this instant."

Rory rounded on her. "She's drunk every last drop of the patients' brandy. And I'll bet she's lied about why she left her last hospital—I'll bet it was because they were scared she'd go off with a bloody great bang if someone lit a match—"

"Carlington!" Beech's voice deflated Rory's tirade like a scalpel. "If this was a regular hospital, I would dismiss you on the spot. I won't tolerate such behavior. Get back to your duties, and don't let me ever hear you speaking to a superior in that manner again." She turned to Harrow, with a look that would have iced the equator. "Sister, I'll deal with you later. Allbright, make her a pot of strong coffee— we can't manage without her."

Madge led Harrow away into the kitchen, and Rory, her heart still thumping with fury, followed Beech back to the ward. She was expecting a continuation of the lecture, and was surprised when Beech shoved a tray of iodine, disinfectant. and bandages into her hands. "You saw how Sister did the dressings?"

"Yes."

"I know you're only a VAD, but needs must when the devil drives. Clean out the tissue thoroughly, and wrap the limb in the stockinette afterward—not too tight, leave it room to breathe. Write the time of the dressing in the notebook."

"Yes, Doctor."

Rory was ashamed of her outburst. She took a deep breath to steady her hands, and willed herself to apply the swab of Lysol in long, thorough strokes. The patient, one of the French soldiers, held out his mangled arm stoically. She paused to smile encouragement at him, and he managed to smile back. Oh God, she thought, he might be Muttonhead. As she soaked the square of gauze in the iodine solution, she tried not to wonder where Muttonhead was now.

At five o'clock, when the makeshift hospital ward had settled into something like a routine, Monsieur Dupont appeared, wearing a frock coat and his Mayor's sash, and requesting a conference with all the nurses.

"Madame Doctor, you must move these men."

"Move them? They've only just arrived!"

"Please, madame. The Germans are on the march. It will not be safe here. For them, or for you."

"Even the Germans will respect the Red Cross," Beech said.

Rory's stomach was turning somersaults, but she nodded agreement. They were not much use as nurses, unless they were prepared to care for patients behind the lines. "We're not thinking of our own skins."

Monsieur Dupont's face was creased and baggy with anxiety. "With respect, ladies, you don't know the Germans. When they entered my brother's village, they rounded up twenty men, including the Mayor and the priest, as hostages. When they found weapons hidden in one of the cellars, they shot them all. Anything that looks like resistance, they interpret as an act of war. It must not happen when they come here."

"But, my dear monsieur," Madge said coaxingly, "we're only women, and we're taking care of the sick. I positively know they won't think we're resisting. The minute they come, I shall send in my card to their Commandant. I got to know so many of them at the Kiel Regatta—"

"Allbright," Beech snapped, "if you don't shut up about your German connections, I shall have you arrested as a spy." She turned back to the Mayor. "Obviously, we have to think of the patients. How much danger is there?"

"Madame, in a few hours they will be in the middle of a battlefield."

Frowning, Beech looked down the two rows of beds. "Where can we take them?"

"There is a convent, *La Sainte Union,* near Wépion, about eight kilometers from here."

"Well," Beech said, "we're under your authority, monsieur, and if you think it's best—"

She was silenced by the rumble of a shell, which burst near enough to make the floor leap under their feet. Harrow, who had been sagging into an intoxicated doze, suddenly jerked up her head and began to scream.

Beech—to Rory's secret satisfaction—smacked her hard across the jowls. "Pull yourself together, woman!"

Instead of bringing Harrow to her senses, the blow finally drove her out of them. She erupted into a shrieking, flailing fit of hysterics, crashing against the furniture and upsetting a tray of instruments. Rory and Isola grabbed her arms, and held her fast until she subsided into long, low wails of terror.

Meanwhile, two more shells crashed down, all the patients began shouting at once, and Madge burst into tears on Monsieur Dupont's shoulder, sobbing: "It's all my fault, I should never have engaged her. I only wanted to help and now everything's gone wrong!"

Beech collapsed into a chair, pulling off her glasses and massaging her weary eyes. "This is a disaster. We were relying on Harrow to drive the ambulance. What on earth are we going to do now?"

Rory had been waiting for someone to think of this. "I can drive it."

"Don't be harebrained, child. This isn't the time for false heroics."

"Honestly, Doctor—I know I can do it. I tried it several times in Brussels, and I was a sight better than Harrow, even when she's sober."

Beech's lips twitched. "All right. I haven't the strength to argue."

Their final task, once patients and equipment were loaded, was the crating of Sister Harrow. Monsieur Dupont himself helped her up to the front seat of Ambulance Two. He then amazed Dr. Beech by kissing her hand, just as she was cranking the starting handle, thanking her profusely, and comparing her to an angel of mercy.

"I hate leaving him," Beech admitted to Rory. "There's something so noble in his ridiculous civic pride. I really believe he'd die to preserve that village. King Albert himself couldn't have a stauncher sense of duty to his subjects."

Rory was loving the sensation of the ambulance thrumming under her hands. She had known it would respond beautifully.

"Slowly," warned Beech. "Remember the patients." She ducked through the canvas flap to look after them. "Some of these poor boys are very bad."

It took them more than an hour to reach the convent—a stomach-twisting hour, listening to the Belgian forts on the other side of the town pounding at the enemy. Rory had been afraid of missing the turning, but half the countryside seemed to be heading for the shelter of the imposing stone building. In the deepening darkness, she drove up the graveled drive to the square of yellow light spilling from the open front doors.

The nuns proved to be both efficient and kind. They

installed the wounded men in the hospital they had set up in their enormous, vaulted wine cellars, and offered the ravenous Allbright nurses a meal in their refectory. Over thick vegetable soup and bread, they discussed the problem of what to do next.

"I could kill giants, now I've had something to eat," Rory said, wiping out her bowl with her crust, "let alone Germans."

Madge had been subdued and deferential since the collapse of her arrangements. "Perhaps we can make ourselves useful here."

"They have legions of nuns, far better nurses than we are," Isola pointed out, "and men to carry the stretchers, and lay sisters to do the scrubbing. They won't want any of us, except Dr. Beech."

Beech snorted crossly. "The doctor I met made it abundantly clear that he had no use for me. He said he wouldn't trust his patients to a woman if she were the last doctor in Europe. Besides, there's Harrow to consider." They had left her in one of the ambulances, snoring on a vacated stretcher.

Madge's head drooped sorrowfully. "How was I to know she'd turn out to be a dipsomaniac?"

Rory and Isola caught each other's eyes and burst out laughing. "Don't blame yourself, Madgie," Rory said. "No use crying over spilled brandy."

"Oh, the elastic spirits of youth," Beech said. "Neither of you unfledged chicks seem to realize the spot we're in. If we stay here tonight, the chances are we'll be behind German lines tomorrow. We can't go back, so we had better go forward. Carlington, give me the map."

They had no idea how near they were to the enemy. It was, as Isola said, "a case of sticking in a pin and hoping for the best."

Rory was conscious of a forlorn pang at leaving the ordered safety of the convent, and striking out into the darkness. Afterward, she was to remember that drive as a feverish Walpurgis Night, with objects suddenly looming out of the black roads like flying goblins. She was glassy-eyed with lack of sleep, but painfully alert in every nerve. Her one comfort was Beech, murmuring encouragement beside her.

It was Beech who insisted they turn west at Profondeville, when Rory wanted to continue heading south. The ambulances chugged along narrow country lanes, past solitary farms, as yet untouched by war, where dogs barked at them. Occasionally, Beech struck a match to study the map.

How long they drove, Rory could never tell. It seemed like all night, or several nights stitched into one. She was aware that the character of the landscape was changing, as she began to see slag heaps and the wheels of mine shafts silhouetted against the horizon. Beech had fallen asleep, with her fists clenched around the map and her glasses bouncing on her nose. Let her, thought Rory. She had not closed her eyes since they were all huddled in the cellar at Chaussonville, and that was already a lifetime ago.

Two figures brandishing rifles jumped out into her headlights. Rory screeched the brakes, her heart swooping.

"Angels must have guided you," the young Lieutenant said. "I can't think how else you got through. It's an absolute miracle." He gazed reverently at Isola. With her rumpled hair and rosy, sleepy face, she made her creased Burberry look as alluring as a silk negligée.

"It's absolute madness," said the Major. "You might have been killed a thousand times over, and you were damned lucky to run into our patrol. Why didn't the Belgians stop you?"

"We didn't ask them," Beech said.

They were sitting around a table under the dirty yellow light of a hurricane lamp in the low-ceilinged cottage, which had been commandeered for Battalion HQ.

"Fellowes nearly had a heart attack, sir," said the Lieutenant. "He took them for a whole division of huns."

"But he couldn't have been kinder," Madge said warmly. "We're really most grateful, Major."

"Hmm." The Major frowned. "You've a lot of explaining to do, Lady Marjorie—quite apart from what you think you're doing in the middle of our forward zone in the first place. What on earth is the matter with that female in the back of your lorry?"

"Not to worry, sir," the Lieutenant assured him cheerfully. "She's only tight, apparently. I say, it must have been quite a bender to make her snore like that."

"Thank you, Waring. That'll do."

The Major, a thin and peevish individual with a gray

mustache, had not been at all pleased to be landed with a party of stray women. In any other circumstances, his annoyance might have made Rory uncomfortable, but it was so heavenly to see whole, healthy men, in clean, smart British uniforms that she almost loved him.

"You certainly can't stay here," he said crossly.

"Oh, we wouldn't dream of being a bother—would we, girls?" Finding herself in a place where she could once more pull her strings, Madge had perked up wonderfully. "We'll find somewhere to set up our dressing-station, and—"

"Good God, you'll do nothing of the kind." The Major looked horrified. "Don't you think I have troubles enough, without a gaggle of lady amateurs cluttering up my sector?"

The Lieutenant asked: "Might I make a suggestion, sir?"

"Well?"

"There's a house outside Maubeuge, sir. Two old spinsters. They threw a fit when we tried to billet men on them, but they can't possibly object to these ladies." He stole another glance at Isola. "Hodges could show them the way."

"I'm supposed to spare a bike, am I? Oh, all right."

"They'll need gasoline—"

"Give them some gasoline, give them anything. Just get them out of here."

"Really, Major," Madge said, "we can't thank you enough. When I next see Sir John French, I shall make a special point of mentioning your kindness."

The Lieutenant, struggling not to laugh, ushered them out before the Major exploded.

Rory climbed back into her ambulance, yawning till her eyes watered and thanking God for the British Army. The chaos she had lived through over the past few days, and the sight of the Belgian and French soldiers reduced to bundles of bloody rags, had made her feel the world was coming to an end. But now the hardy professionals of the BEF had arrived, and they would surely see off the Germans like the legions of the Archangel Michael. It was practically over already.

There seemed to be no such thing as chaos in the British line. The Lieutenant refueled the ambulances, and sent them off behind a dispatch rider on a motorcycle. He led them through slumberous vegetable gardens and darkened villages, to a large brick house at the end of an obscure country lane.

Its owners, two stout sisters in their sixties, with long plaits hanging over their flannel dressing gowns, had a deep objection to men on their territory. Once they had been made to understand, however, that none of these creatures was proposing to pollute their virgin doorstep, they were the soul of hospitality.

Rory, with her fingers crossed behind her back, told them Harrow was *"malade."* She was helped upstairs and dropped onto a musty feather mattress in a spare room so damp and unused that entering it felt like robbing a tomb. While the other beds were airing, the ladies entertained their guests with weak herbal tea, and glasses of sticky *digestif,* which tasted of Collis Brown's Compound.

At last Rory found herself peeling off her filthy uniform for the first time in three days, in the bedroom she was to share with Isola. They managed a laugh over the huge, flapping nightgowns the ladies had given them, then crawled into the double bed, too tired to wash their faces, brush their hair, or do anything but sleep.

Long afterward, Rory was to recognize the next few days as a vital bridge in her life, when she finally left behind the green banks of her innocence. She had seen unimaginable suffering and pain; yet she still assumed, when she woke at the farmhouse in Maubeuge, that some higher force would arrive to set everything right. She was to learn that evil, once set in motion, had no such limits.

But there was no sign of this on the morning after their awful journey, which was as fresh and bright as the first day of creation. Madge, Rory and Isola helped the two old sisters to pick their apples and load them into bushel baskets, while Beech "dealt" with Sister Harrow inside the house. Rory and Isola yearned to know what passed between them. But when the two of them emerged—Harrow very red and Beech very white—the subject of Harrow's disgrace was closed.

They carried the baskets of ripe scarlet fruit to a field beyond a little coppice, where a row of British soldiers were digging a long, jagged trench. Although the two old ladies disapproved of the male sex, they were intensely patriotic. The apples were their special offering, to sweeten the entente cordiale.

Rory never forgot the sight of those tommies, digging in the sunshine in their khaki shirts. They were shouting and laughing as they worked, and making eyes at the local girls, who had come out to gape at them as if they had been exhibits at a fair. The dazzling light, the sweet scent of the fruit mingled with newly turned soil, the tanned forearms of the men, their smiling faces—the scene wove itself into Rory's memory as her last glimpse of British pride before its fall.

The following morning, while the church bells were still ringing for Mass, the battle began. The fields and vegetable gardens shook with the impact of the howitzers firing across the canal at Mons. By dawn the next day, burning villages were bleeding luridly into the sky, and a drizzle of coal dust from the blasted collieries grimed every leaf and blade of grass.

It was hard to believe the terrible news brought by the first refugees, when they stopped to beg water at the gate. They had fled in such confusion that some of them carried the dirty plates from their interrupted meals, hastily bundled into tablecloths. The British Army, they said, had been beaten. Many were dead, and the rest were in retreat.

"The officers were shot first," someone told them, "because their swords flashed in the sun, and made them perfect targets. Hundreds of British officers."

A great, breathless dread froze the blood in Rory's veins. The whole landscape seemed to darken around her.

"Carlington, did you hear me?" Beech demanded.

Rory swallowed, and managed to murmur: "I'm sorry?"

"I said we'd try to get to Le Cateau. If there really are so many wounded, they'll need every pair of hands. Go and help Kentish, and stop woolgathering."

"Yes, Doctor."

Beech's sharp voice softened. "It may not be true, you know. I dare say quite a small skirmish can look like a disaster when you're right in the thick of it. Is there someone you're anxious about?"

"Yes, he's my"—Rory tried to find a definition for her relationship with Muttonhead—"my brother."

"Well, take my advice, nurse, and don't go borrowing

trouble. For all we know, he's perfectly safe." She turned away.

Something made Rory blurt out at her back: "The last time I saw him, I told him I hated him."

When Beech halted and looked around, there was a glitter of amusement in her bright, shrewd eyes. "Did you mean it?"

"No. I'd give anything in the world to take it back."

"I can see I was right not to tell you off for yelling blue murder at Harrow," Beech said dryly. "A temper like yours is its own punishment."

Yes, Rory thought, remorse was the bitterest punishment for letting the sun go down on wrath. If Muttonhead was among those fallen officers, lying dead beside the canal at Mons with his drawn sword in his hand, she would be punished for her bad temper until the end of her days.

As soon as the ambulances left the country lanes and hit the principal roads to Le Cateau, they descended into a whirling maelstrom of confusion, which was to furnish them all with nightmares for several years to come. Here, among the heart-wrenching lines of refugees, were the dirty, unshaven ghosts of the British Army.

Straggling columns of men, glistening with sweat, toiled along behind exhausted officers, their boots slipping painfully on the cobbles. Wounded men, in blood-caked bandages, lay in haycarts or open lorries. The sight of a London bus, towering above a stunted row of French poplars, and still plastered with advertisements for Bovril, made Rory think she was hallucinating. Presently, however, they met vans from Maples and Harrods, requisitioned straight from the London streets. These added a particularly bizarre flavor to the desperate chaos.

It was worse than useless, they discovered, to ask for news, directions or help in any form. The officers they stopped were as confused and ill-informed as they were. Some had only the haziest notion of where they were going, or what they were expected to do when they got there. Others had received no orders at all, because their headquarters had moved on without informing them.

The situation at Le Cateau was no better. The general staff had packed and gone, and left a town preparing for battle. As a sign of how bad things were, even female hands were needed. Rory spent three sweaty hours with a party of local women, helping haggard and sleep-starved tommies to dig a trench.

"You can tell when the buggers are coming," one soldier told her, "because they start singing. It don't half give you a creepy feeling, hearing all them German victory songs floating at you out of the night."

"We'll get 'em this time," another one said. "They was dropping like flies yesterday. I don't see why we couldn't've stayed, and finished the job, like."

The work was backbreaking, but it numbed the mind, and Rory did not want to think. The tommies seemed to regard her as a lucky mascot, and they kindly showered her with precious cigarettes and swigs of rum. She was sorry to leave them when it was time to turn her blistered hands to nursing.

Beech had found a dressing-station in a nearby village, and had been prepared to launch into an impassioned advertisement for women doctors. She need not have worried. The army doctor came out of the makeshift operating theater looking as if he had been in a rainstorm of blood, and Beech had barely introduced herself before he asked: "Got any chloroform?"

"Yes—"

"Morphine?"

"Yes."

"Good-oh. Ever done an amputation?"

"No."

"Now's your chance."

If Beech was nervous, she did not show it. Far into the evening, she worked beside the doctor in that overheated slaughterhouse. Sister Harrow administered the chloroform, dripping it onto the mask with a hand that was—mercifully—as steady as a rock.

Madge, Rory and Isola helped the harassed RAMC orderlies. Nobody quibbled about qualifications, nobody had timie to lecture about the correct way to do things. Rory dragged field dressings off suppurating wounds, cleaned and disinfected as best she could, and only prayed she was not killing anyone.

The patience and stoicism of the soldiers would have touched her to tears, if she had had time to think about it—or to think about anything except the dreadful smell. The stench of some of the wounds was staggering.

"Gangrene," Beech said, probing flesh that was putrefying like bad meat in the sun.

Nauseated, terrified, pouring rivers of sweat, they worked their way along the lines of men who had been left on stretchers in the village street, because every inch of floor space had been filled. Some clutched at their skirts as they passed, begging for water, or whimpering with pain.

Around midnight, the RAMC doctor told them to leave. "I'm grateful for everything you've done, Miss Beech, but we're digging in for a show, and the front line isn't a place for your girls."

"But you need us!" Beech protested. "You need our help!"

"Frankly, God is the only person who can help us now. I could get the order to evacuate the post at any moment. We had to clear out of one yesterday, and leaving the worst cases to the tender mercies of the enemy was enough to break a man's heart. I only got away by the seat of my trousers. No, I'm sorry."

"At least let us take some of them in the ambulances. We can get them to a proper hospital in Amiens, or on a hospital train."

The army doctor, unable to refuse, helped her to choose eight men who might have a chance in a hospital. Rory marveled at their detachment, as they deliberated over which to save. Once again, they set off in darkness, descending to another, deeper circle of hell. Rory drove at a snail's pace, partly to minimize he suffering of the wounded men, partly because an orderly had warned her to watch out for tripwires and roadblocks. In the end, only one fact could be relied upon—which was that nobody knew anything. It was, as one of the patients ruefully observed, "a total cock-up."

Dawn broke, and Rory's ambulance betrayed her by vibrating to a halt. She was out of gas.

"What a bore," Isola said.

They were stranded on a country road in the middle of nowhere. Rory was furious with herself for trying to be clever and avoiding the main highway. The nearest village was six kilometers away. Madge and Isola volunteered to walk there. Rory, Beech and Harrow did what they could for the men.

One, a rather elderly private who had lost a leg, had recovered enough to demand tea and cigarettes. Another, a Sergeant Major who looked perfectly healthy and tanned, was dying.

"Internal bleeding," Beech said. "Don't look so stricken, Carlington. It's not your fault. I don't think our running out of gasoline has made much difference to him, poor chap."

Presently, Madge and Isola returned from the village with a milk churn of coffee, armfuls of newly baked baguettes, two hundred cigarettes, but not a drop of fuel.

"They couldn't have been sweeter!" Madge somehow managed to look as if she had just breezed in from a garden party instead of a long dusty walk. "They were so sorry about the gasoline, but the priest's housekeeper says she'll ask her cousin. It's somewhat tricky, apparently, because they haven't spoken for years—"

Beech astounded them all by breaking into a tinny laugh. "Allbright, you're priceless. If you landed on Mars, you'd know everybody's business in five minutes." She sighed, and pulled off her glasses, rubbing the purple welts they had made on the bridge of her nose. "Well, we'll just have to wait. And God help us all." The sunlight cruelly emphasized the lines etched on her thin face over the past few days. She was utterly spent. "I'm sorry, girls. But like London Bridge, Isabel Beech is falling down. Even if I knew what to do, I wouldn't have the strength to do it."

Rory and Isola looked to Madge for guidance, but she was evidently as bewildered by Beech's surrender as they were. It was Sister Harrow who took charge. Shaking herself all over, as if waking from a long sleep, she went into action like a retired circus horse that suddenly goes through its old paces when it hears a trumpet. The discipline ground into her over years of hospital training had somehow survived being soused in alcohol.

Under her gruff orders, the coffee was reheated on the Primus stove. The healthiest patients were taken out of the ambulance and laid on the grass strip in the shade of the poplars, and given breakfast. She placed the dying man apart from the others and rigged up her umbrella (which had somehow survived their various moves) to protect his face from the sun.

Beech, meanwhile, drank a cup of coffee, smoked one of the brackish French cigarettes, and gradually revived enough to check her patients. Out in the open air, under the kindly sun, they were doing better than Rory had dared to hope.

Some slept. The hardy old soldier who had lost his leg puffed through endless cigarettes, and munched his way through the last of Madge's tinned rations from Fortnum's.

True to her word, the priest's elderly housekeeper eventually drove up in a one-horse gig, bearing two huge cans of gasoline, and milk for *"les pauvres blessés."* She also brought a bottle of brandy, which Beech tactfully took into custody. Rory poured the gasoline into the ambulances, and they carefully loaded the men back into their wooden bunks.

Beech was kneeling on the grass beside the Sergeant Major, holding his limp hand.

"Wait," she said. "He's going."

Rory watched as his last breath rattled in his throat, and the film of blankness settled slowly across his eyes. Somewhere, there were people who loved this man. She tried to imagine them, going about their business at home, never dreaming that their hearts had just broken, or that they were living in time borrowed from grief. What was it like to hear that a man you loved had died on a foreign roadside without moistening a single eye?

The Doctor folded his arms across his bandaged chest and murmured in her dry voice: *"The Lord is my shepherd; I shall not want. He maketh me to lie down in green pastures."*

In the middle of their anxiety and fear, they were still, as if the hectic world had stopped turning.

"Yea, though I walk through the valley of the shadow of death, I will fear no evil: For thou art with me; thy rod and thy staff they comfort me. Thou preparest a table for me in the presence of mine enemies . . ."

At the end, they all murmured "Amen," and were silent until Beech said: "How on earth are we going to bury him?"

It was at this moment that a grimy goblin in khaki emerged through an opening in the hedge a few yards away from them.

"Well, well, what've we got here? Take a look at this, boys."

He gestured behind him, and a dozen or so more of them appeared behind him. Within moments, they had surrounded the group of nurses.

"How splendid!" Madge exclaimed. "Just when we needed you —like the answer to a prayer."

Rory glanced around the ring of unshaven faces. Some

were grinning, but the hostility in their eyes made them look like wild animals baring their teeth. The initial joy at seeing British khaki evaporated. Fear gripped her stomach.

"Pleased to see us, are you?" asked the ringleader. "Yes, I'll bet you are. All alone, and never been kissed. Ooh, what a shame. We'll have to do something about that, won't we?"

Beech drew herself up proudly. "What do you want?"

"Wotcher got, girlie? Mine's a pint."

His companions shouted with laughter.

"We're a Red Cross Medical Unit," Beech said. "Not a canteen."

The self-appointed leader pushed his face toward her. Beech made a visible effort not to recoil.

"We'd like some of them comforts for the troops you've got in there. Go and get 'em."

"Certainly not."

"Not a very nice lady, are you? Me and the boys have been marching the best part of two days. We're hungry, see—and if you won't give it to us we'll take it."

Rory was shaking with fury, but Beech—without shifting her defiant gaze—grabbed her arm warningly. With those cold fingers pressing into her flesh, Rory managed to keep a hold on her tongue.

"Don't you dare touch those ambulances," Beech said, with all the authority she could summon. "We have sick men in there."

"Share and share alike," the man said. "Why should we starve just because we were the lucky ones?"

"I tell you, we haven't anything for you. And you should be ashamed of yourselves, behaving like common rabble, with a dead comrade lying here at your feet."

His face suddenly became hideous with anger. "Don't you tell me about dead comrades—I've seen better fellows than him shot to pieces beside me—so don't you lecture me because I've had enough of bloody lectures and orders—"

"Oh God!" Madge cried out. "They're deserters!"

He rounded on her fiercely. "There's nothing left to desert from. Got that? The war's over, and it's every man for himself."

One of the men pulled aside the canvas flap of one of the lorries. Beech's lips had gone white. Unconsciously, she dug her fingers harder into Rory's arm.

"Leave that alone!"

The leader laughed nastily. His face was now inches away from hers. "Try and stop us, then. We'd love a struggle."

Suddenly he grabbed Beech's shoulders, alert in every nerve. They listened to the sound of a horse approaching the crossroads, which was roughly ten yards from where they stood. All the men fell silent.

Rory's pulse was beating painfully at the back of her dry throat.

"Shit," someone said, more confused than angry, "it's an officer."

Madge let out a sigh of relief that was almost a sob.

"Shut up," the leader said.

Rory boldly turned her head, just as the figure on horseback crossed the road. Something in the set of his back and shoulders made her shake off Beech's arm in a great surge of anguished hope. For a fraction of a second, she thought she was dreaming and her eyes refused to believe what her heart knew. Then she felt she would die if he rode another step away. She had to struggle to find her voice, but when she did, it came out in a scream loud enough to pierce the heavens.

"Mutt! Muttonhead!"

He reined in the horse immediately, flinching as if her voice had been a bullet in his back.

Rory roughly pushed through the men and dashed down the road toward him, holding out her arms and shrieking his name over and over. She never would forget the look of sheer astonishment on Muttonhead's face when she clasped the stirrup and madly kissed his muddy boot.

He had two days' growth of beard, his breeches were spattered with dust and mud, his khaki tunic was torn and stained, and one of his hands was wrapped in a filthy, bloody handkerchief. Typically, once he had got over his surprise, he did not waste words. After saluting toward the other women, he frowned down at the ring of men.

"What the hell's going on here?"

The men shuffled backward, poised uncertainly between rebellion and submission. Muttonhead's frown deepened to a glare. He singled out the self-appointed leader.

"You. Stand up straight, man. And damn well salute."

From the ground, Muttonhead's towering figure in the

saddle was such a graven image of outraged authority that all the men saluted.

"Regiment?"

"North Surreys." Resentfully, the man added: "Sir."

"Surrey tradition, is it, to roam the countryside terrorizing women?"

"We've lost our company, sir."

"No excuse. I've lost mine, too." His face softened a fraction. "Get yourselves into marching order. You can come with me."

"Why should we?" the spokesman blurted out. "There's nowhere to go. It's nothing but a bloody shambles—the war's over—"

"The war is not over. And if you don't fall into line behind me, I'll have you court-martialed for mutiny." He raised himself in the stirrups. "Listen, boys, I know it's a bloody shambles. You're tired and hungry. But you can't give up now. We'll find your company, and get you grub and billets."

By now the men no longer looked menacing—only shabby and weary, evidently glad to let someone else take responsibility. "You and you." Muttonhead nodded at two men who were carrying spades and entrenching tools on their packs. "Bury this corpse." He dismounted.

Madge cleared her throat. "Shall I—would anyone care for—a cup of tea?"

The soldiers hung their heads. There were murmurs of "Thank you, ma'am." One man stepped forward to help her with the Primus stove.

"Poor things," Rory said. "I'm sorry I was so scared of them just now."

Muttonhead had drawn her away from the others. Gently, he raised her chin, and gazed down into her face. There was a pained expression about his eyes, which a stranger would barely have noticed, but which Rory recognized as a rare sign of strong emotion. He was taking her in as if he had never seen her before. It made her oddly uneasy. She wanted to hear him talk.

"Mutt, if I live to be a thousand, I'll never be able to express how glad I was to see you. Weren't you surprised?"

He let out a brief snort of laughter. "I'm not even going to ask what you've been up to. Wouldn't give you the satisfaction."

Rory tucked her hand into his elbow. "We heard the guns at Mons. Were you there?"

"Yes."

"Was it—was it very ghastly?"

Muttonhead's face was grim. "Bad enough. When you get home, tell the Mater you saw me. Don't want her worried by what she reads in the papers."

"If we ever get home."

"Get to Boulogne. Don't let anyone stop you. Get out of this war."

She could not help asking: "Why? Because I'm only a woman, and I can't be any use?"

"For God's sake"—Muttonhead suddenly seized her in his arms—"because I love every hair of your head, you stupid brat."

Rory clung around his neck, boring her face into the cold metal pips on his shoulder. "Please say you forgive me. Please say you're not angry anymore—" Tears spilled out with the words. "I can't bear it—"

Muttonhead held her close. "I was wrong, Rory. Let's have no more skirmishes, eh?" She felt the effort he put behind this statement. He had always hated apologizing.

"Never again," she promised.

He was smiling when he drew away from her. "Till the next time you drive me mad."

It was time for him to leave. Rory watched him lining the men up in the road. Before he climbed back into the saddle, she put a hand on his sleeve and whispered: "God keep you safe, Mutt."

He did not look around as he led his soldiers away. A terrible bleakness closed around Rory, and it was all she could do not to run after him. But she had made up the quarrel, and the happiness of being secure in his affection once more made her feel as if iron bands had been removed from her heart.

Isola was beside her, also watching Muttonhead.

"That," she said deliberately, "is the most divinely gorgeous man I have ever seen in my life."

"And if he's your brother, Carlington," said Beech, "then I'm the Empress of Germany."

Aurora

Letter to my Daughter, 1935

Late that autumn, the remains of Muttonhead's regiment were posted to the Ypres salient. Every day, I pored over the terrible reports in *The Times,* and the long lists of casualties, and thanked heaven we had made up our quarrel. I knew he liked getting my letters, and I wrote him reams. Every week, regular as clockwork, he sent back a few laconic lines to me, and to the Mater, to tell us he was well.

Any woman of my generation could tell you about the sickening anxiety of waiting for letters from the front. I would look at the date at the top, wonder what had happened since he wrote it, and live in a constant lather of worry until the next arrived. We had agreed to use certain code phrases, and when he wrote that he was "hoping for a few days' hunting," meaning he was being sent "up the line," I was frantic.

There was no letter the following week, nor the week after. We made up excuses for him to each other, blaming the postal system, the weather—anything to deflect the heart-stopping fear of the telegraph boy's ring at the front door.

Then, one afternoon, Miss Thompson came upstairs, to tell me that Tertius was waiting for me in her drawing room. One glance at her face, which wore an unfamiliar look of sympathy, and I knew. A moment later, frozen into a trance of dread, I was gazing into Tertius's scared eyes, and hearing him say—as if from a long way off, like a figure in a dream—"Rory, it's Mutt."

Two

Aubrey's Bentley halted on the graveled driveway of the large, mock-Tudor mansion overlooking Wimbledon Common. Rory and Tertius leaped out before the chauffeur had time to open the door, but Fingal had to be helped. The sickening anxiety of the past hour lifted enough for Rory to register how awful he looked. There were hollows under his eyes, and the flesh around his mouth had a ghastly, bluish tinge.

"Fingal, are you all right?"

"Don't fuss. You're as bad as Aubrey." Fingal shook away the chauffeur's arm. "It's my asthma, that's all. The telegram brought it on."

They rang the bell, and a VAD let them into the hall. The officers' hospital still had the appearance of a private house, but the underlying smells of ether and disinfectant struck them all into awed silence. The VAD showed them to a polished wooden bench, and asked them to wait. A large mirror opposite reflected their strained, pale faces.

"Honestly," whispered Fingal, "you two look like a couple of tramps. Tershie, where on earth did you get that ridiculous overcoat?"

"Jesus, what does it matter?" Tertius whispered back crossly. "I grabbed the first thing that came into me hand."

"Lord knows what they'll think of us."

"Who cares?"

"And Aurora, you might have worn a hat. You really might."

"I've got enough on my mind, without perching a hat on top of it all." Rory listened to the shining hospital stillness. In the frozen quiet, she could hear her own pulse thrumming in her ears. "How —how bad will it be, do you think?"

Brisk footsteps broke the calm, like stones dropping into

a well. The Matron, a Queen Alexandra nurse, formidably starched, and smiling behind rimless glasses, took them all in. She settled on Fingal as the most respectable.

"Captain Carey's family? Yes, you may see him, but only for a few minutes, I'm afraid. Will you come with me, please?"

They followed her up the huge, carved wooden staircase. Rory stared at the knot of ribbon between her shoulder blades, on the back of her cape, and clutched Tertius's hand for courage.

"You must be very proud of your brother, Mr. Carey," the Matron said to Fingal. "Goodness, didn't you know? Telegrams don't say much, do they? He risked his own life to save his subaltern. After he was wounded, he crawled ten yards under enemy fire, with the boy on his back, and pushed him into a shell hole. Oh yes, you should be very proud indeed."

In the dark passage upstairs, a girl was weeping on a chair outside a door. She glanced up when they approached, the tears making silver tracks on her fresh pink cheeks. The long pheasant's feather in her hat trembled pathetically.

"Now, my dear," the Matron said, "I hope you didn't show that face to him. Sad faces don't do anyone any good, do they?"

A VAD appeared on the landing, carrying a bundle of linen.

"Nurse, take Miss Yates down to my office and give her some tea."

"Very good, Matron." She took the girl's arm gently enough, but as if she was taking her into custody. From the hall below, they heard the girl breaking into loud, frightened sobs, which were suddenly extinguished behind a door.

For the first time, the Matron looked directly at Rory.

"If you're going to cry, my office is the place to do it. The patients' feelings have priority here, and I won't have them upset."

"You don't have to worry about me," Rory assured her, "but can't you tell us how he is?"

"His leg took the worst of it. The bones are badly splintered by bullets, right up to the hip."

Rory remembered the men she had seen in France. "Is

there any infection?" She knew, as Fingal and Tertius did not, that if Muttonhead's leg was gangrenous, it would have to be amputated. Even then, he would be likely to die.

The Matron raised her eyebrows slightly at the question. "No. The doctors think the leg can be saved. Whether or not he'll be able to walk on it again, we shall have to see. His chances are good, but don't expect to find him looking well." She pushed open the door, and said, in a different voice: "Look who's come to see you, Captain."

The room was bare and clean, with pale spaces on the walls where pictures had been in the house's former life. A fire was burning in the grate. Muttonhead lay very still, watched by a nurse. The bedclothes above his leg were draped over a high frame, so that he seemed to be lying in a tent. His face was gaunt, with shadows under the cheekbones and an unnaturally blank forehead. He looked very young.

The nurse stood up and nodded to Rory, who slipped into the chair beside the bed, and took Muttonhead's hand. His lids fluttered and his dark eyes rolled toward her. With incredible relief, she saw the gleam of recognition, and smiled.

"Hello, brat," he said.

Fingal and Tertius immediately began to cry. They retired to the door, in a flurry of sniffs and nose-blowing, sharing Fingal's handkerchief because Tertius had forgotten his own.

"Oh, Mutt," Rory said, "what a time you've had. I'm so glad you're home now. We only heard an hour ago or we'd have been here sooner. My poor darling, we'd have walked on broken glass to see you. The Mater's coming, and you're not to worry about the money, because Fingal's Mr. Russell has paid for the boat, and she'll be staying in the flat with me."

With an effort, Muttonhead said: "Farm—"

"Papa's agent will see to it. No, don't scowl, darling. He isn't as bad as you think."

"Drinks."

"You don't know that. You can't convict a man on the evidence of a red nose."

His lips curled into a faint smile. "Don't argue."

The smile brought a lump to Rory's throat, which she gamely swallowed. "All right. I'll save it till you're well."

Tertius, wiping his eyes with the back of his paint-smeared hand, said: "It's grand to see you in one piece, Mutt."

"If there's anything you want—anything at all," Fingal said huskily, "you're to say, and you mustn't fret about cash. The one thing we can't afford is to lose you, old boy."

The Matron was beckoning them away. "I'm sorry, you must leave him to rest now."

Rory kissed his forehead, and laid her cheek briefly against his. "We'll be back tomorrow."

When they were on the other side of the door, the Matron said, "Well, my dear, you've certainly brightened him up. He hasn't spoken two words since he arrived."

Rory laughed. "He's not much of a conversationalist."

"You'll have to teach us the knack of drawing him out." She patted Rory's shoulder kindly. "He'll pull through, never you fear. You've been as good as a dose of tonic."

"Matron, who was that poor girl we saw just now?"

"Ah, that was the sister of the boy your brother saved. He's here too. He'll live, but he's paralyzed, I'm afraid. She simply wasn't prepared for the shock of seeing him."

"Poor thing," Rory said.

"Yes, indeed. Poor thing. But I do wish relatives wouldn't weep all over the patients. It only makes a bad situation worse." She glared at Tertius, who was rubbing his nose on his sleeve. "Really, Mr. Carey. Can I get you a handkerchief?"

Muttonhead was written up in *The Times* under the headline "Gallantry of an Irish Peer." Lady Oughterard bought twenty copies to send to her friends at home.

"This'll be one in the eye for Emma Billinghurst," she told Rory, chuckling. "She'll have to eat all those things she said when Lucius joined the Volunteers."

The Mater had been in a dreadful state when she arrived in London. Rory had scarcely recognized the shrunken, haggard woman who had fallen off the train into Tertius's arms. However, as soon as Muttonhead began to improve, she bloomed. Her blue eyes became as sharp as ever, her stocky figure recovered its energy, and her trumpeting voice made Miss Thompson's sober house echo to the eaves.

Every day, she drove to the hospital in Aubrey's Bentley. He never sent the car around without some offering of fruit or wine for Muttonhead, and he often took her out in the evenings because he thought she should see a few sights while she had the opportunity. Thanks to Aubrey, Lady Oughterard was having the time of her life.

"Just fancy, I've been to a cinema," she would tell Muttonhead, busily eating through his grapes. "And there was the King—large as life—scuttling about inspecting dreadnoughts. And yesterday, we went to Selfridges and bought a hat, and you should see the ladies' lavatories—well, I don't suppose you ever will—but the marble basins nearly made my eyes pop."

"Hope she's not too much of a nuisance," Muttonhead said to Rory, one afternoon when they were alone together. His leg was still immobile under its tent, and his eyes were dilated with drugs, but he was sitting up, and had resumed his pipe. "Bit of a handful in a flat, I should think."

Rory swore that she adored having the Mater in Jenny's bedroom. It was nearly true, and she was not going to worry Muttonhead with complaints. But the Mater's heroic untidiness had come as a shock. Rory, who was not exactly house-proud herself, had never seen anything like it.

That evening, while Lady Oughterard was out at the Globe Theatre seeing Rider Haggard's *Mameena,* she took a stab at reducing the chaos. Crumby plates and sticky glasses crowded every surface. The gas ring on the landing was invisible under a heap of crusted saucepans. Lady Oughterard's patched drawers were drying on a chair in front of the gas fire, and she had trailed her knitting wool into such extraordinary places that Rory half expected to find a Minotaur at the end of it.

Someone knocked on the door. Miss Thompson, I'll bet, Rory thought. Just what I need. She whisked the damp drawers under a cushion. "Come in!"

It was Tom.

He was thinner than she remembered, and shabbier. Under the feeble electric light, beads of rain sparkled on his shoulders. He stared at her, breathless and tense, shivering slightly. At the first sight of him, Rory had instinctively backed away with her hand to her throat, fending off the pain of their last meeting. When she met his hot gray eyes, however, she found he had lost his power to hurt her. That first love had died in agony, but it had died.

"Good God," she said.

"You alone?"

"Yes."

He shut the door, and sat down beside the fire. "Get us a drink, love. I'm freezing."

"Oh, how charming, Tom. Is that the best you can do? What about 'Hello'—or is that too bourgeois?"

"And something to eat, if you've got it. Bloody hell, it's good to be out of the rain."

"You're drenched. Take that jacket off." Rory helped him remove his threadbare, inadequate tweed jacket. His boots were giving off a light steam.

She gave him a glass of brandy, and the remains of a tapioca pudding. He attacked the food voraciously. She watched him, thinking how odd it was to have him back in the flat, and to feel hardly a tremor in his presence.

Eventually, he said: "You're a good lass, not to bother me while I'm eating." His eyes crinkled up in one of his rare, disarming smiles. "Now, you want to know why I've come."

She could not help smiling back. "I do, rather."

"Don't worry. I won't take advantage. It's money I'm after."

"I've given you enough of my money."

"Come on, Rory. Get off your high horse. This is an emergency, or I wouldn't ask. There's a warrant out for my arrest and I'm going underground for a few weeks."

"Not here, I hope."

"Don't be daft." He became severe. "It's a right mess, by the way. You should learn to use a duster."

"What have you done this time?"

"Written a pamphlet against recruiting. I've been selling it at factory gates, and I've been nailed under DORA."

"Oh, Tom!" DORA stood for the Defense of the Realm Act, and Rory visited the Berlins frequently enough to know that falling foul of it meant serious trouble. "They'll put you in jail, for sure."

"Not yet, they won't." Tom helped himself to another glass of brandy. "It's the most important work I've ever done, and it's not over by a long shot. Someone's got to point out the lies and tell the working man he shouldn't give himself for cannon fodder in a rich man's war."

Rory did not agree with him about the war—how could she, when Muttonhead had nearly died for it?—but she was conscious of a deep respect for Tom. In his way, according to his lights, he was as brave a man as any of them.

"I've only a few pounds," she said. "I wish I could give you more."

"That'll do me. It's good of you, hen. I'd have gone to Joe Berlin, but he's got the police breathing down his neck as it is."

Silence yawned between them. He cleared his throat several times, before saying: "I read about that lord of yours in the paper. How's he getting along?"

She was touched. "Better. They say he'll walk again."

Tom laughed suddenly. "He didn't half give me a bashing. I thought he'd broken my jaw."

"He was very angry—but that's all forgotten now."

"I'm glad." He took her hand, and held it between his own. "I shouldn't have behaved as I did."

"Oh, Tom, please—"

"No, let me say it. I probably deserved that wallop he landed on me. I didn't mean to hurt you. I loved you a sight more than I ever let on."

She smiled up into his face. "But that wasn't as much as I wanted, was it? You didn't have time for romance, and I guessed that deep down. It wasn't your fault. I dare say it's all worked out for the best."

Tom picked up a strand of her hair so that it caught the light. "Any other man would tell me I was mad to let a girl like you get away. Are we friends?"

Before she could reply, a great voice bellowed: "Cooee!" from the bottom of the attic stairs.

"Oh God," murmured Rory.

The Mater's feet were bounding up the stairs. "Darling, it was absolutely splendid—all about a mighty African chieftain, and they did the most priceless Zulu wedding dance—" Waving her moth-eaten silk shawl over her head, and singing a tribal chant, Lady Oughterard did the Zulu dance as she burst into the room. "Aubrey and I nearly killed ourselves laughing—oh! I'm terribly sorry—"

The shawl slithered to the floor. She had seen the astonished face of Tom.

"Mater, this—this is Mr. Eskdale." Rory was puce with embarrassment.

"How do you do?"

Tom stood up, hastily thrusting his arms into his jacket. "I'd better go."

"Goodness, not on my account, Mr. Eskdale—"

"Here, Tom." Rory emptied the money box into his pocket. "Let me know how you get on, if you can."

"Thanks." He started for the door, then turned back to kiss Rory's forehead. "Take care."

And he was gone.

Rory could not bear to look at the Mater. She could feel those keen eyes burrowing into her, and that busy brain sifting all the possible explanations for a strange man in her adoptive daughter's flat.

"Darling," the Mater said tenderly, "I'm sorry about the dance. Was it very awful?"

This was too much. Rory howled with laughter until her ribs ached. The Mater laughed too. The pair of them rolled about in agonies of mirth, and when they had got it out of their systems, the Mater made cocoa with a dash of brandy.

She had taken off her one disintegrating evening dress, and put on her familiar blue dressing gown. Muttonhead had sent it to her ten years before, when he was a subaltern out in India. The sight of it gave Rory a comfortable feeling of home.

"I haven't stayed up this late in ages." The Mater sat down on the hearth rug next to Rory.

"You deserve some fun, Mater. You've had such an anxious time with Mutt."

"Rory, I'm not a total fool." Her voice was gentle but determined. "I know there's something between you and that man, and I think it's connected to the row you had with Lucius."

Rory sighed, and decided to avoid an interrogation by telling the whole story. She did not leave anything out. The Mater listened attentively, with a skin forming across her cocoa. She twitched with dismay when Rory confessed to the physical side of her relationship with Tom, but did not interrupt.

At the end, she said: "My poor girl, you've been badly hurt. I quite see." Her eyes were soft.

"I couldn't endure Muttonhead thinking of me like that," Rory said. "He looked at me as if he despised me—as if I was dirt. I knew he could never like me in the same way again. I've never seen him so furious."

"But of course he was furious!" the Mater exclaimed, with a sudden burst of energy. "Do you honestly mean to tell me you don't know why?"

Rory was taken aback. "No—"

Lady Oughterard sighed heavily. "Probably just as well. But nobody would think you had eyes in your head at all. Stone-blind!"

Three

Jenny had never been so tired in her life. It was a relentless, dragging tiredness that seeped into the marrow of her bones. She was tired in the dark December mornings, when she got up at a quarter to six and attempted to wash in a jug of cold water. She was tired on the tram to the hospital, tired when she fell into her bed in the VAD hostel at ten. Her red, chapped hands looked as if they had lived for a thousand years—they had certainly scrubbed a thousand miles of floor. Her feet were swollen and throbbing as a matter of course, and putting on her shoes was a daily torture. All the VADs were martyrs to their feet after a few days of dashing around the wards—the common room at the hostel was a wailing wall of lamentations.

Today Jenny's chilblains were giving her hell, but she was so angry she almost forgot the discomfort. She strode toward the sink room with her tray of soiled dressings, loathing Sister Bacon with all her heart and soul. Bacon (known as "the Sow") was a professional nurse who deeply resented the untrained VADs, and never missed an opportunity to humiliate them. She had just shouted at Jenny for daring to express an opinion about one of the patients: "I am not interested in the thoughts of lady amateurs and do-gooders. Try to remember that you are only here to assist the qualified staff."

It had been Jenny's bad luck to end up with Bacon. She had a particular hatred of the prettier VADs, and was convinced they had volunteered solely to flirt with officers. "You will not be assigned to the officers' huts in the grounds," she had told Jenny on her first day at the hospital. "This is not a marriage bureau." As if, Jenny thought, anyone would have the energy or inclination to flirt with a man when the contents of his bedpans were at least as familiar as his face.

Out in the corridor, she took a few steadying breaths. What a day she was having. A convoy of wounded had arrived the previous night, and the number of beds in the surgical ward had doubled. Sister Bacon was in a frantic temper, and to cap it all, there had been that awful letter from Edinburgh. Jenny had no idea how to reply, and solving the problem would probably destroy the whole of her precious afternoon break.

In the sink room she found Gladys Melrose in floods of tears.

"Oh, Dalgleish! Don't tell on me!"

Jenny tipped the dressings into the pail for the incinerator. "What are you doing here? Shouldn't you be on your ward?"

Gladys, who looked like a haddock gasping on a slab, had been risked on an officers' ward. Her damp, adenoidal presence was unlikely to arouse any dangerous matrimonial tendencies in the patients.

"I wish I was dead—I do, really!"

"Don't be silly."

"I can't bear any more of it! I upset the tea trolley during prayers, and Sister said I was clumsy in front of everyone, and I'm so tired, and nobody's nice to me—the broken rib cage in bed six calls me 'HF' and I found out it stands for 'Horse-Frightener'—and it's Christmas, and I've never been away from home before—"

Jenny listened to this litany of woes with rising impatience. When Gladys paused to draw a soggy breath, she said: "Do dry up, Melrose, for heaven's sake. It's just one of those days. We're all having one. The longer you hide in here, the worse hot water you'll get into. You'd better get back and eat humble pie."

Gladys blew her nose. "I'd give anything to go home, but I've gone and signed the contract now—six whole months! Have you signed yet?"

"No." Jenny did not wish to think about her contract. "My probation isn't up till the end of the week."

"Lucky beggar! Oh, Dalgleish, I never should have come here! Mother warned me—"

Jenny was already halfway out of the room. "I'm sorry, but your mother is the least of my worries."

Sister Bacon liked a silent, sterile ward, with all patients lying rigidly to attention, and nurses gliding about on velvet feet. Today, with the beds crammed together cheek by jowl, the gramophone going full blast and the new patients groaning, this ideal was impossible. It did not stop her trying.

"Nurse! Fix that bedspread! Nurse! Tidy those screens! Take away that dirty cup. Rearrange that dressing tray this instant!" The moment Jenny appeared, she shouted: "Dalgleish, build up that fire!"

Jenny shoveled more coal into the huge grate, ignoring the complaints of the man in the nearest bed:

"Have a heart, Nurse—I'm roasting!"

"Nurse!" someone else called. "Be a dear, Nurse, and change the record. We're fed up with bloomin' carols."

"The First Noel" was mooing to a halt on the gramophone. Jenny wound up the machine, and put on "Where My Caravan Has Rested."

"The nurse is not your dear, Corporal," Sister Bacon said. "Dalgleish, I want you. It's time for number eight's irrigation."

"Yes, Sister." Jenny helped her pull the screens around number eight's bed. He was a middle-aged sergeant with a gangrenous leg, and his dressings were Jenny's lowest point of the day. The disgusting smell curdled her stomach, and the only way she could endure the sight of the suppurating green and scarlet wound was to remind herself how much worse it was for him. Besides, it was a matter of pride not to show squeamishness in front of Bacon.

Number eight moaned piteously when he saw them. "Not again, for the love of God—"

"We'll be as quick as we can," Sister Bacon said. "Don't moon around, Nurse. Take off the bandage, and hold his leg steady."

The wound was wrapped in a waterproof cover, to hold in moisture. Every two hours, the rubber tubes sticking out of it had to be injected with a saline solution, and the dressings changed. Jenny saw the gray-white bone, and prickled all over—but the man's leg was easier to bear than his face. All the soldiers made heroic efforts not to cry in front of the nurses. Number eight clenched his jaw until the veins stood out in his neck.

"Steady, I said! Really, Nurse—"

Jenny tightened her grip, feeling she would scream if Bacon sniped at her once more. Normally, she pretended to be deaf, but her mother's letter had pierced her skin. Mrs. Dalgleish had had enough of "procrastination and shillyshallying." She did not approve of gentlewomen slaving in hospitals—everyone knew that nurses, as a class, could not be called ladies. The experience was bound to coarsen them. Furthermore, Mrs. Dalgleish and her husband had been under the impression that Jenny was engaged to be married. What was Alistair playing at? This was her ultimatum: Jenny must either get married immediately or return to Scotland.

Jenny had been a perfect daughter for so long that she was unprepared for the surge of rebellion this letter awakened in her. It was true, she and Alistair were no nearer the church door. But Jenny was not ready to be married yet. Why should she immure herself in marriage when there was so much to be done, and so much life to be lived?

As for going home—well, it would be lovely to sleep in a soft bed for as long as she liked; and to be waited on by the maid instead of washing up all day. Hospital life was far harder than she had expected, and part of her was tempted by an excuse to give it up.

As soon as she pictured herself in Edinburgh, however, Jenny felt suffocated. She would be expected to join her mother's knitting circle, and help her father with parish correspondence. No—she had grown out of that dutiful mold, and it was too late to squeeze herself back into it. Her mother would have to understand that she had other duties now.

"Dalgleish, pass me that kidney dish, and stop woolgathering! Dear me, the energy I waste, pulling you girls into line!"

"Sorry, Sister." Even as she mentally cursed Sister Bacon, Jenny realized, with a stab of surprise, that she could never give up her work here. How could she have considered it? Yes, it was hateful and exhausting. But no matter what Bacon said, she knew it satisfied something in her that nothing else could reach.

When the dressing was finished, number eight suddenly caught Jenny's wrist, and whispered: "Don't you mind her, love. You're a game little lass, and the best nurse of the lot, for my money."

Jenny's tiredness and depression lifted like a black cloak. What other job in the world had such rewards? Now, she knew exactly what she would write in the letter to her mother. This, for better or worse, was where she truly belonged.

The ward was quiet over Christmas, and Jenny was given a day's leave. She changed her uniform for her gray suit and pale green crepe-de-chine blouse, and went to eat her Christmas lunch at the MacIntyres'. Alistair had been dropping hints about an "extra special" present, and as she rang the bell of the house in Hyde Park Gate, she found herself hoping it would not be a date for the wedding.

What was happening to her lately? She hardly recognized herself sometimes. Only a short while ago, her sapphire and diamond ring had been her most important achievement. She had found it easy to submerge her own desires for the sake of a secure future—to be "sensible." Yet more and more, she found herself tormented by stubborn desires that were the reverse of sensible. Naturally, it was important to make a good impression on Alistair's family, and a coup to be invited for Christmas. But if only she could have accepted Mr. Russell's invitation instead. Wistfully, she thought of Rory, Tertius and Q, and dear old Lady Oughterard, wearing their funny hats and pulling crackers, with no Mrs. MacNeil sitting there, like a Banquo in shawls, to spoil everything.

She felt ashamed of herself when Effie and Inkerman rushed out into the hall to meet her. Effie's childish face glowed with an affection that was irresistible.

"Merry Christmas, Jenny darling—oh, you angel, to get a day off. Look at the sweet gold bracelet Alistair gave me this morning—Inky, stop it! Down!"

Jenny handed her parcels to the footman, to put under the tree, and went to join the family in the drawing room. Cornelia's husband, Hamish MacIntyre, had just been commissioned as an officer in the Black Watch. He was a tall, egg-shaped man, with sparse red hair, and he wore his new uniform with self-conscious pride. His eldest son, Donald, was also in uniform. He had left Dartmouth, and was now a midshipman, due to join his ship in January. Donald was only seventeen, and seeing him romping with his two schoolboy brothers, Willie and Hugh, Jenny felt a twinge of sympathy for Cornelia.

"Where's our presents? We want them now!" Meggy and

Peterkin, their mouths already smeared with chocolate, were pawing her skirts with sticky hands.

"Rude little blighters," Alistair said. "Pipe down." He kissed Jenny's cheek, whispering: "Merry Christmas, dearest."

"Hello, Alistair." Jenny was glad to note that she felt fond of him. He couldn't bother her too much with his wet tongue in such a full house.

Mrs. MacNeil was enthroned by the fire, wrapped in fewer shawls than usual. She extended her hand to Jenny, with surprising tolerance, if not courtesy. "Miss Dalgleish. So glad you could come."

"Happy Christmas, Mrs. MacNeil."

"Happy! Well, we shall see. Cornelia, can't you keep these children under control? What has Peter got in his mouth?"

"Don't annoy Granny, darlings," Cornelia said. She looked harassed. "And no more chocolate, Peterkin. Not till after luncheon. Donald—stop playing with that dirk. Someone will get hurt."

Jenny laughed. "Poor Cornelia, cumbered with many cares. I shouldn't have given you an extra head to worry about."

"Oh, you're no trouble. Honestly, it's a relief to have a sane person to talk to. The children have been behaving like barbary apes since dawn."

Cornelia seemed to have forgotten that she had ever opposed her brother's engagement. She had searched her heart, and found she preferred Alistair to her mother. Now she was a staunch ally, and Jenny's gratitude had warmed into genuine liking.

"Donald looks well in his uniform," she said.

"Doesn't he?" Cornelia glowed, then her forehead wrinkled anxiously. "He's awfully young. Just a baby, really. Hamish says I fuss too much."

Jenny squeezed her hand. "I dare say you do. The navy's probably the safest place to be at the moment."

Alistair put his arm around Jenny's waist, and said: "I'm a selfish hound today. You're my Christmas present, and I'm not going to share you with anyone."

Jenny glanced toward Mrs. MacNeil. Alistair's demonstrations of affection usually brought on her palpitations. Today, possibly as a concession to the season, she was ostentatiously pretending not to notice. By her standards, she was in a remarkably benign mood.

Alistair drew Jenny aside. "Sweetheart, you're tired."

"I was up till all hours decorating the ward and singing carols."

Gravely, tenderly, he scanned her face. "I don't like it, Jenny. They're simply taking advantage of you, working you to death for a few pounds a year—but I'll spare you the arguments. You know how I feel."

"We've been through it so many times. I can't sit around sewing a fine seam when they need me."

"I know." Something was chafing at his sense of honor—Jenny knew the signs. "I must talk to you," he said. "I'd like to give you your present in private."

"All right."

She allowed him to lead her into the dining room, where the big table was laid for luncheon, gleaming with silver and bristling with holly. Was he about to put a date to the end of her freedom? In theory, this would be the triumph of all her plans, the key to her happiness. In practice, the prospect filled her with panic. But she kept her head and let him speak first.

She was taken aback when he put a flat leather case into her hand. She opened it, and gasped out: "Oh, Alistair—no!"

It was a diamond necklace, fine as a cobweb. The stones trapped the light like drops of dew.

"Do you like it?"

She was appalled. "It's beautiful. You shouldn't—"

Alistair's lined face was full of tenderness. "I ought to have given it to you months ago. You see—well, it was meant to be your wedding present."

"I don't understand."

"Jenny, when I think of the way I've treated you, and how patient you've been, I utterly despise myself—no, don't say anything. I wanted you to have the necklace now, as a pledge that I love you more than ever—that from the moment I saw you, you've been the center of all my hopes and dreams. My feelings can never change. But the world has changed." His neck was red, and his eyes brimmed. "Which is why we'll have to wait a little longer. I—I've enlisted."

Amazed by the force of her relief, Jenny could only say: "Oh."

"I had to do it. Everywhere I go, I see those recruiting posters"—he laughed shortly—"you know, 'Thirty-nine last birthday, and sound as a bell'—"

"But Alistair, it was splendid of you!" Jenny exclaimed in a rush of warmth for him. "You surely didn't think I'd be against it?"

"I wanted to marry you at once so that we could have a little time together before I join my regiment. To tell the truth, I'd set my heart on it."

He was both grieved and crestfallen. Jenny felt the familiar charge of resentment as she recognized the influence he was under. "But of course, your mother wouldn't hear of it."

"No."

Her pride was smarting, and she did not care how hard she sounded. "She'd rather give you to the army than to me."

"Jenny—oh God, she was so dreadfully ill when I told her!"

"She didn't look the least ill to me just now. In fact, she seems remarkably well. Another reprieve—that's the best Christmas present she could have, isn't it?"

"Don't. Please." He was wretched.

Jenny relented. "I'm sorry. I know you're right. I mustn't criticize you for sacrificing your own wishes."

"My darling!" He took her in his arms and cupped his hand gently around her head. "I sacrificed your wishes too. If you refused to wait for me any longer, I'd understand. I wouldn't blame you."

Jenny was very still. He was giving her a chance to undo her promise. A sudden, perverse longing to be free beat inside her like a trapped bird. But the force of his misery and yearning was too great for her to bear. She could not hurt him without hating herself forever.

"I'll wait for you," she said, "until the end of time."

As if she had uttered a spell, Alistair's anguish dissolved. His arms tightened around her and he buried his lips in her neck. "Jenny Dalgleish," he murmured, "I'll need another hundred years of life to make myself worthy of you."

Jenny was suddenly cold. She clung to him fearfully, trying to fight off an oppressive sense of foreboding. For a fraction of a second she tasted the cup of the future, and found it full of sorrow.

Four

Eleanor caressed the cream silk and lace dressing gown Lorenzo had sent for her birthday so many months before, as if its cool folds could ward off the pain that tore into her spine. The Harrods van had brought it to the door, with an impersonal note stating that it had been charged to the account of Sir L. Hastings. She had never worn it—even then, she had been too stout—but it was the only gift she had ever received from her husband. At Christmas, he had sent a laconic few lines, hoping she was well. It was now February, and she had heard nothing from him since.

The loneliness she had endured in her marriage was worse than any amount of pain. It wasn't that she was physically alone. Francesca, Jenny and Rory had been endlessly kind. Her cook and maid, somehow scenting the misfortune at the heart of Lady Hastings's household, treated her with the gentlest consideration. She was surrounded by a guard of devoted women. But Lorenzo's neglect lay across her world like a great frozen continent.

Lately, she had begun to hunger for the baby. He had danced and kicked under her heart, awakening a hope that he might be a substitute Lorenzo, who would accept the love his father scorned. He was to be called Laurence, and he was to be exactly like his father—the obstreperous personality of the alien creature squirming in her womb had convinced Eleanor of this. A new, reborn Laurence Hastings, to redeem the past.

Everyone accepted the child was a boy. The cook, Mrs. Bintry, a widow with a grown-up son in the police force, said it was a boy for certain. "It's the kicking, ma'am. You can always tell. I was black and blue when I was carrying." Lady Oughterard, visiting with Rory the previous week, had taken one look at Eleanor's stomach, and said: "I hope your bassinet's blue, my dear. Look at the way he's lying—

just the same with my three. The poor old Pater got it into his head that Tertius would be a girl, but I knew."

Being surrounded by women meant enduring a great deal of advice. The unborn bulge had acted as a kind of magnet, drawing yet more females into Eleanor's circle. Mrs. MacIntyre had called, to deliver a monologue about Peterkin's colic. Mrs. Carr-Lyon had told her to breast-feed for at least six months. Monica Templeton had told her not to breast-feed at all—"because they either lose their shape, darling, or they disappear." Eleanor listened, knowing privately that the infant Lorenzo inside her would do exactly as he pleased.

She gasped aloud, and Lorenzo's gift slipped from her hand to the floor. Her waters were breaking. The monthly nurse had warned her about this, but she was unprepared for the violence of the flood. The silk dressing gown lay in the spreading puddle of fluid, and she could not bend to pick it up.

When the nurse came, she said cheerfully: "So he's on his way at last. You are a silly girl not to call me earlier. Let's get you into bed, and I'll telephone the doctor."

"Well, she's started," Mrs. Bintry told the house-parlor maid in the kitchen. "Poor little dear, all alone at a time like this. Honestly, Ethel, I know her husband's in the army and all, but it don't seem natural. Not so much as a word for weeks, and there she is crying her eyes out because she's ruined that dressing gown he sent her."

Eleanor spent the next twelve hours in a delirium of agony, at the mercy of her body's vicious demands. She had not imagined pain like this, and could only lie passive while all her defenses were battered from within. The baby was a monster, so ravenous for life that he was ready to kill her. At last, when the lamps were lit, and the streets outside were silent, Lorenzo's child was hauled out into the world.

Eleanor lay back, limp and gasping, while the nurse washed away the bloody mess between her thighs. Distantly, she was aware of the doctor clearing the baby's mouth with his finger. He gave it a light slap on the leg. The little gray-blue creature flushed angry scarlet, and let out its first breath in a piercing wail of outrage. Eleanor only felt a mixture of resentment, because he had made her suffer, and relief that the suffering was over.

The room was full of women. Rory and Francesca had been waiting in the drawing room, protected from the obscene mysteries of birth. Mrs. Bintry and Ethel crowded in behind them.

"Oh, the precious!" breathed Francesca, her eyes alight. "The angel!"

Rory whispered, "Ugh! Isn't it hideous?"

"Shhh! They all look like that, don't they, Nurse?"

The nurse had wrapped the screeching infant in a towel. She bent down toward Eleanor, and said in a hectoring voice: "Come along now, Lady Hastings. It's all over, and you've got a lovely little girl."

"Girl?" Eleanor echoed dully. This was not right. There had been a mistake. Lorenzo would not want a girl—he would never love her if she had failed to produce his son.

"Yes, dear. And what nice strong lungs she's got!" She laid the baby in the crook of Eleanor's arm. "Don't you want to look at her?"

No, she did not. She wanted to sleep for a hundred years. She had not been through all this just to get a girl. But she turned her head. The baby's squashed face, still slimed and waxy, was inches away from her own. Her mouth was stretched in an O of indignation, her tongue vibrated like the clapper of a bell. Her tiny, perfect fists punched the air, and Eleanor felt the little body tensing with the force of each furious scream.

Love crashed over her in an ecstatic wave, sweeping away all the frozen loneliness of the past nine months. The baby was beautiful, extraordinary; a stranger she already knew better than any person living. She was enslaved, awestruck, aching to soothe her daughter's rage. Gently, she pressed her lips to the wet tufts of hair that clung to the baby's purple skull, and murmured: "Laura."

Francesca stood in the doorway for a moment, watching Mrs. Braddon. She had asked not to be announced, and Sharp—guessing why she had come—had nodded her toward the morning room, whispering: "Is everything all right, Miss Garland?"

"Yes. It's a girl, and they're both well."

"Thank you, miss. I'll tell everyone downstairs."

It was Mrs. Braddon's business hour. She was scribbling away at her inlaid desk, too absorbed to realize she was not alone. She looked older, Francesca thought. Or perhaps it was only because she had not seen her since Eleanor's marriage. She had hated taking sides. Mrs. Braddon had been so good to her. More than good—she had been a rock of constancy, ever since the day Francesca had first crept into her house, the nestless waif from Eleanor's school. Of course, Francesca had had to choose Eleanor. But the familiar sight of Mrs. Braddon at her desk brought out a pang of the old, dependent affection.

"Aunt Sybil—"

Mrs. Braddon started, and cried out "Francesca!" with unguarded yearning. She recovered herself at once, however, and stood up regally. "I wasn't expecting you."

Francesca hung her head. She did not know how to begin.

"Are you well?"

"Yes."

"I'm glad." Mrs. Braddon's spine stiffened. Her lips tightened stubbornly. She was not going to help Francesca, though she must have known the reason for her visit. Only her quick, shallow breathing betrayed her agitation.

"I—I've come about Eleanor," Francesca blurted out. "She doesn't know I'm here, but I couldn't bear you not knowing."

There was a silence. The gold locket on Mrs. Braddon's breast rose and fell rapidly. "Well?" she said.

"She had her baby last night—a baby girl. The doctor says she's recovering beautifully. She's very happy."

"And is the child—is it healthy?"

"She's perfect."

"I see."

"Please, Aunt Sybil, I wish you'd visit her—"

"It's out of the question." Mrs. Braddon sat down at her desk again, and picked up her pen. "I guessed there would be something of this·sort once the child was born. As if the actual presence of a baby might soften my brain. Of course, I'm glad it has ended well. But nothing has changed. Eleanor is not to imagine any connection between her daughter and Viola's. This child has nothing whatever to do with my family."

Halfway through this speech, Francesca had begun to sob. She stood in the middle of the room, hugging her sealskin muff and weeping, while Mrs. Braddon pointedly turned her attention back to her letter.

"Can't you forgive her now?"

"Don't make me angry, Francesca." She refused to look up. "You mean well, but you're too much of a child to understand. If you had a shred of sense, you'd see it goes far beyond anything that can be forgiven. Eleanor deliberately betrayed us. She knew exactly what she was doing when she disgraced herself with that man. And that is all I have to say on the subject."

She was iron and steel, armored in pride. No power on earth would move her. Francesca's stomach chilled with fear. Aunt Sybil had been one of the few people she had trusted, and she could not bear the sensation of being beyond her love. Her first impulse was to beg at her feet: please don't hate me, too. Let me be your little girl again.

But being a little girl meant never judging your elders, and Francesca knew Aunt Sybil was wrong. For the first time in her life, she dared to weigh a figure of authority in the balance, and find it wanting. Unconsciously, she realized, she had been assuming that the woman must have some kind of justice on her side—not to do so would have meant doubting the very foundations of her world. And because of this, she had allowed a shadow to fall across her love for Eleanor. Hadn't she assumed, deep down, that poor Eleanor had done something wicked, when her only crime had been to love too much, and the only person injured was herself? Francesca's self-reproach—and the amazing discovery that the sky did not fall down when she dared to condemn the mighty Mrs. Braddon—gave her courage.

"Eleanor hasn't disgraced herself," she said. "She's married now, and she's the mother of a lovely little daughter. You—you should be proud of her!"

The pen trembled in Mrs. Braddon's hand, but she remained in obdurate profile, glaring at the paper on her blotter.

"Aunt Sybil, you've been awfully kind to me, and I'm ever so grateful. But if you won't forgive Eleanor, I can't forgive you."

Mrs. Braddon jerked up her head angrily. "I won't be held to ransom, Francesca. You know perfectly well I've loved you as if you were my own child. But I don't love you enough to contaminate my family with that man's blood." She let out a short, bitter laugh. "And if Eleanor really is so happy, she doesn't need me."

Five

When one was bidden to a military wedding at a few days' notice, it was good manners to pretend it had been planned for ages, and to turn a blind eye to recycled hats and visible tacking on the bridesmaids' gowns. People no longer spoke of the war being over in a few weeks. Neither did they voice the fear that the only real advances were being made in the columns of *The Times,* where the lists of casualties seemed to grow longer every day. Wedding speeches contained the usual prescriptions for long life and domestic bliss—it would have been bad taste to mention a young bride's true destiny of partings on station platforms, gnawing loneliness, and a neurotic dread of telegrams.

But the knowledge lurked behind the gaiety, a canker at the heart of the orange blossom. It was this that made Rory and Jenny so anxious to find good omens in the smallest details.

"A really perfect spring day," Jenny said, admiring the delicate blue sky for the umpteenth time that morning. "The first we've had this year without a single cloud to spoil it—so lucky."

Rory agreed, privately thinking that Francesca and Stevie needed all the luck they could lay their hands on. The wedding had been arranged in a furious hurry, when Stevie got embarkation leave. Within a week, he would be in France.

"I do feel an idiot in this frock," she said.

Jenny laughed. "Nonsense, you look lovely. Poor Tertius can't take his eyes off you."

"Well, I've trussed myself up in stays and gloves for Francesca's sake, not his. The little darling, I'd do anything to make her happy today."

They were waiting outside St. James's, Piccadilly, in their bridesmaids' dresses of pale yellow silk, and huge hats of blond straw trimmed with white ribbon. The outfit gave

Rory's tall figure a willowy elegance, when she remembered not to stand with her hands on her hips or fan herself with her bouquet.

Jenny was worried. "I do wish Eleanor would hurry up. What's keeping her? Everybody else is here."

Inside the church, the flower-decked pews were thronged with fashionable millinery. Hilary Twisden, in his new officer's uniform, and Aubrey Russell, in morning dress, were acting as ushers. Windrush had appeared, unrecognizably tidy in his blue Red Cross uniform, on leave from his American Ambulance Unit in Belgium. Dinah Curran and Cecil Scott had arrived, in a high state of new gloves and white corsages.

Tertius, Quince and Fingal had come early, to bag a good place for Muttonhead's wheelchair. His shattered leg, encased in plaster, lay rigid in a special trough attached to the chair, and got in everyone's way. Francesca, who was never afraid of men when they were ill, had visited Muttonhead in the hospital several times. He had grown fond of her, and insisted upon seeing her married. Everyone wanted to see the wedding, as if the youth and beauty of the couple contained magical properties that could ward off sorrow.

Even Viola Fenborough had turned up, though it meant she would have to acknowledge her sister, and they had not spoken for months. Gus, stout and rubicund in his staff officer's uniform, was making up for her haughty silence by cracking loud jokes.

Rory and Jenny had not seen Eleanor since Lorenzo had arrived home on leave. He had initially booked himself into Brown's Hotel in Dover Street but, under pressure from Stevie, had agreed to move in with his wife and baby daughter. Rory was desperate to know how they were getting on. She could not imagine Lorenzo as part of a family.

"Thank goodness!" Jenny exclaimed. "Here they are."

A taxi had drawn up at the curb, and Lorenzo was helping Eleanor out.

"Ye gods!" Rory said. "What's she done to herself?"

Eleanor's left arm was strapped up in a sling. She wore a hat with a thick veil, and when she drew it back to greet her friends, they both gasped with horror. This was not a good omen at all. Her face was grotesquely swollen, dragged out of shape by puffy green and black bruises across the cheek and jaw.

Her eyes, however, were alight with happiness. Eleanor had always been transparent, and there was no mistaking her radiant joy. There was no mistaking the reason for it, either. Her good arm was twined around Lorenzo's, and he held her hand protectively. Outwardly, he was as stiff and sour as ever, but he caressed her gloved fingers with a kind of casual physical familiarity. Rory instantly divined that they were sleeping together.

Eleanor was laughing at their shocked faces. "I know— don't I look awful? Lorenzo wanted me to stay at home with Laura, but I couldn't miss Francesca's wedding."

"What happened?" Jenny asked.

Eleanor glanced up at Lorenzo. "We were motoring to Maidenhead, and we ran into a ditch when a tire burst. Lorenzo wasn't hurt at all, but you know my talent for calamity."

Lorenzo smiled at her, almost tenderly. "Come on, let's get inside, so I can hide my fright of a wife behind a pillar."

As he led her into the porch, his arm circled her waist.

Jenny began: "Well, whoever would have thought—"

There was no time to discuss this unexpected improvement in Eleanor's marriage. The Templeton Rolls-Royce had arrived, and was disgorging Archie and Francesca.

Rory, not normally sentimental about weddings, had to swallow several times so that she would not cry. Francesca looked adorable. Her dress was white silk-satin, fine as spun sugar, and her brown eyes shone through a mist of white lace. She was very nervous, but bore herself with a new dignity that lent special grace to her fragile beauty.

Jenny and Rory kissed her, and fell into step behind her as they proceeded into the church. The organist struck up the wedding march, and the congregation rose. Stevie waited in the aisle, his hand resting on the hilt of his sword. A watery ray of sunlight fell across his shoulder, turning his Lieutenant's pips into discs of molten gold.

Handkerchiefs fluttered all over the nave as this handsome young soldier claimed his fairy bride. Marian Carr-Lyon stood sternly to attention, devouring her boy with eyes that burned with pride. Monica Templeton broke into audible sobs when Stevie placed the ring on Francesca's trembling hand.

Please, Rory found herself praying, let them be happy. Make everything all right for them. The sun burst out fulsomely just as the Vicar pronounced them man and wife, and the black clouds of war parted for a moment to reveal something rare and radiant, immune to the ravages of time.

It had not been thought politic to expose the guests to Monica's hospitality in Half Moon Street. The guests made their way through the April sunshine to the Ritz, where Archie had compensated for the social awkwardness with lavish amounts of food and drink. Marian Carr-Lyon had let it be known that she would not stand in a receiving line with Monica, so Francesca and Stevie handed themselves around alongside the trays of champagne.

Rory watched them, leaning on Muttonhead's chair. "Aren't they lovely? Poor things, just look at them clinging to each other as if they were afraid it was all a dream."

Muttonhead tucked his champagne glass into the trough beside his bad leg, and took the pipe from his mouth. "Wouldn't have put you down for a romantic, miss. Is all this giving you ideas?"

"Don't be ridiculous. Marriage is only for girls like Francesca, who can't do anything else. And who would have me, anyway?"

Gus came up to them, holding Viola's elbow. Viola was too dignified to be dragged, but every line of her expressed reluctance.

"Well, Oughterard." He had been at school with Muttonhead. "How's the leg?"

"Nuisance," said Muttonhead.

"That was a fine piece of work you did at Neuve Chappelle. Wish I'd joined up in time to be there."

"Thanks, Fenborough. I like your brass hat." He gestured at Gus's scarlet tabs with his pipe stem.

"Yes, I'm on Rawlinson's staff. I'll put in a word for you, as soon as they let you out of that chair."

"I'm glad to see you looking so well, Lord Oughterard," Viola said.

"Thank you, Mrs. Fenborough."

"And Aurora. What a charming dress."

"Isn't it?" Rory disliked Viola intensely, and knew the feeling was mutual. "I must say, Vi, I wasn't expecting to see you. Francesca must be so pleased."

"Gus made me come," Viola said. "He says I have to start speaking to Eleanor again, if not her ghastly husband."

"Make an effort," Gus urged her. "It's no reason for sisters to quarrel, whatever your mother says."

"All right, but it's extremely embarrassing when she looks such a horror. So typical—she's forever tumbling into things, and out of things, and making herself absurd." Her chill voice became chillier. "And she's monopolizing Tertius. Come on, Gus, I do want to speak to him before we go."

On the other side of the room, Eleanor was cheerfully telling Tertius: "—her eyes are a little darker every day, and I'm sure they're going to be just like Lorenzo's. He says she's hideous and he won't pick her up—but the nurse says lots of men won't hold little babies, and he did buy her an ivory rattle—"

She faltered and looked frightened when Gus brought Viola to her side. Gus, however, was the soul of tact, and neatly folded their reconciliation into a general conversation about babies. Viola, made gracious by the presence of Tertius, ended up sitting down beside her and promising to call at Clarges Street the following week. "And then you must come to me. I want you to see the drawings Tertius has done of Fleur."

Stevie pointed the group out to Francesca. "I take the whole credit. Our wedding has brought everyone good luck." He kissed her lips briefly. "We're so much in love, we can't help spreading sweetness and light."

Over by the buffet table, Monica had pinned down Colonel and Mrs. Carr-Lyon.

"I say, Marian, isn't this a screech? Who on earth would have thought we'd ever be related?" She wore a suit of dove-gray, which fitted her like a skin, and showed her neat ankles. Her large dark eyes were glittering, but the black paint around them had begun to spread. "Of course, I couldn't be happier to have darling Stevie in the family—though I shall find it awfully hard to think of him as a son. You'll have to give me some of his baby pictures so I won't get too carried away."

She held out her glass to a passing waiter. "Or perhaps I should just hang a sign around his neck—'Hands off!' "

Colonel Carr-Lyon chuckled. He thought Monica was an absolute hoot.

His wife was not amused. "We're delighted with Francesca," she said sternly. "Such a charming child, and so eager to please. She'll be staying with us once Stevie goes back to his regiment. It doesn't seem worthwhile to set them up in a house when everything is at sixes and sevens. Naturally, we'll make ourselves scarce on his next leave."

Monica laughed. "Won't that be cozy? You needn't worry that my little girl will give you any trouble. Why, you'll hardly notice Stevie's married at all—I wish I could forget it as easily."

Archie had caught the end of this. He took her arm, none too gently. "I want a word with you."

"Not now, dearest. I'm busy being a proud Mamma."

"Now."

Keeping a tight grip on her, he hustled Monica through the crowd. People stared as they passed. Monica, undaunted, clutched her champagne glass, and blew kisses at her friends. When they were out of the room, Archie pushed her against a potted palm on the deserted landing.

Her face, stripped of its smile, was scornful. "What's the matter with you? I suppose you've been at the spirits again. You smell like a distillery."

"Don't you dare," Archie said, baring his teeth. "Just don't you dare. That kid has had a hard enough life—I won't let you ruin it, do you hear? I don't give a damn who else you fool around with—but if you lay another finger on that boy, so help me, Monica, I'll flay you alive."

When Francesca changed her dress, her mood changed with it. She became deathly pale, and clung to her friends as if imploring them for help. Now, when it was time for everyone to sweep up the confetti and go home, she realized that she belonged to Stevie. It was nobody else's business where he took her, or what he did to her.

In the car, she wore a motoring veil over her hat, and Stevie was, in any case, too busy driving to look at her properly. But when he stopped in a quiet street, to remove the "Just Married" placard from the back bumper, he discovered that she was weeping.

"My darling—what is it?"

"N-nothing!"

An awful sense of helplessness stole over him. His wife
was his responsibility. He could not hand her on to someone else when he did not know what to do with her.
"You're tired," he suggested gently. "We'll be there soon."

"Yes." She tried to smile.

The doubt expressed in the smile wrenched Stevie's
heart. He took her hand, stroking it patiently until she
stopped trying to pull it away. "You mustn't be frightened
of me, you know. I won't eat you."

"I know."

"It's been a long day for you, sweetheart. You'll feel an
awful lot better when we get to the house. And Nanny
Stack will be there to take care of you."

They were spending their honeymoon at a house belonging to the Carr-Lyons in Sussex, which was run by Marian's
old nurse. She had been Stevie's nurse too, and he found
himself comforted by the thought of her. As he drove, he
kept up a stream of cheerful conversation, pointing out
landmarks and telling amusing anecdotes. Francesca relaxed a little, but by the time they reached Calcutta Lodge,
Stevie was exhausted.

Nanny Stack, a spry old lady, despite being bent with
arthritis, was standing in the rose-covered porch to meet
them. The whole of the substantial white cottage was covered with early rosebuds. The smooth lawns around, blue
in the dusk, were scattered with apple blossom. It was a
honeymoon paradise. Stevie bent down to hug Nanny
Stack. Her long-remembered smell of liniment and cough
sweets gave him a sudden, intense longing to be a little boy
in her nursery again, drinking hot milk and watching her
humped shadow on the wall.

"Goodness, Master Stevie, how tall you do grow. And
what a picture you are in that uniform. Mummy must be
as proud as punch."

'Well, Stackie, here she is." He put his arm around Francesca's waist. "Darling, this is the dreaded Nanny Stack,
and if we don't eat our pudding, there'll be hell to pay."

Nanny curtsied. "How do you do, Mrs. Carr-Lyon. And
don't you listen to none of his nonsense. In you come, now.
Supper's all ready by the fire, and then I'll love you and
leave you. The boiler's going, madam, if you want hot
water."

Francesca drew off her gloves, glancing timidly around

at the white-painted paneling, and polished, old-fashioned furniture. She was still nervous, but evidently reassured by Nanny's presence.

Supper was laid out on a card table in the drawing room. Nanny only knew how to make one sort of food. Their first meal as a married couple was a sort of glorified nursery tea of ham, boiled eggs and bread-and-butter pudding with raisins. Nanny, possibly sensing that Francesca was not ready to be left alone, stood beside them while they ate, asking about the wedding and regaling Stevie with obscure bits of family gossip.

At last, she took the plates back to the kitchen, and bade them both goodnight, as if they had been married for ages. Stevie let Francesca go up to bed first, staying to smoke a cigarette beside the dying embers of the fire. His hands were freezing, and his heart was thumping uncomfortably.

He'd never be able to do it. Francesca would think he did not care for her. How was he supposed to get up the courage to touch her? He thought of the times he had kissed her. Never once had he had an erection. He had assumed, he realized, that it would happen automatically once they were married.

He turned out the lights, and in the darkness unbuttoned his fly. His penis was limp and soft. Hating himself, he tried to masturbate. Think of the last time—Monica, on the first night of his leave, taking him into her mouth in the upstairs bathroom at Half Moon Street. It had been horrible. He had closed his eyes, so he would not see her kneeling like a dreadful goblin at his feet, but her fierce sucking had filled his mind with all kinds of illicit filth. For a moment, remembering this, his penis swelled a little.

Then he thought of Francesca, and pulled his hand out of his trousers. He could not defile her with filth. The idea of plunging into her, and turning her sealed opening into a gash like Monica's made him slightly sick. Yet this was his duty. All his life, the necessity for purity and decency—which meant, of course, not frigging or having sexual intercourse—had been drummed into him by his elders. Now, they were all expecting him to be impure and indecent because he had made some vows in a church.

He went upstairs, to the bedroom where his sacrificial lamb was waiting. Francesca had put on a long white nightgown, which covered her from neck to ankle. Her rich

chestnut hair flowed down her back. She looked so beautiful, he could hardly breathe. But was this meant to excite
him into violating her?

She sat on the end of the bed, staring at him. Her eyes
were saucers of terror, yet she seemed to have made a
brave decision to put herself in his hands—she trusted him
and was prepared to yield. Stevie took her awkwardly in
his arms. Being married had not taken away his fear of
hurting her, or breaking her. He kissed her eyes and mouth,
full of the tenderest love for her, but knowing this was
impossible, and possessed by a dreadful loneliness.

"I'm sorry," he said desperately. "I can't—" He began
to cry.

Francesca gazed at him, with a kind of puzzled astonishment that gradually turned into equally puzzled relief.
"Stevie, are you sorry you married me?"

"Oh God, no!" he sobbed. "I adore you, I worship you,
but I can't—"

She drew his head down to her breast, kissing his hair,
and wrapping her arms around him. "Darling, poor darling,
it doesn't matter, as long as you love me."

He did love her. Their happiness was perfect, after all—
white and immaculate, never to be smirched by shame.
Stevie spent his wedding night crying himself to sleep in
his wife's arms.

Stevie's mind lingered on his honeymoon when he returned
to camp on the eve of his battalion's departure for France.
It had been divine—really, love among the roses. After the
awfulness of that first night, he and Francesca had spent a
week in paradise, wandering among the lanes and fields
like Adam and Eve before the fall. Parting with her had
cut him to the heart.

But now that he was back among his men, he felt he
could draw a proper, independent, adult breath for the first
time in ages. What tremendous lads they were, and how he
had missed them. The first sight of Lorenzo's surly face
nearly made him weep with joy.

"Good honeymoon, was it?"

"Rather."

"Lucky devil."

"What about you?"

Lorenzo laughed bitterly. "My delayed honeymoon was

spent in a flat with a screeching infant, a wife with tits like milk jugs, and two of the ugliest female servants that can be got for money."

"Are they well? Eleanor and the baby, I mean?"

"I suppose so. Eleanor made one of her scenes at the station. God, it was embarrassing. Don't paw me about, Stephen—" Irritably, he shrugged Stevie's hand off his shoulder. "Too much affection makes me want to throw up and I've had a bellyful."

Stevie chuckled, not at all offended. He could tell Lorenzo was pleased to see him.

That evening there was a concert in the mess tent. The string quartet who had enlisted straight from the Kardomah entertained the Company with Schubert's "Trout" Quintet, and Lorenzo played the piano part. Stevie watched him, lulled and warmed by the quiet certainty that he was home at last.

Six

Aubrey was seriously annoyed. He had been sitting for one solid hour over a bottle of Burgundy in this obscure French restaurant in Greek Street, and there was still no sign of Tertius.

"It's no use you making excuses for him, Aurora. I'm coming to the end of my patience. He's spent all my cash, and now he's avoiding me because he hasn't done a stroke of work."

"I don't know what's the matter with him," Rory admitted. "It's not like him to miss a free meal."

"He won't get a meal. I shan't feed that ungrateful boy another morsel until he shows me the color of a painting."

Quince was wistfully sniffing a fragrant omelette at the next table. "Not so long ago, I used to wake up in the small hours, and find him daubing away like fury. Nowadays, he doesn't even get up till noon."

"Aubrey, darling, please don't be cross with him," Rory coaxed. "You've been so good to him, he'd never let you down."

"He's a lazy young wastrel." Aubrey was softening. "I might as well have thrown my money into the Thames. God knows, I don't wish to hurry the artistic process, but I've booked space in the gallery and tipped off all the critics—"

"Look, here he is at last," said Quince. "What the bloody hell kept you?"

Tertius, disheveled and smelling of beer, kissed Rory's cheek. "Sorry I'm late," he said cheerfully. "I had some business to settle. Have you eaten yet? I'm starving."

"I've got some business too," Aubrey said. "Where are my canvases?"

"Now, Russell, don't be petty. Times like these call for grandeur of mind and munificence of gesture."

Rory snatched the wine bottle out of his hand. "You really are appalling, Tershie. You keep poor Aubrey hanging about like the smell of gas, and all he's trying to do is arrange your exhibition."

"I'm afraid you'll have to postpone it," Tertius said calmly, taking the bottle back.

"Are you out of your mind?" brayed Quince.

Tertius smiled around at their shocked faces. "I'm taking up a different line of work."

He fished in his pocket, and produced a shilling piece, which he laid carefully on the tablecloth.

"What on earth's that for?" Aubrey demanded.

"The King gave it to me. I've enlisted."

There was a long, appalled silence, during which Tertius knocked back a glass of wine.

Eventually, Rory said: "But you can't have—"

"Oh, indeed, miss, and why not? I suppose you think they wouldn't have me—but the recruiting Sergeant said I was the finest specimen he'd seen all week." He broke into a laugh. "They put down my occupation as 'house-painter.'"

"No, Tershie, you're not serious." Rory's lips had gone white. "You can't be! What'll Mutt say?"

"He'll be all for it, I expect. But it doesn't really matter what he says—I'm Private T. Carey now. I've got to report at the depot tomorrow."

"Well," Aubrey said, "I can't criticize a man for doing his duty. I'd better give you something to eat, after all. Waiter!"

Tertius was in high spirits during the meal, and he gradually infected Quince and Aubrey. Rory, however, could not join in the laughter and drinking. The thought of losing Tertius to the army chilled her to the heart.

Later, when Tertius was walking her home through the dark streets, he said: "Stop sulking, Rory. A lot of girls would be proud of me."

She halted under a streetlamp, and turned to face him. "Don't give me that old nonsense. You don't care about duty, and you're not in the least patriotic. There's something you're not telling me."

He grinned ruefully, not denying it, and Rory felt the hated barrier rising up between them.

"Tershie, don't keep secrets from me—not now."

"I might have had my private reasons." He put his hands on her shoulders. "Perhaps I've got duties at home that I can't manage anymore, and I'm running away from them."

"Who is she?"

His shadowed eyes were tender. "You know you're the only woman I'll ever love. I'm not running away from you."

"You're not getting a kiss out of me."

"Just one, to ease my poor aching heart when it's all covered in khaki—"

"Oh, Tertius, why did you do it?" Rory let him see her tenderness for him. "Everything was going so well for you—"

"Trust me. It's for the best. You're not to worry."

"How can I help worrying?"

"Just remember, I always fall on my feet." He was grave. "I'm idle and conniving and a born coward. I won't get into any danger."

Rory had learned her lesson about parting in anger. She put her arms around him, and held him close. "Don't you dare. I've counted all your fingers and toes, and there'd better not be a single one missing when you get back."

"I promise."

They walked the rest of the way arm in arm, and Rory allowed him to kiss her on the lips when they parted.

For the next few days she was dreadfully depressed. There was a great, gaping hole in London where Tertius should have been, and she took to going around to the studio to be morose with Quince, who was moping like Madame Butterfly.

"I don't half miss him, Rory. It's as quiet as a bloody tomb without him."

A fortnight after his departure, Tertius sent her a letter:

> *Dear Rory,*
> *You've never had less reason to worry about me. Life in the army is as peaceful as a rest-cure, once you get used to shaving every day, and cleaning everything in sight. We sleep in wooden huts, go marching, peel potatoes and tilt at sacks of hay with bayonets, and generally have a rare old time. I am the only Irishman in the Company, so it stands to reason I have been rechristened "Paddy"—but the other lads are good sports.*

*Us private soldiers never have to make a single deci-
sion—they even tell us when to cut our hair and wipe
our noses. We go out and drink beer, while the officers
sit up cramming all night long, and worrying about the
state of our feet. I tell you, Rory-May, I wouldn't be
an officer for the world. The two public school dandies
in my hut have already been whisked away for training.
Luckily, nobody could mistake me for a gentleman.
Give my regards to old Q etc.*

Love and kisses, Tertius.

A drawing fluttered out of the envelope. Rory unfolded
it, and burst out laughing. It was a cartoon of Tertius on a
route march, in his khaki tunic and puttees, with all kinds
of objects falling off his pack into the road. Underneath it,
Tertius had scribbled: *He's an absentminded beggar and his
weaknesses are great ... And he's left a lot of little things
behind him.*

Seven

"If only one could get to Italy," Fingal said. *"Oh, for a beaker full of the warm south.* London is so damp in summer—I'm sure that's all it is." His voice was a wheezing shadow of itself. Listlessly, he drew his silk dressing gown around him, with his spectral, blue-tinged claws. "But this silly war will keep getting in the way. Look what it's done to you, Aurora. Why must they make such guys of you girls?"

Rory had recently joined a VAD Ambulance Unit, ferrying the wounded between Charing Cross Station and various London hospitals, and she had turned up at Fingal's bedside in her new blue serge uniform.

"Wait till you see the hat," she said. "You'll hate that even more." She did her best to speak cheerfully to hide her horror at Fingal's appearance. She had not seen him since Francesca's wedding. In six short weeks, he had become so shockingly white and thin that it was no longer possible to accept his dismissals of his illness. Now Rory was amazed at herself for being able to ignore the evidence of her own eyes for so long. "Fingal, I do wish you'd told me you were stuck here in bed. I'd have come ages ago."

"It wouldn't have been patriotic when you're so busy with the war effort."

"But what about the Mater, and Muttonhead—do they know?"

"Know what?" Fingal challenged crossly. "The Mater can't be spared from the farm, and I'm not whining to Muttonhead when he's only just getting back on his feet."

"I only meant—isn't it fearfully dull for you here, darling?"

Fingal's fleshless face creased into a smile. His eyes rested on Francesca, who was curled on the squashy eiderdown beside him. Rory had been surprised to see her. "I can't possibly be dull when the lovely Mrs. Carr-Lyon comes to cheer my pillow every day."

Francesca stroked his hand with a tenderness that made her childish face very lovely. "I do have such fun here," she said. "It's so much nicer than Stevie's mother's War Orphans' Committee."

She did not seem at all affected by Fingal's blue lips and shallow, panting breathing. Rory wondered if she had even noticed. Francesca was a great one for never looking beyond what she was told.

"I brought you some lilies of the valley," she was saying. "Aubrey's putting them in water now. And a lovely little jar of quails' eggs from Fortnum's. You said you thought you could eat them."

"What a thoughtful creature you are," Fingal croaked. "You see, Rory, how spoiled I'm getting?"

Aubrey came into the room, carrying a bottle of champagne and four glasses. "Time for your medicine, dear one, and I think we'll all join you."

Rory watched him narrowly as he adjusted Fingal's pillows. He was brisk and breezy, but his smile did not extend to his eyes.

"I mustn't!" Francesca was laughing. "You'll send me home tipsy and then what will Stevie's mother say?"

"She'll suspect you've been corrupted," Rory said. "And she'll be perfectly right."

It was a dismal stab at levity, but Fingal chuckled, and a look of gratitude briefly crossed Aubrey's blank eyes. He opened the champagne and gave them each a glass. Fingal took one small sip, then sighed fretfully as if the effort had been too much for him. Without comment, Francesca took the glass from his hand.

"I was telling the girls," Fingal said, "how we're pining for Italy."

Aubrey sighed. "Yes, I'm thinking of writing a stiff letter to the Kaiser—doesn't he think it's high time he stopped all this nonsense and put Europe back where he found it?"

"We discovered the perfect villa, too," Fingal said. "A paradise in Rapallo, my dears, fragrant with roses, and with the most divine young serving boy—an absolute Ganymede. He was a very tiger for guarding his virtue, but I mean to conquer him next time."

"You probably won't want to by then," said Aubrey. "He'll be a great lout with a mustache."

"Well, never mind. It'll be enough to smell the wild thyme and watch the lizards scuttling across the terrace. And to bask in the broiling sun. One so yearns to be really warm."

"Soon, dear boy, I promise." Aubrey suddenly put down his glass and left the room. "I forgot Francesca's flowers," he said over his shoulder. "They smell too heavenly."

Fingal stared after him for a moment with a fleeting expression of wounded sadness, which Rory had never seen before. Then he smiled again. "I say, Rory, isn't it splendid about Muttonhead?"

She seized the subject gladly. "Rather. Did they tell you, Francesca? He's landed a plum posting to Haig's staff. He'll sit behind a desk in a French château, airing his scarlet tabs and eating off solid gold plates, I dare say."

"Poor Muttonhead, he deserves it after that horrid wound," Francesca said. "I don't know how he could have been so brave. Would you like some more champagne now, Fingal?"

"All right."

"And perhaps you'd try some of those dear little quails' eggs, to please me?"

Fingal laughed scratchily. "I believe I'd eat the park railings to please you."

"I'll fetch them," Rory said. She wanted to know what was keeping Aubrey.

She found him leaning against the drawing room mantelpiece, under the violent Bomberg abstract. He had his back to her, and his head was bowed, as if in deep thought. In one hand, he held a crystal vase of lilies of the valley, white and waxen among their dark green leaves. Their scent filled the whole room, and intensified the atmosphere of stillness.

Rory held her breath, feeling that it would be intrusive and somehow vulgar to disturb him.

He let out a dry, suppressed sob. The convulsion slopped a splash of water out of the vase. She found the courage to move toward him, and gently put her hand on his arm.

"Aubrey—"

Slowly he raised his face. It was glistening with tears. "You see it, don't you?".

Of course she saw it. Finally, she let go of the last absurd hope, and her lingering fear turned into hard reality. She could only nod dumbly.

Aubrey pulled out a scented silk handkerchief, and hastily mopped at his swimming, bloodshot eyes. "I didn't tell you because he wouldn't let me. It's been breaking my heart by inches and I'm almost glad we can't pretend anymore. He's dying—and quickly, too. He knows as well as I do that he'll never go back to Italy. Oh God, I'm sorry. He gets furious when I cry—" His thin lips worked convulsively and he sobbed out: "Help me, Rory. How shall I live without him?"

Aubrey did not allow his emotions to run away with him again. Fingal, stubborn to the last, was facing death with a tremendous show of defiance. Though the consumption was galloping into its final stages, though he coughed gouts of scarlet, foaming blood and fought for every breath, he regarded any reference to illness as an insult.

This made visiting him a trial. Rory came as often as she could, but was almost driven mad by the effort of hiding her feelings. Fingal watched her beadily, and lashed her with a tongue of acid when she showed signs of sorrow or pity.

"Go away," he would say. "Your viperous ugliness depresses me, and I'm not a bit amused by your so-called cleverness. You never were as smart as you thought, in any case." When they were children, he had been jealous of the affection the Mater had lavished upon Rory. This old grievance, buried for years, was suddenly fresh again, and he seemed determined to punish her for it. "Why do you bother coming, anyway? You're not related to me. I'm far too tired to keep up this sentimental fiction that you're my sister. I never had a sister and I never wanted one."

Rory hadn't the heart to strike back at him and that was worst of all. He was going out on a tide of bile, but she sensed the dreadful fear that lay underneath.

Fingal was often unkind to Aubrey, too. "What a time I might have had if I hadn't holed myself up with the oldest pansy in the border. It suits you, doesn't it, to have me chained to this bed? You always wanted me to be your prisoner. I hope you're satisfied now."

Aubrey had aged ten years in as many weeks. He nursed Fingal with unfailing kindness, sleeping on a couch at the foot of his bed and never showing when the shafts had hit their target.

"He isn't always like this," he assured Rory, after one particularly vicious onslaught. "When he snipes at me, I feel like the Spartan Boy, my dear—keeping my countenance while the fox tears my heart out underneath my shirt. But he does love me, you know. Sometimes, in the night, he begs me not to leave him and tells me what I've meant to him. And then I feel I can bear anything."

Only Francesca possessed the knack of drawing out Fingal's sting. She continued to call every day, spending long hours with him when he had driven everyone else away. Alone with Francesca, Fingal was gentle and calm. Aubrey and Rory puzzled over the relationship, failing to see that Fingal needed Francesca because she needed him. She had fallen into the habit of confiding in him and this had become an addiction. She had never opened herself so completely to anyone.

It was Fingal she told about the invisible strains in her relationship with Marian Carr-Lyon—her sense that Marian treated her as an addition to her nursery and not as a married woman with rights of her own. Francesca was doing her best to grow up and had no one to help her. Fingal seemed to be the only person who did not have an interest in her remaining a helpless child. He encouraged her in the dangerous game of making judgments and discovering her own opinions.

"Do I tire you?" she asked him one day. "I often feel very selfish when I think how much I've talked about myself."

"You don't tire me, darling. Your troubles are my one remaining link to the real world. Everyone else treats me as if I were already in my grave." He had to pause after this, to catch his breath. Francesca opened her mouth to speak, but he silenced her with a feeble motion of his hand. She recognized that he had something important to say to her. "Francesca, do take hold of life while you have the chance. Don't waste it."

"Am I wasting it?"

"You're not living."

"I have everything I could wish for"—she hesitated—"I think."

"You want a child."

She was surprised. "Do I? How do you know?"

"I listen to you talking about Eleanor's baby and I hear the longing in every word."

"Oh no, I love to play with Laura, but I'd be far too frightened—"

"All the same," he said.

Francesca bowed her head. "She's quite an ugly baby, really—scrawny, with a big nose, and she screams all the time. I would never know what to do with her. But when I hold her and she stares back at me with those weird black eyes, it gives me such a strange feeling —as if I might cry."

"You must have one of your own," Fingal wheezed. "That'll put the Colonel's Lady in her place."

He had hit the bull's-eye. Her eyes were filled with tears. But she shook her head. "I don't think I ever will."

"Why not? You should make some plans for Stevie's next leave."

"Oh, Fingal, I can't," she said wearily. "I don't know how other women can."

He reached for her hand. "Can't what? Tell me, darling."

Francesca took a long moment to consider this, then began carefully, "I mean that I can't do what—what married people are supposed to do. When men kiss you and touch you, you're meant to like it, aren't you? And to want them to go on doing it?"

"That's the general idea."

"Then I'm afraid there's something wrong with me. When men look at me—you know—in that way, it makes me so scared I feel sick. I don't like going to parties, in case I get looked at." She put a peculiar energy into the phrase "looked at," and Fingal understood that she was trying to convey something terrible.

He asked: "What do you think they might do to you?"

"I don't know exactly. Touch me." In a whisper, she added: "Kill me."

"My sweet girl," Fingal said, very gently, "who on earth would want to harm you?"

She made a visible effort to gather up her courage, before blurting out desperately: "It's me. It's my fault. There's something about me that's bad, and makes people do bad things. When I was little, when Mummy ran away with Uncle Archie, my father—my father started to l-l-look at me—how can I say? Not as if he loved me, though he said he did, but angrily. And sort of hungrily." Her words were falling out rapidly now. "I tried very hard to be good. But I obviously wasn't, because I couldn't stop him. He looked at me as if he could see something wicked. And he came and t-t-t-touched me in my bed!" This came out as a quivering cry of outrage. Francesca was not used to raising her voice, and she stopped, appalled at herself, listening to the echo. She finished quietly, and with infinite sadness: "I thought it would be different when I married Stevie. I do love him—I love him more than anyone. I tried so hard to prepare myself and to tell myself I'd be able to bear it when it happened because it was him. But he could see something wrong with me, too."

Unable to speak, they sat hand in hand, listening to the laboring of Fingal's breathing. Eventually, he whispered: "Oh my God, the things men do."

"You mustn't think it's Stevie's fault in the least."

"Dear God. You poor girl."

They fell silent again. Francesca was used to this, knowing Fingal liked to save his breath and retreat into his own inner landscape occasionally. She was always perfectly happy to wait.

"I was thinking," he began.

"Yes?"

"I was remembering how I was sad once because I thought I wasn't normal and would never be happy. I was remembering that awful loneliness and shame, and how you think everyone else must be able to guess."

"It's a thing that nobody talks about, that's very rude to mention," Francesca said, "but it's a very important thing, isn't it?"

Fingal smiled. "A wonderful thing. I discovered that when I met Aubrey." His voice became firmer. "And so will you, when Stevie comes home."

"Oh no—"

"Don't shake your head, darling. How can you refuse me?"

His eyes glittering feverishly, he shook her hand for emphasis. "My angel, you must learn to take risks, and overcome those terrors of yours. I shall die with a better grace if I know you've made up your mind to live."

Once more, Lady Oughterard made the melancholy journey across the Irish sea, to sit beside the sickbed of one of her children. This time, she had no hope to comfort her. Sorrow bent and bowed her, and further grayed her hair. She could not bear to let Fingal out of her sight, and watched him as if she had reclaimed a lost treasure.

The moment he saw his mother, Fingal let go of his anger and bitterness, and fell into a state of childlike contentment. His rage was spent, and he no longer railed at Aubrey or Rory. When he was not dozing, his greatest pleasure was to mull over the past—the remote past of his childhood at Castle Carey.

As much for herself as for Fingal, Lady Oughterard poured out her memories until her voice was a hoarse murmur, and the tears rolled silently down her face.

"What a long time ago it is now, and yet as clear as yesterday. There I was, a young bride, stepping out of the carriage in the drive—Una was waiting on the front steps, and all the servants—and I remember how my heart sank to think I was mistress of such a dilapidated old pile. But before he took me inside, the Pater led me away into the garden to show me where the snowdrops had come up. And he had planted them all in the shape of my initial—G for Grace, printed all over the grass in white snowdrops—"

"Don't cry, Mater."

"He was a fine man. There isn't an hour of my life I don't miss him. Lucius is terribly like him—that's how God compensates us mothers." The smile froze on her face as she looked down at Fingal, and remembered that God was about to rend her motherly heart into shreds. "Oh, Fingal—"

"Tell on. Tell some more."

"I can't." For the first time, Lady Oughterard broke down completely. "It's too sad to remember old happiness," she sobbed, "and it makes me dwell on other things too—the mistakes I made. I expect I was a very foolish, headstrong woman." Wistfully, she gazed into Fingal's wasted face. "Was I an awful mother to you?"

"What a silly," Fingal whispered. "You were never awful."

"Did you know that I always loved you? Even when you were far away, or when I seemed a little cross or distant?"

"Always, always," he comforted her. "And I loved you, though I didn't come home as often as I might. So do stop howling, Mater. Your Wandering Boy will never roam again."

The days wore on, and Muttonhead and Tertius came to say goodbye. Muttonhead sat like a great brick wall, staring at Fingal as if photographing him with his eyes, and clenching his fists around the handle of his walking stick. Afterward he stood, silent and motionless, while his mother wept and wept in his arms.

Tertius arrived in his uniform, and Fingal was greatly amused by his appearance.

"Oh, Private Carey—how appallingly tidy you are—and isn't your hair short?" Painfully, he raised a shaking, skeletal hand, and stroked Tertius's hair. "You poor shorn lamb. You Croppy Boy. There, there," he added, as his touch brought Tertius out in tearing sobs, "don't take on so, Tershie. It isn't becoming in a soldier."

Finally, there came a day when Fingal dozed with his eyes half-open, seeing and hearing no one. The minutes stretched into hours without change, and Rory and the Mater fell asleep in the drawing room. It was the small hours, and Rory had just come off her shift in the ambulance.

Aubrey watched in the bedroom alone, and was glad he was alone. He sensed a difference in the atmosphere, and guessed that Death had arrived to stake his claim. After the weeks of taking care of Fingal, Aubrey had gone beyond exhaustion, to a kind of calm elation; a heightened awareness.

He stared at Fingal's face, already that of a corpse— sharp nose, sunken lips, eyes dulled and flattened. There was very little left, he thought, of the boy who had so captivated him at Cambridge, the day he had come up for the meeting of the Apostles.

Eerily, as if answering his thoughts, Fingal suddenly said: "Tea and whales." His eyes were open, and were fixed on Aubrey.

"Yes," Aubrey said. "I was just thinking of it. The day we met." "Whales" was slang for tinned sardines, a staple ingredient of those meetings. "You were running along Trinity Street in front of me, like a young hart or roe." Alight with life and energy, he wanted to add, and arrogant, as if your youth would last forever. "And there you were beside the fireplace when I arrived."

Fingal's lips formed the word: "Grand."

Aubrey smiled. "Perhaps I seemed so, but I was as nervous as a schoolboy with his first crush. I so desperately wanted you to like me—it was all I could do not to lay siege to you by sending you every single orchid in London." He stroked Fingal's cheek with the back of his finger. "When you came to live with me, I simply couldn't believe my luck. It was worth the risk and the fights—it was worth everything."

Fingal, by a series of barely visible noises and movements, let Aubrey know that he wanted to be raised. Aubrey, bleeding with pity for the body he had once lusted after so desperately, slipped his arm under Fingal's shoulder blades. Marveling that the bones could still hold together with so little flesh on them, Aubrey drew Fingal toward him and circled him in his arms.

Quite clearly, Fingal whispered: "Love," and the spirit seemed to move away from the space behind his eyes, leaving them as blank as shuttered windows.

"Don't leave me," Aubrey said. He held him more tightly, though he knew that Fingal had gone, and he was alone.

Eight

The meeting had splintered into a free-for-all. Fists were flying all over the hall as angry pacifists defended themselves against the flag-waving roughs.

"Comrades! Brothers!" Tom bellowed above the din. "Why put your might behind the forces of oppression? What'll you get out of being turned into soldiers? If you want a fight, go and fight the politicians and generals who got us into this bloody stupid war in the first place—"

Several jeering youths were kicking through the "No Conscription" placards around the platform, and making a rush for Tom's lanky, unprotected body. Joe got there first. He dragged Tom off the stage, and down some steps into a dusty boiler room.

They leaned against a tangle of hot-water pipes, getting their breath back and listening to the thuds and yells above them.

"That was a close one," Joe said.

Tom lit a cigarette. "What did you want to stop me for? I was going great guns."

Joe let out something between a laugh and a groan. "I shouldn't let you do it. The police are still after you. It's sheer madness for you to appear in public now."

"What's the bloody point if I don't?" Tom demanded coolly. "I've got to show them they can't gag me, or I might as well be in prison."

In the dim, cobwebby light, his face was all pits and hollows, and Joe noticed the way his thin shoulders shivered when he cupped his hands around the cigarette, as if for warmth.

"All the same," he said, "maybe you should lie low for a while. How are you off for cash?"

Tom shrugged. "I get by."

"You don't look well, old chap. I wish we could take you in, but the police are watching our house as it is."

"A fine thing," Tom said, "when refusing to kill people constitutes a crime and a threat to the state."

"Here." Joe pulled a sovereign out of his pocket, and pressed it into Tom's cold hand. "Try and get something warm to wear, eh?"

"Thanks, Joe. You're a good mate."

"Never mind that. You'd better get out, before this place is swarming with coppers.

Joe had cased the building thoroughly before the meeting, and he led Tom to a back door, which opened into a murky alley. They clasped hands briefly before Tom vanished into the shadows.

When he returned to the hall, Joe found the crowd scattering to the music of police whistles. The fun was over and the members of the No Conscription League were left nursing their swollen jaws and bloody noses. Most of their public meetings ended in this way, and Joe was resigned to the fact that none of the louts who came to disrupt was ever arrested. A police van waited in the street outside. He watched helplessly as one of his fellow committee members was bundled into it. Another one. How soon would it be before they were all behind bars?

"Hold on, driver!" someone sang out facetiously. "Room for one more inside!"

Two plainclothes men emerged from the alley, dragging something heavy between them. It was Tom, unconscious and bleeding from the head. His scuffed boots bounced against the cobbles.

Joe could not help blurting out: "What've you done to him?"

"He was resisting arrest." The detective eyed Joe narrowly. "What's it to you?"

"N-nothing—" Joe turned and stumbled away blindly. Unable to face going home, he lost himself in the side streets of Hampstead.

What a damned coward I am, he thought. Too cowardly to fight, too cowardly to go to prison with Tom. He had gone into the No Conscription League full of high ideals and fierce convictions, but there was something wrong. Why had he ended up despising himself?

If only he could see things in clear black and white, as

Tom did, instead of torturing himself with the other side of the question. This was the trouble with having a liberal mind—there always was another side. Tom saw just one. It never occurred to him that he might be only half right, or even wrong.

Joe halted on the pavement outside New End Hospital. Three motor ambulances had drawn up in the narrow street. There was no private entrance to shelter the patients from the stares of passersby. Half a dozen dirty little boys stood gaping while the VADs and orderlies unloaded the stretchers. Joe, against his better nature, gaped too.

The first man, motionless under his khaki blanket, appeared to have some sort of black cloth covering the lower part of his face. Then Joe looked again, and saw that the black cloth was a yawning hole where the man's jaw and nose should have been. He had to close his throat to stop himself retching—he hadn't known wounds like this existed.

One by one, he stared at the men as they were carried past him. Their bloodied stumps and crushed limbs seemed a living reproach to his own wholeness and strength. At that moment, Joe hated himself with all his heart. What were his arrogant ideals and convictions compared to this?

The little boys had begun to nudge each other and giggle. "Yeucch—look at 'im, all covered in strawberry jam. Where's yer legs, mate?"

"Go away!" Joe shouted, hitting out at them in a sudden passion of fury. "Get out of my sight, you little bastards. You're not fit to look at them—"

The urchins ducked away from his flailing fists, and dashed off down the street with derisive war-whoops. Joe was left clutching a lamppost, trembling with the aftereffects of rage. Two of the orderlies were looking at him curiously. He knew why when he put his hand to his eyes, and realized he was crying.

"We did everything we could," Frieda said. "Nothing short of a miracle could have saved him."

Rory took off her Red Cross hat, and dazedly smoothed her hair. "If we'd raised more money—"

"No, my dear. It wouldn't have made any difference."

The Berlins had brought Rory home with them after Tom's trial at the Old Bailey. He had made a stirring speech in his own defense, the public gallery had cheered him loudly, and the judge had given him eighteen months' hard labor.

"Sit down, Aurora," Berta said kindly. "You should have something to eat before you go on your shift."

"I'm all right, honestly." But Rory sat down. Although she was no longer in love with Tom, she had turned as pale as death when he was led out of the dock. The Berlins had not liked to let her go straight back to her empty flat.

Dorrie brought in the tray of coffee and sandwiches (Becky had left to make munitions), and Joe roused himself enough to hand around the cups. He had been abstracted and strained for several days. Frieda watched him covertly, her eyes full of anxiety. She loved him too much to nag him, and knew he would not shut her out of his confidence for long.

She was relieved when he positioned himself on the hearth rug and said, in an unnaturally loud voice: "Girls, there's something I've got to tell you."

Rory said: "I'll leave—"

"No, don't." He smiled bitterly, his eyes pinned to Frieda. "I think I'd like you to be here when I break their hearts."

Berta and Dorrie looked toward Frieda in alarm. Frieda sat very still, her body tensed as if expecting a blow. "You needn't worry about our hearts," she said softly.

The bitterness melted from his face. He was pleading for understanding. "Eldest, I—I'm joining the army."

Frieda did not move, but a shadow seemed to fall across her face. The lines around her mouth deepened, her eyes dulled, and she froze into an old woman in a single moment. Berta and Dorrie, still gazing up at Joe, each took one of her hands. He was right, Rory thought, with a shudder—he had broken their hearts. Their beloved boy, only son of the great Dr. Berlin, had betrayed their most sacred beliefs.

When she spoke, Frieda's voice was as gentle as ever. "I know you are unhappy about some aspects of our work. And you were upset to see wounded men in the street. But are these reasons to sacrifice your principles to a war you know to be wrong?"

"I think we set too much store by our principles," Joe said. "Those men made me feel like a traitor to my generation. Why should other chaps of my age be blown to bits, just because they weren't high-minded enough to have principles? Oh God, Eldest, I wish I could make you understand. Ask Rory!" He gestured wildly toward her. "She'll tell you why she spends all her nights driving the wounded across London like the ferryman on the River Styx. It's because it's too late to stand on the sidelines and disapprove. The war's all wrong—of course it is! But it's a fact, and I've run out of excuses for not doing my bit."

Frieda murmured: *"Du lieber Gott!"*

"After the hospital," Joe said, "I went walking on Hampstead Heath—I suppose I was waiting for some sort of sign. And I suddenly remembered the passage from Socrates: *If you have enjoyed the benefits of the laws of your country, you must not refuse obedience to them, even when you think they are mistaken.* That was what I needed. I wrote to the Oxford OTC the same evening. They've accepted me. I'm to be commissioned."

"And you tell me this after watching a man get eighteen months for putting his opinions into print!"

"I'm not like Tom. He's a brave man, but I choose to take my chance with the majority. I'll loathe myself forever if I don't." Impulsively, he flung himself down on the carpet at her feet. "I know what I've done to you. I won't blame you if you never speak to me again."

Frieda forgot her principles and politics in an aching rush of love. Remembering only that he was her adored little brother, she sobbed: "Oh, Joey darling—how shall I live if they hurt you?" and folded him tightly in her arms.

Nine

The Channel crossing had been stormy, and the battered stomachs of the twenty young VADs were beginning to bay for hot coffee and fresh rolls. Delicious smells were wafting out of the hotel kitchen toward them. Not one of them, however, would have confessed to the weaknesses of fatigue or hunger. Pride that they had been chosen for active service overseas, and a burning desire to prove themselves worthy, kept their attention fixed to Sister Constance Gleadow.

"Great trust has been placed in you," she was saying. "Many trained nurses will resent your inexperience. But you will earn their respect by showing that you can submit yourselves to the same discipline."

Gleadow was a Queen Alexandra Military Nurse, who had served in South Africa during the Boer War. They all knew what an honor it was to arrive in Boulogne under the starched wing of such a seasoned old campaigner.

"Active service is not a continental holiday. Nor is it an excuse to escape the restrictions of domestic life. Blind obedience must be your motto."

Despite Jenny's efforts to concentrate, Gleadow's handsome, square-jawed face was drifting out of focus. It was silly to be superstitious, but she could not help feeling that her journey to France had begun with very bad omens. First, there had been the letter from her father—railway ticket enclosed—insisting that she return home to Edinburgh immediately. Jenny, with barely a twinge of conscience, had sent back the ticket, and had heard nothing from her parents since. Did this mean she had been disowned?

Then, the previous day, something far worse had cast its shadow across this new phase in her life. She had called at Hyde Park Gate, and found the MacIntyre house in mourn-

ing. Donald, the young midshipman, had died of cholera
out in the Dardanelles, and poor Cornelia was half-mad
with grief. Jenny, whose instinct was to heal, was haunted
by the memory of that incurable wound.

"... you will be expected to use your initiative in an
emergency," Gleadow lectured. She had a beautiful, husky
voice, contrasting oddly with her austere appearance. "You
will work as and when you are needed, and remember that
no task is too menial for you. The comfort of the patients
comes first at all times. The men you will be taking care of
have, in many cases, come almost straight from the battlefield. Your face should tell the patient that he has arrived
at a place of comfort and safety, even if it is very evident
to you that he is near death."

She paused to take in the awe-stricken faces of her audience, then smiled. Sister Gleadow had a disarmingly childish
smile, which showed small teeth and pink gums. "But all you
nurses come to me with excellent reports from your hospitals,
and I know I can rely upon you. Now, the Railway Transport
Officer tells me our train leaves in an hour and a half. In the
meantime, I have ordered us a hot meal—"

She stopped abruptly, as the door at the other end of the
long, bare dining room swung open. Six officers, obviously
waiting for the leave-boat, threw themselves down on the
wooden settles around the stove. After removing their caps
and nodding politely to the nurses, they instantly, as one
man, fell asleep.

The VADs stared at their blank, exhausted faces, and at
the trench mud still clinging to their boots and uniforms.
Some of them glanced uneasily at Gleadow. She had strict
standards of male behavior, and had delivered a fearsome
lecture to two subalterns on the train, for "sprawling and
lounging in front of ladies."

Now, however, with a face full of compassion, Gleadow
put her finger to her lips. Jenny understood that here in
France, the normal rules worked in reverse: women were
to be considerate, and the men who bore the burden of
fighting were to be tenderly considered. The nurses ate
their meal in monastic silence, while the officers around the
stove slept like the dead.

No. 49 General Hospital, Etaples, was a vast city of match-
wood and canvas. Rows of wooden huts and drab khaki

tents stretched away over the horizon. Jenny found herself sharing a tent with one Polly Shilton, a plump, easygoing person with a plain, freckled face and engaging smile. Their new home had a floor of rough duckboards, two camp beds, two collapsible washstands and two small metal lockers.

There was no time to settle in. Jenny and Polly barely had time to pin on their caps and aprons before reporting for duty. Exactly half an hour after arriving, they were down on their knees, scrubbing out a hut that had contained cases of PUO—pyrexia, unknown origin, or "trench fever."

"I hope we don't catch it," Polly said. "We'd feel such awful frauds when we've never been near a trench."

Polly worked with marvelous speed and efficiency, and was able to talk nineteen to the dozen at the same time. Jenny learned that she was, like herself, a vicar's daughter. She had three brothers, two of whom were in the army. She was engaged to be married to a young solicitor, also in the army—but this was a secret, and Jenny was not to tell anyone.

"What about you, Dalgleish? Are you engaged, or anything?"

Jenny was shocked by her impulse to say no. "Yes."

"Army or navy?"

"Army—the Borderers."

"I say, how splendid. Denis is in the 7th Tooting and Clapham—not nearly so glamorous. My mother will faint when she finds out I'm getting married—poor thing. I'm her right hand. As I told them when I applied for this posting, any girl brought up in a huge London vicarage should be able to manage active service with one hand tied behind her back."

Jenny laughed. "I can just picture you behind the urn, at some Sunday school junket."

"No laughing matter, Dalgleish," Polly said, grinning. "I've spent my life typing, tea-brewing and sorting charity clothes. If I were a curate, at least I'd be paid for it."

When they had finished cleaning the first hut, they were shown to another one—and another after that. By the time they sat down in the mess hut to their meal of tinned pork and beans, Jenny was almost keeling over from weariness.

"Not a single patient, not even a peep at a proper ward,"

she complained. "Have they brought us over here just to skivy? I was hoping to be given some real work."

"That was real enough for me," Polly said, busily scraping her enamel plate. "Now, do let's turn in. I haven't been so utterly dead tired since last year's Band of Hope picnic."

Jenny's longing for "real" work was very quickly satisfied. The following day, she found herself in charge of a hut full of twenty wounded men, with only an orderly to help her and a Sister to run to in emergencies. None of the wounds was serious, but the heaviness of the responsibility was both thrilling and appalling.

While Polly spent her off-duty moments eating biscuits and reading the sentimental novels of Florence Barclay, Jenny pored over medical books, searching for any clue that would help her to understand her "cases."

"You're getting too involved, old thing," Polly told her. "You really mustn't fret over the patients so much. Not that I blame you, because it's awfully hard not to get fond of them. There's such a darling little chap on my ward, not a day more than seventeen, and even Sister pets him."

"It's not the men themselves I'm involved with," Jenny said, as soon as she could get a word in. "It's the wounds. I want to be ready for the complications that can happen, so I don't have to run to Sister every time. It might mean a man's life one day."

"You mustn't expect to save them all. Sometimes it will be beyond any human effort."

She was kind, and Jenny was fond of her. But Polly's lack of interest in this sort of discussion made her yearn for Rory, with her sharp curiosity and inability to let any matter rest. "At least I'll know I did everything that could be done."

Polly crammed in another biscuit—the old ladies of her father's parish deluged her with the things—and said: "Too much dedication is bad for the complexion" so solemnly that Jenny threw aside her book in a burst of laughter.

Polly need not have worried. Despite her hunger for medical knowledge, Jenny was equally hungry for any pleasure or diversion that could be snatched from the grim daily routine. The VADs were penned up like nuns, never permitted to leave the camp alone, and generally cut off from the company of healthy males. They spent their few leisure moments brewing cocoa in tents or mess huts, and gossiping wildly about the hospital.

Certain characters attracted all kinds of romance and speculation. Then there were those godlike, endlessly fascinating creatures, the doctors. Jenny's favorite was Dr. Buchanan, a young Glasgow man who gusted through the wards like a healthy sea breeze, galvanizing everyone with his energy. Unlike his colleagues, he noticed the VADs, and even joked with them; he called Jenny "Edinburgh," and mimicked her accent.

Buchanan was what her mother would have called a "black Celt," short and slight, but with whipcord muscles, and dark eyes very sharp and bright in his gaunt face. He was a passionate researcher, and had spent his last leave writing a paper about new techniques for blood transfusions, which had been published in the *Lancet.* Wherever you found him, he was always about to fly off somewhere else, glancing at his watch, and muttering: "Two o'clock, and no' 'a pinny on the wean!'"

It was Dr. Buchanan who persuaded the hospital authorities to allow the nurses out to a camp concert. The VADs were herded out in a line, with an armed guard of Sisters, and marched down to a huge tent full of soldiers, walking wounded and cigarette smoke.

The amateur entertainment was as good as a dose of tonic, and Jenny, who would normally have turned up her nose at such crudity, laughed until her ribs hurt. The chaplain sang "Devon, Glorious Devon," and was encored twice—more a tribute to his popularity than his talent. Then, three soldiers came on in nurses' uniforms, and sang:

> *Three little maids from school are we,*
> *Proud of the title VAD—*
> *Three little maidens, never idle,*
> *Filled with a mania homicidal . . .*

The undisputed triumph of the evening, however, was Dr. Buchanan's imitation of Harry Lauder. In a kilt and scratch wig, he did "Stop Yer Ticklin' Jock," and was not allowed off the stage until he had sung it three times.

The next time Jenny saw him, he was wearing a rubber apron over a gore-spattered white coat, working on a factory line of amputations at the operating table. The day after the concert, orders came through to clear as many beds as possible. Although nobody said it in so many words, everyone knew this meant a big battle. Any patient who could be moved was sent back to England. Many of the more experienced nurses, including Jenny's superior, Sister de Souza, were sent up the line to the casualty clearing stations.

Those left behind were expected to "rise to the occasion," as Sister Gleadow said. Jenny was placed in sole charge of three huts, with only two orderlies to help her. She was working to the limits of her strength, but was glad of it. In her spare moments, she was crushed beneath a terrible sense of helplessness.

The first convoy of wounded arrived at one in the morning, in a line of ambulances that seemed endless. Extra space had to be made in the huts by placing stretchers between the beds. The operating theaters were soon overflowing.

"So much for organization," Sister Gleadow said bitterly. "Look at these poor fellows—sent straight down in their first field dressings, and wallowing in filth because they've been lying unattended for hours. The clearing stations must be swamped."

Within an hour, the tragedy of the Battle of Loos was known all around the hospital. The wounded were kilted Cameron Highlanders, and they babbled of walking into a tempest of machine-gun bullets singing "The March of the Cameron Men," while their comrades were slaughtered around them. Some of the Germans, they said, had stopped firing on the retreating survivors, out of sheer pity.

Jenny found the familiar Scottish accents of the men almost heartbreaking. Seeing the bloody kilts made her think of the lines of Scott her mother had made her learn as a child: *"No stinted draft, no scanty tide—the gushing flood the tartans dyed."* God help the Highland villages, soon to hear that they had lost all their young men. God have mercy on the towns and cities that would be hushed in mourning, like Edinburgh after Flodden.

Nothing had prepared her for the chaos of a hospital so near the fighting. The men stank, and their clothes were full of fat gray lice. Jenny's first job was to cut off their filthy uniforms with an immense pair of scissors, and she sheared her way from stretcher to stretcher until her fingers were numb, exposing wounds that made her catch her breath.

The horror went too deep for ordinary pity. She was only stunned by a kind of sick despair for the evil of the world. Yet there were isolated moments that thawed her frozen spirits. She glimpsed Sister Gleadow soothing a terrified boy, her face unrecognizably gentle. She saw the chaplain taking water, cigarettes and human comfort into the "moribund" tent, where the hopeless cases were left to die.

A middle-aged Highland man closed his grimy fingers around her sleeve, and whispered hoarsely: "You a Scot, miss?"

"I am." Jenny removed his hand and went on with her work—she was picking threads of bloody khaki out of a wound in his chest. "Lie still, now."

"D'you know 'The Land o' the Leal'?"

"Yes."

A slow tear made a track through the dirt on his cheeks. "I wish you'd sing it, miss."

Jenny wondered what significance the song had for him. Still working on the filthy wound, she sang very softly, her voice no more than the hum of a fly in the racket of yells and moans:

> *"I'm wearing awa', Jean,*
> *Like snow when it's thaw, Jean,*
> *I'm wearing awa'*
> *To the land o' the leal.*
>
> *There's nae sorrow there, Jean,*
> *There's neither cauld nor care, Jean,*
> *The day is ay fair*
> *In the land o' the leal."*

The man drank in the song like medicine, with the tears dripping down his face. "Thanks," he said. "I've heard worse and paid for it."

"Dalgleish!" Sister Gleadow had caught the last part of the song. Her face was flushed and angry. "What on earth do you think you're doing? Where do you suppose you are? This is not a variety bill. Get on with your work at once! I'll speak to you later."

Jenny had not stopped working, but it was not a VAD's place to argue with a superior. "Yes, Sister."

"There are those who would say that the nurse was doing the best work on the ward." Dr. Buchanan emerged from his makeshift operating theater behind the canvas curtain. "Sing another!" he ordered. "But something rousing this time—and let every man who can join in!"

Oblivious to the amazed faces of the nurses, he retreated behind the curtain, and began to sing, in a fine baritone:

> *"A highland man my love was born,*
> *The lowland laws he held in scorn,*
> *But still was faithful to his clan,*
> *My gallant, braw John highland man!"*

Man after man—some barely able to breathe—took up the tune of "The White Cockade" until the whole hut rang with it. Jenny, in her exhausted and despairing state, thought it the most beautiful thing she had ever heard in her life.

PART FIVE

Winter 1915—Autumn 1917

Aurora

Letter to my Daughter, 1935

All through the dreary winter of 1915, my life was dominated by my work for the VAD Ambulance Unit. Every
evening, I reported for duty at Charing Cross Station. Here,
on a silent platform, roped off to keep out the public, we
met the long hospital trains, with their freight of wounded
from France and Flanders.

Sometimes we waited for hours, drinking tea from the
stalls run by various well-meaning ladies, or playing patience. And sometimes, when the fighting had been severe,
we were driving to and fro all night—slowly to the hospitals, to spare the patients, and hell-for-leather back to the
station for the next consignment.

While the men lay in the back of my ambulance, they
were my responsibility, and the burden haunted my dreams.
Each one wore a label containing medical information, and
I had a particular dread of the "red stripe" cases who were
liable to hemorrhage. It was such a relief to hand them
over at the hospital door. They were signed for, I seem to
remember, like parcels.

At last, in the chilly gray dawn, another yawning girl
would appear to take over my ambulance. I would walk
down to a coffee stall on the Embankment—dancing and
stamping to get the life back into my perished feet—and
watch the sun stealing up over the Thames. Altogether, it
was a sad enough existence, but everyone of my age was
more or less miserable. The war had become such a fact of
life that you simply took it for granted, and lived from one
day to the next.

There was one spark of joy as the year drew to a close.
Both Tertius and Muttonhead got Christmas leave, and the
Mater spent her (and my) last ha'penny coming over from

Ireland to join them. Mutt, being a staff officer, entered London in a special dining carriage with little shaded lamps and white cloths on the tables. Private Tertius made the same journey in a third-class corridor, sitting on a pile of kit bags. But this false gulf between them vanished when the Mater held them both in her arms and wept for the aching absence of Fingal.

Loss is harder to endure at Christmas than at any other time, and we all missed Fingal keenly—especially poor Aubrey, who was shattered and gnarled with grief, like a tree that has been struck by lightning. But as he said himself, there was hardly a family in the country that had not lost someone, and one's duty these days was to the living.

Having both the boys at home was bliss. For a short time we did our best to forget the war. Consciously or not, when someone you loved came home on leave, you worked hard at being jolly to lay by a store of happy memories in case you needed them later. Aubrey gamely summoned up a smile and treated us all to a theater—*Chu Chin Chow,* a musical comedy that ran right through the war. I don't think it was quite Aubrey's cup of tea, but he was rewarded by the enjoyment of the Mater, who loved every moment, and drove us mad for the rest of the holidays by endlessly warbling "The Cobbler's Song" and "Kissing Time."

On New Year's Eve I was feeling low, since I was to lose Tertius and return to my ambulance the following day. However, Muttonhead insisted upon opening two bottles of champagne and making us drink to the year ahead. He said it would bring us good luck. We drank the toast in devout silence as if praying.

In fact, 1916 began disastrously. One freezing, stony-hearted January morning, I returned from my shift to find a message from the Berlins asking me to go around at once. I found Berta and Dorrie in tears. Frieda, very gently (God bless her, how kind she was) told me that Tom was dead.

I had had a hard night's work, and the news turned the whole room upside down. The ceiling cornice came rushing at me and I was plunging into the pattern on the carpet. There was a space, then a cup of tea appeared, apparently out of nowhere. I drank it lying on the sofa, feeling half ashamed of my own reaction, and half stunned by this unexpected gap that had opened in my life.

When I could bear to hear it, Frieda explained that Tom had died of pneumonia in the Prison Infirmary. Oh, how dark and still the world became as I took it in, and how amazed I was by the earthquake of crying that took hold of me. I could not shake off the image of poor Tom dying all alone, without one loving word or friendly face to send him on his way. I think I had a strange sort of guilt, too, as if I had killed him by ceasing to love him.

Joe Berlin was also hit very hard by Tom's death. He pulled his parliamentary strings to get the body released for burial, and on the coldest and dullest of London winter mornings, we followed it to Highgate Cemetery. Frieda paid for the funeral, and for the grave plot. It was the last of her many acts of generosity toward him—a clay bed, all he ever owned, where he would sleep forever.

There was a stranger waiting for us at the graveside; an elderly clergyman, rather elegantly turned out. We were sure he had come to the wrong funeral, until Joe and I remembered the Vicar who had sent Tom to Oxford. And so it proved to be. Afterward, he introduced himself as the Reverend Alban Greer, and made a heartbreaking little speech to us about what Tom might have been. Tom, I knew, had treated Mr. Greer with shocking ingratitude and rudeness, yet the poor man still mourned him like a son.

Mr. Greer told us something that altered my perception of the forces of law and order, and made me very bitter against them for a long time. Tom had named him as next of kin—the tears trembled in the old man's eyes as he said this—and he had traveled down to the prison just in time to miss Tom's last moments. He had gone into a side room at the Infirmary, and seen all that remained of poor Tom, still warm and waiting to be laid out. Some officials from the prison had burst in a few minutes later, and had been very angry with Mr. Greer for going in without permission. They hustled him out—but Mr. Greer had already seen that Tom's face, neck and torso were covered with bruises in various stages of healing.

Joe, incongruously smart in his officer's uniform, went behind a stone statue of an angel to cry silently with his leather glove in his mouth. I found him and cried, too. We passed a cigarette between us, saying nothing and not caring that we were keeping the others waiting in the cold.

"He died for what he believed in," Joe said eventually. "They couldn't even beat it out of him. He was too big for us, Rory. For my money, he's the bravest hero of them all."

One

Jenny had decided to spend her leave in London. Her parents had now forgiven her for nursing in France against their wishes, but she found she could not face the northern chill of Edinburgh. The daffodils would still be out up there, while the London parks were already bright with summer flowers, and the trees were in full leaf. The sun warmed her bones after the long winter of cold and discomfort. It was paradise to wear real hats and frocks again, instead of that everlasting uniform, and unutterable luxury to have no responsibility that afternoon other than choosing which pair of gloves she should buy.

She had spent half an hour of intense happiness at Marshall and Snelgrove's glove counter, stroking the soft kids, and delighting in the delicate pastel colors.

"Well, madam?" The girl behind the counter was getting impatient.

Jenny held up the two pairs, pearl gray and pale green. The pearl would be useful, but the green would be such fun with her new coat and skirt.

A male voice suddenly growled, right against her ear: "Buy 'em both, and devil take the expense."

She dropped the gloves and whirled around furiously to see Dr. Buchanan, laughing and looking very pleased with himself.

"Hello, Nurse—miss, I should say. You are the lass from Edinburgh, aren't you? I hardly knew you under that hat."

"Yes, I'm Dalgleish. How nice to see you, Doctor." Jenny recovered herself, and held the gloves out to the salesgirl. "I'll take both pairs, please."

"Very good, madam."

"I'm sorry if I startled you," Buchanan said, while they waited for the gloves to be wrapped. "But I couldn't resist. You looked as if you were deciding the fate of the nations."

"I didn't know I was being watched."

"No, it was very ungentlemanly of me. But I had to make sure it was you. If you want the awful truth, I've been following you for the past hour."

Jenny knew that she ought to have been annoyed, but there was something so honest and cheerful in his manner that she found herself smiling, and saying: "You must have better things to do. This is your first leave for months—we all thought you'd spend it shut up in a library, writing a tremendous article for the *Lancet*."

"Who is included in 'we'?"

"The other nurses, of course. Surely you know that we gossip about you, Doctor?"

"It never occurred to me. I'm far too modest."

"We assumed you'd spend your leave at home in Glasgow."

"And I assumed you'd be at home in Edinburgh. We're two exiles, standing in tears amid the alien corn." He offered his arm as Jenny took her parcel. "And we really should stick together."

This was how Jenny ended up walking out of Marshall and Snelgrove clutching Buchanan's arm as if she had intended to meet him all along. Outside, she was too busy thinking how unexpectedly attractive he looked to take her hand off his sleeve. Most men, she supposed, looked more or less handsome in an officer's uniform—she had never seen Buchanan so spruce. In fact, she realized with a slight shock, she had hardly ever seen him at all without his white coat and rubber apron. They halted on the pavement, and she took him in properly. No, you couldn't call him truly handsome. His face was too bony, his eyes were too small, his upper lip was too long. But there was a kind of quickness and humor about him that made him impossible to ignore.

She went on staring at him, until it dawned on her that he was staring back at her with equal curiosity. Her cheeks became hot and she said: "Well, I should be on my way—"

She tried to pull away her hand, but he kept hold of it. "Don't, Miss Dalgleish. I throw myself on your mercy. Grant me just half an hour of sensible Scots conversation, and you'll be paid handsomely with a cup of tea."

"Oh, I really don't think—"

"Please," he begged, still smiling but more than half serious. "My leave's been a washout so far, and I haven't spoken to a living soul in days. Don't go all prim on me!"

"Very well, then. I shan't struggle." And she was allowing him to lead her along the street, without the faintest idea where he was going. It was highly irregular, and probably against hospital regulations. But there's a war on, a little inner voice reminded her; haven't you slaved and suffered enough? Why should you worry about silly conventions, when you have done your duty in the front line?

He took her to a fashionable, white and gold teashop off Piccadilly, full of officers and their womenfolk.

"I've never seen London so crammed with khaki," Jenny remarked. "Who's minding the war?"

"Perhaps we imagined the whole damned thing."

Jenny carefully arranged her bag and gloves on the marble-topped table. "Is it wrong, do you think, for us to be together? I mean, what would the hospital authorities say if they saw us?"

"I don't care," Buchanan said promptly. "None of their business. I'm too glad to see a friendly face to let you go."

"Are you really having such a lonely time?"

"Yes, utterly desolate. And I'll tell you the reason if you promise not to laugh."

"I swear!"

He leaned toward her, his face sober but his eyes crinkled with amusement. "There's a woman in the picture—or rather, there was. You'd better get your handkerchief out because this is a heart-rending tale of love and betrayal. Assuming a certain young lady had encouraged my attentions, I arranged to spend my leave with her in London."

"But you didn't see her after all?"

"Oh, I saw her, all right—this morning, at St. James's, Spanish Place. She was marrying a chap in the Flying Corps." He smiled wickedly at Jenny. "Go on. Laugh if you want to."

"How awfully sad—"

"Oh, nonsense. My heart seems to be healing remarkably quickly. Now, I hope you're not easily shocked, because I'm about to commit an act of terrible extravagance." He beckoned over the waitress, and ordered lavishly. When she had gone, he said: "If my poor old mother were here, she'd have to be revived with smelling salts—'Och, Jamie, is tea sae dear in London?' Now, I'd never tell that to an

English girl—I won't let them laugh at us for being canny. But I know you understand."

"I do indeed, Dr. Buchanan. My own mother would never dream of eating a scone she hadn't made herself, let alone paying for it."

They both laughed, and by the time the tea arrived, they were deep in conversation about the hospital. Buchanan quickly sniffed out Jenny's interest in the scientific details of wounds and their treatment, and became almost incandescent with enthusiasm. Jenny watched, fascinated, as he demonstrated the growth of gangrene bacteria with cake crumbs. Only the presence of the waitress, looming above them with the bill, brought her back to the present, and the realization that they had been talking for an hour and a half.

"I had no idea. I do hope I haven't kept you—"

"Kept me? You've saved me." He laid his hand across hers. "And you can do something else for me."

"Can I?"

"I have a spare ticket for the theater tonight—a damn fine seat it is too, in the stalls, carriage trade only. Awful shame to waste it."

Jenny feebly began: "Thank you, but I don't think—" And knew, before the words were properly out of her mouth, that she meant to say yes.

"It's *The Bing Boys*—you know, with George Robey— and it's all the rage. Tell me where you live and I'll call for you."

"Do people always give in to you?" she asked, laughing. "Don't they even try to struggle?"

"Will half-past seven be too early?"

And it was settled. Nice young women—especially when engaged—did not, as a rule, go to theaters with men they barely knew. But there was a war on. *The Bing Boys* was the most popular musical comedy in town, and it would be a pity not to see it. And Dr. Buchanan was a colleague from the hospital. Altogether, nothing could be more innocuous, and there was no reason to deny herself this treat.

Jenny worked all this out with a comfortable sense of virtue. Buried deep inside her was a sense of breathless heat, as if someone had set a hot coal smoldering, ready to shoot into flames. Yet she managed to ignore it, and to imagine that she was being perfectly rational when she stopped at a very expensive florists on the way home, to buy an evening corsage of pale pink camellia japonica, at a ruinous price.

"Gorgeous flowers," Rory said, nodding toward the corsage, which lay fragrantly in a dish of water. "I had no idea Alistair was in town."

"Alistair?" The name made Jenny flinch. "Of course he's not. He's still with his regiment." She made a superhuman effort to keep her voice cool, and kept her back to Rory, to hide her crimson cheeks.

"Oh. Well, why are you getting all dolled up?"

"For heaven's sake, it's only evening dress! I ran into a chum from the hospital, who had a spare ticket for *The Bing Boys.*"

"Lucky thing," Rory said, drifting out of the room with her mouth full of bread and dripping, to pull on her blue serge uniform jacket. "I'll be spending most of my evening slouching about on a station platform. It's been so quiet lately."

"Rory," Jenny called after her, "which do you think— the white or the blue? And is the velvet cloak too heavy for June?"

Rory came back into the room, frowning. "Darling, what on earth has got into you?"

"I don't know what you mean." Jenny became very busy with the clothes brush, unable to remain still under Rory's level green gaze.

"Nonsense. You've been running around like a woman possessed ever since you came home. You've drenched yourself in eau de cologne, and you're wearing damp silk stockings, because you won't go out in cotton lisle, even though nobody will see them under your dress."

"You know me," Jenny said, with an attempt at a laugh. "I always was fastidious about my appearance."

"Hmmmm." Rory was skeptical. "Have a good time, then. I hope it all lives up to the stockings."

Left alone, Jenny was angry with herself, and ashamed. Why, if everything was so proper and decent, hadn't she told Rory the simple truth? Because, she decided a minute later, Rory might put the wrong construction on it, and think all sorts of things. Better for her not to know.

Cheering up immediately, Jenny devoted all her attention to dressing. She had washed her hair the previous day, and it rippled around her face in soft waves and curls. She put on a white dress, long white gloves, white satin shoes and the pink corsage. Then she threw her pale blue velvet evening cloak around her shoulders and studied the effect in Rory's small mirror. She was lovely. Her cheeks were tinged with color, her eyes had a moist clearness, and youth and happiness glowed around her like a halo. She could have crowed aloud with exultation. Somewhere in her head, a sensible voice was warning her that it would all be in rags by midnight—but that was hours and hours away.

Buchanan called for her at precisely half-past seven. Jenny was waiting for him at the front door, so as not to arouse the curiosity of Miss Thompson. And the moment she saw him, she blushed, because she realized that there was a change between them. By agreeing to go out with him in the evening, she had stepped over an invisible line, and their relationship was charged with awareness of this.

He inspected her solemnly, and with unmistakable admiration. Jenny knew, by the reverential way he handed her into the taxi, that he thought her beautiful. For herself, she was unprepared for the little electric shock of pleasure when she caught his brisk, clean scent.

The Bing Boys was very amusing, and Jenny enjoyed it enormously. Afterward, however, she found that her strongest impression was of Buchanan's arm on the plush rest beside hers, and the unsettling warmth of his body. At the end of the show, they stumbled into the street, dazed and enchanted.

Buchanan cleared his throat, and said: "You're not going to like this, but I can't take you home."

"Why not?"

"Because I've gone and booked us a table at the Criterion."

"You haven't! How dreadful of you! I ought to hail a taxi this moment, and insist that you see me home at once." She was laughing, and clinging to his sleeve as he steered her through the crowds of theatergoers. No nice girl would have permitted such a liberty, but—well, there was a war on, for one thing. And she felt so free and lighthearted, strolling through the warm summer night, among other people as young and happy as she was.

At the Criterion, officers and ladies were talking at the

tops of their voices in a gaudy fog of cigar smoke and music.

"This is much, much worse than the tea," said Jenny. "What would your mother say now?"

Buchanan smiled into her eyes with an intimacy that sent a warm flush sweeping across her breasts and neck. "Something about only being young once, and not being a doctor absolutely all the time."

"I wouldn't want you to stop being a doctor," Jenny said. "I can't think of you without your work."

"Am I very boring about it?"

"No! I like to hear you. I want to learn." She was genuinely interested, but seized upon the subject now to steer him away from anything more personal. He began to tell her about his training in Scotland, diffidently at first, then working up to that blaze of energy that ignited him whenever he talked about his ruling passion.

"After the war I shall go back to Glasgow and set up a clinic in the Gorbals. Poverty is the worst enemy of health, and I've never forgotten my first glimpse of the slums—the filth, the degradation. That surely won't be allowed to go on when this is all over."

In the normal way of things, Jenny would not have cared to think about the slums, crawling with ringworm and venereal disease. But Buchanan's passion was contagious. The way he spoke showed her that running a clinic for the poor was the noblest and most exciting calling on earth. They were still talking furiously when the taxi drew up outside Jenny's door.

The house was dark, and Miss Thompson's rooms were shuttered and silent. Buchanan took her latchkey and opened the door for her, following her a little way into the shadowy hall, where one dim gas jet sputtered.

Jenny's heart was thumping so violently that she felt dizzy. She held out her gloved hand. "Thank you. I've had a wonderful evening."

Buchanan stared down at her hand. Then he seized it, stripped off the glove, and pressed his hot mouth into her palm. Jenny had to bite her lip, to stop herself moaning aloud.

For several minutes, they were silent, listening to one another's shallow breathing.

"Tomorrow," he said eventually.

"Yes," she whispered. "Where?"

"I'll call for you. Ten o'clock. Good night."

"Good night."

Slowly, Jenny climbed the stairs to the attic, glad for once that Rory was out, for she desperately needed space to think. She did not feel guilty. If anything, she was only guilty because she felt no guilt. She was bewildered, a stranger to herself, unable to grasp the enormity of what she had done—and totally unrepentant when she thought of what she was going to do next.

He called for her next morning in another taxi. He had prepared a picnic hamper, which was strapped in beside the driver, and told her they were to spend the day in Oxford. Jenny said yes, that would be lovely—eager to get away before anyone in the house thought of looking out of the window.

Both were silent and awkward, sizing each other up covertly, waiting to recapture the magical urgency of the previous night. Jenny was congratulating herself, because it appeared that she could still be saved. Nothing need happen, she told herself. She was simply enjoying a day out with a friend. She was perfectly in control.

By the time they reached Paddington Station, however, and dashed for the train, the constraint between them had melted like early-morning mist before a noon sun. Jenny had been too tense to eat any breakfast, and too afraid of waking Rory. Now, she discovered that she was starving, and they opened the hamper to sample some of the potted meat sandwiches and bottles of lemonade.

Buchanan was marvelous company, and it was only too easy to forget one's duty while laughing at his jokes and stories. The laughter was so healing, and felt so harmless, that by the end of the journey, Jenny had somehow slipped into the habit of calling him "Jamie," without thinking it at all strange.

Oxford turned out to be as full of khaki as London, since most of the students were away at war, and most of the colleges had turned themselves over to officers in training. No amount of khaki, however, could quite dispel the air of ancient calm, or spoil the sweet, mellow voices of the bells, which called to each other every hour, high up in the spires. Jenny and Jamie strolled through chapels and cloisters, and

around emerald squares of grass, until it was time to re-
claim their hamper from the stationmaster and find somewhere to have luncheon.

They took an obscure branch line to a tiny, rural stop, a
few miles outside the city. It had no name; when Jenny
remembered the place afterward, she saw it as a piece of
paradise, which angels had rolled up like a magic carpet,
the moment they left.

Here, in water meadows of a rich, luscious green, they
ate the rest of their picnic, while the black-and-white cows
plodded serenely through the clover in the fields nearby,
attended by clouds of gnats. Jenny leaned back on the tartan rug, watching Jamie light a cigarette, and thinking how
perfect this was. When she was with him, everything
yielded pleasure. He had a knack of finding it everywhere
he looked—while she admired the imposing façade of a
college, he had spotted wonderful gargoyles hidden in the
shadows, and imitated their expressions until she was nearly
sick with laughter. Although this was not like her, and her
friends would hardly have recognized her behavior, in
Jamie's company she was—for the first time in her life—
truly herself.

Jamie blew out a plume of smoke, and said what young
people all over England were saying on that perfect summer day:

"You'd never know there was a war on, would you?"

"I don't think it reaches as far as here," she replied.
"Some things are still sacred."

"This place can't have changed in centuries," Jamie said.
"I wouldn't be surprised to see Matthew Arnold's Scholar
Gipsy leaning over that gate, with his long cloak and
staff—"

"You said a moment ago that you were too full of walnut
cake to be sentimental. And anyway, you're far more likely
to see a Zeppelin."

He chuckled. "You're good for me, Jenny. You won't let
me get away with any nonsense."

"It doesn't stop you trying."

"We always end up talking about the war, don't we?"
Jamie crushed out the cigarette. "Even when we try to
forget it. Do you mind me going on about my work to
you? Honestly?"

"Of course not," Jenny said. "It's my work, too. Funnily enough, I find I think about it more when I'm not there."

He frowned, and began digging a little grave for his cigarette butt in the dark soil. "I sometimes feel that if I don't talk about it, I'll go crazy. That's another reason why I didn't go home to Glasgow this leave. My mother and my aunts ask me what I've been doing, then change the subject as soon as I start to tell them. I'm made to feel disgusting."

"Oh, I know," Jenny assured him. "My mother always claims she wants me to tell her everything, but her last letter was full of complaints about gory details, and why can't I write something she can read aloud to the sewing circle? They like to hear about smoothing fevered brows and gliding around with basins of broth, but they don't understand about the reality—and they don't want to understand. Do I sound very sour to you?"

Jamie edged closer to her on the rug, and took her hand. "Here we are, working and suffering and giving up our plans for God knows how long—and on top of all that, we're expected to spare the feelings of those who stay at home. I sometimes wonder if I'll have anything to say to my mother when the war's over. We already seem to inhabit different worlds. She complains to me about the price of coal, and the paper shortage, and the meatless days, and wants me to sympathize—and you know, Jenny, I spend my time wading through corpses, and seeing my generation mangled and slaughtered, until I wonder if there's a whole, healthy young man left in the British Isles."

He paused, and tightened his hold on her hand. They listened to a cricket moving along the hedgerow and the gnats mourning under the trees. "I'm afraid of what I'll become," he said. "I'm afraid of what the war will make me. I'm sickened and disgusted by what I see—but I'm terrified of being able to bear it, of getting used to it. I don't want to be a butcher, who sees those poor fellows as so many lumps of bloody meat." There were deep furrows in his forehead, and threads of gray in the dark hair at his temples, but he looked very young. "That's not why I became a doctor. So if that's what happens to me, my whole life will have been thrown away." His jaw hardened. "But who the bloody hell am I to whine about the waste of my life when I see chaps who'll have to live another thirty years with no arms, or no legs—"

"Don't." Jenny put her hands on either side of his face, and held them there. They gazed at one another, trapped and half frightened. With a heavy sigh—almost a groan— Jamie flung his arms around her and pulled her toward him. She felt his heart thudding against his bony rib cage, and inhaled his sharp, clean scent. Her lips were already parted for his kiss, and she shuddered with pleasure when he plunged his tongue into her mouth.

This was pure ecstasy, and at first she wanted the kiss to last forever. But her body wanted more. Her breasts were tingling, and she cried out with longing when his fingers touched her nipples. More than anything in the world, she wanted to feel his touch between her legs—the wanton desire to stroke her most secret, shameful place was the only reality left in the world.

Jamie pushed her down into the grass, and rolled on top of her. He was shuddering, and stabbing his groin against her thigh. She felt the hard outline of his erection, and was scared by her sudden, savage determination to have him inside her. Blindly, instinctively, they clung together, until Jamie suddenly tore himself away from her. They lay a few feet apart, breathless and aching.

"My God," Jamie said quietly, sitting up.

"Shall we go home?"

"Yes, let's—"

Very softly, Jenny murmured: "My friend will be out when we get back. She works at night." She was blushing so painfully that she could not look at him while she said this. When she did glance up, he was gazing at her with a radiant tenderness that made her want to cry.

"Are you sure? I mean, do you really want to?"

"Yes," she said. Once more, they were locked into a ravenous mutual stare, afraid to touch each other in case they lost control.

In silence, they packed the luncheon basket and walked along the winding lanes back to the station. Above the chaos in her body, part of Jenny's mind remained surprisingly clear and calm. She had gone too far now to retreat, and she could not feel that she was doing anything wrong; if anything, it would have felt wrong to reject this heaven-sent chance of bliss.

They talked very little on the way home. Facing each other in the empty compartment, they became almost

choked with desire. The movement of the train chafed at
Jenny's clitoris, until she was driven mad by a desire to rub
away the itch of urgency. This was a part of her body she
had hardly known she had, and suddenly she was at its
mercy. As if she had never known the meaning of modesty,
she stared at the bulge under Jamie's fly and fell into a
trance of carnality.

On the way to South Kensington, they sat at opposite
sides of the taxi, grim and nervous now that the hour was
approaching. Jamie asked the driver to stop, and went into
a chemist's shop. Scorching with humiliation, Jenny cow-
ered behind her hat veil, and would not look at Jamie until
they had reached the house. Motioning for silence, she led
him past Miss Thompson's closed door.

Then they were facing each other in the dusk, and the
whole thing seemed impossible—sordid and cheap. Jenny
was about to say so, when Jamie whispered: "My dear
love—my sweet girl—"

He was tearing off his clothes, and she was not trying
to stop him. She was tearing off her own clothes, tugging
impatiently at buttons and hooks.

"Now, please—" He was almost sobbing. "Let me
now—"

With shaking hands, he pulled on the condom he had
bought at the chemist's, and entered her with a groan of
relief, which quickly built to the yells of his orgasm.

Jenny was aware of the fierce pain, and the indignity of
being pried open, like an oyster. But there was pleasure, too,
in holding Jamie's warm, pulsing body in her arms, and
feeling the smooth rubber loosening as he shrank inside
her. He kissed her, and hardened again. This time, he
moved slowly and gently, arching his back so that he could
brush her clitoris with his finger. He was very patient,
allowing the rhythm to flow through her until she came,
and his own climax melted into hers.

He held her in his arms, cradling her head against his
naked chest, and running his fingers through her long waves
of hair. "My darling."

"I can hear your heart," she said.

"It's all yours."

She smiled, in her haze of contentment. "And mine is
all yours."

"Is it? What about your fiancé?"

"No!" Jenny flinched as if he had hit her. "This has nothing to do with him—and how did you know?"

"You VADs aren't the only people at the hospital who gossip."

"Oh God," she said, "so you've known all the time?"

"Yes."

"Oh, Jamie, what an evil, faithless woman you must think me!"

"Come to that, what a cynical seducer you must think me. But I've never done anything like this in my life. I was stuttering with embarrassment in that damned chemist's, and me a doctor."

Jenny had been on the point of tears. Now, she began to laugh. "What have we done? What's happened to us?"

He kissed a strand of her hair. "I know what's happened to me. Lord knows how or when, but I've gone and fallen in love with you."

And Jenny snapped back to a full sense of reality, as if someone had switched on a powerful light. She had betrayed Alistair. She was lying naked in bed with a man she hardly knew, and it was too late for regret, because she was wildly, passionately, deliriously in love with him.

Two

Early in the morning of July 1, the British barrage lifted, and in the moments before attack, a blissful silence fell across the sweet summer landscape. Lorenzo, waiting to go over the top with the first wave, stood in the trench with his foot on the scaling ladder and his eyes on his watch.

Above him, the sky arched, a perfect, delicate azure. It was already warm, and promised to be a brilliant day. The blessing of the guns' silence and the scented morning breeze had instilled a kind of holiday atmosphere, despite wretched dry throats and thudding hearts.

Lorenzo was annoyed because he was feeling guilty. This could very well be the day of his death, and he had not written a letter to Eleanor. The previous night, he had found himself so unexpectedly attached to life that he had not trusted himself to put pen to paper without being unkind. For if I do die, he thought, I shall be jealous of that poor woman, as if she had stolen my life like a witch. And yet he ought to have made an effort. What would his true feelings matter when he was lying in his grave?

Stevie, of course, had sat up all night, scribbling page after page by the light of a candle stuck in a wine bottle. Lorenzo had watched him, and seen the tears running down his face, as he tried to put his deepest feelings into words for those he loved. Being Stevie's feelings, they could bear the light of day—he would never have to lie. Lorenzo could just imagine the heart-rending gallantry of those letters. He had an awful feeling poetry had been quoted in them, if not actually composed.

But his own feelings for Eleanor had better die with him. All he could have said was the truth—that their marriage was a hopeless failure, even if she refused to see it. The more he pitied her, the more savagely he resented her. Her goodness was a constant reproach to him. Their ill-begotten daughter looked like some sort of hideous goblin change-ling, and Lorenzo loathed the sight of her. She was a little wild thing, always biting and screaming, and he shuddered to think what might be wrong with her.

At his lowest point the previous night, Lorenzo had de-cided that dying would be his best option. His life was miserable, and he made other people miserable. God knew what would happen, if he was forced to put up with Eleanor and the child for any length of time.

This morning, however, with the sun above him and en-ergy pulsing through his body, he felt that it was a fine thing to live. Earlier, he had looked over the parapet, through a periscope, at the land he was to lead his men across. The barbed wire had been beaded with dew; the young grass and frail, scarlet poppies had quivered in the breeze. Then, a fat pheasant had waddled majestically across his line of vision, somehow pressing home the message that life was a thing to cling to and struggle for.

I will come back, Lorenzo told himself, listening to the shallow, nervous breathing of the men around him. Over their heads, a lark soared with the sun on its wings, pouring music into the clear air.

Stevie would never get used to the sense of being in a dream that swept over him when he went into battle. It took him by surprise every time—the aching intensity of his senses, the feeling that a thick, dull, everyday skin had been peeled away, leaving him exquisitely tender and alive. Life changed its shape. Lorenzo, Francesca and his parents faded to the back of his mind, and his love for them became theoretical. His orders and the importance of carrying them out to the letter filled his horizon. Through the ecstasy of being in action at last, he was aware that the great plan appeared to be going wrong.

After forming with his men in front of the British wire, he was to advance at a steady walking pace over the rough, shell-damaged ground for 900 yards until he reached the German trench that was his first objective. This, he as-sumed, would have been stormed and taken by the first wave of men—Lorenzo among them. Stevie was simply to regroup here, and then go on to another trench, 1,000 yards away, to await further orders.

But there had been a mistake somewhere. The enemy,

who were supposed to be crushed and decimated after days of shelling, were horribly hearty, and spewing out a tempest of machine-gun fire. No-man's-land was strewn with bodies, and with wounded men trying to crawl home.

Within sight of the first objective, Stevie cast around for his men. The bullets were swishing past him, so close that their breath kissed his cheeks, but he was too frantic to care.

"Ayres," he shouted desperately, "where are the boys?"

"Get down, sir!"

In disbelief, Stevie counted the remaining heads of his flock. "Where are the rest of them?"

"For God's sake, sir, get your head down!"

Around him, Stevie saw men being mown down like grass. *Man that is born of woman hath but a short time to live,* he thought distractedly; *He cometh up, and is cut down, like a flower* . . . A great kick of pain knocked him backward, so violently that his feet left the ground. The landscape swirled around him like a diorama, before the deep night fell across it. He landed in a tangle of rusted German barbed wire, twitched, and was still.

In the last of the light, no-man's-land was full of sighs and cries, and fleeting shadows.

"That's him, sir, over there," Sergeant Ayres murmured into Lorenzo's ear. "I'm as sure of it as I can be."

They had allowed themselves just enough daylight for Ayres to see the landmarks he had passed earlier. Cautiously, they had picked their way through the landscape of bodies. The wounded grabbed at their ankles as they passed, and they had muttered guiltily about stretcher-bearers. Some of the men had wept at the sound of another voice, others had shrieked and sworn at them: "Bastards! Don't leave me here, you fucking bastards!"

Lorenzo held his revolver ready, for there were other shapes moving around them—probably just as wary of him as he was of them, but it was best to be careful. He was aware that Ayres was watching him narrowly. He thought Mr. Hastings had gone barmy, and was about to run amok.

Perhaps I am, Lorenzo thought. He was still staggered to have survived the day without a graze when so many had fallen around him, and the news that Stevie had not returned had filled him with a determination that was half-crazy. The wrong man had been taken, and he could not live unless he did something about it. The unfairness was insupportable.

"Sir," Ayres said, "don't expect to find him alive."

"Did you see him die?" Lorenzo demanded feverishly. "Did you stop to check that he was dead?"

"Well no, but—"

Lorenzo made an effort to control himself. "This is very decent of you, Ayres. If ever we get back in one piece, I'll recommend you for a medal as big as a breakfast gong." He put away his revolver.

Both men took out wire-cutters, and began clipping and pruning their way through the barbed wire, toward the black shape Ayres had pointed out. It looked like a fly, lashed to the web of some huge spider.

"Oh, dear God," groaned Lorenzo.

Half of Stevie's head was plastered with clotted black blood; a thick layer of slime. The other half of his face was gray and motionless.

Ayres said, as gently as he knew how, "He's had it, sir."

"No—"

"Shall we turn back?"

"No!" Ferociously, Lorenzo hauled Stevie's body out of the wire. "We're taking him with us. It should have been me, not him. I'm not leaving him here."

"All right, sir." Ayres thought it best to humor him. He offered to take the feet, but Lorenzo insisted upon carrying him alone.

"He's warm," he said.

The body let out a low wail, guttural and inhuman, and opened its one eye.

"He's alive! My good God—Stevie, it's me—"

Stevie wailed again. Out of one corner of his mouth, he mumbled: "Leave. Please."

"Oh, no. I'd rather die myself."

"You're hurting him, sir," Ayres said, in an anguished voice. "He'll cry out—"

"He can scream blue murder, for all I care." Lorenzo's nostrils were full of the sweetish, sickly smell of blood and corruption. His shoulder was warm and wet, where Stevie's blood was oozing through his tunic and shirt. Keeping his eyes on Ayres's back, he stumbled across the dark, pitted landscape. Stevie weighed like lead in his arms. His shrieks of pain faded to whimpers, then to silence. Lorenzo did not know whether he was unconscious or dead. He did not care if the weight of the body pulled his arms from their sockets. He was alight with rage at the injustice of it, and the frustration of being unable to take on Stevie's pain himself.

Their own lines were in view now, and Ayres was snipping a path through the wire. Yards from the heaps of sandbags, he whistled the signal he had arranged with the sentry. Lorenzo was taking his final steps to safety when a burst of sniper fire sliced into his rib cage. He fell with a roar of fury that filled his mouth with the metallic taste of blood.

Three

Francesca leaned wearily against the rail of the veranda, watching the first scarlet leaves skating across the lawn of Calcutta Lodge. The last few months had worn her out, body, mind and spirit, and when she glanced down at her hands, she was surprised to see how old they looked. She had grown up a great deal during those long nights of sitting with Stevie.

But the whole country had grown old and sad. Francesca shuddered at the memory of the ghastly hush that had fallen across London when the casualty lists came in from the Somme—column after column of *The Times*, each lost life the end of a dozen others. The place-names tolled through the imagination like funeral bells. Fricourt, Mametz, High Wood, Martinpuich, Bapaume. She would never hear them again without hearing the voice of Rachel, weeping for her children.

And she had been lucky. After an agony of waiting, during which Marian had delivered awful lectures about the duty of a soldier's wife, the telegram had arrived, with the news that Stevie was alive. Marian had shouted at the parlormaid, for giving the telegram to Francesca, instead of to her. She was the true Mrs. Carr-Lyon, and the only one with any rights over Stevie.

During the tense weeks at the nursing home, when Stevie hovered between life and death, his mother had taken up a permanent sentry post beside his bed. Francesca had been reduced to waiting for permission to see her husband—because he must not be distressed or tired, Marian said. Apparently, more than a few moments of Francesca's company were enough to distress him.

Stevie had lost his left eye. There was now only a scorched, puckered socket where it had been. A huge scar plunged from above his eyebrow through the socket and cheekbone, pulling the flesh slightly out of shape. He had been lucky, for some of the shrapnel had pierced his skull. People could not tell them often enough how nearly he had died. Francesca was sure he had been spared because she was learning how to love him in the right way. She had ached to be near him, but Marian had always found reasons to chase her away. She did everything for Stevie, as if he had been a baby, and became bright-eyed and rosy while Francesca grew pale.

So it might have remained, if Colonel Carr-Lyon had not been posted from his desk in France to a more important desk in London. On his first visit to Stevie, he had found Francesca sitting meekly outside the room, like a servant waiting to be interviewed. He had taken her inside, and they had all had a very jolly visit. Stevie had been roused by his father and a VAD had brought them tea.

That night, however, Francesca had heard her parents-in-law shouting at each other through the bedroom wall. Both had loud, barking voices. The Colonel's, in particular, made the bedsprings vibrate.

"What are you playing at, leaving her to hang around in some drafty corridor?"

"If she wants to come in, she only has to say—"

"Nonsense. She's scared stiff of you."

"A child like that is no earthly use in a sickroom. You know what she's like."

"She's his wife, Marian. You're only his mother."

"Only! Only his mother! What does she know about a mother's love—that little chit, that wax doll? How can her love be half as good as mine?"

"Well, I wonder what you'd have thought if my old mother had shoved her oar in, that time I was laid up after Magersfontein."

"That was different. Stevie needs me."

"So you've always said—trying to turn him into a damned mother's boy."

"And you've always tried to make him grow away from me!"

"I don't want any more fuss, Marian. You'll leave the boy to his wife from now on. And that's an order."

Since then, Francesca had spent nearly all her time at Stevie's side. She had a natural tenderness for sick people, and her love for Stevie deepened when their roles were

reversed, and she was the protective one. Two weeks ago,
she had brought him to Calcutta Lodge, to convalesce. He
was now well enough to lie on the sofa, or sit on a basket
chair on the lawn. Strangely, the disfiguring scar had the
effect of making him look handsomer than ever, since the
other half of his face was more unblemished and angelic in
contrast. He was very good-tempered and cheerful, and
often joked about the piratical figure he cut in his black
eye patch. But he still suffered terribly from headaches,
and when Francesca sat with him in his darkened room,
endlessly applying ice to his forehead, she felt her youthful
energy draining away.

Oh, cheer up, Francesca scolded herself. Today was a
festival occasion, and she had absolutely no right to feel so
low. Stevie's parents were motoring up from London.
Nanny Stack and a girl from the village were preparing an
elaborate meal, and Stevie himself had gone down to the
cellar to choose the wine. He had felt well enough that
morning to dress in flannels and a jersey, and was now
sitting in his chair on the lawn, throwing a ball for the
gardener's cocker spaniel.

Francesca was a little hurt by his cheerfulness, for the
reason was obvious. The luncheon was being held in honor
of Lorenzo. This would be the first time the pair of them
had met since the day they had been wounded. Of course,
Francesca was immeasurably grateful to Lorenzo, but
something in the quality of Stevie's happiness made her
afraid.

She was also jealous of Eleanor, because she had a child.
Her marriage might have been stormy and full of pain, yet
Francesca could see it had a vitality her own marriage
lacked. Although she made every allowance for Stevie
being ill, she did wonder why he avoided touching her
whenever he could. Every day, no matter how sweet and
kind he was to her, Francesca felt plainer and duller, and
less visible. She could not shake off the idea that it was her
fault; that there was some flaw in her that disgusted him.

"Madam!" Nanny was calling from the dining room.

"All right." Francesca smoothed her hair, and straightened the cameo at her throat. The senior Carr-Lyons were
in the drive, being helped from their car by an ancient
chauffeur. Stevie received them in the sunny garden, with
almost exuberant cheerfulness, but Francesca noted how

feverishly he waited, and how he flinched and blushed at the sound of another car in the drive.

Eleanor had driven them cross-country from Rotting-dean, where she had recently leased a cottage. Lorenzo appeared on the veranda leaning on her arm, wearing a uniform with a wound-stripe sewn to his sleeve. He was very thin, and his black eyes glittered more fiercely than ever.

There was an awkward moment, when Marian showed an inclination to fall upon his shattered breast and weep. Deterred by his tremendous scowl of embarrassment, however, she merely kissed his cheek, and said: "Laurence, we can never be grateful enough."

Francesca decided this was as good a time as any to get the frightening part over. She gave Lorenzo her hand, whispering: "Thank you."

He kept hold of her hand for a moment, gazing down at her, as if something in her face surprised him.

Stevie struggled out of his chair, and laughingly embraced Lorenzo. He had been keyed up and nervous, but now that they were actually together, he was almost his old self again.

"Poor old Larry, what a scene—I bet you wish you'd thrown me back. Someone might at least offer you a drink."

"Yes, by God," the Colonel shouted, relieved. "And congratulations, Hastings. Very well deserved."

Lorenzo had been mentioned in dispatches, and awarded the Military Cross. He looked most annoyed at having it mentioned. Stevie, with his usual tact, changed the subject by insisting that it was time for luncheon.

Afterward, he took Lorenzo out on the veranda to smoke. The Colonel fell asleep under *The Times,* and the women gathered around the drawing room fire for coffee.

"Nanny never could cook to save her life," Marian announced, "but she can make decent coffee." The occasion, and a glass of champagne, had mellowed her.

Eleanor was looking through the sealed French windows at Lorenzo and Stevie. "Will they be warm enough out there?"

"Shall I ask them?" offered Francesca.

"Heavens, no! Lorenzo will bite your head off. He

loathes being fussed over. It's terribly awkward, when he's been so ill."

"Darling, you do look tired. Has it been dreadful?"

Eleanor sighed. "It's not Lorenzo, it's Laura. Mrs. Bintry has her today—but I dread to think what I'll find when we get home. I hate being parted from her, no matter what she does."

"Gracious," Marian exclaimed, "what's wrong with the child?"

Eleanor reddened, but answered levelly: "She has such an impossible temper, every little thing brings on a fit of screaming. And she—she hasn't quite got used to Lorenzo."

Francesca scrutinized Eleanor's forearms. "Did she give you those frightful bruises?"

"No, of course not!" Eleanor laughed. "Nobody gave them to me. I managed to fall down the cellar steps. You know how clumsy I am." Francesca seemed to want to say more, but she hurried on. "I do wish you would both come to see the cottage. It's paradise, and I'm turning myself into a real country wife. I have three beehives, you know, and a flock of geese. Mrs. Bintry is going to show me how to make goosefat embrocation for Lorenzo's chest." Her eyes were radiant and beautiful with love. "Every day, I tell myself how lucky I am to have him at home with me."

Marian asked: "Will he have to go back?"

"Yes, but not until well after Christmas. The war might be over by then, mightn't it? What about Stevie? I mean, obviously he can't go back. What will he do?"

Out on the veranda, Lorenzo had asked the same question.

Stevie leaned back in his chair. "No idea. I might get a desk somewhere if Dad can pull the right strings."

"At least you'll be out of it."

"Don't say that! I can't stand it."

"Don't tell me you're sorry! I know you're a tiger for duty, Stevie, but you've given them enough."

"Oh, I shan't miss the beastly parts—the noise and the cold, and never getting my boots off. But I have dreams about Ayres and the lads. They're always calling to me to save them."

"I know," Lorenzo said. "I waste half my time wondering how my chaps are managing without me."

"Have you heard any news?"

"Yes, but I shouldn't tell you. Eleanor's been lecturing me about how delicate you are. You'll only cry, or something equally frightful."

Stevie turned his one, cloudless blue eye toward him. "I won't," he said seriously, "because I can't. Isn't it weird? I've run out of tears."

"Perhaps it's just as well. Too many being shed these days." Lorenzo lit another cigarette, from the stub of the last. "My Kardomah string quartet is reduced to a duet. One is in the hospital, I believe, and one is sawing away in the Paradise Philharmonia. Two of the shopwalkers have gone west. And did you hear about Bubble and Squeak?"

"No."

"Can you bear it?"

"Tell me."

Lorenzo sighed. "I hardly know how, without saying 'Rosencrantz and Guildenstern are dead.' Though actually, only Bubble's dead. Killed out in Mesopotamia. Squeak's merely gone barmy. He was in an institution in Scotland for a while, now he's at home in Northumberland. He gets up at dawn, and goes into the garden with binoculars and tin hat, for stand-to."

"Oh God."

"Pots at encroaching cows with an air gun."

"Oh hell. Poor old Squeakie."

"And they were going to live forever," Lorenzo said, on a sudden surge of bitterness. "Do you remember? Christ, Stevie, this is all so awful. Why won't we admit it to ourselves? Life is utter shit, and we'd all die now if we dared."

Stevie smiled. "You only see the awful part."

"And you only see sickening sweetness and light." Lorenzo softened. "But I'm glad you can still see anything at all."

"Do you like my eye patch?"

"No, because it isn't fair. You're the type who deserves the full quota of limbs and features, and so on. I wouldn't have missed an eye—I've only the one ear, as it is. It should have been me."

Stevie laid a hand on his sleeve. "You've had a bad enough time, by all accounts."

"Rather. Eleanor and that kid of hers are worse than the enemy barrage. They'll drive me into an early grave."

"Come on," Stevie coaxed, "it can't be so bad."

"Can't it?" The frown melted from Lorenzo's face. He gave Stevie one of his reluctant, lopsided smiles. "This is obviously why you were spared; to keep the peace in my unfortunate family."

"Sorry. I don't mean to interfere."

"Yes, you do. Look, you're not to worry about us. I dare say we'll struggle on somehow, until I get sent back to the front." Briefly, he stroked Stevie's hair. "I'll miss you."

Such demonstrations were very rare. Stevie shivered with pleasure, and murmured: "Everyone's thanked you but me."

"You don't have to," Lorenzo said. He leaned forward long enough to kiss Stevie on the forehead, just above his scar. "I owed you a life."

Four

A log cracked loudly on the fire, and Lorenzo woke with an anxious rush of adrenaline, in time to hear the drawing room clock chime five. His heart racing, he lay back in the armchair. There was a cold cup of tea on the small table beside him. Mrs. Bintry had not dared to wake him. The woman treated him like Jack the Ripper—ugly, self-righteous, spying old cat that she was—but she was the only servant they had managed to keep. He wondered what strange masochism kept her in his miserable household when she could have earned twice as much in a munitions factory.

He glanced out of the latticed windows at the rain-blotched view of fields and orchards. The country was supposed to be good for his health, but it only made him nervous. He could not look at the opposite ridge without expecting to see a gun emplacement, and when he lay awake at night, he drove himself nearly crazy planning raids on the farm next door. The silence reminded him too forcibly of the lifting of the barrage moments before an attack.

Naturally, Eleanor loved this place. She adored tending the hives, storing the apples, bottling and canning all the plump produce of the garden. Lorenzo also suspected her of hoping that out here, the child would somehow become normal—she had a stubborn aversion to the truth when it happened not to suit her. He stretched painfully, cursing the dragging, eternal weariness that kept him in his wife's custody. The moment he was strong enough to get to the station unaided, he would escape to London.

Outside, he heard the local taxi spluttering in the lane. She was back. Lorenzo hated himself for not wanting to see her. Against the orders of his doctor, he poured himself an enormous whiskey. From the window, he watched his wife and daughter, thinking how odd it was that they should belong to him.

While Eleanor paid the driver, Laura tottered busily around the front lawn, pulling up fistfuls of flowers. At only twenty months, she was as knowing and agile as a monkey. Her father's tar-colored, heavily lashed eyes dominated a sallow, peaky, ugly little face. She was, as dozens of departing nursemaids had informed them, ungovernable and impossible. Lorenzo could not look at her without a shudder of antipathy, and the feeling was mutual; the child had been ten times worse since he came home.

Eleanor's face was covered by her hat veil, but every line of her body expressed dejection and exhaustion. She called, in a high, strained voice: "Laura! Laura!"

"You idiot," Lorenzo groaned to himself. "What's the bloody use of shouting at her?" He downed the whiskey in one angry gulp.

Laura saw him at the window. Her tiny body froze—she had a way of appearing to bristle all over and bare every tooth in her head, like an animal at bay—and she burst into ear-splitting yells of terror and loathing.

Mrs. Bintry came out, said something to Eleanor, and bore the screaming brat away toward the back door. Predictably—and for some reason this made him furious—Eleanor's first concern was for her husband.

The moment she stepped through the drawing room door, she asked: "How are you, darling? Did you manage to sleep at all, this afternoon? I do hope Laura didn't disturb you." She removed her hat in front of the mirror, lifting the veil to reveal a swollen, sorrowful face.

"Well?" he demanded. "What did this one say?"

She pretended not to hear. "I bought you a new bottle of iron tonic and—"

"Eleanor, for God's sake. You took the child to a specialist. What did he say?"

"Oh"—Eleanor twisted her wedding ring—"the same. Exactly the same as all the others, but—"

"There you are, then. Now will you accept the truth?"

"But, Lorenzo," she said eagerly, "he didn't know her, none of them do. She wasn't behaving, that's all. I tried to explain that she was only being naughty."

"You idiotic woman, this is the third man you've seen—

the most eminent in Europe, apparently. Why won't you face facts? The child was born deaf."

"No! I swear she heard the tuning fork, she just refused to turn around."

"Listen to me!" he shouted. "Listen to me, you imbecile. Your daughter is deaf, incurably and profoundly deaf. Which is why she won't respond to a call or a shout, or a clap of thunder—and why her crying sounds like a sawmill going at full pelt, and tears my bloody nerves to shreds!"

Eleanor, exhausted after weeks of nursing, mothering and keeping the peace, dissolved into frightened tears. Lorenzo saw what it cost her to part with her last hope. He loathed himself for not being able to pity her.

"I don't know what to do," she sobbed. "How shall I ever manage her now? My poor little lamb—"

"A marvelous piece of irony," Lorenzo said, pouring himself another whiskey, "when you think of all the things that might have been wrong with her. Do you want a drink?"

"No, and you shouldn't either." Eleanor wiped her eyes distractedly. "I asked him if it could be connected to what your mother did to you. It isn't, of course. And then I asked if it could have been because you were drunk when we—when Laura was conceived."

"Thank you very much. Did you ask if it had anything to do with the appalling selective deafness of her mother—her inability to hear sentences like 'I don't love you' and 'I don't want to marry you'?"

"Oh, please! I had to find out! I'm so afraid it was something I did while I was expecting her—that I might have injured her, when I love her so much—"

"I always said there would be something wrong with it," Lorenzo said. "You refused to hear that, too."

"Don't—oh, don't!"

"Well, now you see I was right, you can take responsibility for her—you can damned well stop nagging me to like her, because I never will."

"Don't, Lorenzo! Don't be cruel! She's your daughter! She shouldn't have to beg for your love!"

"Put her in an institution."

Eleanor, failing as usual to detect the irony which underlined nearly everything Lorenzo said, screamed: "No! I

don't care what you do to me—but you can't take away
my baby!"

Lorenzo opened his mouth to reply, and saw Mrs. Bintry
standing in the doorway, hands folded primly over her
apron. She had a habit of suddenly materializing wherever
there were raised voices. "Excuse me, madam. At what
time shall I serve dinner?"

She addressed Eleanor, but looked malevolently at Lorenzo. He longed to hurl his glass at her. A sickening exhaustion took hold of him, and he collapsed suddenly into
the armchair.

Eleanor was kneeling at his side immediately. "My darling, I'm so sorry. It's been too much for you and I could
only think of myself. Mrs. Bintry, we'd better eat as soon
as possible, and would you bring Sir Laurence another cup
of tea?"

"Very good, madam."

Lorenzo, through his miasma of nausea, read in her face
a desire to lace it with arsenic, and half wished she would.
He was trapped, imprisoned in a sick body, a remote cottage, a soul-destroying marriage. Eleanor's affectionate
hand lay on his knee with the weight of a millstone.

The pianist had played his final encore, and the auditorium
of the Queen's Hall was emptying rapidly. Only the officer
with the dark hair remained, motionless and listing slightly
to one side. Rory, several rows behind, had been watching
the back of his head for the past hour.

Aubrey stood up, searching his waistcoat pockets for his
cloakroom ticket. "May I give you a lift anywhere, darling?
I'd adore to buy you tea, but alas, I must retrieve my hat
and fly."

Rory kissed his lined cheek. "Go on—and thanks so
much for this divine concert. I can't leave until I've braved
the lion's cage."

"Are you sure that's your friend's husband? He seems
perfectly innocuous. I expected a fanged ogre, at the very
least."

She laughed. "I don't believe he's dangerous, just rather
too full of vinegar. And he was badly wounded, poor thing.
I ought to make sure he's all right."

When Aubrey had hurried off, she made her way through
the sea of plush toward the young man she had recognized

as Lorenzo. He was deeply asleep, and she allowed herself to study his face at close quarters. It was thinner than when she had seen it last, and lined around the thin, tense lips. But so young, she thought, with an unexpected stirring of sympathy. Young and exhausted, and lonely.

She shook his shoulder. Very slowly, his spiky black lashes lifted. Still and silent, he was staring at her with eyes so dark, they seemed to have no pupils. Rory stared back, suddenly intensely curious.

"Hello," he said, after a moment or two.

She sat down beside him. "Hello. Aurora Carlington."

"Yes, I know who you are."

"I thought you might have forgotten me."

"How could I possibly?"

Rory smiled. "I saw you in the interval, and knew you almost at once. You slept through the Debussy."

"Any good?"

"I thought so—but I'm so starved of diversions these days, I become excited if I hear a barrel organ. Are you all right?"

"Yes."

"What are you doing in London? I thought you were living in a pastoral idyll."

"If it's any of your business," he said dryly, "the idyll bores me."

"It's supposed to," returned Rory. "Eleanor leased it especially for your convalescence. What did you expect—a casino?"

Lorenzo was beginning to thaw into amusement. "I've never understood why a view of wet fields is thought to be good for invalids. Unless it's because it fills one with a savage determination to get well as quickly as possible."

"You look tired," Rory said.

"Oh God. Not you too! Every woman in the world feels she has a right to tell me how I look."

She ignored this. "You need something to eat. The Langham Hotel is just across the road. Tell you what, you can take me out to tea."

For the first time, he smiled properly. "I say, that's awfully generous of you."

"Well, I'm famished, even if you're not, and I haven't a bean. Eleanor would be absolutely livid, if she heard that you met me, and wouldn't buy me a cup of tea."

"All right, all right. Blackmailer." He held out his hand. "Help me up."

His hand was warm, and he kept his fingers twined around hers a second longer than was necessary. "I still get breathless," he said. "I always imagined a bullet going in with a sort of piercing sensation. Actually, it's more like being kicked by a horse."

He did not offer her his arm as they left the Queen's Hall. Rory knew he was walking a little way apart from her to watch her. She was out of uniform, wearing a tailored coat and skirt Aubrey had had made for her, of conventional cut, but the color of a sapphire held to the light. Despite the chilly autumn weather, she was hatless. A newsboy outside the church in Langham Place shouted: "Ullo, Carrots!" at her, when she strode past.

Totally unconcerned, she led Lorenzo into the tearoom of the Langham Hotel, a cavernous room with a dusty chandelier and painted ceiling, full of officers. Behind a row of potted palms, a female piano trio, all arrayed in dim cretonnes and noisy ropes of amber beads, were plodding through a medley from *The Crinoline Girl.*

"Khaki everywhere," Lorenzo commented, glancing around suspiciously. "I wonder what we all did with ourselves, before the war?"

Rory poured them both tea. "We can't have been as happy and idle as we like to think now. We've just got too used to being miserable."

He turned his attention back to her. "Are you miserable?"

"Frightfully. In a month's time, my feet will be two huge chilblains, and I shan't see daylight for weeks on end." She put his tea down in front of him. "I wouldn't stand it for a moment, if there wasn't a war on."

He was eyeing her intently. "Carrots," he said.

"I'm sorry—?"

"I was just thinking how inaccurate he was. You have the reddest red hair I've ever seen, and a carrot is orange. It's more like a ripe tomato."

She was taken aback, and a little disturbed, but she managed a laugh. "Or the worst sort of pelargonium—the kind they put in municipal floral clocks."

"You wore a green and scarlet gown once," Lorenzo

said. "And the scarlet in it was almost the same color as your hair."

There was something intimate in the way he said it which made Rory's cheeks warm. "My Russian Ballet gown. What ages ago it seems."

"I meant to ask you to dance that night. But you had a tremendously jealous young man hanging around you." His eyes soured. "And I, of course, had Eleanor hanging around me."

Eleanor's name ought to have sounded warning bells, but did not. "I remember you staring at me," Rory said. It seemed overwhelmingly important to tell him this.

"I thought you were stunning. That's why I was so furious when it was you that turned up in Devonshire with Stevie." He chuckled softly. "And you had the supreme cheek to tell me I should have used a French Letter. I could have killed you."

They were both laughing, with the color rising in their cheeks, and their eyes locked together.

"Our tea's getting cold," she said.

"I know."

Neither of them moved.

Rory said: "I shouldn't have been so angry with you. I don't think it was fair."

"My feelings didn't matter. I did the right thing, even though it was perfectly clear to me that it would be a pretty awful marriage."

"And—and is it?"

"For God's sake, Rory. You must know it is."

"You shouldn't tell me," she said uneasily.

"Why not? Nobody else will listen. We were doomed from the start because I couldn't make Eleanor happy."

"Did you try?"

"No." Lorenzo took out a flat, gold case, and lit one of his Turkish cigarettes. "What would have been the point? Only one thing would ever make her happy. She wants me to love her—and I can't. I tell you, Rory, I'm bloody tired of being made to feel wicked because I can't love to order." He leaned across the table toward her. "Have you ever been in love? Madly, desperately, so that it was the only thing that mattered in the world?"

"Never." Rory realized, for the first time, that the true center of her heart had never been touched. "I thought I was once, but I was wrong. I found I could live without him quite easily."

"Where is he now?"

"Dead."

"I'm sorry. Where was he killed?"

"He was a pacifist. He died in prison." She smiled reminiscently. "How he would have disapproved of you, with your title and your MC."

"You don't disapprove though, do you?"

"Oh, no—"

"Not even when I freely confess to making your friend wretched?"

"I don't think you're as bad as you make yourself out to be."

"I can't breathe at home," he said suddenly. "That's why I'm here. You're right, I'm not well yet. But that coven of women—that gruesome baby, that vortex of reproach in the shape of a wife—" His eyes suddenly brimmed with tears, and he seized Rory's hands across the table. "Thank God, Rory—thank God I found you today. You know we have to meet again."

"Yes," Rory said. "When?"

Seeing Lorenzo again was as vital as breathing or drinking. Her existence before this afternoon had been a slow, dull, sepia-tinted affair. Now, everything had color and meaning. Without fear or guilt, she plunged willingly, hungrily, into the catastrophe of her life.

Five

There was still time to turn back. Rory had thought of it a thousand times, and it was all that had kept her from panicking, on this long, cold journey from London to Norfolk. She was now on a branch line running between Norwich and Cromer, telling herself she could not go through with it, and in a fever of anxiety, in case she missed the station.

The train halted just long enough to disgorge Rory and her carpetbag, then pulled away, leaving her alone, marooned in an immensity of flat, brown fields. The red November sun had dipped below the horizon, and the vast sky was darkening into twilight. The sound of the departing train was gradually overwhelmed by the deafening silence of the wintry countryside.

The only light came from one feeble lantern, nailed to the door of the station office. Rory drew her coat around her, shivering in the salt-tasting wind. Oh God, she thought, I should never have come.

She saw him then, leaning against the fence in the shadows, like the proverbial tall, dark stranger lurking in a crystal ball. She was conscious of fear, shame and longing, but mainly of a dreadful embarrassment.

"Lorenzo?"

"Hello." He stepped into the circle of light, and she saw that he was as nervous as she was; how close had he come to changing his mind?

They were careful not to touch. He took her bag, and she followed him to a muddy two-seater, parked in the lane outside. Quickly, before he could offer to help her, Rory climbed into the passenger seat. The oddness of it all was like a dream. Lorenzo was out of uniform, in unfamiliar tweeds. When he got into the car beside her, the heathery, musky scent of his clothes set her overcharged nerves jangling. She folded her gloved hands in her lap, so he would not see them shaking. He drove with an air of being only just on the right side of graciousness. Was he glad she had come, or did he despise her? And where on earth was he taking her?

After twenty minutes or so, Lorenzo swerved through a tall pair of wrought-iron gates, past an empty lodge with its windows boarded up. He took them slowly down a gloomy, neglected avenue, and they emerged in front of a long, square eighteenth-century manor house. In the last of the light, Rory made out a gray stucco façade, and a portico lashed with the gnarled, sinewy tendrils of very old wisteria.

Lorenzo got out of the car, grabbing her bag.

"Come on," he said over his shoulder.

Doing her best not to appear too cowed, Rory scuttled after him. The house, as far as she could see, was in reasonable repair, yet one could somehow tell that no one had lived in it for decades. The unlit windows had an extinguished look, like the eyes of waxworks, and the front door was heavily padlocked.

They used the back door, which opened into stone-flagged sculleries and servants' quarters. For one moment, they were overwhelmed by the mildewy desolation of an empty house. But Lorenzo opened another door, and Rory found herself blinking in the light of a clean, bright kitchen, with a fire roaring in the range. A battered old sofa, draped in faded patchwork quilts, had been pushed against one wall. There was a large box of groceries on the table, and two bottles of claret were warming on the hearth rug.

Rory spread her hands to the blaze. Lorenzo poured the wine, and his fingers brushed hers as he gave her a glass.

"You're cold."

The gesture warmed Rory more than the fire. "Where are we?" she asked. "You've been so mysterious. Whose house is this?"

"Mine. I don't let on that I own it, and I haven't been here in years. There's not a servant in the place. I gave the caretaker a holiday. You don't mind being alone, do you?"

"Oh no—"

"Good. That was rather the point, after all, wasn't it?"

They lowered their eyes, unable to break through the awkwardness.

"I want to show you something," Lorenzo said suddenly.

He took away her wineglass and picked up an oil lamp from the table.

She followed him out of the kitchen and into an eerie world of shuttered windows and shrouded furniture, on the other side of the baize door. Pictures and ornaments loomed at them, as the light struck the faded walls. Rory gasped: "My God!", catching a menacing gleam of eyes and teeth.

"Don't panic," Lorenzo's voice said dryly. "It's stuffed."

The chilly air took on a breath of lavender and ancient woodsmoke. They were in a drawing room, under a great chandelier wrapped in brown holland. More eyes gleamed—painted eyes, dark and melancholy.

"My mother," he said.

Rory drew in a sharp breath, realizing he was showing her something uniquely private. She studied the portrait curiously. Lady Elizabeth Hastings posed in her white court dress, with white feathers in her dark hair. She bore a marked resemblance to Lorenzo.

"She was Lady Elizabeth Dalton when that was done," Lorenzo said. "The usefulness of prussic acid as an antidote to marriage had not yet been revealed to her."

"Don't—poor woman, I'm sorry for her. She must have been so unhappy to do what she did."

"I'd like to have had the chance to ask her about it," he said slowly, in the rusty and reluctant voice he kept for admissions. "I've always longed to know exactly what was in her mind that night."

Rory shuddered. "This wasn't the house where—"

"No, of course not!" He swung the light away from the portrait, half irritated and half amused. "Good God, Rory, as if I'd take you there. Give me some credit."

"I never know what you'll do."

"And yet you've trusted me this far. I'm a hopelessly bad host, aren't I? Let's have something to eat."

The kitchen was warm and welcoming. Rory breathed a little easier. "Shall I cook something?"

"You don't have to."

She began to rummage through the box of groceries, wondering how long they would be able to endure this excruciating politeness. So far, they had behaved like two desert island castaways, making the best of each other's company because they had to.

"I hope you didn't invite me for the sake of my cooking," she said, "or you're in for an awful disappointment."

Quietly, he said: "You know why I asked you here. Did you have trouble getting away?"

Unable to concentrate on the labels of tins, Rory reached for her wineglass. "Not really. I was owed some leave from the unit, and I don't have to answer to anyone else." She tried to sound casual. "What about you?"

Lorenzo replied: "I simply told her I was going away for a couple of weeks. She never makes a fuss. I think the kid is easier to manage when I'm out of the way."

Rory could not bear to talk about Eleanor and her child for long. She was bitterly jealous, and so guilty that she was almost angry with Eleanor for being innocent and wronged. "What about tinned peas and sausages?"

"Damn the sausages."

"Scrambled eggs, then."

"Rory," Lorenzo said gravely, "stop being angry."

"I'm not. Not with you, anyway. With myself."

"Do you wish you hadn't come?"

He was standing very close to her. She could not look him in the eye. "I had to come. But I wish we'd never met. You know it can't lead to anything except trouble."

"Don't think about the future. You have to learn to live inside the moment." He threw his cigarette into the fire, and pulled her face around toward his. "I haven't kissed you once—not in all the times we've met."

"I thought you didn't want to." Rory was afraid, but possessed by a peculiar, delicious languor.

"I wanted to desperately. But I was afraid of wanting too much more. That's why I had to find a private place for us, where we could be alone."

Rory's blood was drumming in her ears. She had waited all this time for him to touch her. Very tentatively, his mouth found hers. The second their lips fused, it was as if they had been struck by lightning—those weeks of frustration had stoked their desire into frenzy.

Lorenzo tore open his trousers, and they both fell to the floor. He was inside her before she got more than a glimpse of his erection. Eyes half-closed, she focused on the animal pleasure of his hardness moving inside her. He came quickly, with painful, savage thrusts, shouting her name. They lay in silence, breathless and pulsing.

A hot coal dropped onto the tiles behind the fender. They rolled apart and stared at one another in amazement. The barrier between them had been ripped down. They were one flesh now, and the sudden closeness was frightening. Rory was aware of his muscles and nerves, as if they had been an extension of her own.

She lay on her back, her legs spread. She was calm, basking in the warm glow that had its center between her legs. She could not move. The lips of her vagina felt gorged and fiery.

Without taking his eyes from her, Lorenzo drained his wineglass, and began to take off his clothes. He left his shirt until last. His chest was heavily embossed with a network of fading scars, like the branches of a tree, where they had ripped him open to pull out the pieces of lead.

When he was naked, he knelt over her, and placed a finger lightly on her wet clitoris. Watching her with a kind of brooding curiosity, he began massaging the delicate skin around it, until it hardened to an aching ridge. Rory had no idea what he was doing to her. It felt dangerous, but irresistible. His strokes became harder and rougher, and she ground herself against his hand, arching her back in her desperation. When, for the first time in her life, she climaxed, she felt the explosion in every atom of her body.

He was hard again. Sighing with bliss, he thrust himself back inside her. They made love slowly and dreamily this time, relishing each sensation, until they were satisfied and exhausted.

Still twitching with the afterpangs of his orgasm, Lorenzo said: "I love you."

"Lorenzo, I love you."

He propped himself on his elbows. "I've done it again."

"Done what?"

"No rubber. Don't laugh. What's so bloody funny?"

"Serves me right for lecturing you last time."

"For God's sake, what if—?"

"It doesn't matter," Rory interrupted him. "I'm not afraid, whatever happens."

He kissed her forehead. "Whatever happens, I adore you, and I'll take care of you.

They lay twined in each other's arms, until Rory announced that she was starving. She cooked the sausages and tinned peas, and they finished the second bottle of wine. They talked until nearly two in the morning. Finally, Lorenzo took her to a squashy brass bedstead, and fell asleep curled around her.

Rory always thought of the next two weeks as the happiest of her life. Even at the time, however, she knew this was not strictly accurate. Happiness implies contentment, and she was living at the highest pitch of emotion, flying higher and higher, yet always knowing there would be nothing to catch her when she fell.

They made love at all hours, in all kinds of places. Last thing at night, and first thing in the morning, Lorenzo fucked her in the cozy embrace of the brass bed. During the day, when she stood at the range or the sink, preparing one of their picnic meals, he would pull up her skirts and take her from behind. She loved the tremor that ran through him when he came.

Out in the fields, they satisfied their eternal mutual hunger on stiles and in hedges. He impaled her against the trunks of trees, ramming into her with swift, selfish thrusts, then kneeling to lap away his own sperm. She discovered the delight of taking his penis into her mouth, and exploring his tenderest places with her tongue.

The bouts of lovemaking, however, were only physical manifestations of a love that grew deeper and more interdependent every day. They were living in a dream, barely sleeping because they had so much to tell one another. Sometimes, they walked, reveling in the brisk, cold air. They lay together in the huge cast-iron bath, drinking wine from steam-fogged glasses. One day, Lorenzo put on his uniform, and they drove into Swaffham; ostensibly to place orders at the shops, but really to savor the joy of their isolation among crowds of other people.

Lorenzo took the cover off the piano in the drawing room, and tuned it. The tone was a little warped by damp, but good enough to play. On wet days, he serenaded her with Chopin, Brahms, Schubert and Schumann—the Romantics he had despised before he fell in love.

They laughed, they argued, they walked, or they simply sat reading together, in companionable silence, while the bare branches tapped against the windows, and the ash fell softly in the grate.

On Rory's last day, they went out shooting and gathered a handsome bag of wood pigeon. Rory plucked, drew and

roasted the birds, while Lorenzo searched in the cellar for
the oldest and rarest wines. Both felt, though neither said
anything, that this should be a special occasion. Rory threw
herself into the extra work, glad of anything that would
take her mind off tomorrow. Separation lay at the end of
this evening like a great gray wall. She could not bring
herself to think of what lay beyond it.

They sat on cushions, on the floor of the bare dining
room. A log fire roared in the grate. Candles flickered in
empty wine bottles, and moonlight streamed in through the
long, uncurtained windows.

"We should have had more candles," Rory said. "I can't
see to get the shot out of these birds."

"Dammit, that reminds me—I nearly forgot." Lorenzo
pushed aside his plate, and dug in his jacket pocket. "It's
a present for you. It came this morning."

Rory was no longer hungry. There was a stone in her
throat. "That was one of our rules. No flowers or gifts."

"I know, but this is different, I swear." He was deadly
serious, and his eyes had a compelling glitter in the flick-
ering light. "Please, Rory."

Reluctantly, she took the small, velvet-covered box out
of his hand. On the lid, she made out the gilded name of
a Bond Street jeweler. Inside it, on a bed of white silk, lay
a large gold brooch, set with sapphires and diamonds—
sapphire forget-me-nots with diamond hearts. Rory stared
at it, not knowing what to say. Any woman who cared for
such things would have been delighted, but Lorenzo should
have known she did not. This was not a lover's token, but
an emotionally neutral piece of portable property.

"Press the catch at the side," Lorenzo said.

Tilting the brooch toward the candle, she found the
catch. The jeweled front sprang open, to reveal a heavy
nugget of gray metal, and an inscription: "A.C. from L.H.
Nov 1916. Omnia vincit amor: et nos cedamus amori."

"Virgil," Rory said, in a shaking voice. "Love conquers
all, let us, too, surrender to love."

"The lump of metal is one of the bullets they pulled out
of me at the casualty clearing station." He was smiling.
"The one that went in closest to my heart."

She closed her fist around his gift, and began to cry.

"Rory—" He had never seen her in tears. "My darling—"

"I'm sorry. But I can't bear to think of its being over."

Lorenzo scrambled to her side, crashing through the ruins of the supper. "It's not over!" He held her chin, so that she was forced to look at him. "It never will be while there's breath in my body! My sick leave isn't up yet, and we'll see each other when you get back to town."

"What about Eleanor?"

"I've told you a hundred times, I've never loved her. You're taking nothing from her."

"Oh God, I wish I could believe that!" Rory wiped her face on the sleeve of her jersey. "You don't love her—but I do. And I hate myself for taking away the only thing that means anything to her." She could not speak through her racking sobs. Lorenzo took her in his arms, and they clung together fiercely, as if they could press their two bodies into one.

"I won't let you blame yourself for this," he said. "I wanted it to happen, because I fell in love with you. Don't you know what you've done for me? Over these two weeks, I've tasted happiness for the first time in my life. The world has some meaning for me now, and some hope for the future, thanks to you."

"Help me, Lorenzo!" Rory sobbed out. "I'm too selfish to let you go! I think I'll die without you!"

Instinctively, they reached for the comfort of each other's flesh, and made love with lingering slowness, until they were both sore and sucked dry. Afterward, they lay beside the dying fire, feeling the hours and minutes pass.

In the sober light of the following morning, Lorenzo drove Rory to the station. They had hardly exchanged a word since waking, and waited for the Norwich train in grim silence. When it arrived, Lorenzo kissed her briefly, whispering: "I love you," and in a few short seconds, Rory was speeding away from him.

The compartment was empty, and she wept. Her period had started, and there was a barb of anguish mixed with the relief. She had tempted the Fates and got away with it, but suspected they had another punishment in store for her. The love that had become the center of her life could only be continued in an atmosphere of secrecy and lies. She would have to extract what happiness she could from hurried furtive meetings, and they would always end in tears like these—doubly bitter because she was alone.

Six

"Lovers should be excused winter," Jamie shouted above the wind, huddling into the collar of his army greatcoat. "I came here to sit beside you, whispering sweet nothings, and it's too damned cold."

Jenny was ahead of him, pink-cheeked from the sharp salt breeze, and holding down her hat. "Isn't this perfect?" she called back at him. "So fresh and clean—"

He laughed. "You stormy petrel, you love bad weather. But I just wish the medical authorities could bring themselves to admit the amorous goings-on among hospital staff and give us a special recreation hut with stoves and beds."

"Jamie!"

"Well, I'm sick of laying gunpowder plots just to get five minutes alone with you. It's fairly driving me mad, when I see you a dozen times a day, and have to hide the fact that I want you so badly, I can barely hold a scalpel."

By huge diplomatic efforts, they had managed to get the same day off. Jamie had borrowed a car from one of his colleagues, and they had driven to Le Touquet—not because it was especially attractive at the end of January, but because they were unlikely to meet anyone they knew.

The place seemed to have forgotten its character as one of the liveliest resorts in Europe. More than three years of war had frozen the hotels and casinos into shuttered ghosts of themselves. The only shelter along the desolate plage was a wrought-iron hut, open on three sides. They dived into it gratefully.

Silver-gray sand had blown across the wooden floor. The hut smelled of damp seaweed and pin-mold, and the voices of the wind and sea roared around its flimsy roof. Jenny opened the leather satchel slung over her shoulder. "I brought a Thermos of tea, and Polly gave me some of the everlasting biscuits she gets from home."

"My good Jeanie, this is excellent." He pulled a pewter hip flask out of his pocket. "It wants but a drop of whiskey to be absolutely perfect—Highland malt, old as Methuselah. My mother sent it at Hogmanay."

"I shouldn't. I'm on duty at seven."

"Doctor's orders."

Jenny laughed and held out her tea cup. "Why do I always do as you say? What makes me surrender my dearest principles without a murmur?"

His face, close to hers, was suddenly serious. "I only wish you would."

"Oh, darling. Don't spoil it."

"All right, all right. Tell me about your leave."

"I did some shopping. I caught up with my friends." She could not meet his eye. "It was—pleasant."

"Pleasant?"

"Oh, Jamie—it was awful."

"You saw him."

"Yes, all the time. I could hardly avoid him. We—he took me to a dance on New Year's Eve, at the Fenboroughs'. And we went to the theater. He wanted to take me to *The Bing Boys,* and I had such a time persuading him to see *Tonight's the Night* instead."

"And?"

Jenny risked a glance at Jamie's lowered eyes, and saw the effort he was making to keep his mouth steady. She loved him so intensely that tears surged to the back of her throat. There was no point in hiding her true feelings from him. "He wanted dreadfully to kiss me." She always avoided saying Alistair's name. "And he thought me very modest when I fought him off. I despised myself for deceiving him, but I couldn't let him spoil what I have with you. It's far too important."

Jamie took away her cup, and gathered her into his arms with a moan of frustration. "I went crazy while you were away. I nearly killed myself with jealousy."

"You mustn't. You know how much I love you—"

"I can't sleep for wanting you. I can't bear to think of another man even being allowed to hold your hand."

Jenny drew a steadying breath, and said: "I know what a terrible thing I've done to him, by falling in love with you. But seeing him face to face made me realize what a mistake it would be to—to carry on as we are."

Jamie seized upon this eagerly. "Don't think about him. Think about us, or we'll neither of us know another second of happiness. Jenny, this situation is turning us both gray before our time!" He grabbed her shoulders, and his imploring face was inches away from hers. "This isn't some abstract question of morals. I'm talking about our future. I won't have it made into a burnt offering because of your sense of honor. You want to marry me, don't you?"

"More than anything!"

"You want to work beside me—to use what you've learned in this slaughterhouse to help build a better world after the war—"

"Yes, but how can I live with myself if I hurt him?"

"How can you live with yourself if you break my heart?"

They fell upon each other's cold lips, and their warm tongues writhed together. The squalor and anxiety of the hospital, the endless war, the problem of Alistair—all melted away before the sublime reality of their love.

"The promise of a life with you is all that keeps me sane," he murmured into her hair. "If I lose you, I lose everything."

"Give me some of your courage," she said, stroking her face against his shoulder. "I'm going to tell him the truth, and ask him to release me. I'm writing the letter tonight."

Alistair only had time to glance at the envelope, but he recognized Jenny's handwriting as he tucked the letter into his inside pocket. For a moment, his anxiety lifted—he only had to think of her to feel stronger. What luck, he thought, I shouldn't have got this for days, if Niven hadn't gone up to HQ.

Niven was Alistair's fellow subaltern, a boy of twenty, easily young enough to be his son. Alistair had long resigned himself to fighting alongside rosy-cheeked infants who looked as if they should have slingshots sticking out of their pockets.

"Any trouble?" he asked.

"Name it—crumps, whizz-bangs, all popping like fireworks. And it was ruddy cold, too."

"Bad show." Alistair turned his attention back to the map spread across the table. "Look here, is this thing up to date? I can't find the supply dumps marked anywhere."

Niven looked over his shoulder, and pointed out several red triangles. "You need reading glasses, old man."

"Don't be saucy."

"I call it cruel, sending out chaps your age. They should leave you to your pipes and slippers."

"Shut up, Niven, there's a good boy. I'm not ready for the breaker's yard just yet." Alistair laughed suddenly. "Though I'll probably never get over the oddness of taking orders from a captain younger than my eldest nephew. And I saw a major the other day who was scarcely shaving—are you sniggering at me, you callow little brute?"

"Gosh, MacNeil, as if I would. I say—Inkerman's scratching. Shall I let him in?"

"I suppose so. He must have given my batman the slip. That animal is an absolute Houdini."

Inkerman bounded joyously into the room. His wiry coat was full of mold, and a rat's tail drooped from his jaw; as far as he was concerned, it was a lovely war. Niven threw him a square of chocolate.

"You're spoiled," Alistair told the dog, slapping his flank affectionately. "Still, if the Royal Welches can have their regimental goat, why shouldn't the Borderers have you?"

"He'll make one hell of a row when we go up the line," Niven prophesied. "What will you do with him?"

"Poor thing, I shall have to chain him. He chewed right through the rope last time. I can't make him understand that he can't come with me." As usual, Alistair carried at the back of his mind the possibility that he might not return. I must arrange for someone to keep an eye on him, he told himself—terrible to think of Inkerman waiting in chains for a master who would never come.

In the event, though he tried hard not to appear too sentimental about his dog, a lump gathered in his throat when he left him. He seemed to epitomize the heartbreaking vulnerability of all the helpless creatures left in the wake of the army. There was no place for any of them in the assault upon the Sailly-Saillisel ridge, marked on his map as Hill 153.

The bleak February winds found their way right into his joints, and twinges of his lumbago added to all the other miseries of marching up the line. Niven's right, he thought, I should be dozing beside a fire. Or sitting in some cozy office. I'm too damned old for this, and nobody would have forced me to join up. What on earth am I doing here?

He summoned the vision he kept in one sacred, separate compartment of his mind to comfort him at times like this—Jenny, in a white dress, singing "Auld Robin Gray." The bride of his dreams, who had been wearing out her engagement ring for three and a half years. An, Jenny, Jenny—the world has grown old and ugly since then, but not you.

Next leave, he swore by all the gods, he would put his foot down and insist upon marrying her. Mother knew she had had a good run for her money, and all his sisters had been nagging at him for ages. Jenny could give up that nursing business, and then, what bliss. His white-robed angel had promised to be his forever, and despite being old and tired and lumbago-stricken, Alistair considered himself a lucky man.

There had been a song in the show they had seen on his last leave. "And when I told them how beautiful you are," he sang to himself, "They didn't believe me—" In the midst of all his discomfort and anxiety, he smiled, for he hardly believed it himself. Jenny was the last figure to rise up before his eyes, on the cold slope of Hill 153.

Out in the freezing darkness on the captured hill, bloodcurdling howls floated toward the moon. They could be heard for miles, and some of the men thought it was a ghost— the White Sergeant, whose awful pallid form was said to appear to a man before he died.

The stretcher-bearers could not afford to believe in such stories, though they were well acquainted with the Dashing White Sergeant whose name was Death. Two of them followed the unholy keening, and found a rough brown terrier, dragging a length of chain from his collar.

"Where did you come from, mate?"

"Wait a bit. There's something sticking out of the soil behind him."

"Well, bugger me, it's a body—one of the jocks."

It had been the last thing Jenny expected to hear. She had been keyed up, waiting for an answer to her letter, when Sister Gleadow called her out of the ward.

"I don't know the details, Dalgleish. But the person who

telephoned seemed to think it was serious. As a nurse, you will know what that can mean." Her brisk voice softened suddenly. "We can spare you, dear, if you would like to go to him. He is in a hospital in Boulogne."

"Thank you, Sister."

Jenny went to her tent in a trance of unreality to remove her apron and fetch her coat and hat.

Polly dived in, long enough to hug her, and say breathlessly: "Awfully good luck, old thing. There's a newish fruitcake in my tin, in case he's up to eating."

The kindness and absurdity of this thawed Jenny almost to tears. If Alistair had received her letter, eating would be the last thing on his mind. Where was Jamie, when she needed him so desperately? One loving word from him would have given her the courage she needed. But he was in the theater, and there was no way of getting a message to him.

By the time she reached the large, well-appointed hospital in Boulogne, Jenny was giddy with apprehension. The cheerful Sister who met her, however, only noticed her uniform.

"You'll find us jolly dull, after Etaples. I did six months there, you know, when the camp was first built. I left when my hand went septic—and was I glad! This is a converted hotel, and I'll never get over the heaven of having proper hot water. Did they tell you anything about your fiancé?"

"No."

"Well, the main thing we tell them is to keep cheerful. He was a little down at first, but he's coming around wonderfully. And the dog is a perfect darling—won't leave his master for a moment, and we've broken every rule in the book to keep them together."

In her anxiety, Jenny was having difficulty picking out the important pieces of information. "I'm sorry, Sister—cheerful, did you say?"

The Sister paused in front of the door to the ward. "Rather. Keeps us all in stitches."

"Does he know? I mean, is he expecting me?"

"Oh, yes. He's been imploring us to summon you, almost from the moment he could speak. He says he has something important to say to you, which he wants to get off his mind. It may be a good notion to humor him."

"Yes, Sister."

For the first time, the Sister scrutinized her properly. "Gracious, nurse, you're as white as a sheet. I suppose it's different, when it happens to someone one knows. I'll get one of the VADs to bring you a cup of tea."

"Oh no, really, I—"

The Sister opened the door. "In you go."

For the first few moments, Jenny actually felt faint. I'm a murderer, she thought; he has read my letter, and I shall die of shame.

The room was large and warm, with busy hotel wallpaper. Jenny registered three beds. One was empty, one was occupied by an inert figure, whose every limb appeared to be in traction. A nurse was sitting beside him, reading a magazine. It was not Alistair.

Having braced herself for something harrowing, Jenny was almost angry when she saw him. He was sitting up in bed, perfectly well and rosy. Except for the square of gauze taped across his right temple, you would never have known there was a thing wrong with him. She stood in the middle of the room, waiting for him to acknowledge her. He went on staring vaguely at his hands.

He can't bear to look at me, she thought.

Then Inkerman ran out from under the bed, and began to lick her hands in greeting. The noise made Alistair turn his head toward the door, but his eyes gazed straight past her.

"Alistair—"

"Jenny!" His blank face sprang to joyful life, and his eyes wandered uncertainly in the direction of her voice. He held out his arms to the empty air.

The room was suddenly very cold, and her scalp prickled with apprehension. "Yes." Her voice came from a long way off. "I'm here, dear." She managed to get to the chair beside the bed, and put her freezing, trembling hands into his.

"My sweet girl," he said gently. "Didn't they tell you I was blind?"

"N-no—"

"Idiots. I begged that addle-brained Sister to warn you— darling, your hands are like ice."

"What happened?"

Alistair chuckled. "Ask Inky. If he hadn't somehow cut loose and followed me, I'd be a goner."

"And will you—what do the doctors say?"

He stroked her fingers tenderly, as if she were the one who would have to bear the worst of it. "Not a chance, I'm afraid. The optic nerve has gone, and I shan't see again until Judgment Day. We'll have to make the best of a bad job. Now, I know you've had a shock, but Jenny, we must talk about the future, and—well, how this changes things."

"Yes." Even though he could not see her, Jenny could not look at him.

"Darling, there's no reason to wait anymore. When can you leave your hospital?"

On the table beside him, on top of a small heap of his belongings, was the letter she had written about Jamie. It had not been opened. He had not read it—and now, of course, he never would. A ghastly, paralyzing feeling of helplessness and dread stole over her. She could never tell him now. She picked it up and put it in her bag.

"Wish I could see you," he was saying. "What are you wearing?"

"My uniform."

"An, yes." His fingers meandered clumsily over her starched cuffs. "Funny, I can only imagine you in that white dress you wore on the day we first met."

The tear splashed on the back of his hand, before she could wipe it away.

Alistair's voice became unbearably tender. "Darling, you mustn't cry—"

"I'm sorry. It's selfish when you have so much to bear."

"But you mustn't worry about me. You'll be my eyes now."

Jenny's head sank down to the bed, and she almost choked on the bitterest sobs of her life.

He caressed her shoulders. "Why, I'm a lucky man. The only thing I really couldn't bear to lose is you. You're dearer than sight or sound to me, and while I have you, I have more reason to live than most. Oh, Jenny, don't cry so terribly."

Inkerman, making a noise like a kettle just beginning to boil, thrust his muzzle against Alistair's hand.

He laughed. "I say, isn't this odd? When you saved Inky's life that day, you were saving mine as well."

She remembered perfectly how the hand of the future had gripped her that afternoon. Now, she almost wished she had left the dog to die. For if she had thrown herself

into the chasm and broken her neck, she could not have
ruined her own life more disastrously.

"You mean you didn't tell him!"

"Oh, Jamie, how could I? Can you see me doing it when
he said I was his reason for living? It would have been
worse than taking out a knife and stabbing him."

"What about my reason for living? Did you think of me
at any point during this touching scene?"

Jamie was not bothering to keep his voice down, though
they were within earshot of the outer rim of the encamp-
ment. Jenny had arranged to meet him behind a screen of
poplars just beyond the wire fence. It was wildly against
the rules, and neither of them cared.

Jenny was weeping so wretchedly that she could scarcely
get the words out. "He—he said I was his eyes now—"

"Jenny, listen, listen." He grabbed her arms. "You're
more than that to me—you're my heart and soul—"

"Don't!"

"You can't sacrifice yourself to a lifetime of fetching and
carrying for a blind man!"

"He's depending on me."

His grip tightened until he hurt her. "You do intend to
tell him eventually, don't you?"

"Please, try to put yourself in my place. I had to think
of his feelings—"

Jamie flung her roughly away from him. His face was
hard and furious, but his wet eyes and lashes betrayed him.
"You didn't dare, that's all. You obviously don't give a
damn about me. Fine bloody fool I made of myself, planning our future."

"Darling, you have every right to be angry," Jenny said.
"I love you more than anything, but I can't desert Alistair
now. I made him a promise long before I met you, and it
must be honored." She scrubbed at her swollen eyes with
her handkerchief, and her voice took on a slightly firmer
note. "There isn't any other way. Don't imagine I haven't
looked for one."

"So, you've made up your mind!" Jamie shouted. He
punched the trunk of one of the trees. "And I don't count,
because you're nothing but a shabby-genteel Edinburgh
snob, afraid of losing caste! You never wanted to work in
a slum clinic beside me."

"That's not true—"

"Was it his money that got you in the end? Would you have ditched him if I'd been the one with the castle? If you'd been honest and true in the first place, if you hadn't sold your soul for the sake of filthy lucre, you wouldn't have to destroy our lives now!"

"You're right, it's my fault. I deserve this," Jenny said. "But Jamie—please believe me—I love you so terribly, I feel as if I should bleed to death if you were taken away from me."

"Oh God—" He suddenly snatched her in his arms, and burst into tears. Jenny stroked the back of his head, appalled by his terrible male sobs. For the first time, she saw the situation in terms of what she had done to him—the innocent bearing the punishment of the guilty.

"I must do what's right," she said sadly. "You'll see that eventually."

"Of course," he murmured into her neck. "And I'm sorry. I didn't mean any of it. You must keep your word, and we must both endure it. But oh, God, I had such hopes for us!"

"So had I."

"God bless you, Jeanie—be as happy as you can. There won't be a day that I don't think of you."

"I love you—I love you—"

"I love you, Jenny. I'll love you forever—"

"Jamie—"

He was gone, and she was left alone, every nerve aching for him. As the seconds stretched to minutes, the pain bit deeper. This was where her cleverness had brought her. She could not get over how carefully, how thoroughly, she had sealed her own fate. Three days later, in the middle of an operation, Jamie suddenly asked the Sister what time it was.

Slightly surprised, she told him it was half-past two, and watched a shadow settle across his face.

At that moment, in Boulogne, the hospital chaplain was joining the hands of Jenny and Alistair and pronouncing that they were man and wife.

Seven

Men were dying in the thousands, for slices of ruined land that were indistinguishable from the ruined land around them. For nearly a year, Tertius had spent every spare moment, and all his last leave, obsessively painting these mudscapes and their haggard inhabitants. He created black seas, from which charred tree stumps and fragments of buildings rose like the bones of dinosaurs. As he saw it, this was a world literally turned inside out by the impact of the mines.

It was said that the explosion of the nineteen underground mines, during the capture of the Messines-Wystchaete ridge, had been heard on the South Coast, and felt in Number Ten Downing Street. As if, Tertius had thought, earth's crust had broken enough to give Lloyd George and his cabinet an unexpected whiff of hell.

Tertius felt himself becoming, like so many others, hardened and bitter. Painting helped to keep him outside the horrors, but he knew now that the day had come when he could no longer keep his vision separate.

It was early July, and he had been sent with a message to HQ. Messages these days had a way of dying in your pocket en route—before the ink was dry; the officer who sent it could be dead, and HQ in another place. Summer rains had turned the land into an evil-smelling swamp. Tertius was sinking into the mud with every step. His boots were made of lead. His heart somersaulted with fear, whenever he stumbled off the crude road of duckboards slung across the mire. Night was falling, and the sky began to flicker with star shells and Very lights.

Statues made of crusted mud loomed at him out of the dusk—an abandoned gun carriage, submerged up to its axles, and a bloated dead horse in the shafts. And all for what the newspapers would describe as "A slight advance on the Messines front," if they mentioned it at all.

Tertius was mortally afraid, feeling himself the only living speck in this nightmare. There were no roads, no signposts. The map, with its carefully marked copses and farmsteads, was worse than useless. They had all been blown to perdition months ago.

The suction of the mud made him think of infernal hands, tugging eagerly at his heels to drag him down to his tomb. You could go crazy here. Many did. "Holy Mother of God—" Tertius prayed, as he had heard the Catholic boys praying at home.

The mud suddenly yielded beneath him. He had planted his boot in the stomach of a corpse. As he stepped on it, the air rushed from the body with an angry grunt, and he was overwhelmed by a stench of putrefaction that made his ears sing and his eyes water.

Where was the victory in staying alive? The mud was cold and greasy at first, but it soon became warm and numbing, even soothing. He had thrown himself into the bosom of the brown ocean, before he realized, with a thrill of horror, what he had done. The demons were pulling him down, the mud was closing over his head.

He was heaved up roughly by his shoulders, and shaken mercilessly until he woke, choking. Feeling crept back into his body, and Tertius realized he was still clinging to the sides of the deep shell hole, where eight of them had lain for a night and a day. He had fallen asleep, and slithered down into the filthy water at the bottom of the crater. Now, the second night was coming on fast.

The sky was full of flashes, and there was no sign of rescue. Mr. Drayton lay dead, with both his legs torn off and his stomach blown open like a burst pillow. They had left him where he fell, at the crater's rim, his service revolver hanging uselessly in his hand.

Later Tertius would be sorry, and miss the poor little fellow. At the moment the situation was so awful that he lived from second to second, postponing all emotion until he could endure it without going crazy. He had come close, when he fell asleep and dreamed of that night on the Messines front, and treading on the grunting corpse.

Stupid with fear and fatigue, he did his best to shake himself awake. "Thanks, Alf."

Alf, the other surviving member of the foursome that had been halved at the Somme the year before, only said:

"I'd give a year's pay for one dry fag."

They had all tried to coax sparks from the sodden matches and cigarettes in their pockets. Tertius idly wondered what luxury he would give a year's pay for—a cup of tea, a glass of whiskey—before he realized he had started a dangerous train of thought. Never mind a year's pay, he would give five years of his life to lay his head upon the Mater's breast now, or to know that Muttonhead's quiet, steady presence was nearby. He could have died quite happily, he thought, for one smile from Rory.

But he must not think like this. He put out his tongue, and distracted himself with the taste of the salt in his tears. They had all eaten their iron rations hours ago, and he was hungry. How long did it take to starve to death?

From outside the shell hole, soft but distinct against the racket of artillery, a voice began to call.

"Paddy—Paddy—"

Tertius thought he had finally gone mad until he saw the appalled faces of his comrades. His scalp prickled. "Jesus, it's not possible—"

"Paddy—" it sighed. "Paddy!"

"Sir!" he shouted.

"Oh, don't leave me," mourned the voice. "Oh, Paddy, don't leave me here—"

"I'd never have thought he could last more than a couple of hours," someone said. "Not with his stomach gone like that."

"Oh, Paddy—please, please!" Drayton's voice somehow rose intact from his mutilated body, gaining volume. The anguish in it lashed Tertius to a frenzy.

"I'm here!" he roared. "I'm coming!" The sides of the crater were slippery. He clawed his hands into the mud to get a hold.

"Here, are you off your onion?" Alf grabbed his leg, and pulled him down again. "Where d'you think you're going?"

"I've got to get to him. Can't you hear him calling for me?"

"You can't do nothing for him," the corporal advised kindly. "D'you want to get yourself blown up too?"

"Oh!" Drayton screamed. "Paddy! Paddy! Paddy!"

"Fuck off. Let me go." Tertius went wild, cursing and shouting, and hitting out at his friends.

They proved stronger. Alf pinned him down, full of compassion, but determined to keep his friend's beloved head below the line of fire. Every time Drayton screamed, and Tertius thrashed wildly to be free, he would say: "You'll thank me for this one day."

Tertius, under this restraint, could barely summon the breath to reply to his officer's terrible swan song. He remembered a fragment of his classical education—Mr. Phillips telling him and Rory about the fall of Troy. Inside the Trojan horse, one of the Greek soldiers had thought he heard his wife outside, calling to him lovingly. But it had been a trick. The others, afraid of betrayal, had stifled his cries so effectively that they smothered him.

Gradually, the screams faded, and the overworked angel of death at last got around to gathering Mr. Drayton. About an hour after this, they managed to leave the shell hole and head back toward their lines. It was too dark to see the young officer's body, yet Tertius carried away an impression of it in his mind—so clear that he could have drawn it. The face, as he saw it, was untouched and streaked with tears.

Alf said he was daft, but Tertius could not escape from this picture of Drayton in his last hours, crying up at a cold sky for a friend who would not come. His hands began to tremble and sweat, and he could not sleep without seeing Drayton and the groaning corpse, which had somehow struck up a relationship in his unconscious.

A week later, they were sent to rest billets behind the lines. Tertius and Alf—the only two men left out of the original battalion—had been here before in the weeks before the Somme. It had become busier and less peaceful through dealing with a constant flow of soldiers, but it was still essentially a quiet country place. The river where they had bathed was the same, and the barn, where they had been inspected by the Prince of Wales.

Apart from higher prices, the local *estaminet* was unchanged. In the speckled mirror above its zinc counter, Tertius caught a glimpse of his own face, and remembered how it had been the last time he was here. He had done a self-portrait in pastels around that time—a picture of a bright-eyed boy, brimming with vitality and good humor.

That face was irritable and mournful now. There were tense lines around his mouth, and a streak of gray in the lock of hair across his forehead. It would be interesting, he thought, to do another self-portrait as a companion piece, to illustrate the ravages of war.

But it was out of the question. The interest faded when he looked down at his hand, and saw it trembling so persistently that he was shaking drops of beer out of his glass. No use thinking of paintbrushes and charcoals, when it took all his concentration to hold his razor steady while he shaved.

Eight

The orchard was dappled with afternoon sunlight. Wasps hummed industriously around the ripe apples in the long grass. Under the fruit-laden boughs Lorenzo and Stevie lounged in wicker chairs, yawning over their coffee and cigarettes. Eleanor, Francesca and Laura could be heard playing on the lawn behind them, throwing an old tennis ball for the sheepdog puppy that Stevie and Francesca had brought for Laura. They had driven down to Rottingdean from London, where they now had their own small house in Chelsea.

Stevie sighed luxuriously. "Isn't this perfect?"

"You've only got one eye," Lorenzo said. "Are you sure you can see everything?"

"Oh, don't be so crabbed. I've had a damned good lunch—ten times better than one ever gets in town these days—and I won't let you spoil it."

"Eleanor does have a gift for household management," Lorenzo conceded. "Inherited from her mother, one assumes."

"You'll miss all this when you go back."

"Not at all. She showers me with parcels. Our mess keeps the best table in the sector."

"Are you dreading it?"

Lorenzo shrugged. "I'm well aware that the odds against me shorten every time I go back. But the war has been the business of my life for so long now, I simply take it for granted." He leaned closer to Stevie. "I even think I'm rather good at it, though I'll never possess your gift for inspiring worship in the ranks."

"Do I take it that Captain Hastings is still known as a tartar?" Lorenzo had been promoted, shortly after his return from sick leave.

"Absolutely. I'd rather have a well-run outfit than popularity. You know I never did care to be harassed with too much love."

Stevie's thin hand involuntarily went to his black eye patch. "I wish—this is mad, but I wish I was going back with you."

"My poor young Stevie, it's nearly a year since they invalided you out," Lorenzo said, with mocking affection. "Haven't you come to terms with your good fortune yet?"

"I don't feel properly alive yet. Perhaps I'm being sentimental, but from where I'm sitting, it'd be a fine thing to be well and strong, and drinking claret at the officers' club in Poperinghe. Is it still there?"

"Yes. Pop's just the same, except that the prices have gone up."

"God, Larry, I've missed you this past year," Stevie said softly, trying to cover the depth of his emotion with a wan smile. "Worse than I've missed my eye."

In the past, this kind of admission would have irritated Lorenzo into a stinging display of sarcasm. It was a sign of how much he had changed lately that he only smiled, and said thoughtfully: "I suppose it's the longest time we've ever been apart, since we were kids. And I've neglected you this leave, haven't I?"

"Oh God—n-no—" Stevie stammered, thrown into confusion by the unexpected gentleness of Lorenzo's manner. "I wasn't reproaching you. You only have seven days—"

"All the same." Lorenzo's dark eyes were serious. "I've missed you, too. I hope you know it."

A wisp of cloud trailed across the sun. For a moment, the light shining on Stevie's fair hair dimmed, and it was possible to see how pale and gaunt his face had become.

"You might not like me saying this," he said, "but there's something on your mind, isn't there?"

"Hmm." Lorenzo frowned, instantly on his guard. "That obvious, is it?"

"You're different." Stevie knew the exact tone to adopt—coaxing but humorous. "Only half with us, while the rest of you wanders heaven knows where."

"Well, I'm sorry."

"Actually, it's rather an improvement."

It worked. Lorenzo laughed, then softened again, and said: "I'd tell you, if I could. You won't be in the dark forever. Someday you'll see everything."

"All right. I trust you." Stevie smiled, at the exact moment the sun emerged, and drenched him in its syrupy gold light. "But you must tell me one thing. Are you happy?"

Lorenzo turned the question over for a few seconds. "Yes. I think—I'm happier than I've ever been in my life."

"Then I'll be satisfied."

Lorenzo's brow cleared. He lit them both fresh cigarettes, and refilled their coffee cups from the heavy silver pot. "Come on, now. You mustn't encourage me to go on about myself. You should give me a recital of your own grievances."

"I never have any."

"Nonsense. You haven't told me anything about your health, or why you look so ghastly."

Stevie let out a delighted shout of laughter. "Thank you so much. Don't let the girls hear you. You're meant to say how much better I seem."

"Well, you don't. What's the matter with you?"

"Oh, it's all taken longer than everyone thought. But I'm nearly well now, except for the occasional headache."

"And have you decided what you'll do?"

"Let's be honest, it isn't really worth talking about." Stevie's cheerfulness was forced, and he could not meet Lorenzo's eye. "I'm pretty useless now."

"The world's full of chaps with bits missing. You could operate a hurdy-gurdy. Or play a mouth organ on street corners—but you really need a wooden leg for that."

Stevie smiled dutifully, but his one, tearless eye was full of sorrow. "Larry, I never should have lectured you about marriage. Not when I'm making such a hash of my own."

There was a silence between them, during which they listened to the happy, indistinct chatter of their wives.

"Francesca looks well enough to me," Lorenzo said. He took a robust view of other people's marriages, failing to see how they could be worse than his. "She's vastly less silly than she was this time last year. You've improved her."

"No." Stevie shook his head. "I can't make her happy."

Lorenzo brooded over this for a long time, staring down at the cigarette between his fingers.

"Happy?" he echoed eventually. "Who on earth knows what will make a woman happy?"

*   *   *

Eleanor's eyes were a clean, honest gray beneath her sun-whitened fringe. "I want to tell you now, Lorenzo, before you go, how happy you've made me."

"Have I?"

Eleanor smiled. "Don't look so suspicious. I mean it."

"Because you've seen so little of me this leave?"

"You expected me to heap you with reproaches, but I don't want us to have that sort of marriage."

They were on the deserted, flower-decked platform of the country station, beside a pile of Lorenzo's polished leather suitcases. He was in uniform, beginning to feel the heat of the late summer sun. Eleanor wore an old dress of washed-out blue linen. Her bleached hair was bundled under a plain straw hat, and her rosy, tragi-comic face was dusted with freckles. The happy unself-consciousness of her appearance made Lorenzo pay closer attention to her than usual. The phrase *sancta simplicitas* came to him—holy simplicity, sacred innocence. Her goodness, which had always repelled him, now seemed endearing instead of formidable.

"You look pretty today," he said, on impulse.

The compliment brought tears to her eyes, but she was too welltrained to draw attention to this. "What," she said lightly, "in my gardening rags?"

"I never did like to see you dressed up."

"You—you said I reminded you of a milkmaid, once."

"Did I?" He surprised her, by taking her hand. "I can't get over the way you treasure up my kind words. I suppose they are somewhat rare."

Eleanor took this as a witticism, and laughed. "All the more valuable."

"It takes so little to please you. I should make the effort more often."

"My darling!" She was radiant. "You do please me—I know how hard you've tried. I noticed it last winter, when you were home on sick leave. You seemed more settled and more—that is, less angry with Laura and me. It started before Christmas, when you went off for a fortnight alone—do you remember?"

"Yes."

"Don't be angry! I never breathed a word of complaint about it, and I never will. I understood that you needed some time to yourself. I missed you, but you were so rested and calm when you came back—"

"So much more like a human being," he said harshly.

"No! I didn't mean—"

He interrupted her. "And have I been as good this past week? Do you forgive me for spending so much time away from you?"

"Lorenzo"—love made Eleanor radiant—"I refuse to tie you down. I shall always be here when you want me, but you are a free man."

"Free." His voice was bitter.

Eleanor did not notice that she was causing him pain. "I begin to see how our marriage must work," she went on. "In the past, I've been selfish and wrong, because I wanted so much of you."

"Oh, Eleanor, for God's sake." He was more irritated than angry. "Don't be so bloody noble."

"Listen!" She stroked his hand. "In future, we must try to live as we have done this past week."

Lorenzo searched her face curiously. "Have you really enjoyed it so much?"

"Yes, because you have."

"Christ! You have a talent for making me feel a swine!"

She was puzzled. "But I'm not criticizing you at all, I'm saying how sweet you've been. When the war's over, and we're together all the time—"

"Let's not discuss the future, eh?"

"No. All right."

There was an awkwardness between them. Both had realized this might be the last time they ever saw each other, and they did not know how to get over the moment.

Mercifully, the train appeared around the bend in the track. "On time, for once," Lorenzo said. He transferred his attention to his luggage, beckoning over the doddering old porter.

Eleanor sadly feasted her eyes upon him, while he could not see her and accuse her of staring. "The same look," she murmured, "like the day we met." The relief of getting away from her.

"What did you say?" She had got his deaf ear. "I can't stand it when you mutter."

"Only to be careful with the small valise. I put in the jar of pears in brandy."

"Oh."

The train halted at the platform, bathing them both in

steam. Eleanor bit into her lower lip to stop herself crying, and raked her eyes over his face, in a last panic-stricken attempt to print every detail on her heart.

"God bless you, Lorenzo. God keep you safe. I'll be thinking of you every hour, darling." She longed to tell him how much she had loved him for the past four years, and what joy he had given her, in spite of everything. But she absolutely must not make a scene. "I'll send you the marrow jam the moment it's ready."

Lorenzo's luggage was stacked in a first-class compartment.

"Well—" he began.

Usually, he gave her one brief, chilly kiss on the cheek. This time, he put his arms around her, and his lips touched hers with real tenderness. "You never deserved to be landed with a husband like me," he muttered quickly. "Forgive me, Eleanor."

She never could bring herself to say the word "goodbye." Making a supreme effort, she kept smiling and waving as the train pulled away—for by some miracle, Lorenzo was still leaning out of his window, watching her.

For several minutes, she stood motionless, following the progress of the train until it was nothing more than a smear of white steam on the ripe, golden landscape. Then she blew her nose vigorously. It would be ungrateful to cry now, when—at long last—all her prayers for her marriage appeared to have been answered.

Lorenzo, meanwhile, sat back upon the dusty plush seat, brooding over the sun-striped figure of that sweet woman in her blue gown; as wholesome and innocent as the fields and orchards around her. She belonged in that smiling landscape, with her bees and flowers, and he could not love her because he was not good enough.

Then he thought of someone else; someone who belonged among mist-shrouded mountains and windswept stretches of heather. His wild colonial girl, Rory of the Hills. His blood caught fire, and Eleanor was blotted out of his mind as if he had never met her.

This seven days' leave had been the climax of the underground obsession that had kept him alive since he returned to the front the previous January. After their fortnight in Norfolk, there had been several weekends, and many meetings in London when Lorenzo was supposedly seeing his doctor. Parting from Rory had been torture. At last he understood what made some of the men in the mess so white and silent in the first hours of their return to camp.

They had been living through their letters. Lorenzo wrote to her every day, if he could—in restaurants, in dugouts, under the lees of great guns, which blew his candle out every few minutes when they fired. Everything connected to her was precious to him. Someone had pointed out Major the Lord Oughterard, dining one evening in Poperinghe, and his heart had even leaped at the sight of that granite peer eating his way through a huge beef stew.

On the first day of his leave, Lorenzo had arrived in London several hours earlier than he had told Eleanor. He had leaped into a taxi and gone straight to Rory's flat, so excited that he had had to keep one hand in his breeches pocket, to restrain the shameless bulge of his erection.

They had fucked fully clothed on the attic stairs. Rory had clamped her black-stockinged legs across his back, and he had roared out her name, over and over, as he came. Then they had wept some voluptuous tears as they re-learned the scents and textures of each other's bodies. Twenty minutes later, they had been at it again (Lorenzo grinned involuntarily at the memory) standing up, and pressed against the landing wall. There had not even been time to get up to the sitting room.

Their frantic couplings had been interspersed with equally frantic talk. Rory had opened a bottle of excellent champagne, hoarded for this very day, and they drained it, just as they had drained Lorenzo's groin. Much later, he had taken the train down to Rottingdean, and submitted to Eleanor's adulation with a far better grace than usual.

He had not wanted to fuck Eleanor, but knew she expected it—there had been no mistaking her look of mingled longing and fear. For the sake of a quiet life, he had fisted up another erection when they went to bed. He had intended to thrust into her for a while, until he grew bored with her sighs, and then withdraw without coming. Halfway through, however, he had imagined that he caught the smell of Rory on his skin, and the memory shattered his control. Eleanor, poor girl, had almost died of happiness when she felt the force of his orgasm.

She had floated around the house and garden on a cloud of bliss for the entire seven days. Lorenzo had discovered

that if he fucked her occasionally with a show of enthusiasm, she did not seem to mind that she only saw him last
thing at night and in the early morning.

Now, while Eleanor thought he was on his way to the
coast, he left his luggage at the station, and hastened to
spend his final, priceless hours of freedom with Rory. She
was waiting for him at the front door.

There was no need to speak. As soon as Rory's own
door was shut and bolted behind them, they fell ravenously
upon each other's mouths. Lorenzo fought to keep control
of himself, because he wanted to take her in all his favorite
positions; to stamp himself all over her body, so that she
would carry the memory of him in every cell.

Throughout the past seven days, their lovemaking had
been wild and animalistic. Today, it was almost savage—
they clawed and bit, bruising each other's flesh. Lorenzo
made Rory lie on the floor with her legs spread. Kneeling
over her, he flicked his tongue around her clitoris until it
was aching and swollen. She sobbed and arched herself
toward his mouth, but he would not allow her to come.
Instead, biting the insides of his cheeks, to stop himself
squirting too soon, he pinned down her arms and pushed
his erection slowly into her, watching her face as the pressure from his strong, rhythmic thrusts in her vagina finally
exploded her inflamed clitoris into orgasm.

The force of her spasms made him thrust more violently.
He withdrew and reentered her from behind, his face buried in the soft red hair at the nape of her neck. Then he
rolled over on his back, and Rory sat astride him. This was
a position she adored. While she rode him, he massaged
her wet clitoris with his finger, and she came again.

Finally, lying on top of her, Lorenzo abandoned all self-
control, and gave himself to one of the volcanic, deathlike
climaxes he had learned to build with Rory. She wrapped
her arms and legs around him as it thundered through him.

Afterward, when he lay dazed and exhausted, she held
his head protectively between her breasts. They were both
weeping silently, partly from physical repletion, partly from
the bleak sense of their approaching parting. There was
very little time left. Wordlessly, Lorenzo disentangled himself from her arms and began to retrieve his clothes.

Watching him dress was unbearable. The face he made
at himself in the glass, as he drove the pin into his collar,

was a dagger in her side. Quickly, she wrapped herself in her kimono, and opened the last bottle of the excellent champagne.

"Thanks." He finished fastening his Sam Browne belt, and accepted a glass. "This is frightfully good stuff. I've been meaning to ask where you got it."

"My friend Aubrey Russell. He believes youth should have its fling." It was hard to make light conversation with a throat full of barbed wire.

"Good for him. Did you tell him about me?"

"Everything except your name—though he's no fool. I dare say he's guessed."

"And do you mind him knowing?"

She managed a crooked, unnatural smile. "Oh no. I have to be able to talk to someone, and I can't tell anyone else. If Muttonhead found out, I think he'd kill me."

Lorenzo put an arm around her waist. "Because I'm married."

"Of course."

"Rory, darling, I've put you in an impossible situation."

"I love you, and I have to let you go. That's the only impossible thing about it."

His beautiful ebony eyes were gentle, and full of deep, unstinting love. "You witch, you've cast a spell on me." His hold on her tightened. "And nobody is going to make me let you go."

"Lorenzo, please—"

"I know what we agreed, but I don't care. I'm leaving her."

"No!"

"What's the point?" he asked sadly. "If she were honest she would admit to herself that I have never loved her. She sets so much store by my happiness—or says she does—that she ought to let me go."

"No, Lorenzo," Rory said, in a wretched, breaking voice. "You don't understand her. Isn't all this enough for you? She doesn't know, and ignorance is bliss—"

"You're not happy, though, are you?"

She could not lie to him. "I don't deserve to be."

"Well, I bloody deserve to be," he said, with sudden anger. "For the best part of three years I've been frozen and scorched, shot at, shelled, and nearly torn limb from limb. I've only got one life, and once this war is over I'm going to live it just as I choose. Do you love me?"

"More than anything."

"Say you'll marry me then. Give me that to look forward to."

His passion and intensity hypnotized Rory, and numbed her conscience. She only had to gaze into the face she loved so terribly, to push aside all her misgivings and say "Yes."

"Oh God, Rory—" He locked his arms around her. "How the hell am I going to leave you?"

The tears she had tried to suppress spilled out, staining his khaki shoulder. "Is it time?"

"Promise me, you'll always think of me at my best. No matter what happens."

"Lorenzo, if anything happens to you," she blurted out desperately, breaking all their rules, "if you don't come back, I don't know how I shall live—"

Tenderly, for the last time, he sifted her hair. "You'll bend, but you'll never break," he said. "You have too much strength and vitality. Besides, I'll always be with you. I'll never leave you. If I'm killed, I promise to come back and haunt you. You won't scream or run away from me, will you?"

She smiled. "Not even if you're carrying your head under your arm."

"I promise, Rory. Remember, I'm always with you."

"Goodbye, darling. God keep you."

She fought to keep smiling, as he left, so that he would not have to remember parting with a weeping female. When he was gone, however, and the sound of his footsteps on the stairs had faded, she lay down on the floor where they had made love, and cried herself half-blind, while the night closed in around her.

Nine

Lorenzo held up his hand, and the column of men behind him shuffled to a halt, slithering on the widely spaced wooden duckboards. They were struggling through a black, featureless sea of mire, in lashing rain. Ahead of them, the enemy shells sent up great slimy fountains. The men's boots were encrusted with pounds of clinging mud. They wore waterproof capes over their packs, and looked like a line of wet snails.

"No going forward or back," Lorenzo said to his Sergeant. "We'll have to wait it out again."

"Yes, sir."

"We began by crawling out of the primordial soup," Lorenzo remarked, trying to light a cigarette behind the collar of his sodden Aquascutum, "and it looks very much as if the world will end with us all plopping back into it."

"Yes, sir." Sergeant Ross was used to the ironical asides Captain Hastings came out with to distance himself from despair, and found them soothing. "Except I thought the end of the world would be drier. We could do with a flame or two."

It was the last day of October. The previous day, the British had attacked in the Ypres salient from Poelcappelle to Passchendaele. Lorenzo and his men were marching forward now to relieve men who had been driven back from Passchendaele. The rain had been pouring down for weeks, turning the whole devastated sector around Ypres into a treacherous swamp.

The misery of it could scarcely be believed, Lorenzo thought, finally abandoning his attempt to light a cigarette. Water dripped off the rim of his helmet, and sluiced down the back of his collar. His feet were aching with cold and damp, his boots weighed like lead, the old scar on his chest throbbed painfully.

"This," he said bitterly, "is the Ten Plagues of Egypt all over again. We have provoked the wrath of Jehovah, and now we're getting it in the neck—lice and boils a specialty."

"And the crops dying, sir." Ross was a countryman. "And the flax and barley smitten."

"The plague of locusts."

"Who, sir—the Huns?"

"All of us, sweeping across what was once a perfectly decent stretch of land, and devouring every speck of green. We've seen the rivers flowing with blood, too, just like the ancient Egyptians. And—what was the last plague?"

"Death of the firstborn son, sir."

"My God—we've certainly had that. I begin to feel rather sorry for the Pharaoh."

Lorenzo glanced up at the leaden banks of cloud, streaked here and there with lurid fissures of light. He then peeled back his wet leather glove, long enough to check his watch.

"We're late," he said. "We'll have to tell them we became so captivated by the beauties of the landscape that time mattered not to us."

"That's right, sir."

The bombardment appeared to have stopped, and Lorenzo could not risk making targets of his men any longer. Slowly, cautiously, they began to inch forward.

When the shell came screaming at him, Lorenzo was not thinking of Rory or Eleanor. In the seconds before his body took the impact, he was preoccupied only with the logistics of getting the men under his command from one point to another, and with the wretched wetness of his feet.

The shell tore him open from throat to groin. Sergeant Ross found Lorenzo wallowing on his back, with his intestines bursting out of the bloody pulp of his stomach, screaming in agony like Prometheus on the rock.

In his dazed state, the Sergeant had a blurred idea that Lorenzo's body was a trap, and his soul was an animal caught by one heel, fighting desperately to be free. With a trembling hand, he put the muzzle of his service revolver to Lorenzo's temple.

"There you are, sir," he said automatically, though he knew he would never be heard. One shot, and the trapped soul had soared free. With his deaf ear, Lorenzo was listening to the humming of the Pleiades.

*   *   *

The sickening pain in Stevie's head intensified for a moment, then suddenly lifted, leaving him with a feeling of lightness and freedom after hours of torture. He sat very still in his armchair, watching the firelight shifting on the wall.

Without turning around, he knew there was another person in the room—standing in the doorway behind him, as if looking in on the way to somewhere else.

Smiling at the fire, Stevie murmured: "Larry?"

Francesca found him half an hour later. He was slumped awkwardly in the chair, his one eye half-open, his face wearing an expression of amused surprise.

PART SIX

Winter 1917—
Spring 1918

Aurora

Letter to my Daughter, 1935

I read about it in the casualty lists in *The Times,* which I scanned anxiously every morning. Killed: Hastings, Capt. L. G., Royal Wessex Infantry. That was all, but it was enough to turn the landscape of my life into a blasted heath of desolation.

Jenny wrote to me shortly afterward, to tell me that Eleanor had been very ill since she received the news in a telegram from the War Office, and that poor Stevie had died of a brain hemorrhage on the same day. "Francesca says she takes comfort from the fact that he was able to follow Lorenzo out of the world," Jenny wrote. "She says she does not think he could have lived without him."

I could not live without him either, but fate had not been kind enough to kill me, too.

Remorse poisoned every breath I drew. Jenny wrote that we needed our schoolgirl vow more than ever, because two of us were widows, and that twisted the knife cruelly, for hadn't I broken that vow and betrayed one of my dearest friends?

Don't ask me how I got through. I only know that, limping from hour to hour, I somehow did. I managed to write letters of condolence to Francesca and—yes—to Eleanor, which made me cry until my nostrils and eyelids were raw. I went on driving my ambulance, even on the night after I heard about Lorenzo's death. Perhaps the work helped me. At any rate, none of my superiors seemed to notice I was dragging around a heart as heavy as a marble tombstone. My commandant called me into her office one night, but it was only to ask me to consider applying to command one of the new VAD Ambulance Units they were setting up in

France. I was valuable, apparently—strong, experienced, and good at mending temperamental old engines. Yes, I said, I'd consider it. And I went home, as usual, to howl myself into a stupor.

The loneliness was the worst thing. The tears come to my eyes now to remember it. I longed for a kind word, and often dreamed I was running for the last ever boat to Ireland, to find comfort with the Mater. But no one I loved had any idea what I had done, and how I was suffering for it now—and they would be so angry, I thought, if ever they found out. Only Aubrey Russell knew, and he was far kinder to me than I deserved.

Aubrey escorted me to Stevie's funeral, where Francesca's mother embarrassed everyone by screaming, when the clergyman read out the text: "David and Jonathan were lovely and pleasant in their lives, and in their deaths they were not divided." Mr. Templeton had to lead her out of the church, and Aubrey made surreptitious tippling gestures at me to show his diagnosis of her condition.

Francesca had changed. She was thinner, and pale as a lily, and her sparkling prettiness had matured to a sweet, grave beauty. I have never seen anything as poignantly lovely as her face that day, under the wide brim of her black hat. She would not disfigure herself with a veil, but showed us all her dark, sorrowful eyes, calm as if she was mourning something she had lost a long time ago.

I was the only one of her three friends to attend. Jenny, who was expecting a baby, was in Scotland. Eleanor was still too prostrate with grief to go out in public. You can imagine what a relief that was to me.

You can also imagine, I dare say, my dismay when Eleanor turned up on my doorstep about a week later. I heard a light knock, and there she stood, a slight figure in deep black. It was awful to see the pain in her innocent blue eyes. I felt myself to be hideous with evil, and jerked my head away brusquely when she kissed me. Of course it was selfish, but the thought: Why has she come? chased around and around my brain like a frightened squirrel.

"I should have telephoned first, or sent you a postcard," she apologized breathlessly. "You see, I still do things on impulse."

I sat her down in the basket chair beside the fire, and made us tea, giving myself time to gather my strength. I should say that far from doing anything to make me nervous, Eleanor was carrying her bereavement with great courtesy and composure.

"It's worse for Francesca," she told me, when I had brought in the tray. "At least I have my baby to remember him by. And Rory, she grows more like him every day. You've no idea what a comfort it is. Seeing traces of him in her face makes the separation seem less permanent—oh! I'm sorry—" Her voice had suddenly faltered and broken. She set down her cup and saucer, and took a black-edged handkerchief from her bag. "This is why I had to come. I simply had to see you."

I was too scared to reply. It was all I could do to breathe.

Eleanor blurted out: "Does your aunt still hold her meetings?"

"You mean her séances?" I was astounded. "You're not serious."

"We had only just begun to understand one another, before he—Rory, I think he was trying to tell me something important when we last parted."

It was impossible to refuse her, though my misgivings were powerful. However, the sheer tenacity of her love for him swept all objections aside, and I duly escorted her to Aunt Hilda's next Tuesday séance—turning scarlet with anger and mortification when it was my turn to put my half-guinea into the basket that was taken around beforehand.

After more than three years of war, business was booming. Besides the usual, dingy circle of regulars, there were two black-clad women—both trembling, one clutching a photograph of a boy in uniform. We sat around the table in Aunt Hilda's parrot-scented dining room, and the parlor-maid drew the curtains.

The Polish medium, Madame Gerlinska, spread her fat hands facedown on the chenille cloth. We all joined hands, and I had one moment of absolute terror, which left my upper lip prickling with sweat. Madame began by rocking and wheezing, and muttering in Polish to her spirit guide. Then she cleared her throat, and began.

"Someone in this room has known great sorrow."

Well, you could have made the same statement on any crowded bus, and been right. The odd thing was, though the whole thing reeked of humbug, my eyes filled with tears.

First, Madame concentrated on one of the women in black, and we heard that her son was very happy on the other side of the veil, and had met up with his deceased father. Then the old charlatan cried: "I am gettink ze letter L, a name zat sounds Italian."

And Eleanor cried out, with her whole soul in her voice: "Lorenzo!"

"Yes, it is Lorenzo."

As we came in, we had all been told to write our questions for the other side on a slip of paper. Madame had made a great ceremony of putting these on the fire, but I strongly suspected she had found time to read them. I refused to notice the pounding of my heart. This was not Lorenzo.

"He has a message for you," Madame intoned.

"Yes?" Eleanor breathed, and I felt her fingers tighten around mine.

"You alone had his heart. He loved only you. Yours was a very great love. The bodily change we call death cannot destroy it."

The liar, the wicked old liar—I was the woman Lorenzo loved. I was glad of the darkness so that no one would see the tears cascading down my face.

Afterward, Eleanor rose from the table with an air of calm radiance. "I can carry on now," she told me, out in the street, "because I know that our love has been purified in death. It is as perfect as it was always meant to be."

She returned to Rottingdean in a cloud of exaltation.

I returned to my flat, and broke into sobs of desperate loneliness and anger. Damn him, he had promised to haunt me when he died—where was he? How could I stay in this place, where everything reminded me of Lorenzo—and reminded me, too, that the yearning for him could never be satisfied? His death felt like the ultimate desertion. That evening, I reported for duty a few minutes early, to tell the commandant to put my name forward for service in France.

One

When Tertius came home on leave in January 1918, he found himself the talk of fashionable London. Aubrey Russell had decided that the time was ripe for his exhibition. With his shrewd instinct for the prevailing taste, he sensed the hunger for a new perspective on the war. And, as he had foreseen, the stark, ferocious and oddly beautiful paintings Tertius had been sending him for the past three years caused a sensation. Every newspaper and magazine had acclaimed the exhibition at the Swan Gallery as the debut of a genius; the spirit of his generation. The narrow Mayfair street was jammed with the sleek motor cars of the rich and influential, and tickets were changing hands at extraordinary prices.

The only flaw in all this was Tertius himself. He had refused to visit the show until the last day of his leave, and his response to the extravagant reviews had been distinctly sullen. Aubrey could not understand it.

"But do you like it?" he asked for the dozenth time. "Have I done your work justice? It can hardly be called a success unless you're pleased."

"Of course he's pleased!" roared Quince. "Aren't you, boy?"

Tertius, Aubrey, Quince and Rory were touring the gallery late in the afternoon. Catalogs rustled as Tertius passed. His self-portrait of 1916 had been widely reproduced.

"You've done me proud, Russell," he said. "It makes me wonder who on earth this Tertius Carey can be—nothing like me, I'm sure." There was a bitterness in his voice, which grated on the ears of Quince and Aubrey, and made them exchange troubled glances.

"I've never seen such a triumph," Aubrey said. "The

gossips are already saying my gallery will be too insignificant for your next show."

For some reason, this made Tertius wince irritably. Hooking an arm around Rory's waist, he touched the gilt frame of the portrait described in the catalog as "The Hon. Mrs. Augustus Fenborough, 1913"—Viola, before her wedding, in all her glacial splendor.

"Never expected to see this again."

"Mrs. Fenborough was most generous about lending it," said Aubrey. "Though she couldn't come to see it on display. She's down in the country, nursing a new baby. A boy, I believe."

"I heard," Tertius said dully. "I'm glad for her."

Rory was gazing at the large painting of Fingal, monocled and morning-coated; his supercilious elegance captured for all time. "Your dearest possession," she murmured to Aubrey.

"Yes. And I had a struggle before I could persuade myself to expose it to the public gaze. Not that it's for sale. I wouldn't part with it for all the pearls in the ocean. Which reminds me, Tertius, we really must talk a little business—"

Tertius did not seem to have heard. He was staring at a full-length portrait of Rory, as if seeing it for the first time. It had been done in Ireland, when they were in their teens. Rory stood against a backdrop of mountain and lough, proud and slender, with the skirt of a shabby riding habit looped over one arm, and her short red hair blowing across her laughing face.

"Where did you get this?"

"Your mother sent it over in the crate of family pictures I asked for. I had no idea you'd mind."

Tertius glanced at the catalog, then back to the painting. "Why'd you give it a title?"

"I, dear boy? You're the one who did that. It was chalked on the back of the canvas: *Rory of the Hills.*"

"Rory-of-the-hills," he gave her a rough squeeze, "what d'you think of yourself?"

"She ought to be madly vain." Aubrey tried to lighten the tone. "You've been hailed as one of the beauties of the decade, darling. I'm besieged by court photographers pleading for sittings. They've been so disappointed, to hear that you're driving an ambulance on the other side of the channel."

"They wouldn't know me for the same woman," Rory said.

In her austere blue uniform she was as thin and sharp as a metal file under the blazing gallery lights. Her eagle's profile was more pronounced, and though the tilt of her head was as proud as ever, there was a bitter set to her mouth.

"Anyway," Aubrey cut in, with rather forced briskness, "I've had to turn down some ridiculous offers for it. Which brings me back to the prosaic but necessary topic of business. You're not to run away from me again, Tertius, before I've had a chance to—oh, damn the boy, he does this every·time." Aubrey turned in exasperation to Quince, as Tertius led Rory away into the next room. "He wouldn't even come to his own exhibition before today. I simply cannot pin him down."

Quince (who had proved first too old, then too asthmatic to be called up, and had been working as a volunteer hospital orderly) looked at the spot where Tertius had been, with baffled affection. "Perhaps if you put Rory onto him?"

"No. I know it worked in the past, but the poor girl is as changed as he is. Can't you see it? She clings to him, Q, and she never used to. I found her in tears the other day, because she couldn't bear to see his gray hairs. I suppose she thought he'd be a boy forever."

"Can't say I blame her," Quince said sadly. "That's what I thought, too."

They followed Rory and Tertius into the gallery's second room. Here, Aubrey had gathered all Tertius's war work: sketches, cartoons and paintings of haunted faces and shattered landscapes. His dramatic 1916 series "Howitzer Studies" hung along one wall. Another was dominated by lowering, semiabstract oils of the Menin road, and the ruins of Ypres. These, above all, were the paintings that had made Tertius's reputation.

The room was crowded with people, and very quiet. Soldiers, often with wound stripes sewn to their sleeves, contemplated Tertius's interpretation of their shared tragedy—the Aid Posts, supply dumps, dugouts and firebays of their world. Women stared, wide-eyed, at the barbarity from which they had been shielded for so long.

"Tertius"—Aubrey touched his khaki sleeve—"do I have to chloroform you or will you come quietly?"

Tertius grinned briefly. "All right, you win."

Aubrey kept an office on the first floor of the narrow Georgian house: a comfortable, square room, with a red

Turkish carpet, a Chinese cabinet, a shelf of morocco-bound ledgers, and a large mahogany desk. There was a leather chesterfield against one wall, and a generous fire burning in the grate. Mr. Forbes-Hardy, the gallery manager, had drawn the velvet curtains against the bleak January afternoon, and set the decanters neatly on the desk.

"Irish whiskey." Aubrey pushed a glass into Tertius's hand. "Procured—with enormous worry and fatigue—especially for you. Cigarette?"

"I'll have one of me own, thanks. I only smoke Woodbines now. All the boys do, and you get used to 'em."

"As you wish, my dear." With a delicate shudder over the coarse smell of Woodbines, Aubrey sat Quince and Rory down with their drinks, and faced Tertius across the desk. "To business."

"If we must."

"You have gathered that this show has made you famous. You don't seem to realize, however, that it could also make you rather rich." He leaned forward, and said, separating each word for emphasis: "I could have sold every picture five times over, for a king's ransom."

Tertius shrugged impatiently. "So? Is there a problem?"

"Far from it. The Tate wants the howitzers, by the way." He left a pause, for Quince and Rory to make impressed noises. "All that has to be cleared up is the question of ownership. Obviously, some of the portraits are already spoken for. I own twenty-four of the prewar abstracts, under the terms of our first agreement. These, I am free to sell."

"I don't dispute it, Russell."

"But what do you want me to do with the others?"

"Others?"

"You're being deliberately obtuse." Aubrey was beginning to sound annoyed. "All the other work belongs to you. You could sell it for a small fortune."

"I see." Tertius drained his whiskey, and put the glass on the desk with exaggerated care.

"Shall I make the arrangements? Of course, I shan't charge commission—"

"It's very decent of you," Tertius interrupted, "but they're not for sale."

Rory and Quince exclaimed in unison: "What?" This could not be their Tertius, who set so little store by his paintings that he had once given one away to a tram conductor who admired it.

Aubrey, equally astonished, managed to keep his voice casual. "Have you any particular plans for them?"

"No. I just know I won't sell any."

"In that case, would you like me to store them for you?"

"Why ask? You always store them."

"It's not as simple as that," Aubrey snapped, losing patience. "Suppose a zeppelin dropped a bomb on my head tomorrow? Where would you be without some legal proof of ownership? For heaven's sake, Tertius, stop being such a nuisance! There is nothing on this earth worse than a young artist who lets success turn his head."

"Sorry." An expression of such deep, dumb misery crossed Tertius's face that Aubrey was instantly mollified.

"I'm here to help you, so let me. You haven't sent me any work for the last six months."

"They keep me too busy."

"Precisely. And how too absurd, when you could serve your country far more effectively by using your true talents. So I have been making inquiries to see if I can get you onto the list of official war artists. Like John, you know, and Spencer. They'll give you a commission, and you can daub away as much as you like. Thanks to your success here, I'd say it can be very easily arranged."

Rory let out a cry of delight, but Tertius showed neither gratitude nor enthusiasm. He simply sat, nursing the butt of his cigarette, his face hardening into stubborn anger. After a long silence, he said: "No."

"No!" Quince could not let this past. "Have you gone mad?"

"I don't want to be an officer."

"Oh, for God's sake!" bellowed Quince. "Of all the awkward little buggers—what does that matter if it means you can be an artist?"

Tertius said: "I don't want to be an artist."

It fell in the room like a bombshell, making Rory gasp painfully, and striking Quince dumb. Aubrey was the first to recover.

"Perhaps we should discuss it a little later."

"You won't change my mind."

"Quince is quite right about your awkwardness—are you this much trouble to the army?" There was a knock on the door. Aubrey allowed himself a moment to wrestle down his irritation and anxiety. "Come in."

It was Mr. Forbes-Hardy. He was a thin, bald young man, who spoke softly because he had been badly gassed at Ypres in 1915. Aubrey had taken him on out of compassion, and now found him invaluable.

"I beg your pardon, Mr. Russell. Some ladies downstairs are asking for Mr. Carey."

"You didn't have to tell them I was here," Tertius said.

Mr. Forbes-Hardy looked pained. He did not know exactly how to deal with Tertius. Brother of a peer and brilliant young painter he might have been, but he wore a private's uniform, and Mr. Forbes-Hardy had been an officer. "They claim to be old friends of yours—the Misses Berlin."

"Berlin! Oh, that's different. Thanks, Forbes-Hardy." Tertius was suddenly his alert, friendly, prewar self. "C'mon, Rory."

The three Berlin sisters were among the portraits, solemnly ranged in front of a pastel head-and-shoulders of Joe. They turned when Tertius and Rory appeared, followed closely by Quince and Aubrey. Frieda stepped forward as spokeswoman.

"Tertius dear." She touched his cheek briefly, as if to assure herself of its youth and strength. "How well you look."

She had aged noticeably over the past few months. Her face was crisscrossed with fine lines, like a piece of crazed china.

Tertius took her hand. "I was so sorry to hear about Joe."

Her cordial smile wavered. "Thank you. We don't think it right to make too much of our grief, when so many are suffering. But it has been hard for us."

Behind her, Berta and Dorrie nodded sadly.

"Where did it happen?" Tertius asked.

"At a place called Polygon Wood. Perhaps you have heard of it?"

"Yes."

"We mean to go there when the war is over—we think actually seeing the place where he died will help us to bear it. His commanding officer wrote that he was out on patrol, and that right to the end, his only concern was for the safety of his men. We have heard that they sometimes make up things to write to families when reality is too horrible," she added. "But this sounds so like our Joey, we know it must be true."

Dorrie suddenly let out a muffled sob, and had to fumble in her bag for a handkerchief. Frieda, however, kept her composure. "We had to come here when Cecil Scott told us of your portrait. She said it was beautiful—and it is, Tertius. We would so much like to buy it."

"It's not for sale." His face was gentle. "It already belongs to you."

"Oh, but we—"

"Please. I want you to have it."

Joy flashed across the three ugly faces. Berta and Dorrie turned back to the portrait with welcoming smiles of ownership.

Frieda kissed Tertius's cheek. "I hardly know how to thank you. It's almost too much—"

He was watching her curiously. "Does it honestly mean such a lot to you?"

She replied simply: "It is like getting a piece of him back."

Aubrey, sensing that too much melancholy was bad for his star artist, decided to brace up the mood. "Mr. Forbes-Hardy, will you make a note of the transaction?"

"Certainly, Mr. Russell."

One by one, in order of seniority, the Berlins kissed Tertius and Rory, and filed out of the Swan Gallery into the cold dusk. They were the last visitors. With unhurried precision, Mr. Forbes-Hardy tidied the stacks of catalogs, pulled down the blinds and put on his overcoat and bowler hat. He stood, keys in hand, waiting for the others to leave.

Aubrey took his gold watch from his vest pocket. "Q, I hope you'll be my guest for dinner. And Tertius, if you and Rory would care to—"

"No thanks," Tertius cut in. "We have a prior engagement—last night of my leave, and all that. Haven't we, Rory?"

"Oh—" For one fraction of a second, Rory looked confused. "Yes, of course—"

They left arm in arm. Aubrey stood at the window, watching them huddling together as they wound their way along the busy pavement.

Quince was still in front of the portrait of Joe. "He was a good sort. So many of them are. You wouldn't think a country would want to go on chucking chaps like that away."

"It's too late," Aubrey said. "Our youth has already been poured out and lost. Look at Tertius and Rory—I'm not a kind man, Q, nor a sentimentalist, but the pair of them break my heart."

"You were awful quiet in there," Tertius challenged Rory. "I thought you'd bite my head off."

"I don't bite people's heads off anymore."

"Didn't you care that I turned down a free dinner, when we're both broke?"

"No. I'd rather be alone with you."

"So you can nag me about being a war artist and selling my work to the Tate."

"No."

They were climbing the narrow stairs to her flat. Since Tertius had invented the prior engagement, they had ended up buying two mutton chops and two bottles of stout, and settling for an evening of quiet domesticity.

"Jesus, the price of these chops," Tertius complained. "You'd think they'd been carved off a frigging unicorn."

"Everything costs a fortune nowadays." Rory stooped to put a match to her gas fire. "Miss Thompson moaned to me about it for a solid hour the other morning. We young people out in France have no idea how elderly civilians are suffering at home."

"Rory."

"What?"

"Look at me."

Reluctantly, Rory looked at Tertius. "Well?"

"Rory-May, what's happened to you?"

She felt her back stiffening defensively. This was the question she had been dreading. "Nothing."

"Come on," he urged. "You've changed. Is it driving the ambulance?"

"The work's an awful lot harder out in France than it is here. Not to mention the diggings and the grub." She began to bustle about in the landing kitchen, unwrapping the meat and melting lard in the frying pan. Tertius followed her, blocking the doorway, and watching her critically.

"You're not going to tell me. You're acting as if you were a thousand miles away, and you don't think I'm worth an explanation."

"Tertius, that's not fair! I've spent every moment of this leave with you."

"Sure you have. But you're holding something back."

There was a dangerous glint in his eye. "It's a man, isn't it?"

The chops slid from her hand, and flopped to the floor. She turned on him, furious that he had guessed so easily, and made her grieving sound so cheap. "Damn you."

"Who is he?" Tertius shouted. "I want the bastard's name!"

"There isn't any bloody man!" Rory shrieked back at him. The bleak truth of this brought a sour taste to her mouth. "You're wasting your stupid jealousy on nobody!"

The demented edge to her voice shocked them both into silence. She put her hands to her burning cheeks, and breathed hard to regain control of herself; she had fought her grief for months, and refused to sink beneath its weight. "There isn't a living soul with any claim on me except you," she began, in a breathless approximation of her normal voice. "So it's silly of you to accuse me. You know how lonely I'd be without you." She gazed down at the chops, suddenly tearful and exhausted. "Oh God, what shall I do with these?"

Tertius took her in his arms. "I'm sorry, sweetheart," he murmured. "Don't cry." The anger had faded from his face. "Not for the sake of a couple of chops." He kissed her cheek, picked up the chops, rinsed them under the cold tap, and slapped them into the pan. "I'll take care of them."

"No, really—"

"Who does it better? You're such a great cook, I suppose?" With a surge of his old spirit, he gave her a friendly smack on the bottom. "Open the bottles."

Rory obeyed him, blowing her nose. Of all people on earth, Tertius came closest to healing the terrible void in her heart. She must not allow herself to give way or she would start thinking about the parting tomorrow. "This isn't much of a last night for you," she said, handing him one of the large black bottles of stout. "We should have done something special."

He was concentrating on the frying pan. "You don't know the sorts of things we hanker after out there. I'll bet you anything that this is what I'll remember about my leave when I get back just being here with you. It means a hell of a lot to me, Rory-May."

They ate the chops with Worcester sauce, warmed-over bubble and squeak, and the remains of a Fuller's cake.

Afterward, they settled themselves on the hearth rug, and Rory produced a carefully hoarded two inches of brandy, and a huge, vulgar box of chocolates.

"Aubrey sent it, the day I came home. He thinks it terrifically funny to bombard me with chorus-girl presents."

"He's fond of you," Tertius observed.

"Yes. He's been very kind."

"He knows what you're hiding from me."

Rory hung her head wearily. She could not cope with this. The wound was too raw, and she loved Tertius too much to tell him what would hurt him. To her surprise, however, he lifted her chin gently with one finger, and softly said, "I won't pester you. But you've been unhappy, haven't you?"

"Dreadfully."

"I hate to see it, that's all. Wish there was something I could do."

She was warmed by a rush of love for him—nothing like the love she had felt for Lorenzo, but something comforting and wholesome, from the innocent past. "You only have to be here to make me feel better."

"That's not what you used to say."

She smiled. "I'm not the woman I used to be. I hope I've grown out of squabbling with you now. I know your value too well."

In the dim yellow light from the lamp, Tertius looked young and very sad. There were poignant hollows under his cheekbones. She leaned forward to stroke his hair, pulling his lock of gray through her fingers with special care. "You've changed, too."

"I know."

"Why were you so odd with Aubrey? I'm not reproaching you, darling. I only want to understand." She shifted, so that she could draw his head down to her shoulder. "You say I've been distant, but you've been as remote as the Andes. Let me reach you."

His heart beat hard against her arm. She kept up her rhythmic stroking of his hair, wishing her arms could make a whole world for him and keep him safe. The idea that he might be lost or damaged chilled her like death. If Tertius were hurt, it would be an outrage against all the laws of heaven. "I love you so much," she whispered.

"Oh, Rory—oh my God—" His lips fastened on hers and he pushed his tongue into her mouth.

Rory was taken by surprise. She had not thought of sexual pleasure since the death of Lorenzo, except to decide that he had taken all her desire with him to the grave. Her extinguished body felt nothing for Tertius. But if this was what she must do to keep him, to save him—

He was fumbling with the buttons on her blouse and skirt, his fingers ruthless and clumsy. His breathing was hoarse, and his desperation alarmed her. With an overwhelming sense of unreality, she helped him to peel off her clothes, and his own. Her mind refused to connect with the extraordinary fact that she was lying naked in Tertius's arms, feeling his flesh against hers.

He fingered her breasts with mounting panic, as if trying to decipher some code written on her body. It was only when she moved her leg, and brushed against the damp softness of his genitals, that she realized he had no erection.

"Shit!" He pushed her roughly away, and sprang to his feet. "Shit! Shit!" Grabbing the brandy bottle, he smashed it against the mantelpiece, then buried his face in his hands.

Stunned, Rory lay sprawled across the rug, watching the dregs of the brandy dripping into the grate, and not daring to move, even to brush away the broken glass from around Tertius's bare feet.

"Don't say anything," he warned, through gritted teeth. "Not a word." His face emerged so transformed by bitterness and anger that Rory was seriously afraid. This hard, menacing man, with his gray-streaked hair and restless hands, was a stranger to her. He was staring down at her now, raking his eyes over her body with a coldness that made her flesh crawl. "You're not to move," he said.

She had no intention of moving. Her pulse throbbing uncomfortably, she watched him searching the room for pencil and paper. When he had found them, he sat down beside her. The pencil trembled wildly in his hand. The effort to keep it steady brought the sweat out on his upper lip.

His hand faltered on the page, and was still. He made a second attempt to mark the paper, and the pencil flew from his shaking grasp.

"There," he said, holding up the spoiled piece of paper. "The latest Tertius Carey, worth a king's ransom."

The anger in his eyes shattered into a childlike look of helpless anguish. Ducking his head and reaching out blindly toward her, he burst into tears. She flung her arms around him as if snatching him from the jaws of death. She was weeping with him, cradling his head against her thin bosom.

"My darling, let me help you—"

"Nobody can."

"Tell me, tell me."

With a mighty effort, he blurted out: "Rory, it's all over. I can't work anymore. You saw how my hand shakes when I try to draw. I'll never work again."

"But surely after the war, when you've had a chance to rest, and—"

"No! It's not only my hands. Something else has gone too."

"What?"

"I don't know. Whatever drove me to work in the first place—I'm an orphan without it—" Sobs overcame him. Rory tightened her grip on him, bracing her body to absorb his convulsions. "And I'm a success," he sobbed out furiously. "Now I'm a fucking success—when I don't have a thing left in the world."

"You've got me, you'll always have me, I'll never leave you." Rory murmured this over and over, like a spell, until the wildness of his distress subsided.

"Honest to God," he said, "if I didn't have you, I'd break in pieces."

"Me, too, Tershie. I've been pining for you these last few months."

Tertius pulled away from her slightly, so that she could see his eyelashes, spiked and clogged with tears. "We need each other. We belong together."

"Yes," Rory said evenly, "I believe we do."

They stared at each other, weighing up the implications of her admission.

"Does that mean"—he began—"do you mean you'll marry me, at last?"

And Rory, again caressing his lock of gray hair, replied: "Yes."

He collapsed in her arms, like a marionette with broken strings, and this time, he cried from sheer tiredness and relief. In deep love, and deeper sadness, they fell asleep.

* * *

In her dream, Rory was a traveler, arguing with someone about directions. Of course I know which way to go, she was saying angrily. The other person pointed out that her way was cold and unpleasant. No, she insisted, I know I'm right. What other way is there?

She woke shivering, to find herself alone. It was still dark outside, but the darkness had the quality of early morning, and she could hear the milkman's horse and cart down in the street. The gas fire was barren and dead, a sooty draft hissing through its clay teeth. The meter had run out of shillings. Rory sat up stiffly, hugging herself.

"Tertius?"

The solitary sound of her voice scared her. There was a piece of paper propped against the gas pipe, and it was just light enough for Rory to see that it was addressed to her in Tertius's new, galvanic handwriting. She struck a match, to read: *Dear Rory-May, I ran because I couldn't face you. Bless you, my darling, but you don't have to marry me. I know you only said yes to be kind. Your loving, devoted T.*

He had gone. He had left her to go back to the war. Rory's heart swooped with panic. He didn't understand—she had to see him—which station? What time was it? Seven o'clock. She still had time if the gods were on her side.

She flung herself into her clothes, not even bothering to brush her hair; not noticing when she cut her foot on a shard of the broken brandy bottle. She only knew hours later, when she found her stocking and shoe glued together with dried blood.

By some miracle, she met a taxi almost outside the front door, which rattled her to Victoria Station. By an even greater miracle, she had money enough in her pockets to pay for it.

Inside the station, she could have howled like a dog with frustration and despair. The place was seething—how on earth would she find him? Suppose he climbed on his train and went away from her without knowing how near she had been? Every platform seemed to be a solid mass of khaki. There were women and children and old men milling around to see them off. There were charitable tea stalls, handing out thick white cups and hefty sandwiches.

Rory stood absolutely still in the middle of it all, focusing every atom of her mind on Tertius. If she thought about him hard enough, she would find him. She shut her eyes, and when she opened them again, she caught a glimpse of his profile in the distance, beside one of the stalls.

The joy of seeing him hurt more than the suspense of searching for him. Rory had no idea what she meant to say to him, only that touching him once more was the most important thing in the world. Not caring whose feet she trampled, she barged violently through the crowds toward him.

He saw her approaching. For a couple of seconds, his face was expressionless. Then he rushed to meet her. They fell ravenously into each other's arms, speaking at the same time:

"Tertius! Why did you leave me—"

"Rory, I'm sorry I was such an idiot—"

"You frightened the life out of me," she said, with a shaky laugh. "Don't you ever sneak away like that again."

"I didn't have the guts to wake you. Oh, Rory, Rory!" His breath was warm on her neck. "Thank God you're here."

"You do want me really?"

"I was cursing myself just now, because I wanted you so much. I nearly sent Q to get you when I went back to the studio for my things."

"I still mean it," she said. "We belong together, and I won't let you change my mind."

"Oh, darling—" Gently, he disengaged himself from her arms and stroked her cheek. "I know you're as staunch as steel, but I won't hold you to it."

"But Tershie, I—"

"We'll talk about it another time. What's this?" He smiled—the old, familiar Tertius smile. "You're not crying? I'm ashamed of you. What kind of face is that to send me off with?"

"I love you."

"And I love you, Rory-May."

Tertius kissed her mouth, swung his kit bag over his shoulder, and was gone, with one backward glance and one brief wave. An icy fist closed around her heart as she stood gazing after him, bruised and buffeted by the jostling crowd. This parting from him was only a shadow. The real Tertius had left her a long time ago.

Two

The fog was thickening. Gray wreaths and drifts of it swirled in the gutters and muffled the streetlamps. No air raids tonight, anyway, Francesca thought, trying to dispel the fear that chilled her worse than the bitter cold. It was foolish of her, she knew, to be afraid of the blind loneliness at the heart of the fog, and the distant, unconnected sound her own feet made on the pavement.

She only had to walk the length of Sloane Street and cross the square, and within minutes, she would be safe in the little Queen Anne house Stevie had bought for her—her own house, in her name, which nobody could take away. Ivy, her cook-general, would have made scones for tea. There would be a fire waiting in the sitting room. The same fire, she thought, with a contracting of the heart, that Stevie had watched as he died. Her kindly, merry, beautiful young husband, whom everyone now spoke of as some species of angel.

Francesca wondered what Stevie would have felt about her keeping their house, against the wishes of both sets of parents. Marian Carr-Lyon had wanted her to move down to Calcutta Lodge, where she could be a comfort—these days, she clung to Francesca as a living souvenir of her lost boy. And her own mother was nagging her to sell the house and move back to Half Moon Street.

The thought of Monica hardened Francesca's tender heart. After Stevie's death, certain things had become apparent. Monica had, as Archie put it, "hit the jolly old bottle somewhat." And under the influence of the jolly old bottle, she liked to hint at things she had kept hidden from her daughter. Archie had done his best to protect Francesca, while Monica taunted her for her innocence. But it was obvious she knew something about Stevie. Francesca's delicate nature shrank from probing any further.

If there was any purpose to her sad, isolated life of mourning, it was the determination not to become like her mother. This had given her the strength to defy her elders and betters. She had also found herself some worthwhile work, even if it was only sorting old clothes for soldiers' widows, in Lady Madge Allbright's Knightsbridge ballroom.

I'm a soldier's widow, too, she had thought that afternoon. How would she have coped if losing Stevie had reduced her to wearing these mangy, camphor-smelling cast-offs? She had money. She was lucky. She had no right to think her life was ruined. Then, she had picked a baby's dress out of the pile, and all the old pain had come flooding back.

Out of the four of us, she was thinking now, I'm the one who has failed. Eleanor and Jenny have their children, Rory has her freedom. I have one house, where I live like a little old crone in a fairy tale, untouched and withering away. Nobody would ever know how widowhood had only continued the sterility of her life.

There were brisk footsteps behind her. Francesca's pulse fluttered, and she smartened her own pace.

As she stepped into the light of a streetlamp, a male voice cried breathlessly: "Wait!"

Very frightened, she clutched her bag with both hands and hurried on.

"Stop, for God's sake!" The voice was urgent.

Hard fingers grabbed roughly at her arm. He pulled her around to face him. "Monica—don't pretend you don't know me—"

She saw the stern glitter of his eyes, before the fog swelled and darkened and she plunged from terror into blackness.

Gradually, she became aware of a soft warmth, spreading through her frozen hands and feet. She lay floating in the rose-scented dark, listening to voices, hundreds of feet above her.

"You are a fool, Jim," a woman was saying. "Did you have to charge at her like a rogue elephant?"

"D'you think she'll be all right?" The man's voice was anxious. "I don't know what took hold of me—only that she looked so like her."

"There is a resemblance," the woman conceded, "but it's no excuse. Look at the cut of her coat, and the stones in her ring. She's probably a young viscountess or some such, and her husband will horsewhip you. Or you'll be sent to prison for assault."

"Mother! She'll hear you."

"Poor little thing, she hardly seems old enough to be married."

Francesca floated to the surface, and repossessed her senses. To her utter amazement, she found herself lying on a strange bed, in a strange room, with two strange people. The room was beautifully warm, with a glorious fire, as if there were no such thing as a coal shortage. Leaning over her was a young man, in a uniform that looked wrong, until she realized that it belonged to the United States Army.

In her state of dreamlike bewilderment, she registered that this American officer was very handsome—tall and gracefully made, with nut-brown hair, dark gray eyes and features of an aristocratic fineness. He was agitated, and tried unsuccessfully to speak to her.

The woman came to his rescue. "Lie still, my dear, and don't be alarmed. This is the Cadogan Hotel, and we're not a pair of kidnappers. My idiotic son mistook you for someone else in this frightful fog, and you fainted. Fortunately, only a few yards from the door." She was like him, with the same porcelain refinement of feature; the same patrician grace stamped upon every movement. Her creamy skin was the source of the scent of roses. "I am Peggy Redmond. The barbarian is Captain James Redmond. Would you care for some tea?"

"Yes, please." Francesca wondered why she was no longer afraid, and cautiously stole another glance at Captain Redmond when his mother went to the table beside the fire to pour the tea.

He cleared his throat and managed to say: "I'm dreadfully sorry. Please accept my apologies."

She suddenly remembered what he had said before she lost consciousness. "Did you call me Monica?"

His ears reddened. "Yes."

"That is my mother's name."

"Your mother?" He was amazed. "Oh no, she couldn't possibly have a daughter old enough—"

Mrs. Redmond whisked around, holding the big silver teapot. "Are we all talking about Monica Templeton? Married to Archie? The same Monica Templeton whose necklines reach down to her knees, and whose face contains more paint than the average Rembrandt?"

Francesca felt herself turning scarlet at this description. "Yes," she said.

"There you are, Jim." Mrs. Redmond turned to her son with grim triumph. "I always said that woman lied about her age."

"I don't understand." Francesca sat up on the bed. "Are you friends of my mother's?"

The Redmonds exchanged uneasy glances. James said, too quickly: "I hope you can forgive me for my rudeness, Mrs.—"

"Mrs. Carr-Lyon."

"Is there anything we can do for you, Mrs. Carr-Lyon? Perhaps call up your husband, to let him know you're all right?"

"No, he's—I'm a widow."

Mrs. Redmond handed her a cup of tea. "That's too bad. You're too young to know such things exist."

"Please, Mrs. Redmond, I wish you'd explain what all this has to do with my mother. You mustn't be afraid of upsetting me," she added firmly. "I know she tells lies."

James's ears flared redder than ever, but Mrs. Redmond appeared to approve of her directness. She sat down on the end of the bed. "So you also know how she steals men?"

"Will you let me do this, Mother?" James sounded firm now, though there was a hint of humor around his well-bred mouth. "We came to know Mrs. Templeton a few years ago, when she spent a winter in Boston—"

"And managed to weasel her way into our circle," interrupted Mrs. Redmond. "Lord knows how."

"Mother, really!"

"They say a weasel can slip through a wedding ring, and Monica sure knew how to do that."

"Mother!" He snapped the word out angrily. "Mrs. Templeton and I—" Frowning, he searched for the right words.

Francesca said: "You fell in love with her."

"Me!" He drew himself up proudly. "My younger brother. You mustn't think too badly of him—he knew that what he was doing was dishonorable, but he was crazy about her. He lost his head. The whole family got dragged into it, and—well—I'm sorry to involve you, Mrs. Carr-Lyon, if you didn't know."

His boyish sincerity reminded her of Stevie. The lurking suspicion itched at the back of her mind, and she put another black mark against her mother's name. Mrs. Redmond sensed this, and her manner become warmer, and more alarmingly frank.

"If you were a mother yourself, my dear, you'd know the anguish of standing by while someone like Monica breaks your son's heart. But you mustn't mind what I say— Jim will tell you how many times this tongue of mine has reduced polite Boston to rubble. I don't know why they still call on me."

"Because there's no one like you," he said, relaxing into a smile. He was very fond of her. Francesca decided she liked the woman, too.

"I always say," Mrs. Redmond continued, "that vulgar honesty is the best policy. So I'll tell you that I never cared for your mother at all. All right, it's the duty of every young man of good family to have his fling before marriage. But she wasn't 'fling' material—too fast, too old and too damned scheming." She eyed Francesca shrewdly. "Do you want to know any more?"

"Yes." She was suddenly avid to know everything.

"I've never told you this, Jim, but you might as well hear now—it took fifty thousand dollars of your father's money to buy Monica Templeton off poor Will's back."

James drew in a sharp breath. "You—you offered her money?"

"She took it, dear. That's the point."

"Perhaps this isn't the time—"

Francesca was trying to digest Mrs. Redmond's incredible claim. It simply did not make sense. "Mummy wouldn't need to take your money. Uncle Archie has plenty."

"Oh, really? That's not what the man from Pinkerton's discovered when he investigated their finances."

James's head jerked up sharply. "Did you and Dad put a detective on her?" He was shocked, and shot Francesca a side glance of embarrassment.

"Well, of course," Mrs. Redmond said coolly. "And he told us the Templetons didn't have a nickel between them. They got by in style because Archie had a run of lucky wins at poker—too lucky, some said. Anyway, they certainly went home with well-lined pockets." She addressed Francesca. "My husband can afford it. His family sailed over on the *Mayflower,* and they're one of the richest in the country. But just because we can afford it doesn't mean I'm happy to let Monica Templeton shimmy off with our fifty thousand dollars."

Francesca was busy remembering various events from her childhood, and trying to interpret them in the light of what she had just learned. There had never seemed to be any shortage of money. Hadn't Archie always heaped her with cash and expensive gifts? And yet—it was falling into place now—there had been one or two odd delays with the school fees. And they had been remarkably keen to leave her in the custody of Sybil Braddon. They had only returned to London and set up their ménage at Half Moon Street on the strength of the Redmonds' fifty thousand dollars—blood money, the price of a broken heart. Burning with shame, she swore she would never speak to either of them again. The anger poured strength into her. It was as if she had cast off a weight she had been dragging around all her life.

"Mrs. Carr-Lyon"—James briefly touched her hand—"you must think we're both crazy. We shouldn't have told you all this. It doesn't seem decent, somehow."

"Oh, you sound so much like your father!" Mrs. Redmond exclaimed. "Thank heavens you don't look like him, too. You can probably tell, Mrs. Carr-Lyon, that I'm not exactly old Boston myself—far from it. That's how I took the measure of your mother so fast. Grand and English she may be, with legions of titled friends. But I was in a chorus line with a girl just like her, when I was in burlesque—and she'd have flayed the stockings from right off your legs."

James's embarrassment suddenly dissolved into a shout of laughter. "Mother, you're impossible. Mrs. Carr-Lyon, I'm so sorry—"

Francesca drained her tea. "Do stop being sorry, Captain Redmond. I asked to know everything, and I'm glad you told me." She gave them both an uncertain smile. "It has been a very peculiar afternoon for me, but a very important one."

Francesca had not been sure about the propriety of seeing the Redmonds again. She was less sure when she found herself having lunch in a fashionable French restaurant alone with Jim. Suppose she was seen by one of the Carr-Lyons' numerous friends—what on earth would they think?

Her awkwardness lasted only a moment, however. Jim was very easy company, and his every movement and action was designed to show her that he respected the distance between them. Strangely, this made her want to confide in him. While the food congealed on her plate, she told him about Stevie. It was odd, she thought, describing him to someone who had never met him.

"I knew he was dead the minute I went in," she finished, twisting the rings Stevie had placed on her finger. "The maid ran for the doctor, but I knew. The room felt—vacant."

There was silence between them. Jim's fine gray eyes were full of sympathy. "And afterward?" he prompted.

She raised her solemn eyes to his face. "There wasn't any afterward. I mean, there isn't. That was the end."

He seemed pained. "Forgive me, Mrs. Carr-Lyon, but I can hardly bear to hear you talking as if your life were over. You're too young."

"I'm nearly twenty-five. Older than I look. And I feel a thousand, sometimes." Francesca took a sip of wine. "You're very kind to be concerned about me at all, when my mother treated you all so badly."

Jim smiled. "We recovered. It wasn't such a tragedy. My brother is a resilient little fellow. Mother says he has the kind of heart that bounces when dropped."

"She's well, I hope? I thought she would bejoining us."

"So did I." Jim was apologetic. "Then she rushed off at the last minute, to inspect some zeppelin damage in the East End. She prides herself on her vulgar curiosity. When she told you she wasn't 'old' Boston, she was putting it mildly."

"Where did she come from?"

"Irish Boston, Mrs. Carr-Lyon, which might as well be in another galaxy. And she was on the stage, too."

"A real actress—how thrilling!"

This made Jim chuckle. "She was a New York burlesque queen—Peggy O'Connell, the Bowery Belle. Unlike Ethel Barrymore or Eleanora Duse, she could sometimes be persuaded to entertain at bachelor parties—and that's how she met my father. She jumped out of a giant pie, straight into his lap."

Francesca stared at him for a moment, scandalized, then saw the absurdity of their two mothers pitted against each other, and burst out laughing. At the back of her mind, she knew she had not laughed so much since long before Stevie died.

Delighted and touched by her reaction, Jim went on to tell her that the real joke was the grandeur of Peggy's appearance, when his impeccably bred father looked like a well-dressed dockhand. He told her of his war experiences; how he had worked as a driver with the Harvard Medical Unit, until the United States had entered the war the previous year. He had got a commission in the U.S. Army, he explained, but seemed to have spent most of his time since then recovering from a bad leg wound.

He also told her that he meant to see every sight in London before they shipped him home to Boston, and over the next few weeks, Francesca discovered that his appetite for tourist attractions was indefatigable. He dragged her to the Tower, Madame Tussaud's, Westminster Abbey, the Houses of Parliament and Buckingham Palace.

Sometimes, Mrs. Redmond joined them, but she was usually busy, buying what she called "curios" to take home to her friends. Francesca became used to being alone with Jim. When not being a tourist, he would stroll with her through the chilly parks, making her laugh with stories of his life at home. Before she was aware of it happening, his friendship had grown into the single most important fact of her life.

But was friendship the right word? One evening, while preparing to dine with the Redmonds at their hotel, Francesca found herself staring at the reflection in her dressing-table mirror. The bedroom behind her had not changed since the day she and Stevie had moved in, and she had the sudden, uncanny feeling that he was about to emerge from his dressing room, pulling on his dinner jacket, as she had seen him do so many times. He would see how she had changed.

Above the sober collar of her black velvet dress, her face had a secret animation. Her skin, though still very pale, had regained its bloom. There was color in her lips. She shocked herself, by thinking for a moment that she had returned from the dead. Had James Redmond done all this?

She tried to imagine being alone with him in this room. A deep, hard shudder of fear swept over her. Jim was not safe, as poor Stevie had been. But did she want him to be safe? She remembered the times when he had casually taken her hand or brushed against her shoulder, and the fleeting, nervous excitement this had stirred in her. It was all incredibly confusing. Every cell in her body leaped in gladness at the merest sight of Jim. Yet he was more than a friend—or was it less?

He was always more than polite. His warm, genial courtesy toward her never faltered. Beneath it, however, she sensed an insistent heat, which both attracted and repelled her. It surged to the surface one afternoon in early March, in the musty shadows of the Whispering Gallery at St. Paul's Cathedral.

They were moving around the edge of Wren's great dome, staring at the broad shafts of sunlight which pierced the nave, hundreds of feet below. Francesca unconsciously clung to Jim for the murmurs in the air around them seemed to creep through the very roots of her hair like voices from the invisible choir of the dead.

Two little girls and their governess had been pressing their lips to the walls, to try the whisper, but now their feet were clattering away down the wooden staircase, and Jim and Francesca were alone. He placed both his hands on her shoulders.

"Francesca."

She looked at him from under the brim of her hat, feeling the physical urgency beneath the gentleness of his manner. It made her terribly nervous, but she did not want to hurt him by moving away.

"Do you remember," he whispered, "how I told you I came to Europe to find the missing piece of my heart? Darling, I found it, the day I met you. It's kismet, or destiny, or whatever you want to call it. I only know I've felt like a cork being swept over a waterfall—don't care where I'm headed, as long as it's near you." The grip of his fingers tightened slightly. "You're trembling. Are you all right?"

"Y-y-yes," she said, between chattering teeth. She was not all right, but she would force herself to bear it.

"Do you—Francesca, I realize it's only a few months since you lost Stevie, and this sounds like fearful cheek—but do you think you could ever fall in love with me?"

"Oh, yes." This was true. She already loved Jim with all her soul. It was her body that held back.

"I wish I understood you," he said, frowning as he searched her face. "I always get the idea that you're holding something back. Don't be anxious—if you are holding a dark secret, I won't try to wrest it from you. But I think you like me, and I think you're scared. And I want you to know that I'd do anything in the world for you. If you say you'll marry me, I'll make sure nothing scares you ever again. No,'—he added quickly, seeing her look of alarm— "I won't take an answer now. I won't even hear you if you try. Think about it, until I ask you again."

Still holding her shoulders, he lowered his face and kissed her on the mouth, just brushing her parted lips with the tip of his tongue. Her heart seemed to leap up to meet it. But before she had time to be afraid, he had released her, and was making for the door of the gallery, as if the conversation had never happened.

Think about it. As if she could think about anything else. Francesca had shut herself into her bedroom earlier than usual, to grapple with Jim's astonishing question. Perhaps she was very stupid, but in her wildest dreams she had not imagined that he would want to marry her. Since Stevie's death, she had avoided thinking about the future, but she could not do this now.

In an effort to relax, she had soaked in a long, hot bath—recklessly and unpatriotically squandering huge amounts of precious coal to heat the boiler. Warmed and scented, but not in the least relaxed, she was pacing restlessly. Saying no would mean the end of Jim's friendship. Saying yes would bring her face to face with her deepest fears.

She did not see how she could go through all that pain and humiliation again. Other women managed to be happy with husbands and children, but she had something terribly wrong with her, she was sure. Of course, Stevie had never mentioned it. The ethereal innocence of their marriage was proof enough. It must have been her fault—at least, if she was not to commit the appalling crime of blaming her dead and sainted Stevie.

Their wedding photograph, elaborately framed in silver, stood on the mantelpiece. Francesca picked it up. How ironic, she thought, that they had kept this in their bedroom, when Stevie had always slept in the dressing room next door, and nothing remotely connubial had ever occurred in the large double bed. Why hadn't they been ashamed? It had been an unwritten article of faith between them never to mention the ghastliness of their wedding night. The photograph had mocked them, every other night of their joint lives.

She replaced it, blinking away a rush of tears. Darling Stevie. It was wicked to think of him with anything but unqualified love. But she was finding it harder and harder to recall him as a real, living person. He was retreating away from her, into a golden, prewar summer that belonged in the land of myths and memories.

If only she could follow him there. Standing in front of the long cheval glass beside the fire, she slipped off the long silk robe she had put on after her bath, and made herself look at her naked, virgin body, flushed by the pink glow of the flames.

It seemed so starved and pitiful, so childish and sterile that she covered herself again immediately, shaking with sobs. Jim would never want to touch her. She could not risk spoiling his life, as she was sure she had spoiled Stevie's. All her newfound determination was melting away. She was not fit to be out in the world. She would give in to Marian Carr-Lyon, retreat to the house of mourning at Calcutta Lodge, and take her place as one more relic of her dead husband.

There was no more hope left. Curling herself on the bed, she wept for the dead and the living—herself and Stevie, Eleanor and Lorenzo, Rory and Tertius, and all the youthful dreams that had turned to ashes.

Three

"I'm so glad you were able to come, Major Carey. It will mean the world to him. He hasn't stopped asking for his family." The Sister was a serene-looking woman in her thirties, with soft, grave eyes swimming behind thick spectacles. "I should warn you that he doesn't always know where he is. Sometimes he thinks he is at home." She glanced aside at Muttonhead's bad leg and walking stick. "Please tell me if I'm going too fast for you."

They were walking along the corridor of a large, ugly, neo-Gothic convent on the outskirts of Amiens. The French nuns had vacated it for the English nurses, but a religious hush, like a faint smell of incense, lingered beneath the brisk hospital atmosphere.

"He can hear you, and he can talk to you." The Sister did not seem to mind Muttonhead's silence. "His eyes are still bandaged, so I'm afraid he won't be able to see you. The gas burned him badly, and his breathing is very poor." She stopped at a door, and paused to say: "It won't be long now. I do hope you can stay."

Very quietly, as if she had caught some of the stealth of the absent nuns, she opened the door, and led Muttonhead into a small, whitewashed cell. A barred window looked out onto cloisters and a square of lawn. The walls were bare except for a small wooden crucifix hanging on a nail above the bed.

Muttonhead's pulse missed a beat as his mind took in what his eyes showed him—that the burned, tortured body struggling for each breath was Tertius. There was a bandage around his eyes, and his mouth was a mass of cracked, red sores. A plump young nurse sat beside him, holding one of his hands. When she saw Muttonhead, she gently laid the hand down, and left the room.

"Press the bell, Major, if you see any change." The Sister closed the door behind her, and they were left alone.

Feeling massive in the tiny room, Muttonhead sat down and took Tertius's hand. He wanted to speak, but—as usual—found that his feelings had sealed his throat.

Tertius whispered, "Mutt, is that you?"

At last, he found his voice. "Yes, old chap."

Tertius's hand twitched and closed around his. Muttonhead was assailed by a sudden memory of putting his finger into Tertius's tiny palm on the day of his birth. "He's your new baby brother," the Mater had said, "and you must take very good care of him." He saw himself as a sturdy ten-year-old, carrying his little brother around the farm on his back, proud to be trusted with something so precious. Oh God, this would kill her.

"I knew I was getting near home," Tertius wheezed. "Is the Mater coming soon?"

"Yes," Muttonhead said, not knowing what else to do.

"If it wasn't for the hill, you could see the house from here." There was a pause, while he gasped for air. "Terrible rain—we left the boat out on the lake. Now it's filled with water—"

"Doesn't matter," Muttonhead said.

"Honest? You're not mad?"

"No."

The silence stretched into minutes. Tertius fell into a doze. Muttonhead froze to the stillness of marble, not daring to move. He listened to the sound of Tertius's breathing, and the occasional footsteps and voices passing in the cloister outside. After nearly half an hour, Tertius stirred, and said more clearly:

"Mutt, are you really there?"

"Yes."

"I dream so much—don't know what's real—"

"This is real." Muttonhead briefly touched his hair. "You're in a hospital. In Amiens. The Mater will come as soon as I can send for her."

"Rory—"

"Rory, too."

There was another silence. Tertius's sore lips moved, as if he talked to himself. Presently, he said: "They won't be in time."

Muttonhead winced, but kept his voice steady. "They will, don't you worry. Everything's fine."

"Rory—" Tertius was getting agitated. "Tell her not to mind—it wouldn't have worked—she was right all along—"

"Yes, yes." Muttonhead spoke soothingly, but this revelation that Tertius and Rory had reached some kind of understanding startled him. Conscious of pain, he could not decide if it was because he was glad or sorry.

"Take care of her, eh?"

"Leave it to me." Muttonhead laid his hand across Tertius's cold forehead, and it seemed to calm him.

This time, he dozed for forty-five minutes, by Muttonhead's watch, which seemed to tick unnaturally loudly. He counted every breath that Tertius drew, willing him to gather strength for the next one. In one corner of his mind, he was aware of the scarred muscles in his bad leg cramping painfully, but it did not seem important and he did not move.

The nurse came in briefly, to put a cup of tea on the small cabinet beside the bed. Muttonhead acknowledged it with a nod, and shook his head when she asked if he would like her to take his place for a while.

Tertius's hoarse whisper broke the silence. "Mutt—"

"Yes?"

"Don't leave me."

Muttonhead was scowling with the effort of keeping the pain out of his voice. "Rather not. I'll stay as long as you want me—all night, if you like."

A shadow of a smile briefly twitched Tertius's mouth. "I don't smell your pipe."

"It's against the rules."

"Wish I could see you. Can I—touch your face?"

His hand trembled on the counterpane, but he was too weak to lift it. Muttonhead carefully wiped away the tracks of his tears, so he would not feel them, and raised the chilly hand to his cheek. He held it there until Tertius sank into another sleep, and only lowered it when he was sure he would not disturb him.

Tertius's lips were working anxiously as he slept. There was something disturbing him. Muttonhead learned what it was, when he croaked out two words: "Vi—Fenborough."

"Yes? What about her?" Instinctively, Muttonhead bristled. A lady's name had been mentioned—the wife of one of his friends—and he did not wish to hear that his brother had done anything to stain her reputation.

His disapproval must have bled into his voice, for Tertius groaned and said: "Sorry—sorry—"

"It's all right, old boy." Muttonhead pulled himself together, realizing that his old code of chivalry now belonged to the age of the dinosaurs, and that there was nothing more important than Tertius's peace of mind. "I'm listening."

When the nurse returned to remove the cold cup of tea and light the gas, she heard Muttonhead say: "Don't worry. I'll take care of everything."

"Thanks." Above his bandaged eyes, Tertius's forehead became smooth.

Dusk fell, and Muttonhead kept up his vigil, half believing he could save Tertius with his own strength, but already wondering how on earth he was to break the news at home.

The chapel clock struck six, and Tertius's lungs cracked like sheet ice on a lake. Suffering and afraid, he used his last reserves of energy to cling to Muttonhead. His rib cage bucked and heaved under the covers as he fought for air.

"Nearly there—" he gasped. "Mamma—Rory—"

Muttonhead tightened his grip on his hand, refusing to let him go. Very slowly, Tertius's agonized body relaxed, and a look of peace stole over his face. Gradually, his hand froze between Muttonhead's palms.

The Sister, when she came in, saw the stricken slant of Muttonhead's broad shoulders, and the waxen stillness of the figure on the bed.

"Major Carey—" she began.

"He's sleeping," Muttonhead interrupted sternly.

She thought he was unaware of what had happened, until she saw his face. His jaw was set stubbornly, but his eyes—never had she seen such a look of dumb anguish.

"Yes," she said gently, "He giveth His beloved sleep."

Lady Oughterard stayed out on the terrace longer than she had intended, staring at the gold bar of sunset above the black mountains. All day, she had been trying to overcome a peculiar sense of unease, almost foreboding. Una had seen something in her tea leaves, too—all nonsense, of course. Superstitious nonsense. She retreated into the drawing room, bolting the French windows against the dusk.

It was only restlessness, and work was the cure for that. There were the month's accounts to be done—enough to make anyone uneasy. Lady Oughterard took the oil lamp over to her walnut desk, and sat down briskly. The ledgers and bundles of bills were in front of her, yet she could not begin.

Her attention was snared by the large silver-framed photograph she saw every day and knew by heart—herself and the Pater on the steps of Castle Carey, with Lucius and Fingal. Below them, Paddy Finnegan stood beside a jaunting car that contained two small, laughing children in sailor suits and straw hats. Rory and Tertius.

Seized by a sudden sense of urgency, Lady Oughterard pushed the ledgers aside, and began rummaging in the drawers and pigeonholes of her desk. She sighed with relief as her fingers closed around the ribbon from Tertius's sailor hat, which she kept among her private clutter of milk teeth, baby curls and tiny kid shoes. The strip of Petersham was stiff with age, but the letters were as clear as ever—"HMS *Audacious.*" Where was her audacious boy now?

A rushing sound, like a heavy sigh, filled the room, making the flames of the peat fire leap up, shedding a momentary, lurid glare into the twilight. Lady Oughterard's pulse was hammering even before she heard it—a long, low moan in one of the disused rooms upstairs. It soared louder and higher, until it shattered into staccato sobs, which echoed all over the house. Some huge creature—a bird or a bat— was blundering around above her, beating its gigantic wings against the walls and rafters.

Lady Oughterard sat stock-still at her desk, paralyzed with terror. The voice started up again, wailing and keening; the very epitome of despair. The sound of it seemed to claw her heart to rags. A black wave of grief flooding through the house. Before it engulfed her, she leaped up, crying: "Una! Una!"

The terrible sobs rose to screams, and the huge wings seemed to be in the room with her. Lady Oughterard covered her ears, frantic to escape from the sound, and the awful message it sent into her bloodstream.

"Una!"

"I'm here, my darling. Una's here—" Una was in the

room, weeping as she folded her arms around her. "Don't be scared. She loves you, so she does. She's dying of sorrow for you—"

"No!" Lady Oughterard squeezed the sailor ribbon in her fist.

The sounds died suddenly, as if they had been nothing more than the wind. In the silence, she whispered: "Tertius."

Frieda rose, detaching herself from the background of her overfurnished drawing room, and took Muttonhead's hand. It made her own look like a mouse's paw. She had to tilt back her head to meet his eye.

"Major Carey."

"Miss Berlin." As usual, Muttonhead came straight to the point. "How is she?"

"Poor child," Frieda said, "they sent her home in a dreadful state. She does nothing but cry for him, until we've been quite frightened for her. We offer all the comfort we can, but we know this is a pain that has no cure." Her keen black eyes seemed to burn through his reserve. "We're so sorry," she added softly. "I can hardly believe it—so much life, so much talent and promise—"

"All gone," Muttonhead finished for her bitterly.

She shook her head. "Fixed and preserved forever, where they can never fade. That is what we tell ourselves about our brother." She pointed to the pastel portrait of Joe. "Tertius gave that to us only a few months ago. I can't tell you what a comfort it has been. It's beautiful—but even Tertius never could have created anything half as beautiful as himself. We loved knowing him."

Muttonhead whisked around to glare out of the window, and Frieda waited patiently while he blew his nose.

"My sister will bring Rory," she said, when she judged him ready to talk again. "We thought it best not to tell her you were coming in case there was any delay. It would have been so awful to disappoint her."

Muttonhead turned back to her, squaring his shoulders and evidently preparing to dredge up some difficult words. "Miss Berlin, I must thank you for taking care of her like this."

"We could not have allowed her to go back to that lonely flat."

"I mean—I know how good you've been to her, and to—to my brother." The color deepened in his tanned neck. "Look here, in the past, I've been less than tolerant—I've disapproved of your influence over Rory. It was entirely wrong of me."

Frieda was deeply touched, but she could not help smiling. Major the Lord Oughterard was so huge, and so magnificent, blazing away in her drawing room in his staff officer's red tabs. There was something rather comical in his climbing down, when his high horse was so very high. "It doesn't matter."

"Forgive me, but it does," Muttonhead said gruffly. "I hope the war has taught me to be wiser and less of a pompous ass. Then at least I'll have come out of it all with something."

Frieda went to the mantelpiece, which had been turned into a shrine to Joe. Photographs of him at all ages were crowded, two and three deep. She touched them proudly. There was Joe in her arms, as a motherless infant; Joe as a small boy, leaning against the patriarchal arm of his ancient father; Joe in knickerbockers, trundling a hoop; and in tweeds on the river at Oxford. Finally, Joe in his uniform, taken on his last leave.

"What has really hurt me about this war," she said, her voice unsteady, "is seeing young people suffer so terribly. This is not the right way around. When I think of young bodies tortured and maimed, and young minds warped by bitterness and grief, I can hardly endure it. You should be mourning for us. Not us for you."

"Mutt!"

Rory was in the doorway. She was painfully thin. Her colorless face was swollen from endless crying. For a moment, she simply stood and stared at him.

He held out his arms. "You knew I'd come to you."

"Oh, Mutt, I wanted you so much—" She flung herself at him, sobbing stormily.

He picked her up and carried her over to the sofa. "All right, brat. Here I am."

Frieda caught the expression in his eyes, as he cupped his great hand around her head.

"Of course!" she whispered to Berta, nudging her toward the door. "How silly we've been!"

Four

Francesca was out in the garden, cutting the first white roses for the drawing room at Calcutta Lodge, when Nanny Stack came hobbling out across the veranda toward her.

"Mrs. Stevie—someone to see you, dear."

Francesca was known as "Mrs. Stevie," to distinguish her from her mother-in-law. "It'll be Mrs. Perkins, I suppose, about the fish," she said calmly. Tradespeople were their only callers these days, because Marian insisted that they were still in deep mourning. "Ask her to wait."

"No, dear. It's a gentleman. An officer."

A wild hope, with fear treading on its heels, surged through Francesca. Her hand shook, and she clumsily decapitated one of the blooms at its neck. "I—did he tell you his name?"

Nanny ignored this. Her wrinkled old face was disapproving. "I tried to tell him you weren't receiving. But he wouldn't take the hint and go away. Wanted you to tell him yourself. What Mummy will say, I can't imagine."

"Mrs. Carr-Lyon." Jim stood on the veranda, framed by the French windows. "Mayn't I see you, just for a moment?"

Francesca blushed fiercely, prickling all over. A few years ago, she would simply have sprinted out of the garden, leaving someone else to deal with him. Now, though her heart had given a terrifying leap of longing at the sight of him, she knew she owed him at least an explanation.

"Yes, of course. Nanny, this is Captain Redmond. Will you bring us out some tea?"

Nanny looked stubborn. "I don't like it, Mrs. Stevie."

Francesca could be stubborn too, when she chose. "And some scones. I know you've just made some."

"Well, all right, madam. If you say so. But I don't—"

"I'm not asking you to like it, Nanny. Now, do leave us alone."

Nanny did so. Jim's lips twitched as she passed him. "I didn't realize you'd be under house arrest. My God, it's like trying to visit Rapunzel in her castle."

Francesca smiled, in spite of herself. "Oh, Jim—I'm so sorry if she was rude. You should have told us you were coming."

"Would you have seen me, if I had?"

The smile faded. "You're very angry with me, I know you are. I hope you'll forgive me, for treating you so badly—it seems to run in my family, doesn't it?"

He joined her on the lawn, taking the basket of roses from her hand. "Can we get something straight, right now? I'm not angry, and I didn't come all this way to complain to you. I simply had to see you again."

"How did you find me?"

"I asked your friend, Lady Hastings."

"I—I hope I didn't hurt you, Jim, when I ran away like that, without a word to you."

"Of course you hurt me. I thought you cared for me."

"I do—that is, I did."

He took her hand, wrapping his own firmly around it, but she did not try to pull away from him. His touch was warm, and seemed to pour energy into her. "It was my fault. I scared you. That's why I'm here." His grip tightened. "I've got to have an answer to my question." Catching the unmistakably wistful look in her eyes, he pressed home his advantage. "I can't get on without you. I don't care what you're hiding from me. I'll take you on any terms."

"No, you don't understand—"

"Make me understand, then. I'll keep right on asking, until you convince me you don't love me."

Francesca felt this was unfair of him. He must know she was too worn down by misery to lie. And there was nobody she could turn to for help—he was forcing her to take responsibility for her own future. Unconsciously, she returned the pressure of his fingers. She could not bear this, but she would die if he left her here, among the groves of sepia photographs and the smell of grieved old age.

Very gently and slowly, he let go of her hand, and put

his arms around her. She did not resist, but the shaking had begun, and she could only gaze at him helplessly.

He stroked her back. "Why are you so afraid?"

"I don't know."

"I swear, you can trust me. Do you believe me?"

"I—I don't know—"

She loved Jim. She knew she had to trust him, though the black fear was swirling around her. She held her breath, and found that the touch of his mouth on hers did not kill her. It was like coming out of the cold, into a warm room. Her tensed muscles relaxed, as if a cord had been cut, or a spell broken. Suddenly, she was clutching at him, opening her lips. His tongue brushed her teeth, and the shock turned the warmth to delicious, languorous heat.

She had never wanted Stevie to kiss her like this.

Horrified by the sacrilegious ache of desire she felt for Jim, she struggled out of his arms, and dashed blindly toward the shelter of the house.

"What's all this, Francesca? Turning the place into a canteen for Yankee officers?"

Colonel Carr-Lyon's loud voice made her jump like a startled rabbit. She put down the pile of Stevie's letters, and shrank defensively into her chair as he strode into the drawing room.

He surprised her by chuckling. "Don't worry. Not going to bite your head off. Had enough of that from the Memsahib, I should think."

"Yes." Marian had been furious with her. All the old resentments had come flooding back, to increase the bitterness of Francesca's remorse.

"Nice chap, is he?"

"Yes." Her eyes widened in bewilderment.

"Wonderful fellows, those Americans. Wish I'd been around to meet him." He gave one of his sudden barks of laughter, and bellowed: "Kissed you, did he?"

If she blushed any harder, she would go up in flames. "Honestly, I didn't mean him to!"

"Course not. Shy little thing like you." Another bark.

"Marian thinks I asked him to come—and I didn't, truly." Her voice thickened with the threat of tears. "I wish you'd make her see."

"Don't you worry about her." He became grave. His red

face, when softened, bore a fleeting reminder of Stevie.
"She was wrong to be angry with you, Francesca. And so
I told her. If you want to ask this chap down again, you
ask away."

"Oh no, I won't do that."

The Colonel cleared his throat—a signal that he was
changing gear into something approaching tenderness.
"You know, it's a tremendous comfort to Marian, to have
you here."

"I hope so."

"She can't help it, you know. He was the only child we
ever managed to have, and we couldn't have loved him
more."

"I know."

"But he's gone, and there we are. He wouldn't want you
to chuck yourself on his funeral whatsit. This isn't any life
for you—going through his letters, staring at photographs,
letting Marian bore you with his school prizes. When the
war's over, that'll be my job. You should be thinking of
the future."

The tears spilled out, blotting the old letter in her hand.
"There isn't any future."

"Nonsense!" He sat down beside her, awkwardly patting
her shoulder. "Francesca, I couldn't have wished for a better son. But that doesn't stop me knowing Stevie wasn't
much of a husband to you."

She was amazed to hear such heresy, in this house, from
Stevie's father. "He was a perfect husband."

"My dear, he told me."

"Oh." She hung her head.

They sat in silence for a few minutes, listening to the
clamor from the blackbird's nest outside the window.

Presently, Colonel Carr-Lyon murmured, "He was very
unhappy about it. When Marian told me about your Yankee, my first thought was that if you got yourself settled,
then my poor boy could rest in peace."

Francesca looked down at her left hand, so pathetic with
its shining wedding ring. Yes, she thought, it was time to
leave Stevie to rest. Suddenly, she remembered, like a sign
from heaven, Fingal Carey saying: "I shall die with a better
grace, if I know you've made up your mind to live."

PART SEVEN

Summer 1918— Summer 1919

Aurora

Muttonhead had some leave before he was due to take up his promotion to the War Office in London. He used the time to take me home to Ireland. Tertius came too, in a lead-lined coffin. Half the countryside turned out to follow the hearse. Poor things, they had suffered losses, too. Only one of the boys Mutt had taken off to war had come back.

It was the saddest homecoming you can imagine. The Mater held up her head proudly in front of the villagers and neighbors, because that was what one did, but her crisp hair had turned iron gray—there was not one thread of ebony left in it—and Muttonhead had to support her up the steps of the Protestant church. Mr. Phillips read the service with the tears pouring down his ruddy face.

And so we laid our beloved Tertius to rest in the mildewy family vault, alongside Fingal and the Pater, and he became the fictional character you were brought up to know—a creature from the great, golden legend of the world before the war.

I stayed on in Ireland after the funeral. Muttonhead told me the Mater needed me, and that I wasn't even to think of going back to work; and for once in my life, I simply gave in to him. I was so deathly tired, I didn't even have the stamina to argue. After Lorenzo's death, I had pushed myself too hard, and the loss of Tertius had proved too much for me. For the rest of that spring, and into the early summer, I let the peace of Marystown and Castle Carey heal my shredded nerves.

Eventually, I could remember Tertius and speak of him without my every muscle seizing up in agony. Mutt had told me what he had said when he was dying—that it would never have worked. At first, it only made the pain worse.

I would have married Tertius a thousand times if it would have brought him back. Later, however, I began to see his wisdom, and bless him for it. Darling Tertius—to this very day, missing him is like missing my right hand. But we were never meant to marry.

While I was working all this out, I did what I could for the Mater. The sheer weight of her grief bent her shoulders, and she hobbled about from fireplace to fireplace, wrapped in threadbare old shawls like a little old lady. Una told me she had been in this state since the night they heard the crying of the banshee.

As the weather got warmer, however, she regained some of her old briskness, and began to show heartening signs of interest in other people's business. "So help me," one of the village women said, "I'm glad her ladyship's up to interfering again."

She took a renewed interest in the war, and in the evenings, she and Una would knit khaki balaclavas beside the kitchen range, while I read aloud from the newspaper. These were horribly worrying months. The Germans went on and on advancing, and everyone knew how bad things were when Sir Douglas Haig sent a special message to the forces: "Every position must be held to the last man; there must be no retirement. With our backs to the wall, and believing in the justice of our cause, each one of us must fight on to the end."

Una and the Mater had quite an argument over the message. The Mater said it would fire her blood, and fill her with inspiration. Una said all that stuff about "backs to the wall" was depressing, and that if she were a soldier, she would be scared stiff. My own reaction was that the tired old nation-next-door needed every spare pair of hands. It was time to go back to London.

I found a city full of poor, hungry, black-clad people, worn down by the unrelenting hopelessness of a war that had lasted nearly four years, and showed no sign of ending. There were shortages of everything. Meat, sugar, butter, margarine and lard were rationed—you were given a book of stamps to take to the shops. Jam, bread, cheese, coal and paper were about as plentiful as pearls, and certainly as expensive. You could be fined huge sums for hoarding food, or obtaining it illegally. I don't think anyone actually starved under the system, but it increased the general atmosphere of weariness and gloom.

I went to see a kind old soul at VAD headquarters, who forgave me for leaving my post in France, and wangled me a place in my old unit at Charing Cross. This time, I took the day shift, and was shocked by the lack of respect shown to my ambulance on the streets. In the beginning, a red cross could bring the traffic to a standstill. Now, people no longer seemed to care about the wounded. The country was holding on to its collective sanity by a thread, with precious little compassion to spare.

There was one rainbow of hope that summer. In July, Francesca married her handsome Yankee officer. It was not yet a year since Stevie's death, but everyone had urged her not to wait. Though James was still on sick leave, there was no knowing when he would be sent back to the front.

Much as I had liked Stevie, I was all for grabbing happiness with both hands. Love had made a new woman of Francesca—she was confident and resolute, with only a shadow of her old shyness. She asked Muttonhead to give her away, because she was no longer speaking to her parents. Monica had apparently done something unforgivable—to this day, I don't know what, except that it must have been pretty horrific to make sweet Francesca so obdurate.

They were married in St. Peter's, Eaton Square, on a lovely sunny day. Francesca wore a very plain coat and skirt of dove gray, and carried no flowers, but I could not help thinking of the magical little sugar bride who had fluttered down the aisle with Stevie, three years before. I suspected that she had suffered more than she let on, and prayed that the future would bring her peace and plenty.

Eleanor had not lightened the mourning she wore for Lorenzo, but her face was rosy and serene above her black frock. She had just returned to her flat in Clarges Street because the lease had expired at Rottingdean. Soon, she said, she hoped to buy a country place of her own. Lorenzo had made a desert of her life, but she had managed to find an oasis of something like contentment. She had his child, of course, as I reminded myself, with a pang of jealousy.

Jenny now had a child, too. She had installed herself in Cornelia MacIntyre's London house to give birth to her stout son. Alistair was in seventh heaven, and Jenny was the heroine of the whole family. She adored being a mother, and she and Eleanor spent the entire wedding reception having the most boring conversation about babies.

I was conscious of being an outsider. The presence of the other three reminded me that I was the one who had broken the vow. I wasn't good enough to be with them. Fortunately, they attributed my altered looks and manner solely to the loss of Tertius, and did not bother me with too much attention.

Anyway, once the excitement of the wedding was over, I struggled on through the summer and into the autumn. In my spare time, I saw a good deal of Muttonhead, and realized the true value of his friendship. He had mellowed, and could hear about radical politics without turning purple and bellowing for a horsewhip. I found him infinitely good and infinitely wise, and thought what an ungrateful little hoyden I had been in the past to rebel against him.

The balance between us had altered. I still looked up to him, but not as a child. We were man and woman now, and he treated me with a respect that was flattering and oddly disturbing. If anything could make me laugh in those dark months, it was Mutt's gruff humor. But even he could not cure the black chill that lay at the core of everything I did. As far as feelings went, I was a burned-out volcano; all ash and no ember.

I couldn't even rejoice when the great day finally, finally came. I heard the news when I drove into the station from some hospital or other, and found the other drivers in tears. An Armistice had been signed, in the eleventh hour of the eleventh day of November, 1918. Peace had broken out. The war was over.

I have to say, my first reaction was annoyance. We had a train in, and dozens of injured boys to take care of. I had to inch the ambulance down streets crammed with people dancing and hanging bunting; in their wild joy, nobody cared about my poor soldiers.

I spent that evening sitting on the floor of my room in the dark, flicking cigarette ash into a saucer, and listening to the cacophony of celebration in the city around me. I was too bitter to celebrate. For God's sake, celebrate what, anyway? Victory?

To this day, I don't know who "won" the war, or what their prize was supposed to be. I could only count the cost, and reckon up who was dead and who was only changed. I was in no mood to bawl out jingo songs and swill champagne when I thought of Lorenzo and Tertius. My life was in ruins. My punishment seemed greater than I could bear—and I had more sorrow to come.

One

The Great War was over, but at the beginning of December 1918, Rory was working harder than ever. A deadly plague of influenza was sweeping across Europe, killing soldiers who had survived battles and hardships, and raging through their families at home. Hospital trains kept arriving, and nearly half the women in the ambulance unit had fallen ill themselves—four had died. Rory, who had managed to escape without catching so much as a cold, was so tired that she often flung herself on her bed fully clothed when she dragged herself home from her shift.

Late one afternoon, while she was toiling up the stairs to her flat, Miss Thompson ran out into the hall, holding a telegram at arm's length.

"It's the second today, Miss Carlington. Someone must be very anxious to reach you."

The war had implanted a national horror of telegrams, and Rory automatically turned white as she ripped it open, and read: *Lady Hastings ill stop come at once.*

Anything to do with Eleanor was sacred. Shaking off her exhaustion, Rory crammed her hat back on her head. "Could you possibly lend me some money for a taxi, Miss Thompson?"

"Well, I don't know—"

"It's an emergency—my friend Lady Hastings."

Love of a title was one of Miss Thompson's weaknesses. She emptied out her camphor-smelling purse, and produced ten shillings. Within twenty minutes, Rory was ringing the bell at Clarges Street.

Mrs. Bintry opened the door. She was breathless and perturbed, and wearing her hat. "Thank heavens you've come, miss. I couldn't think who else to send for. I can't stay another minute, and I'm at my wit's end."

"Is it the influenza?"

"Indeed it is, Miss Carlington, and she's ever so bad with it. I wouldn't leave her, but my son's wife and kiddies are down with it too, and he needs me."

"Wait—Mrs. Bintry—you can't mean you're going?"

"You won't be alone. The in-between maid is here to look after Miss Laura."

"But what about a professional nurse?"

"I tried, miss. None of the hospitals can spare anyone until tomorrow."

"Did you try her family? I know they don't get on—"

"They've got it, too." Mrs. Bintry had one foot over the threshold of the door, and was tying a rabbit-fur tippet around her neck. "The butler told me Mrs. Braddon is poorly, and Miss Braddon, and most of the servants. Oh please, miss, do let me go!"

Rory pressed her fingers to her temples, to force her thoughts into some kind of order. She felt hopelessly out of her depth, but Eleanor needed her, and her sense of duty in this quarter was particularly stern.

"Of course you must go, Mrs. Bintry. You've been a brick to wait so long. What does the girl answer to?"

"Dobbs, miss." Hope and relief were dawning on Mrs. Bintry's strained face. "She's on the simple side, but Laura minds her as well as anyone. If you could give her ladyship some—"

"Thank you, I know what to do. I've seen hundreds of cases. When is the doctor calling again?"

"First thing in the morning, if he can."

"All right, off you go. I hope your son's wife and children will be all right."

"Oh yes, Miss Carlington—thank you." Mrs. Bintry fled.

Rory removed her hat and coat, resigning herself to the fact that she had taken on a heavy night on top of a hard day. At least Eleanor's flat was warm—there were times when it helped to be rich. What must it have been like to live here with Lorenzo? Rory shivered, and forbade herself the painful luxury of thinking about him.

She went into the kitchen, and found the in-between girl hunched awkwardly at the table. Dobbs was eighteen or nineteen, with a vacant, adenoidal appearance. She gaped expectantly at Rory, waiting to be told what to do.

"I am Miss Carlington," Rory informed her. "I've come to take care of Lady Hastings. Where is the little girl?"

"In the nursery, miss, fast asleep."

"Good. You're to have total charge of her because I shall be far too busy to have anything to do with her. Do you understand?"

"Yes, miss."

"Now, make me a pot of strong coffee."

"There's only Camp, miss."

"Damn and blast." Rory examined the bottle of coffee essence gloomily. This would not be enough to keep her awake. "Never mind. Tell me what you have for Lady Hastings—beef tea? Chicken?"

"Bovril, miss."

"Excellent. Make her a cup of hot Bovril and milk." When it was ready, Rory took it from her. "Well done. Now go back to the kitchen. Fetch me a large pan of cold water—as cold as possible—and a pile of clean linen cloths."

"Yes, miss."

"And practice closing your mouth, Dobbs, or someone will post a letter into it."

Rory softly opened the bedroom door and went inside. The thick brocade curtains were drawn, and the only light came from one electric lamp and the coal fire. The first thing she saw, when her eyes adjusted, was a large, angry-looking photograph of Lorenzo, beside the bed. Eleanor lay limply on a heap of lace-trimmed pillows. Her breathing was shallow, and her cheeks were two solid wedges of purplish red.

She murmured: "Mrs. Bintry?"

"No, darling. She had to go home." Rory spoke as lightly as she could, though Eleanor's hectic appearance made her very anxious. Surely the doctor ought to come again before morning? "I've dropped by to sit with you."

Eleanor's eyes were glazed with fever. "You can't—you mustn't—I shouldn't dream of it when you work so hard—"

"Nonsense, I'm as fit as a flea, and I'd far rather be in your gorgeous flat than my beastly one." She sat down beside the bed. "I've brought you something to drink."

"No, thank you."

Rory took one of her hands, and her concern deepened when she felt how hot it was. "It'll make you feel stronger."

Eleanor stared at her, then said, as if imparting an amazing secret: "My throat hurts, and I ache all over. I feel so awful! But it's not serious, is it?"

"Goodness, no! You'll be better in no time."

"Laura—"

"She's asleep. And as well as possible." Rory hoped this last piece of embroidery was true. It was extraordinary, the bold-faced lies one told to invalids. "Now, drink up."

She raised Eleanor's head, and put the cup to her lips. Her struggles to get the liquid down her sore throat were heart-rending, but Rory knew how important it was to make her take nourishment. She had heard nurses saying this influenza was like a forest fire, destroying every scrap of energy in a matter of hours. Water was important, too. When Eleanor had taken the Bovril, she fed her a large glass of water, which she gulped thirstily.

Dobbs brought in the pan of cold water, and a pile of towels. Rory stripped the nightgown from Eleanor's burning body, and packed it in freezing wet cloths. Eleanor moaned a little at first, but soon fell into a light-headed sleep. Rory told herself she looked more comfortable, and hoped the cold water treatment was bringing down her temperature. She wished she could sleep herself, but it was out of the question. No effort should be too much, however, for the friend she had betrayed. She chose the least comfortable chair for the long night ahead.

And it was very, very long. Several times, Rory checked her watch against the big clock in the drawing room, because she was sure the hands were standing still. Gradually, the sounds in the street below faded to the deep, London silence of the small hours—as if the city's heart had stopped beating, Rory thought morbidly.

Every half-hour, she rose to give Eleanor water, and apply fresh towels. Her temperature was still high, but did not seem to be climbing. Occasionally, she would wake for a moment, to mumble out an apology for being a nuisance. She even tried to be cheerful, with attempts at smiles that lacerated Rory's heart. Mostly, however, she slept, with her limbs in an ungainly huddle.

Rory began to find the mementos of Lorenzo oppressive. There were references to him strewn all over the room, which only revealed themselves by degrees. It was not enough to avoid the black gaze of the photograph at Eleanor's bedside. She kept recognizing small objects she had seen in his pockets—cherished by Eleanor, of course, for that very reason. Unable to resist, Rory moved quietly through the room, touching everything Lorenzo had once touched, communicating with him one last time. His cigarette case stood on the mantelpiece, alongside a silver penknife. Rory caressed this covetously, brooding over the memory of Lorenzo using it in Norfolk, to carve their initials in a tree.

Moving to the dressing table, she found several pairs of cuff links, a set of pearl and gold dress studs, and a round box full of khaki collars. These were impersonal objects, which might have belonged to anyone, and she did not envy Eleanor for possessing them. When she found his wristwatch, however, she almost cried aloud with the unfairness of it. She had seen him fasten it, moments before they parted forever. The brown leather strap had darkened with accumulated sweat, and the smell of it made her shudder with longing for him. He must have been wearing it when he died—and he would have been thinking of her, not his unloved wife. What right did Eleanor have to something that had been so much a part of him?

"They sent it back with all his other things."

Rory jumped as if prodded by an electric wire. Eleanor was watching her, with eyes that glittered in her flushed face. She felt her guilt exposed, in all its hideousness.

But Eleanor only said: "His clothes, too. Some had blood on. I burned them."

Rory, her heart still racing, returned to her post beside the bed, and poured a fresh glass of water. "I didn't mean to wake you."

"This is so kind of you, Rory. But I feel such an impostor—I'm not really ill."

"Of course you're not. Have a drink." She held the glass to her lips. Though she was as parched as the Sahara, Eleanor could no longer swallow without intense pain. When she had finished, she fell back against her heap of pillows with a look of relief.

The heat of her body had dried some of the cloths. Rory could hardly believe such a thing was possible, but she did her best to hide her dismay as she sponged Eleanor down again. I'm all alone, she thought—alone with Lorenzo's wife. I could kill her now by telling her about him and me, and only the bar of heaven would know what I had done.

The sense of her own wickedness made meeting Eleanor's trusting eyes virtually unbearable. To make it worse, she had become talkative.

"I wish you'd go and rest, Rory dear. It's frightfully late and you look so tired."

"I'm fine." It annoyed Rory to be considered so selflessly by the woman she had wronged. Did Eleanor have to be so virtuous all the bloody time? Then she remembered, with an agonizing twinge of guilt, that this was precisely what had angered and alienated Lorenzo. Eleanor was an angel, and he had hated to be reminded how little he deserved her—when he hadn't even asked for her in the first place.

"I thought keeping his things here would make him seem nearer," Eleanor murmured, "but he gets a little further off every day. I can't hold him."

Rory could have told her how well she knew this feeling. She took Eleanor's hand. "Don't try. Let him go."

"I know you always disapproved of poor Lorenzo," Eleanor continued, with no idea that she was inflicting death by a thousand cuts on Rory's aching conscience. "So did Jenny. I never told you, but that day when you went off with Stevie, she begged me not to marry him. She said it would be better to have my baby in secret—anything, rather than marry him. I knew she was right, and I didn't care. Even if I was miserable I couldn't face being without him." Her fevercrazed eyes widened solemnly. "Rory, I loved him so much. It's the only thing I've ever been sure of in my whole life. The moment I saw him, I had to make him take me, on any terms."

"I know—I'm sure he loved you, darling," Rory said, desperate to reassure her. "In his way."

The calm confidence of Eleanor's reply surprised her. "Oh yes. I learned that toward the end, when he was so much kinder. On his last leave he tried so hard to make it up to me—but I understood him by then. I'd already forgiven him for what he had done to me."

"What? What did Lorenzo do?"

Eleanor mistook the reason for Rory's urgency. "You mustn't be angry with him," she begged. "It isn't fair when he's dead. Everything is forgiven where he is now."

Through the rush of blood in her ears, Rory registered

that Eleanor was not talking about her betrayal, and was giddy with relief.

Eleanor asked: "Who was that man we learned about at school—whose arrows could never miss, and whose open wound could never heal?"

"Philoctetes," Rory said distractedly.

"How clever you are. That's the sort of thing he would have known, too." She squeezed Rory's hand feebly. "If I tell you, you must think of Phil—of that man. Lorenzo hurt me, but only because he was so badly wounded himself."

How typical of Eleanor, Rory thought; she'd tie herself in knots to be magnanimous.

As if the fever had sharpened her faculties, Eleanor seemed to hear this. "I just want you to understand him." Her hand twitched restlessly in Rory's, but her face was calm. "I was scared of him at first. When he came home for Francesca's wedding, I thought he was going to kill me. That's when it started."

"When—what?" Rory's hackles rose defensively. She did not want to hear any more.

"When he started to hurt me. The bruises and the broken ribs, and the split lips—"

"But you were in a car accident!" Rory protested harshly.

"I lied. I told Lorenzo nothing would make me miss the wedding. And in any case, he was sorry by then. I got good at lying when he did it again next leave, and every other leave. And I was surprised at first, when you all believed me. But eventually, I started to believe it myself—that I was a clumsy idiot who kept falling down steps and walking into lampposts."

By digging her nails into her palms, Rory managed to keep up an appearance of composure. Her first impulse was to scream that Eleanor was a damned liar—that this was not the true Lorenzo she knew—that he would have told her because he told her everything.

But Eleanor never lied. A picture flashed into Rory's mind, of the man she had loved so desperately, inflicting terrible injuries upon his helpless wife. This was a new Lorenzo, capable of violence and cruelty. If his death had hurt, this shattering of her idealized vision of him was torture. "Why did you let him?" she raged at Eleanor. "Why did you stay with him?"

"Because afterward he used to make love to me," Eleanor said simply. "And I couldn't make myself stop wanting that."

"Oh dear God!"

"He was always, always sorry. And he never harmed Laura. Believe me, Rory, if he had done anything to my baby, nothing would have kept me with him. Please believe me."

The child must have been well aware of what was going on, Rory thought, fitting the pieces together. How many times had Lorenzo talked about the way his daughter screamed at the sight of him? Casually, too, as if he had not known the reason.

"You're shocked," Eleanor said sadly. "But toward the end, he was so much better, I know it would have been all right, if he had lived. When he was recovering from his wound, after the Somme, that was the worst time. We found out about Laura's deafness, and it made him so angry. Mrs. Bintry begged me to leave him, and I wondered if I ought to—but he was so ill and weak—"

"Strong enough to hit you."

"He stopped as soon as he was well enough to spend his days in London. Then he went away by himself a few times. It suited him to be free, and the more freedom I allowed him, the nicer he became. On his last leave, I really began to think I had found the key." She sighed, and glanced toward the photograph of Lorenzo beside her. "But it doesn't matter now. When we meet again, we'll be able to love as we were meant to."

Perhaps it was the fever, but the happiness in her eyes seemed to come straight from the celestial city, and Rory was afraid.

"Darling, that's enough talking. You must close your eyes and go to sleep. I'll be here—I won't leave you."

"Yes, I—yes, I'll just rest for a minute," mumbled Eleanor. She was soon asleep.

Rory kept hold of her hand, feeling that she had reached the bitterest moment of her life, the inevitable punishment for her besetting sins of pride and willful blindness. Her love for Lorenzo seemed purely selfish now. Could she have known the truth if she had wanted to? Her Lorenzo had been wonderfully charming—but how much of that charm had depended upon his having a wife at home to soak up all his cussedness?

And all that time, she had actually plumed herself, because she had won his love where Eleanor had failed.

Merciful God, she prayed, give me a chance to make it up to her. Show me a way to atone for breaking our vow.

Dawn came, and Eleanor slept on. Faint from emotion and sleeplessness, Rory made herself some tea, and drew back the curtains in the bedroom to let in the gray light. The morning bustle of tradesmen's vans was beginning in the street outside, but it made her feel lonelier than ever.

From somewhere in the flat, she heard the harsh squawks of Eleanor's little deaf child. The sound appeared to trouble Eleanor's sleep, but it did not wake her. She grew hotter and hotter, and when Rory sponged her limbs, they felt somehow heavier, and less coordinated.

At half-past seven, the doctor arrived. He was rushed off his feet, he explained. His partner in the practice was ill, and he had not closed an eye the previous night. Rory felt a surge of optimism, as she watched him taking Eleanor's temperature, and listening to her chest. He was bound to write out a prescription for something that would help her. She could send the girl to the chemist's immediately.

The hope was short-lived. He beckoned her over to the window, where they were out of earshot, and murmured: "It looks as if the influenza has developed into bronchial pneumonia. Keep the child well away from her, and give her plenty of fluids."

Rory saw him packing up his thermometer and stethoscope, but could not believe he meant to desert her. "What if she gets worse? What about the pain? You don't understand—I'm here on my own!"

He sighed. "You could send Lady Hastings to a nursing home or hospital—if you could get an ambulance, and if you could find a vacant bed within ten miles. But even then it would make very little difference to her. She would probably be more comfortable here, in her own home, surrounded by familiar faces."

"She will be all right, won't she?" Rory clutched at his sleeve. What shall I do if she—oh God, it can't happen!"

The doctor was very weary, but he found the strength to pat Rory's hand quite kindly. "She may get through. But

I'm afraid it's up to you to be brave, and to help her as much as you can. I'll try to call again, some time this evening."

When he had gone, Rory panicked. She went out onto the narrow balcony, smoked two cigarettes, tore at her hair and chewed her nails. Then, because she had to, and because she could not afford to despise herself any more, she pulled herself together. She telephoned her ambulance unit, packed Eleanor's stricken body in fresh towels, and fed her more Bovril and milk with a teaspoon.

All the time, she told herself that if she was vigilant enough, and loving enough, the nightmare would be over. God had put her through so much, He surely could not do anything else to her. She refused to face the possibility. It wasn't just because of her guilt, and the broken vow. As the time crawled by, Rory realized she could not imagine her life without Eleanor's grace and sweetness. Her friendship was a treasure, abused and taken for granted, and when Rory reflected that she might never have a chance to make it up, her remorse was overwhelming.

Dobbs came and went, with cups of tea and fresh jugs of water. Rory heard her taking the child out in the afternoon, and bringing her back just as the lamps were being lit. She was reeling from lack of sleep, but far too pent up and anxious to rest. Eleanor had slipped from the loquacity of the previous night to a state of incoherent groans and mumblings. Her temperature went on climbing, and her face turned the color of a ripe plum. It was as if she were being devoured by a ferocious internal fire.

Oh God, if the doctor would only come back and do something—Rory hated having to sit and watch, while the disease tore the life from her friend.

When it was dark, the change came. Eleanor had been showing signs of distress in her sleep. Now, she opened her eyes, looked directly at Rory, and said quite clearly: "What about Laura?"

Rory thought she was asking to see her. "She can't come in. They're afraid of infection. Shall I bring her to the door?"

"No, no. I mean, who will love her?" The anguish in her voice made Rory's eyes fill with tears. "If I have to leave my baby, will you take care of her?"

"Of course, of course." She did not know what she was saying.

"Oh, my baby—and you must love her! Please love her! She can't live without love!"

Rory would have cut off her right arm to comfort her. "She won't have to, darling, I promise."

"Really?"

"Honor bright. I'll take such good care of her."

"Thank you, Rory—" Eleanor sighed, and subsided back into a less troubled sleep.

Rory allowed herself to hope that the fever was passing, until there was no mistaking the shadow that deepened across Eleanor's face. In perfect peace and tranquillity, with the trustfulness of a child, she died.

Laying her cheek against the dead hand, Rory wept and wept, until the first sharpness of grief had blunted slightly, and she was left with a hollow feeling of resignation. It was time to take up her burden.

Some instinct must have told the child what had happened. Before Rory reached the nursery door, Laura broke into a terrible, orphaned wail. Rory found her cowering against the wall, with her arms locked around the neck of a sheep dog almost as tall as she was. Her mouth was stretched in a howl, and behind her tangle of dark hair, she glared at Rory with eyes uncannily like Lorenzo's.

This wild, afflicted little gypsy, with the dirty face and torn smock, had witnessed suffering and violence in her three and a half years. Now she was motherless, and the only source of gentleness and hope in her silent, isolated life was gone. Rory was full of pity for her.

But Eleanor had made her promise more.

Her spirits sank hopelessly. It was the chance she had prayed for, yet she could never bring herself to love Lorenzo's misbegotten child.

Aurora

Letter to my Daughter, 1935

Now you see, Laura, you are the ghost of Lorenzo, come
back to haunt me as he promised.

Two

The Braddon house was somberly decked in formal mourning. All the front windows were shuttered, and the front door was hung with black crepe. Rory found it deeply ironic, and not a little insulting to Eleanor's memory. Not one of them had spoken to her in years. She had not had one word of love or forgiveness from them to send her to her rest. Yet they still thought the outward form important—presumably, in case the neighbors read the announcement in the paper.

Rory had a good mind to turn away, there and then, but knew it would be wrong. Blood was supposed to be thicker than water, and Ma Braddon had always been a tremendous stickler for duty. There would be trouble, if she did not at least endure this meeting.

Sharp ushered her into the hall. He was noticeably older and more cadaverous. But good God, Rory thought, catching her own hollow-cheeked reflection in the mirror, aren't we all?

"Hello, Sharp. Are you well?"

"Thank you, Miss Carlington, yes."

"You were expecting me?"

"Yes indeed, miss." He paused, taking the temperature of the words, before he said awkwardly: "We were all very sorry to hear about Miss Eleanor. A dreadful tragedy."

"I understand you had the influenza here, too," Rory said.

"Yes, Miss Carlington. Mrs. Braddon and Miss Flora. Mrs. Braddon is improving, but unfortunately, Miss Flora passed away."

"Oh, I'm sorry. I always liked Miss Flo."

"There was quite a drama attached to it." Sharp lowered his voice, unable to resist gossiping. "Miss Flora's will turned out to be quite unsuitable. She left all her money, some sixty thousand pounds, to Margaret."

"The parlormaid?" Rory snorted with laughter. "Bully for her. Margaret was so kind to the poor old dear, and I bet she was sorriest when she died."

Sharp lapsed into disapproving silence, leaving Rory to inhale the monied smells of wax polish and potpourri she had once known so well. She had not realized it would be so sad to return to the house in which Eleanor had been a happy, hopeful young girl.

Sharp knocked on the door of Mrs. Braddon's bedroom, opened it, announced: "Miss Carlington, madam," and discreetly withdrew.

"Come in, Aurora."

Rory was startled to see the magnificent Mrs. Braddon reduced to yellow skin and bone, and huddled over the fire in a bundle of shawls. "I didn't know you'd been so ill. It's good of you to see me."

"You're thinner, and you look older," Mrs. Braddon observed. "You wouldn't cut such a figure in a backless ballgown nowadays, I dare say."

"I wasn't planning to." Rory's lips twitched. The old bat would never forget that Russian dress. "We've all changed rather, since then."

"I heard about Tertius," Mrs. Braddon said, with a momentary melting of her implacable eye. "Such a waste. It must be terrible for his mother."

"It is," Rory said stiffly. "I don't think she will ever recover."

"No. Mothers never do recover from wounds inflicted by their children. Sit down."

Rory perched on the extreme edge of the boudoir chair on the other side of the fireplace. "You received my letter."

"I did." Mrs. Braddon was iron and steel again. "Please ask Lord Oughterard to send the bill for the funeral to me."

"He wouldn't dream of it," Rory snapped. "We were both glad to do anything we could for her."

This was a bad beginning, and she was annoyed when she saw that her show of temper had given Mrs. Braddon an advantage.

"Really, Aurora, don't be so dramatic. You know perfectly well what happened between Eleanor and myself. It was by no means all on my side. I might have forgiven her if she had shown any sign of repenting her gross immorality. But she willfully and deliberately cut herself off from me the day she married that man."

Rory swallowed her pride, and said in what she hoped was a meek voice: "I didn't come here to talk about Eleanor, Mrs. Braddon, but about little Laura Hastings."

"Well?"

"Well, Eleanor left her in my care. However, since she is your granddaughter, I thought you might wish to be consulted about her upbringing."

"You hoped you would be able to fob her off on me," Mrs. Braddon said.

There was a grain of truth in this, and Rory reddened angrily. "Eleanor made me promise to take care of her, and I wouldn't betray that trust for the world. But I have to consider what's best for her. I'm not married, nor ever likely to be, and I don't believe I could ever provide the ideal surroundings for a child."

Mrs. Braddon's gaze slid toward the fire, and she was silent for what seemed like ages. Eventually, she asked: "Was there any money left?"

"Yes." Rory had been surprised to learn how much. "Besides Eleanor's fortune, the Hastings estate turned out to be a great deal larger than Lor—than Sir Laurence had led anyone to believe. Laura will be a rich woman. Which is another reason why I thought I should consult you."

"And you did right." Mrs. Braddon was freezing over. "I don't doubt that you mean well. But I won't have that child in my house. I won't have anything to do with her. She is not a member of my family."

"No, thank God she's not!" Rory sprang up, letting her anger off the leash. "I'm glad you don't want her—I wouldn't give her to you if you begged me! And if you ever try to interfere, I swear, I'll take you to court!"

Mrs. Braddon was trying to appear cold and indifferent, but there were unhealthy spots of color in her sallow cheeks, and painful twitchings around her nostrils. "All very fine, but how do you propose to manage her? The child is a deaf-mute."

"She can think and feel, and tell the difference between being wanted and being rejected, even if she can't hear." Rory was surprised by the depth of her own conviction.

"You'll climb down off your high horse when you get tired of struggling with a congenital idiot—"

"Laura is not an idiot!" shouted Rory. "There's nothing wrong with her brain."

"Put her in an institution."

"Never!"

"You wait. You'll be crawling back here on your knees inside a month."

"I will not! I'll never come here again—and you've just lost your chance to have anything to do with your grandchild. You broke Eleanor's heart, but you won't hurt Laura!"

Rory flew out of the room and down the broad staircase, shaking with rage. Yes, she had been nurturing a hope that someone would relieve her of the terrible burden of Laura. But unattractive as the child was, she would not dream of bundling her away in some dreadful asylum for the deaf. If she could not love Laura, she could at least give her a better home than that.

Outside the tragic Braddon house, the keen winter wind blew energy and resolve into Rory's veins. She had taken on a fearsome responsibility, but what else did she have to do? The ambulance unit had been disbanded, and there was not much hope of finding paid work. London was swarming with idle unmarried women, now that the war was over.

How odd, she thought wryly, that all her high-flown ambitions should come to this. Here she was, lonely and obscure, devoting herself to the care and education of a deaf orphan. And she had never even liked children.

It would have been easier to tame a lion cub. Freed from Eleanor's roving but smothering restraint, Laura was impossible. She sat for hours in the middle of the nursery floor, literally snarling, with her little teeth bared. If Dobbs or Rory approached, they could expect bites or kicks. Mrs. Bintry fared slightly better, but at the end of January, she left to look after her son's family.

Rory was utterly exhausted, marbled with bruises, and so close to despair that only her determination to prove Mrs. Braddon wrong prevented her from sending the child away. Laura hurled her food, tore her clothes, and screamed for hours at a time. A week after Mrs. Bintry's departure, Dobbs walked out, saying she could endure no more. A special governess, who had had successes with deaf children, resigned at the end of three days, claiming that Laura was beyond hope. Rory was alone in the gloomy flat, terrified of the child's valnerability and frailty. She was tiny for her age, with bird bones that seemed ready to break through her transparent, blue-veined skin. The doctor said she must be kept as warm and as quiet as possible, and prescribed a malt tonic, which Laura threw through the dining room window.

Anxious about her constant sniffles and wheezing chest, Rory kept the flat as hot as a furnace. Her days were spent clearing up after the little creature's tempests of rage. The only times she was relatively calm were the visits of her sheepdog, given as a puppy by Stevie and Francesca, and christened "Whizz-bang" by Stevie. Whizz-bang was no longer a puppy, however, and he knocked Laura about in a way that brought Rory's heart into her mouth. She paid one of the chauffeurs down in the mews to look after him, and decided to ration his appearances, until Laura gained strength.

Sometimes, she found herself looking at the child and almost hating her. It was not only because her youth was draining away. Laura looked remarkably like her father, and Rory had not forgiven Lorenzo for making Eleanor's life so wretched. It was difficult not to think of him, when she saw the rage sealed in the war-baby's piercing black eyes.

Or was there something besides plain rage? She became so hysterical when any man entered the flat that she had to be shut away in another room. Rory dismissed this as nothing more than bad temper, until one afternoon when Muttonhead called. Rory leaned over to kiss his cheek, as she always did, and Laura flew at him with an inhuman shriek, sinking her teeth into his hand, and trying to push him away.

Rory managed to pry her off, and retired behind the sofa with the child struggling in her arms. "I'm sorry, Mutt—"

He was amused. "Plucky little thing, taking on a chap my size. Must have thought I meant to hurt you."

"Of course—oh, what a fool I've been!" At once, Rory realized that the look on Laura's face was not anger, but fear. "It's not you, it's your uniform! She thinks you're

Lorenzo!'' How many times had she witnessed Lorenzo
mistreating her mother? With a sudden rush of pity, she
braved the flying fists, and hugged Laura tightly. "Poor
baby—poor little baby!''

Laura could not hear, but she seemed to sense the feeling
behind the gesture. She had never accepted Rory's caresses
before—perhaps because she guessed how half-heartedly
they were offered. Now, her yells subsiding into sobs, she
curled up on Rory's knee, and glared at Muttonhead from
the shelter of her arms.

Something yielded in Rory, as she felt the delicate little
bones, and inhaled the warm scent of Pears soap from her
straight dark hair. She had overcome the barrier of Laura's
deafness, and glimpsed the wounded but fiery spirit that
lay behind it. The hardness at the very kernel of her heart
that had chilled her since Lorenzo's death, melted away
now that she held his child. She remembered how it felt to
love, and forgave him.

After this, Laura stopped fighting Rory, and clung to
her instead. She continued to have moments of spectacular
awfulness, but was largely content to hang on to Rory's
skirt, and to scramble into her lap whenever she sat down.
It became possible to keep help again, and Rory engaged
an energetic Irish girl, grandly named Agnes Moncrieff,
whose Kerry accent made her terribly homesick.

"Come home with me," Muttonhead said.

Rory sighed. "I can't. I haven't the freedom to scoot to
and fro across the sea, as I used to.''

Muttonhead was making arrangements to leave the army,
and resume management of the farm. Busy as he was, however, he found time to call at Clarges Street most days.
Rory had her hands full with Laura, but managed to notice
a change in his behavior. She would look up to find him
watching her broodingly, with an ominous dark frown. At
first, scared that he had found out about her affair with
Lorenzo, she asked him what the matter was. The frown
always vanished immediately, however, and he assured her
everything was fine.

His silence and stillness gradually won Laura's trust. Intensely curious, she would inch closer and closer to his
chair, gaping at him, until she stood right between his enormous, polished riding boots. One day, Muttonhead lifted
her onto his lap, and to Rory's amazement, she sat there

quite peacefully, tugging curiously at the insignia on his cuffs.

"You look so funny together," she said, laughing, "like a buffalo and a kitten—the perfect pairing of dignity and impudence."

"Scrawny little tyke," Muttonhead said. "She could do with country air and decent grub. Bring her home to Ireland."

Rory might have known she had not heard the last of this. "How can I? She needs such special care. The doctor says I must keep her indoors. A howling wilderness like Castle Carey would be the death of her."

"Never did us any harm."

"We were all born to it. And we weren't delicate—or deaf. For the last time, we're not coming to Ireland."

In February, it was Laura's fourth birthday. Rory bought her a plush rabbit, and a box of picture-bricks, each side printed with the fragment of a painting. She was taken aback when Laura knelt down on the nursery floor, and deftly joined the bricks into a gaudy farmyard scene.

"I thought it would take her weeks to work out!"

"You underestimate her, darling," Aubrey told her. "She's as sharp as a cartload of monkeys." He doted on Laura, and had bought her a tricycle, ignoring Rory's worries about bruises or broken bones. "Now, little one, here's something else for you." He put a carved toy—two red bears on a yellow seesaw—into Laura's hand.

"Aubrey, really! I said one present—"

"Shh. I want to see what she does with it."

Her shoulders tense with concentration, Laura examined the toy. Her long, sensitive fingers pushed the seesaw, and her eyes widened with surprise when it sprang back into place. She carried it over to Rory, with an air of puzzled fascination.

"Look, darling." Rory pressed the wooden levers at either end, and made the seesaw fly up and down. Laura snatched it back to try for herself. After staring at the bears with a pocket edition of Lorenzo's scowl, light poured into her face, and she let out a peal of laughter.

Rory had never heard the child laugh. The sound brought tears to her eyes, and healed something painful, deep within her. A child's laugh, she thought, was the most hopeful sound in all the world.

It was at this moment that Muttonhead came into the nursery. Rory smiled at him with brimming eyes, over Laura's head. He turned to stone, and stared at her with a look she could not fathom—as if she had done something to hurt him. It only lasted a few seconds. He was dragging Whizz-bang on a lead, and the dog created a diversion by knocking Laura over.

"Don't fuss," Aubrey said, picking her up. "She's not hurt."

"What's he doing here?" Rory demanded, though it was difficult to be annoyed when Laura was so pleased. She was hanging around Whizz-bang's neck, undeterred by his rough greeting.

"Goodish day," said Muttonhead. "Thought we'd take the kid to the park."

"But it's freezing cold—"

"You protect her too much."

"Yes, because she needs special protection."

"Oughterard is quite right," Aubrey said. "You can't keep the child wrapped in cotton wool until she's old enough to be presented at court. I know you want to shield her from the rough world, darling. But the best way to do that is to expose her to it."

Rory looked at Laura, and saw the way her body seemed to quiver with suppressed energy. She was fragile, but not weak—she had all Lorenzo's intensity. Perhaps, thought Rory, she would take the risk, this once.

Agnes Moncrieff dressed Laura in a thick coat, buttoned gaiters and a tam-o'-shanter, and Muttonhead escorted her, Rory and Whizzbang to the park. He produced an India rubber ball from his pocket, and showed Laura how to throw it for the dog.

"Badly trained animal," he commented, through a mouthful of pipe stem. "Have to lick him into shape, when we get back to Ireland."

"When we get back to where?" Rory could not help laughing. "I thought I'd settled that—I'm not coming."

"Don't be so stubborn."

"Me! It's you that refuses to listen to reason. We can't possibly come to Ireland."

"Why not?"

She wondered why she was not angry. "It would be too much for the Mater, for one thing."

"Nonsense," Muttonhead said. "Just what she needs. Something to occupy her. Stop her pining for Tertius."

"Do listen to reason, Mutt. Eleanor would turn in her grave, if I let that baby run wild among the bogs and lakes. She's so frightened of strangers, and strange surroundings—"

"Is she?" Muttonhead asked. "Look at her."

Rory looked. Laura was pelting across the cindery, wintry London grass, crowing with joy. Her nose and cheeks were pink with the cold, and she only laughed—for the second time that afternoon—when she tripped and fell over.

They arrived at Castle Carey—Rory, Muttonhead, Laura, Agnes and Whizz-bang—a fortnight later, in the middle of the night after a long drive across black countryside and unmade roads. Lady Oughterard was in the hall to meet them, and Rory realized how much of the bounce had gone from her step since Tertius died. Muttonhead was right, she was pining for him. Her hand had a slight tremor, and her blue eyes were webbed in fine wrinkles. She would pine slowly into old age and the grave unless she had something to distract her.

"Here she is, Mater." Rory held the sleeping child toward her.

Lady Oughterard's face melted into tenderness as she gazed at Laura's odd little face. "Well," she said eventually, "there's always room here for a motherless little maid. She's as welcome as you were, darling, and I hope we can make her happy."

Rory's last doubts were settled the next morning. It was March, but the weather had a springlike softness. The mountains were green beneath a pale blue sky, and the lake was as smooth as glass. Laura stood at the top of the steps of Castle Carey, and stared at this new world as if her eyes would jump out of her head.

At first, Rory thought she was afraid. But she suddenly sprang down the steps and raced across the endless, rolling carpet of young grass, flinging her arms wide, as if to embrace the whole vista of sky, mountains and silver water.

Nothing in this paradise was safe from Laura's prying eyes and fingers, and for the next few days, it took the combined efforts of Rory, Lady Oughterard, Agnes and Una to keep her out of trouble. Once she had settled into some kind of routine, however, Rory had leisure to ride around the countryside, and spend time with her father over at Marystown.

With Muttonhead in charge again, the Castle Carey farm returned to its prewar efficiency. Marystown, however, was visibly neglected and run-down. Justus, when challenged with this fact, became maddeningly vague. Muttonhead had been warning him of the hopelessness of his English agent, John Boon, for years, but he hated to be bothered with prosaic agricultural details.

"I don't care how old-fashioned or inefficient Boon's methods are, he told Rory peevishly, as long as he gets on with it and keeps out of my way."

"Muttonhead wouldn't speak badly of the man without a reason, Papa."

"Oughterard is as obstinate as a brick wall; my dear. Just like his father. Once an idea lodges in that stony skull of his, nothing can blast it out. First, it was Boon's drinking. Now, he says the man is unpopular with the natives—as if they didn't always loathe a land agent on principle. I wish he would run his own farm, and leave me to run mine."

Rory knew Muttonhead would never interfere, unless he was seriously concerned. She was not surprised, a few days later, to hear Mr. Boon's voice in Muttonhead's gun room, shouting angrily. She could not make out what he was saying, but she was just inside the front door when he charged up the hall, and rudely pushed past her, without a word. His heavy-jowled face was mottled red and purple with anger, and he galloped off on his horse as if he had the devil at his heels.

"What was all that about?"

Muttonhead had come out on the step behind her. "He's a fool, and I told him so. He's been shooting his English mouth off about the boys who didn't volunteer for the war, and today he chucked a couple of men off the farm because he thinks they're Fenians."

"How ridiculous! I'll go right over, and tell Papa to take them back."

"Rory, wait." He caught at her arm. "Leave it. Stay clear of Marystown for a few days."

"Why? I'm not afraid of Boon."

"It's not Boon. Just stay clear, Rory, eh?"

He was as guarded and controlled as ever, but the solemnity in his dark eyes made her take the caution seriously. Why, she wondered, was Muttonhead getting into such a stew about the idiotic doings of Boon and his farmhands?

She was woken in the middle of the night by Laura, who was standing on her bed and kicking her shoulder. Grumbling and bleary, she allowed the brat to drag her to the window, and saw the hot glow in the sky, over the hill to the west. It took a moment for the reality to sink in.

Marystown.

Hurriedly pulling on riding breeches, boots and a jersey over her nightgown, she ran down the passage to hammer at Muttonhead's door.

"Fire! Marystown's on fire! Marystown's burning!"

Muttonhead opened his door so quickly that she almost knocked on his hard, bare chest. He was pulling a jacket over an unbuttoned shirt.

"Damn them." He was thunderous. "I should have guessed."

Rory barely heard. "Oh, Mutt—suppose Papa didn't smell the smoke in time? There's only him and Mrs. MacNamara, besides Boon."

Despite his bad leg, Muttonhead could move very swiftly when he chose. He was already loping down the stairs, and he roared over his shoulder: "Bugger Boon!"

Lady Oughterard heard this as she emerged from her room. She seized the back of Laura's nightgown to stop her running after them. "Lucius, really! For once, I'm thankful this child is deaf."

Frantic with anxiety, Rory followed Muttonhead into the dark stables. "They won't see the smoke from the village," she babbled breathlessly. "I'll wake Paddy Finnegan, and tell him to get some men—"

"The men won't come." Muttonhead was putting saddles across the backs of two old hunters, Orpheus and Eurydice. "And neither will Paddy, if he has any sense."

"What are you talking about?" She stamped her foot impatiently. "How else can we put out the fire? My father could be burned to death and you don't even care!"

"Stop that shrieking and do as I tell you." It was his sternest voice, and not even Rory had ever dared to disobey it. "You'll take Orpheus."

Rory muttered: "You're not in the bloody army now," but began to fasten Orpheus's saddle, with feverish clumsiness.

As they mounted, Muttonhead said, more gently: "Trust me, Rory. I can't help you or your father unless you do."

There was a glint of metal at his waist. Rory saw that he was wearing his service revolver, and her blood chilled with fear. The familiar home surroundings suddenly seemed full of sinister omens. "Yes, Mutt. I trust you."

Muttonhead knew every stick, stone and blade of grass between the two houses, and Rory kept her eyes on the outline of his broad shoulders, as they galloped across the estates. Nearing Marystown, the glow in the sky intensified to an amber glare, which shed a lurid imitation of daylight on the surrounding trees and hedges. There was a bitter flavor of smoke in the air, and a steady drizzle of cinders falling from the sky like black snow.

When they emerged from the copse of trees on the edge of Marystown's parkland, the horses reared in terror. The west wing of the house was a vast torch, shooting flames twenty feet into the sky. The windows were cracking in the heat, and the fire was licking ominously across the roof.

Coughing in the acrid air, Muttonhead and Rory tied the horses where they could not see the flames, and dashed across the lawn to the house. The soot-streaked grass was crowded with bedding, silver, furniture, books and startled-looking family portraits. Mrs. MacNamara was at one of the ground-floor windows, hurling out boxes of tarnished cutlery.

She screamed when she saw them, then laid her hand on her bosom, and exclaimed, "Your lordship! Thank God it's only you! I've saved what I can—"

"Where's Papa?" Rory demanded.

"Library," Mrs. MacNamara said shortly. "All he wants is his blessed books."

"Get him out," Muttonhead said. "The house is a goner, and the roof's about to cave in."

The library opened onto the terrace, and Rory was able to enter through the open French windows. Immediately, her chest rasped, and her eyes watered. The room was hazy with smoke. Wildly, she looked around for her father, and was relieved when she saw him staggering outside, his long arms filled with books.

Wheezing alarmingly, he dropped the books on the lawn. "Aurora!" He was only faintly surprised to see her. "How opportune. I've saved all my Greeks and Romans, and my early Irish folios, now let's start on the Germans—"

"Papa!" Rory hung onto his sleeve. "You're not going back in there! You'll be killed!"

"Don't be ridiculous."

"If you try, I'll fetch Muttonhead!"

"Oughterard is a splendid young man, and a most excellent neighbor, but he's a hopeless judge of a good book." Justus choked suddenly, and dropped to his knees. Recognizing this mad speech as a sign that he was overcome by smoke, Rory managed to lead him away from the house, to lie in the relatively pure air among his piles of salvaged books.

"Is he all right?" Muttonhead's long, wavering shadow fell across the grass.

"I think so." She glanced up. "Dear God, what've you done to yourself?"

His face was striped with soot, and he was dripping with sweat. "Broke into the farm office, to get Boon."

Justus raised himself on one elbow. "You were right, Oughterard. I should have listened to you. Where is he?"

Muttonhead gestured toward a still figure nearby, hastily covered with one of the drawing room curtains. "Drunk when the fire started. Dead when I found him."

Rory had never seen her father looking so chastened and helpless. "Do you think they meant to kill him?"

"Doubt it. They only wanted the house."

"You're surely not saying it was torched deliberately?" Rory felt stupid, as soon as the question was out of her mouth. This was why Muttonhead had brought his revolver. From babyhood, she had heard of the terrible things that had happened to agents and landlords who fell foul of the ribbon-societies, Land-Leaguers and hillside men. But this was her home, these were her people. "We know everyone for miles—nobody around here would do such a thing to us! They're our friends!"

Justus and Muttonhead exchanged sober glances, and were silent for a few moments, while Rory looked anxiously from one to another.

Muttonhead wiped his sweating forehead with his shirt-sleeve. "They're fine people. But if you want to live here in peace, remember you're a foreigner."

The idea of not belonging among her own kind was so painful that Rory longed to protest and argue, but she had not the heart, when Muttonhead looked so sad. He loved this land and its people very deeply, and she understood his anguish as clearly as if he had communicated it in words.

There was nothing more to be done in the house. They spent the next few hours carrying the articles that had been saved into the shelter of the stable block. Just after the first streaks of dawn to the east, they stood at the edge of the park, and watched as the blazing roof of Marystown imploded, in a firework display of sparks.

"Ashes to ashes," Justus said. "There goes your inheritance, my dear."

"Never mind, Papa."

"That's a sensible girl. And we saved all the best books—would have saved more, if you hadn't been so hysterical."

"Well, I like that. You'd be crêpes suzettes, if it wasn't for me."

Daylight revealed them as a haggard crew, amazed by one another's black faces. At Castle Carey, Una and Lady Oughterard were waiting with supplies of thick, stewed tea and hot water. They drank the tea laced with rum, which Muttonhead said reminded him of stand-to in the trenches.

Una graciously entertained Mrs. MacNamara in the kitchen, while Lady Oughterard fussed over Justus. This chance to lavish her threadbare hospitality made her face glow. "You shall have the big chamber, with the four-poster bed. It's the grandest room in all Ireland—as long as you don't mind a little whiff of mildew."

Rory took a can of hot water up to her room, and scrubbed off the smell of smoke with lavender soap. She should have been sorrier about the house, she supposed. But it had never been a home to her, and the land was the thing. And though Boon's death was horrible, she was thankful her father was safe. Invigorated and hungry, she dressed in her short black skirt and a clean jersey, and went in search of something to eat.

The door of Muttonhead's room stood open. In the middle of the bare floor, his tin bath of cold water stood, surrounded by damp towels and huge wet footprints. He was in his shirtsleeves and braces, shaving at the round mirror beside the window. His cuffs were turned back, and Rory saw angry red blisters on his wrists and forearms.

He had risked his own life in an attempt to save a man he despised. Could she, could any of them, ever fully appreciate the depth and breadth of his goodness? On impulse, without knocking, she walked over to the window, put her hand on his sleeve, and said:

"Mutt, darling, you must let me put something on those burns, before—"

She did not finish the sentence, because Muttonhead did an extraordinary thing. Dropping his razor, he swept her into his arms—so roughly that he almost squeezed the breath from her—and pressed his lips to hers.

It was so astonishing that Rory would have fallen over, if his arms had not pinned her against him. When the astonishment subsided, however, it left no resistance. Being kissed by Muttonhead seemed the most natural and delicious thing in the world. Warmth flooded into her. Her body, petrified since Lorenzo's death, sprang back to pulsing, yearning life. She was aware of nothing, except the sheer animal pleasure of feeling his great, lean, sinewy body against hers, and the pagan desire to be fucked senseless.

Reluctantly, he drew away from her, just far enough to gaze at her with his solemn brown eyes. Rory held herself very still, stunned by the revelation of their mutual longing.

"I had to do that," Muttonhead said breathlessly. "I couldn't go on being a gentleman anymore. I love you, Rory. I've been in love with you for years."

The words were barely out of his mouth before she realized, on a surge of elation, that she was in love with him. Of course she was. This was far more than simple physical passion—it was the first right thing she had done in ages. What an idiot she had been not to see it until now.

She did not need to say anything. He would understand if she waited, with parted lips and yielding body. But instead of kissing her again, he said: "I want to marry you."

Instantly and painfully, Rory fell back to earth. The blessing had come too late. Muttonhead did not know about her affair with Lorenzo. He would loathe her for it, and she would never have the courage to tell him. But that stain on her past made marriage impossible.

"I—I can't."

"Why?" His hands gripped her shoulders. He would not surrender easily.

"Let me go."

"Don't you love me?"

She lacked the strength to tell him she did not—and in any case, he had always known when she was lying. Tears spilled down her cheeks. "It's not that. I can't explain. Please don't make me!"

His face was unbearably tender. "Is it because of Tertius?"

"No!" The sound of Tertius's name made her sob in good earnest. "Please let me go, Mutt! If I told you, you'd see I was right—"

He released her, with an expression of pain that made Rory feel she had never known the true meaning of punishment until now.

Three

Muttonhead did nothing to betray his unhappiness, but Rory felt it, running like a subterranean current under his every word and gesture. She hated herself for being the cause of it. She hated herself for the torments of desire she suffered, at the daily sight of his powerful, massive beauty. With every nerve aching for his touch, she did not trust herself not to weaken and deceive him. She had to get away from Castle Carey.

Seizing upon a vaguely worded invitation in one of Jenny's letters, Rory left Laura in the care of Lady Oughterard and Justus, who was immersed in teaching her to read, write and lip-read, and fled to Scotland. Here, she was sure, under Jenny's calming influence, she would find the courage to plan some kind of future.

She arrived at the MacNeils' on a cold, rainy evening. The manservant showed her into a vast, baronial hall, its stone walls bristling with antlers and claymores, and covered with dark paintings of Alistair's tartan-clad ancestors. She could not help smiling to herself. Jenny had always dreamed of being chatelaine of a great house, but this was surely beyond even her wildest dreams—a genuine castle, with facilities for dousing enemies in boiling oil, and turrets and dungeons innumerable. The fact that old Mrs. MacNeil, thoroughly vanquished, was now living permanently in London, only brought it nearer to perfection.

When she approached the huge fire—in which several trees appeared to be burning—Rory discovered she was not alone. A small girl jumped up from the folds of a bearskin rug.

"Hello."

"Hello," Rory said, scanning her face curiously. The child was absolutely beautiful; a cherub with a dirty face. "Who are you?"

"Flurry."

"Flurry who?"

"Fenborough. It's my birthday very soon, and I'm nearly five. I strongly think Daddy's going to get me a pony."

"Good for you," Rory said automatically. This, she was thinking, is Laura's cousin; this graceful sprite is first cousin to my poor little monkey-face. How unfairly the gods had divided their gifts.

There was something else. The shape of Flurry's eyes, blue as delphiniums beneath a fringe of golden-brown curls, gave Rory a painful stab of recognition. It was followed by amazement—no, it wasn't possible, he would have told her—and hardened into certainty when Flurry gave her a wicked, dimpled smile. Oh God, she thought, her heart in ribbons, if the Mater could only see this!

"Are you crying?"

"No." Rory quickly wiped her eyes with her glove. "I was just thinking about someone."

"Rory—I'm so sorry—" Jenny hurried in, looking every inch the laird's wife in a perfectly cut lovat tweed skirt and silk blouse. She kissed Rory warmly. "I was upstairs in the nursery. Donald is cutting a tooth, poor little chap, and he won't let me leave him for a moment. Fleur," she added, glancing down at the angel child, "Nana wants you. It's past your bedtime."

Rory gazed after the bold little figure, scampering up the stone staircase, fearless in the shadowy gloom.

"What a darling."

"A minx," Jenny said, smiling. "Don't let her see that you like her or she'll make a slave of you. Gus and Charlie are putty in her hands."

"I didn't know you were on such intimate terms with the Fenboroughs."

"Now, don't purse up your mouth like that, Rory. Alistair likes Gus, and Viola has improved with age and motherhood. And they were properly invited and sent for. They didn't simply descend at a day's notice."

"Is it very inconvenient to have me here?"

"Madly." Jenny was teasing, her hazel eyes gentle and affectionate. "But I'm so glad you haven't lost your talent for doing things on impulse. You look as if you need a rest. It was so splendid of you to take on that poor little scrap of Eleanor's, when Viola and her mother refused to have her."

"I'm not conferring any favors," Rory said sharply. "Laura and I suit each other very well."

"Do you? I felt awfully guilty about not taking her in myself, but—"

"But you have Alistair to take care of, besides a child of your own, Rory finished for her. And I have nobody.

"You might marry one day."

The bleakness of her situation made Rory's eyes smart with the first storm-warning of tears. She dug her nails into her palms. "Oh no, that's all gone by. I'm destined to be a spinster of this parish—one of those surplus women you read about in the papers."

Tactfully, sensing the wildness and instability of her mood, Jenny changed the subject. "Dinner is in half an hour. Do put on something decent."

The room allotted to Rory turned out to be large and rather depressing, with wormy paneling and awful tartan hangings, but Jenny had placed lamps and bowls of spring flowers where they would give an impression of light and warmth. She had found the ideal setting for her natural graciousness and good taste, Rory decided. Funny, how they had had their doubts about Alistair, when he and Jenny were first engaged. Obviously they were excellently suited, and Jenny was the very model of a contented wife.

Trying not to envy her, or to pity herself too keenly, Rory put on her only surviving evening dress, a draped emerald chiffon she had last worn to go out to dinner with Tertius. The waist had to be tightened with a safety pin, because she had become so scrawny in the past year. It did not show, however, and on the whole, she felt civilized enough to face Viola.

She found the MacNeils and their other guests already assembled in the great hall. Alistair stood with one hand on Jenny's arm, and the other resting on the impatient, inquisitive head of Inkerman. His lids drooped languidly over his unused eyes, but his manner was brisk.

"Well, Aurora. What a surprise." For Jenny's sake, he was making an effort to be welcoming, though he clearly disapproved of her as much as ever. She was fixed in his mind's eye as the girl who wore flimsy gowns and was a Bad Influence upon his beloved.

"How thin you are," Viola said. "It can't be healthy."

Rory noticed that Viola, although still in the high noon of her amazing beauty, had definitely put on weight around her waist and breasts.

"Nonsense!" Gus exclaimed heartily. "She always was the beanpole type. Rory, have you met my brother, Charlie?"

Charlie's loud laugh and exuberant jollity acted as an antidote to Viola's frostiness. He had a tin leg, and was constantly tripping on rugs and knocking over furniture. Rory, wincing as the hollow limb crushed her foot, assumed that he was not yet used to it, and was surprised to learn that it had been fitted after the battle of Cambrai, back in 1917.

Gus seemed proud of his brother's natural clumsiness. "If he hadn't tripped and fallen flat on his face, he'd have been blown to smithereens," he told her over dinner. "Now, how's old Oughterard these days? Can I expect to see him in London again, or does he mean to hide in the wilds forever now that the war's over?"

"I don't know." Rory felt herself turning to stone at the mention of Muttonhead's name. "You'll have to ask him."

Gus addressed the whole table. "I've been telling him for years, it's high time he got married. He's just the type."

"And there's the title," Alistair said, feeling across the cloth for his wineglass. "He should take steps to get himself an heir, now that both his brothers have gone west."

"But who on earth will he find to marry, out in that Irish wilderness?" asked Viola. "He's a very good match, even without any money, but I'm sure there isn't a single suitable female within miles—is there, Aurora?"

"No," Rory said, scarlet-faced, loathing Viola. "Nobody is good enough for Muttonhead." With a shaking hand, she reached for her glass of water, and swept it straight into Charlie's lap. "Oh, what an idiot—I'm so sorry—"

Charlie brayed with laughter, as he mopped at his trousers with a napkin. "Won't hurt me to get a taste of my own medicine for once."

"Viola, have you seen the view from the top of the cliff? We must take the children up there tomorrow." Jenny changed the subject with cool firmness, and Rory knew she had divined at least part of the truth. She would expect to be confided in, but Rory did not feel ready for her astringent wisdom.

She spent the next two days tramping through the coniferous woods and shallow braes of Glen Ruthven, blinking the thin rain off her eyelashes, and trying to exhaust herself into submission to her duty. It was so hard, when her conscience pointed one way and her heart another. She must take Laura away from Castle Carey, and make a home for her. Any decent person would tell her so. She could not stay there, dying of love for Muttonhead, though he was dying of love for her. God, what a mess she had made of her life. The best she could aim for was a totally unselfish future, devoted to the child of the marriage she had violated. And this virtuous prospect was perfectly hateful to her.

Late in the afternoon of the second day, Rory did not get back to the castle until well after tea. Damp, shivering and incredibly hungry (she had lunched on bread, cheese and whiskey), she went into the great hall expecting to find it deserted.

"Rory. I'm glad you've come." Gus jumped out of one of the leather armchairs. "We were just talking about you."

She was staring at the mighty, broad-shouldered figure beside the fire. "Mutt! What on earth are you doing here?" She could not kiss him in the old way. They gazed at one another, both turning red, trapped in awkwardness.

"I had some business with Fenborough," Muttonhead explained stiffly. "And Mrs. MacNeil was kind enough to invite me."

"Have a sandwich," Gus said, helping her off with her raincoat. "Jenny had them made for Oughterard."

Belatedly, Rory remembered her manners. "You're talking about business, and I shouldn't intrude."

"I think it's your business, too." Gus looked sad. "Would you say so, Oughterard?"

Muttonhead nodded. "It's about the kid."

"Fleur," Gus said. "Tell him what she's like, Rory."

Rory heard the pain mingled with the pride in his voice, and was intensely sorry for him. "She's adorable. The most impudent little witch you can imagine, and"—she hesitated, but had to say it—"she's the living image of Tertius. I'm sorry, Gus, but I nearly fainted when I saw her."

"No, you're quite right. I'm not so blindly doting that I don't notice it." He grinned unhappily. "The thing is, I was terrifically fond of Tertius, too."

Muttonhead growled, as a way of expressing emotion, and lit his pipe. "I would never have brought it up, only Tertius made me promise I'd give some of his paintings to the child—they're worth a small fortune now, apparently."

"He was a talented beggar," Gus said, his eyes moist. "I always knew he'd be a success."

Rory strove to speak lightly, but could not hide the tremor in her voice. "He should have left them to you, darling. God knows, he owed you enough money."

"Oh, I never expected to see the color of that again." Gus cleared his throat vigorously. "I knew about their—his relationship with Vi. I think she wanted me to find out. She wasn't entirely settled in marriage at first. And I guessed about the baby soon after she was born. It didn't matter. I love Flurry as much as my own two little sons." He squared his shoulders. "And she loves me. I want to make it clear, I won't surrender any of my rights as a father. If she belongs to anyone, she belongs to me."

Muttonhead said: "Understood."

"As for the paintings, you said I could sell them now, and put the money in trust—and I'm sorely tempted. She'd get it when she was grown up, and never know where it came from. But it doesn't seem fair. She ought to have a chance to decide what to do with them. So I'll propose something else. Keep the paintings until she's twenty-one, and then let her wonder about the truth herself."

Gus was not a noble-looking man, but Rory's admiration of him now amounted to awe. Not one blot of meanness or selfishness marred his determination to protect the changeling foisted on him by his wife.

"Sounds reasonable," Muttonhead said. "What do you think, brat?"

"I think Flurry is a very lucky child, Gus, to have you as a father," Rory said. "I wouldn't change things for the world—but if Tershie's mother could only see her once—"

Gus laughed suddenly. "Of course Lady Oughterard must see her. She's not a state secret. I'll find some excuse to bring her and the boys over to Ireland. And here she is," he added, as Flurry herself came sprinting into the hall. He could not keep his feelings out of his face. "Come over here, missy, and meet one of Dad's pals."

Flurry tilted back her head, to take in Muttonhead's height. "*Cor blimey*," she said.

"Language, Flurry. What would Mummy say?"

Putting her lips to Gus's ear, she whispered loudly: "He's very big."

"He won't bite. Give him your hand."

She stood at Muttonhead's feet, staring solemnly into his intense dark eyes. He made no attempt to lower himself to her level, but stood stiffly to attention. Rory thought him a forbidding figure, yet something about him must have reassured Flurry, since she offered him one grimy paw.

Muttonhead laid down his pipe, grabbed the child and whisked her up in the air, holding her out at arm's length. She was only startled for a moment, before she began to delight in being so high. Swinging her legs, she favored Muttonhead with a grin so like Tertius's that he suddenly clutched her to him, covering her curly head with his hand, as if sheltering her from some danger that only he could see.

"Rory, why are you so angry with me?" Jenny asked.

"You know perfectly well. You sent for Muttonhead without asking if I'd mind."

"I didn't send for him. Gus asked if he might come. It never occurred to me that you'd mind."

The day was fine, and they were sitting in a relatively sheltered part of the castle's grounds. Jenny's baby, Donald, lay sleeping in her arms, dribbling onto her sleeve.

Rory absently picked at the lichen on the weathered stone seat. "I came here to get away from him."

"I think you're being a fool."

"You don't know anything about it."

"I know that you're in love with him." Jenny wiped the baby's mouth. "I've lived with you. I ought to recognize the signs by now. And Lord Oughterard is so desperately in love with you that it would be comical to watch if it wasn't so sad. How you can eat your dinner, with those great, eloquent eyes pinned to you, I can't imagine."

"Don't!" Rory covered her face with her hands. "I can't bear making him so unhappy!"

"Then why do it? Why not just get married like a normal person?" She was serene, but steely. "I won't stand by while you chuck your best chance away."

"It's too late." When Rory took her hands away, there were tears on her face. "I haven't any chances left."

"Oh, Rory! I knew you came here to confess something. What have you done?"

She could not look at Jenny while she told the story of her illfated passion for Lorenzo. Fixing her eyes on a patch of bald, green hillside in the distance, she poured out the story judging herself as harshly as possible, because she was sure Jenny's verdict would be severe.

"I knew I was being wicked. I knew I was betraying Eleanor." She turned back to Jenny, her thin body shaking with sobs. "I remembered when we made our vow at school. You saw then that one of us would break it—and it was me."

"Yes," Jenny said ruefully, "I knew it would be you."

"You—you did?"

"I didn't say so. It was your last night and I didn't want to spoil it. Besides, the future seemed so far away."

Rory dug her handkerchief out of her sleeve, and blew her nose. "I can't understand why you're not furious with me. In any case, you see why I can't possibly marry Muttonhead."

"No. As a matter of fact, I don't."

"What?" Rory was astonished, and outraged that the verdict she had reached so painfully should be questioned.

Jenny pulled the blanket more securely around her sleeping baby, and carefully laid him in the pram, which stood beside them. "Have you told Lord Oughterard about Lorenzo?"

"Are you mad? Of course not."

"I think you're unjust when you assume it'll make him stop loving you." Jenny's voice was quiet and deadly serious. "You say yourself, his attitudes have softened."

"Never—never!" Rory hiccuped. "The shame would kill me!"

"Oh, I see. We're talking about your shame, and not Lord Oughterard's disapproval. My poor dear"—Jenny took her hand—"stop punishing yourself. It isn't fair, when it means punishing him too. Why should he suffer, because of what you did?"

"But I'm doing this for his sake!" Rory protested. "Are you saying I'm being selfish?"

Jenny sighed. "You confessed your wicked secret. Now I'll confess mine."

Clutching Rory's hand, she told her about Jamie Buchanan. Her manner was impersonal and brisk, but Rory knew her well enough to sense the terrible wound it covered. When she had finished the recital, they were both silent for a while.

Then Rory said: "I'd never have dreamed of it. I thought you were so happy. I envied you."

Jenny's eyes, which had been staring out at the horizon, traveled back to her sleeping baby, and lost their strained, wistful look. "But I am happy now. Having Donald changed everything. He made me see Alistair properly—he's a wonderful father, Rory, and you can't imagine how brave he is about his blindness. I thought my heart was broken after Jamie, but I've come to be so thankful that I let him go. Passion is one thing, rightness is another." She put heavy emphasis on the word "rightness." "Alistair is the right man for me, and if I hadn't been so silly, and so selfish, I'd probably have known it all along. I suspect Lord Oughterard has exactly the same rightness for you."

"I've loved him all my life," Rory said, "and now it's more. If he brushes against me, I tremble for an hour afterward. When we're apart, I can barely see the point of living."

"Then, for God's sake," Jenny urged, "grab at him with both hands! Don't let anything stand in your way—not decency, or your wrongheaded morality—nothing!"

In the fine, sharp spring evenings, Muttonhead liked to stroll outside before dinner, smoking his pipe and letting the breeze stir his hair. Rory found him pacing on the terrace, in his threadbare, prewar evening clothes. His back was as straight as a ramrod, and his head rode high, but she knew he was as desperately unhappy as she was. Jenny was right: this could not go on.

He was so preoccupied that he was not aware of her presence until she fell into step beside him and took his arm. Immediately he halted and glared down at her. She had rehearsed several brilliant and eloquent speeches, but when it came to the point, she could only gaze at him helplessly, shivering the want of him.

Muttonhead thrust his pipe into his pocket, circled Rory in his arms, and kissed her savagely. The taste of his hot tongue in her mouth made Rory so reckless with desire that she forgot all caution, and pushed her groin against his. He groaned, his arms tightened around her and for one tantalizing moment, she felt the bruising and seemingly endless outline of his erection.

With a long, low growl of frustration, he wrestled down his sexual violence, and drew away from her. They were both breathing heavily. Rory's clitoris felt so swollen and sensitive that the lightest touch would have brought her to swooning, reeling orgasm.

She was afraid he would be angry with her, but he only said, after a long silence: "Don't ever run away from me again."

"It wasn't you I was running from. I love you so much, Mutt—but I didn't trust myself."

He stroked her hair, and briefly kissed her throat. "Now, are you going to tell me what all this nonsense is about?"

Turning away, toward the darkening hills, Rory told him. Actually making her confession seemed the final goodbye to the old, headstrong, prewar Rory, and brought her pride to its knees.

Afterward, his silence stretched into minutes.

He despises me, she thought. Yet she was oddly calm. She had stripped away his assumptions about her, and showed herself in her new colors. She had a powerful and almost liberating sensation of an era coming to a close.

He said: "I see." Another silence. "Rory, look at me."

She faced him. "You're not angry?"

"You thought I would be?"

"I've smashed all your rules, Mutt. And I knew I was doing it. I'm a fallen woman."

"So you thought I'd stop loving you?"

"Yes."

"Once, I might have done," he said gravely. "But I've never loved you as much as I do this minute. I've changed too. I don't live in the age of chivalry anymore. You won't hear me talking about preferring death to dishonor. I've seen too much death."

He held out his arms. Giddy with happiness and relief, Rory launched herself into them.

"Stop crying," he said. "You'll take all the starch out of my shirtfront."

"Mutt darling, I'll never leave you again."

Jenny pulled Alistair away from the glass door. "Not outside."

"What are you doing? Why can't I take a stroll on my own damned terrace before dinner?"

She surprised him by suddenly kissing him, and twining her arms affectionately around his neck. "Because you'll spoil everything."

He smiled at the satisfaction in her voice. "Spoil what?"

"Rory's engagement."

Four

Rory wondered if everyone's wedding day felt like a dream. It was so intensely odd, she thought, to have all this ceremony and dressing up for something essentially private—the joining of herself and Muttonhead, body and soul. The happiness was almost too intense to bear. She felt as if she had swallowed the sun, and all her deepest emotions seemed to be pinned to her sleeve. She had wept a dozen times that morning.

Fortunately, everyone around her was weeping too. Even stony, disapproving Mrs. MacNamara had shed a tear when she pinned Rory's veil. Lady Oughterard had hugged her tightly, murmuring: "I think of my lost boys this morning, darling. I know they'd bless you, if they were here." Una had sobbed extravagantly as she buttoned Rory's ivory kid gloves.

Now Rory was sitting beside her father in a horse-drawn brougham—driven by Paddy Finnegan, who wore a white favor in his rusty top hat, and white ribbons on his whip. She was wearing the wedding gown that had belonged to her Carlington grandmother, a full-skirted cream silk, beautifully embroidered with pale yellow daisies. The blaze of her red hair was muted beneath the ivory silk and lace wedding veil. Mrs. MacNamara had found these treasures in a bundle of the linens she had saved from the fire.

"Well, Aurora, you look—you look very—" Justus was doing his best, but found the whole situation most bewildering. "You remind me of your mother."

Rory laughed. "You remind me of a scarecrow, Papa. You might have borrowed a morning suit that fitted."

"My dear girl, I can hardly be blamed for the shapes of our neighbors. I was lucky to find a spare suit at all."

"It looks as if you dug for it in a pile of Saxon remains."

"You won't be so saucy once you're married to young

Oughterard. He always did have the knack of bridling your tongue. You've chosen a very fine man." Justus sighed, as they passed the turn for Marystown. "And perhaps he'll be able to get my land into some kind of order, now that he's managing both farms together. I'd still have a roof over my head, if I'd listened to him."

Rory squeezed his hand affectionately. "You'll adore building yourself another house—but you're welcome to stay with us as long as you want."

Lady Oughterard was waiting in the church porch, with Laura and Flurry, in a glossy new lavender silk dress. She had put off her mourning for Tertius in honor of the day.

"Darling, you look simply lovely—" She embarked on a stream of loud incoherences before Rory was out of the carriage. "I couldn't be happier—I'm the proudest woman alive—"

Flurry, cherubic in pink tulle, tugged at Rory's skirt. "Laura bit me. I've got toothmarks on my arm."

"Oh, Laura!"

Laura was also in pink tulle, but looked more devilish than angelic. Trying not to smile over the belligerence of her two little bridesmaids, Rory kissed them both, and trusted Lady Oughterard to keep them in order. From this moment, she had eyes and ears for no one but Muttonhead.

He stood at attention in the aisle, extraordinarily handsome in a new and excellently cut morning suit. A stranger might have thought him too stiff-backed and stern, but Rory knew how to read him. Scarcely noticing the nods and grins of Gus Fenborough, who had volunteered himself as best man, she took her place beside Muttonhead at the altar rail. It felt entirely familiar and natural—and yet so strange. She could not help stealing glances aside at him, relearning his features as if they had just met, though she knew his every pore like the palm of her hand.

"Dearly beloved," began Mr. Phillips, his fleshy red face wreathed in smiles, "we are gathered here in the sight of God, and in the face of this congregation, to join together this man and this woman in holy Matrimony—"

Through her trance of joy, Rory heard Muttonhead saying: "I, Lucius Alexander, take thee, Aurora Mary, to my wedded wife . . ."

She heard her own voice, a very long way off: "I, Aurora Mary . . ."

Then Muttonhead was placing her mother's gold ring on her finger; Mr. Phillips was pronouncing them man and wife. They were in the vestry, signing the register, and everyone was pressing around to kiss her. She was impatient to be alone with Muttonhead, but there were social obligations to fulfill before other people would allow them to belong to one another entirely.

Emerging from the church into a blizzard of rice, they returned to Castle Carey, where a feast had been laid out on the park lawns, and the best fiddler in the county was already tuning up over a glass of beer. Muttonhead had invited everyone for miles around, and after speeches had been made, and toasts formally drunk, the bacchanalia began. The new Lady Oughterard—still feeling a total impostor whenever anyone addressed her as such—walked around on the arm of her husband accepting congratulations and yet more kisses.

Much later, after Rory had nearly jigged her feet off, the guests departed, and the Castle Carey house party sat down to a supper of poached salmon and champagne.

This was oddest of all, Rory thought. Gus, the Mater and her father were all yawning and chatting, as if the day was over. How could they fail to notice that she was mute and trembling with anticipation? Whenever she caught Muttonhead's eye, her heart swooped fit to leap out of her dress.

At last, her embarrassment hidden among the general goodnights, Rory was walking upstairs to bed, as she had done a thousand times before. The difference this time was that she passed her old door and followed Muttonhead into his bedroom, which had been repainted and given new curtains in honor of his bride.

With unhurried calm, as if they had been married for ages, he loosened his tie, laid his shirt studs on the mantelpiece in a military row, and knocked out his pipe against the windowsill.

Rory stood awkwardly beside the bed, clutching its mahogany post. Slowly and deliberately, Muttonhead came to her, and took her in his arms.

"My turn to kiss the bride," he said.

She opened her mouth to his. He had kept his distance during the month of their engagement, saying gravely that he could not trust himself to keep control, and Rory was starving for him.

His fingers were on her spine, unhooking her wedding dress. She stepped out of it, and stripped off her stockings and petticoats. In the first chill of exposure, she felt ashamed of being so thin, and tried to cover her small breasts. She quickly forgot everything else, however, in the stunned contemplation of Muttonhead's nakedness.

He was magnificent—towering and firm-fleshed, every muscle molded perfectly. She stared at his huge penis, growing by the second as it hardened to an iron bar, and wondered how on earth she would fit the colossal thing inside her. By now, her desire had built to such a pitch that she did not care if he split her in half.

He picked her up, laid her on the bed, and knelt over her. Silently, he began to kiss her body, starting with her neck. Rory sensed that he wanted her to be still, but it took all her effort not to writhe and cry out when his tongue flicked her nipples. With exquisite, tantalizing slowness, his mouth traveled downward—how like him, she thought, not to hurry. She felt his hot breath in her pubic hair, but he passed her mound, and began feasting on her thighs, working closer and closer to her clitoris until she was ready to die for him.

For one maddening instant, his tongue parted the lips of her vagina, then he suddenly took his mouth away, and substituted the tip of his penis. It felt so enormous, stretching her tender skin, that Rory gasped in shock.

Muttonhead gently pushed himself in further, and then a little further—she could hardly believe how much of him there was. At last, their pelvises were locked together. He was buried inside her to the hilt, and she was overwhelmed by a feeling of fullness and completion.

As soon as he started to thrust in and out of her, Rory opened out to him and surrendered herself to waves of ecstasy, which built to a gasping, racking orgasm.

Its aftereffects tore away Muttonhead's last shreds of control. Tremors like the onset of an earthquake ran through his massive body. He came in an explosion of passion that shook his habitual stillness to the core, and revealed to Rory—if she had ever doubted it—the full heat of his love.

She lay with her head resting on his chest, listening to the steady drumming of his pulse.

"Must do something about this bed," Muttonhead said. "Can't have it clattering like a damned stagecoach, every time we make love."

Rory laughed. "Oh, Mutt. I do adore you." She had traveled such a distance, she thought, only to discover that the right man had been next to her heart all along.

Reading her mind, he stroked her hair, and murmured: "It's been an awfully long road. I'm glad we're home."

Epilogue

1920

"Marriage hasn't changed you," Rory told Francesca, with mock severity. "You're as much of a ninny as ever. Now, stop that giggling and let me take a lock of your hair—quick, before the men finish guzzling their port."

Francesca was trying to muffle her shrieks of laughter in the sofa cushions. "No! You'll take too much, and I'll look silly!"

Jenny patted her shoulder soothingly. "Don't get so worked up, darling. It's not good for the baby."

Francesca's longed-for pregnancy had only just been diagnosed, during this brief visit to London, and her figure was as slight and delicate as ever. Rory, in contrast, bulged fulsomely under her beaded chiffon evening dress. Her first child was due in less than a month. She was standing over the sofa, snipping at the air with a pair of Jenny's embroidery scissors.

The three of them were in the drawing room of the MacNeils' London house. From the dining room across the hall, they could hear the rumbling conversation of Alistair, Muttonhead and James.

"There. I've done it anyway." Rory made a lightning pass at the back of Francesca's neck, and sliced off one chestnut curl. "Oh dear, I've ruined it. Sorry. You're practically bald now."

"What!"

"Nonsense, your hair is perfect," Jenny said. "Don't pay any attention to Rory—you know it makes her worse."

Rory laid Francesca's ringlet beside the two locks of hair, red and light brown, in the empty cigarette tin on the table. "Now we have to sign the paper."

Francesca stopped giggling, and became sober. "In blood?"

"Not this time," Jenny said. "We're too old and dignified."

"Speak for yourself." Rory picked up the sheet of paper, and read out the words they had composed jointly, over coffee and petits fours:

> *We, the undersigned, do most solemnly renew and reaf-*
> *firm our ancient vow of eternal friendship. From this*
> *day, May the 3rd, 1920, we vow to love one another*
> *until the ends of our lives, and to be true to the memory*
> *of our departed friend, Eleanor Hastings. We undertake*
> *to help one another at all times and in any circum-*
> *stances, even if we are at the four corners of the earth.*

They were silent for a few minutes, each remembering the first vow, all those years ago, and the hopes and wishes of their former selves. Then, seeing each other's grave faces, they burst out laughing.

"I spared you another poem," Rory said. "I didn't have the heart now that the four maidens are only three, and nobody could say we were in the spring of life."

They signed the vow, and Jenny ceremoniously fastened the cigarette tin with string and sealing wax.

"Hurry up!" Rory urged. "It'll all be ruined if they barge in while we're doing it."

Jenny opened the French windows, and led them down narrow cast-iron steps into her dark town garden. "Careful, mind the flowerpots."

Rory stamped the ground, searching for a soft place. "This'll do."

"My only herbaceous border!"

"Really, darling. You have miles of herbaceous border in Scotland. Let's not be petty." She knelt down, without a thought for her dress, and began digging vigorously.

"What are you digging with?" demanded Jenny.

"One of your pudding spoons."

"That's my best silver service!"

"And a lovely service it is, too." Rory was chuckling wickedly. "It was all I could do not to pinch the whole place setting, and sneak off to the nearest pawnshop. Why didn't I have the sense to marry money?"

"You sold all those paintings of Tertius's," Francesca pointed out. "They must have brought in something."

"All swallowed up, my little angel, in rebuilding Castle Carey before it collapses on our heads." Rory sat back on her heels, massaging her back. "That should do it."

The other two helped her to her feet, and Jenny finished the work of burying the tin, with her customary neatness and dexterity. Back in the drawing room, she poured them each a tiny glass of precious old Tokay.

"What shall we drink to?"

"Our children," Francesca suggested, her eyes filling.

"Absent friends," Rory said. "All of them, and Eleanor in particular."

"I have the eeriest feeling," Jenny murmured, "as if she were here with us."

"I wish she was," Rory said. "I wish we could turn back the clock to when we all made our vow together."

Jenny put an arm around each of her friends' waists. "Don't brood over the past. Whatever happened then, the three of us have found peace and hope now." She smiled. "Weeping may endure for a night, but joy cometh in the morning."